# SINNERS
# &
# ANGELS
# DUET

# Sinners & Angels Duet

## LUNA PIERCE

Editing by Tori at Cruel Ink Editing & Design
Proofing by Cady at Cruel Ink Editing & Design
*First Edition 2025*
*ISBN 978-1-957238-19-7 (paperback)*
*ISBN 978-1-957238-20-3 (hardback)*
*ASIN B0F2BV6ZDV (ebook)*

# Untamed Vixen

## A MAFIA REVERSE HAREM ROMANCE

# UNTAMED VIXEN

## LUNA PIERCE

# playlist

JOKE'S ON YOU - CHARLOTTE LAWRENCE

SILENCE - MARSHMELLO, KHALID

THE BEGINNING OF THE END - KLERGY, VALERIE
BROUSSARD

PANIC ROOM - AU/RA

WAR OF HEARTS (ACOUSTIC) - RUELLE

FEEL SOMETHING - JAYMES YOUNG

HATE U LOVE U - OLIVIA O'BRIEN

COUPLE OF KIDS - MAGGIE LINDEMANN

CASTLE - HALSEY

SO BAD - BRANDON COLBEIN

SHADOW PREACHERS - ZELLA DAY

YOU SHOULD KNOW WHERE I'M COMING FROM -
BANKS

HEARTBREAK - MDWS

MY HEART I SURRENDER - I PREVAIL

SKIN - RIHANNA

DEVIL SIDE - FOXES

PLAYGROUND - BEA MILLER

# Dear reader:

The contents of this book contain graphic material meant for mature audiences. Some situations and scenes are triggering, and I urge you to read through this list of triggers and make sure this book is suitable for you.

Attempted sexual assault. Planned homicide. Murder. Mention of domestic violence. Assault. Kidnapping. Stabbing. Attempted murder. Torture. Witnessing an overdose. Mention of drugs.

For a more comprehensive list of WHERE the triggers are located (spoilers), please visit https://www.lunapierce.com/triggerwarnings

*"They say all's well that ends well, but I'm in a new Hell, every time you double-cross my mind." — Taylor Swift*

# CHAPTER 1

## *June*

The paper-thin walls of my shared apartment provide me no shelter from the blaring noise coming from my roommates. At any given time, someone is either arguing, fucking, or playing video games. Right now is no exception. I yank my pillow out from under my head and shove it across my face, muffling an exaggerated groan.

"June, keep it down in there." Carter bangs what I can only assume is his fist against the meager drywall between us.

Out of all of them, I hate him the most. He's not even on our lease, but for no good reason, he's here every single fucking day.

The no good reason is Heather, his girlfriend. One of the four names signed to the piece of paper legally binding us to this dump of a unit.

Desperation is the only excuse for why I'm here. And no matter what I do, there seems to be no escaping this shit hole and the people that live in it. Hell, I can't even escape myself.

I can't afford to leave, and if I could, there aren't many other options available. Finding a landlord that'll rent to a single, twenty-one-year-old with a spotty job record is next to impossible. Plus, it's not like I'll be coming into a large sum of money anytime soon, either.

So, for the foreseeable future, I'm stuck here, unless I can find a crossroads demon to sell my soul to for a little peace and fucking quiet.

I toss the pillow to the side and drag my legs off the edge of my bed, dramatically slamming my feet onto the cold, hard floor, and storming toward the door. I swing it wide and glare at my target.

He flinches at my sudden appearance.

"One fucking hour," I say through gritted teeth. "That's all I asked. You can't give me that?"

Carter glances at his bare wrist. "Sorry J, the boys are playing a live match."

Because apparently, his gaming sessions are more important than me getting any sleep before pulling another night shift at the bar.

"You're an asshole."

Carter shrugs and continues thumbing the buttons on his controller. "I can't keep track of your schedule. It's not my fault you have two jobs."

"Three," I correct him.

If I stand any chance of ever making enough cash to get out of this dump, I had to take a semester off from school and focus on working, hence the additional gig I picked up. I keep telling myself it's only the one skipped term, but at the rate I'm going, I have no clue when I'll be able to go back to college. Most of my waking hours are devoted to various income-earning endeavors with slivers of sleep in between. But with the increased workload, I can't remember the last time I actually got any rest.

Carter flits his attention from the flat screen to me. "Oh, you're still here." He slides his gaze up and down my body. "Listen, if you want me to give you something to whine about..."

I cut him off. "Eat shit and die." Turning on my heel, I go back into my room and slam the door shut behind me, wishing like hell it would rattle the TV off the fucking wall.

He mumbles a few choice words but I tune them out, not letting him have another second of my time.

What Heather sees in him, I'll never fucking understand. He's a man-child, sitting around playing video games and having her wait on him hand and foot. She even went so far as to tell me he's a bad fuck. The whole situation makes no sense. She's a grown-ass woman, and who she chooses to keep around is on her, but with each passing day, it becomes more and more my problem, too.

The only reason I come to this place is to sleep and shower, so I might as well do one since I can't do the other. Maybe if I'm lucky, I can start my shift early and make a few extra bucks.

I rifle through a stack of clothes piled on a chair in the corner of my room and do a sniff test to make sure they're clean. Once I've managed to find a decent outfit, I grab my shower caddy from my dresser. My reflection stares back at me as I consider how long it's been since I've washed my jet-black hair.

Was that yesterday? Maybe the day before? Each day blurs into the next.

I run my fingers along my scalp to reveal that it doesn't seem that greasy. With a little dry shampoo, I'll be good as new. It's just my bar shift anyway. Those guys are too drunk to take their eyes off my tits long enough to notice my hair anyway.

Which reminds me, if I want tips tonight, I need to swap out my shirt for something a bit more revealing. It's not the noblest of career paths, but it pays the bills, and right now, that's all that matters.

After a quick shower, a pinch of blush and mascara, and enough eyeliner to make me look more dangerous than I really am, I slide into my sexy but practical combat boots.

I pass through the common room, ignoring the seething eyes of my roommate's creepy boyfriend, and make my way out the front door, not bothering to tell anyone where I'm going. Not like any of them care anyway.

At one point, what seems like forever ago, we were all friends. High schoolers who couldn't wait to graduate, get our own place, and do the whole college thing together. Since then, though, we've all grown apart. *Drastically.* Whether it was booze, drugs, or bad choices, none of us have much of anything in common anymore, and other than the occasional rent check drop off, or forced small-talk coming or going, we don't really speak.

If I'm being honest, I'm not bothered by it one bit. They're not my people. They're just the humans I'm currently stuck living with. I've made other friends here and there—Cora being the only one that doesn't annoy the shit out of me— but I typically spend most of my time outside of work and school either alone or fulfilling my need for physical contact with a stranger. All of which I'm totally okay with. It suits me. And I've learned that if you're the one who does the leaving, you can't be left. Not that I've ever felt the need to stay. No one has ever caught my attention long enough for me to even consider it.

I make my way the few blocks to the shitty dive bar I've worked most of my evenings at lately. It's run down, and the pay sucks, but on occasion, a high roller comes in and makes it worth my while in tips. I scan the patrons upon entering the smoke-filled establishment, noting the few regulars and the new faces littering the place.

"You're early," Jack says from his spot behind the bar. He stops counting the till and cranes his neck to get a look at the clock near the shelf of booze.

I bite my lip and tilt my head in my weak attempt to feign sweetness. "Thought you could use the help?"

"I could give you something to do," a sloppy drunk man slurs from his spot at the bar.

Jack ignores him, rolling his eyes at me. "Right." He sighs and nods to the drink Sarah had just set next to him when I walked in. "Corner booth."

"Thanks, Jack." I let out a breath and grab the glass from the counter, immediately noticing the aroma of the top-shelf bourbon in my grasp, meaning only one thing.

I settle my sights on the person it belongs to. The same guy who has spent countless hours in here the last couple of weeks. Drinking the same expensive liquor. Always alone. Not speaking to anyone. Just brooding in his own little zone, not bothered by the world around him.

I approach, taking in his broad shoulders and pressed black suit, the jacket folded neatly and resting on the table. His cuffs unbuttoned, his sleeves the most haphazard thing about him. His salt-and-pepper hair is neatly swooped back, with that long on the top, but short on the sides thing going on. His scruffy but well-kept beard matches him perfectly.

He's significantly older than me, but there is no denying that he's a sight for sore eyes.

The man drains what's left of his dark-honey-colored drink and holds it out to me to replace with the fresh one. I do my best not to stare at his lips as he licks the remaining liquid off them.

"Can I get you anything else?" I know damn well not to make small talk with him.

He's been coming in here long enough for me to realize he's a hell of a lot different than the rest of the people who frequent this place. He doesn't fuck around. He doesn't treat me the way every single other douche in this bar does. His gaze doesn't linger on my tits and I don't feel his stare when I walk away. He's just... him. We co-exist. I do my job, he pays his tab, always leaving way more than I deserve. And that's that. I enjoy his presence because it's nothing like what I deal with daily.

Maybe I should take offense to that, because I do make it a point to put my body on display for the extra cash, but I don't. Not with him. He comes in here to escape and that's what I allow him to do.

Sarah told me a few days ago that I'm his favorite but I laughed and said she was out of her mind. He hardly speaks to me. According to her, it's somehow much more attention than he gives anyone else who's served him.

"You can get me something, sweetheart," the drunk guy calls out from behind me.

I ignore him and focus on the dark and mysterious older man in front of me, paying close attention to the way his jaw tensed slightly when the guy spoke.

Mystery man slowly tilts his head toward me, his dark brown eyes piercing through me. "That'll be all. Thank you." His gaze doesn't falter, doesn't slide down my body, but yet stays directly on mine.

This should be the part where I feel intimidated, break eye contact, anything other than match the intensity of his stare. But I don't. I let the wave of adrenaline rush over me and revel in the blissful decadence of it.

It's him that looks away first, turning his focus back on the empty seat across from him.

I hide the smirk that wants to creep its way across my face and head toward Jack to see if there's anything else he wants me to do before taking up my usual post behind the bar.

A loud group of college-aged guys walk in and steal everyone's attention.

"Gonna need to see some IDs," Jack spits out the second they get close enough.

The guys laugh, slapping each other and making the simple task much more drawn out and dramatic than it needs to be. Two of them drop their wallets, burst into laughter, and bang their heads together when they both reach down at the same time.

It's hard to tell whether they're all drunk or just really fucking stupid.

I let out a sigh, waiting for them to get the show on the road.

"It's my buddy's twenty-first," one of the guys tells us. He grabs the birthday boy on the shoulder and shakes him. "A round of shots for the bar on me."

This seems to shift everyone from being annoyed to intrigued by the newcomers. Everyone loves free booze. Well, everyone except you know who.

Mister tall-dark-and-handsome doesn't give so much as a blip of interest their way. All the while, most of the other patrons crowd around and wait for their handout to be served.

I slip behind the bar, doing my best to help Jack and Sarah maintain order to the newly introduced chaos erupting around us. I count the heads that appear, reaching under and pulling out glasses to go with each one.

"Cash or card?" Jack asks the guy standing in front of him.

The dude pulls out his wallet and flashes a few hundred-dollar bills. "I'm good for it, don't worry."

The tension in Jack's shoulders loosens and he steps out of the way to let me and Sarah do our thing.

I extend a shot toward the obnoxious drunk who called me sweetheart.

Somehow, probably with the liquid courage, he has the audacity to grab onto my hand and hold it in place. He forces me to look at him, his eyes red and glassy. "Do one with me."

"I'll pass. I don't drink on the job." It's everything I can do to not deck him right here, right now. But I can't exactly afford to get fired for punching a customer.

One of the wild younger guys latches onto the drunk dude's shoulders, stealing his focus from me, resulting in him loosening his grip enough for me to pull away.

"Come on man, join us," the birthday boy says.

The drunk guy eyes me but decides to go along with the fun, probably realizing I'm not worth the trouble.

I catch a glimpse of one of the group members approaching the loner mystery man, a second later he raises his hands and backs away like he might actually be afraid of him. I smirk at the endless possibilities of what could have been said.

Jack leans down and whispers into my ear. "Hey, when they settle down, can you service the ladies' room? The machine is out of plugs."

I shake my head and elbow him gently. "Tampons, Jack, they're called tampons."

After a few noisy minutes of celebrating, everyone floats back to their respective booths and tables and the guys find a corner of their own.

I make quick work of helping Sarah clean up the giant mess that was made from the sloshing of booze all over the countertop. Once I'm confident she's got everything under control, I pop around the side and head toward the storage closet.

I fumble around for far too long to find the box of *plugs*, tucked on the highest shelf where I can barely reach. I stand on my tiptoes and use a random pencil to drag the thing closer for me to grab.

"Let me get that for you."

My skin crawls at hearing the drunk guy's voice, to feel his breath so very close to the back of my neck.

The volume to the jukebox gets turned up, and a small crowd forms around the make-shift dance floor.

"I've got it." I snatch them off the ledge and shut the door. I stroll away from him, turning down the dimly lit hallway where the bathrooms are located, hoping for the millionth time that he'll get the hint and leave me alone.

Guys like him are a bit dull though, and no matter how many "no thanks" vibes you put out, they don't fucking get it.

I disregard his words and go straight to the women's restroom in a desperate attempt to get the hell away from him.

Only, a second later, he follows me inside, twisting the lock and positioning his body in the way to block the exit.

"Listen, if you needed a tampon, you could have just asked." I attempt to make light of the situation, unsure of which direction he's going to take things.

He steps forward, giving me a better look at his build. He's wide, but in an *I go to the gym way too much* kind of way. The steroid-induced testosterone flowing off him with his arrogance. "I'd fuck you on your period, baby."

"Um, no thanks."

"Grant, you can call me Grant." The words slip off his tongue lazily.

"Grant." I crack open the box and try to go back to my job. "I'm all for gender fluidity, but I'm not sure you should be in the women's restroom."

Grant reaches over and latches onto my arm, pulling me toward him. "I'm all man, baby." He jerks me toward his groin and tries to place my hand on him.

"Get your fucking grimy hands off me." I jerk my arm to no avail.

His grip tightens and he bores his hazy stare into me. The stench of booze pours out of him as his words slur together. "You know you want it."

I swallow and try to figure a way out of this.

Grant takes his free hand and runs his fingers up my thigh, tracing under the hem of my skirt. "You wouldn't dress like this if you didn't."

If only he knew I dress like this for his money, not his repulsive cock.

The door rattles, a knock following. Sarah must be coming to check in and see what's taking me so long. But her voice doesn't follow to ask if everything is okay.

Grant brings his hand up to my face and steps closer. "Such porcelain skin." He trails my bottom lip. "And a fuckable mouth."

It was probably the worst thing I could think of doing, but the second he brought his digit near me, I knew I had to do something. And that's why I latch my jaw around his finger and bite down as hard as I can, using my hand to punch him in the throat, too.

At the same fucking time, the door to the bathroom flies open with force, a tall man appearing from the shadows. He turns toward me and Grant, his eyes focusing on me for only a second before stalking forward, grabbing Grant by the collar and away from me.

He doesn't say a word, he just throws Grant across the room and into the door, slamming it back shut.

I stand there, frozen in place, watching this completely cryptic man toss this semi-buff dude around like a ragdoll.

Grant groans. "Ah, come on man, I'll share her. We can take turns." He brings himself to his feet. "I'm sure her pussy is..."

But my savior doesn't allow him to finish. Instead, he slides his large hand around Grant's throat, tugging him toward him. His other hand forms a fist, and within a second, it lands across Grant's stupid fucking face.

Over and over and over again.

So many times that blood ricochets with every punch. Until he finally stops and lets Grant's limp body drop to the dirty bathroom floor.

Slowly, he turns toward me, red covering his face and somehow making him look sexier than he ever has.

I finally step away from the wall, careful not to move too quickly. Not because I'm afraid, but because I don't want to startle him.

His dark gaze narrows, as if he's trying to read my mind, figure out what the fuck I must be thinking after watching him beat the shit out of this stranger who tried to force himself on me.

The only thing I'm certain of is that I want this man standing in front of me.

I have from the moment he stepped foot in this bar weeks ago.

So, I do what I do any time I see something I want, I take it.

And unlike the man lying here beaten senseless, I only force myself on willing participants. The look in this mystery man's eyes is enough to tell me exactly what I need to know.

I bridge the gap, reaching down and taking his hand in mine, studying his bloodied and swollen knuckles, and then looking up at his stern face.

I should be scared. I know I should. This is one of those deer walking into the lion's den kind of moments, but no matter how dangerous and terrifying this man in front of me is, I feel it in my gut that he wouldn't hurt me. Not unless I wanted him to. And damn do I want him to.

His lips part, like he's going to say something, probably a warning to stay away, that I'm safer that way, but I've never been the kind of girl to stray from a little danger, especially when it's this good-looking.

Instead of letting him talk his way out of this, I stand taller, reaching around his neck and dragging him down to press his lips onto mine, completely disregarding his blood-soaked face. The second our mouths touch, his resolve completely shatters, his body melting into mine like we've done this dance a million times before.

His palm spreads across my back, gripping me closer to him, our tongues gliding feverishly against each other, telling me that he might need this release as badly as I do. A second later, he wraps his arm around my waist, lifting me from the ground and pulling me to his body.

I wrap my legs around his strong torso, and run my fingers along his neck, and into his once well-kept hair.

His hands grasp my ass, which is practically out by now considering I'm wearing a short skirt.

He slams me against the wall, and I use the extra support to reach down and glide my hand over his growing erection.

He stifles a moan against my lips, pulling away and breathing heavily. "We can't."

I tighten my grip around his cock and stare at him. The red splatter on his cheeks only makes his dark eyes even darker. "Do you want to?"

His jaw clenches and he sighs. "Yes."

"Then fuck me." I give him the smallest window to back out, but he surprises me by forcing his lips onto mine and greedily kissing me.

"What about a..."

Before he can continue, I cut him off with my mouth on his.

I dig into my pocket, pulling out the handy-dandy condom I keep in case of emergencies like this. Never know when you'll want to bone down, and getting knocked up is not something on my to-do list.

With one of his hands holding me up, we work together to unbutton his pants and wiggle them over his throbbing erection. It springs free and I nearly gasp at the size of it, quite possibly the biggest I've ever been with. I slide my hand down the length of it, circling up and spreading the bit of precum from the tip. Oh what I would give to drop to my knees and take him into my mouth right now, but at the rate we're progressing, getting down to business is our main priority.

He continues kissing me, somehow multi-tasking like a mother fucker as he takes the condom I open for him and secures it in place, then drags his hand up my waist and quite literally rips my panties off of me and tosses them onto the floor next to the beaten body.

He pauses, his hand around his cock, gliding it up and down my wet and eager slit. "Are you sure?"

And that's all it takes, ladies and gentlemen. Three fucking words to confirm consent. If this brutal as fuck man can do it, when I'm practically begging to be fucked, any man can.

I grab hold of him and guide him toward my entrance.

He stops me from going any further. "Say it." His stare turns serious, his voice a bit gravelly.

"I'm sure."

The slightest hint of satisfaction rolls over his face. "Good girl."

Little does he know, I'm the furthest thing from it.

He positions himself to enter, slow at first, filling me with ease, until the length of him completely stuffs me full. Then he rocks his hips and thrusts me up and down on his shaft. My tits bounce, nearly freeing themselves from my revealing top.

Pleasure and pain consume me at the sheer thickness of him opening me in ways I've never felt before. I continue on this rollercoaster ride wherever it takes me.

He backs us away from the wall, and a bit of disappointment washes over me as I worry that this is about to be over all too soon. He plops my ass down onto the cold countertop and props my feet up on the edges, grabbing me by the waist and pulling me toward him, continuing to thrust through every bit of this.

When I instinctually move my legs, he grunts, grasping both of my ankles and spreading me wide.

My head tilts back, slamming into the mirror, my eyes rolling with the control he has over me.

He pivots his hips in the best ways, hitting every single nerve like he's a pro at fucking. It's when he slows and pulls out that I nearly lose all my calm.

"Fuck, man."

"Shh." He replaces his dick with his hand, sliding three digits along my slit and then shoving them inside of me. Kneeling down, he brings his face to my pussy, gliding his tongue around my clit.

"Don't tell me to *shh*." I rear up my foot and gently but firmly shove him away from me, hopping off the counter and turning around to face the mirror. I bend at the waist, resting my elbows in front of me and arching my ass toward him. "Come on."

He narrows his gaze, almost in disbelief at me regaining that control. He takes his overpriced shoe and nudges each of my legs apart, dropping down between them once more to get a taste of me from behind. He rolls his tongue from the front, all the way to the back, using his hands to pry me apart with each inch he moves. He teases me with his thumbs, both on each side, caressing and massaging my hole.

I rock my body toward him, desperate to feel him fill me once more.

He obliges, standing and sparing no kindness when he shoves his cock into me with a force that drops me from my elbows.

I spread my arms across the counter to steady and pivot myself for him.

He runs his large hand along my ass, up my back, and into my hair, raking his fingers along my scalp and grabbing a fistful of my hair. He yanks my head up, but in a way that is almost all pleasure, no pain.

"Harder," I say through gritted teeth, feeling my climax rise with each pump of his cock.

Most guys, when they hear the word harder, they think *faster*, but no, this man with no name knows *exactly* what I mean when he starts thrusting deeper and to a different tempo, sending me spiraling over the edge and into oblivion.

"That's it," he moans, slamming into me and blowing his own load into my pulsating hole.

My body shakes from the insane rush of pleasure, my pussy tightening around his throbbing cock as our orgasms wind down together. I lay there, against the cold counter, panting and trying to catch my breath. I close my eyes and revel in the pure fucking bliss, knowing damn well that reality is about to set in.

Slowly, he pulls out of me, and from the sound of it, he tugs the condom off his dick and tosses it into the trash can to my left. It's his zipper I hear next, but then, something I don't expect. Him stooping behind me to blow cool air on my exposed area.

I don't dare open my eyes, hoping like hell I can keep this dream lasting for as long as possible.

He continues to surprise me by reaching up and rubbing the palm of his hand against my clit. He nips at the back of my thigh with his teeth, leaving a trail with his tongue up to my crease. He presses his lips against mine, sucking and biting and teasing me once again.

I let out a moan and arch myself in his direction, ready for whatever he's willing to give me.

How is it possible to be so incredibly fulfilled, but want even more?

*Need* more.

He slides a couple digits inside me, while keeping another rocking gently against my clit, his thumb resting near my asshole. Wasting no time, he picks up his pace, paying close attention to the way my body reacts to him, heightening my pleasure like he can read my fucking mind.

His beard bristles up against my leg and he blows more air on me, then dives back in for another taste. "Now," is all he says.

The way the vibration of his voice rattles against me, and the sheer power he has over my body, I succumb to his beautiful torment, climaxing for the second time.

I bring my hand to my mouth to suppress the whimper that threatens to leave my lips and continue to shake against his grasp.

He steadies his grip until he's certain I'm done, and pulls away, standing and washing his hands in the sink beside me.

It's then that I remember he's covered in blood. Luckily, he finger fucked me with the cleanish hand.

"Are you ambidextrous?" I ask him.

He shuts the faucet off, grabs a paper towel from the holder, dries his hands, and faces me. "What?"

I step closer, take the semi-damp thing from him and blot the blood off his cheek. "You know, can you use your left and right—"

He cuts me off. "I know what it means."

"Oh." I continue to help clean his face. It's the least I could do after the mind-blowing double orgasm.

He grabs my hand, stopping me in place. He stares into my eyes with those seriously deep, dark orbs of his. "I've got this." He nods behind me, toward the door. "You should get back to work."

I glance over my shoulder at the limp body on the floor. "What about that?"

"I'll take care of it."

"I can help."

"You've done enough." His resolve softens just barely, and he brings his hand to my face, thumbing my bottom lip softly. He scans my features, and I wonder what the hell he must be thinking. But in an instant, he hardens. "This can't happen again."

I huff and grin. "Don't worry. I'm not that kind of girl." I drop the used towel into the trash can and turn on my heel, fully prepared to do what I always do—not get attached.

# CHAPTER 2

# Dominic

"Dominic, hello, are you fucking listening?" Bryant waves his tattooed hand in front of my face.

I blink and look at him, snapping myself back to this dreadful reality. "Yes, you fucking idiot." I smack him away and adjust the cuff of my shirt, pivoting my body toward him. "Shipments are running slower. Numbers are down. Total anarchy. I get it." I take in an annoyed breath. "Tell me something I don't already know. What can we do to fix this mess?"

Bryant looks to Hayes. Hayes raises his brows and shrugs.

I rub my temple. "What good are you two for anyway?"

Hayes speaks up. "You don't know what it's like out there. The guys are scared. They don't know which side to choose."

I cut him off. "Then draw a line in the sand. Force their hand. If they pick Beckett, put a bullet between their eyes."

Bryant side-eyes Hayes, clearly skeptical of my order. "You want us to kill anyone who defects?"

"Did I stutter?"

For someone covered in ink head to toe, appearing like a total badass, Bryant sure is a fucking softie. Had I known that from the get-go, I would have thought twice about hiring him. In our line of business, there is no room for weakness. Everything about right and wrong blurs, and suddenly, you understand, it's a dog-eat-dog kind of world out there. And if you want to survive, to thrive, you must be more ruthless than the other guy.

That alone is why I always come out on top—why I will win this war and claim the throne that is mine for the taking.

It should have been simple. An easy transition.

Our leader was taken out, and I was supposed to be named the successor by his wife, who no longer wants to oversee the operation. The obvious choice. It's what I've spent most of my adult years working toward. I sacrificed everything for this career. Gave up having any kind of life outside of this, and never once put my needs above it. But, with so many hungry up-and-comers, it's no surprise that the normal order was challenged. Not by one, but by many. Most have been handled, but there are still a few that threaten to take what is rightfully mine.

Simon Beckett is my biggest concern.

He's a child. Barely legal drinking age, and somehow, he dares to assume he should gain control over the largest criminal enterprise on the west coast instead of me.

I know the ins and outs of our organization better than anyone, hell, possibly better than our previous leader. I was his apprentice, often leading when he would be out of town on business. People know me, respect me.

What does Beckett know other than being an arrogant, spoiled little boy? He spends most of his time driving around his Lamborghini, flaunting his money, and buying bottle service. How could he possibly be better equipped for this position than I am? His status is based on his blood connection to some of our council members, not because of his management skills.

Why would anyone in their right mind want *him* to oversee things?

"If that's what boss wants, that's what boss gets." Hayes finally speaks up.

I tip my head at him and bring my hand up to rest against my jaw. The same hand I had buried inside that woman from the bar. It's a shame I've cleaned up numerous bodies since then, otherwise, I might be lucky enough to have her scent still on me.

I swallow the lump in my throat and replay the event through my mind.

I was certain she would have freaked out. Absolutely convinced that nearly beating that man to death would have terrified her, but instead, she walked straight into my arms and did something not a single person has ever done before. She saw me, for the brutal and sick man I am, and she didn't run away.

I shouldn't have intervened. I should have let things play out the way they were going to, but I couldn't bring myself to sit back and watch that piece of shit objectify her the way he was. I had watched it too many times. I've spent more nights than I can count in that dive bar the last few weeks, my meager attempt to escape the chaos and think with a clear head. I witnessed countless guys try to pick her up, but not once did she give in to their demeaning ways.

I could sense her confidence, and despite wanting to step in all the other times, I knew she could handle her own. It wasn't until that douche bag followed her into the bathroom that I was certain he was about to take things too far.

And I couldn't let that happen. Not to her.

I was sure it would ruin whatever image she had of me. That she would finally fear me for the twisted man I am. But that was the furthest from what actually happened.

I should have stopped there. Let her walk out of that bathroom and go about cleaning up the mess I had made, but no. I had to lose all my control and fuck her like there was no tomorrow. Even going so far as to make her climax a second time, just because I could.

God, what I would do to bury my face in her and smother myself to death with her tight little...

"Dom, buddy. Where the fuck do you keep going?" Bryant snaps his fingers in front of me.

"I'm going to chop that fucking hand off if you put it in my face one more time," I snap at him.

He brings it to his chest and pouts. "Dude, this is a nice hand. Come on, now."

Hayes leans back in his chair, folding his fingers together and propping them behind his head. "I'd like to see this happen. I'm thinking machete. What about you, Dom? What would be your weapon of choice?"

Leave it to Hayes to actually daydream about maiming someone.

"You're both fucking psychos." Bryant glances at both of us

Hayes grins his pretty-boy grin. "Thanks, appreciate that."

Bryant slowly takes a step backward. "I'm sleeping with one eye open tonight."

"Just tonight?" Hayes tilts his chin.

"I hate you so much right now." Bryant bumps into the wall behind him. "I'm going to go hide all the weapons."

Hayes exhales dramatically. "And I'll find more. Trust me. I'll get creative if I have to."

"Can you two focus a little more on winning this war instead of fucking with each other? If we lose the lead to Beckett..." I trail off, thinking of the endless scenarios that would follow if he gained ultimate control. Things are rocky enough as it is, there's no telling how quickly we would crumble in his hands. "Trust me, it'll be bad."

We're being hit hard from all directions. The east is coming at us with immense pressure, given they took out our leader. The story is still a bit unclear on what the hell happened, but the second we got wind that he was down, complete mayhem ensued. Honestly, it's a genius plan on their behalf. Sit back and watch our empire crumble, then swoop in as the dust is settling and take full and utter power. They'd rule the two biggest markets, the east, and the west, and have a solid foothold if they wanted to push in any other direction.

My only saving grace is that their leader was taken out, too. Causing issues on both sides with who will grab onto the reins and steer away from total annihilation. I'm not sure how dire things are going on their end, but if it's anything like what we're going through, it's enough to keep them busy while I regain my authority here.

I'd like to think I'm well equipped to overcome whatever is thrown my way, but I'd rather handle one massive problem at a time than two.

Both looking more and more like my demise with each passing day.

"They're afraid of you," Bryant adds from his spot far away from us.

"Your point?" I ask him.

Before he can elaborate, the buzzer to our front door goes off.

I immediately shift to Hayes and wait for him to tell me who it is.

He fumbles with his phone, nearly dropping it. "Sorry man, had it on silent."

I narrow my gaze at him. "You're the lead point on security, Hayes. Need I remind you that if you provide no value—"

Bryant pushes the button to our gate, letting whoever it was in. "Come on up." He turns to us. "It's just take-out. Chill."

I sigh, running my hand through my hair and seriously considering why I ever took either of these idiots in.

Loyalty, that's what I remind myself.

An impossible to find trait. Unfettered, absolute, loyalty.

They may get on my nerves, do the dumbest shit ever, but never once would I question whether they had my back. And in this line of work, that is a rarity to have. I am their boss, but we are a team. A dysfunctional one, but a highly effective unit that has managed to climb the ranks and never once question each other.

I tap my fingers across the table and check the time on my watch.

Hayes jumps from his spot and rushes over to Bryant, stealing the bags from his grasp. "What did you get, dude? I'm starving."

"You two are always hungry."

Like toddlers. Or a pack of wild dogs.

Bryant reaches into the sack and pulls something out. "Heads up." He tosses the thing to me. "Chicken wrap, extra bacon, hold the onion."

At least he's good for something.

My stomach growls quietly but I don't give him the satisfaction of knowing that I haven't had lunch yet. "Thanks."

I stroll over to the first-floor kitchen a few feet away to wash my hands. I pop open the fridge, only to realize the drinks I had him stock for me are on the second-floor kitchen. The one downfall of living in such a massive house, you forget where you leave stuff. The price you pay to maintain privacy while keeping your closest associates around. The reason we work so well as a team is because we're practically an extension of one another. We each have our roles and we stick to them to keep things running smoothly. Well, for the most part.

It wasn't always this way, the living together. But a few years ago, it was the obvious choice if we wanted to continue on our path to the top. It's not like any of us had other family or friends to be concerned with the shift in dynamic. We're all loners, but even more, we're all aware that those types of relationships only threaten to ruin what we've worked hard for.

The sound of feet clobbering the stairs steals my attention, and when I turn around, Bryant is setting three glass bottles on the table.

Okay, he's good for two things.

"You were saying." I pick up where we left off prior to the interruption.

We take our spots around the large oak dining room table.

"Face time," Hayes adds.

I raise my eyebrow at him, wishing one of them would just fucking elaborate already.

Hayes bites off a chunk of his hamburger, chewing it quickly and bobbing his head as if that will somehow make him finish quicker.

"Yeah," Bryant continues, popping a fry into his mouth. "If people see you out in the field, knocking heads and enforcing shit, I think it would get them on board. A fear-induced vote."

"I knock plenty of heads," I tell them. Two today, actually.

"Discreetly. Because that's your thing, you're like a shadow. A ghost. They're afraid of the *idea* of you, not necessarily you. Give them a reason to step back in line." Bryant reaches into the take-out bag and pulls out a packet of ketchup.

I hate to change things up. To be a different version of myself. To stray from the one that has proven effective for countless years. But if I don't do *something*, I may lose everything. And I can't afford to do that.

Hayes shrugs. "It's worth a shot."

"You think this will garner support?" I look between them, reading their energy and the smallest tells they give off. I might be the boss of us, but at the end of the day, I do value their input, because it's what's gotten us this far.

"If they *see* you in action, and word spreads, there's no doubt they will either run for the hills or bow down and pledge their allegiance." Bryant pitches a pretty good case.

"You said you wanted to draw the line in the sand," Hayes reminds me.

So that's what I will do. Step out from the darkness and show everyone just how brutal and ruthless I can be.

---

Hayes and I walk side by side into the dimly lit corridor of the packaging warehouse where today's shipment is being processed.

Security pinged a potential situation, and I figured, what better time than now to test the new theory.

Tension rises the second we enter the room. Heads turn our way, eyes widen, and stare, only to avert once they realize they've been spotted. Everyone falls into line, not wanting to draw any unwanted attention to themselves. Too afraid that what they've heard about me might come true.

They recognize me, and they've heard the stories about where I go, destruction and death follow. Only usually, it's from whispers told, no one ever really witnessing it firsthand. Because no one typically makes it out alive when I show up unexpectedly.

There must be thirty of them, in rows of five or so, weighing and bagging up product, placing them in cardboard boxes to be picked up from the workers waiting to double-check and seal them off for shipping.

Armed guards stand posted on the north and south wall; rifles slung over their shoulders.

I approach the man in charge of today's outfit. A chubby fellow with thick glasses and bags under his eyes. He reeks of coffee and nicotine. His face glistens and he does his best to wipe his brow with the handkerchief from his pocket.

Hayes exchanges a few discreet words with him while I scan the group of men at work before me. Ages ranging from barely legal to mid-sixties. Body shapes and sizes vary between each of them. The only thing they have in common is the look of terror they're all trying to hide.

One man sweats a bit more than the rest, and without hearing a bit of the conversation going on behind me, I know that's the guy I came here for. I lock my gaze on him, noting the way his jaw tenses, and his hands shake.

I wonder if people can sense when the end is near? When their time is almost up?

I unbutton my fitted jacket, sliding it off my arms and folding it in half. It cost me a pretty penny, and I refuse to allow it to suffer because of a little occupational hazard. That's how you keep nice things, you take care of them. No one appreciates genuine Italian craftsmanship anymore.

I keep my stare glued to my target as I hand off my jacket and glide across the room. I stop in front of his spot and roll up each of my sleeves. "Stand," I order him.

Silent tears roll down each of his cheeks, telling me everything I need to know about him being guilty.

"Empty your pockets."

He fumbles his hands around, flipping them inside out to show me.

When each of these workers arrive, they are to put all their belongings in an allocated bin, only to collect them after they have clocked out for the day. They are searched, then granted to do their job, then checked again before leaving. It's how we keep product loss to a minimum. But sometimes, things slip through the cracks. The workers get smarter, think up new places to stash their stolen goods to smuggle them out.

"Take off your pants," I say calmly. A bit too calm, considering.

The man's bottom lip drops. "What?"

Someone calls out from behind me. "You heard him."

The man flits his gaze as if to consider he has any other alternative than to comply. He chooses wisely, gripping the waistband of his cheap denim jeans, unbuttoning and dropping them to the floor. He trembles but remains firmly in place.

"And those." I point to his boxers, not caring that we're in a room full of people.

"I'm sorry?"

I let out an exasperated sigh, reaching into my own waistband and pulling out one of the handguns strategically placed on my person. I grip the slide, tugging it back and loading one into the chamber.

This seems to get the man to cooperate. The second his eyes land on my weapon, he starts blubbering and whining, a bit of his piss trickling onto the concrete floor.

The men around us tense but stay in place. For good reason, because with my rising annoyance, I'd shoot anything that moved at this point just for the thrill of it.

My suspicions are confirmed when the man exposes himself. His shriveled-up cock and balls covering the few small bags taped to his upper thigh.

We had been tipped off that someone had been exceptionally fidgety in their seat tonight. This man and his stolen goods no doubt being the person of interest.

"I—I can explain."

I perk up my brows at him. "Oh, you can?" I fold my arms across my chest, waiting for him to tell me how the product got strategically placed in his nether region.

"Well, um..."

But if there was a legitimate reason, he would have already said it by now. So, I choose to waste no more time with this pathetic excuse for a human. Before he can spit out another word, I uncross my arms, extending the one holding my gun, point it at him, and pull the trigger.

His mud-colored eyes go wide, shock rattling his features as the bullet is expelled from my gun and impaled in his forehead.

Blood splatters and his body falls back into the table behind him. A collective gasp fills the room.

I tuck the barrel into the holster on the back of my tailored suit. "Someone clean that up."

People move in my peripheral and begin the job that I have assigned.

Making my way to the front of the group, I clear my throat to silence the mild disorder. I steal a glance at Hayes, a sadistic grin across his cheeks.

"Thievery will not be tolerated. Dishonesty. Disloyalty. Not a part of our business motto." I turn, facing the remaining terrified faces. "The pay is generous. Isn't it?" I tilt my head at a young man in the front row.

He avoids eye contact like I might have the power to kill him with one look. "Yes, sir."

"I am not an unreasonable man. If needs arise, I expect you to come to me. But I will not take to this..." I wave my hand toward the scene that's being tended to. "Treachery."

Hayes comes to stand at my flank, as if to show his support of my words.

I continue. "If you do not agree with my ways." I point to the door and keep my hand held in place. "If you wish to join the opposing side. Go. No one is stopping you." I flit my gaze at them, sensing a small shift in energy.

A man from the third row moves, stepping around his line-mates and mumbling under his breath. "Fuck this shit. Beckett doesn't..."

I don't quite catch what he says, but it doesn't matter either way. He crossed that line in the sand and sealed his own fate.

In one swift motion, I yank my weapon back out and plant a bullet in his dome before he can even comprehend what hit him.

His body hits the concrete with a thud, and the second the gasps from the men conclude, a pin drop could be heard from how quiet the room becomes.

I put my gun away once again. "Have I made myself clear?"

CHAPTER 3

## June

Have you ever been dicked so good that all you can think about is getting it again? I'm talking instead of cloud nine, you're riding the cloud dick train. Dick that makes you ache between the legs, both from the experience itself, and wanting it badly again. It turns everything you do into a potential dicking. Do the dishes? What about getting railed from behind? Take a shower? Slam me against the wall. Check the mail? How about a little exhibitionism? I wake up thinking about that thick, juicy cock, and I go to sleep wishing I could manifest it into my ravenous hole.

I swipe through the matches on my phone, none of the guys putting off the type of vibes I'm fiending for. I even up the age parameters, hoping like hell I'll come across the guy from the bar. Not that I've ever been the type to chase down a lay like that, but desperate times call for desperate measures. And just imagining the adrenaline I felt that night, laced with the insane pleasure, it has me doing nearly anything to track that thrill down again.

It's been a week. Seven days of working multiple jobs and dealing with my idiot roommates, and I haven't seen the mystery man once. Every night, I wipe the tables down and glance over at the corner booth he would usually reside in and wonder where the hell he is. Not because I caught feelings or anything like that. I'm game with keeping things strictly professional, in an X-rated kind of way. It's clear that he doesn't want to be found. He went from being in the bar a few times a week to nothing at all.

I don't even have to know his name. I'm good with anonymity.

Does he regret hooking up with me? What if he's in jail for beating up that guy?

But instead, I'll settle for trying to match with someone random and hope that it's enough to satiate my desire.

29

"You want to leave early?" Jack asks me. He props his elbow up on the counter. "Pretty slow and doesn't look like it's going to pick up anytime soon."

I straighten up and glance around. "I mean, you're the boss." Forty-five minutes isn't going to make or break my already depleted bank account and there's a slim to none chance that any of the people in here will tip me anyway.

"Yeah, get out of here." He nods to the kitchen area. "I can pull help from there if I need it."

"Thanks." I slide off the stool, grabbing the bottle of well vodka nearby and putting it back in its place on the shelf with its brothers and sisters.

"See you tomorrow, June." Jack tosses the rag he was using to clean the counter over his shoulder.

He's a decent man. A bit awkward when it comes to menstruation, but what guy isn't? He was kind enough to take me on when I needed another job, and he's been considerate to let me flex my hours when my other two jobs demand more of my time. This shitty dive bar is exactly that, a shit hole, but it's my favorite place to work, and trust me, I've been around the block.

Literally.

I make my way out the front door, sidestepping a couple that drunkenly walks by and almost knocks me down.

The two hang on each other, slurring gooey sweetness about loving each other.

I shake my head and turn in the direction they came from. The Haven District.

AKA, a fuck ton of bars jam-packed in a side of town where booze can be carried to and from in open containers.

Stay in the Haven, you're good to go. Leave the Haven, bye-bye alcohol.

I pull out my phone and send a quick message to my potential date for tonight, letting him know that I got off work early and can meet him sooner, rather than later.

Fingers crossed that it works out, because I'm ready to bang my last lay out of my system and hopefully get his cock out of my mind.

I could text Cora, see if she wants to hang out in the meantime, but considering I have a one-track thought process lately, I don't want to bother her just to ditch her for a dude. I'm planning on seeing her tomorrow night anyway, so I should just ride solo tonight.

"Excuse me," I tell a group of guys standing near the entrance of the bar I'm trying to get to. When they don't move, I speak up louder. "Get the fuck out of my way."

Their eyes widen and they collectively stare at me. A murmur of, "Sorry," then the shuffling of feet as they comply with my demand.

"Bitch," one of them says.

I stop in my tracks, a few different scenarios playing out in my head.

There are five of them. One of me. They're piss drunk. I'm too sober.

I could easily throat punch one or two of them before the others get involved. But then that would cause chaos, potentially ruining any chances I have of getting laid tonight. I sigh, settling for the safest option.

I grip the handle and swing the door wide, smacking it into one of them. "Oops," I say, as if it was an innocent accident. I don't bother listening to the rest of what they spit out, yet continue into the booming bar.

I weave my body through the crowd, putting those douchebags in the past and silently praying the guy I'm meeting isn't that big of a tool.

It takes me fucking forever to wiggle up to the bar, finally squeezing myself into an open section and attempting to draw the attention of the nearest bartender.

A person bumps into me from behind, sending me into a patron sitting at the bar. "Shit, I'm sorry." A legitimate accident this time.

I put my hands out to steady myself, and my victim reaches over to stop me from tumbling over completely.

"Are you okay?" His cobalt blue eyes glance up at me through his dark lashes, something so fucking familiar about them. About him.

My gaze trails down to his lips, to the freckle just barely visible above his chin.

No, it can't be. It isn't possible.

My memory flashes back to the summer before seventh grade. I was maybe twelve years old. I couldn't fathom the idea of starting junior high school without having my first kiss. I thought people would somehow be able to tell. See me as the girl who had never been kissed. In comes the sweetest, most thoughtful boy I'd ever met. We had been best friends since childhood before that, but upon telling him about my virgin lip worries, we crossed that boundary together, taking our friendship to the next level. I was infatuated. Completely in puppy love with him. That entire summer was full of sneaking out of the house, stolen smooches under the night sky, breaking into the local ice cream shop for a midnight cup of java chip, and dancing in the rain.

It was the shit you see in movies. Raw. Real. Innocent.

And it was over in the blink of an eye.

One day, we were holding hands on the rooftop of our favorite pizza shop, the next, we were saying goodbye through the window of his dad's run-down truck as it drove away.

I'll never forget that moment. Watching that stupid pickup sputter and kick up gravel and dirt with each inch it got further from me. I could feel the pull of my heart, the connection I had with him being severed the bigger the space between us grew.

He hung out the passenger window and once it became no longer safe to do, his dad pulled him inside and he pressed his hand against the back glass.

I never heard from him again. And with each passing day, my heart grew cold to the love that had been lost. I had always heard stories of heartbreak. Whispers of a pain unlike no other. But I never knew what it meant to have a broken heart until that moment. It was swift, ruthless, and unforgiving. It came with no warning, and forced itself with no regard. That was the first and last time I would ever allow myself to be vulnerable enough to feel that way. I knew the only way to overcome that horrible feeling was to flip the switch and power through. And that's exactly what I did. I got myself to the other side, and I haven't looked back since.

I hadn't even thought of him in years. Not until now, as I trace the shape of his features with my gaze, wondering if any time had passed at all.

"Coen?" His name rolls off my tongue like a question, despite being certain that it really is him holding onto my shoulder to steady me.

His brows pull together. "J?" He calls me by the nickname he used all those years ago.

It's then that I snap out of the stupor, shaking his hand off me and standing firmly on both feet. "June."

He is not the same person I kissed on the beach at night under the stars. Because I am not the same girl who wept for days when he disappeared from her life.

That Coen and June died almost ten years ago, and I refuse to ever resurrect those pieces of me.

It made it all that much easier when I went back to school that fall and everyone was certain I lost way more than my first kiss to that boy a few years older than me. I went from being worried they would think I was inexperienced, to defending that I still had my virginity intact. It became a fruitless effort, and eventually, I decided I might as well embrace the girl that everyone accused me of being.

It wasn't that difficult, considering all the boys paid much more attention to me than the other girls. Not to mention, I quickly realized how damn enjoyable sex could be. Trust me, I've had my fair share of lousy experiences, but I discovered quickly just how much I liked exploring my sexuality. And as long as partners are consenting, and safety is being practiced, there's not a thing wrong with getting in touch with your wild side.

"You look good," Coen says.

Of course I do. I have my *please tip me well* outfit on.

"You, too," I try to reply with as little intrigue as possible.

Clearly, he's still gorgeous. With that surfer boy long shaggy blonde hair and stupidly blue eyes. His features are more defined, obviously, given all the time that's passed. Despite being in the sitting position, I can tell he's taller, wider, with a healthy layer of muscle on his body making his plain navy tee hug him in the best of ways.

If we didn't have a past, I'd definitely consider putting him in the queue of prospects for my bang therapy. But we do, so I need to keep my game face on, and not let him see how rattled I am by his existence.

His gaze flicks to his glass, then to me. "Have a drink with me."

I swallow, a bit surprised by his invitation. By this whole fucking interaction. "I'm meeting someone."

"Then just until they arrive." He pauses then adds. "Please."

I fall right into his trap, unable to resist that alluring appeal. It's not like I've heard back from my date yet, and I could really, really, really use a bit of booze running through my system. Maybe he'll have better luck flagging down the bartender than I will on my own. It's only a drink. I'm free to walk away whenever.

What's the worst that could happen? Famous last words of many, and somehow, I let them float through my head and convince me this will be totally harmless.

"Fine, but good luck getting the—"

The second his fingers raise in the air, the cheery red-faced woman glides over. "Ready for another?"

I tilt my head at him, sizing him up and wondering if he somehow developed magical powers during all these years apart.

"Not yet." He grins and focuses on me. "Whatever she's having."

Oh, right. Duh. "Bourbon. Two fingers. Neat. Something cheap."

Coen holds out his hand to stop the woman from reaching toward the bottle she's already grabbing. "No. Give her what I'm having."

The older lady raises a brow at him. "If you say so." She pulls a bottle out from under the counter, a short but wide bottle with a golden fluid sloshing around inside.

I spot the black label, eyeing the name, my heart nearly stuttering at the recognition of the insignia.

Double Hawks Mark. Easily a thousand dollars for a bottle alone. Coming in around one hundred per shot.

We have the same kind at our shitty dive bar, just in a different shaped bottle, reserved for one very elusive and exclusive client.

"No, really, I'm good with the well stuff." I point toward the shelf of liquor behind her.

Coen rests his hand on my forearm. "I insist. Really. It's the least I could do."

For leaving me and completely breaking my heart? Yeah. You're right. A two-hundred-dollar drink is definitely the least you could do.

I stop resisting and pull the glass toward me after she sets it on the counter. "Thanks," I tell her. I bring the thing to my nose to waft in the glorious aroma. Thick and strong and somehow a bit sweet.

A girl screams from behind me, almost like she's being attacked.

Only when I turn, she's yelling at her friend, "This is my jam."

Coen picks his own glass up, pivoting in his chair to face me partially. "Cheers?"

I let out a chuckle. "Yeah? What are we cheersing?"

Coen sighs, a weird weight seeming to lift and lower on his shoulders all at once. "Is it too cliché to say 'fate'?"

Fate—that sick bitch.

"Definitely," I tell him. "But I have a feeling that won't stop you."

"You know me too well." Coen extends his glass. "To fate."

At one point, I thought I did know him, but when he left and never once reached out again, he proved that theory wrong, reinforcing the belief that the only person I could count on was myself.

"To fate," I say anyway, clinking my glass against his. "Did you know if you break eye contact during a cheers, you'll be cursed to seven years of bad sex?"

Coen grins, his gaze locking onto mine. "Can't have that now, can we?"

We both take a sip of our bourbon and I pause to let the flavor wash over me. A hint of vanilla with a pinch of something else.

"Nutmeg," Coen tells me as though he can read my mind.

"It's delicious." And expensive.

He pats the empty seat next to him. "Sit."

I pivot, glancing into the thick crowd of rowdy people. My phone still hasn't buzzed, so there's no real reason I can't join him for a little while. I sigh and comply, climbing onto the stool and settling in.

Coen doesn't take his eyes off me, almost like he's afraid I'll disappear into thin air.

"So." I twirl my glass and wait for him to say something, anything. Maybe apologize for disappearing from my life. But even then, what good would it do? I don't think I have it in me to forgive him anyway.

"Sorry, I'm just..." He brings his hand to his neck and rubs it. "I can't believe it's you."

I shrug, taking another slow swig of the decadent liquid. "Surprise," I mutter unenthusiastically.

"Tell me about you." He snaps his fingers. "You're an actress, right?"

I chuckle and turn to him. "I was twelve when I said that."

"Yeah, but you were so passionate about it. I was certain you'd make it happen."

And I was certain about things, too. But time proved us both wrong.

"Nope, business major." I omit the *drop-out* part. He doesn't need to know my struggles.

"Gross. That sounds horrible. Practical, but horrible."

"And you? You don't exactly strike me as living out of a van, traveling the country kind of guy."

Coen exhales. "I guess we both missed the mark on what we wanted to be when we grew up."

I reposition myself on my seat and prop my boots onto the metal wrung around the bottom. "What are you doing then?"

"Security."

"What, for like the mall?" How can he afford this bourbon on that kind of salary?

Coen shakes his head. "No, private security."

Sweet, innocent Coen is doing a potentially dangerous job? I find that hard to believe.

If my experience with the past Coen has taught me anything, it's that he's not telling me the whole truth. Luckily for him, I'm not in the mood to pry. If he wanted me to know, he'd say whatever he isn't saying.

Coen slides his phone out of his pocket, pushes a sequence of buttons, then shoves it back inside. "Sorry about that, work thing."

"Right." This awkward small talk is getting more difficult by the moment. "How's your dad?"

He doesn't skip a beat. "Dead."

"Wait, what?" Did I hear him wrong over the loud music?

"Yeah, not long after we moved."

All those years ago?

"Christ, Co, I'm sorry." If I knew I would have never brought him up.

Coen picks up his glass and brings it to his lips. "It's fine, really."

Another lie.

He cautiously sets the cup down, his voice barely audible. "I think I was so mad at him, for..." Coen flits his gaze over at me. "You know." He sighs. "That it was difficult for me to be sad about it. To properly grieve him."

Finally, a truth. One that eats away at my soul.

He shoves his wall back in place, his entire demeanor changing in an instant. "But, that's a thing of the past. Where are you going to school?"

"Co..."

Suddenly, it's not the now version of him sitting in front of me, it's the ten-year-old boy that I met at the cemetery, picking dandelions to put on his mom's grave.

"Don't do that," he tells me.

"Do what?"

"Pretend like I didn't ruin everything."

"Hey," a new person calls out, their hand gripping my shoulder and nudging me away from Coen.

Before my mind can fully wrap around what has happened, Coen is on his feet. He grabs the guy by the arm, twisting it behind his back and slamming his face into the counter.

"Fuck man, what the hell," the guy calls out. "Let me go."

Coen, his eyes wild, like nothing I remember of him, turns to me. "You know this guy?"

I squint to get a better look at the dude with the smashed face. I nod slowly, baffled by his knee-jerk reaction. "Yeah. He's my date."

"Oh." Coen releases the guy immediately. "My bad." He smooths out the folds in his victim's shirt. "Sorry. Honest mistake."

The guy rubs his wrist and side-eyes Coen for good reason. "Psycho." He focuses on me. "Is he your boyfriend or something? I'm not into being a third."

"No," I reassure him, despite the strange defensiveness rising. "He's an old friend. We were just catching up."

"Are you done, or should I give you a minute?"

Jason, I think his name is. I'll have to double-check my messages.

Coen speaks up. "No, that won't be necessary." He reaches over and grabs his drink, tossing it down his hatch and leaving the empty cup on the counter. He raises his finger at the bartender. "Whatever they're having, on me. Give yourself the usual tip."

"That isn't necessary," Jason interjects.

The flushed lady nods and smiles. "Thanks, I appreciate it."

"Of course." Coen sidesteps Jason and plants his feet in front of me. He grips my shoulders, looking deeply into my eyes before pulling me into an unexpected hug.

I stand there like a statue, in complete disbelief of having his warm body wrapped around me; a chest locked and shoved deep inside of me rattling, threatening to break open at his touch.

Coen presses his lips to my cheek briefly. "Enjoy yourself, J, you deserve it."

And without even letting me gather my thoughts and form a proper response, he turns around and disappears into the crowd, my heart aching like I was back on that road ten years ago watching that old pickup drive away, never to be seen again.

"June," Jason waves his hand in front of me.

I blink and look at him. "Jason."

He sighs and shakes his head. "Jeremy."

"Oh, right. Yeah, I knew that. Sorry." That's what I get for not double-checking prior to opening my mouth. "Weird night."

"I'd say." He points to the two open seats. "Shall we sit?"

"Sure." I run my fingers through my hair and tuck it behind my ears, glancing over at the place Coen vanished into.

How is it possible that with all the time that has passed, he was able to stir up so many emotions with such ease?

A strong part of me wants to hate him, because that's how I've felt for a while now, but there's also this lingering sadness, a dull ache that tells me there's more to the story than I could even begin to imagine.

I take a long swallow of the bourbon Coen ordered for me, noting just how strange it is that both of the men I can't seem to get off my mind drink the same damn thing. That can't be a coincidence, can it? What are the odds they know each other though? Coen is a few years older than me, and the mystery guy that fucked me in the bathroom was easily twice my age.

"So, are you a student or...?" Jeremy picks up his bottle of cheap beer, I must have missed him ordering, tipping it back, and looking around us.

His features are soft. Attractive. But a bit boring. And if I'm being honest, I'm not sure why I swiped on him. Maybe because he looked nice. That maybe I was subconsciously seeking the direct opposite of the mystery man, in hopes that it would get him out of my system.

Whatever I was thinking, it's not working, because my mind is anywhere but on the decent guy sitting beside me.

"Yeah," I answer him. "Well, no. I'm taking a semester off."

"Right on." He nods. "What are you going for?"

"Business."

This conversation is as dry as the spot between my legs.

"Sick, I'm a business major, too."

I grip my glass, spinning it around and realizing how pointless this is. "Listen, Ja —Jeremy." That was almost too close. I turn to him. "You seem nice and all, but this," I motion to the space between us. "Isn't going to work." I down the remaining bourbon in one fell swoop.

Jeremy opens his mouth to speak but stops himself, like he's accepting his defeat.

I hop off the stool and pause. "Good luck."

And with those parting words, I leave him behind, making my way through the crowd and out the door, not for a second regretting my decision to put a fork in tonight's quest to bang a stranger to help me forget another stranger.

It takes a couple minutes of walking to get out of The Haven, my lungs grateful to breathe in the fresh crisp night air once I'm far enough away from the chaos.

I sigh, checking my phone for the time and wishing like hell I didn't have an apartment full of roommates to go home to. I was banking on the ability to crash at my random hookups tonight, freeing me from having to deal with those idiots for at least a few hours. Maybe sleep sound somewhere else and recharge my batteries enough to get me through the weekend.

It's pathetic, really, that I dread going home, but they make living there pretty much unbearable. They're slobs. Loud. Obnoxious. Inconsiderate. It's impossible to have any level of privacy or quiet with them around. And with the way my mind is right now, I can't afford to be near that chaotic energy.

Which brings me to where I am now, a small park on the outskirts of town, peaceful enough to give me a little bit of calm in this crazy storm called life. I probably shouldn't come here this late, in the dark, considering I'm basically painting the setting for a horror movie to unfold. But I do it anyway. And I do it often. About once a week I come and sit here, alone. I drown in the serenity of it. Listen to the music that nature provides, and relish in the fact that not a single other person is around to bother me.

I sit on the same bench I've sat on many times before, and tilt my head back, closing my eyes and taking a deep breath in and out, grounding myself to the here and now.

Maybe if I can think clearly, the universe will provide me some guidance on what the hell is going on with my life.

# CHAPTER 4

# June

"Maybe she's dead," someone whispers.

"Here, use this stick," another person chimes in.

I peek through one lid, squinting through the blaring sunlight. How did I not notice that already?

A teenage girl gasps and steps back. "Sorry, we..."

I rub my eyes and sit up, stretching and yawning. "What time is it?"

The boy with the stick in his hand points at the bench I'm on. "Did you sleep out here all night?"

"No, I woke up really early to come out here and take a nap." I stand, pulling my phone out of my pocket and pushing the touchscreen. *Great.* It's dead. "What does it look like?"

The two of them exchange a cautious glance.

"Are you...homeless?" He says the last word like it might give him cooties.

"Do I look homeless?" I motion to my body and then at the overpriced phone in my hand.

"I mean, you slept on a bench...in a park..." He crosses his arms. "Are you on drugs?"

"Yep. The shit that makes you kill stupid ass kids that won't tell you what time it is." I flit my gaze toward the trail. "No one is around to hear your screams for help."

"Tommy," the girl tugs the boy's arm. "Let's get out of here."

"Chill, Lizzy." He shrugs her off and checks his smartwatch. "Ten after seven."

"Shit," I mutter. My shift at the diner starts in less than an hour and my likelihood of having time to take a shower beforehand is decreasing with each passing second.

How the flying fuck did I manage to sleep all night on this hard ass bench? And how was I not murdered by some weirdo who preys upon dumb girls who pass out in parks? Don't get me wrong, I'm pretty reckless, but this takes my carelessness to a whole new level.

With all that aside, if I knew it was this easy to get some rest, I'd have brought my pillow and blanket a long time ago.

---

I shove my key into the lock, dreading the impending doom of stepping foot into my apartment. It's half-past seven and there's already music playing inside. Homemade rock garbage by Carter and his lame buddies. I'm all for creativity and following your dreams, but the stuff they produce sounds like raccoons were attacking them and they were using their instruments to scare them away. At first, I thought that maybe I was being overly critical, that I hated Carter too much and it was blocking my ability to listen without an overly biased ear. But no, the only people who ever pretend to enjoy the sad excuse for music are Heather, and Carter's dirtbag friends.

The water valve to the shower shuts off, and someone fumbles around in the bathroom.

I continue on my path to my bedroom to grab my supplies and hope whoever it is hurries the hell up.

A second later, my door is shoved open, Carter standing there with his towel clinging loosely around his waist. Water beads all over his body like he didn't bother drying off at all. Knowing him, he probably didn't. I doubt he cleans behind his ears, let alone his balls.

I turn my nose up at the thought of his nasty man parts.

"What do you want, Carter?" I shuffle through my pile of clothes, snatching a clean tank off the top.

He leans against the frame, eyeing me up and down. "You and me." Carter flits his gaze behind him briefly, like he gives the slightest shit if someone—aka Heather —hears him. "What do you think? I have needs. You have needs." He sighs and licks his lips.

"You're disgusting if you think I would ever consider having sex with you."

"Don't be so harsh, J." Carter crosses his arms over his chest. "I know that's where you spend most of your nights. In the bed with a random stranger."

"What I do and who I do it with is none of your business." I gather my last remaining items and make my way toward him.

He stands in my path, blocking me from going any further. "Think about it."

"No. Now get the fuck out of my way before I'm late for work."

"June," Heather calls out from behind him.

And with that, he changes his demeanor and steps aside.

"Yeah?" I ask her while pushing past him.

She rubs her sleepy eyes and yawns. "I need your portion of the rent."

I stop dead in my tracks, turning to face her. "What?"

Heather tugs her brown cardigan around her tighter. "It was due a few days ago. You're late."

I blink, replaying the memory of putting my money in the same envelope I do every month, and setting it in the same spot it always goes in. "No. I paid it last week."

She sighs and shakes her head. "You must have forgot, the money wasn't in there." Heather pauses then adds, "You've been late before."

"One fucking time, because I was sick with food poisoning."

Carter strolls around me and goes to Heather's side, putting his arm across her shoulders.

She shrugs him off. "Stop, you're wet."

"If you need me to spot you some cash," Carter suggests.

I narrow my gaze at him, knowing damn well his klepto hands were the ones who took my rent money in the first place. Unfortunately for me, there's no proving it. Only his word against mine, and with him wrapped around Heather's stupid little finger, she'd never believe me over him. I'd be wasting my breath even trying.

I'll get even with Carter, but for now, the bigger issue at hand is how am I going to come up with six hundred dollars in a day, when I barely make enough to feed myself.

"No, Carter, I'll figure it out." I go into the bathroom and close the door, making sure to lock it behind me.

"I need it by tomorrow to avoid the late fee," Heather says loud enough for me to hear.

"Got it." But do I? How in the hell will I pull this off? It was hard enough to scrape the money up the first time, let alone once again. And even if I do, there's next month's rent I need to scrounge up, too.

I'm working my ass off, barely having any time between jobs as it is. There has to be something I can do that pays a little better than the part-time gigs I have now.

Maybe I could ask Cora to loan me some cash, just until I get paid. She lives at home with her parents and from what she's told me, she has a hefty nest egg she's been nurturing since she was a kid. I hate to bring it up, but unless a grand opportunity presents itself in the next twelve hours, I'm not sure I'll be able to come up with that kind of money that quickly.

I shouldn't have to. Mister sticky fingers out there should fess up to his crime, but I'd be better off taming a wild cheetah than getting him to take responsibility for anything he's ever done.

I'll figure it out, it's what I always do. For now, I need to focus on taking the quickest shower of my life and getting my ass to my first job of the day.

I turn the faucet, stripping down and waiting impatiently for the water to warm. But it never does. Instead, it runs cold, barely lukewarm, telling me that Carter probably used what was left of the hot water. Because why would he do anything other than ruin every aspect of my life?

"You're late," Rosco says, not bothering to glance up from his morning paper.

"I'm sorry, sir. There was an..."

He holds up his hand to stop me. "I don't want your excuses. I want you to show up on time."

"I understand. It won't happen again." The same line I've given him a handful of other times. It's not that I mean to be such a shit employee, it's just hard to juggle closing at the bar at night and opening at a bakery the next morning.

Although, randomly sleeping in a park and dealing with an idiot roommate didn't necessarily add to my punctuality. Plus, the occasional night out with friends. Is it a crime to have a social life?

"You're right. It won't." Rosco finally looks at me, staring dead into my eyes. "You're fired."

It's as if I was punched in the gut, the wind being knocked out of me and the likelihood of me making enough money in time being stripped away completely.

I step forward, my mind half telling me that I should drop down on my knees and beg for forgiveness. "Sir, please. One more chance. I need this."

"If you needed it you would have been here ten minutes ago instead of showing up late." He flips his hand toward me. "Looking like that." He exhales. "Now go, before you waste any more of my time."

My mouth hangs open, words unable to form properly.

Could this day get any fucking worse?

I step out into the morning air, swallowing the lump in my throat and glancing both ways, wondering where the fuck I should go now. The pizza shop I work the day shift at doesn't open for a few more hours, and the bar doesn't open until this evening. It would be pointless to go home, given how badly I fucking hate that place and how the idea of spending the rest of my life in prison for murdering Carter doesn't sound too appealing either.

So, I wander, letting my feet take me west in hopes that the universe will stop being such a cruel bitch and throw me a bone for once. In only a few minutes, I pass the university I should be attending, watching the students pass between the buildings, and carry on with their college lives.

It's not that I enjoy school, because who in their right mind does, but I was working toward something. A goal. A purpose. A potential opportunity to advance myself and get the fuck out of this shit situation I'm in. But no one really prepares you for how expensive being on your own is. And trying to cover living expenses and tuition without anyone else's help, it's fucking hard.

Some people have parents, partners, scholarships, or even government assistance. Me? I have nothing other than what I'm able to provide. And boy am I spread pretty fucking thin.

To the point where I'm concerned I may have to start being a little more like Carter if I'm going to make it through these dark days.

I walk a couple more blocks, scoping out the windows for help-wanted signs in my desperate attempt to save myself from petty theft or selling drugs. Both of which I'm certain Carter does when he's not slumming it on the thrifted couch in our shared living room. Leave it to him to have his hand shoved into a criminal cookie jar.

An older man climbs off a ladder and stares up at the building. He glances over at me and smiles kindly. "You look lost." His hair is mostly salt and pepper, but nothing like my mystery guy from the other night.

Lost might be the understatement of the year. But I'm not about to tell this stranger that.

"I was just..." But instead of finishing my sentence, I blank.

The guy nods, folding his ladder and putting it over his shoulder. "I've had plenty a morning like that in my time." He tips his head toward the diner we're standing in front of. "You want a cup of coffee?" And like he can sense I'm about to protest, he adds, "On the house."

Honestly, it's not a terrible proposition. I could use a minute to catch my breath and figure out what the fuck I'm going to do next. And a free cup of coffee sounds divine. But what's the catch? People don't do nice things without expecting something in return.

Something in my gut urges me to take him up on his offer though. Like the universe might actually be throwing me that bone I had asked for.

"Yeah, that would be nice," I finally say.

The man grins and opens the door, the bell on it chiming as he holds it for me to step through. Immediately, I'm graced with the heavenly aroma of freshly baked donuts and brewed coffee. I've been in here a couple times before, but I don't recall it smelling this damn good. Maybe it's the lack of having had breakfast and the desperation of needing a little bit of caffeine in my system for this chaotic day.

Claire used to work here, part-time, before her boyfriend was gunned down in the alley next door and she packed everything up and moved back to the east coast. I hadn't known her long, she was only here a handful of months but in that time, Cora and I had become decent friends with her.

It was tragic, what happened to her man, Johnny, especially after everything Claire had gone through with her toxic as fuck ex-boyfriend prior to him. I guess the dude went psycho and tried to kill her, and ended up falling down a flight of stairs. I had only heard that story once she was gone, rumors spread around school like wildfire when not only Johnny, but a couple other students were found dead from apparent gunshot wounds in a short period.

It smelled gang-related, but common folk know better than to put their noses into mafia business unless they want to meet the same fate as the fallen.

"Do you take cream or sugar?" The old man asks me.

I shake my head and climb onto an open stool at the counter. "Black is fine, thank you."

He points to the glass case full of bakery items. "Donut?"

"Coffee is plenty. I appreciate it." Not to mention if I still plan on going out with Cora tonight, I have to save every penny I can to drown myself in booze.

"I insist," he says. "Blueberry or plain?"

I try not to narrow my gaze at him, but his kindness feels incredibly unfamiliar and suspicious.

He lets out a chuckle. "I'm harmless, I promise. I've been around the block long enough to see someone in need, that's all."

So what, he's like my fairy freaking godfather?

I soften my demeanor. "Surprise me."

He plucks one from the cabinet and places it on a plate next to my steaming cup of coffee. He extends his hand toward me. "Bram."

I blink at him, then let my gaze wander to the branding all around the diner, letting the puzzle pieces fall into place. "Oh." I give him a firm shake. "You're like *the* Bram."

Bram rolls his eyes. "You make it sound like I'm famous."

"Sorry, it just makes a bit more sense now." I realize I never gave him my name. "June." I bring the mug to my lips and inhale the boldness before taking a careful sip.

"Nice to meet you, June." Bram grabs the towel draped over his shoulder and wipes up a bit of orange juice off the counter at the spot two seats down from me. "What has you wandering around aimlessly this morning?"

I set the cup down and spin it around. "Um, well. I just got fired."

Bram nods like he understands completely, which makes no sense at all. "I see."

"I'm sort of in a pinch, financially, so that definitely threw a wrench into my day. It's not like I blame the guy, though. I was late, and it wasn't the first time. I have two other jobs, but they don't start until later, and I don't exactly want to go home and deal with my roommates." I sigh and break off a chunk of the donut this man offered me. "Which brings us to where you found me, looking for anyone hiring."

He raises an eyebrow at me. "You have three jobs?"

I bob my head and pop the chunk of donut into my mouth. "Trying to save enough to move out. At this rate though, it's not looking great." Especially when Carter is stealing my hard-earned rent money when no one is watching.

"That's tough." Bram crosses his arms. "It's no wonder you were late. When do you sleep?"

"Here and there." I don't mention the random park bench from last night.

"Are you a student, too?"

I bite at my lip, a bit of shame rising up at admitting the truth. "No. I'm taking a semester off."

Why am I telling all of this to a complete stranger?

"Sounds like you need a job that understands the lengths you're going through to overcome this situation you're in."

"Yeah, wouldn't that be nice?" The closest I have to that is Jack, but even then, he's still a selfish asshole at times.

A girl about my age walks up to the register, pulling Bram's attention to her. "Can I get a large mocha to go?"

Bram pushes a couple buttons on the machine. "Anything else? Maybe a banana nut muffin?"

The girl flits her gaze at the plate in front of me. "What's she having?"

I put on my best salesperson face. "Blueberry old-fashioned. It's heavenly. Ten out of ten recommend."

"I'll have a half dozen of those, too. To-go. Please." She hands Bram a piece of plastic and he inserts it into the card reader.

I sit in polite silence, eating the rest of my donut and sipping my coffee while Bram completes her order. It doesn't take him long; working around the place like he could do it with his eyes closed.

The girl leaves and he tops off my mug. "Thanks for the assist there."

"Happy to help." It's the least I could do after his generosity.

"I could use a hand around here." He refills the sugar packets in the holder near the register. "If you're looking to replace that job you lost this morning."

"You're kidding." I stare at him, utter disbelief consuming me.

"Nope. I'm totally serious. Flexible hours. You could do deliveries if you want. There are some decent tips in it. I don't usually offer delivery but when I do, it's pretty popular."

Why does it sound like he's pitching me the job instead of me selling myself on the position?

"Um, yes. Absolutely yes. Whatever you need." I hop off the stool, damn near ready to give this man a hug for potentially saving my day. "When can I start?"

He glances over at the clock behind him. "I mean...now?" Bram focuses back on me. "Unless you're busy."

I let out a laugh. "Not at all." I point to the remaining packets that need to go in the holder, shifting to see the same kind at all the tables. "You want me to fill all of those?"

Bram nods, "Yeah."

It's then that I notice a sort of sadness about him. Like something is missing. Something silently torturing his soul and causing his heart to ache. For such a good man, I hate that for him. Granted I've known him for a total of twenty minutes, but in that short time, he's already shown me more kindness than most other people have.

I make quick work of completing my first task, shuffling around the room and restocking the napkin holders, too. "Hey, hand me that broom," I ask him when I've finished, taking it and cleaning up the mess under the booth in the corner.

"Your first delivery." He sets a bag on the counter. "Can you ride a bike?"

"Yep."

"Good. I'll bring it around to you." He points for me to go out the front door.

I latch onto the bag and meet him where he told me to. My gaze is drawn to the dark alley where many have died.

Bram appears from the shadows, pushing a bicycle beside him. He shifts his attention to the dimly lit area briefly like he's looking for a ghost.

I want to ask him about that, but I don't want to intrude. It seems like the deaths in this alley might be more personal than the fact that it's just beside his place of business, and we haven't really known each other long enough for me to pry.

"This one isn't too far." He presses his finger against the basket on the back. "You can put the order in here." Bram hands me a small device. "This has the tracking on it. It's pretty self-explanatory. Just have the customer fill out the receipt section and sign off on it. You'll make the full tip, whether it be cash or card. You can clip it on here for hands-free while you ride." Bram scratches his chin. "I think that's it."

I climb onto the seat. "And you're not worried about me stealing your bike and credit card machine thingy?"

Bram shrugs. "I guess if you're that desperate, you probably need it more than me. We can work out the formalities later for payroll."

I might be a morally grey person, but I don't think I could ever bring myself to harm this man, not when he radiates such damn goodness.

"Okay then, wish me luck." I grip the hand brake to get a feel for it and put my feet on the pedals, taking off the direction the GPS is telling me to go.

The breeze floats across my skin, careening my black hair behind me. A newfound sense of hope lingering in my core. A feeling I'm too afraid to cling to just yet, given my history with bad luck.

I pass a couple houses I've gone to parties at, dodging the other people on the sidewalks and stopping at all the red lights. I enter a neighborhood I've never been to before, with homes much larger and more expensive than I could ever imagine.

It doesn't take me long to get there, a feat that would have sucked majorly on foot. I slow to a stop in front of the massive home. I glance down at the GPS again to verify I'm at the right place. It's something out of a modern architecture catalog, with its sleek edges and crisp design. Big, beautiful windows with a large balcony wrapped around the entire second floor. The landscaping is lush, but well maintained, only continuing to confirm whoever owns this place is loaded. To maintain greenery like that in this west coast heat is a challenge in itself. A tall, black metal fence goes all the way around the property, making it difficult for anyone that's unwelcomed to step foot inside.

I approach the entry, pushing the button to ring whoever is home. I climb off the bike and fumble with the kickstand while I wait.

A buzzer sounds, and a voice comes through the speaker. "Come on up."

A man. But I'm not at all surprised by that.

Probably some rich doctor or lawyer who decided to let their in-home chef have the morning off.

I pull the bag from the basket and make my way into this uncharted territory. The closer I get, the larger the house becomes. It's like I'm about to crash some reality TV show or an episode of MTV Cribs.

I raise my hand to knock on the front door, the one that's twice the size of anyone else's.

But instead of tapping my knuckles against it, the thing swings open, revealing nothing I would have ever imagined.

It's a man, for sure. Covered in tattoos. Not too much older than me. A smile lighting up his face.

"I've never seen someone so happy to get their food," I spit out without much of a filter.

"Well, when the delivery girl looks like you..."

I narrow my gaze and tilt my head. "Uh-huh."

He leans against the large doorframe, his white tee bunching over his ink-covered biceps.

I guess we're both enjoying the eye fucking.

He draws his bottom lip into his mouth and slowly lets it graze against his teeth before speaking. "You want to come in? I'll share."

And just like that, the impossible happens, my mind rearranging files and instead of getting the mystery man or Coen out of my head, all three of these men consume my thoughts.

In an instant, I've already daydreamed about dropping this bag of food, latching onto his decadent lips with mine, and letting him ravish me on that fancy table behind him in his foyer.

But I can't. Not because I don't want to, but because I can't afford to lose this job if I stand any chance of making enough money today to cover rent.

So instead, I sigh, holding the take-out to him. "Maybe next time."

The smile drops from his face, but not completely. "Fair enough." He grabs hold of the bag, his fingers gliding along mine. "I had to try."

Where was he twelve hours ago when I was trying to bang the older man out of my system?

# CHAPTER 5

# June

"Two twenty-three," Bram says from his spot behind the counter. "Plus, your hourly."

"What?" There must be a mistake. There's no way I made that much in the few hours I've been here.

He scrolls through the little device I took with me on my deliveries. "Five bucks here, six there, another five, another…" He pauses, his eyes widening. "There we go. Your first delivery. The customer tipped you two hundred."

"Dollars?" My mouth drops open.

"Yep."

"That can't be right. He must have hit the wrong button."

Bram holds the thing out for me to see. "He put a wink face next to his signature. I'd say he knew what he was doing."

I settle my sights on the doodle, then shift to the name. *Magnus.*

It's oddly fitting.

"Anyway." Bram lifts the cash box out of the register and pulls a few bills out from underneath. "You did great work today." He holds them out to me.

I eye the cash then him. "That's more than what you owe me."

"Not by much." He adds, "Consider it a welcome bonus."

"Are you sure?" Why does this all feel way too good to be true? Did I actually get murdered on that park bench last night and now I'm living some weird lucid dream?

"Positive." He remains totally serious.

"Thank you." Although those two words come up massively short on how thankful I really am.

The rest of my workday went nothing like what I hoped for.

When I woke this morning, stiff and running late, I had a hunch shit would go bad. And with the rent money situation, Carter weirdly propositioning me, the cold ass shower I rushed through, and getting fired, my worries were confirmed.

But upon meeting Bram, and having that golden opportunity present itself, I thought the universe really was helping me out for a change. Not to mention the hot piece of tattooed eye candy.

Really, it was just teasing me with the idea that I might pull this miracle off, with no chance of making that happen.

My second gig of the day fell flat. Typically, I make decent tips, but it was crickets because of some stupid construction down the street making it nearly impossible for anyone to get in or out of there. Not to mention, customers probably thought we were closed. The only people that came in were the dirty workers, who tip like shit and get their fill on grossly checking out the waitresses.

At job number three, I wasn't at all surprised when Jack let me go two hours into my bar shift, telling me that it was a slow night, and he could handle it on his own. At first, I was mad. But he has to pay his bills, too, and if the bar isn't making money, neither of us are getting paid. I had hoped the mystery man would show up, if not to bang me in the bathroom, but to leave a fat tip like he normally does and get me a little closer to meeting my sizable goal.

That didn't happen. And now here I am, walking into the Haven to meet Cora and drink this shitty day away.

My problems will still be there tomorrow morning, that's for sure. Tonight, I will drown my sorrows and do my best to forget them, even temporarily.

"Hey, slut," Cora greets me from her tall table. She has a round of shots and a pitcher of beer ready, almost like she can read my mind on how fucked up I'd like to get this evening.

"Where's Steff?" I ask her, glancing around the noisy place to spot her fiery redhead.

"She said she'd be here later; she has a *thing*."

I raise my eyebrows. "Oh? Is she hot?"

Cora shrugs, her blonde hair rolling in waves off her shoulders. "She's being all secretive about this one. She must like her."

"About time." I climb onto the stool beside her and grip one of the shot glasses. "I need this."

"That's what you always say." Cora takes the other in her grasp, holding it out to me.

"Bottoms up." I clink mine against hers, making sure to maintain eye contact. Can't afford a curse of bad sex over here.

I down the contents of the cheap tequila, the burn tingling down my throat and chest. I push a mug over to the pitcher for Cora to fill. "How was your week?"

We're not always the best at it, but we try to meet once a week to catch up. We've grown apart a few times before, but after what happened with the random college students being killed around here, we started valuing our friendship a bit more.

Cora and I have only known each other since freshman year, but I've considered her one of my best friends, despite only a few years having gone by. She's one of the few people that don't judge me, or at least, make it obvious that they do. She accepts me how I am, and doesn't try to change me. It definitely helps that she has a dark sense of humor that matches mine and on occasion can drink me under the table.

It's a beautifully broken dynamic that works well for us.

"Meh." Cora fills her own mug and takes a healthy swig. She wipes her lip and continues. "You're lucky you dropped classes this semester."

Luck had nothing to do with it.

I go along with it anyway. "I bet."

"How's the roommate thing?"

I shake my head. "Terrible. The dude tried to get me to sleep with him this morning."

Cora gasps and rests her head in her hand to focus on me. "Carter did?"

"Yep." I leave out the part about him stealing my money. Or at least that I think he did.

What other explanation could there be for it? That Heather did? Or my other roommates, Tommy and Sadie. Those two pretty much only leave their room long enough to shower, go to work, or grab take-out when it arrives. They keep to themselves, and while they're not exactly the ideal roomies, they're a hell of a lot better than Carter. Honestly, Heather wouldn't be that bad if she would just get rid of that douche.

"Gross," Cora bunches up her nose. "What a pig."

I refill what I've already drank from my mug and wish there was some way to magically refill our shot glasses. My tolerance to booze has changed the last few months, and it's going to take a lot more than this to remotely have any impact.

"I got fired this morning," I say nonchalantly.

"Holy shit, J. What happened?"

"Showed up late. It was my fault." I cross my legs and reposition myself. "You know that place Claire used to work? Bram's?"

Cora shifts her stare like she's recalling a memory. "Yeah. Over by..."

She doesn't finish her sentence, but I know what she's getting at. Where those people were gunned down.

"Yeah...I got a job there."

"Damn, girl. You move fast." She climbs off her chair. "Hold that thought, this calls for celebration, or something."

Cora leaves me behind as she rushes over to the bar, finding a spot between other customers and flagging down the bartender. It doesn't take her long before she's on her way back, one glass in each hand.

"More tequila?" She shoves one of them toward me.

I gratefully accept it, noting the weight of the contents. That's definitely more than a double.

"To...new beginnings," Cora says over the loud music that starts playing.

"When one door closes, drink tequila."

Cora laughs and taps her glass against mine. "Yeah, that."

I revel in the burn that floats down my throat, inviting it to numb my senses. "You want to play pool?" I dip my head at the newly opened table.

"Um, yes." Cora grabs the pitcher of beer. "Get our mugs."

I comply with her orders and follow her over to our new spot. Our old table being quickly taken by a couple that was looking for a spot to sit.

I dig in my pocket to pull out a single dollar and get change from the machine. It's not much, but at least I can provide us with a little entertainment on my limited income.

"Who's breaking?" I ask her as I shove the four quarters into the slot and release the balls from their restraints.

"Me if I stand any chance of winning."

I smile and roll my eyes, grabbing the rack and setting it up for her. "It's only because alcohol makes me better and you worse."

"Mmhm. Sure." Cora fingers the sticks on the wall, deciding on a sleek red one. She dusts the tip of it with a bit of chalk and blows the debris away. Getting into position, she lowers her body and leans over the table, causing any dude with a pair of eyes to look her way.

I climb onto a stool and wait for her to do her thing.

Cora cracks the cue ball perfectly, sending balls spiraling all over the felt table and landing one in each of the far corners. "Solids," she announces, and then sizes up her next target. She pockets one more and misses the next, giving me a chance to catch up.

"Thought you were about to clean house on me," I tell her when we pass.

I eye the table and quickly strategize my plan. There are three easy shots available, but those can be sunk anytime. People often lose at pool because they play the short game, not the long one. You have to be able to anticipate where the cue will land, and what you'll do next. Failure to prepare often leads to piss poor performance. I decide on my mark, sinking it on the opposite end of the table and setting myself up perfectly for my next shot. I drop it into its home and clear one more of the stripes away. I put too much English on the cue, and it ends up in the wrong spot, setting me up for failure on my next play.

Now, my only move will be strictly defense, by placing the ball where Cora won't have any openings and making it harder for her to advance. I tap my ball, barely moving it but technically having a legal shot.

"You bitch," she says when she realizes I screwed her from having a decent move.

I laugh and raise my shoulders. "It was my only option."

"My ass."

"It's a good one, I won't deny that." I smack her butt playfully on the way over to my seat. I drag my mug to my lips and drink it down while she stews over what to do.

"You screwed me." Cora pouts as she walks from one side of the table to the other. "Fine. I'll do the same damn thing." She nudges the white ball, hitting hers by a hair and putting me in a rather crappy spot.

But not crappy enough.

"Sorry, boo." I tilt the stick toward the ceiling and jam it down, popping the ball off the table momentarily, up and over hers to crash into mine, sending it exactly where I want it to go. I lean across the edge, the stick behind my back, and softly knock my next one in, too. I clear the rest of the stripes, leaving the eight ball in the corner. I point at the pocket I'm aiming for and without hesitating, I sink it into its new home.

"You're literally the worst." Cora puts her hands on her hips and sighs.

I dig another dollar out of my pocket and hand it to her. "Beginner's luck."

She swipes it away and goes to work making change.

I slide onto my seat and gulp the beer in my glass.

A chill runs up my spine, like I'm being watched. But not in a bad way. I scan the crowd until my eyes land on him, that familiar smirk and ink-stained skin. I let out a sigh, the spot between my legs warming at just the sight of him.

He leans on his elbow against the bar, staring right at me.

"Do you know that guy?" Cora asks me.

I shake my head. "Nope, not really."

"Looks like he knows you." Her words slur a little.

I hop off the stool.

"Where are you going?" Cora calls out to me.

"I'll be right back," I tell her. I point to the table. "Your turn to rack."

I head straight toward him, not caring at all about the group of girls I have to push through that are trying to get his attention.

"Magnus." His name rolls off my tongue like honey.

He grins wider. "You know my name."

"Excuse me." One of the groupies grabs at my arm.

I shake her off. "Don't fucking touch me." I might be intoxicated, but I will fuck a bitch up if they get too handsy.

"Rude," she says under her breath, but not quiet enough.

I turn to her, taking in her minimal clothing choice and the thick layer of makeup on her face. Don't get me wrong, I'm all for female empowerment, but what's happening here is sheer desperation and frankly, it's pathetic.

"What's rude is you practically begging for attention from someone who clearly isn't interested in you. What is it, the bottle service you're after? His money?" I point to a group of older men in the corner. "You'd have better luck over there, sweetheart."

"I—I..." She frantically tries to come up with a response.

"Listen, I see girls like you every day—"

But she doesn't let me finish. She huffs, turns on her heel, and storms away toward the bathroom.

"Feisty one," Magnus says from behind me.

"Guess so." I face him.

"I was talking about you, not her." He continues leaning against the bar, his eyes not daring to look away from me. "Let me buy you a drink."

I chuckle. "That's not why I came over here."

"Then why did you?" His tongue darts out to wet his bottom lip, reminding me of just how badly I wanted to jump his bones earlier.

"To tell you, that you overpaid me earlier."

A random patron bumps into me, nudging me closer to Magnus.

His hand reaches forward and lands on my waist, steadying me. His liquor-soaked breath dancing in my face.

"What are you drinking?" I step back and out of his grasp.

He picks up his cup and holds it out to me. "Here."

I take the glass and bring it to my nose. "Hawks Mark?" What are the fucking chances?

"The girl knows her bourbon." Magnus smiles, exposing those beautiful teeth of his.

How is it possible to be attracted to such a thing? There's just something about the bubbling energy that pours out of him. There's this darkness, this bad boy nature with all the tattoos, but then this giddy, happy layer that contradicts it all.

"You could say that." Plus, the fact that the last two guys I've interacted with have drank this same, very specific, incredibly expensive brand.

"Want one?" He raises a brow.

"Too rich for my blood."

He holds his hand out to call for the bartender.

"No, you don't have to do that."

But it's too late, he's already ordered me a drink of the same thing he's having.

"I insist."

"That's not why I came over here." The last thing I want him to think is that I'm anything like the girls lurking around him.

There's nothing wrong with having guys buy you drinks, but the way these chicks are going about it, it's like they're vultures waiting for their moment to strike.

"I know," he says confidently.

"Do you?"

He changes the subject. "I didn't get your name."

"I didn't offer it."

Magnus beams. "Making me work for it. I like it."

"I have to get back to my friend."

"How about a wager?" Something wild sparks in his blue eyes.

"Excuse me?"

"Play me." He nods where I came from. "I win, you tell me your name."

I chuckle. "And when I win?"

"Solid choice of wording..." Magnus winks at me. "Name it. Your wish is my command."

Oh, the endless things that I would love from this man.

I extend my hand. "You're on."

He grabs onto me, giving me a solid and firm shake. His touch is electric and has me ready to skip over the formalities and straight to the part where we rip each other's clothes off.

"Your friend, does she have the same taste as you?"

It takes me a second to realize he's referring to booze, not men.

Both of which vary from time to time.

"Beggars can't be choosers."

Cora might have more money than me, but we're still broke college students who drink cheap alcohol.

"Very well." Magnus signals for the bartender again. "Here," he gives me the expensive drink he ordered for me. "I'll meet you over there."

I take it from him and make my way back through the crowd and to an eagerly waiting Cora.

"What the hell was that about?" she asks me the second I'm close enough. "What is that?"

"Um, so..." I hold the drink out to her. "He's buying us a round. And he challenged me to a game of pool."

"What's the wager?" She takes the cup from me, sniffing the contents and sipping it. "Damn, this is smooth."

Because it's a hundred dollars a pour.

I glance over my shoulder at him, watching him approach. "He wins, I tell him my name."

Cora laughs. "Seriously?" She climbs onto the chair and spins the cup around. "I am here for it." She leans forward. "What do you get when he loses?"

I smile at her, having faith in me that I'll beat him. "I haven't decided yet."

"Oh, this is going to be interesting."

"Princess." Magnus advances, giving me my drink.

"I'm sorry, what?" I shake my head. "No."

He reaches forward, twisting a strand of my hair around his finger. "You won't tell me your name, what else should I call you?" He brushes his thumb against my cheek. "It's fitting though. Don't you think?"

"Hardly." I glare at him through my lashes.

He turns to Cora. "Hi, princess's friend. I'm Magnus."

"Cora." She holds up her cup. "Thanks, for this. It's delicious."

"Of course."

I eye the drink in my grasp. "How do I know you didn't roofie this?"

"You don't." He takes it from me, pressing his lips against the rim and sipping it. "But, if I did, we'll be drugged together."

I shudder a sigh at his lush mouth on the glass, wishing it was pressed against my body instead.

"Shall we?" He points to the ready table.

"You in a hurry to get your ass kicked?" I grin at him and wait for his smart-ass reply I know damn well is coming.

"Cocky little shit, aren't you?"

"You scared?" I savor the taste of the bourbon and set the glass next to Cora's before I stride past him and pick up my pool stick.

"Never."

And with that one word, it's like he's saying so much all at once. There's a darkness about him, just hovering under the surface, and I am dying to explore it.

"Go ahead, princess." He walks by me to get his own stick from the wall.

"You're going to regret calling me that," I whisper on my way around him.

"Don't tempt me with a good time." He plucks one from the selection and turns to watch me break.

I get into position, eyeing him for the slightest second before cracking the stick into the cue ball. It makes a thundering sound and sends balls all over the table, but none of them land in a pocket.

*Fuck*. That never happens.

Of course, when I actually need to win, I play a shit game.

I maintain my composure, going over to where Cora sits, and sipping my drink.

"What the hell, J?" she says quiet enough for only me to hear.

"It's fine." Although maybe the booze really is affecting my skills negatively.

Magnus raises an eyebrow at me, a stupid grin on his face like he's eating this up. "I'll go easy on you, princess."

"I wish you wouldn't." Oh wait, did I say that out loud?

He glides over to the side, sinking two solid balls back-to-back without much effort. I study the shape his ink-stained body takes with each move, wishing he'd work me like he is that table.

Magnus takes his time on the third but manages to land it, too, positioning himself perfectly for the fourth. Only, instead of knocking it in, the ball taps the edge of the pocket and bounces away from the hole. That's what he gets for being overly confident.

His jaw tenses but he doesn't give much else away. "Your turn, princess."

His persistence with the pet name is a weak attempt at getting under my skin. It's annoying, just not enough to take away from my desire to beat him.

I analyze my options, playing through them in my mind, and coming up with the best strategy. The safest, most aggressive one I can manage.

Magnus comes up from behind me and places his hand on my waist, leaning down to whisper into my ear. "You need some help?"

I turn to look up at him, his gorgeous face only a breath away from mine. "I could ask you the same thing."

For the smallest second, it's me and him, and no one else. Not the loud music blaring in the background, or the wandering eyes of the drunk people. Not even Cora, who I know is watching us intently from her spot half-boozed up a few feet away. I'm weirdly drawn to him and I can't really explain it.

It's not like me to get hung up on a guy. Let alone three men. In a matter of a few days.

Magnus brushes his lips against my cheek. "Better do your worst, princess." He steps back, giving me space to take my shot.

And that I do.

He thought he would unravel me with his seduction, but all it did was focus me.

I sink the first ball with ease. Then the second. And the third. Each time, flicking my gaze at him. A silent reminder of who's in charge here. I float around the table, making sure to pause and think things through before I act. I pocket the fourth, noting the way he blinks from his spot sitting next to Cora, as if he's finally realizing he may have met his match.

Cora smiles like a proud mother would at watching her child win whatever it is that kids play. Or it could very well be the copious amount of alcohol running through her veins, causing her cheeks to flush and a perma-grin to stick on her face.

I continue to clear my balls, not for a second doubting my ability. "Eightball, corner pocket." It's a bank shot, and a little riskier than I would usually try to manage, but I do it anyway just because I can. The black ball kerplunks into its designated pocket and I hold my breath as I watch the white one get dangerously close to falling into another.

Time slows and I wait for it to stop moving toward my sudden loss.

Magnus leans down and starts blowing on the ball dramatically.

"Hey, that's cheating!" I grab his arm and pull him away.

"You want to talk about cheating?" He raises his brows. "That was some hoodoo shit if I've ever seen it."

"I won fair and square, and you know it. Don't be a sore loser."

Magnus leans against the table and runs his fingers through his hair. Tattoos line the top of his hands and each digit.

I strain to make out what they are, but without him holding still, I can't quite place them.

"I'm telling you, princess. You could make a pretty penny hustling pool."

I point to the sign posted near the sticks, where it clearly states that monetary wagers aren't allowed in here. Only friendly bets, like having to buy someone a beer or telling them their name.

Magnus rolls his eyes. "That doesn't mean shit. Plenty of other places where people exchange wads of cash."

Cora strolls over, staggering between us. "You two, are just...adorable. Here." She shoves both of our drinks into our chests, nearly falling down in the process.

Magnus and I reach out to steady her at the same time.

"Whoa there, lightweight," I tell her.

She leans her head on my shoulder. "I love you, Juney B."

Magnus cocks his head sideways to look at me. "Juney B?"

I take a sip of my bourbon and pat Cora's shoulder. "She's drunk."

"Am not," Cora protests.

"Shh. There, there, sweet thing." I notice a group of girls eyeing the pool table like they want to play. "Hey, let's move her out of the way."

Before I get my arm under her, Magnus takes control and steers her to the high-top we were at.

"I have a car," he says. "I could have my driver get her home."

"Sounds like the start to a horror flick where my best friend gets murdered and I'm the next victim."

"You have trust issues, don't you?"

"That obvious?" I spot the empty pitcher of beer and Cora's equally dry glass. "Dude, did you drink all that yourself?"

She lifts her head, her eyes drooping. "I was thirsty."

It's no wonder she's piss drunk.

"Cor," I steady her to look at me. "Have you eaten today?"

She mumbles something unrecognizable.

"I need to get some food in her system, try to sober her up."

Magnus nods. "Yeah, definitely. Pizza? We could order it from my place, there's a good joint like a block away."

I narrow my gaze at him.

He throws his tatted arms in the air. "Harmless, seriously. Just trying to help. You don't even have to tell me your real name."

I let out a breath. It's not like I don't already know where he lives. And the neighborhood is pretty respectable. What kind of friend would I be if I dropped her off at her parents' house in this condition? And bringing her to my apartment isn't in the cards, either. I wouldn't put it past Carter to try to make his move on her while she was inebriated. Fucking slimeball.

The best option is standing in front of me, six-foot-something, a total dreamboat with baby blue eyes, and that irresistible bad boy aesthetic who's actually a charming sweetheart.

"Fine," I finally say. "But I will shank you if you step out of line." It's not me that I worry about, it's Cora. If something happened to her, I'd never forgive myself.

Me on the other hand—I was born broken; nothing can break me.

"I expect no less from you." Magnus puts his arm around Cora and nudges her off the chair. "Can you walk?"

"Yep." Cora stands up straight, blinking wildly and glancing all around. "Did I hear someone say pizza?" She makes a beeline through a group of people, leaving us behind.

Magnus latches onto my hand, weaving his fingers around mine and tugging me in their wake.

It's like there's a collective gasp from the girls who were hoping to shoot their shot with him tonight. Does he realize he could have had his pick from any of the females, and probably some of the males in this bar? Why fixate on me?

I mean, don't get me wrong, I'm a hot piece of tail, but I'm nothing special in the grand scheme of things.

I follow the two of them out the front door and bask in the fresh air of being outside.

"Cora," Magnus lets go of me and stops her from going the wrong way. "Over here." He guides her gently back in the correct direction, to a waiting blacked-out SUV.

The engine roars to life the second we approach it.

"Uh, this isn't creepy at all." I glance between him and the vehicle. "What, are you in the mafia or something?"

Magnus laughs. "Something like that."

He opens the back door and Cora climbs in without question.

"After you, princess," he extends his hand for me.

I pause in front of him, peering up at his stupid gorgeous face. "I know what I want, for winning that game of pool."

He tucks my hair behind my ear. "Anything."

"Stop calling me princess."

Magnus bunches up his nose like he's wincing. "Anything but *that*."

"What?"

"A car, a house, hell, a trip to the moon, but you're not getting that."

"You're literally the worst." I glare at him.

His lips turn into a grin. "And here you are, getting into an unmarked vehicle with me."

I climb inside. "I've done stupider things."

"Again, I would expect nothing less." Magnus slides in next to me and shuts the door. "Home," he tells the driver hidden behind a sheer wall. "Think she's going to puke?"

I look at the beautiful blonde resting her head against the window. "I hope not."

The sexy man sitting inches from me pulls his phone out of his pocket and pushes a few buttons. "What do you want on your pizza?"

"Pineapple," Cora perks up and announces.

Magnus bobs his head while hovering his finger over the screen. "What else?"

"Pineapple," she says again.

He elbows me, "What do you want?"

"Whatever you're having." I don't mean for it to come out as sexual as it does, but the way his sapphire eyes meet mine, it's enough to make a million erotic thoughts rush through my head at once.

A small part of me thinks he's having the same damn thoughts.

We drive the short distance to the house I delivered food to this morning, only instead of going in the way I did, we go around the back, and enter through a gated area that leads to a garage under his mansion.

Yep, we're definitely about to get murdered. But why go through the trouble of ordering us a late-night meal? Maybe it's a ruse, or some sick game he plays before ending his victims.

Oh well, it was fun while it lasted. I guess if I'm going to die, full of expensive bourbon and greasy pizza, by his hands it doesn't seem like a terrible way to go.

# CHAPTER 6

# *June*

"I'm not going to murder you." Magnus pokes me in the ribs.

"What, you read minds now, too?"

"No, but I read people. And your cards are exposed." He shifts in his seat. "Speaking of, you play poker?"

"Texas hold 'em?"

"Yeah."

I shrug. "A little bit."

"Oh man, I'd love to take you some time. The guys wouldn't know what hit them."

Our SUV finally comes to a complete stop, the doors unlocking once it's in park.

Did he just sort of ask me on a date? In the future? I don't do dates, or the future. As friends, maybe. But nothing more. If he's trying to make plans, I have to keep this strictly platonic. How the hell am I going to do that when he's out here looking like he does?

He even smells sexy, with his cedar cologne and bourbon breath.

Magnus hops out the side and holds out his hand to me. "Princess."

I smack it away and shake my sleeping friend. "Cora, wake up, we're here."

She sucks in a breath and glances around wildly. "Where's here?"

"Magnus' place. He's going to feed and provide us shelter."

"You make it sound like I picked up a pair of feral cats." Magnus waits outside the door for us, his arm resting on the roof, exposing his tattooed skin.

*Friends, June. You can do this.*

My mind immediately goes to the gutter, thinking about stripping that t-shirt over his head and running my fingers down his chest, straight to unbutton his black jeans and revealing what he's working with.

"Or maybe I have." Magnus winks, reminding me about the whole reading people thing he mentioned.

*Whoops.*

"Wait, did someone say something about pizza?" Cora fumbles for the handle of her door, popping it open and stumbling out.

"Do you always bring home strays?" I ask Magnus while climbing out after Cora.

"Not usually, it's actually against the HOA rules." He steadies Cora and points her toward the entrance to his house.

*Rules were meant to be broken.*

Magnus places his hand on my lower back, guiding me, too. "Rules were meant to be broken."

A chill runs up my spine, both from his touch and the repetition of the exact words I spoke in my head only seconds prior to his.

"Holy shit." Cora's mouth drops open and she turns to Magnus. "I think we're in the wrong house."

He chuckles and leads us through a hallway and into a massive open area. A gigantic living room, with a couch bigger than anything I've ever seen, and a flat-screen to match the overall theme of go-big-or-go-home.

I notice his nervous energy, almost like he's embarrassed, and become more in tune with that than the enormousness of his place.

"This kitchen is..." Cora runs her finger along a giant slab of granite, or marble, I can't really tell the difference. "Any housewife's dream."

"Or househusband," I add.

"House-partner." She spins around to take it all in.

Magnus pauses next to me, his arm hovering barely against mine.

I lean into him gently and glance up at his face, all the alcohol from the night making my head spin just a bit.

Damn is he pretty, though. Like in a photoshopped kind of way.

A buzzer dings somewhere in the distance, snapping me back to reality.

"Be right back." Magnus points to Cora. "Don't let her touch any of the guns."

"Guns?" I call out after him.

Cora strolls over and plops down on one of the stools tucked under the counter. She leans her head on her hand and pats the spot next to her.

I join her, tucking her wild waves behind her ears. "You're a mess."

She smiles a toothless grin. "I know."

"What are we doing here, Cor?"

"Listen, J, if I wasn't this drunk, I'd probably be asking the same thing. But I am, and it seems like a pretty okay place to be." She pivots at the waist and looks around. "Please marry this man."

"Money isn't everything, Cora."

She turns to me, her gaze locked onto mine. "You're right, it isn't. But have you seen him? Heard him talk? Watch the way he walks? Have you noticed how damn sweet on you he is? He's a fucking gentleman, J. Much better than all the other tool-bags you spend your time with."

"Touché."

"Yeah, yeah, you don't do relationships. Whatever. You're a lunatic if you don't at least give him a shot."

Footsteps tread against the hardwood floor, Magnus appearing a second later with two boxes in his grasp.

"That smells heavenly." Cora nearly drools at the sight of food.

"My ears were burning." Magnus plants them on the counter and goes across the kitchen to get a few plates.

"Can I help?" I offer.

"I've got it, princess. Just sit there and look pretty." He opens the door to the large refrigerator. "Water, tea, lemonade…" Magnus glances at Cora then at me. "Beer?"

"Water is fine, for both of us, thank you."

Cora side-eyes me but is more focused on pulling a slice of pizza out of the box than disagreeing with me about the drink I chose for her.

That girl needs to hydrate, not consume any more booze.

He slides the bottles across the counter toward me and claims the seat to my right. He grabs a plate, and points to the two open boxes. "Which do you want?"

"I can get my own."

"I'm aware. Would you like to decide, or should I?"

I narrow my gaze at him and reach for my plate.

"Both it is." Magnus places the largest pieces from both boxes on my plate and puts it in front of me. "That wasn't so hard."

"She hates when people do stuff for her," Cora says with a mouthful of pineapple pizza.

"I've noticed." Magnus gives himself a slice of each and wipes his fingers on a napkin. "You going to eat, or do you want me to feed you, too?"

I sigh and take a bite, doing my best to hide the fact that it's fucking delicious.

"Good girl."

The same thing the mystery guy had said to me in the bathroom before he screwed me senseless.

What the hell is going on? Why are they all weirdly reminding me of each other? And why do I like it so much?

This isn't going to end well. Not for me. Not for them. Not for any of us.

We eat in silence for a few minutes, the only sound aside from our chewing is faint music playing throughout the house.

"What is that?" I point to the ceiling. "That noise."

Magnus swallows the bite in his mouth before speaking. "Instrumental. Mostly piano. You want me to change it?" He reaches for his phone.

I stop him, my hand resting on his arm. "No. It's nice."

"Peaceful." His blue gaze meets mine.

"Yeah."

Cora clears her throat. "I think I'll leave you two to bone, now." She hooks her thumb toward the living room. "Can I crash on the couch?"

Magnus stands, his chair scooting out behind him. "No, you can stay in one of the guest rooms."

Of course, he would have *multiple*.

"I'll be right back, princess."

It's starting to sound more like the actual name he has for me than it does a way to get under my skin. I should just tell him already, but that would mean giving him another piece of me that I can't take back. I'm not sure if I'm ready to do that.

It's not that I have anything against admitting it to him. I mean, he already knows one of the places I work, which would make it relatively easy to locate me if he wanted to. I guess without much effort, I try to make it harder for people to find me once we've run our course. The little information I give them, the less likely they are to find my social media or track me down and attempt to stick around. I don't do long-term. I never have. And going through the trouble of blocking people repeatedly is exhausting when they refuse to stick to just being friends.

Ladies, if you want a boyfriend, act like you don't. Then they won't leave you alone.

It's some kind of weird science. They want what they can't have.

I guarantee the second I switched things up, they'd all run for the hills. I'm doing everyone involved a favor by keeping myself out of their reach.

"Miss me?" Magnus slides into the seat beside me again.

"You wish." I sip the water he had given me, glancing at the unfamiliar bottle, and setting it down.

Not at all surprised that he has fancy H2O.

"Cora is all set up, in *heaven* she says." He even uses air quotes to detail the word.

"She doesn't come from much, so she gets excited about shiny objects easily." Cora's only saving grace is that her parents are still together, meaning some stability in her life, despite their financial situation.

Her mom is a nurse, who works crazy hours at the hospital, and her dad recently got laid off from his corporate job doing who-knows-what. Their house is high stress, but it's still completely different than anything I've known.

My mom died when I was two, leaving my dad a blubbering mess, drowning his sorrows in whatever vice he could get his hands on. He wasn't a mean drunk, just a neglectful one. Home was never something I looked forward to going to, which is funny considering my current living situation. I must be drawn to unsafe and volatile environments.

"Me, too," Magnus says quietly. "I grew up without money, so this," he points his slice of pizza at the room around us, "is strange to me. It's nice and all, don't get me wrong. But it's weirdly uncomfortable, if that makes sense."

"Yeah, it does." I push my plate forward, resting my napkin on top of it. I want to ask questions, figure out how he evolved into this version of himself, where his abundance came from. But I keep my mouth shut because that's how feelings get caught. The more layers you peel back and expose, the higher the chance of connecting with someone on a deeper level.

The only way to avoid that is to keep those walls up and refuse to ever let them down.

"What about you?"

Shit, I knew this was coming, the whole him wanting to get to know me thing.

"What about me?"

"Why do you do that?" His question surprises me.

"Do what?"

"Deflect."

"I don't," I lie, shifting a bit in my seat.

He rubs his finger under his chin. "You forget I can see straight through you."

"Oh? Then tell me, what do you see?" I cross my arms over my chest.

"That, right there." He points to what I just did. "A tell that you're worried I might actually be on to something here. You're blocking me out, even if it's subconscious."

I unfold and drop them onto my lap. "Am not."

He stares into my eyes like he's looking directly into my soul. "You have a tortured past that's followed you into your present. You don't trust anyone; you barely trust yourself. If I had to guess, I'd say because someone left you. Someone you opened up to. And that's why you refuse to ever let yourself feel that way again. It hurt. And you'd do anything to never experience that again. Even if that means keeping everyone at a distance and pushing people away."

My heart pounds wildly in my chest and I will it to stay still and not give him any more insight than he's already managed to figure out.

"I don't fault you for that." His features and voice soften. "It's commendable, really. To have the willpower to build and maintain those walls."

I don't say anything. Too afraid that would confirm what he's saying to be true. If I didn't know better, I'd wager he was speaking from experience, but maybe he's really that good at reading people.

"Not everyone will leave. Not everyone is a bad person."

"It's not you I'm worried about." I hate that I don't catch the words before they leave my mouth.

"Oh, princess. You are far from being bad."

Little does he know I've never been good a day in my life.

"You're wrong," I tell him with little conviction.

"Prove it, then."

How can I prove something that he is absolutely spot on about? Why should I let this complete stranger in when I have refused time and time again with everyone else?

"Or don't, that's okay, too." Magnus breaks eye contact, taking with him a little piece of me I didn't authorize.

What was that? The fleeting possibility of a connection hanging in the balance?

I clench my jaw, hating myself for making this so fucking difficult.

"June." I pause. "My name is June."

Magnus turns to me, bringing his hand with him to trace the side of my face.

*Fuck, what have I done?*

"June." He tries it out on his tongue. "It's nice to finally meet you." He grazes his thumb against my bottom lip, tugging it softly. "I want to kiss you."

I lean forward, not wasting any more time, and press my mouth to his. Something I wanted to do the second I saw him and only intensified with each passing moment.

Screw being friends, I want this man and I want him now.

He wraps his strong hands around my cheeks and deepens the kiss to match my intensity.

I climb off my chair and right onto his lap, straddling him and feeling just how badly he wants me, too. I sink into him, grinding my body against his growing member.

He moans into my mouth and pulls me closer, bringing his fingertips down my back and up under my shirt, his skin sparking every nerve ending in my body on fire.

I reach the hem of his tee, gripping and pulling it over his head in one swoop, only breaking contact long enough to strip him of his top, and notice that the ink covers his entire torso, too.

"Hold on, princess." Magnus stands, backing us away from the counter, only for him to drop me on the edge of it and stay between my legs.

Our tongues dance in a frenzy of lust and passion.

He makes a path from my lips, down my neck, nibbling on my collarbone and tugging my shirt down to get a better vantage point on my nipple, freeing it before putting it between his teeth. Magnus sucks on the sensitive area and runs his hand up my thigh, dragging his thumb under the fabric of my shorts.

My body comes to life in a way I wasn't sure I'd experience again after my last sexual encounter with the mystery man from the bar.

I unbutton my bottoms, frantic to feel him touch me with less clothes on.

"Lay back." He grips the sides, pulling them down and over my ass along with my panties, leaving me completely exposed on the cold expensive stone.

I sit up on my elbows and watch him lick from my knee to where the faded line of last year's tan barely remains.

"This," he tugs on the triangle-shaped section of hair I left growing wild. "Is sexy." Magnus swirls his tongue around it and slides over my clit.

My head and my eyes roll back at the pleasure, a moan escaping my lips.

He's just getting started, and I don't know how much more of this I can take. I want him inside me like yesterday.

"Magnus," I breathe.

"Yes, princess?" He widens his tongue and dips it along my slit, taking his time to taste every bit of me that he can.

"Fuck me."

"Patience, princess." Magnus continues to lick and suck my entrance, even bringing a tattooed digit up to tease me that much more.

I rock my body against the single finger, wishing like hell it would turn into his cock, which must be throbbing with want by now. I ride the wave of pleasure that builds, desperate for release.

But it doesn't come, and neither do I.

Magnus withdraws his hand and face. "Flip over." He licks his lips, my desire all on him.

I comply, turning on the hard surface and bringing myself into the doggy position.

He grips my ass, running his thumb along the edge of my crease. "You taste better than I imagined you would." He brings his mouth back down, hovering over my pussy and flicking his tongue against me.

I quiver at his touch, but he keeps going, sending me climbing that mountain once again.

This time, he slides not one, but two fingers inside of me, arching and rocking them back and forth.

I tighten around him, the end of this beautiful torment so very near.

But like he can sense the very moment of no return, he stops his movement and steps away. I'm about to protest, to get mad, and finish myself off, but I hear him unbuttoning his pants, and positioning a condom in place.

What a shame I didn't get to lick and suck and tease him the way he did me. Hell, I didn't even get a look.

"Off," he tells me.

I plant my hands firmly and climb down from the counter, my back still to him.

Magnus swipes the hair away from my neck, kissing the spot he cleared and stroking his cock against my ass.

I reach around, dying to grant it entry to my soaked hole. "Give it to me."

He presses on my back, leaning me forward to gain a better access point. Magnus dips his two fingers into my slit again and then replaces them with his sheathed member, filling me entirely without getting the whole thing in.

"Fuck," I moan at the fullness.

He rocks himself slowly to stretch me further.

Pain and pleasure dance dangerously between us.

We stay this way for a little while, a quiet tempo of labored breaths and soft whimpers. We're barely moving and yet I continue to climb the pleasure mountain once more.

I chase it, hoping he doesn't notice and stop me from climaxing, but he's more in tune with me than I realize, pulling out and flipping me around to face him.

"It's not time yet," he says against my lips. Magnus kisses me and rubs himself along me.

"You are so frustrating."

He smiles, guiding our puzzle pieces back in place. "Now you know how you make me feel."

I arch myself toward him and let him fill me.

His phone buzzes on the counter and he glances down at it. "Fuck." Magnus wraps his arm around my waist, picking me up with his dick still inside me, and carrying me out of the kitchen and up the stairs.

"Are you married?" My first thought blurts out of my mouth.

He shakes his head. "No. It's a work thing." His eyes meet mine. "I swear."

And without another doubt, I believe him. Which is fucking strange.

Magnus presses his lips to mine and shoves us through the threshold of a room. "I wanted to make this last all night." He lowers me onto a king-sized bed in what must be his bedroom. "I wanted to make you beg for it."

Aren't I already?

He pins my hands above my head with one of his, thrusting himself in and out of me. Magnus reaches up under my shirt, taking my nipple between his fingers and twisting it.

"Please," I whimper.

He fucks me harder, deeper, bringing his face down to kiss me.

He releases me and I immediately drag my nails across his back, digging them in and pulling him closer. I widen my legs, an open invitation to give me all he has.

He grinds right up against my clit, the vibration of his body taking me higher and higher.

"I'm close," I tell him, almost like I'm seeking the approval he's yet to give me. Why I want it this time, I'll never understand. Maybe I like the game he's playing.

"I know." Magnus wraps his hand around my neck, applying the softest pressure and then tilting my chin to look up at him. "Come for me."

And with those three words and his steady rhythm, I climax harder than I ever have before, a moan escaping me as my pussy pulsates around him with the sweet release.

"Good girl." He keeps his eyes trained on me, lengthening his pace and following my lead into his own orgasm. Magnus throbs inside of me, intensifying and prolonging my pleasure until we ride the wave to the end together.

I drop my arms to the side and relax into his bed. "Fuck, that was…"

Magnus grins and plants his lips on my sweaty cheek. "Incredible."

"To say the least."

"And to think, that could have happened this morning." He climbs off me and strolls across the room and into another.

I notice the sound of a faucet being turned and water running.

Magnus pops his beautiful head out of the doorway. "You want a shower?"

I hop off the bed and go over to him. "Is this your subtle way of telling me I stink?"

"Far from it, princess." He kisses my nose. "I have to run out, to do a work thing. Thought I better not go reeking of sex."

"Oh right, you're in the mafia."

"Or something." Magnus winks and goes over to the closet in the corner to grab towels. "There are clothes in here. Take whatever you want. The bed is comfortable, and if you can't sleep, the nightstand on the right side has a remote that will bring out the TV."

I take in the large bathroom with a soaking tub and a shower big enough for a group of people to fit into. "Bring it out? Where is it?"

"Hidden." Magnus steps under the running water.

"Wait, are you really leaving?" I strip the rest of my clothes off and follow him in.

He tilts his head back, letting the stream crash over his face and glisten along his tattooed skin. "I won't be long."

"Aren't you worried I'll rob you?"

Magnus chuckles and grabs my hand, pulling me closer to him. "That's the least of my worries." He presses our lips together briefly and rests his forehead against mine. "I do have to hurry though." He finishes rinsing off and kisses me one last time before stepping out and drying himself off.

I crank the temperature up hotter and sit on the tiled floor, letting the water cascade over me. Cora was right, this is heaven, especially compared to the hell of a shower I had this morning. The muscles in my body relax and I savor the momentary relief they bring. This day may have started terribly, but at least it's ending well.

And tomorrow will be another shit storm, considering I only have a little over half of the money I needed to make for rent. I'll have to woman-up and ask Cora if she'd be willing to loan me the rest until I can pay her back. I wanted to avoid it at all costs, because then I'd have to either admit I'm bad with my finances or tell her that Carter stole the cash I had set aside. I don't really have any other options available though, unless I find someone who wants to buy a kidney in the next twelve hours.

"Princess." Magnus pokes his head into my steamy oasis. "Help yourself to whatever you need, in here, but don't wander too much. I'm not hiding anything, but...well...consider it my occupational hazards."

"I have no idea what that means," I tell him. "But don't worry. I'm probably going to pass out when I'm done here."

"Okay," he says with a sad smile. "I'll join you soon."

I stay in the water for longer than I probably should, but there's no knowing when I'll have another chance to bathe like a queen, so I bask in the glorious opportunity. I even use his fancy products, shampooing and conditioning my hair with something that smells like the angels themselves created it.

I dry off on a towel that must have been made of fluffy clouds, and moisturize with the lotion I found in the first drawer in his vanity. I peek into the closet he told me to get clothes from, my eyes widening at the size of it. I'm pretty sure my entire bedroom at my apartment could fit in there.

Rows of white, black, and grey tee-shirts hang on one side, with various shades of dark jeans under them. I open a drawer to find his boxers, and another with socks. It's the next one where I locate a few pairs of sweatpants. I pull the first from the top and slip into them, grabbing a white shirt and putting that on, too. Hanging my towel on a hook in the bathroom, I finish and shut the light off.

His room is cozy, in a dark and neat kind of way. Lots of similar colors to those in his closet, but with a splash of green from a plant here or there. I climb into his plush bed and wiggle myself under the covers, only to realize I forgot to turn the bedroom light off. I wouldn't be surprised if he has some nearby button or clapper for that, but considering he isn't here to ask, I get up and settle for the switch near the door.

It only takes a second before I'm back in bed, letting out a breath and sinking into the high thread count sheets.

---

I fell asleep hard, without much effort, only waking once when a warm body snuggled in behind me.

He was a little wet, like he had taken another shower, but because I was out of it, I didn't put too much thought into it, just melted into his embrace and conked back out.

I squint through my achy eyes and feel around the now empty bed. Light pours in through the window, telling me that it must be morning, or afternoon for all I know. I reach for my phone, but it's not there. I must have left it in the kitchen during our sex-capades.

Is Cora awake? She must be wondering where the hell we are, given how wasted she was last night. With the headache I have, she's probably in worse shape than I am.

I sit up on my elbows and blink a few times to clear up my vision, settling my sights on the tall glass of water sitting on the nightstand with a couple pills. I scoot over and down them both gratefully, and sigh at how thoughtful this seemingly hard exterior man is. I guess that saying really is true, don't judge a book by its cover. Graphic designers and marketing teams might think otherwise.

I snatch the small fuzzy throw blanket on the edge of the bed and put it over my shoulders, making my way to the door. I crack it open as quietly as possible, and peek out into the hallway.

For all I know, she could be behind any of those closed doors, and the one thing Magnus told me was not to wander around. I at least owe him that courtesy after how generous he's been to me.

I step into the hallway and try not to make a sound. If I listen carefully, maybe I can hear her rustling around and find her that way. Perhaps she's even waiting for me downstairs where we had pizza last night. I'll check there first prior to playing detective up here.

I tiptoe across the rug-covered floor and stop near the steps when I hear chatter float up to me.

"You have to stop ordering so much take out," a man, definitely not Magnus, says.

"Dude, it's fine. I have it under control. I'm not an idiot," Magnus tells the person.

"Do you?" The guy sighs. "These are trying times, Bryant. You're going to get yourself killed."

Bryant? Killed? Who and what the fuck are they talking about? He's going to get offed by a delivery person?

I lean against the wall, clinging to the blanket wrapped around me. I try to listen closely and figure out what it is I've stepped into.

"Hayes agrees with me, you're being careless."

Who's Hayes? And Bryant? And the dude who seems to be in charge? And why does his voice sound familiar?

I rack my brain, trying to place it to a memory to figure out how I know it. I deal with so many people daily that it could literally be anyone.

My foot slips and I don't catch it in time before it thuds against the step.

"What the fuck was that?"

Bryant speaks up. "It's fine, don't wor—"

A golden blond-haired man appears around the corner in a flash, his hands out in front of him, a gun pointed directly at me. His expression shifts from a tight hardness to a softer look with bunched brows. "June?"

"Don't shoot her." Magnus rushes into my line of sight, skidding to a stop beside the man with a gun. "Wait, you know her?" He flits his gaze between us.

"Who's June?" The other man calls out on his way over.

"Coen?" I say to the man who I thought I once knew.

"Coen?" Magnus continues to feign confusion.

The third guy finally steps around the corner and my stomach drops at the sight of him.

"Fuck." The word slips out of both of our mouths at the same time.

It's him, the mystery man from the bar, who fucked me so good I couldn't think straight for days, standing next to the tattooed hottie who kept me on the brink of orgasm last night, and the boy who stole my first kiss many, many years ago.

I shift my gaze to each of them and pinch my arm, hoping it'll wake me up from this strange fucking nightmare I just stepped into.

But it doesn't work, and I'm left here, gawking at these three completely gorgeous men who appear to be riddled with the same level of bewilderment I'm experiencing.

To add to it, a door creaks open behind me, sending Coen's arms a little higher to aim at his new target.

"June?" Cora whispers.

"Down here," I respond while stepping forward to place my hand on Coen's wrist. "Please don't shoot my best friend."

His blue eyes lock onto mine and it's like he's desperately trying to silently communicate to me, to tell me what the fuck is happening here. But like I had sensed it the other night when I ran into him, he's changed. Both of us have. The gun in his possession, confirming that the sweet boy from my childhood is no more.

Coen tucks the thing into his waistband before Cora steps into view, joining us for this awkward reunion of sorts.

"I'm dying for some coffee," she says.

Oh, what choice words to use, Cor.

"Yeah, let's do that." I weave my fingers around hers, thankful for the escape from whatever reality this is.

"Hi." She smiles and nods politely at the men, she has no idea who they are.

I can't exactly admit I know them any better either. Other than the fact that I've slept with two of them and made out with the other. Okay, maybe I know them a tiny bit.

"We have coffee," Magnus offers.

"June," Cora whines. "Let's stay." She drops my hand and holds it out to Coen. "Hi, I'm Cora."

Coen takes a breath in, glancing at me and the rest of the guys. "Coen Hayes."

"And you are," she turns to the mystery man with the sexy as hell salt and pepper beard.

His jaw tenses and if I'm certain of anything, it's that he wishes she would just disappear.

Magnus smacks his shoulder. "Ah, come on Dom, don't be rude."

Dom?

"Bryant," Dom sneers at Magnus.

"I thought your name was Magnus," I add.

Magnus winks at me. "Magnus *Bryant.*"

Bryant. Hayes. I get it now. This whole time, they were using their last names.

"Dominic." Mr. McDreamy shakes Cora's hand and focuses on me. "*June*, a word please."

My memory flashes to that night in the bar. The blood splatter all over his face. The danger, the adrenaline spiking through my veins that fueled me to step forward and boldly press myself against him in what was probably the best decision I've ever made.

But that was then, and this is now. And whatever this is, is way more than I bargained for.

"Sorry," I mutter, latching onto Cora again. "We have to go...do a thing." I slide the blanket off my shoulders and hand it to Magnus. "Thanks, um, for...you know."

"Wait, don't you—" Magnus calls out as I pull Cora around him and make our way into the large open main floor.

I spot my phone, snatching it and looking for a way out. "Where the fuck is the door?"

"Uh, J, are you okay?" Cora follows me anyway.

The men mumble things, but I don't bother to try to listen to them. The only thing on my mind is getting the hell out of here.

I recall Magnus disappearing to grab the pizza last night, and decide to go that direction, sighing when I spot the front door. The same one he stood and offered to share the take-out I had delivered to him.

I pull Cora with me through the massive entrance, hurrying down the steps and stopping at that stupid gate. "Fuck." I turn back to the house but before I can ask to be granted exit, the thing buzzes and cracks open.

I don't know which of them let me out, but I'm fucking grateful for it either way.

For a second, I thought I was going to have to go in there and have the most awkward conversation of my life.

"Dude, I am way too hungover to be rushing around like this." Cora wiggles out of my grasp once we round the corner and are out of sight. "What the hell is going on? And what are you wearing?"

I glance down at the stolen sweatpants and t-shirt, laughing at how baggy they are on me. "I'll explain everything, just come on."

Hopefully, the walk to Bram's will give me enough time to figure it out myself.

# CHAPTER 7

# *Magnus*

"What the fuck was that?" Dom raises his voice at me.

Which is never a good sign. Actually, with Dom, the raising or lowering are both equally bad news. Luckily for me, we have a strict *no killing each other* rule in the house.

Once I step outside though, that's another story.

"Um, that was June." I walk away from him and into the kitchen to refill my coffee. "And her friend Cora." I stir some sugar into my cup. "Nice girl."

"You let them *into* the house?" Dom follows me in, Hayes right on his tail, shadowing him in the weirdest way.

He's got a *I want to kill you, too* look on his face that's creeping me out a bit.

"It's fine. Everything is fine. Why are you freaking out?" I bring the cup to my lips and take a drink.

Dominic's big brown eyes widen. "Did you forget we're in the middle of a fucking war?"

"A *fucking* war, that sounds fun."

He exhales, clearly not appreciating my humor, but how could he with that stick shoved so far up his ass.

"Yes, Dom, I get it. But seriously, I was careful." I point to Hayes. "How do you know her?"

And thank fuck he did, because I wouldn't have put it past him to put a bullet in her and her friend just for being in our home. I should have probably thought that one through, but I didn't expect them to arrive prior to her leaving, especially after the mess we made last night. Me and the guys, not me and June. That clean-up should have taken longer than it did. Our crew is getting it down to a science with the latest increase in casualties.

If I thought June had trust issues, Hayes would give her a run for her money. Sometimes I wonder if I'll wake up to him strangling me to death.

Psycho little shit.

Which is hilarious, because everyone thinks *I'm* the intimidating one, having most of my body covered in tattoos. Nope, it's the sweet, pretty surfer boy you have to worry about. Don't underestimate any of us though, our body counts are nothing to be proud of. But in our line of work, it comes with the territory. We've all seen more death than the inside of a funeral home.

Coen shifts his attention to Dom. "You seemed pretty familiar with her, too."

Great, the girl of my dreams has already caught the attention of these two knuckleheads.

Which isn't all that surprising, given we share an exquisite taste for the finer things in life.

"It doesn't matter." Dom places his hand on the counter. "I forbid any of us from seeing her again."

I set my mug down and do my best to settle the rage building inside of me. "You can't do that."

Dom flares his nostrils. "I just did."

I shrug, trying to make light of the situation. "Well, I override your order."

He tilts his head and stares at me. "Hayes."

"Yes?"

Obedient lap dog, that one.

"If Bryant here so much as reaches out to June, I want you to put a bullet in her head." Dom doesn't take his eyes off me in his attempt to confirm just how serious he is. "None of us, and I repeat *none*, are to have any contact with her." He turns to Hayes with that same intense look. "That goes for you, too." He runs his hand through his hair, which is something he only does when his emotions are heightened. "Otherwise, that girl will be the end of us."

But the thing about me, why they keep me around—aside from my handsome exterior, obviously—is because I can read people, and Dom...he's fucking bluffing.

Whatever his experience with June is, he wants her as bad as Coen and I both do.

He's not wrong though, she very well could be the end of us.

Dom shoves a pizza box across the counter toward me. "And clean this fucking mess up."

My gaze settles on the edge of the counter, where I pressed my face into her warm, tight, decadent pussy and tasted her sweet lust. If I would have known how short-lived that moment would have been, I would have stopped and savored her even more.

Hayes appears at my side, his eyes boring into me. "Did you fuck her?"

Oh, did I ever. And what I wouldn't give to do it again. And again. And again.

If I keeled over with my cock buried inside her, I'd die a happy man.

"I'd never kiss and tell." I reach for the box, but he grabs my wrist, turning it over and yanking me toward him.

"So help me god, I will—"

Dom steps between us, practically sandwiching himself in the small space. "Enough."

Hayes, with his murderous stare, releases me.

"See. You're proving my point right here." Dom plants his palm on both of our chests and pushes us away from one another. "This is pathetic, over a girl, really?"

He knows damn well this isn't *any* girl. It's *the* girl.

I knew it the second I saw her, my heart practically leaping out of my chest to get closer to her. And it was confirmed that evening, watching her across the bar, simply existing. I wanted her. But more importantly, I needed her, like she was some lost limb, a piece of me that I could no longer live without. That I didn't know I required until she stepped into my path. I could sense her soul—the darkness and the light dancing painfully as one, matching mine.

Love at first sight is a foolish sentiment until you experience it yourself. The way our lips melded perfectly together has me convinced I've kissed them in another life. That they belonged to me. And I would stop at nothing to make them mine once again.

Nothing will prevent that from happening.

Not Dominic. Not Hayes. Not a goddamn war.

---

We ride in silence to a warehouse on the outskirts of town. Dom in the front with the driver, me and Hayes on separate ends of the back seat, both peering out the window in an attempt to not have to look at each other.

I lean forward to readjust the pistol strapped to my ankle, one of the few weapons strategically placed around my body. A person can never be too prepared in times like these.

Our mission should be simple—interrogate and eliminate.

In a typical situation like this, we wouldn't *all* need to be present. But with the war we're currently waging, the only people we can really count on are each other.

Funny, considering the budding tension between us.

Hayes and I will stand guard, and Dom will have a chat with the rival member. Once he's sure he's got all he can get out of him, we finish the job and have a clean-up crew come in.

Easy peasy. Same shit different day.

Our main goal is to gain input on Beckett's attempt to claim control over our organization in our quest to eliminate him completely.

Why don't we just kill him, you might ask?

The exact reason he doesn't off us. We're smart. We've all been around the block long enough to have protection wider than what you see on the surface and we know how to wiggle around the grey areas and stay safe. There's this unspoken agreement about public executions, too, meaning waltzing up into a bar and shooting each other is off-limits.

We're ruthless, but we have some level of decency.

We have cops in our pockets and enough power to evade most trouble, except for a few things.

That's where the balance of our little trio comes in handy. I read people, and being able to suss out threats comes naturally to me. Hayes is strategy and lead of security, always keeping us in the loop on the latest and greatest new weaponry. And Dom, he's the brains of the entire operation, the level-headed one that terrifies every person he walks past because of his constant resting bitch face and the stories of how brutal he is.

We're a team, but Dom typically calls the shots, making him the one in charge. And to be honest, that's fine with me. I don't want that type of responsibility. Nor would I have any clue what the fuck to do with it if I did. Although, him attempting to tell me who I can date might be stepping on my toes a bit.

Since knowing either of these guys, which has been a long time, none of us have had a relationship longer than a few wild nights in the sack. Up until now, that's been working well. There's been no room for anything more. Our lifestyles are dangerous and to bring someone into that would be selfish. But what if for once I want to be greedy.

Am I a fool for desiring a human connection that lasts more than a quick fuck?

With the uncertainty of this war we're in, I don't want to meet my maker without having pursued the aching in my chest to be with this woman.

But what if chasing this phantom feeling ends up bringing her into something she can't escape, and she meets a fate so many others have fallen to?

Maybe I should listen to Dom. Stay away. If not for me, but to keep her out of harm's way. If I care about her the way I think I do, I owe her that.

Will Dom and Coen both be able to keep their distance though?

Our driver pulls into a narrow section between the industrial buildings behind a modest four-door sedan and cuts the engine.

Coen and I hop out of the vehicle and draw our guns.

He points his weapon toward the side. "You check in, I'll check out."

I nod and go right to work on my task. One thing is for sure, we're all damn good at playing our parts, even if there is shit going on between us. That's how we've managed to advance ourselves the way we have and why we will win this war and gain control of the west coast sector. Staying alive is just an added bonus. Or a curse, depending on what way you look at it.

I keep one hand on my weapon and use the other to open the door to the building we've arrived at.

Two pistols greet me, trained right at my chest.

"Just you three?" I enter, not giving too much attention to the guns. I've had enough of them pointed at me to not sweat like most people would. It's not like they're a threat anyway; they're only doing their job.

"Yes, sir," the taller one with a shaky hand says.

*Nerves.* It's what's going to get kids like him killed over.

He doesn't appear much over the age of twenty, and clearly in over his head on his choice of occupation.

Most of us are, in the beginning. But then the weak are thinned out, either by a bullet in the head, a knife in the back, or simply biting off more than you could chew and crawling home with your tail tucked between your legs. That's when the true colors are shown, and you commit yourself for life, or hope like hell you can make a clean exit.

These two guarding our hostage look like they're still in the trial period of figuring out which direction they'll take.

I do a quick, but thorough sweep of the contents of the building, checking behind containers and in any potential hiding spots. All points of entry are sealed, aside from the unlocked door I came in moments prior. I steady my gaze on the man tied to the chair, the single bulb above him swinging gently and casting a glow around the bloodied area.

His eyes focus on me, the vessels in them broken. His brow is split open and seeping a steady trickle of red that has dripped down the side of his face.

I approach and verify his restraints are tight.

The man sucks in a breath and attempts to spit on me, but I shift my body and avoid his pathetic effort, the gob landing on the concrete floor near my shoe.

A triple knock sounds on the metal side of the building—a signal from Coen that the coast is clear.

I walk a few feet over, indicating from my end that we're good to go, too.

"You're excused," I tell the guards, noting the way the one stays quiet and avoids eye contact with me.

It could very well be nothing but intimidation, but there's *something* off about him.

"You," I point at him.

He stops and glances from his co-worker to me. "Yes?"

It's a damn good thing he's talking to me and not Dom or Coen. The lack of using the term *sir* would have been enough to end him right there. I'm all for respect, but those two are a bit extreme with their demands. This kid could easily be nervous and forget the formality of ranks.

I stroll over, stopping only a foot away. "Your name?"

"Frankie."

The taller guy clears his throat and nudges him, his eyes bulging a bit as if he's trying to communicate via telepathy.

"Oh, Frankie, *sir*. Sorry." He blushes, something anyone else would deem embarrassment, but to me, it's different. Almost like he's faking the shame to cover his ass.

The door creaks open and I glance behind me to spot Coen and Dom making their way inside. Coen with his gun in hand, trained forward but low, ready to strike at a slight notice. Dom with his resting bitch face intact, practically gliding across the floor. That dude is deadly, but with an elegant grace.

"Leave," Dom tells all of us. He pulls a shiny pair of brass knuckles out of his pocket and slides them in place.

I focus back on Frankie, my internal meter scanning him once more.

He takes Dom's demand as a saving grace from whatever I was going to ask him next and goes straight toward the door.

Coen and I follow them out, watching them intently while they climb into their burgundy car and drive away.

"What was that all about?" Coen asks me.

"I'm not sure. Had a weird vibe." One that I couldn't quite pinpoint, especially with my shortened interrogation.

But we have more pressing issues at hand, and Dom needs to do his own questioning if we want to get in and out of here without one of Beckett's teams coming after us. Beckett doesn't exactly take kindly to us kidnapping and torturing his men, but we do what we have to do to advance the likelihood of our win. These aren't really the type of situations you can dawdle in.

"Should we call it?" Coen's gaze skims the close proximity.

"We should be fine."

"Should?"

"I don't fucking know, man. Christ. It was a *vibe* for fucks sake."

"Isn't that your specialty? To recognize threats."

It could be very possible that I'm off my game. The tension between us boiling up and over into my professional life. The fact that I can't get June off my mind is not helping one bit at all. Separating the idea of her moaning my name and identifying if a couple of nervous kids are a risk or not is more difficult than I thought it would be.

I hate when Dom is actually right about shit.

Hardly any time has passed at all and I'm already slipping up at work.

A work that consumes my entire life and could easily determine if I live to see another day.

"It's nothing we can't handle." I straighten my posture and keep my eyes trained around us. My hand eagerly rests against my gun.

A scream pierces through the building and out to us.

Dom doing what he's best at, inflicting pain on people. It's no wonder he's a fucking natural in our professional world. He was bred to take control, to lead, to dominate. Half the time though, the dude really just needs a hug. He puts up a hell of a front, but he's as broken as the rest of us. Unlike everyone else, I notice it, given my specific expertise. He'd never admit it, and I'd never bring it up. He might have a hidden soft side, but I'm not the one to go poking around on that one.

Coen glances over at me out of the corner of his eye. "You going to listen to him?"

"The fuck you talking about?" Although I know exactly what he means.

Coen exhales. "Don't make me say her name. Not here."

There's a piece to the puzzle I'm missing. A concern for her safety unlike anything I've ever seen from Coen. On the outside, he's the sweet and innocent one, but at the end of the day, he's probably the deadliest out of us. The sleeper that everyone underestimates. Which makes him a great asset and one hell of a flight risk.

"Why does it matter?" I'm well aware he cares but I want to hear it from him.

"Because I don't want to have to kill her."

"You won't."

"You don't know that."

"I do."

"What makes you so fucking sure?" His jaw clenches, continuing to give away all his raging emotions.

Another scream from inside the building, then Dominic's low laughter.

That sick fuck is enjoying himself, which in turn will hopefully reduce the stress at home.

"You already gave yourself away. A dozen times. I think you forget who you're talking to right now. Even the simple statement of, *I don't want to have to kill her.* When the fuck do you ever not *want* to kill someone?"

Coen's nostrils flare, and for a second, I worry he'll shoot me just to end this conversation, but he keeps his arm lowered, his finger off the trigger.

I shouldn't, but I continue. "You won't hurt her, and neither will Dom."

"Stay away from her."

"I'm not going to hurt her either."

"That's not what I said. I said to stay away from her."

"Yeah, I heard you the first time." I turn to face him. "But why? Who is she to you?"

"It's none of your business."

"It is when you make it my business." I sigh and run my hand through my hair. "You and Dom think you own me. Control me. Get to call the shots. Get to dictate who I fuck."

Coen's expression hardens. "You will *not* use that tone with her."

"Yeah? And what are you going to do about it? You going to stop me? I was already all up in that sweet...sweet..."

But before I can finish pushing Hayes' June button, he raises his arm, pointing his gun directly at me.

I stare down the barrel, a wicked grin forming on my face at having pushed him this far. "Do it, I dare you." Hell, he'd be doing me a fucking favor. What's the point anymore if all I am is some puppet in a game that's out of my control? If I can't even pursue one damn thing I want, then why go on? If I'm going to go out, I'd rather it be at Hayes' hand than anyone else's.

Hayes steadies his grip, and pulls the trigger on his exhale.

Like a coward, I flinch, closing my eyes and letting the loud vibration rattle through me. A slight wind passes my ear along with a cracking sound, then the brief groan of a person and a thud on the ground.

I peer through my lids at Coen as he shoves past me to examine the lifeless body.

"Holy fuck, I thought you were going to kill me." I chuckle despite the humor of the actual dead person nearby.

That's when I notice the blur of a figure come around the side of the building. My muscles go into autopilot and retrieve my weapon, aiming it, and eliminating the target in one fell swoop.

"Two more, coming from the east." Coen rushes over, pressing his back against mine.

"And the west."

"Protect the entrance, at all costs."

"At all costs," I confirm.

We're stormed on both ends, more armed men running toward us in haste. My breathing steadies as the call of duty settles over me, knowing that other than Dom, I wouldn't want anyone else with me than Hayes. He might be a total lunatic, but so am I, and we work well together. Almost like we're one extension of the other, a deadly duo that even freaks me out from time to time.

We move gracefully, removing threat by threat, dodging bullets, and circling our way through this attack. The bodies keep coming, one by one, along with the reverberation of gunfire, filling the night sky with a smoky haze and the scent of gunpowder and death.

"Fuck," Coen shouts.

I take my eyes off the incoming men for a second to see the tiny blip of blood on his upper arm.

"Bastard nicked me."

"You good?" I drop the magazine and reload quickly, not wanting to waste even a moment of time.

"I'll be better when I kill the asshole." Coen shoves off from the spot and goes straight into the line of fire, emptying every single round into the man who shot him. He presses the release and shoves in more ammunition, turning it on the next victim in his rampage.

I drop two more, the herd thinning and retreating from where they came from.

"You think you can kill *us*?" Coen shouts, spit flying from his mouth. "You'll have to try harder than that."

I rush to his flank, facing the opposite way of him to keep all our viewpoints covered.

Bodies litter the ground; blood splattered all over. A sight I'm all too familiar with. One that *should* bother me but doesn't. I'm well aware of how fucked up that is. Nothing I can do about it now other than embrace the darkness that has consumed me from within.

"We had to try," a voice calls out from behind me.

"Come out and face me like a man," Coen calls back.

A shape appears in front of me. I flit my gaze to see one in front of Coen, too.

The two dumbass kids that were guarding our hostage. They must have been working for Beckett this whole time, playing the role of double agent. What a foolish errand he had them on.

They stroll closer, taking their time, almost like they know they're walking into their demise.

"Why?" I ask the dude heading in my direction. The taller, more nervous of the two. The other was obvious with his disobedience, this kid though, gave me a different vibe altogether. Guilty for sure, with something else underlying.

"We had to." He keeps his gun to his side; his arm slack against him.

"Who cares why?" Coen wastes no time, pulling the trigger and dropping the guy approaching him.

Frankie, I think is his name, muffles a cry.

Coen continues forward and pops two more bullets in him, ending the poor sucker's life.

The kid in front of me flinches with each round. "I had no choice." His eyes water with tears ready to be shed.

"You could have come to us," I tell him, my gun still aimed at his chest. "We could have figured something out."

"I—I..." he struggles to find his words.

Anxiety, fear, and pure regret bubble out of him. He's aware he screwed up, that he picked the wrong side. That he knows his chances of survival are slim to none. Because if it's not us, it'll be Beckett that ends him.

"You're getting soft." Coen pushes past me, moving quicker than I have time to react, planting a bullet in the kid's chest, and one in his head for safe measure.

"Seriously?" Wide-eyed, I exhale. "You're such an asshole sometimes."

"Like I care what you think." Coen walks a few feet to another body, nudging it with his foot to verify it's dead. He shifts his gaze around the quiet lot and settles on me. "Isn't it your job to anticipate this?"

"I told you it was nothing we couldn't handle."

And handle we did. Over a dozen bodies, their life force draining out and staining the ground around them.

Coen pokes the wound on his arm. "I got fucking shot."

"It's just a flesh wound. Don't be such a baby."

The door to the building we were guarding creaks open. "What are you idiots doing?" Dom steps through, surveying the mess we made. "You two sure do know how to throw a party, don't you?"

I nod toward where he came from. "What about you? You have any fun?"

"Not as much as you did." Dom walks over to our SUV, leaning against the top of it and peering inside. "Really? Our driver?" He sighs and pulls his phone out of his suit pants pocket, turning to face us. "One of you move him while I call this in."

Hayes and I extend our fists, using our other hands as a table to rock-paper-scissors who gets to play clean-up duty. I throw paper; Hayes throws rock, only adding to how pissed off he is at me.

Whatever. Maybe if he'd grow up and learn how to communicate like a fucking adult, I'd be more considerate to the weird claim he's staked on June. But until then, she's fair game, and I will stop at nothing to make her mine.

# CHAPTER 8

# June

"**I** still can't believe you slept with both of them," Cora whispers from her spot at the bar. "Okay, no, I totally can. What I can't believe is that they know each other. That they *live* with each other." She pauses, her eyes going wide. "What if it's a father son type situation. I would *so* not put it past you."

I roll my eyes and dry off a glass, setting it in its respective home next to the other cups.

"Old-fashioned and a *whatever is on draft*," a round-faced waitress barks off a table's order.

"We have six beers on draft." I point to the selection.

"They said to surprise them."

"What am I, a fucking magician?" I pluck a sugar cube from the tray and swipe the bottle of bitters to get started on the first of the two. It doesn't take me long until I finish, topping it with an orange slice and reaching for a mug. I decide on pouring them a Floki, mainly because it's my personal favorite out of our collection. An international pilsner with a crisp hop flavor and well-balanced sweetness. A solid crowd pleaser for most palates.

And if there are any complaints, they can fuck off, considering they gave me nothing to go off of to help sway my decision.

I set the drinks on her tray and go to work cleaning up the small mess I made, preparing for the next order.

"Have you heard from them?" Cora reaches over and plucks a cherry out of the little holder.

I narrow my eyes at her. "You're going to get me fired."

Cora grins. "I'm the least of your worries, babe."

She's totally right. There are countless reasons why my employment should be terminated, specifically the brutal beating and the wild sex in the bathroom. Not exactly going to be winning employee of the month anytime soon.

"No. I haven't," I answer her.

"It's been what, a week?"

"Mmhm." Six days to be more precise.

And as much as I try, as hard as I push the thought of each of them away, they play on a steady loop in my head, not seeming to fade one damn bit.

It's annoying, really. I haven't thought this much about one man, let alone three, since...ever. Even years ago, when Coen left me, it was this sad overwhelming loss I couldn't comprehend. Now, it's an untamed lust for a trio of guys who I can't have. Because how the hell would I ever choose? I can't pick just one, and I wouldn't want to anyway. I don't do long-term. That much is certain. So, I do what I do best, I move forward, move on, and push them into my past where they belong.

*Best* is a loose term, given I'm struggling to have a single thought without any of them in it.

"You know where they live." Cora rests her chin on her hands, her elbows propped up on the counter.

"And they know where I work."

"True, but maybe they're waiting on *you* to make a move since you barged out of there like a madwoman."

"You're enjoying this way too much."

She smiles. "Let me live vicariously through you, please."

The older man at the end of the bar clears his throat. "I'll be seeing ya, June." He pulls out his wallet, rifling through his bills until he finds the one he's looking for. "Keep the change."

"Thanks, have a good night." I smile politely and wait for him to walk away before going over to his spot.

"Damn, he left a twenty."

"Is that good or bad?" Cora asks me.

"He only owed seven-fifty for his drink."

I close out his bill on the register, make change, and hand Cora ten of it, pocketing the rest. "That makes one-forty that I owe you."

"You can wait until you have it all to pay me back."

I shake my head. "Makes me feel like I'm making progress if I do it this way." Not to mention, I don't trust that Carter won't break into my room and steal my money if I stash it in there. I don't exactly like to walk around with too much on me in case I get mugged. One can never be too sure. After losing what I did and having to scramble to recoup it, I can't afford to take any other unnecessary risks.

I hated having to ask Cora for a loan; the sooner I get the balance squared away the better. She's my friend, and I know she cares, but there's this weird, unsettling feeling about being in someone's debt that I can't seem to shake. I've gone my whole life without asking anyone for a damn thing, I don't want to start now.

Getting Carter to admit to taking my money is still on my to-do list, but I have more pressing matters. He'll get what's coming to him sooner or later if it's the last thing I do.

"When does your shift end?" Cora swirls the straw around the remnants of her vodka and diet.

I glance at the clock. "Another hour or so, depends on if it picks up at all."

She swivels around in her seat. "Not looking promising."

I scan the dying crowd, the likelihood of making more money tonight dwindling with each passing minute. Thank god for tippers like the last one. He was my ideal patron. Quiet, keeps to himself, doesn't eye-fuck me in an overly creepy way, and leaves me more than his spare change.

"I'll meet you there if you want to go ahead. I probably won't be much longer." I wipe the counter in front of Cora and take the almost empty cup from her. The only remains are the last few ice cubes that melted into a gross mess of soda flavored water with a hint of booze.

"Are you sure? I don't mind waiting." Cora hops off her chair at the first sign of me giving her approval to leave.

"No sense in both of us being stuck here." I swat at her with my towel. "Go before I change my mind."

The waitress from earlier approaches. "Booth six wants another round."

I glance at her nametag, never quite registering what the hell it is every time she pops up. Granted, she's only been here a week, you'd think I'd remember it by now. "Same thing?"

Jane nods. "Yep. And could I get a seltzer for the guy in the corner?"

My gaze darts across the room to the man she's referring to. An unfamiliar face, although that's not at all surprising around here. We have a handful of regulars, but typically there is a *type* that comes into this establishment. Random couples, rowdy college kids, the old grumpy men who like to sit at the counter, and the exception of the sexy as hell silver fox who fucked me silly in the bathroom.

This guy is none of those. Middle-aged. Not terrible to look at but nothing eye-catching. Very plain. But with an ex-cop vibe about him. Simple clothing, a dark t-shirt with a black jacket over it. No labels. A close haircut and a put-together without much effort aesthetic. He's alone which isn't a big deal, but he hasn't once checked his phone or gotten out a book or occupied his time more than sitting there, sipping his drink at a snail's pace. He's in a bar. Drinking carbonated water.

It just doesn't fit.

But who am I to judge?

I make all three drinks and set them on Jane's tray, ignoring the watchful gaze of the questionable man and chalking it up to him checking me out like all the other straight dudes in here. Maybe I remind him of someone. Or there's the possibility that he's not looking my way at all, and I'm a little too self-absorbed for my own good. Whatever it is, it doesn't concern me. I'm not interested, nor do I have any room to even consider it anyway. I've got my mind full of three other men at the moment, and my failed attempt at banging the first one out of my system led to a complete and massive fail on my behalf.

If I'm going to shake my lust for them, I'm going to have to do it without climbing onto another cock.

Three is enough. I can't begin to imagine any more.

Jack lifts the partition and steps behind the bar with me. "Clean up and you can go. Things are getting pretty slow."

I knew that was coming. This place is a ghost town lately with the opening of a couple bars nearby. Popping nightlife is all the craze, and most investors have tailored their businesses to suit the booming college crowd. Jack hasn't adapted to the newest fads, meaning his old-fashioned tavern-style place with a beat-up jukebox in the corner isn't cutting it anymore. People want craft beer and artesian platters, but Jack refuses to succumb to the trends, insisting that going against the grain will eventually be the new thing.

He could easily get a few other beers on tap, hire an indie live band to come play, and serve some tacos and people would flock in to throw their cash around. It's not like I'm a business major or anything and have any formal education on how to properly adjust to the changing times.

Silly me.

I do as he asks, wiping down the counter and tidying up our station, making sure all the bottles have found their way back to their spots. Once I'm confident it looks better than when I arrived, I toss my towel into the bin with the other dirty ones.

"You want me to start a load of laundry?" I point to the nearly full crate.

"No, I'll have Jane get it before she leaves."

"Okay. Anything else you want me to do?"

"That'll do, June, that'll do."

"See you tomorrow night," I tell him while making my way to the customer side of the counter.

Jane waves at me from the booth in the corner she's clearing. The one my mystery man had staked claim to for weeks on end. Now he's less of a mystery and gone forever. I almost wish I could turn back time and enjoy those moments again when we were nothing more than a server and a customer. A bit of sexual tension between us in those few word interactions.

I make my way out the door, side-stepping an older couple that is entering Jack's place. "Excuse me." I force a customer service smile and continue on my path.

The night air is cool and refreshing, a welcomed change from the thick mustiness of the bar. Bright lights illuminate the sidewalk, leading me to my destination.

A tickling chill runs up my spine, a strange unsteady feeling coursing over me.

I turn, glancing behind me and studying the people going to and from, trying to find anything peculiar. Cars scurry by, one pulling into a parking spot a few buildings down, another across the street. I'm being paranoid, but why? I've walked through here more times than I can count; why am I suddenly tuning in to some strange sensation?

Maybe I'm hyper-fixating; my mind playing tricks on me in its weak attempt to distract me from all the issues popping up in my life. That must be it. Because what else could it be? Someone following me? For what reason?

I shake it off and go the rest of the way into the Haven, spotting the place I'm supposed to meet Cora at for our night out together. I cross the street between two cars and dart into the bar without taking another look around. If someone really was trailing me, they're going to have to wait me out because I don't plan on leaving anytime soon.

I scan the crowd, my sights settling on the beautiful blonde chatting with a guy near the bathrooms. Her body language is telling me she's not interested, but his is showing that he's not quite ready to give up. Guys really can be oblivious at times.

I push through until I'm beside her, sliding my hand around her waist. "Hey, honey. Sorry, I'm late." I kiss her cheek and focus on the newly puzzled guy. "Thanks for keeping my girl company while I finished up at work."

He blinks a few times as if he can rid me from his vision if he tries hard enough. "Wait, you're..."

I cut him off. "In a committed relationship?" I nod and slap his shoulder. "Afraid so, bud. You'll have to try picking up a different chick tonight."

"I—I didn't realize." The rather boring guy struggles to find the words to say.

"Honest mistake." I grab her left hand and rub my thumb along her ring finger. "I really need to wife this one up."

The man takes a swig of his beer and steps away. "I guess so."

Once he's out of sight, Cora can no longer hold in her laugh. "That was incredible. You're my favorite human on the entire planet. He had me cornered for ten minutes telling me about his fantasy football league."

I wink at her and position the straw of her drink to have a sip. "Your taste in alcohol is really a deal-breaker though, sweetheart. Maybe I'll have to throw you back to the wolves."

"You wouldn't." She weaves her arm around mine and pulls me toward the bar. "Let's get you something a little stronger, my hero. It's the least I could do after you pretended to be my girlfriend."

"Hey, what are friends for?" And with the monetary exchange, it's almost like I'm her hooker, too.

Cora orders us each a double of tequila, our go-to to get wasted, and a pitcher of Floki.

"You going to pace yourself tonight or black out on me again?"

"You going to flirt with another tattooed hottie and make me the third wheel?" Cora grins and hands me the two tall shot glasses.

"Those days are behind me, I'm going celibate."

Cora narrows her gaze and rolls her eyes. "Fat chance. Hell is likely to freeze over first."

"You have no faith in me." I slide onto a stool and set our drinks on the table, shoving one in her direction.

"Oh, I do. Just not in that department. Especially with those three on your radar." She picks up the glass, holding it out in front of her. "To all of June's sexy admirers. May she leave some for the rest of us."

"I am not cheersing to that."

"You will, and you'll like it." Cora reaches over and raises my arm for me, clinking the two shots together. "Down the hatch, girlfriend."

I tip it back and swallow the golden liquid—the burn of it lacing down my chest and into my belly, spreading out through my body. Cheap, but efficient. Nothing at all like the stuff Dominic, Coen, and Magnus drink. Now the strange coincidence makes sense, considering they know each other in such an intimate way.

*Roommates.* If I didn't see it for myself, I'd never believe it. Those three couldn't be any more different than they already are. Dominic, the salt-and-pepper man who could easily kill someone with just one stare. He's serious and a total enigma. Magnus, the inked baddie with such a bubbly personality. Adorable with a hint of darkness about him. And Coen, my blast from the past. Handsome surfer boy wielding a handgun and a darkness about him that is nothing like what I remember.

What the hell was that about anyway?

Never in a million years would I have imagined Coen that way. Protective, sure, but not with a weapon. Not with something so...deadly. His sights were trained on me, ready to shoot first and maybe bother with questions later. The Coen I remember was soft and gentle, and kissed me with such caution like I might break if he was too rough.

Cora sighs, resting her head in her hands. "Which one are you daydreaming about? The hot older dude? What was his name again?"

"Dominic."

"God, it's so fitting." She releases her hold on herself and drags an empty mug over to fill it with beer. "Wonder where I can find a trio of men that sexy?"

"You do realize they're not actually mine, right?" It's like Cora has made up this imaginary universe where I'm dating all three of these dudes.

"Shh. You're ruining my fantasy." Cora slides my full drink.

I take it gratefully and down half of it in one swig, muffling the burp that rises.

"Ladylike."

"You know me." I should have been born a dude, between my manners and insane sex drive, I can pretty much out drink and fuck any guy. Which makes for one hell of a first impression, not to mention the last, considering I don't stick around long.

"I was thinking..." Cora raises her brow, the figurative light bulb going off over her head.

"Yeah?" I glance around the noisy place and then focus on her.

"What if, when we finish with this," she points to what's left of the pitcher. "We go next door."

She leaves out the last bit, but I know exactly what she's alluding to. "To the Fox Hole?"

Cora presses her palms together and brings them close to her chest. "Please, please, please." She even goes as far as jutting out her bottom lip.

I sigh and lean back in my chair. "I am not drunk enough for this."

Her green eyes go wide. "Really? We can go?"

I shake my head. "How could I ever deprive you, especially when you pout like that?"

"You're the best." She reaches across the table and squeezes my forearm.

"That's debatable." I down my beer, while saying a silent prayer to the universe to lift my high tolerance and let me feel a little bit of a buzz.

---

The Fox Hole is packed, just as I expected. Loud music blares and bodies become one on the massive dance floor.

Cora practically squeals when we enter the place, making any reservations I had about coming in here go away. To see her smile, be happy, it's enough to get me to do nearly anything. She's a hell of a good friend, and accompanying her to dance her little heart out is the least I could do. We've been there for each other through some dark times, so it only makes sense to let some light in for once.

"I'll get us drinks," Cora yells over the chaotic noise.

"You sure?" I shove my hand into my pocket. "I can pay for this round."

But before I can give her the twenty I pull out, she takes off toward the bar, leaving me standing here looking like I'm talking to myself.

The song ends, another one picking up where it left off. The throng of people jump to the beat, the DJ doing his best to pump up the crowd.

I mentally prepare myself to join them. To become one of the many thrusting myself like a wild person.

I'll fuck a stranger in a bathroom, but dancing in public is what throws me for a loop.

It's not that I don't enjoy it, either thing actually, I just prefer to be inebriated when I'm doing it. The fact that I always seem to make questionable choices when I get drunk enough to dance is why it happens on a more selective basis.

Cora reappears beside me, two of our usual in her grasp. "Here."

"To bad decisions." I clink mine against hers, keeping eye contact with her the whole time.

We down them and leave the empty glasses on the nearby table with other discarded drinkware.

Cora weaves her fingers around mine and tugs me toward the gathering of tipsy folk.

My head swims, the alcohol finally starting to take effect. An alternate cool and warm feeling taking over me in the best way. Like a temporary weight is lifted from my shoulders, the worries of my life being carried away on a train that will hit me full force with a hangover tomorrow morning. But for now, I'll embrace the freedom and the carelessness it provides.

With each step, the choice to go out on the dance floor evolves more into my decision rather than Cora's. Or maybe it's just the liquor doing the talking. Either way, I'm here for it.

I shove my phone into the pocket of my tight black jeans and hope that no one steals it. The concern should be higher, but my mind is doing that thing I asked for —caring less. I slide in behind Cora, fitting into a small gap around a bunch of other people.

The EDM beat fades and a Cardi B song comes on. Cora's eyes light up and she beams, her body shifting provocatively from side to side. She grabs my hands and pulls me closer, giggling and grinning the entire time.

We get lost in the sound, in each other, in forgetting the world exists outside this dance floor. Two best friends allowing all their troubles to be ignored for the shortest blip in time.

Another song, then another, until we're out of breath and blending in with every single other person shaking their bodies in an attempt to free their minds. A few girls join us, and we take turns spinning circles around each other. It's strange and wonderful how easy it is to make friends when you're drunk. People you would never imagine you'd get along with, yet are shaking your hips in tune together.

And let's not mention how it's much more common in the bathroom. Girls are psycho, me included, but throw us in a confined space with too much booze running through our veins and a full bladder, and we'll be sharing stories and braiding one another's hair in minutes, ganging up on some guy Chad who wronged Elizabeth over in the third stall.

Given my typical closed-off nature, it's nice to let myself fall victim to the typical ways of women. Especially with how temporary it is. There are no long-term promises in the bathroom of some dance club. No obligations to stay in contact. Just you and a stranger, a good time, and the ability to walk away and not think twice about looking back.

I'm grateful for Cora, but she's all I need and more than I'm prepared to commit to.

I'm not even sure how it happened, us lasting longer than one drunken night, but if I'm going to stick around for anyone, it's going to be her.

"I'm going to get us some water," I tell her over the music. I might be wasted, but I'm not a complete idiot. From the sheen covering our skin and the panting breaths, we could use a little hydration.

She nods and continues dancing, her energy bubbling out of her. Cora and a short brunette take each other's hands and bounce up and down to the hip-hop blasting through the speakers.

I wiggle through the crowd, glancing behind me to see if there are any identifying people to remember to find my way back to her. The one downfall of splitting up in a place like this is figuring out how to get back to your person.

The intoxicated version of me shrugs it off and reminds me that I'll cross that bridge when I come to it.

I make a beeline for the bathroom before heading to the bar for water. The line isn't too long, but it's still out the door.

Men pop in and out of theirs, and for a split second, I consider going in there instead to relieve myself.

I decide to eavesdrop on the conversation in front of me instead.

"He's so hot." The taller of the two girls grips the short blonde's arm, nearly dragging her down as she stumbles against the wall, her words slurring.

"Yeah, but so are *you*."

"Um, you both are," I blurt out, because how dare they think any less of themselves because of some man.

"Oh my god, shut up, that is *so* sweet." The tall one reels me in, quite literally, pulling me by the arm over to her. "What's your name? I'm Faith, and this is Sav. Short for Savannah, obvs."

The line moves and we take a few steps closer to the door.

"I'm June."

"June," Sav gasps. "Are you a Gemini?" She latches onto me to hold me at an arm's length. "Wait, don't tell me."

Faith brings her thumb and finger to her chin, her eyes narrowing to examine me. "I'm not getting twin vibes. Not completely. I bet Pisces."

I shake my head. "Nope. I'm a Cancer."

Sav widens her stare. "You know the FBI ranked Cancers as the most dangerous of all the zodiac."

"Is that true?" I let out a laugh and step out of the way of a girl coming from the bathroom. With her exit, we're able to go inside and escape the loud area.

"Yep," she lowers her voice to accommodate the quiet but still muffled space. "You're probably a Slytherin, too. I'm a Hufflepuff if you can't tell. Capricorn to a T."

Faith nods obediently, going along with everything Sav is saying. These two are best buds and it shows.

"Here." Sav opens her clutch and digs around for a moment, pulling out a partially transparent stone. She shoves it into my hand. "I'd sage that the first chance you get, but keep it on you."

I eye the glistening blue thing and admire its soft and milky appearance. "What is it?"

"Moonstone, silly. Your birthstone. It'll bring you balance, clarity, and help amplify your Cancer traits."

I raise an eyebrow at her. "Even my dangerous ones?"

A stall opens and Faith latches onto Sav and tugs her toward it, the two of them disappearing inside, full of giggles.

A girl with a bright red dress confidently strolls out of the next one and makes her way to the sink.

I shove the shiny thing in my pocket and go in to relieve myself. I hurry in an attempt to recoup some of the time lost from standing in line. Cora is either totally fine, dancing her heart out, or is worried, wondering what is taking me so long. I'm going to assume the former.

The second I stand from the toilet, my head spins, reminding me how much alcohol I've consumed tonight. I accept the fuzz with welcomed arms, ready to intensify it with another round. If I know my friend, she's probably done for the night—shimmying to the beat of her new form of intoxicant. For me though, I need something a bit stronger.

I exit my stall, giving another female the opportunity to tinkle. Washing my hands, I glance behind me at where my bathroom friends had gone in together and consider whether I should tell them bye. I decide against it, knowing this territory doesn't have set rules and the chances of them already forgetting who I am being high.

The music assaults me when I exit the bathroom, a loud thumping in my ears. I go straight to the bar, moving easily around the tipsy people going to and from.

A handsome bartender approaches. "What can I get you?" He continues to shake the drink in the tumbler between his hands.

"Two bottles of water and a double of well vodka."

He glances at the stamp on my hand and nods. "Anything else?"

"No. Thank you." A little common courtesy goes a long way in a situation like this. Too many drunk inconsiderate assholes disrespect servers all the time. Being one myself, I do my best not to be on the giving end of that rudeness.

The guy strolls out of sight, and I take the opportunity to scan the crowd and try to find Cora.

"Here you go." He plants the waters on the counter and a glass of golden liquor.

"What's this?" I ask him, knowing I'm not that drunk. Vodka is definitely a clear liquid.

He flips his head in the other direction. "Some dude covered your tab. Said to tell you you're too pretty to be drinking well."

"Who was it?" I strain to look down the counter at the faces littering the area.

"Didn't catch his name." He walks away without another word, helping a customer a few seats down from me.

I sigh, not having a clue who would have bought this for me. I pick up the glass, bringing the thing to my lips and taking a sniff.

What I sort of expected to be bourbon, is actually tequila, throwing out the idea that it could have been Dominic, Coen, or Magnus, considering that's their signature drink. Is this just a completely random patron who decided to be nice? What are the chances of that happening? Especially when the few people I call my friends tell me I'm not exactly approachable with the constant resting bitch face. I guess they didn't approach me, though, they used the bartender to play middleman. But why not wave, say hi, or at least give me some opportunity to say thank you.

I take a sip, swirling the booze around in my mouth and letting the warmth flow through me. It's not a fierce burn like the cheap stuff Cora and I shoot, instead it's smooth and steady, a note of citrus in it. It's good, that's for sure. But way out of my price range.

And probably something I'll never have the privilege of drinking again, unless, obviously, I somehow come into a bunch of money. Which doesn't seem at all likely with the way my life is going.

I drink the rest of the tequila, hating that I have to down it so quickly. I'd rather sit here and appreciate it a bit more, but my friend is alone and intoxicated, and probably in need of the water I promised her.

Sober me would have put more thought into who treated me to such a specialty but drunk me is ready to get back out on that dance floor.

I stand a little taller on my way back in my attempt to peer over the crowd and spot Cora's blonde hair. I scan the yellow shades, coming up empty, until I do a double-take. I was looking for a single white female with maybe some other girls around her, but nope, Cora has managed to secure a man as her dance partner this time.

*Atta girl.*

I weave through the bodies with ease, finding gaps to wiggle through and make my way to Cora. "Here, drink this."

She twists the cap off, downing the entire contents of the small bottle of water in one motion. "Thanks." Cora wipes at her lip, not missing a beat the whole time.

I do the same, pointing at the dude grinding up against her when I'm finished. "Who's that?"

She shrugs, a smirk on her face.

I shake my head and chuckle. She's clearly been hanging around me too much, my bad habits are rubbing off on her.

"Hey," one of the short, dark-haired girls we made friends with yells into my ear. "Want me to take your empties? I'm going to the bathroom."

"Yeah, sure, thank you."

"Thanks," Cora chimes in, immediately going back to her partner.

With my newly freed hands and the high of the alcohol settling in, I join them, swaying my body without any care who might be watching. We stay like this for the rest of the song, then another, until time has lost all meaning and I'm not sure how long we've been like this.

"Does he look like Damon Salvatore or am I really that drunk?" Cora whisper screams into my ear.

I slow my rhythm and squint my eyes to get a better view of him as he approaches.

He grins when he slides past me, grabbing my hips and settling his body against mine.

Am I dreaming or is the bad boy doppelganger grinding up on me?

I turn to face him, continuing to move to the beat. "Um, hi."

"Hi." His dark gaze leaves a hot trail from my eyes to my lips, flicking down to my breasts and back up to my eyes again. He's decked out from head to toe in designer clothing, and reeks of expensive booze and cologne. Tequila to be exact.

It immediately sets my Spidey-senses off, alerting me to something I'm not sure of yet. Between his intoxicating stare and the alcohol flowing through my veins, I can't tell if it's a bad or good feeling that's consuming me.

I want to ask him his name. To see if he's in any way connected to the three men I can't get off my mind. To confirm he's not a fourth roommate in the weird lust triangle that is my life. But if he's not, I don't want to exchange any more information than I have to.

Instead, I spin myself back around and face Cora.

Her eyes are closed, her arm reached over her head and wrapped around the dude behind her neck. Their bodies sway to the beat. His fingers resting against her waist, rocking in tune with her.

"You are something else, June." the guy mutters.

It takes me longer than I'm proud to admit to notice that I never told him my name. I flip to face him once more. "Who are you?"

He licks his lips, tugging the bottom one with his pearly white teeth. "Just a man, dancing with a girl."

There's an evil glint in his eye, and don't get me wrong, usually I'm a fucking sucker for danger, but this, this is something else.

"I asked you a question," I say through gritted teeth.

"And I gave you an answer." He reaches up, running his thumb along the side of my face and cupping my chin. "I see what they see in you."

I shake him off, his touch having the opposite effect that he wants. Or maybe the correct one after all. "Who?"

"You know who, June." He winks and twirls a strand of my black hair, still keeping to the steady thump of the blaring music.

"Is this supposed to intimidate me or something?" I grab his hand, dropping it and putting mine on his shoulder, moving to the melody.

He reaches for my waist, pulling me closer. "You don't find me threatening?"

"Not at all." I tend to go head-on into the fire any chance I get. My soul is called to the darkness.

"And that is why..." He leans in, his warm cheek pressed against mine, his breath lingering on my skin. "One way or another. You will be mine."

The song stops, my heart with it, the lights going off in a flash and the heat of his touch being replaced by the sweaty air filling the dance floor. The next tune comes on, along with the strobes illuminating the sheen-covered faces of the crowd. My hand hovers where his body once was; now it is nowhere to be found. Gone quicker than he arrived, leaving me with a pounding in my chest that could only mean one thing.

Things are about to get even more interesting.

# CHAPTER 9

# *June*

Cora and I close out the bar, along with a crap ton of other people, including her random dude.

We all funnel out onto the sidewalk to say our goodbyes. Dozens of bodies go in each direction, leaving a few stragglers behind.

"You sure you're okay?" Cora hugs me tightly and almost falls over when she lets go.

"I could ask you the same." I narrow my gaze at the guy waiting patiently for her. "You hurt a hair on her head, and I'll find you Liam Neeson style and end you."

The seemingly plain but attractive guy holds his hands up. "Drunk doesn't mean consent."

Maybe he's not so bad. But it could be a front to convince me otherwise. Or maybe I'm being paranoid, and a little overprotective of my friend.

Their ride pulls up in front of the bar and he points to it. "This is us."

Cora steadies herself to face me. "You have one coming?"

"I'll order one when I get outside the Haven. Rates are cheaper." I point to a few buildings down where the Haven ends, knowing damn well that I'm walking home from here. I spent more than I should have on booze and if I stand any chance of balancing the budget, I'm going to have to opt out of transportation tonight.

It's not too far, but in my somewhat drunken state, it should make for an interesting stroll home. I have half a mind to crash on that park bench again, just for the sake of not having to deal with my idiot roommates when I show up at three something in the morning.

But, as much as I hate them, I love my bed more, and boy does she sound hella good right now. If only teleportation was a thing.

Cora presses a sloppy kiss against my cheek. "Love you, bitch."

"You, too, skank." I grab her shoulders and steer her toward her new man. "Take care of her."

"Of course." He gently helps her into the back seat, shutting the door behind her and going around to the other side. "Have a good night."

The silver car takes off and when I glance around, I'm the last one standing here. The rest of the throng fluttered out their respective directions.

I take a deep breath, grateful to finally be alone after that rather hectic evening. Don't get me wrong, it was fun, quite a bit actually, but now I'm drained, mentally and physically, and not having anyone around to drain any more of my energy is a welcomed blessing.

I go past the bar we were in, casually making my way out of the Haven, each step guiding me further, toward my apartment. It's strange to be simultaneously in a hurry but want to take my time, too. I could use this window in between human interaction to attempt to regulate my next encounter. Going from an enjoyable evening to that hell hole I call home is a massive mindfuck.

A car approaches from my rear, and I shift to look at it. It slows, turns down an alley, and disappears from my line of sight. I focus back on my path, crossing the empty street and stepping into a lesser lit area. The Haven is bright and inviting, making everything around it seem much drearier and unappealing.

It's clever, really. Like a moth to a flame kind of thing they have going on. Drawing people in with the lively vibe it puts off. Although now, with not another soul in sight, it's a bit eerie.

I pick a leaf off a tree I pass, flipping the foliage between my fingers and breaking off little pieces of it. Raising my arm up, I take a whiff of my armpit. I could definitely use a shower but considering how late it is, that's going to have to wait until I can get a few hours of sleep. It's laundry day tomorrow anyway. Or well, today, if we're being technical.

It's the one day a week I only have one job to work instead of three, leaving me a small window of time to get my errands done. It's a financial hit I hate taking, but if I didn't, there would be next to no way for me to get anything done. And truthfully, I need the break. As little as it is.

Another car passes, snapping me out of my distracted mindset. I watch it drive a few blocks and put its turn signal on before I stop concentrating on it.

A sound to my right catches my attention but I react too slowly. My vision goes dark from something that's put over my head.

This can't be real. This can't be happening.

I throw my arms, elbowing anything I possibly can in an attempt to get away from my captor. "Get the fuck off me," I blurt out, but it's no use.

The person latches onto me, pushing the fabric against my nose and mouth, forcing me to panic and breathe in whatever is lining the thing covering my face. I power through despite the effects taking hold; my world growing even fuzzier than it already was.

My knees buckle out from under me, dropping me to the ground. Pebbles impale my skin, and my palms scrape against the pavement. That's going to leave a mark. But it's the least of my worries given the circumstances.

I fight the uncontrollable drug overriding my ability to function properly. I grip the ground, willing myself to get up on all fours and crawl away. Anything to escape.

"You're making this harder than it has to be." The person finally speaks, reaching down and pushing the bag into my face again.

I hold my breath, but it doesn't matter, there is no dodging the drug-laced fabric.

My head spins and with one final thud to the ground, everything fades to black.

I wake to the sound of screaming.

Only instead of settling my sights on who's making all the noise, I realize it's me that's causing all the commotion.

A man standing in front of me, a cigarette butt pressed between his fingers. He flicks it to the ground. "Nice of you to join us." He leans against the wall, crossing his arms over his chest.

My forearm burns painfully. A round welted mark at my wrist where he had pressed the hot thing to my skin. Both of my arms are tied to the wooden chair I'm sitting in. My legs are unrestrained. Only one other person is here with me in this poorly lit room.

A guy in his mid-thirties. Thick, but not overweight. Brown shaggy hair matching his scruffy beard. Definitely taller than me, but from the angle I'm in, I'm not sure exactly how much more. Scars litter his face, predominantly across his brow and cheek. A faded, blown-out tattoo peeking out from under his shirt sleeve.

"What do you want?" I ask him. I do what I can to trick my mind into forgetting the searing sting from his assault.

"I thought we could have a little fun." He reaches into his pocket and pulls out a switchblade, flicking the thing into the open position. Pressing it into his index finger, he spins it gently, a bit of blood coming to the surface despite the lack of pressure. "Are you a fan of Halloween?" He raises a brow at me.

I don't respond, because I know exactly where he's going with this train of thought. No, my mind is elsewhere, looking for any potential way out of this torture chamber.

"I am." He kicks off the wall and takes a step forward. "You know my favorite part?" He doesn't wait for me to answer. "Carving pumpkins." He flits his attention to the blade. "There's something about jamming a blade deep into the meaty flesh...over and over...until you create something magical."

I check my peripheral, noticing the bare wall behind me. The lone doorway is the one in front of me, and behind the man. One that appears to be a hallway from what I can make out.

"People are no different, you see." He continues, hovering in front of me with the blade inching nearer. "A fresh canvas at my disposal, only to wither away when I'm done with them. Just like a pumpkin would." He puts the thing against my cheekbone, pressing it until the sharpness pierces my skin.

I tilt my head as far as I can to get out of the line of danger, but being restrained, there's only so far I can go. I am at his mercy, and he knows it.

He drags the edge against my skin, an evil grin forming on his face with every bit of torment he causes me.

Warm liquid rolls down my neck and puddles at my collarbone.

"Why me?" I fumble with the rope around my arms, the tautness stopping me from breaking free.

Obviously. Like it would be that easy.

I beg the universe for something, anything to help me out of this fucking nightmare.

"Oh." He wipes the bloody blade on his dark pants, inspecting it when he's done. "That wasn't my doing. I'm only the worker bee, following orders from up the chain."

This wasn't a random attack? What chain is he referring to? I might be a bitch, but I don't have enemies.

*Unless.*

What if it was the guy Dominic had beaten up in the bar? I never did confirm whether he was alive or simply unconscious. What if he had the power to do this in an act of twisted revenge for what happened to him? Or it could be countless other guys I've turned down and somehow pissed off enough to kidnap and torture me. Carter is the person I argue with the most, but I can't fathom he would ever do something like this. Nor would he ever have the power to pull it off. He might be into illegal shit, but he doesn't have this kind of authority. And what would he gain? He's the one who stole from me—if anyone should be punishing anyone, it would be me doing it to him, not the other way around.

"Then who?" I ask him although I doubt he'll tell me. My chair squeaks under me when I shift my weight.

Whoever is pulling the strings, I don't care to stick around and find out, because if I spend much more time alone with this psychopath, I won't live to tell the tale. That much I know for sure.

I reposition my footing and pause, settling my gaze on this man and waiting for my chance to move. I very well could die here in this dreary room, but I won't go down without a fight.

"You picked the wrong side, little girl." He pulls another cigarette out of his pack and puts it between his lips. He pats his pocket for a lighter but it's not there.

He turns his back to me, and I realize, if I'm going to act, I have to do it now. This might be the one and only opportunity I get to move with any level of an upper hand. Even if that means merely a second of knowing he's distracted.

With the chair still attached to my arms, I force myself to my feet, rushing away and shoving myself into the wall behind me with force.

The wooden chair buckles against the impact, creaking and struggling to stay together.

"You bitch," he calls out. The cigarette dropping out of his mouth and falling to the floor.

He rushes toward me, but I pivot and turn quickly, smacking him with the chair I can't seem to break free of.

I groan and slam him once more, throwing us both to the floor and shattering my wooden confines.

He swings his arm, landing a punch across my forehead, crashing into my brow, and dropping me further onto my ass. Blood trickles down and I wipe at it with the shoulder of my shirt.

It's then that I catch sight of the shiny thing that sliced my chin open, laying discarded and unoccupied. We both lock our gazes on it at the same time, flitting a glance at one another and both of us leaping for it at the exact same moment.

I've never moved quicker, and with such a serious intensity in my entire life. Because I'm fully aware that whether I make it out of this depends on if I make it to the blade first. I reach for the handle, holding my breath and summoning it into my grasp, barely grabbing onto it and ripping it from his reach in time.

I draw my arm back and sink the knife into his thigh with as much force as I can muster, rising to my feet and not giving another thought to the antagonizing yelp he lets out. I push past him, using his weakened state to knock him over and get as far away as possible. I burst through the door, blinking quickly to adjust my sights to my new surroundings, scanning for a potential escape. I spot the front entrance, running to it and fumbling with the lock. I shift my gaze toward where I came from, not wanting to become another one of those clumsy girls who die because they couldn't get a fucking door unlocked.

I twist the deadbolt and fling the thing open, rushing out and across the yard, not giving another thought to the house or man I'm trying to put distance between. I bolt down the street, my shoes hitting the pavement and not slowing until a few minutes later when I'm out of breath and finally sure of where I am. I cross through backyards, hop fences, and dodge barking dogs, putting one foot in front of the other.

I skid to a stop in front of my apartment complex, running up the steps two at a time until I reach the top. I shove my key into the lock, twisting it and almost snapping the thing off inside. I yank it out, turning the knob and slipping inside, shoving it shut and collapsing onto the floor in the somewhat safety of my home.

"Uh," a voice floats out to me. "You okay?"

I settle my sights on Carter sitting in the chair in the corner of our living room. A man I despise but honestly could kiss right now. Not because of anything he's done, but because it means I made it, I escaped from my abductor—I'm safe. Whatever that means.

"Yeah." I bring myself to my feet, dusting my pants off and realizing just how insane I must look to him right now.

"Don't bleed all over the floor." Carter yawns and stretches his arms, turning and closing his eyes.

I could have probably walked in here missing an arm and he wouldn't have put too much effort into helping or caring about me one bit. His main concern is solely on getting back to sleep.

So very typical of Carter to be a self-centered prick.

I grab a paper towel from the counter and clean up the red handprint I left behind on our linoleum-tiled floor and make my way to the bathroom, snatching a clean towel from the closet. I dig around under the vanity to locate any kind of first aid supplies.

Standing at the sink, I catch a glimpse of myself in the mirror. Mascara blurred around my eyes, a solid goose egg on my brow with a bloodied wound to go along with it. A small cut along my chin where he had taunted me with his blade.

I've seen better days, that's for sure.

I hold my wrist out and clench my jaw, pouring the peroxide over the cigarette-sized hole in my skin and onto my tattered palm. It bubbles and I fight through the intense pain. I let the water from the sink trickle over it and repeat the steps a few more times. I grab a round cotton pad from Heather's makeup section and douse it with alcohol. I dab it along the damage that was done to my face and toss the blood-covered thing into the trash can. I'm sure there are more bumps and scratches on my body, but I manage to half-ass the major ones.

I turn the shower on and unbutton my jeans, tugging them down and peeling them from my bloodied and bruised knees. I step out of them and drag my shirt over my head. I strip down naked and step into the shower, grateful that there's a decent amount of hot water. I sink onto my ass, pulling my legs to my chest and hugging them as the water rids me of what happened tonight.

I should go to the hospital. Call the cops. Do something in some official capacity. But I know how the system works. They'll ask me what I was wearing. How much I had to drink. They'll have me recall the events that led up, and what happened during, and after. If I knew the man. They'll file a report. Take my name and number. And all it will boil down to is nothing more than an embarrassing waste of time that I'm not willing to sacrifice.

Instead, I sit here, the hot liquid cascading over my skin, both helping and hurting me at the same time. The wounds on my body take turns sending spikes of pain throughout my body. From my head to my toes, I am one solid throbbing being.

My throat aches with the rawness of the scream I had woken up to. The memory of my skin sizzling and the scent of burning flesh lingering in my mind. I force away the thoughts, remind myself that I am safe, that I am far away from the man who hurt me.

My wet black hair sticks to me and I don't move to get it out of my face. I use it as a shield, a protective barrier from the world.

Surely, there had to be a mistake. Maybe he confused me with someone else. Someone who had pissed off someone in power. Someone who deserved what he did to me. But he seemed so sure, so confident, that I was the one he was supposed to target.

I recall the man in Jack's bar tonight, the one who lurked without saying much. Was he the same guy who assaulted me? I think back to their features, noting how different they were.

"No," I whisper to no one. Not the same person.

Must have been a weird coincidence.

But didn't I sense someone following me when I left the bar to head to the Haven? Was that in my head or was there something to be aware of? And what about the random drink I was gifted with...and the new mystery man who approached me, and told me I would be his.

Was it him?

None of that makes sense.

Why would someone buy me expensive tequila and then try to kill me? And why would the Damon lookalike flirt with me and then order me to be kidnapped and tortured?

Is it possible that it was Dominic, Coen, or Magnus? That they wanted so little to do with me that they would rather have me murdered than deal with me in the future?

Dominic literally beat a man nearly to death when he threatened me. That doesn't really put him at the top of my suspect list. And Coen...he'd never hurt a fly, let alone me.

But with the recollection of the gun in his hand, pointed straight at me, and then at Cora, anything could be possible. Still, though, I'd never believe it was him unless he really was upset that I had slept with Magnus. It's been years though, what right would he have to stake such a claim after all this time has passed.

Leading me to Magnus. The dark and dangerous bad boy with the soft and gentle inside. No fucking way it was him that ordered this to happen.

Which pretty much gives me no insight on what the hell went down, further making me certain that I was caught up in someone else's war—that I was never meant to be the target of such aggression.

I lean back, resting against the tub and extending my legs. The water runs murky with a mix of dirt and blood.

Whatever it was, what transpired, it's over, and I will do with it what I do with everything else—I shove it into a folder deep in my mind and put it where it belongs, in the past.

# CHAPTER 10

# Magnus

I t's been too many days since I've seen her.

Yesterday, I went to her work in an attempt to settle my sights on her, but she never arrived while I was there, lurking in the shadows for a glimpse of her beautiful face.

I'd go to her house but I'm not sure where she lives, and it's not like we exchanged phone numbers. Shit, she barely gave up her name.

I could ask Coen more details to find her, but then that goes against the whole *leave her alone* thing that Dominic has ordered. So, I take the little bit I do know about her, and use it to resolve the ache in my chest and pit in my stomach caused by her absence.

I lean against the building across the street, just hidden enough in the darkness not to be seen by passersby. I wait and hope for her to be in there today, to fuel my addiction and stave off the craving I have for her.

It's dangerous to linger like this, but I do it anyway without a care of what might happen.

Seeing her is somehow more important than my continued existence.

A feeling I've never had about a woman in all thirty-two years of my life, which only makes me chase the high that much more.

The owner of the diner, Bram, an older man with kind yet sad eyes lifts the partition to the counter and steps through, a carafe of coffee in his grasp. He glides to a booth, pouring a cup and going to the next and topping another off. A teenage waiter cleans off a table and wipes it down. Typical business as usual. The same thing I witnessed yesterday until I was finally called away to my own job, no longer able to ignore the buzzing of my phone.

My heart lurches out of my chest, almost like it spots her before my eyes do. But when I focus on her, my stomach drops, my jaw with it. My pulse picks up and I move from the shadow, out onto the sidewalk. I step into the street, a car blaring its horn at me as it skids to stop itself from hitting me. I continue, completely disregarding the peril around me.

I scan her, my gaze trailing from the injuries on her face to her wrapped wrist and hands. A rage building within me, unlike anything I've ever known. My hand itching toward the gun at my waist, ready to end the life of whoever laid a finger on her. My soul is pulled to her, begging to wrap around and protect her from any other threats. To nurture and care for her while she heals from this terrible attack.

I press my palm against the glass, peering into the diner, still unnoticed by her.

She stands at the end of a table, taking the order of an elderly couple, jotting the details onto a small pad of paper. Her frail fingers gripping the pencil. She offers them a smile and walks away, pulling off the sheet and sliding it across the counter to Bram.

He nods and attaches it to the clip for the line cook.

June flexes her left hand, almost like she's working out a cramp in it, and I ache to be there, to offer whatever aid I can. But right now, the one thing I'm wired to do is eliminate the cause of her despair.

I power walk the entire way home, not giving two shits about being out in the open like this. By the time I arrive, sweat has accumulated on my brow and the anger inside me has continued to fester at an insane rate.

I swipe my badge at the gate to grant myself access, and rush up the stairs and into the house. Immediately, I draw the gun from my hip and the other from my waistband, securing them in both of my hands.

Bursting into the kitchen, I train them on both of my targets.

"Whoa, buddy, what the hell?" Hayes raises his palms in the air.

"Which of you?" I look between them. "Who fucking did this?"

Dom stands, his chair scooting back behind him. He reaches for me, but I shake him off, straightening the gun I have pointed toward him.

"I swear to Christ, I will kill you both if someone doesn't start talking."

We have a strict no killing each other in the house rule, but that went out the door when they laid a finger on her.

"We can't tell you if you don't explain to us what happened." Dominic crosses his arms over his chest, a bit of irritation at my disturbance settling into his features.

"June." The word leaving my mouth raises the tension in the room.

"What about her?" Hayes' nostrils flare, the possessiveness of his tone telling me he's innocent, at least when it comes to the harm that was done to her.

I tilt my head at Dom, shifting my body and shoving both pistols in his direction. "You sick fuck." My head spins, my heart pounding wildly.

The three of us have gone head-to-head in the past, but I never actually thought I'd end the life of either of these men. Especially Dom, my mentor, the man who took me in and gave me a chance when no one else would. He believed in me when I didn't believe in myself.

But none of that matters now. Not with her involved.

"Maggie." Coen tries to gather my attention. "What happened to June?"

"I went to her work." I grit my teeth. "I know I wasn't supposed to. I wasn't going to say anything. I just wanted to see her. To verify she was okay."

"And...?"

I flit my gaze to the floor, recalling the cut across her lip and brow, the bruising on her cheek, the bandage wrapped around her wrist and hands. The same intense anger I felt then only continues to grow.

"Someone." I point the gun in my left hand at Dominic. "Roughed her up."

Dominic's expression changes, his arms dropping to the table, his fist slamming into the wooden surface. A low growl escapes him. "What?"

Either he's a damn good actor, or it wasn't him who hurt her. Telling me that someone *outside* this house got to her. Which might mean several things. June could have enemies of her own, or our rivals could very well know how important she is to us and are using their easy access to her to their advantage. Somehow that will only end poorly. For them, or for us.

The latter is much more likely given our dire circumstances.

But how would they have known?

They must have eyes on our house and saw her leaving the other morning. Or one of the men standing in front of me might have gone against Dom's order and saw her, putting her even more at risk.

"Tell me, exactly, what you saw." Dom stares at me with an intensity that I feel within my bones.

Hayes drops a magazine from his gun, checking to make sure it's full and shoves it back in, pulling the slide and putting a bullet in the chamber.

Dom grabs my shoulder, shaking it and snapping me out of my stupor. "Focus, Bryant."

"Her face." I motion to mine. "It was all fucked up." I hold up my hands, the guns still gripped in them. "She had bandages on both, and her wrist." I replay the image of her in my mind. "She was limping, nothing drastic, but definitely noticeable."

Dom's entire exterior hardens, and he exhales, taking a step away.

"Where are you going?" I call out after him.

"To find her, to see who did this, so I can end him."

"What happened to the *no June* rule?"

He slides the gun off the table and secures it in his holster like a person would grab their keys before leaving. "Null and void. If anyone is going to kill her, it's going to be me."

Without thinking, I raise my weapon at him once more. "Don't you fucking dare."

Dom swats at me as though I'm a fly in his face. "I'm not going to, you idiot."

"I'm coming," Hayes chimes in.

"Wait a minute." I position myself in their way so they can't leave. "First of all, neither of you know where she is. Secondly, what makes you think she wants to see either one of you?" I nod at Dom. "She fucking took off the other day when you tried to talk to her." Then at Hayes. "And you, she looked like she saw a ghost." I cross my arms, the gun still in my hand. "If anyone should confront her, it should be me. The one person she doesn't hate."

The two of them look at each other, then at me.

I add my last point. "And all three of us storming into her work doesn't sound like a solid plan."

For once, Dominic is speechless, his mouth parting briefly then closing.

"I've known her the longest," Hayes blurts out.

Dominic rubs his temple. "Two months." He points to me. "You?"

"A week." He clearly has me beat on this one.

We both pivot to Hayes, waiting to see if he'll win this one or not.

"Over a decade."

"What?" I'm not sure if it comes from me or Dom.

"It should be me." Hayes runs his fingers through his surfer boy hair. "She trusts me. I'll get her to tell me who did this to her. Then we can take turns torturing them."

"She doesn't trust you. June doesn't trust *anybody*." Because if I learned anything from my short but sweet time with her, she's got mad trust issues.

"This, right here, see." Dom raises his voice. "This is why we can't get involved. We're in the middle of a fucking *war* and we're completely focused on something else."

Hayes stares right at him, a look that could kill. "She isn't just *something*."

It's like he took the words right out of my mouth.

"I know, damn it do I know." Dom reaches into his pocket to pull out his keys. He hands them to Hayes. "Hurry back so we can end this."

"What the fuck." I stand my ground. "I get no say in this? I'm the one who found her. If she's going to talk to anyone, it'll be me."

"How about this?" Hayes grips my shoulder. "You can come with me, stay in the car. If she kicks me out, I'll send you in."

"Can you two shut up and come on already?" Dom snags his keys back and shoves me out of the way to open the door. He stops in his tracks. "Wait, you said you saw her at work? Where?"

I hesitate, not wanting to give away my precious secret just yet. Like having it to myself means I somehow know her more intimately than they do.

"I thought she worked at a bar." He glances at his watch. "Last time I checked, bars aren't open this early."

"Definitely wasn't a bar." I bite at my lip, hating what I'm about to say—the tiny detail slipping from my grasp. "It was a diner. Bram's, over on—"

Dom cuts me off. "I know where that is. Come on."

"Shotgun," I call out.

"What the fuck." Hayes stomps behind me.

We climb into Dom's SUV. A Mercedes AMG G 63, fully tailored to Dominic's specifications. Obsidian black exterior, Nappa leather inside, blacked-out rims, and bulletproof accents. It cost a pretty penny, but it's totally Dom's style. It's quick, it's sleek, and it sticks out like a sore thumb. We could have easily taken one of the unmarked vehicles, but knowing how I feel right now, Dom doesn't care about someone spotting him either. Almost like he's inviting them to him, to summon the war and go on a rampage, ending anyone in sight.

It doesn't take long to get there, especially when Dom blows through stop signs and goes the wrong way down a one-way to cut across quicker.

Hayes hops out as soon as we park, shoving his gun into the back of his pants and pulling his shirt over it.

I watch his every step with precision, my fingers digging into my thigh with the desire to trade places with him. To be the one to confront June. In a loving but attentive way. The Hayes I know is rough, brutal, and not the comforting type. How he thinks he's more equipped for this job than me I'll never understand.

Hell, Dom might be better suited and he's a fucking psycho.

Hayes claims he and June go back over ten years, yet he's never once mentioned her name. She's important enough to invoke a rage inside of him and a fierce posses-siveness but not actively have her in his life?

My gut tells me he's going to make this entire situation worse than it already is because he can't handle a woman like June.

She's strong, resilient, powerful, and if I had to guess, she's fully capable of handling her own. I mean, she's back at work with minimal downtime after what-ever happened. A second job at that. And from the looks of it, she was fucking tortured. What other person, aside from those in my line of work, operates that way?

In addition to her strength though, there's this broken part of her. The wreckage that created her toughness and forced her to push everyone away.

She needs someone in her life that sees her. That understands her. That shows her a bit of kindness and actually means well. That won't use or abuse her. That will treat her with caution but give her the ability to flourish and treat her like the princess she really is. And most of all, won't break her trust and leave her once she's finally opened up. Maybe that man isn't me, but it sure as shit isn't Hayes.

That's when it dawns on me. The dynamic between Hayes and June. The raw ache I felt between them. The tragic story that was unspoken and yet still heard by my soul.

Coen Hayes is the person who abandoned June.

I grip my thigh harder, the anger inside of me bubbling nearly out of control while I watch him reach his hand out and touch her shoulder to get her attention.

No, it wasn't Hayes who inflicted the recent injuries on June, but his damages run much deeper than any surface-level wound. And for that alone, it puts him at the top of my kill list.

# CHAPTER 11

# *Coen*

"June." I approach her from behind while she's cleaning off a table.

She flinches, dropping the tray in her hands. A partially empty coffee mug falling to the ground and shattering. "Fuck."

"Shit, I'm sorry." I cower and pick up the pieces, ignoring the stares of the few patrons I can feel glancing our way.

June shuffles to get them too but I stop her.

"No, let me. It's my fault. I shouldn't have snuck up on you." I grab onto a shard and it slices at my palm. I ignore the pain and continue to clean up the mess I made. If only life were this easy to fix, too. But in a way, it is, the pieces and remnants never able to go back together the way they were, often bits left behind despite the rigorous attempt to sweep them all up.

Who am I kidding though? I never once tried to repair things with June. The single most important person to me and I couldn't bring myself to face her. To tell her the truth and explain why I was stolen from her and where I had gone. I was ashamed. A large part of me thought that she wouldn't understand, that she wouldn't forgive me, that I wasn't worthy of her. So, I stayed away. I kept my distance. I told myself she was better off without me, because I truly believed that.

But seeing her again, it was like I was brought back to those days together. The way she chiseled away at my walls and stole my heart without anything stopping her. We were kids, but it was powerful. Real. It was the shit they talk about in movies. And I have never once remotely felt close to another person the way I did with her. I've never even given it the chance, too afraid that it would taint what we had.

I've kept my relationships short, and strictly sexual, never attaching any feelings to them. Not just on purpose, but because I couldn't. I've had nothing left to give —all my love being taken by the girl with beautiful brown eyes and jet-black hair.

The one who was patient and kind and didn't judge me for spending time in the cemetery visiting my mom. She was strong but broken like me. She knew loss and yet still gave me her heart. She was reserved, selective with who she let in, but somehow she chose me, and I will forever be a better man because of the love she gifted me.

But we both broke that day we were unwillingly pulled apart. Shattered onto the earth like pieces of a fallen glass. Separated. Irreparable. Unfixable. Forever changed by a force we could not control. We were young, and there was no stopping what happened. Maybe if I had known, I could have snuck out the night before. I could have gone to her, told her what was going on and devised a plan to stay together. We could have run away.

We didn't get that chance. Because our separation was just as much a surprise to her as it was to me. And it transpired quicker than I could fathom, the moving parts giving us whiplash at how fast it went down. I blinked and she was gone. A fading speck on that gravel road until we turned out of sight, my heart was left behind in the hands of a girl I thought I'd never see again.

"Co." June steadies my hands with hers. "You're bleeding."

My gaze meets hers, taking me on a journey to that beautiful summer we spent together. We had been friends since childhood, but we took things to the next level that year when a sad girl let me kiss her and changed my life forever. The biggest change of all was when she was taken from me. Turning me into a cold, heartless version of myself. One that was shaped into the dark and twisted man I am today. The reason why I'm so damn good at my job, is because of the empty pit in my chest.

"Is there a problem over here?" An older man with a broom appears above us. He steadies his attention on June.

She stands and takes the thing from him. "No. I'm just a bit jumpy. I've got it under control."

He stays put, eyeing me seriously. "You sure?"

I don't hate how protective he is of her, his reaction telling me that there is someone else in her life in tune with potential threats that might arise. He's not wrong to keep his stare locked on me given my history with death and violence, but little does he know, I'd rather die than lay a finger on her. And I would kill anyone who even thought about harming her.

Bryant and Dominic included.

They might be the closest thing I have to family, but June exceeds any level of loyalty I have to them.

"Yeah, sorry Bram. You can take it out of my check."

I reach into my pocket and pull out my money clip. I slide a fifty from the top. "Here, that should cover it."

"That won't be necessary, young man." Bram pivots my extended offering toward June. "If you'd like to compensate anyone, it should be her." The two of them make eye contact. "If you need me, I'll be finishing up the orders. I won't be long."

She goes to work sweeping up the discarded fragments left behind. "I don't want your money, Coen."

"Please, J. I created more work for you. It's the least I could do."

She rolls her eyes. "Don't get me started on the *least* you could do."

I sigh and sweep my hair off my brow. "June." I reach for the broom, slipping it out of her grasp and replacing it with the money. "I insist." I nod to the booth. "Sit, let me do this."

For some unknown reason, she listens to me, slipping into the cushy seat and crossing her arms over her chest. "Whatever."

I make quick but efficient work of cleaning up the one mess I'm capable of mending, hoping like hell it isn't the last one she lets me try to fix.

There's such a wall between us that it pains my soul, even more, to know she no longer looks at me the way she used to, all those years ago. I don't blame her, but it still hurts all the same.

I set the broom against the wall and climb in across from her. "Can we talk?"

"I'm at work, Coen. This isn't exactly the time or place to clear whatever is on your conscience." She flits her gaze to the few customers in the diner and at the other waitress taking care of them.

"You're right." It's not often I say those words and mean them. "That's not why I'm here."

June raises a brow. "Then what is it? You want to place a carryout order?"

I shake my head, my inner child laughing at her smart-ass remark, reminding me of the June from so many moons ago. Reaching across the table, I hesitate, not wanting to get too close and surprise her again. "Who did this?"

She blinks in surprise, a blank but startled look on her bruised face. "What?"

I motion to the wounds, repeating my question. "*Who* did this?"

"I—I don't...wait. Why?" Her expression hardens. "Why do you want to know? Why does it matter?"

It's everything I can do to not jump out of my skin and strangle any person potentially responsible for doing this to her. Sitting across from her, I can fully see the darkened marks on her face. The cut on her brow that is poorly covered by a bandage, the wound along her chin.

"It matters." Of course it does. How could she possibly think otherwise?

She lowers her voice. "You lost the right to care about what happens to me a long time ago, Coen."

I match her tone. "That doesn't mean I stopped."

"You sure have a shit way of showing it."

"I'm sorry." Those two words leaving my mouth mean much more than they allude to.

June rocks her head back and forth slowly. "Sorry doesn't cut it."

The simple fact that she's still sitting here gives me the tiniest bit of hope I need. Confirming that despite how badly I fucked up, maybe I can gather the broken pieces of us and put them back together.

All I can do is try. My first task is ending the life of whoever did this to her.

"You can be mad at me. You can hate me. You can wish whatever ill will you want on me. I accept that. I deserve that. Truthfully, I do. But I need to know, June. You have to tell me. Who hurt you?"

"You mean other than you?"

Her words slice through me, cutting me deeply. My lips part, but I come up short for what to say. I don't fault her for treating me this way, but it won't help me bring justice to those worthy of it.

She reaches across the table and pulls a napkin out of the holder, extending her hand and grabbing onto mine. "You're still bleeding."

I savor the touch, basking in how sweet it is. Temporary, fleeting, and a blaring reminder of what I lost. No matter how much time has gone by, I never cared for her less, my love for her never withering in the slightest.

I clung to it desperately. The last remaining shred of my humanity fading into memories of a time far in the past but never forgotten.

Once I had thought maybe I was crazy. That she was a figment of my imagination I created in a weak attempt to stay sane through the darker days of my life. That maybe I idealized the perfectly imperfect girl who prefers sunsets over sunrises, could eat her weight in popcorn, and who I taught how to play pool.

But seeing her, feeling her skin against mine, looking into the same mesmerizing eyes I had peered into day after day, I realize she's exactly what I remember—only now, she's no longer mine. Not that she ever was, because June can't be captured, not really. She's one of those things that if you want her to stick around, you have to accept that she will remain wild, free, and completely untamed.

I gently place my palm on the top of her bandage-wrapped hand. "June, I need you to tell me."

Her gaze meets mine. Steady, interrogatory, like she's trying to see through me.

The bell on the front door chimes, alerting us to new patrons entering the diner.

"I have to get back to work." June pulls away and scoots out of the booth. She offers the older couple a fake customer service smile. "Have a seat wherever you'd like."

They walk past us and take up residency at a nearby table.

June pushes me toward the door. "I don't need your pity, Co. I'm a big girl. I've handled things on my own for this long, I don't need your help now."

But it's not about pity. It's about getting even. Inflicting the same or more pain on whoever thought they could touch her and get away with it.

"J..."

"No." She continues shoving me, her warmth pressing through the back of my shirt. "I can't talk about this here." June pauses. "Is that your ride?" She points to Dom's over-the-top SUV.

"Maybe."

"Is that Magnus in the passenger seat?" She squints to take a better look. "And Dominic driving?"

"Um."

"Go." She grabs the handle and yanks it open. "All three of you. I'm fine, seriously. I don't need any of your help."

And with a final push, I'm out onto the sidewalk. Alone and with none of the questions I came here for answered, plus a fuck ton more of them piling up.

She's still that same firecracker I remember—hellbent on waging this war called life on her own and not relying on a damn person for anything.

Magnus rolls his window down, his head hanging out of it, waiting for me to fill him in.

I walk over, careful to glance around and check out anything suspicious on my way. Climbing into the back, I sigh and run both hands through my hair.

Magnus turns to me. "Who do we get to kill?"

Dominic stays silent in anticipation of my directions on where to go.

"She wouldn't tell me."

"I fucking knew it." Magnus slams his fist against the dash. "God, no one fucking listens to me." He points at me. "You're the reason she's so cold and shut off."

This grabs Dominic's attention. "What? What did you do to her?"

I shake my head, dropping it into my hands. "Nothing."

"You're lying." Magnus is certain he knows what he's talking about, and unfortunately for me, he is.

He's a damn good people reader, the best I've ever been around, but that means he can read us, too. He's the master at calling people on their bullshit and that's exactly what he's doing right now.

"Enough, you two." Dominic glances at me. "Did she say anything? Give you any clue who could have done it?"

"No. Not a word." I recall the marks on her skin. The discoloration. The poorly taken care of wounds, almost like she didn't seek medical care at all. I process all the information I was given, despite how little it was. I've had less and managed to figure shit out, why would I let that stop me here? "Her chin."

"What about it?" Dom's interest is piqued.

"There was about a three-inch-long thin gash along it." I focus on the details, not on the victim, because if I picture it being June, I'll spiral out of control and not be able to follow through with solving the mystery of who did this. "Must have been a blade of some sort. Who do we know that works with knives?"

A chill runs up my spine, a thought I hadn't fully processed until now.

When we do interrogations, not a single person makes it out alive. And typically, that's how it goes in our line of business. The casualties pile up one after another with minimal regard to the lives lost. With that being said, how the fuck did June get away with her life still intact? Does that mean the game has only just begun? That instead of a quick assault, this would be a long, drawn-out torture, not just for her, but for the three of us sitting here? Is this a twisted game to distract us from the war we're trying to win? A sadistic distraction to gain the upper hand? Is her life now hanging in the balance because of us carelessly involving her? Something we can no longer stop now that it's in motion.

"I have a few people in mind," Dominic announces.

I center my sights on Magnus. "Get out of the car."

"What?" His brows bunch together.

"Someone has to keep an eye on June." And considering how upset she is with me, I'm not the best suited for the task. No, my skills are better suited for something else entirely. "Dom and I will investigate."

AKA, slit every throat around town until someone confesses to hurting our girl.

# CHAPTER 12

# June

What gives Coen the right to come into my work and ask me questions about what happened to me? He's been absent for *years* and he shows up out of the blue being all protective? How the hell did he even find out?

Out of the three of them, Magnus was the one who knew I worked at Bram's. Why wasn't it him that confronted me? Especially since he was waiting out in that ridiculous SUV the whole time Coen was inside trying to pity me.

I saw it in his eyes, the way he looked at me, like I might fall apart at the seams like that stupid fucking broken mug. I don't need his sympathy, or anyone else's for that matter. I'm fine on my own.

Did they agree that because I've known Coen the longest that he would be the best to talk to me? Well, they were wrong. Because none of them fit that description.

"June." Bram hovers near me while I refill the salt and pepper shakers.

"Yeah?"

He sighs, his posture stiffening a bit. "Listen, I don't want to pry, and I know you already told me what happened. But if there's anything else going on, I hope you can put your trust in me to help if you need it."

I haven't worked here long but Bram has absolutely shown his trustworthiness. Definitely a too-good-to-be-true situation, still I'm rolling with it as long as I can.

"Thanks, I appreciate that. I'm fine though, really. Just an isolated mugging incident is all." At least, that's the story I'm telling him and anyone else who asks, because the real version is too fucking unbelievable, especially the part where I managed to get away.

Bram lowers his voice. "Don't look now, but there's a guy, across the street.

He's been there for a little over an hour. I don't want to alarm you, or bring concern to something coincidental, but do you know him?"

I shift my attention from the task at hand to Bram's concerned face. "The man that was in here earlier?"

He shakes his head. "No, taller. A bit rougher around the edges. Tattooed arms and neck."

I exhale and go back to my duty. "He's harmless. Probably just keeping an eye on me since…" I hold up my bandaged hands. "This."

He shouldn't be here, lurking in the shadows, but it's better than him being the man who kidnapped and tortured me. I'm convinced it was a random mix-up, but I'm still on edge about the whole thing. At least it's Magnus and not Coen. I'm not sure how much more of his sad looks I could take.

"Okay." Bram relaxes a bit. "I guess I should call off the cops then."

"You called the police?" I wide-eye him.

"No," he chuckles. "They're on speed dial though if you need me to."

"I'll let you know if I change my mind." I grab the shakers and put them on their allocated tables, glancing at the clock and realizing it's almost time to leave.

"You can go if you want. I'll mark the whole hour." Bram wipes off the counter and grabs the coffee pot. "Want one to go?"

"You sure?" Where's the catch? Why is he so damn nice? It's like it's ingrained in this man's DNA, unlike the majority of the population who prefer to only do nice things when they can get something in return from you.

"Absolutely." He pulls a takeout cup off the stack and fills it to the top.

"Could I have another?" I point outside. "For my stalker." I reach into my pocket. "I'll pay for them."

"On the house. Consider it a thank you for him looking out for you." Bram pours another cup full and secures the top. "I worry about you kids."

I ask the question that has been on my mind since I met him. Something that I probably should just keep my mouth shut about. Curiosity striking me too hard at the moment.

"Did you know them? The college students who got shot."

Bram's shoulders tense up, telling me the answer without a word. He confirms it anyway though. "Yes."

"I'm so sorry." It's one thing to have a tragedy strike so close to home, and another for it to be personal.

The sadness I see written across Bram's face every time I'm in here and the burden he carries daily making much more sense now that my suspicions are confirmed. Whoever he lost in that doomed alley next to his shop meant something to him.

It's been a month or so since the accident, the wound still fresh in his memory, in his heart, in his soul.

"I was friends with Claire, one of the victim's girlfriends." I'm not sure why I say this.

A spark seems to light in his eyes. "Really?" He tries not to make himself too obvious, but I already noticed the shift in his demeanor at the mention of her. "Have you heard from her?"

"No." It wasn't like she and I were the type to keep in contact though. We were buds through association, through Cora. When I notice the minimal brightness in him dimming, I add, "She might be in touch with a mutual contact of ours though. I could ask and get back to you."

"Yeah. That would be nice. Thank you."

And if that's any indication, the person who Bram lost would have been Johnny, Claire's boyfriend. I wonder how the two of them knew each other. Maybe they were related, or perhaps Bram took Johnny under his wing like he seems to do with other lost and broken people he stumbles across. The goodness in his heart spilling out and making him incapable of watching someone suffer and not do something about it.

"She worked here, right? Claire?"

"Best help I ever had," Bram smiles, a genuine one. "No offense."

I laugh. "None taken."

"You give her a run for her money though." Bram shoves the two cups across the counter. "I better not keep you any longer. Your bodyguard might worry."

I take them from him and mentally prepare myself for whatever is going to happen when I step foot outside. Will Magnus grill me? Pity me? Shame me for getting myself into such a situation?

"See you tomorrow morning," I tell Bram.

A middle-aged woman walks in and holds the door for me so I can walk through.

"Thank you," I tell her and step onto the sidewalk outside. I stand there, waiting for Magnus to cross, but he doesn't.

Does he think I don't know he's there? Is this him trying to be inconspicuous?

I lean on my hip, putting my weight on one of my legs. "Come on, Magnus," I call out in his direction.

He appears from the shadows, slowly at first, but then jogs across the street to me.

I shove the coffee toward him. "Here."

He looks at it with furrowed brows. "You got that...for *me*?"

"If you don't want it I can—"

Magnus cuts me off. "No, of course." He takes the cup from me. "Thanks."

Has no one ever given him something before?

I pop the lid on my drink and let the steam float out. I want to take a sip but I'm rather fond of my taste buds remaining intact. "Why are you here, Magnus?"

He goes right for the kill, flipping the opening and drinking some of his. "Shit, that's hot."

"I have to go to work." I point the direction I need to head.

"Work?" Magnus nods toward Bram's. "You just came from there."

I shake my head. "No, my other job."

"June..."

I sense the judgment coming in his tone.

"How many places do you work at?"

"Today?" I pull my phone out of my pocket to check the time. "Three."

He stares at me like I just grew a horn out of my forehead.

"Not everyone can be rich like you." I don't mean for it to come out as harsh as it does. But with the mood I'm in and the last few days I've been having, I don't apologize.

Magnus's expression shifts through surprise, to concern, to understanding in a matter of seconds. "I'll walk you."

That, I did not expect.

"What? It's like four blocks."

"Then we better get moving so you're not late." He places his tattooed hand on my lower back and guides me in the general area I had insinuated I needed to go.

His touch is warm and cool all at once. A strange comfort I didn't expect given my current and ongoing annoyance with the human race.

I let him move me, because I really do need to get to work. I'm exhausted already from working at Bram's but there is no rest for the wicked, or well, more realistically, the broke.

"You never told me, why are you here?"

"What? A guy can't walk with a girl?"

I glance over at him, ignoring the shape of his jaw, the subtle arch of his nose, the dark, wispy lashes that extenuate his beautiful eyes. God damn, he is a sight for tired eyes. "The lurking in the alley across the street is a bit much. You going for a *Joe Goldberg* from the show *You* type of vibe?"

He raises that bushy brow of his, a grin forming on his face along with it. "That guy had game though, no denying that."

I exhale and take a cautious sip of my coffee. "I'm fine, really. I told Coen that. I don't need your pity, or whatever this is."

"You think this is pity?"

"What else could it be? Coen shows up out of the blue with that sad look written all over his face. Then you're creeping from across the street like I can't be left alone. What's next? Dominic showing up, too? My boss almost called the cops on you."

"It would have been fine I know a—" his train of thought changes. "Never mind. No, you've got this wrong, June. It's not sadness we feel toward you. I mean, yeah, we hate that you got brought into this. But what you're not picking up on is the rage, the anger, the pure desire to make whoever did this to you pay."

I glance at him out of the corner of my eye. Am I hearing him right? They want *revenge*? For what happened to *me*? Why? I'm just some girl to them. I mean, maybe not to Coen, but to Magnus and Dominic I'm a random one-night stand.

Did Coen put them up to this and the two of them are forced to tag along on his weird quest for vengeance? But even then, why would he care? He's been gone for years and years and never once cared what happened to me.

"Why?" I finally ask.

"Believe it or not, you matter to us."

"Sure do have a weird way of showing it. Coen disappears from my life for a decade. Dominic after one night. And you…" I gaze at him briefly, recognizing the preemptive hurt on his face. "I guess you're the only one who hasn't shown their true colors yet."

His resolve softens, my blow not hitting him as hard as he had prepared for. "I'm sorry, on behalf of them and the entire male population."

"That's a heavy burden to carry." I pause my stride, waiting for the signal to turn green and give us permission to cross the street. Without turning, I can sense Magnus looking at me.

I hate to admit it, but his presence made the walk to my second job much less stressful. After what happened the other night, I'm on edge. Which is something I've always been, but now, it's at an extreme level. A highly paranoid one that makes me aware of the smallest things.

Like the man standing on the other side of the street in anticipation for the light to change. The other older one approaching Magnus and us from the south. A couple exiting a shop a few doors down. And the teenager sitting at a table in front of the Mexican place. The two cups in his grasp dripping with condensation, telling me that the kid has someone with him, too.

I don't notice everything, but I hope to see enough. Enough to keep me safe. Enough to prevent the same thing from happening again.

We walk a few more minutes, only now it's in silence.

"This is me." I motion ahead to where I'm going.

"You work here? I love this pizza place."

"Yep." I dawdle, unsure how this goodbye is going to go when everything else is so uncertain, too. "Thanks…for walking me."

Magnus grins and pulls me to his chest, wrapping his arms around me and holding me tight. He kisses the top of my head and his body relaxes into me.

"I've got to get in there," I say after an appropriate hug time has passed. "You're going to have to let me go."

"Right. Sorry." He releases me and holds me at an arm's length, his happiness fading a bit when his gaze trails the wounds on my face.

*Pity.*

Magnus strolls forward and latches onto the handle, holding the door open for me.

I step in and stop when he follows me inside. "What are you doing?"

He rubs his stomach. "Can't a guy eat?"

I deadpan. "Seriously? Here? There's that Mexican joint we walked by."

"But I'm already here."

I sigh and glance around. "Sit wherever you want. I'll take your order once I clock in."

The restaurant is empty aside from us and a couple at a table smack dab in the middle of the room. Understaffed, too, but with hardly any customers, I'm not at all surprised. I'll be taking the place of whatever other waitress is working before me, and mentally hoping for a busy but manageable shift. I could use the money, but it's stressful when I get overly slammed. The kitchen help can hardly cover their own work, let alone stop to come assist me if I need it.

I walk across the open area, offering a fake smile to the patrons already sitting down. They cringe a little at my appearance, reminding me for the millionth time that I look like shit.

"Whoa, what the hell happened to you?" Saul, the manager, calls out the second I step into the back.

"Not a big deal, I got mugged." I slide my timecard out of the slot and reach to put it into the machine.

"Hold on there." He puts his hand out to block me from finishing my task.

"What?" The urge to punch him in the throat grows with each passing second he's taking from me. Can't he wait to be a dick until I'm at least being paid for it?

"You, uh, don't look so good, June."

"Yeah, I'm aware." I scrape my card against his hand to try to move him. "Can I clock in? I need to take someone's order."

"Go home, June."

*If he says my name one more time...*

"What? Why?"

He pulls his hand away but not before circling my face with his finger, going so far as to press it above my brow. "This. Not good for business."

I swat him away. "Don't touch me."

"Did you just smack me?" Genuine shock riddles his features.

Did he forget completely about touching my face first? Like my reaction wasn't a normal one to a creepy pimple-faced weirdo getting too comfortable with my personal space.

"Yeah, want me to do it again?" I shouldn't have said that.

He stands up straighter, putting himself fully between me and the time machine. "You're fired."

"Are you kidding me?" Because I called him out on getting a little too handsy?

His gut presses against my torso, pushing me back.

"You disgusting prick." I throw the cardstock in my grasp at him. "I fucking hated working here anyway." That's the God's honest truth. This place sucked. Either it was deadass empty or too busy to manage. Meaning no tips from no people, or hardly any from my inability to juggle ten tables at a time.

This has got to be a record though. Being fired twice within a short period. What's next, Bram and Jack kicking me to the curb, too?

I'd be royally screwed.

I turn on my heel, going back the way I came, shoving the swinging door open and not caring that it slams against the wall.

Magnus is on his feet in an instant, rushing over to me. "What's wrong?"

"Come on. Let's get out of here." I reach the front door and throw my middle finger in the air. "Fuck this place," I call out, hoping it's loud enough for Saul to hear.

"What the hell is going on?" Magnus follows me despite having any clue why I'm rushing out.

I burst onto the sidewalk and angrily walk a few blocks before the rage inside me simmers in the slightest. "Fuck." So much for the money I'm trying to make to get out of the apartment situation I'm stuck in. I can't fucking win. I run my hands through my hair, wincing at the ache it causes.

"June." Magnus reaches out to me. "Hey." He steadies my shoulders and forces me to look at him. "Breathe." He takes a deep breath in and exhales like he's trying to teach me how to.

I peer up at him. "Why are you still here?"

"Where else would I be?"

I shrug. "I don't know. Work or something."

"This is more important."

"Following me around?"

He shakes his head gently. "Making sure you're okay."

"Good luck with that one."

"Here, sit." Magnus guides me to a bench.

It's then that I recognize where I took him. The park. The one I go to in an attempt to decompress from the chaotic world around me. The place I accidentally crashed all night and scared a couple kids into thinking I was dead. I've never taken anyone here.

He lowers himself onto the bench first and pats the spot next to him. "Please."

I comply because what else do I have to do. I'm not due at Jack's until this evening and it's not like I want to go home and deal with my idiot roommates. I was supposed to be working for the next five hours, not wandering around the city pissed off with Magnus on my tail.

"What happened back there?" Magnus leans into the bench, his arm resting behind me.

I have the strong urge to keep my mouth shut, to not burden Magnus with my mundane issues, but I find myself talking anyway, despite my natural tendency to bottle everything up. "Apparently, my appearance was bad for business." I leave out the part where Saul had invaded my space.

"Wait, so let me get this straight. You got fired because of something completely out of your control?"

"Pretty much, yeah."

Magnus runs his hand through his hair. "Damn, princess. I'm sorry."

"It's not your fault." It was mine, for being in the wrong place at the wrong time. For not paying better attention to my surroundings. For walking home intoxicated.

"It might as well be."

"What's that supposed to mean?" I turn and face him, pulling my leg up and resting it on top of the other. I ignore the ache from the bruises on my knees and shin and continue to look at his serious yet gorgeous face.

He flits his gaze at my bottom half.

"It's nothing," I tell him before he can ask.

"If it was nothing you wouldn't have winced."

"You noticed that?" I thought I hid it well enough.

"I notice everything."

Does he see that despite my injuries and how pissed I am about losing yet another job, that I still want to rip my pants off and climb on top of him, sliding myself over his shaft until he's buried deep inside me?

I break eye contact and try to keep that one off his radar. Neither one of us can afford to deepen our already intense connection.

"What happened to you..." Magnus touches my shoulder, bringing my attention to him once again. "It wasn't your fault."

"It wasn't yours either." Why are he and Coen hellbent on making this *their* problem?

"I wouldn't be so sure."

"Stop being cryptic and tell me why you think this is about you. I'm not your responsibility." I take a drink of the coffee I'm still holding in my grip.

Magnus must have left his at the pizza place when I stormed out in a fury.

"I have enemies."

"Don't we all?"

Magnus rocks his head back and forth. "Not like this." He extends his hand, gently tucking a strand of my hair behind my ear. "It's not safe for me to tell you much more."

"If what you're saying is true, and it was your *enemies* that did this." I hold up my bandage-covered hand and circle my face with my finger. "Pretty sure we're past the point of keeping me safe."

"I never meant for you to get hurt, I promise."

I don't mean to, but I let out a laugh. "Stop blaming yourself. It wasn't your fault. It was some freak misunderstanding that had nothing to do with you or Coen or Dominic. How would that even make sense? I'm a nobody to you three. How would they know who I was and better yet, what the hell would be the point? They might as well kidnap and torture your fucking paperboy."

Magnus's jaw tenses at that last bit. "You really don't get it do you?"

"Get what? Please tell me what I'm missing here."

"How important you are to us."

I chuckle again, this time standing up from the bench. "Right. And I'm the Queen of England."

"Princess," he mutters under his breath.

"Whatever." I roll my eyes and fold my arms over my chest. "You guys clearly have some issues to work through, but they don't involve me. I have my shit taken care of. I don't need any of your help." And right now, I should be on the hunt for another job, not dealing with this.

"You think this is a joke?" Magnus rises to his feet in front of me. "There's nothing to laugh about. These *men* are dangerous. They let you go to prove a point, but that doesn't mean they won't finish what they started just to drive it home."

"They didn't let me go," I say quietly.

"What?" His eyes shift back and forth across my face.

"I escaped."

"Did you...did you kill the person? How many were there?"

"No. I stabbed him in the thigh and ran out the door. There was only one of them."

"Christ."

"It had nothing to do with you, Magnus. Stop blaming yourself. How would they have even known to go after me anyway?"

"They must have seen you leave the house."

"I..." My heart picks up its pace when my mind catches up to what he just said. "I wasn't alone, Magnus. I was with Cora."

All the doubts I had, all the moments I blew Coen and Magnus off for their overconcern that could have never been linked to me disappear in the blink of the eye. If what they're saying is true, and that it is their dangerous enemies who attacked me, that means Cora is in danger, too.

And if I don't get to her before they do, she might not be as lucky as I was to escape the twisted ways of the man who threatened to carve me like a pumpkin.

# CHAPTER 13

# June

Is this how the guys feel? This agony in my chest. This aching fear consuming my entire being at the thought of someone hurting Cora.

If it is, there's no wonder why they're reacting the way that they are. If Cora gets hurt because of me, I could never forgive myself. I would stop at nothing to inflict twice as much pain on whoever touches her.

"We'll find her," Magnus calls out from behind me. He catches up within a moment and reaches out to stop me. "June. Please."

"You don't get it." I turn to him, facing him with what must be a wild look on my face.

He tilts his head. "I do, trust me, I do. But reacting irrationally isn't going to do any of us a favor."

"How do you expect me to be rational?"

"A minute ago, you didn't believe me, now you're storming off in a hurry."

"You think I care what happens to me?" I picture Cora sitting where I was the other night. The knife pressed against her cheek, the blade digging across her flesh. No fucking way will I allow her to experience that. But what if I'm too late? What if the damage is already done?

"Obviously you don't. But I do. And I bet Cora wouldn't want you putting yourself at risk to save her."

He's totally right. Cora would be pissed.

"Then what? What am I supposed to do?"

"Where's your phone? Call her." Magnus pats my pockets and pulls the device from the one in the back.

I unlock the thing and click on the last person I had called. Cora. It goes straight to voicemail. "Fuck."

"Send her a text."

I thumb a few words together and hit send, the little bar at the top pausing and not wanting to go all the way through. Her phone is definitely off.

"Where *should* Cora be right now?"

I think back to the last time I saw her, getting into that car with the random dude from the bar. He seemed nice, but isn't that how they trick you? They lure you in and pull the rug out from under you when you least expect it. She had sent me a message the next morning, a few emojis to let me know how bad her hangover was, but other than that, I haven't spoken to her. I was too embarrassed to admit what had happened to me that night after I had left. Here I was worried about her and it was me that got caught up with a psychopath.

I try to process the days, align the details Cora has told me when her classes are and her social calendar. Maybe she's at home, having some quality time with her partially dysfunctional family.

What if she's tied to a chair, bleeding out onto the floor of that house? The one I can't even remember where it was because I was fueled into a self-preservation frenzy to get the fuck out of there as quickly as I could.

"Campus, let's try campus." Because the idea of her sitting through a boring lecture is far more appealing than the alternative.

Magnus nods, pulling out his own phone and pushing a few buttons. "I have a car coming."

"I'm not waiting on an Uber, Magnus." I continue on the path I had taken prior to him stopping me, making my way through the gated area and out onto the sidewalk in front of the park.

A blacked-out vehicle approaches, slowing to a stop near us.

"Me either." He grips the handle and opens the door. "Get in, princess."

I swallow my pride and hop in the back, putting entirely more faith than I'm comfortable giving into this tattooed man I barely know. Desperate times call for desperate measures, and if I want to find Cora, I need all the help I can get.

Magnus's phone buzzes and he answers it, pressing it to his ear. "Yeah?"

I can't make out the mumbling on the other line.

"She's with me." He flits his gaze to me. "She's fine. We're trying to locate the other girl, Cora." He waits while the other person speaks then continues. "If she's important to June then she's important to us. End of discussion." He disconnects the line and steadies his attention out the window.

We drive the few blocks across town in the opposite direction I had come from and arrive at the university's grounds.

I hop out before Magnus can stop me and make my way across the grassy area. It wasn't too long ago that I was a student here and yet it feels like an eternity. Each passing day is a hurdle that grows larger, reminding me that I probably won't overcome the challenges that keep coming at me.

"June," Magnus calls out. "You have to stop."

I round the corner, my heart nearly leaping out of my chest as my sights settle on that familiar blonde-haired girl. I gasp, bringing my bandaged hands over my mouth to hush the noise that escapes me.

Magnus rushes around me, drawing a gun from who the fuck knows where.

I put my arm out to stop him, to disallow him from going any further.

Cora. She's alive. She's smiling, laughing, and gripping the arm of another girl.

I drag Magnus away, going back behind the wall and letting my weight fall against it, savoring the relief flooding through my body.

Cora is fine. Unharmed. And showing no signs of trauma.

"Was that her?" Magnus keeps the pistol in his grip, not quite ready to holster it.

It suits his whole bad-boy appearance but doesn't match with his genuinely gentle nature. His entire existence is a contradiction and somehow, it totally works for him.

"Yes." I steady my breathing and let my heart take a break from thumping wildly.

"Why didn't you go over there? Talk to her?"

"I don't want her to see me like this." I hold out my hands. "If she doesn't *need* to know then I'd rather her not."

Magnus finally puts away the gun, tucking it behind his back. "Why didn't you get proper medical care?"

"Who said I didn't?" Is there anything he doesn't pick up on?

"I'm not an idiot. I've had my fair share of wounds. Those are going to heal like shit if you don't get them taken care of."

I push myself off the wall. "They're fine."

"Where are you going?"

"Home." I turn to him. "Now that I know Cora is safe..."

"Just because she's okay now doesn't mean what I said is any less true. These people aren't fools, June."

"Okay, well, the more I'm seen with you, the higher my chances of being kidnapped again are. So wouldn't it make sense for me to go home?" If I'm lucky, Carter won't be home, and I can take a nap in peace before my night shift at the bar.

"Let me take you then, drop you off."

"And lead them and you straight to where I live?"

Magnus steps forward, closing the gap between us. "God damn it, June. I'm trying to protect you. Don't you see that?"

The million-dollar question rattling through me: why?

"Can't you for one second put yourself in my shoes. What you just felt for Cora, don't you think that's how I *still* feel, and have ever since the moment I first saw you? You were in danger the very second I locked my eyes on you and you will remain in danger until either one of us is dead. I take no pleasure in torturing myself with concern. There's no escaping it now, so please, for the love of all things holy, believe me when I say I'm trying to keep you safe."

I study his face, the concern lining his brow, the tightness of his jaw, set in a hard line. His eyes pierce through me, begging me to understand what he's going through. Maybe he really is speaking the truth. Because why would he lie about something like this? How would *that* make any sense? What would he possibly gain from taking time away from his life to look over me? And given my run-in with that creep from the other night, wouldn't it be smart to have a man wielding a gun lurking in the shadows, ready to leap at the slightest threat?

"Okay," is all I respond.

He swallows, continuing to stare at me. "Okay?"

I nod. "Yeah. You can take me home." I owe him that much after he brought me here. Helped me calm down enough to figure out where Cora was and ease the raging nerves that almost had me running through the streets of this city until I found her.

He breaks out into a grin and lets out a laugh. "I really thought I was going to have to throw you over my shoulder and cart you to my car."

"Is that still an option?" I raise a brow at him and wink.

"Only if you keep tempting me."

We walk to the vehicle at a much slower pace than the one we took away from it. My body is already feeling lighter at setting my sights on Cora and confirming that she was untouched. There's still the chance of something happening to her, but it seems unlikely given the time that has passed. If they were going to, wouldn't they have acted soon after I managed to slip out of their grasp? Maybe Cora isn't on their radar at all, leading me to believe I was right with the original idea I had about it having been an isolated accident. A freak fucking coincidence that I ran into some weirdo who thought I was someone else.

If he hadn't mentioned that a higher-up was pulling his strings, I would have chalked it up to a sick weirdo getting his rocks off on carving up girls. But no, he's a hired hand who gets paid to fulfill his twisted desires.

Magnus opens the door to the black car and climbs in behind me. "Where to, princess?"

*Shit.* I don't really want him to see where I live. Partially because of how private I am, the remaining bits, a heavy embarrassment at the drastic difference from his place to mine. He lives in a literal mansion and I'm slumming it with a bunch of low lives.

"Um, Weber and Sixth," I tell him the closest intersection.

It's not far from here but getting a ride beats having to walk. Especially when danger seems to prowl around every corner.

"What time do you head back out?" Magnus keeps his eyes trained out the window, surveying each person and building we pass.

"A few hours. Why?"

"I'll pick you up."

"That won't be necessary."

"Sure it is." Magnus's features harden again, like he's preparing to fight me on this.

I have half a mind to tell him the wrong time, but I wouldn't put it past him to tear the whole city apart looking for me if I don't show up when I say I will. This might be a battle I'm not capable of winning, given how deadly serious he is about my safety. Perhaps if I humor him, give him what he wants for an evening or two, he'll realize there is no threat, and he can return to his normally scheduled programming. And I can go back to my own life and the issues that keep piling up.

With the Cora scare, I didn't exactly stop and look for help-wanted signs posted in the windows we passed. I was more focused on finding my friend in one piece, and still alive.

"June." Magnus breaks my concentration.

"Yeah?" I blink over at him.

"That job earlier, the one pizza place."

"What about it?"

"How much would you have made during your shift?"

"I don't know? Why?"

Magnus reaches into his pocket, pulling out a wad of cash sufficient to solve quite a few of my problems. He flips through it and slides off some of the bills. "Will five cover it?"

"You're going to give me *five hundred* dollars?" If I made that much at *one* place, let alone all three of them, I wouldn't be struggling to pay my bills. And I sure as shit wouldn't be living in that disgusting dump.

"Is that not enough?" He tries to get more but I stop him.

"No, that's more than I would have made." I push his hand away. "But I can't accept that."

"Why? It's my fault you got fired."

"How many times do I have to tell you? You had nothing to do with it." But I'm beginning to realize there's no convincing Magnus otherwise.

"What if it was—would you take it then?"

"I'm not looking for a handout."

"I'm not giving one."

I could easily settle the debt I have with Cora with that cash, and maybe even breathe easier at having lost that job earlier. It would give me a tiny cushion of time to not rush into another gig, and perhaps find something I don't hate. It would provide a bit of freedom, relief, and offer me a chance I wouldn't have had without it. But then it would make me weak, dependent, and give Magnus the idea that I can be bought, or worse, that I expect that from him.

"No strings attached, I promise, princess." He shoves the money into my hand, folding my fingers around it. "Pretend it never happened."

How can I forget something so small to him but so big to me? It might not be much to him, but it's a life-changing amount of cash to me. With it, plus the fifty Coen managed to force on me earlier, a huge burden has been lifted from my shoulders. Temporary yet monumental.

They say money can't buy happiness, but when it's the main cause of most of your problems, I'd say it's a gigantic contributing factor to having a good or bad life. I'm not after Ferrari's or gold-plated dinnerware, I'd just like a roof over my head that doesn't come with a potential drug-dealing sexist pig using up all the hot water and making passes at me every opportunity he gets.

The car slows to a stop at the intersection I had told them to take me to.

"Which one is yours?" Magnus peers out the window.

"I can walk from here." I reach for the door handle and tug it, but it doesn't budge. "Child-locks, seriously?"

Magnus opens his and steps out, holding his hand for me to take. "I'll escort you the rest of the way."

"No, it's fine, it's just right over there." I vaguely point in that direction.

Magnus sighs. "Will you at least let me put my number in your phone in case you need me?"

I look at him through my lashes, wanting to tell him no. How do I deny such a beautiful man when he's got that puppy dog kind of vibe about him? Well, more like a guard dog.

"Fine." I pull the thing from my pocket, unlock it and hand it to him.

He pushes a sequence of buttons, his own device ringing in response. "And just in case I need you."

"What could you possibly need me for?"

Magnus raises his eyebrow and grins. "I could think of a thing or two."

"I'm sure you could."

He studies my face, the smile on his fading. Magnus leans down, gently pressing his lips to my cheek. "If you need anything, anything at all."

My heart stutters at his softness. "Okay." I meet his gaze one last time. "Thank you."

"I'll see you at..." Magnus turns his wrist over to check his watch. "Eight?"

I don't have to be at work until nine, but I find myself agreeing anyway. "Yeah."

Magnus climbs into the back of the car, hesitating before closing the door.

I wave at him and use the opportunity of space between us to get moving. The direction they're parked means they can't turn down my street, given it's a one-way and that would be illegal. They'd have to circle the block and come down the other end. I'll be long gone by then.

The rustling of pavement lets me know they're driving away, but I don't look back. I keep going, inching closer to this hell hole I call home. It's not far, just a few buildings down from where they dropped me off.

Opening the front gate, I steady my breathing to prepare myself for whatever bullshit Carter is about to lay on me. With his less than legit job, his hours fluctuate. Meaning he's more than likely inside, sprawled out on the couch with a bag of chips next to him and a remote control in his hand. No doubt getting crumbs everywhere like the little leech he is.

I step through the entry of our building. There are four units, two on the left, two on the right. One upstairs on each side, one on the ground level. We live on the top floor of the right in a three-bedroom unit. Immediately, I notice the commotion up the steps at our door. I rush up to them and spot my shit being shoved into a tote.

"What the fuck is going on?" I grab the clothes out of Carter's grasp. "Get off my stuff."

"You've got to go, J." Carter shoves his hand across the threshold so I can't get inside.

"Don't fucking call me J like we're friends you fucking low-life."

Heather stands behind him, her arms crossed over her chest. "He's right, June."

"Someone care to explain why I'm being kicked out?"

"What happened to your face?" Heather asks me, but not out of concern, more like she's trying to prove a point.

"I got mugged, Christ. You're booting me out because of that? How the fuck does that make any sense?" I thought these two couldn't get any worse, and somehow they continue to prove me wrong.

"If that's what you want to call it." Heather picks my shower caddy off the floor and tosses it into the box with my other belongings. She nudges it toward me with her foot.

"Whatever trouble you got yourself into, is none of our business. But you make it ours when the thugs that are after you come by here and threaten us." Carter continues to block my path. "Especially those kinds of guys."

What are they talking about? "Someone came here?"

Heather nervously glances at the ground and nods. "Yep. Luckily Carter was on his way home or who knows what they would have done to me."

I stare at Carter. "You're the one who sells drugs, they were probably here for you."

"They asked specifically for you, June." Heather exhales and places her hand on Carter's shoulder. "We can't have that here."

"You can't be serious. I paid my rent; you can't evict me."

"We can, and we will." Carter grips the handle and starts to close me out.

I place my bandaged palm against it. "Where am I supposed to go?"

Carter shrugs. "You'll figure it out." He shuts the door in my face, not a care in the world that he threw me to the wolves like this.

I reach into my pocket and pull out my key, shoving it into the lock. But it won't slide in, not the way it used to. Fuckers already changed the locks on me. I slam my fist against the door, the ache of my injuries reminding me of my fragile state.

Footsteps approach me from behind, and when I raise that same fist to slam it into whoever is coming toward me, I'm stopped.

Magnus holds me from punching him. "Come on."

"What? How did you...?" That question has multiple meanings.

"Doesn't matter." His jaw tightens and he glances at the place I was locked out of. "You're done here. It's not safe for you."

"It's not safe for me anywhere." I thought the attack was random. I tried my best to convince myself and Magnus of that. I shoved that knife into that man's thigh and ran like hell to get away. I was sure I wasn't followed, that he couldn't have chased me in his condition.

Maybe Magnus was right after all. Because how else would they have found where I lived?

This wasn't random. And if they can easily find me here, what else do they know about me?

That same question rattles my core, the one I've asked myself time and time again.

*Why me?*

I study the remains of whatever possessions I have, half-ass shoved into a cheap plastic tote. The shampoo bottle that is currently leaking onto the few clothes Heather and Carter grabbed.

"Unless it's of sentimental value, leave it." Magnus slides his hand under my arm. "I'll get you new."

"Wh—what?" I let him guide me down the steps one by one, the entire situation still processing in my mind, making my head spin with a plethora of emotions. I glance back, the last few things I owned becoming a blur as we walk out of sight. "I need my..." But I draw a blank. I've had less and survived; do I really actually *need* anything from that mess of a box?

Magnus pauses to listen to me. "What is it?"

"My charger," is the only thing I can come up with.

"I can buy you a new one." He continues to help me down the stairs. "Your phone could use an upgrade, too."

"I don't want—"

Magnus places his hands on my shoulders and forces me to look at him. "You're getting a new phone, a new charger, an entire new wardrobe, and better beauty products than whatever off-brand shit I just saw in that box. You will have a bed to sleep in, a safe place to rest your beautiful head. And for Christ's sake, you are letting our doctor tend to these wounds."

"I don't have health insurance," I blurt out.

"Is that why you didn't go to the hospital?"

"Among other reasons." Can my level of embarrassment rise any further?

"Not a concern. It will all be taken care of."

"You can't just—"

"I can, and I will. Not up for discussion, princess." Magnus settles his palm on the small of my back.

We step out onto the sidewalk, the sun blaring in my face, the realization that I have to start completely over again settling into my core.

I've worked my ass off, and for what, to be kicked out by my piece of shit ex-friend and her sad excuse of a boyfriend? I get their concern for their own safety, but do they seriously have no regard for mine whatsoever? How can someone be so fucking cruel and inconsiderate? Did they even run it by our other two roommates, or did they decide my fate themselves? I wouldn't be surprised if this was all Carter's doing. Hell, I wouldn't put it past him to have bribed a couple of his druggie buds to come by and cause a scene to make it seem like I was stirring up more shit than I really was. The bruises and cuts all over my body making his ruse that much more believable in his master plan to ruin my fucking life.

Magnus opens the car door for me. "Let's get you home."

I climb in and rest my head against the seat, because what other choice do I have?

"I want to kill him," I mutter under my breath, fully meaning the words.

Magnus exhales and pats my thigh. "In due time, princess."

# CHAPTER 14

# Dominic

"We're going to have to set some ground rules." I shift my gaze toward the stairs, where the sleeping beauty rests in our spare bedroom.

I got home a couple of hours ago from doing recon with Hayes to find out that Bryant brought June to our house, with the intention of allowing her to stay here. Whether that is temporary or permanent is lost on me. It was short notice, but I did what I could to get a few things for her to make her time a little more comfortable.

This new arrangement is a mixture of good and bad with the way this situation is unfolding. On one hand, having June in our home means that we can keep an eye on her, and do what we can to maintain her safety. But on the other, it will confirm to all our enemies that she is our weakness, the thing that could potentially be our downfall. Something we all agreed we would not permit. And here we are, each of us experiencing romantic feelings for the same woman.

There is a minimal chance that this will end well for any of us.

Even if we manage to win this war, then what? The three of us will start another over her.

"Toilet seats need to be put down." Bryant is the first to chime in.

I rub my temple. "That wasn't what I meant."

He plucks a grape from the bowl sitting in front of him and pops it into his mouth. "What's wrong with manners?"

"Nothing. Nothing is wrong with that. But I'm referring to more serious matters." Like where she'll be sleeping, the distance we should keep regarding our personal and professional lives, and a general rule of keeping it in our pants. It won't bode well if there is any temptation, and if we establish that boundary now, the better off we'll be.

June appears around the corner, rubbing her eyes but somehow appearing more beautiful than ever. Something about that just woken up look makes me want to cross the space between us and pick her up and take her back to bed. But I don't. I remain stone-faced and still, not moving an inch in her direction.

"You guys talking about me?" She walks barefoot down the steps and into the kitchen with us.

Hayes unglues himself from his phone and plants his gaze on her. A side of him I've never known before. Not much can distract that man from his work.

Bryant meets June halfway, putting his arm around her shoulders and tugging her toward him. "You hungry?"

She shakes her head. "Not really. Do you happen to have an extra toothbrush I could use?"

"Your bathroom has been stocked," I tell her. "Bryant mentioned you didn't have your toiletries, so I sent for them."

"You *sent* for them?"

"Yes. If you find they are not suited for your taste, I will replace them with whatever you wish." Although I can't imagine she'll have many complaints as I had our driver get the best of what was available. "I took the liberty of having your clothes washed. They're hanging in your closet with a few other items."

"Um, thank you. I'll pay you back as soon as I can."

"Not necessary," all three of us guys say at once.

I clear my throat. "You should eat something though. What would you like?" I walk over to the fridge and look inside.

The doorbell rings and I shift my attention toward it.

Bryant exits without a word, and a minute later, he arrives with a bag of food in his grasp.

"Seriously?" I glare at him, wishing I could somehow shake some sense into his empty skull. "That's it. Last one. No more."

"Forever?" He pouts like I kicked his puppy.

"Until this is done."

"Until what's done? Me? I can leave." June folds her arms and takes a cautious step back.

"No, not you," I weakly reassure her. How can I make her understand the severity of our situation without telling her the truth? That would only put her more in danger, and I'm not willing to do that to her.

Bryant pulls container after container out of the takeout bag.

Chinese. He's risking our lives over Chinese.

"Then what?" June's gaze pierces through me.

"It's complicated."

Bryant pulls the plates from the cupboard and reaches in to grab some silver-ware. "What he's trying to say is..."

Hayes smacks Bryant when he walks by him. "Bryant, keep your mouth shut."

"Leave it to you to be okay with leaving me in the dark." June glares at Hayes and I'm grateful that the attention has shifted from me.

I don't want to withhold from her, but it's the only thing I can think of to prioritize her safety.

"Can we eat, in peace, for once?" Bryant opens the first container, revealing fried rice.

"I'm not hungry," June says again.

Hayes approaches the selection of food. Plopping some of the rice, General Tso's, and an eggroll onto a plate. He reaches into the fridge and pulls out one of his Dr. Peppers and strolls over to our dining room table. Dragging the chair back, he turns to June. "Eat."

The two of them have a momentary standoff but then she ends up claiming the seat. Maybe she realized it was three against one and her odds of walking out of this room without feeding herself were slim to none.

We might disagree on a lot, but her well-being is one of the few things we have in common.

Bryant slides a full plate across the counter to me. "Here."

"Thank you." I nod and take his offering. "But I mean it, this is the last time. You'll have to put those cooking classes to use."

June brings her napkin to her mouth, chewing through her bite before speaking. "You took culinary classes?"

Hayes chimes in. "Bryant has taken a course on pretty much everything. Culinary, photography, botany, pottery...pretty much anything that ends in a 'y'."

"Jack of all trades." June opens her drink and takes a sip.

"Master of none." Bryant slides into the seat next to her.

"Better than a master of one." She elbows him and smiles.

I hate the jealousy that courses through me at their interaction. I shouldn't feel that way. She is not mine. She is not theirs. She is no ones. Yet, the envy still slips into my veins at wanting that look of admiration to be at me.

I note the tenseness in Hayes' jaw, telling me he's experiencing a similar emotion, too. Which is exactly why we need to amend the house rules to accommodate our newest member.

"How are your wounds?" I ask her.

Bryant informed me that she did not receive proper medical care after what had happened, and that he had our on-call doctor tend to them when they arrived at the house. I haven't seen the extent of the damage, but with the visible bruising and discoloration, it would only make sense to have a professional care for them.

"Better." She flits her gaze at me.

"Good. Are you in any discomfort?" I haven't had a chance to speak with the doctor about her condition.

"No, he gave me something for the pain and inflammation, and used some fancy antibiotic. Said it would help with healing."

"You should make it a point to get some rest in the meantime, too," I add.

"I took a pretty solid nap." She reaches into her back pocket to pull out her phone. "I need to get to work here in a bit."

"Work?" Hayes and I speak at the same time.

We really must get out of each other's heads.

"Yeah, I have to be there at nine. It's not far, I can walk from here."

"No," all three of us blurt out.

"You better be saying no to me walking, and not me going." June shoves a piece of chicken into her mouth, chewing it and glancing between all of us.

I cool my rising temper. "I think what we meant to say is, you should take the evening off. Spend it in bed, binge-watching television, or whatever it is you enjoy doing. We have a state-of-the-art entertainment room with access to anything you'd like, all at your fingertips. I can send for whatever food or drink you prefer."

"I have to go to work," June insists.

"No." I clench my jaw.

"Am I being held captive here? Against my will?" She stares across the table at me.

"Of course not."

"Then I am going to leave here in twenty minutes and go to work. Either I can walk, or you can have your *driver* take me." She uses air quotes to enunciate the word driver. "This living arrangement, while absolutely appreciated, is completely temporary, and not necessary. As soon as I'm able, I'll be out of your hair and no longer burdening your lives."

Hayes speaks up. "J, you don't understand, it's not sa—."

"Safe?" She cuts him off. "It's not safe for me out there? Guess what Co, I've made it this far without you, I'll be fine on my own." June exhales and places her napkin on her plate. "I'm grateful for your hospitality, I really am. But I won't be in your debt because of the shit storm that is wrecking my life. I've never needed anything from anyone, and I don't plan on starting today."

"That's not what this is about." Hayes stands when she does. "Don't blame them for my mistakes."

"It's too late for that, Co." June storms off, up the stairs and out of view.

"Dude, what the fuck did you do to her?" Bryant asks the question rattling my own mind.

Hayes runs his hand through his hair and slumps down into his seat. It's strange to see him so...disheveled. Especially over a female. Usually, he's mad about not being able to kill someone or the lack of ammunition at our local supply center.

"You wouldn't get it." He leans his head back and sighs. "She'll never forgive me."

"Have you tried..." Bryant stretches his arm across the chair June was sitting in. "Talking to her? Believe it or not, communication is kind of important." He focuses on me next. "This whole keeping shit from her isn't going to go over well for us. I think it's best we just be honest about what's going on."

I shake my head. "No."

"She's not like the rest of them, Dom, she can handle it. The one thing I've learned about her is that she doesn't trust anyone." Bryant nods at Hayes. "I'm guessing because of this fucking idiot." He turns back to me. "We've given her no reason to trust us. Do you really think being secretive is going to do us any favors?"

"No, but—"

"I have followed you for this long, and I would go to the ends of the earth for you. You two are family to me. And I know she means something to both of you. So please, if you care about her, about us, then you'd at least consider what I'm saying to be true." Bryant grabs his plate and June's. "I'm the people person, remember. The one thing I'm a master at. Put a little faith in me."

I hate that a strong part of me thinks he's speaking the truth. That his words hold some value and that confessing to June would be the best thing for us all. But if we do, there is no turning back. She could react poorly, take off and put herself in more danger than she already was. The reality of the situation could be uglier than she imagines, scaring her away forever.

Why would that be an issue though? Why does it matter that we keep her near, when doing so is the riskiest thing of all?

I'm being selfish for wanting her, and in our line of work, that's not a luxury we can afford.

I should have stayed away the first time I saw her and felt that magnetic pull. I should have never entered that random bar ever again. But there was something about her. Something dark that drew me in. A familiar depth to her that had me going in there every chance I could spare. I told myself that if I didn't engage with her, it would be fine. And I managed that. I stole little moments when she wasn't looking, just to be near her. But with each passing day, and each disgusting disgrace of manhood that made a pass at her, a simmering rage built inside of me to be there, *just in case.*

I've never wanted to be wrong more than in that moment I saw him follow her down that hallway and into the bathroom. I could smell his ill-intent like a cheap aftershave, reeking so potently that the only thing I knew to do was to show him who's boss.

I could hear his words when I entered that space, that she had a fuckable mouth. A declaration I knew with certainty was not welcomed in that moment. He followed it up by telling me that we could share, further proving he had every intention of forcing himself on her and solidifying the thirst I had for his blood.

I beat him but held back knowing that she was there. That I was probably frightening her more than she already had been by his sick advances.

I was certain she would fear me, because she had every right to. That's the effect I have on people who know me, and most who just catch a glimpse of me. Ruthless. Cruel. Brutal. Those are the words I hear whispered when I walk by. Let them believe what they want, especially if it's true.

But when June looked into my eyes, it was like she saw past that, or somehow embraced it for what it was. She wasn't afraid. And that's why, when she stepped forward and grabbed onto my face, I lost all control, melting into, and becoming one with her. The only thing on my mind was bringing her every ounce of pleasure she deserved. Because for someone to face something as evil as I am, and to dive headfirst without reservation, I knew I had found something absolutely rare.

And that alone is why I believe Bryant. That June might not react poorly to the truth. She saw plenty of it that night and still wanted me, perhaps even more once she was exposed to the real me. If anything, I should be afraid of her for going against normal human nature to cower in the presence of such darkness. No, she walked straight into the line of fire like the vixen she is.

"Fine," I finally say. "Not now, but later. I'll accompany her to her night shift. In the meantime, you two have work to do."

Hayes perks up. "Seriously?"

"Do you have something better to do?"

"No. I mean, you're going to tell her? Really?"

"Yes. At least, the parts she needs to know." I rise from my seat and take my plate to the kitchen.

Bryant relieves me of it and scrapes the contents into the trash before loading it into the dishwasher. "I think it's a good idea."

"Of course you do, it was *your* idea." Hayes stands again. "I gave everything up. Every*one*. I put it all in the past. Now you're telling me I didn't have to? That I could have been with her this *whole* time?"

"What are you talking about dude?" Bryant wipes his hands on a towel and tosses it onto the counter.

"Nothing, fucking forget it." Hayes shuts us down and takes off in the same direction June had gone, only I imagine he's going to his room, not hers. He's fuming, and between the two of them, there are too many emotions running wild.

"I've never seen him this moody." Bryant closes the takeout boxes and places them in the fridge.

"He'll be fine."

But a part of me wonders if he will. I've seen the things he's capable of. Hayes, the person that he is today, was born in blood—both literally and figuratively. Men like me, we came from the womb cold and ruthless, it was ingrained in our DNA, but Hayes, he was turned into a hardened psychopath by the shit life threw at him. He endured loss after loss until one day, he snapped, something breaking in him that could never be repaired. He's fueled by violence, and it's not that we don't share that in common, but mine is a natural response, where his is a conscious choice. And in a lot of ways, that's a much more potent attribute.

People fear me because I am pure evil.

People underestimate Hayes because he chooses it.

People misjudge Bryant because he looks it.

The three of us combined, a deadly force not many dare to fuck with.

---

The ride to June's work is quiet. She sits opposite of me, her arms folded across her chest like she's pouting that I insisted on escorting her to work. She's going to be even more pissed when I go in with her, and sit out her shift in my corner booth.

I have other things that I need to get done, work that requires my attention, but it will have to wait until I'm certain that she is home and safe. It's not ideal, that's for damn sure, yet I do it anyway, because the thought of something happening to her when I could have prevented it eats away at me.

I'm already furious enough with myself that danger managed to find her. I thought I was doing the right thing by keeping away once I crossed that line with her. But little did I know that Bryant and Hayes had their own thing going with her, too, putting June deeper in the line of fire.

None of us should have gotten involved.

Now there's no possibility of going back. Our enemies wouldn't believe we cut ourselves off cold turkey, and they'd use her as collateral on the chance that it would work. The only way to keep her safe now is to keep her close, and do everything we can to protect her.

"You're not going in there," she tells me when I climb out of my side of the SUV and approach her.

"I am."

"No, you're not."

"Come on." I grip her under her arm and nudge her toward her place of work.

"I'm not a child." June pulls herself from my grasp.

"Then don't act like one."

June narrows her gaze at me and sucks in a breath, her wild eyes telling me she's considering all the things she'd like to do to me...just not in a fun way. Although, fun is a subjective term.

I steady my stare back at her. "Until you are no longer in danger, someone will escort you to and from wherever you please. If you have a problem with that, tough. The alternative will likely result in your untimely death. Now, would you like to step inside or perhaps you don't enjoy being punctual?"

"I didn't sign up for this."

"Neither did I."

"Clearly you did, you're the one enforcing it."

"My apologies for caring whether you live or die."

"I'm going to prove you wrong. This is all one big misunderstanding."

"Uh-huh, sure." I place my hand on her lower back, my other outstretched toward the entrance of the dive bar she spends most of her nights in.

June shakes me off once more and walks to the door, each of her footsteps carrying the weight of her growing annoyance at me.

I grip the handle and pull the thing open, following her into the poorly lit establishment. Without saying another word to her, I mosey over to my booth, unbuttoning my jacket and folding it neatly in half. I ensure the table is dry and free of any other debris, then set it carefully down. All the while listening in on the conversation June is having with the man named Jack who owns the place.

"Did you two come together?" He asks her.

"No," she says firmly.

"Oh. I thought you did." Jack pauses and shifts his tone. "What happened to your face?"

His first thought was to question her about me and not the very visible injuries she sustained? What a dick.

"I got mugged."

"Damn, that's rough. You okay?"

"Other than looking like shit, yeah, I'm fine. I'll be fine."

Despite the bruising and cuts on her skin, June is far from *looking like shit*. She's just too oblivious to notice her own beauty. It's frustrating, really. Her simple yet elegant features. She's aware enough to flaunt her body and use it to her advantage, but I'm not sure she realizes how stunning she truly is, not just eye-catching in the sense of getting extra tips.

"Okay, well, the table in the corner hasn't ordered yet if you want to grab them before Jane does. And obviously, high roller over there."

I settle into my seat and wait for her to arrive.

Does he not realize how loud he speaks and that his voice carries throughout the bar, to the point that anyone who *wanted* to pay attention to what he was saying could?

June makes it a point to go to the other customers first, despite knowing I tip better than anyone in this place. I'm not bothered by it though, I prefer her to do what she wants, so long as she's maintaining her safety.

She drops off their order at the bar and then continues on her way over to me. "Your usual?" Her voice is missing that usual sly flirtatious tone it typically had prior to us fucking in the bathroom. It would probably still be there had I not completely disrupted her life.

"Yes."

Not wasting another second, she turns on her heel and goes to the bar, mumbling my drink to Jack and taking the tray filled with full glasses to the other patrons. She drops off a refill to a lone woman at a table, and slides by the counter again to get mine.

"Thank you," I tell her as she strolls away without exchanging even a glance.

She's pissed and somehow, I love it—my cock throbbing in my pants at having gotten under her skin so damn badly. I shouldn't feel this way, want her this fiercely, but I do, and to think I can sit here all night without doing something about it will be the biggest challenge my self-control has ever faced.

---

The night progresses that way, her floating around to her tables and then dropping off a drink when mine gets low. I cautiously sip the decadent bourbon, savoring each last bit the same way I'd love to do to June.

I shift my mind from remembering our night together, the heated passion we shared in an adrenaline-fueled desire. The tension had been building for weeks but I wasn't quite sure it was reciprocated until she took that step forward and applied her lips to mine. I was completely lost in her, the chaos of the world falling into a slow-motion vortex that I temporarily escaped from. For those fleeting moments of our bodies becoming one, the only thing on my mind was her. Not the war. Not the many threats. Not the possibility that a man half my age might steal the empire I spent my entire life working toward. Just me and her and nothing else.

I knew I couldn't keep her. Couldn't pursue her. That I had to go back to the way things were before. And yet days went by and the thought of her wouldn't leave me. I was sucked in, hook-line-and-sinker. Completely shaken by the idea that something that fucking rare existed. That it was possible for my thoughts to be of anything other than violence and bloodshed.

Granted, that was exactly the thing that led us to that moment.

June was an angel but with tattered wings and a devilish grin, a darkness matching mine I couldn't stay away from.

The same that stands before me today, angry and brooding to and from, as if I'll be bothered by it and leave her alone. Doesn't she realize it only makes me want her more? That defiance, disobedience, that stubborn-headed *I can do it all on my own* vibe she has.

"Stop looking at me like that." June appears in front of me, her hand on her hip.

"Like what?" I should be checking the notifications popping up on my phone, not shadowing her with my gaze. This was obviously a terrible idea coming here tonight. I should have tasked Hayes or Bryant. But even then, would they have been able to withstand her alluring presence?

"You know what you're doing."

"Do I?" I thought I was being discreet but perhaps she's more in tune with my desire than I realized.

"Either fuck me or leave me alone."

I blink at her, a genuine bit of shock consuming me. "Excuse me?"

"You heard me." She remains still, unmoved, completely dead-ass serious.

"Is that option on the table?" My own mouth betrays me by asking the question I should have kept to myself.

June glances over her shoulder then back at me. "Not *literally* the table." She nods toward the kitchen area. "Staff bathroom. One minute. Don't keep me waiting." She takes off in that direction, disappearing out of sight.

Is she really implying what I think she is? Right here? Right now? After everything that's happened? Especially with how mad she is at me?

Who am I to question a woman who knows what she wants?

It would be wrong of me to not fulfill her desires, even if they go against everything I was trying to enforce. Boundaries. Rules. Distance.

To hell with it all.

I slip out of the booth and follow where she had gone, completely acting with confidence that I belong in this employee-only section. Who would dare to stop me anyway?

I knock lightly on the bathroom door, June's healing but still battered face greeting me on the other side.

She opens it up enough to let me in and shuts it behind me, locking it and turning to me. "This means nothing. And it doesn't mean I'm any less mad."

This is the part where I regain control, walk out of here, and put a stop to what's about to happen. Instead, I reach out and pull her toward me. I glance down at her from my position towering over her, taking in her beauty from this angle.

June reaches around, her hand finding my already growing erection through my pants. She grins and stands taller to bring her lips to mine. "Make it quick."

"Oh, love, I'm anything but quick." I run my hand up the nape of her neck and onto the base of her skull, gripping her hair and tilting her head up to look at me.

Our eyes lock onto each other, and I realize, if I'm going to back out, this is the time.

She meets my mouth with hers once again, sealing the fate we already decided when I stepped foot in this bathroom. Hell, when I walked into this bar. I was a fool for ever thinking any differently. June breaks away, flipping herself over and unbuttoning her shorts, tugging them over her delicious ass. She spreads her legs as far as her discarded clothing will allow, and reaches forward to hold onto the single sink basin.

"You going to fuck me, or should I do it myself?" June looks at me through the mirror in front of her.

"You wouldn't."

"Don't tell me what I would or wouldn't do." She raises her right hand from where she was holding on and shifts it toward her pussy.

I reach around and grab onto it as she slides her middle finger down her slit. "Mine," I growl at her.

"Then act like it."

How on Earth is it possible that I am such a feared man and here she is, nearly a foot shorter than me, a tiny little thing, half my age, calling the shots like she runs the place?

And why is it so fucking hot?

I cower behind her, gripping her thigh and grazing my mouth over her wetness. I give myself a quick taste, sighing at how fucking delectable she is. Just as I remembered from our time spent together in that *other* bathroom.

She pulses in response and lets out a sigh. "I don't have all night." June holds a condom between her fingers out to me.

I take it from her, biting off the corner of the wrapper and spitting it onto the ground while simultaneously taking my other hand and gliding two digits against her clit, rubbing in a circle, and dipping them into her pussy.

What can I say? I've always been rather good at multitasking.

Once I'm sheathed, I remove my soaked fingers and step closer.

Her hair brushes against my face, the scent of it a mixture of citrus and honey.

I press myself into her, the tip of my cock aligning with her hole, pushing through the tightness and spreading her to fit me inside.

She lets out a moan, dragging my hand up to her face to cover her mouth.

The other I keep on her hip to steady her into me.

I go easy for the first few thrusts, letting her body get adjusted to the fullness, but the second I sense her tenseness diminish, I pick up the intensity.

June reciprocates, slamming herself down onto my shaft and moaning against my hand.

A knock rattles the door, stopping us completely mid-motion.

"June, you okay in there?" Jack, her boss.

I slide my palm down her lips and rest it against her throat.

"Yeah," she calls out, her voice faltering. "Just changing my bandages. I'll be right out."

"Okay." He lingers for another second. "Mister bourbon neat disappeared, but he left his jacket behind."

Her gaze flicks to me in the mirror. "He could have stepped outside to make a phone call."

I rock myself back until the tip is barely in, and then forward, slowly moving my cock inside her again, not wanting to spare another second because of the interruption.

June tips her head up, enjoying the renewed friction. She tightens around me, her climax building with each steady motion.

I slither my hand along her side and around her front, slipping it under her bra and covering her breast. Pinching her nipple, I place my other palm over her mouth, thrusting deeper into her taut pussy, not caring at all about the man inches away on the other side of the door.

Jack adds, "Yeah, you're probably right."

June moves her body into mine, my cock growing harder in response. She manages to reach for the faucet, turning it on and giving us a little bit of a sound barrier for our forbidden sexcapades.

The sound of Jack's footsteps let us know that he finally walked away.

I lean into her and whisper in her ear, "Come for me." I slow my pace but maintain the depth, sending her spiraling into climax, mine following in tandem, exploding together in beautiful chaos. I ride out the wave with her and pull myself free, sliding the condom off and tossing it into the wastebin.

June pulls up her shorts, securing her outfit and washes her hands.

"Well, that was unexpected," I tell her.

She turns, dropping the paper towels she used to dry her hands with on top of the used rubber. "And meant nothing." She pats my chest. "Don't forget that." June reaches for the handle of the door. "Wait a minute before you follow me out." She leaves me behind without another word, only continuing to show me just how she cannot be tamed.

And further instilling how badly I want to make her mine.

Both a contradiction and yet here I am, willing to do whatever it takes.

# CHAPTER 15

# June

I'm living in a house with three men I want nothing more than to fuck on a regular—unattached—basis, and yet, I'm not supposed to be sleeping with any of them.

"June, did you hear me?" Dominic snaps his fingers in front of my face.

The same ones that were knuckle deep in my pussy last night in the employee bathroom at Jack's bar.

"Yeah, I get it. No banging each other." I point between them. "Does this count for you guys, too?" Partially sarcasm, but one can never be too sure.

"No one, and I repeat, no one," Dominic looks to all of us. "Is exchanging bodily fluid in this house."

"But what about—"

Dom cuts Magnus off mid-sentence. "But nothing."

Magnus crinkles his brows. "I was going to say sharing drinks."

Dom's jaw tightens, something he does regularly when he's annoyed. Or frustrated. Or pretty much experiencing any emotion. "You know what I mean."

Is he trying to convince himself or us? Because I'm pretty sure he was a willing participant in last night's shenanigans. And if what he's attempting to enforce is true, does that mean it's okay for me and him to fuck, but not the rest of the guys?

That's going to be a hard no from me.

It's all or nothing.

Although, despite wanting to strangle Coen for leaving me all those years ago, I'd still like to see if we still have the same insane chemistry we did when we were kids. We never did have sex, even though I wanted to. He was always wary and wanted to make sure we waited until I was older and could think more rationally about such a big decision. Little did we know, we didn't have the luxury of time on that one, and instead, I lost my v-card to some loser I didn't care about when I was fifteen, starting off my sex life with a one-minute interaction that resulted in minimal pleasure on my behalf. Not to mention a sexual hunger that was awoken and pretty much has been insatiable since then.

I've fucked Dom twice and Magnus once, and despite them being the best I've ever had, there's still *something* missing. It's not like I could choose just one of them anyway, nor would I want to. I'm not a solo partner kind of person. I'd never be satisfied tied down and I refuse to settle for anything I don't want.

So, for now, I'll stay in this house, and have sex with whichever will screw me, even if it's a secret from the rest of them.

What they don't know won't hurt them.

"Fine, no fucking. What's next?" Magnus sips his coffee and takes a bite of his bagel.

Something about the way his tattooed arm makes his shirt bulge sends a fire straight between my legs. I stop myself from gnawing my lip and staring too hard. I had a world-class orgasm yesterday and somehow, I'm roaring for more. I unlock my phone, swiping through my apps until I find the one I'm looking for. The screen alerts me that there's only one day left until my period starts, explaining why I'm in ultra-horny mode.

Dom's device buzzes but he ignores it. "I think now would be an appropriate time to fill June in on the severity of the situation."

Coen lowers his mug onto the counter, a bit harder than normal. "Is that really necessary?"

I glance over at him. "What's your problem, Co? You don't trust me?"

His blue gaze settles on me. "Has nothing to do with you, J."

"Then what?" I point to the other two men. "Magnus and Dom have no issue telling me the truth. You're the only one who refuses."

"It's for good reason," Dominic adds in Coen's defense. "I was hesitant, too."

"What changed your mind?" I ask him.

"Your safety is our main concern." Dom's phone vibrates again. "And we can't ensure that if you aren't aware of a few aspects of what's going on."

"What, like that you're in the mafia?" I let out a laugh but none of them join in on the humor.

Instead, their faces show a mixture of surprise and shock, none of them saying anything.

"Oh," I glance at Magnus. "You weren't joking."

Honestly, it makes sense. How else would the three of them have everything that they do? Between the mansion, the private security, their expensive taste in booze, and pretty much everything else, along with the other details I've picked up on but haven't paid much attention to. They have enemies, they disappear at all hours of the day and night, not to mention my very first close encounter with Dominic. What else was I expecting? Him to be a teacher or something?

They're incredibly secretive and if my declaration was true, it's for good reason.

It's not like you can go around telling everyone you're in a dangerous and hella illegal line of work.

I shrug. "Okay, and?" Because that can't be the whole big reveal. Obviously, it's nothing to discount, but there is clearly another layer to this mystery I've yet to unravel.

"I fucking told you." Magnus smacks Coen's arm and glares at Dominic.

"Told who what?" I give Magnus my attention.

"That you wouldn't freak out."

"It's going to take a little more than that to surprise me."

Coen drops his head into his hands, his elbows planted on the counter. "I can't fucking believe this," he mutters.

I ignore him and repeat my question. "But really, what's *actually* happening?"

"We're at war," Magnus speaks up.

Dom raises his hand to cut Magnus off. "Yes, what he's saying is true. There's been a shift in management, and we are set to take over the operation. We're getting some pushback from rivals who wish to hijack that control, meaning everyone in contact with us is essentially at risk."

I nod at him to continue and bring my mug to my lips, drawing in a mouthful of the strong coffee courtesy of Magnus.

"Our enemies have deemed you a weakness, and will use that to their advantage to throw us off and gain the upper hand."

"That explains what that guy said," I recall the evening of my kidnapping.

Coen speaks up, his stare locked onto me. "What was it?"

"Something about choosing the wrong side."

"One of Beckett's minions," Coen tells us.

"What's a Beckett?" I bite off a chunk of the remaining bacon strip on my plate, chewing it and waiting for one of them to tell me.

"Not what, *who*." Magnus comes to my rescue. "Simon Beckett. The leader of the group, trying to overthrow us."

"Ohh." I piece the puzzle together in my head, a part of it not making sense. "What happened to the previous leader?"

"Dead." The three of them say in unison.

Dominic shifts his posture. "I've been training with him for most of my life, as his main advisor, to take over when he retired. The transition was supposed to be seamless. Turns out, he fell before that happened, rather abruptly. His wife has been overseeing most operations since his death, but she wants out." His shoulders tense. "I should have been the obvious benefactor, but Beckett has made it a point to rally troops to claim the throne for himself."

It's amazing how much they'll confess once they get started. A second ago, they were too tense to say a word, now they're answering every question I toss their way.

"Hence the war."

I spin my mug back and forth on the counter. "So, you're not just *in* the mafia, you *are* the mafia. Okay, okay. Boss dies, you take over, Simon won't allow it." Suddenly, an idea dawns on me. "Why not just kill him then?"

Did I really just suggest murdering a man to eliminate their problems? And not be bothered by it at all?

"Don't you think we would have done that if it were that simple?" Coen runs his hand through his blonde hair.

I look at him, finally take him in. The soft features that have been hardened over time. The sweet, innocent boy who is now haunted by a constant darkness I only now noticed. Is this why he never came for me? Was this new life of his more important than the promises we made to each other that summer? I shake my head to rid myself of the thought. What's done is done, there's no going back and changing the past. And if I could, would I even want to?

"What Hayes is saying," Magnus chimes in. "Is that the situation is a bit more complicated. We can't kill Beckett for the same reasons he can't kill us. We're protected, we're smart, and we're dangerous. As is he. Well, for the most part."

Dominic clears his throat. "It's all about strategy. Getting his men to turn on him, sabotaging his efforts, making him look like a bad choice."

"Choice?"

Dom nods. "Yes. The wife that took over, gets the final say on who she wants to hand the reins over to."

"That's fucking stupid."

He shrugs. "I don't make the rules."

"Then why follow them?"

His phone goes off once more, this time pulling his attention from my face. His expression gives nothing away to what the notification might say. It could have been anything from a winning lottery ticket to a death in the family and I'd have no idea.

"You good?" Magnus asks him.

"I need to go." Dom shoves the thing into his pocket.

I glance at the clock. "Me too."

"No," Dom basically growls.

"Excuse me?" I climb off the chair and grab my plate. "I have work."

"You had work last night." He steadies his gaze on me.

"And this morning, and afternoon, and tonight. Well, after my first one today, I'll be job hunting, *then* I'll be at the bar again. Get with the program."

"That's unacceptable."

I slide my dish into the sink and stroll around the counter, slapping Dominic on the back on my way around him. "Good talk." I continue toward the stairs, turning around and glancing between the three men staring in my direction. "Which of you are escorting me?"

They look at each other, their expressions lined with surprise.

"I will." Magnus beams and raises his hand.

I had a hunch it would be him, considering Dom has other plans, and Coen gives off vibes like I'm a ticking time bomb. He's playing a solid game of hot potato and he refuses to lose.

"Wait." Dom steps away from where I had left him and focuses on me. "Magnus will accompany you now. Hayes will join you this evening. But I request that you come home in between shifts."

I cross my arms over my chest and study the gorgeous man in front of me.

Nearly every ounce of me wants to say no, because he's not the boss of me, but on the other hand, he *did* ask nicely. And if I want him to keep fucking me like he did last night, I should probably comply with him occasionally.

Still, though, it's not an option to obey him. I need to find another job. "I can't."

"You can, and you will." His demeanor hardens.

"No." I stare at him, matching his intensity.

Magnus jumps between us, his hands out. "Okay, as much as I'd love to see you two go at it, you're both wearing way *too* many clothes." When neither of us budges, he continues toward me. "I'll go with her, Dom, it'll be fine."

Dominic slowly shifts his stone-cold gaze to Magnus. "It won't, and you know it. You're being naïve and reckless."

"Yeah, yeah, that's my middle name." Magnus reaches my side and stops, his hand resting on my back.

Dominic steps closer, his voice deepening. "I said no touching."

"Actually, you said no swapping fluids, and unless I have a medical condition, I'm unaware of, this is not off-limits." Magnus drags me to his chest and throws his arms around me, smothering me in a hug.

One I didn't realize I needed until I was wrapped in it. It's suffocating, but I relax into it anyway, enjoying it while it lasts.

He releases me a second later, my body itching to be near him again.

I blame those damn pre-period hormones. I'm horny, filled with rage, and desperate for cuddles. All three things are a complete contradiction of one another.

"Don't test me." Dominic tightens his fist and I'm not entirely sure if he realizes he's doing it. "You two will come back here when you're done. End of discussion."

I step around Magnus to stand in front of him. "No, not *end of discussion*. You might be the boss of him, but you're not the boss of me. This living arrangement, it's temporary, and I won't put my life on hold because of it. If I don't pick up another job, it will completely fuck up my entire plan."

Although, not having rent to pay, that makes saving for my own place a bit easier. I shouldn't be this harsh on Dom, but if I don't stand up to him, no one will, and I seem to be the only one he'll back down from.

"How much?" Dominic shoves his hand into his pocket, pulling out a money clip similar to the one I've seen Coen and Magnus have. Engraved, fancy, and stuffed full of cash. "Name your price and you can quit working right now."

"Not going to work, I already tried." Magnus grips my shoulders and rests his chin on the top of my head. "You're wasting your time, Dom."

I glance over at Coen, watching him watch us in silence while he sips his coffee.

"Maybe you didn't offer enough." Dominic takes the entire wad of bills out from under the clip while walking over to us. "Here."

I don't even bother looking at it. "No. You can't buy me." I sense his frustration, my guilt following suit. "But, because my uterus feels like it's about to fall out, I will grant you the afternoon."

The idea of wandering aimlessly scouring windows for help-wanted signs sounds hella unappealing given the current state of my female reproductive system. Instead, maybe I'll use the time between gigs to take a freaking nap or do something I don't do often, relax.

"Are you not at all concerned about the danger you're in?" Dom remains with his hand outstretched like I might actually take his offering.

I reach for it, the clip, too, shoving them back together and into his pocket. "Not really."

"This is serious, June. These men, these people, they'll kill you and not think twice."

Maybe I should be more scared, threatened by the life I've stumbled upon, but honestly, I embrace it for what it is, because what other choice do I have? I refuse to let them think they've rattled me, that I can't handle whatever comes my way. I've never been one to show weakness, and I won't start now.

"Then let them, they'd probably be doing us all a favor." I don't mean for this to come out as melodramatic as it does, but it's the truth.

If the evil they keep trying to warn me about finds me, then it would eliminate the burden of them having to watch over me, the obligation they feel to maintain my safety. They would be free to go on with their lives the way they were prior to my arrival, and focus on winning the war they're battling. It's not like I'd be leaving much behind either, given I barely have two nickels to rub together. Cora would be bummed, that's for sure, but she'd get over it in time.

Magnus shakes my shoulders and turns me around to face him. "That's not true."

I catch a glimpse of Dom, his brows bunched.

"Do you think we do this for fun?" Dom says from behind me. "We don't invite people into our home. We don't *worry* about anyone. And we don't go to the lengths we have to keep someone safe. Whether you want it or not, we are going to protect you, respect you, and provide for you."

Magnus nods his head with each of Dom's words. "What he said."

"Yep," Coen adds.

My heart aches at the rawness surrounding us. It feels so...unfamiliar.

"I understand you want this situation to be temporary, June, but it's not." Dominic exhales. "So, I encourage you to embrace it for what it is. There is no reason for you to want to put yourself in any unnecessary peril to make a few bucks. Whatever you wish for, we can give it to you, without question."

I meet Magnus's gaze, an idea coming to me, something they would never be willing to do in a million years. Something money could not buy.

He seems to read my mind, a grin forming on his beautiful face. "Oh, you little vixen."

I chuckle and shake my head, turning to the rest of the guys. "Fine. I won't get a third job. But I'm keeping the other two. I won't be reliant on a man...or three."

Dominic's shoulders relax in the slightest. "That's acceptable, for now. Although, I do hope you reconsider."

"I'll think about it." I stare at him, my gaze lingering on his hands, his mouth, his strong arms. I recall the private moments we've shared together. The tenderness and consideration he paid my body, despite his polished and serious exterior. I should fear him, I know this, but instead, it only makes me want him more.

"That's all I ask." He pulls his vibrating phone out once again. "I have to go. We can discuss this in detail later."

I should be afraid of each of these men. They're all criminals, dangerous ones who do God knows what during their work hours. And yet here I am, more intrigued than ever, defying them at every chance and growing more attracted to them with each passing moment.

That alone concerns me the most. The attachment I have to them. The fact that despite everything I say and do, I *want* to be here. It's not the potential hazard to my life that freaks me out, it's that the feelings I have for them are developing into something out of my control.

My shift at Bram's goes exactly how I expect—a bit awkward with Magnus lurking around, but overall, it's a relatively easy one. I enjoy working at the diner the most out of all my employment ventures, mostly because of Bram.

There's something about him that my other bosses don't share. Kindness? Compassion? A genuine consideration for his employees? Maybe I'm not used to basic human decency out of a superior, given that most of my managers have been selfish assholes. Which, I totally get, because it's not their place to be more concerned with their workers than the bottom line, but there's a point you'd think fundamental social skills come into play. Like the douche at the pizza place firing me because of my face. He didn't care at all that I was hurt, only that it might hurt business.

Bram on the other hand has tried to offer me paid time off and goes out of his way to do my job so I don't have to. Which literally defeats the purpose of me being here.

I settle my gaze across the diner at Magnus, Bram hovering above him with a steaming pot of coffee. The two of them are chatting and I can't help but wonder what the heck about. I untie my apron and hang it on the hook with the others and exit from behind the counter.

Their murmurs die down when I approach—never a good sign.

I lean against the booth and cross my arms. "What did I miss?"

"Oh, nothing you don't already know." Magnus reaches over and rubs my shoulder with his tattooed hand. "Like how stubborn you are."

I side-eye him. "I like to call it strong-willed."

Bram smiles. "That's it alright." He nudges the pot toward me. "Now that you're officially off duty, would you like a cup?"

"To-go, if you don't mind." I reach for it. "Here, I can get it."

Bram swats my hand gently. "Shh." He looks over to Magnus. "You want one, too?"

"No, thanks though." Magnus slides out of the booth, standing dangerously close to me. His body grazes mine and he peers down at me. "You okay?"

"Mmhm." I force a toothless smile and take a step back to put a little space between us, otherwise, I'm going to get fired for indecent exposure when I rip Magnus's clothes off.

"Come on, princess." He hooks his index finger around my hand and drags me with him.

His touch is cool and welcoming, unlike the nickname he's coined for me. It's starting to grow on me, although I still dislike it. Maybe because it feels so...dishonest, considering I'm nothing close to a princess. If anything, I'm the exact opposite.

A damsel in distress.

Magnus slides a twenty out of his pocket and across the counter, replacing it with the cup of coffee Bram poured for me. "Thanks, again." He tugs me away before Bram turns around.

"Oh, that's not necessary," Bram tells him while holding up the bill.

I smile, knowing that Magnus isn't about to go back and take the money. Finally, someone else gets to benefit from Magnus's seemingly bottomless pockets. "See you tomorrow, Bram."

"About that..." Magnus says while opening the door for me. "You have the day off. Or well, the morning."

I step onto the sidewalk and stop. "What? Why?"

"Bram and I, we agreed that we thought you were a bit overworked and could use a tiny break."

"But I don't. I'm fine. I—"

"June." Magnus stops me from reaching for the handle to reenter the diner. "It's one shift. Enough for you to sleep in. I can bring you breakfast in bed. Whatever you want."

"Did Dom put you up to this? To keep me home? Under his thumb?"

"No? I don't give a shit about Dom. I mean, I do. And he's totally right." He shakes his head. "But no, I'm not fucking around. Up until a couple days ago you had *three* jobs. You were kidnapped, and tortured. And if that isn't enough, you said your period is coming. I care about you, whether you believe it or not."

I don't mean for it to happen, but tears well in my eyes. I don't know if it's because I'm mad at him for going behind my back, or the influx of hormones making me emotional, but I do something unexpected. I reach toward him, tugging his white t-shirt and wrapping my arms around him, resting my head against his chest.

"Are you...um...hugging me? Willingly?" Magnus holds his arms out to his sides, a bit confused at my sudden public display of affection.

"Shh, go with it." I squeeze him a little tighter and close my eyes, breathing him in.

"Right, yeah, duh." He embraces me, patting my head and kissing the top of it. "You sure you're okay?"

I tilt my head up at him. "Aren't you the *people person*? Can't you just read me and figure it out?"

His big, beautiful blue eyes melt into me. "You're not used to someone doing something nice for you, without expecting something in return."

A stupid teardrop rolls down my cheek and he catches it with his thumb and wipes it away.

"Let's get you home." He presses his lips to my forehead.

A moment later, the car we arrived in pulls up in front of the diner.

Magnus leads me over to it, opening the door for me and following me into it. "This is probably too hot." He goes to put my coffee into the cup holder, but I don't heed his warning and reach for it anyway.

I pop the top and take a cautious sip, relieved when it doesn't burn my tongue off. I've been plopping an ice cube in my cup lately, and if I'm not mistaken, Bram went ahead and did it for me. "It's not bad."

Magnus tries it for himself and nods. "You were right." He extends his arm across the seat. "Come here."

I comply, mainly because his presence has been like a salve to my soul lately. I should stop, scoot to the other side of the seat, and put distance between us, but instead, I rest my head on his shoulder and bring my legs up onto the seat.

He drags them over to lay over his. He sighs and runs his fingers over my bruised knee. "Does this hurt?"

"Not really." At least not anymore. I've gotten used to the healing ache, along with the other injuries I obtained that night.

"I'm sorry, for this, and for everything else." Magnus leaves his palm on my exposed thigh. "I hate that you've been forced into this life."

"It's not your fault," I reassure him. Because at the end of the day, it was my choices that led me to them. I didn't have to sleep with Dom. Or go home with Magnus. And I sure as shit didn't have to walk home alone after the bar when I already had numerous bad feelings that day.

"I won't let it happen again. None of us will."

"I don't doubt that, considering none of you will let me out of your sight."

He rubs my shoulder and pulls me closer. "And it's going to stay that way."

But it can't, and I won't allow it. That's not what I do. I don't stay.

It's only a matter of time before I do the thing I do best...leave.

# CHAPTER 16

# June

I open my eyes to a note sitting on the pillow next to me.

It was rather strange to go to sleep without setting an alarm, and having no consideration for when the hell I woke up. And even more so that I wasn't woken up thirty-seven thousand times by my annoying ass roommates.

If anything, my current roomies either have soundproof walls, or they have been tiptoeing around not to disturb me. A thoughtfulness that is totally foreign.

*Princess, text me when you wake. Love, M.*

I climb out of bed, plopping gently onto the plush rug at my side. I slide my feet into the slippers tucked barely away, and head to the massive, attached bathroom. I make quick work of brushing my teeth and splashing cool water on my face to wake me up. I stand up straight, only to recognize the familiar feeling between my legs.

*Shit.*

Instinctually, I start opening drawers, my heart sputtering when the first one is lined with various feminine hygiene products, quite literally saving my day. I grab a tampon and close myself into the little toilet room. Although, there's nothing little about it. It's rather large, almost the size of the entire bathroom at my prior apartment on the other side of town. The one I got freaking kicked out of because Carter is a royal prick.

I finish up, washing my hands and drying them on the plump towel that is somehow already warm. I slip into the sweatpants I had stolen from Magnus and hug my arms to my chest. I could easily rummage through the clothing they got for me to find a sweatshirt, but I'm dying for a cup of coffee.

Making my way down the stairs, I hear rustling in the kitchen. I round the corner to find Magnus with his back to me, jotting something down on a piece of paper.

"Morning, you."

He turns, his eyes a bit wide. "No! Go back up. You were supposed to text me. You had *one* job."

I laugh and continue toward him. "You're literally *right here*."

He juts out his bottom lip and pouts, but pulls me to his chest, wrapping his arms around me.

A person clears their throat behind me, either making their presence known or insinuating we're too close.

Both things I ignore on purpose, hugging Magnus back and relaxing into him.

"Oh, don't look so gruff," Magnus tells the newcomer. He holds out his arm. "Do you need a hug, too?"

"No, I don't," Dominic tells him, making his way over to the fancy coffee machine on the counter. He pushes a sequence of buttons and it quietly comes alive. "I could use your assistance though. We leave in five."

"What the hell, I thought I was on princess duty?" Magnus grips me tighter.

A smirk settles on my face.

"*June* doesn't have work, meaning she'll be home, where she's safe. She doesn't require your surveillance here."

The smile fades. "*She* is right here." I loosen my hold on Magnus and stroll across to where Dominic is standing, waiting for his coffee to finish. I reach for it the second it's done. "Thanks."

Dominic glares at me through his thick lashes before pulling out another mug and repeating the steps again.

Magnus turns away and attempts to hide the laugh that bubbles up out of him. "Oh man, I could get used to you living here, princess."

"Don't get your hopes up," I tell him. "It's only temporary." Although, I have no idea what that even means. How long will their war be going on? What if it never ends? Would that be such a bad thing?

*Yes.* Because this goes against everything I am. I've already stayed longer than I normally would, but given the circumstances, I don't exactly have a choice in the matter. I don't have a place to go home to, and I don't have enough money to go out and get one. Plus, the very real possibility that I'm a walking target that could be eliminated at any moment if I step outside alone. Or maybe that's what they want me to believe, to keep me here.

Dominic checks his watch. "You now have three minutes."

Magnus groans and walks to the fridge. He pulls out a tray with a beautiful assortment of cut fruit with yogurt and granola with various toppings in small glass containers. He places it on the counter beside me. "Your breakfast."

I glance at it, then at him, then at it once more. He made this, for me?

Not caring that Dominic is watching, Magnus plants his lips on my cheek. "I'll see you in a bit." He pulls away and winks. "You look good in my sweats."

I catch Dom's hardened stare out of my peripheral.

"Do not leave this house," he orders me.

"Dude, chill, she's not going anywhere." Magnus slaps him on the shoulder. "Right, princess?"

"Mmhm." I sigh, the heaviness of my period looming over me. If I weren't so fucking tired, I'd leave just for the sake of defying this man who thinks he can control me. I'll have to save that recklessness for another day. "But only because I have nowhere else to be." I point toward the vast open area. "Where's Coen?"

"On a job." Dominic grabs the replacement cup of coffee. "There's more food in the fridge." He nods toward a large double door. "And in the pantry."

Magnus walks into the living room and snatches the remote off the spotless table. "TV here. One in your room. The projector downstairs is pretty easy to use but if you're not feeling tech-savvy, I can show it to you later." Each step he takes, his tattooed muscles bulge the white shirt he's wearing. Black fitted jeans highlight his strong body. It's a simple look, and somehow, it's sexy as hell.

Dominic on the other hand, is the complete opposite. He's got a dapper kind of thing going on. A white collared shirt unbuttoned at the top, revealing a bit of hair on his chest. A sleek dark vest overtop, with a matching set of pressed slacks, and a perfectly polished pair of obviously expensive leather shoes. He slides his thick arms into his jacket, repositioning it at the top. His beard is speckled with grey, and his hair is perfectly in place, like he put careful consideration into every single aspect of his appearance.

It's dramatic, but it's Dominic. Totally fitting to his incredibly serious demeanor. He's all business, with that rough, *don't fuck with me* vibe. And yet, that's all I want to do—disobey him.

He plays it off like he hates it, but I know deep down he loves that I challenge his every move. I'm not afraid of him, not the way everyone else is, and if I had to guess, that's why he's drawn to me. He's not used to being seen as anything other than the ruthless man he presents himself to be.

"If you need me, I'm just a call away." Magnus meets Dominic at the door, pausing to look at me.

I climb onto a stool at the kitchen counter and bring the beautifully arranged tray Magnus put together toward me. "I'll be fine, don't worry. I won't leave, I promise."

"Good girl," Dominic says before walking out.

Did I hear him correctly?

I flit my gaze up as they leave, my cheeks giving away the slightest blush, his words catching me a bit off guard.

They disappear on the other side of the garage door, leaving me alone in the kitchen with my thoughts and this delicious spread. I consider taking it into the living room, but my luck I'd spill something on their expensive couch and that's not a risk I'm willing to take. Instead, I sit here, sipping the coffee I stole from Dom and stirring some berries into the yogurt.

I force myself to slow down, to eat my meal with intention. It's not like I have anywhere else to be, and it's been a while since I've truly felt safe in a space. I never felt welcome around my old roommates. Sure, it was my place, too, but it was never home. There was no comfort, no solitude from the outside world. It was just another layer of my life that was unstable. I was constantly on guard, watching over my shoulder and holding my breath for the next stupid thing to happen. It wasn't like that in the beginning, but I should have seen the red flags go up and get out when I could.

Who am I kidding though? I see blaring red flags and make it a point to go headfirst into them. I'm attracted to all things bad, especially men. Honestly, Cora is probably one of the few good people in my life, possibly the only one.

Which is why I'm certain that it's only a matter of time until the three men I'm currently staying with turn on me. Realize I'm a burden to their life. That I no longer serve a purpose and am only adding to the negative. It's what humans do. They use others and discard them when they no longer need them.

I'm guilty of it, too. That's why I never stay long enough for someone to do it to me.

Loss isn't something I handle well, so I avoid it at all costs. If you don't get attached, there's nothing to lose, no risk of allowing yourself to get hurt. It's rather foolproof.

Until now.

With each passing day, I'm more drawn to these men. I grow comfortable with their existence. It's comforting. Hell, even Coen, who will barely speak to me, brings me some level of contentment. It's like I've been lost at sea, and finally have something to hang on to, regardless of whether it's fleeting and will pass with the storm called life.

I must be cautious though, otherwise, I'll be pulled out too far, unable to make it back to shore on my own.

Finishing the rest of my breakfast, I hop off the stool and scoot my dishes toward the sink. I rinse them off and load them into the dishwasher, careful to pay attention to how it was already organized. The last thing I want to do is make someone angry for putting them in wrong. It's petty, but if I'm going to be staying in someone else's house, I'd like to not fuck with the way they do things. Apparently taking Dom's coffee is acceptable, but messing up the kitchen is not.

I do my best to put everything away with where I think it goes, and wipe off the counter, leaving no trace that I was ever there. I scurry across the silent space, and up the stairs to more familiar territory. I go into my makeshift bedroom and pull my phone off the nightstand.

There are a few missed notifications. One from Cora. One from Magnus. The rest is from social media. I swipe those away and click on the photo of Magnus.

**Magnus: Miss you already xo**

**Me: You've been gone like ten minutes.**

Dots immediately appear.

**Magnus: More like thirty, princess!**

I glance at the time, noting that he's probably correct. I made no effort of rushing when I was downstairs. I should be out looking for another job right now, or perhaps not taking time off from the one I do have. I have a shift tonight at the bar, though, so maybe the guilt of the free morning will dissipate once I'm back to work.

I hold the phone to my chest, my legs guiding me out of my room and down the hall. I press my hand against his door, and the thing creaks open. The scent of Magnus floats out and greets me, inviting me to come inside his space. I comply, the familiarity of that night we spent together coming back to me. I run my fingers across his sheets, recalling the way they felt against my skin. I find myself climbing in and basking in the continued comfort Magnus provides, even in his absence. Resting my head on his pillow, I breathe him in, closing my eyes and relaxing into the bed that doesn't belong to me.

None of this does. This room, this house, the men that live in it. This life, lavish and dangerous. None of it is mine. And the clock continues to count down, reminding me that it won't last forever. But what's the harm in savoring it while it does? Don't I deserve that much? I've been through hell and back, numerous times, shouldn't I allow myself the decadence of pretending that for once, everything might turn out okay?

I pull his blanket up to my neck, settling into the soft, yet firm and inviting mattress.

I can't control everything, nor can I choose the outcome of the future. But right now, I choose to enjoy this momentary peace life is offering me. I have a feeling it will be gone before I know it.

Sleep welcomes me almost immediately, which isn't at all surprising given how deprived of it I've been. If I thought my slumber on that park bench was nice, it's nothing compared to high thread count sheets and black-out curtains.

At some point, warm arms wrap around me and a head nuzzles in behind mine. Lips kiss the back of my head and our legs intertwine. I doze again, pulling Magnus's hand up to rest along my chest. I shouldn't allow any of this, I should climb out of his bed, go into mine, and stop permitting these feelings to continue to build...but how do I resist something that is so damn good?

***

My phone vibrates against the bed, waking me up from my slumber. I pry Magnus off me and reach for the glowing thing. I squint, recognizing Jack's number on the screen. I press the green button and hold the device to my ear.

"Hello." My voice cracks.

Magnus grumbles something and stretches his tattooed arm out toward me.

"June, hey. Are you sleeping? It's like seven o'clock."

I sit up and rub my eyes. "I was taking a nap." Is that a crime? "What's up? Is something wrong?"

Muffling comes through the line. "Put that over there," Jack tells someone else. "No, June. I hate to do this, but I double booked the shifts tonight, so I don't need you to come in."

"Wait, what?" I slide out from under Magnus's arm and hop off the bed. "Who's working instead?"

So help me God if he says Jane.

He hesitates for a second. "Jane is."

"She's been there like three weeks?"

"I know." Jack sighs. "I called her first to cancel on her, but she mentioned quitting and well...I'm sorry, June."

"And what if I quit? Didn't you consider that?"

He covers the receiver again. "No, on the other side."

Magnus rolls over on his back, dragging his forearm over his eyes. What a beautiful sight.

Jack speaks up. "Yeah, I did, but I know you won't. You don't really have another choice." He pauses. "I've got to go. I still have you down for tomorrow night. I'll see you then." He hangs up, not caring if there is anything else I have to say.

*Don't have another choice.* His words cut through me. How dare he think I'm stuck working at his shitty bar. But he's not wrong. He's aware I'm broke as fuck and desperate for every extra hour he throws my way. It would be foolish of me to quit, especially when I'm already down a gig. Working at Bram's has been a saving grace, but it won't compensate for the lost wages at *two* jobs. He has me cornered between a rock and a hard place and he's using that to his advantage.

And here I am, playing fucking house with three dangerous men.

Magnus pats the spot next to him, where I was only moments prior. "Come back to bed."

My head throbs with the mixture of my newest problem and the sleep my body isn't quite used to. "Do you have a medicine cabinet around here?"

He sits up, running his hand to get his messy hair off his brow. "What's wrong?"

"Nothing. Just a headache." I glance at his bathroom. "I can get it if you tell me where it is."

"I've got you, princess." He reaches into the nightstand and pulls out a bottle, popping the top and dropping two pills onto the palm of his hand. Magnus slides off the bed and brings with him the glass of water that was sitting on a coaster, dripping with condensation. "Here."

I take the little white things and down them without the liquid. A habit I formed when I did my best not to leave my room once I was already inside, at my old apartment. The less I had to interact with my roommates, the better. I recall all the shit I left behind. Clothing, books, school supplies. Nothing of real value, but everything left that I owned. It's pathetic that I have next to nothing to show for the years I've been on this planet. Even the one thing I do have, my body, is in shit condition. Bumps and bruises still healing from the asshole who kidnapped and tortured me.

They'll heal, that's for sure, but will I? Shouldn't I be more concerned or traumatized by what happened? Is there something wrong with me because I've managed to shove it into a folder in my mind and not be bothered by it since? Instead of terror or fear, I mostly feel angry, like I want to get revenge on who did this. But mainly, I'm focused on how the hell I'm going to afford this thing called life. I had this morning off, not by choice, and my evening shift was taken from me. I have the money Magnus and Coen gave me, and the little bit I had been saving, but it isn't much. And each workable hour that passes, I start to panic at how I'm going to figure this all out.

"Penny for your thoughts?" Magnus asks me.

I let out a chuckle, considering I'm desperate enough to take him up on that offer. "You wouldn't get it." Because how could he?

He's surrounded by anything and everything he could desire. He doesn't want, not for material things. None of these guys do. They've worked hard for what they have, despite it being less than kosher, and money is the last of their concerns. They're at war to claim a lucrative throne, and I'm wondering where my next meal will come from.

"Try me." Magnus tucks a strand of my jet-black hair behind my ear.

There's a kindness in his expression, like maybe he would understand. But I'm not willing to open up that part of me to him. Not if I stand any chance of ever walking away. The more I give, the harder it will be when things have run their course. For him, for me. It's a reality I don't want to face, but one I'm aware will happen with or without my consent.

A knock sounds on the door. "Maggie."

"Come in," Magnus calls out.

The handle turns and Coen pokes his head around, his face tensing when his sights land on me. "Dinner is ready." He flits his gaze to Magnus. "She shouldn't be in here."

"You guys seriously need to work on the whole talking about me like I can't hear you thing." I cross my arms and walk away from Magnus, bumping into Coen when I exit the room and head toward mine.

"Are you coming?" Coen says to me.

I don't bother turning around. "I'll be down in a minute; I need to freshen up." AKA change my tampon since I accidentally napped for five billion hours. I don't add that part, not because I'm modest, but because I'd rather Coen think that me and Magnus potentially just messed around.

When I finish in the restroom, I sit on the edge of my bed, wondering what the fuck I'm doing with my life. I drag my fingers along my scalp, raking my hair out of my face, and let out a sigh. I pull my phone out of my pocket, clicking on the text that Cora had sent me earlier.

**Cora: Which night are we going out this week?**

Our ritualistic hang out that both of us look forward to more than we probably should. A perfect depiction of how much we dislike our lives outside of each other.

I graze my brow with my fingers, and trail it down to the cut on my lip. They're healing, but they're still fresher than I'd hope they would be prior to seeing Cora. I don't want her to worry any more than she already does.

**Me: How about Saturday?**

I push it out and hope that between now and then, the marks will fade and won't be quite as noticeable.

**Cora: Works for me, boo boo. Text me if anything changes.**
**Me: Will do. You okay?**
**Cora: Yep, swamped with assignments. You?**
**Me: Yeah, I'm good.**

She heart reacts to my response, our conversation fizzling out with the few exchanged messages.

A figure appears in my doorway, casting a shadow into the room. "Everything okay?"

I turn to see Dominic standing there, leaning against the frame. His body practically taking up the entire space. He's not wearing his jacket, and his sleeves are rolled neatly to his elbow, somehow making his already sexy outfit that much hotter.

"Yes." I rise and make my way toward him, but he doesn't move.

"Not very convincing." He studies my face.

"What can I say, I must be a shit actress." I stop in front of him, shoving my hands in the pockets of my stolen sweats, and wait for him to let me through.

"Is there something I can do?" His gaze remains on me.

"Other than step aside?"

Dominic plants one foot forward, then the other.

I crane my neck to look up at him but remain firmly grounded where I am.

He closes the gap, leaving no space at all between us. Not even a hair could fit between our bodies. He raises his hand and glides his fingers along the side of my face, tilting it toward him. "I can't help you if you won't tell me."

"Who said I wanted your help?" There are a million other things I do want from him though.

Dom lowers his face, grazing his lips along my forehead, down my nose, and resting just against my mouth. "You know I can please you in more ways than one." His words are a murmur barely spoken.

My eyes close and my body begs to react. My bottom lip runs up his, hovering barely apart. In a split second, I imagine him guiding me backward, shoving me onto the bed, and climbing on top of me, our tongues frantic to dance their familiar rhythm. I'd rip his white dress shirt off, buttons flying, and I'd trail my hands down his chest and into his pants, grabbing onto his thick...

He breaks away, snapping me out of my fantasy. "But if you don't want that."

If only he knew how badly I wanted that very thing.

Dominic leaves me standing there with the female version of blue balls. He turns when he gets to the door, his hand gripping the wall. "Dinner is ready, you won't be told again."

I remain for only another second before following him out and down the hall, to the stairs. My stomach growls in response to the scent of something delicious wafting in my direction.

Dominic takes his place at the table, across from Magnus, next to Coen, leaving me the open spot across from Coen and next to Magnus. They watch as I approach, not yet touching their food. Were they waiting on me this whole time? Had I known that I wouldn't have had a mini existential crisis.

The second I sit, it's like they come to life, passing things around to each other. Magnus holds his plate for Coen to put a steak on, then over to Dominic for asparagus and sauteed mushrooms. He finishes it off with a scoop of little potatoes that look crisp and tasty. Magnus swipes the empty plate in front of me and lowers the full one in its place.

"You didn't have to do that," I tell him.

Why can't I just be normal and accept something nice being done for me?

I correct myself. "Thank you."

Coen nudges a can of Dr. Pepper toward me, almost like it's a peace offering.

If only he would open his mouth and communicate with me instead of flitting through various stages of ignoring me or pretending I'm not in the room.

"This doesn't happen often, don't get used to it." Magnus nudges me.

"What doesn't?" I ask him.

"A home-cooked meal, together, at the table, at a reasonable hour."

"Oh." I fork a piece of potato, letting the many flavors settle onto my tongue. Salty, earthy, but with a bit of something else, maybe oregano, definitely garlic. Yep, they're as good as I thought they would be. I cut into the steak, relieved when it's pink inside. It has the right amount of char and tenderness, and is seasoned perfectly, although, I'm not at all surprised. Leave it to these three to know their way around a piece of meat.

We eat in silence for a few minutes until Magnus finally breaks it. "What time do you need to leave?"

"About that." I press my napkin to my mouth and finish chewing the bite in my mouth. "Jack called and told me not to come in."

Magnus tilts his head toward me. "Like ever?"

"No. Just tonight. I guess he double booked me and another girl. Ended up giving her priority over me."

"The new waitress?" Dominic takes a sip of his water.

"Yep."

"She's terrible." He slices a strip of steak and plops it into his mouth.

I eye him, watching the way his jaw moves. Something that shouldn't be *that* sexy.

He swallows and continues speaking. "Really. I saw her mess up at least three table's orders. She over-pours her drinks. She's sloppy."

And here I am, chopped liver compared to her because Jack doesn't want to risk her quitting. Wouldn't she be doing him a favor anyway, especially if she's costing him money by being a fuck up?

"I could have a talk with him," Dominic adds.

"What? No." I shake my head. I glance down, realizing that I'm holding my knife in the air toward him. I lower it with my voice. "That isn't necessary." I add, "Maybe not with Jack," under my breath.

"Neither is you working somewhere you're not appreciated." Dominic's jaw tenses.

I shift my attention to Coen, who's eating his food quietly, sadness written across his face. Magnus on the other hand is happily consuming his, practically giddy with each bite. He must have been hungry after our nap together.

Magnus points his fork at Dom. "I agree."

"I can't afford to quit. And it would be great if you didn't get me fired either." I focus back on Dom, doing my best to read his features. I recall when he brutally beat that man in the bathroom with no regard, something I'm sure he'd do again to Jack if I gave him the go-ahead.

Jack isn't at the top of my list though. The man who attacked me is. And Carter follows close behind.

"At what point will you realize that money is no issue?" Dominic glances up from his plate and narrows in on me.

"Maybe when you realize this arrangement is temporary." Even if I were to allow them to help me *now*, it wouldn't be sustainable. What would I do when I go back out into the world, a free woman? With no job, no income, nothing to call my own. I'm already risking too much by not finding a third paying gig and letting shifts slip through my fingers with the others.

"Okay." Dominic pats his mouth with his napkin and places it beside his plate. "If I accept that, will you?"

Is he fucking with me?

He stands from the table, walks out of the room, and around a corner where I can no longer see him. The sound of electronic buttons floats back to us.

I look to Magnus and he shrugs, continuing to eat his dinner.

Coen remains painfully quiet.

Dominic returns, setting a stack of cash next to my plate. A golden band around it noting the denomination. It's much smaller than one would imagine that amount of money would be, but considering it appears to be all hundreds, it adds up. "One month. Will that suffice?"

"You're not serious." I blink at it like it might disappear and focus on Dom.

He goes to his seat and sits back down, taking a drink of his water and not acting at all as though ten-thousand dollars is sitting out here with us. "It's a yes or no, June. Do you require more? Because that could be arranged." Dom scoots his chair out again.

"No." I hold out my hand to stop him.

"Very well then." He picks up a knife and cuts off another chunk of his steak.

"But I...I can't take this." I look between these three men, hoping one of them will speak up and question Dom for his antics.

Dom exhales and plants his hand on the table. "What are your reservations? I have no issue with it. Do you?" He shifts to Magnus.

"Nope," Magnus replies.

Dom turns to Coen. "And you?"

Coen, with his head still a bit lowered, glances at me briefly, then at Dom. "No."

"Then we're all in agreement. The cash is yours to use however you see fit. Although I would advise that you don't use it all in one place, or make a lump sum deposit, unless you want the IRS snooping around. If there is anything else you need, let any of us know and we will provide it. At the end of the allotted time, we will assess how to go on from there, given your safety is still maintained. If you choose to leave, a stipend will be given to you to allow you the opportunity to find proper employment. In the meantime, my only condition is that you quit working until further notice."

"But I..." My words trail off because I'm honestly not sure what to say.

I want to be defiant, tell them that they don't control me, that they can't tell me what to do. To toss the cash across the table and say I cannot be bought. But at the end of the day, can't we all? Doesn't each of us have a number they would do anything for? Ten thousand dollars is a *lot* of money. More than I would make in a month, or six. And the only catch is I have to live here for a few weeks and *not* work. The one thing that causes me the most stress is simply erased with a stack of crisp bills. Wouldn't I be a fool for turning this deal down? They're offering me safety, security, and financial support, not to mention anything else I could ask for.

And yet, there's a pit in my gut opening up and screaming at me to run. I don't stick around, not this long, and sure as hell not a month. This goes against everything I've worked toward to keep myself from being hurt. The man who cut me the deepest is sitting across the table from me, living in the very lavish home I'm supposed to stay in. He barely speaks to me. Hardly looks at me. He's hurting, I'm aware of that, but so am I.

Despite my own issues, I shouldn't let that stop me from seeking solitude and shelter here. Although, the only way I can be okay with agreeing to this arrangement is if I set my own terms.

Dominic waits for me to continue like the gentleman he is. He's fierce, he's brutal, but he absolutely has manners.

"I will quit Jack's, but I want to stay on at Bram's. And I won't look for another job until time is almost up."

Dominic considers what I've said, processing the information carefully.

"Bram treats her well, and I can watch over her there." Magnus delivers a supporting point I am grateful for.

Dom counters. "One day a week."

"Five," I say without hesitation. Always go big and have room to work with.

"Two."

"Three or no deal." The actual amount I was hoping for all along.

"Fine," Dominic concedes.

"And once a week, I'm going out with Cora. Non-negotiable."

Dom clenches his jaw and his nostrils flare slightly. It's adorable, really. "I need at least twenty-four-hour notice."

"This Saturday. How's that for notice?"

"I will do my best to accommodate your request."

"Oh, and one final thing." I make sure to keep my eyes trained on him. "I will *swap fluids* with whoever I want to in this house, and you will have no objections."

He runs his tongue along his teeth, sizing up my latest demand.

Coen tenses from his spot like he's anxiously waiting for Dominic to reply.

"Very well." Dominic pauses as if there is something else he'd like to add, but he keeps it to himself. He pulls his vibrating phone out of his pocket and peers at the screen.

Coen lets out a sigh and stands from the table, taking his plate with him. He tosses it into the sink and makes his way toward the stairs.

Dominic calls after him. "Hayes. We have work to do, don't go anywhere."

Coen stops, his back still to us. His shoulders are tight, his hand making a fist at his side.

A small part of me wants to reach out to him, to take him into my arms the way I had done when we were kids, and hold him to me, telling him everything will be okay. Younger me had no idea that those words were a lie. I meant them though, because I truly thought if we were together, nothing else mattered. We could handle anything that came our way, and we did. Two broken pieces that were an unbreakable pair.

But things out of our control broke us apart, severing that bond we had shared. Leaving us more damaged than we were to start. It changed us into different versions of ourselves and would ensure that we would never be the same again.

I can't even look at him without replaying that last memory of him in my head. Him hanging out of the back window of his father's pickup as it drove away and out of sight. I clung to the hope that eventually, Coen would return. That he would fight for us and prove my belief wrong that everyone leaves. Instead, days passed, and they turned into weeks, months, years. The stolen bits of my heart hardened into cold, irreparable darkness in his absence.

I shouldn't have taken it so personal. We were only kids, drunk on the idea of love. But the feeling reminded me too much of another loss, one I wished I could rid myself of. Coen, being in my life did exactly that. It was a beautiful bandage to the gaping wound on my soul, only to be shattered when he suddenly left. It taught me a valuable lesson, that you cannot rely on another person for those comforts, because people ultimately will leave, and you'll be alone to pick up the pieces left behind.

Why give them the chance in the first place?

Coen was the only man I've ever loved. That I had ever, truly given myself to. I opened up to him, and he did the same in return. We saw the ugly parts of each other and chose to be together anyway. He loved all the little things I hated about myself that I never let anyone else see. We found a home in one another. A dangerous power to give to someone.

It hurt when he left, but it pained me more seeing him doing well, thriving even. Did he never feel the way I did? Never thought to come back to me? Was I nothing to him, especially compared to how much he mattered to me? Did each day pass without his mind remotely wondering how I was? If I was okay? If I missed him at all? If I had moved on?

How could he be so okay with the way things happened when I was fucked up over it?

"Do you need me?" Magnus asks Dom.

"No. Stay here. Hayes and I can handle it."

I avert my attention from Coen to the food in front of me. I push it around on my fork, no longer hungry at all despite everything being delicious. Between the rollercoaster of dinner conversation and the period cramps I'm having, I'd rather be horizontal than sitting here awkwardly.

"June." Dominic folds his napkin and sets it on the table. "Are we in agreement?"

I consider his question for a moment. "Yes."

"Good." He leaves out the girl part. "You mentioned something earlier. About someone needing *talked* to."

"What?"

Magnus leans over and whispers, "Are you done?" while pointing at my plate.

I nod and he takes it, cutting into the steak and finishing off what I left behind.

Dom adjusts the sleeve of his shirt. "I said I would talk to Jack, you said no, but insinuated there was another person. Who?"

"Oh. Nothing. No one."

"As much as I'd like to, I can't read your mind." He moves to the other arm. "This is my expertise. Trust that I would take care of it, whoever it may be."

I shouldn't, but I say it anyway, "I was referring to the guy who kidnapped me."

Dominic pauses, shifting his gaze at Coen, who has now turned around and is leaning against the wall.

"Can you tell us anything about him?" Coen speaks up first, which is surprising since he's usually doing what he can to ignore me.

"Um." I think back to that night. The bag that went over my face, the wetness on the inside that made me weak and unable to get away.

"No detail is too small," he adds. "Any identifying marks, hair color, height, build."

"He was sort of chubby. Definitely not in shape like you guys are." I glance at each of them. "Brown hair, beard. He was chain-smoking cigarettes." I flit my attention to my wrist where he had pushed the hot thing into my skin. I rub the spot and recall the painful burn that had woken me up from my drug-induced slumber. "He had scars, all over his face. And a tattoo, on his arm." I point to the spot on mine, right where the sleeve of my shirt ends. "I couldn't see what it was though."

Magnus places his hand on my upper back and gently glides it around.

"Good, this is all helpful, J." Coen takes in every detail like it's the only thing keeping him alive. "What else?"

My finger trails the cut along my chin. "He had a switchblade. Was talking about Halloween...carving pumpkins. Told me he was following orders but didn't say who from, just that I picked the wrong side."

I sense the energy in the room continue to shift with each detail shared. A combined rage settling through all of us at getting revenge.

"I broke free from the chair he had me tied to, saw an opportunity to take the knife, and plunged the thing into his thigh before getting the fuck out of there."

"Do you remember where you were?" Coen keeps his eyes trained on me.

I shake my head. "No. I just ran, and kept running until I saw something familiar. It was all a blur."

"You did good, J." Coen's expression remains hard but softens in the slightest.

"I want to slice him up the same way he intended to do to me." I don't mean to say this out loud, and yet it slips out anyway.

"You'll get your chance, don't worry." Dominic snatches his keys off the counter. "We'll make sure of it."

Is he serious? How would he ever find the man responsible? I don't have a name, a location, anything of use other than a few vague details about the psychopath. Still, I find myself believing his assurance that justice will be served.

"Hayes." Dominic tips his head for him to come on.

The two of them leave without another word, disappearing into the garage and going to work on whatever task they face tonight, leaving me and Magnus behind.

Magnus gathers the plates, stacking them on top of each other. "How about a movie?"

I help him clean off the table and carry what I can over to the kitchen. I put the salt and pepper shakers back where they belong, and face the cabinets. "Which one has the Tupperware?"

He stops rinsing the dishes to come over to me, wiping his hands on a towel on the way. Magnus grazes his fingers against my cheek. "I can get this. Go sit down."

"Another stipulation of staying: you guys have to let me do stuff. I'm not helpless." I point to the vast selection. "I will climb all over those expensive countertops if you don't tell me which one."

Magnus grins and steps forward, reaching to a top cabinet. His shirt goes up, revealing a section of a tattooed bird on his torso. A phoenix. It's beautiful, just like the man it's permanently marking. "Here."

We make quick work getting the leftovers put away and cleaning up from dinner. It doesn't take long for us to find a groove and accomplish our mission, functioning in perfect harmony.

"About that movie." I lean against the island once we're done.

"Yeah?" Magnus raises a brow at me and glides closer, until he's standing right in front of me. "You up for it?"

"Not like I have anything else going on." Since I'm not allowed to leave, and my shift was canceled. "Actually, hold that thought."

Magnus tilts his head.

I reach into the pocket of my sweats and pull out my phone. I touch the last number in my call registry and push the speakerphone button.

It rings twice then it connects.

"June, listen, I know you're upset, but I can't really talk now."

"Jack, after further thought, I wanted to inform you that I will, in fact, be quitting. Consider this my immediate resignation."

Magnus grins and bobs his head up and down in approval. He presses his thumb and index finger together to make a little circle. "Nice," he whispers.

"What, you can't be serious? You're not even going to give me two weeks?"

"I'm giving you more of a notice than you gave me, so if anything, you're welcome. I got a couple hours, you're getting what, twenty-four?"

"That's absurd, you can't—"

I cut him off. "I can, and I will. I don't appreciate being taken for granted, Jack. I understand you have a business to run, but you chose a shit employee over the best one you have, and that's on you. I'll be in Saturday to pick up my check." I disconnect the line, not at all bothered by anything else he might have to say.

"That was...badass." Magnus raises his hand for a high-five.

I slap it back, a smile spreading across my face. Damn, that felt good. Cutting out crappy people from your life can be hella liberating. A bit scary though, because I rely on them for money, which in turn is how the world goes round. Still, I cherish the blip of joy it brings me to basically tell Jack to shove it.

"Come on, princess." Magnus weaves his fingers around mine and pulls me out of the kitchen and along a hallway I haven't been yet.

It suddenly dawns on me that there are so many parts of this house I have yet to explore, and here I am, committed to living in it for the next month. I guess I have time to get acquainted with it, especially if I'll be spending most of my time stuck inside.

He opens a door, flips a light switch, and leads me down a set of stairs. We go around a dimly lit corner and through another opening.

My eyes take a second to adjust, but when they do, I spot the various cream-colored leather chairs and couches arranged around the room. A bar is located in the back corner, fully stocked and neatly organized like everything else in this house.

He reaches for a remote, pushing a button to illuminate the recessed lighting in the ceiling. Bright white beams out, allowing me to fully see the attention to detail that was taken here.

"It's been a while since we've used this room," he tells me. "Not since, well, you know."

"The war."

"Yeah." Magnus pokes the thing again, turning on the projector. "We've been a bit occupied."

"Do you need to go?" I crane my thumb at the door. "Don't let me keep you."

"Nothing pressing needs my attention." He places his hand on the small of my back and nudges me toward the couch. "You're stuck with me."

I let out a chuckle. "I could think of worse things."

"No kidding." He plops down next to me. "What do you wanna watch?"

I sink into the comfortable, plush sofa, wondering how much this thing costs. It fits the room perfectly, telling me that either the room was designed for the furniture, or the other way around. "Something funny?"

I haven't watched a movie in ages. Between not having a television in my bedroom at my old place and my budget not exactly movie theater friendly, it didn't leave much in the way of catching a flick.

He scrolls through a selection and stops. "What about the new Ryan Reynolds one?"

I shrug, not entirely sure which one he's referring to. "That works."

Magnus side-eyes me. "You sure, princess?"

"Mmhmm." I pull my legs up onto the couch and relax into it. He could put on whatever he wanted and I'd be content. It's rare that I get to do something like this.

"I think you'll like it. It's not out for another three weeks." Magnus clicks another button and pauses the screen. "Popcorn?" He jumps over the back of the couch and glides across the room to an old-fashioned popcorn maker I'm only now noticing. "Something to drink?"

I sigh and rest my face on the cushion, watching him move around with ease. "I'll have whatever you're having."

He finishes up at the machine and walks over to finger a few of the bottles until he finds the one he's looking for. "This is no Hawk's Mark, but it's pretty good."

I squint to take a better look. "Is that Tremblan?"

"Yeah." He holds the thing out toward me. "You ever had it?"

"Once. It's pretty tasty." Not as expensive as Hawk's, but still too rich for my blood.

The room fills with the scent of buttery popped corn as the machine spits out little puffs of deliciousness. Magnus pours two glasses of the brown liquid and brings them over, then goes back to retrieve a bucket of popcorn. He hops onto the couch and tosses a piece into his mouth.

"You ready?" A look of complete contentment settles on his face, telling me that it's been a bit since he's found comfort in such a mundane evening, too.

I take a sip of my drink and nod. "Thank you."

"Of course, princess. Anything for you." With the flick of a finger, Magnus shuts the lights off and turns the movie on.

It doesn't take long for the two of us to polish off our snacks, especially with the mini popcorn war we had at the beginning of the show. He refills our drinks shortly after, and settles into the couch with his arm splayed out for me to join him.

I settle into the crook and bring my legs out to the side on the deep seat. I place my hand to my stomach, resting it on top of my aching uterus.

Magnus kisses my forehead and holds me close. "You okay?"

"Period cramps, I'll survive." Is it weird to be this open with a man I barely know? It hasn't been long, but I feel like we're past the point of awkwardness.

"I hear orgasms help with that."

"This couch would never survive."

"Couches can be cleaned, or even replaced."

This thing looks and feels like it cost more than the stack of cash I left sitting on the table upstairs.

"Oh, speaking of that, I got you something." He sits up. "Hold on. I'll be right back." Magnus pauses our movie and bolts out of the room. The second he's out the door, I no longer hear him. These rooms must be soundproof or something.

I sit there waiting, wondering, curious what he could have possibly gotten me that has to do with bloody couches.

A moment later, he reappears, something in his left hand.

He grabs the remote and holds it toward the projector, pushing a button to dim the light on the screen. "Trust me?" His blue gaze meets mine.

"Yeah," I breathe.

Magnus lowers himself toward me, brushing his lips against mine. They're soft, gentle, and eager. Everything I remember them to be from our night together. Our tongues dance in rhythm, swaying back and forth with ease.

He reaches between my legs, sliding his hand down my thigh and parting my knees.

Just his slight touch has a moan escaping me.

Magnus pulls his hand away, only to come back a moment later with a phallic-shaped thing in his grasp. He continues kissing me, flicking a button on the side, and turning the device on. It vibrates quietly and he rubs it against me. Up and down on my most sensitive areas.

"Fuck," I mutter, my hips reacting to the electric pulses caressing me. I run my fingers up his neck and weave them into his hair, pulling him closer to me to deepen our kiss.

Magnus glides the thing in all the right spots with the perfect amount of pressure.

I shove him away and climb on top of him, straddling his body.

He keeps the thing between us, positioned right where his cock is. Magnus increases the speed, rubbing it a bit harder against me. His other hand makes its way up my frame, along the nape of my neck. Gripping my hair, he tugs me toward him.

I break away, desperate to provide him remotely the same amount of pleasure he's giving me. I drop to my knees on the floor and reach for his waistband, unbutton his jeans and tug them down.

"You don't have to…"

I lick my lips and look up at him. "I want to."

At this, he pivots to grant me better access to getting his bottoms out of the way. He springs out of his boxers, his erection telling me he wants it, too.

I grip the base of his shaft, coming closer and breathing on the tip of him. I swirl my tongue around and taste the precum that builds.

Magnus pats the couch beside him.

I climb up, getting into the doggy position to allow myself access to him still. I spread my lips around his head, and tease him before guiding him further into my mouth. I moan against him when he places the vibrator on my clit again, this time, my desire heightened at feeling him inside me.

His cock hardens and grows, filling my mouth completely.

I do what I can to relax my jaw and take as much of him in as possible. I slide him in and out, touching the back of my throat with every motion.

"God damn," he whimpers.

I swirl my hand up and down against him and widen my tongue.

He removes the vibrator and replaces it with his hand, still over my sweatpants, rocking it side to side. Somehow, the sensation is more intense, heightening my climb to orgasm.

Magnus grips my head and thrusts his hips gently.

My eyes water at the fullness of my mouth, but I don't dare stop. I want this too badly. I need it.

He climaxes first, his warm load exploding in the back of my throat and sending mine into action immediately after.

"That's it, princess." Magnus moves his hand as I pulsate onto it.

I keep mine moving too, slowing the stroke down and taking every last drop he has to offer me while grinding against him. My body quivers and gratification gushes over me. Slowly, I pull him out of my mouth and swallow him down.

He drags my face to his, our lips meeting again. Magnus kisses me, his tongue darting into my mouth. He breaks away, resting his forehead on mine and running his thumb along my bottom lip.

I grin and sit back, giving him space to put himself back together.

Magnus stands, pulling his pants over his hips, and repositioning his cock. He zips everything back up and drops onto the couch, his arm outstretched for me once again. "You feel any better?"

"Absolutely." I grab my bourbon off the table and scoot over to him.

"Good thing you amended that no-bodily-fluid rule."

"Like that would have stopped us anyway?" I take a sip and hand the glass to him, watching as he tips it up to his luscious lips to get a taste.

A thought crosses my mind that no matter how hard I try to ignore it, it keeps bubbling up. One that continues to challenge all the rules I have in place to keep myself safe.

*I could get used to this.*

# CHAPTER 17

# *Coen*

The ride to our destination is quiet.

I sit on the right side, Dominic on the left. Both of us peering out our windows, more than likely the same thing on our minds.

June. The man that hurt her. And the sweet torture we'd like to inflict on him.

But with June's latest confession, it seems Dominic wants to share that pleasurable experience with her.

Can I allow that to happen though? Just because we're used to this world of brutality doesn't mean she should join it so carelessly. I understand she's reacted well to everything she's been shown, but at what point will it have been too much? And then what? Will she truly see us for the ruthless men we are, and finally say enough is enough?

I've lost her once before—can I handle another?

It's better to have her around and hate me, than not at all.

I'm hopeless, that much is given. There is no mercy for me. No amount of Hail Mary's or penance can save my tormented soul from the things I've done. I was broken when she found me, June being the glue that held me together, only for it to all come tumbling down when we were ripped apart. She was the light through the darkness I never thought I'd find. A precious gift from the universe that I treated with more decency than I thought I was capable of, in an attempt to protect her from this cruel world. She saw me for who I was, the broken sad boy, and helped me catch my breath when I felt everything slipping out from under me. I shouldn't have given a single person so much power, but I knew with absolute certainty that she would never take advantage of it. Her intentions were pure, like mine were with her.

The moment she was stripped from me, it felt like my heart was ripped from my chest. I had to get back to her, and I knew it was only a matter of time until I made that happen. I wasn't aware of the lengths I'd go through until I had already gone through them.

Dominic found me sitting in a pile of blood so thick that it coated my entire body. I was only a teenager, and yet I had done more damage than he had said he'd ever seen. I killed ten men that week. Three of their bodies scattered around me, oozing what was left of them out onto the concrete of the building we were in.

His gun was trained at me until he realized that I was unarmed. Just a kid covered in the remains of people who had it coming. I was exhausted, hadn't slept in days. Couldn't remember the last time I had a meal. My only thirst was for revenge, and that's exactly what I got. I ended the life of every person deemed responsible for the death of my father. The people standing in the way of my freedom, my path back to her. My quest was easier than I imagined once I flipped the switch and allowed the darkness to consume me.

"You're safe now," Dominic had said.

But did he mean from the dead people or from myself? Because I would never escape the black cloud looming over my head, the one that was there my entire life. The one that only temporarily lifted the one summer before everything changed. The cloud was gone, a bright beaming light brought in from the blissfully perfect moments with her, only to be taken and replaced by a ravishing storm that would wreck and ruin me forever.

"Your past," Dominic continued. "You keep it there. Anything you knew before this moment, you forget. You cannot return to that life. You made that decision when you carried out this rampage. I can help you, but you must make one last choice. Death, or the cause?"

"What?" I stared up at him, noting the hardness of his jaw. The expensive suit he was wearing. The effortless strength he carried, like people listened to him when he spoke.

"Protection comes at a cost. These men you killed, there are more of them. And they will come after you and anyone you care for. You may have concluded your murder tour here today, boy, but the implications will follow. If you leave this building alone, they will find you. If you hide, they will seek. Anyone you contact, they will pursue. Every step you take will be a trail of death lingering in your wake. Unless of course, there is a force that prevents that. That is something I can offer you."

"Why?" If I was such a liability, why would he ever consider taking me under his wing instead of throwing me to the wolves?

Dominic's gaze had trailed over my face, down to my blood-soaked hands and the bodies that cluttered the space around us. "Because I know potential when I see it."

My mind had fluttered to her face. The ache in my chest pulled at the thought of leaving her behind. It was something I battled with every moment following the one where I was forced into my dad's truck and driven away and out of sight. I didn't realize the man driving the vehicle was running from men like this until we were motel hopping in our attempt to get away from them. The idea of getting back to her was the only saving grace I had. It wasn't safe to break away, not when they would have come for me, and potentially put her in danger. But when they finally caught up to us, and ended my dad's life, I knew what I had to do.

I would kill every one of them and make my way back to her.

It wasn't until I shoved a dagger into the first man's heart that I realized the severity of what I had done.

It was easy. Too easy. And it made me understand just how dark and twisted I really was inside. How I would do literally anything to end this and be with her.

But with each kill, the doubt set in. How would I explain the missing time? Would I tell her what I had done? Would she forgive me for my ruthlessness? Would she fear me? Yet, the only way I would find out was to see it through. And that I did. I shot and stabbed and snapped necks until I collapsed onto the cold, wet concrete in a pile of blood that did not belong to me.

Finally, I could rid myself of this life, and be at her side.

But with Dominic's words, he told me that I was in too deep, and there would be no escaping the world I careened headfirst into. No amount of death or time would protect June from me and the wrath that would follow. In that moment, and each that had followed our separation, all I wanted was her, but she was the one thing I couldn't have. I wouldn't do that to her. I wouldn't risk her life so fucking foolishly. Our beautiful summer would have to stay that, a memory that I would cling to for the rest of my sad existence.

I stood from the wreckage that day a different man. I had shed the skin of a boy seeking revenge and became a man who would give up everything to protect the last remaining good in his life. Even if those two things were the same.

I walked away from her because I was told that was what I had to do.

And now, she's back in my life, but not because of me, because of these two men who insist on putting her in danger. She thinks I abandoned her. That I willingly let her go. Yet, leaving her behind was the single hardest thing I've ever had to do.

It's not like I can explain that. She wouldn't believe me. She wouldn't understand. I couldn't tell her the horrible things I've done to ensure danger would never come her way.

She hates me because I love her. That reality hurts harder than I thought possible.

I always told myself that protecting her was worth it, the smart choice. The noble one.

I didn't want this life for her. That's why I've done everything in my power to make sure she stayed out of it. I acted selflessly, and all she sees is a man that walked away with little to no regard for what she went through.

Dominic and Bryant continue to push the limits, confessing details of our work that I never wanted her to know about. Things that should have come from my mouth, yet I kept it shut to ensure her safety.

They've touched her. Been intimate with her. Shared things with her that I never did because she was too damn innocent and I wanted to maintain that purity.

They are two of the most ruthless, brutal men I know, and they share a bed with the only woman who I've ever given my heart to. I don't doubt that they will fight for her, but how much danger will they bring?

It fucking kills me that she looks at them with more adoration than she does with me. Those same eyes I stared into countless nights under the stars, making up stories of the future together. Hatred lines her gaze when she settles her sights on me. Disgust. Resentment.

And I don't blame her for a single fucking second. I broke her heart. I caused her pain.

How am I supposed to sit across the dinner table from her and pretend I love her any less than the day I was forced away from her? Live with her and not want to take her into my arms and hold on tight and never let her go. Beg for her forgiveness and promise I'll never do it again.

I want to feel her kiss against my lips and forget all the time that has passed between us—pick up where we left off, daydreaming of a time when we would run away from it all. Me and her.

I can't count the number of times I've laid my sights on a short girl with jet-black hair and my heart dropped, thinking it was her. Every fucking instance, a reminder that I would never, could never, let her go. She was a part of me. And I would carry that with me no matter how much it hurt.

Seeing her in that bar, talking to her for the first time in years, it ripped the half-assed stitches I had mended my broken heart with and tore me apart all over again. She's always been just out of reach, a cruelty I was cursed with, never able to be with the person I care most about in this world. Stuck living this life of solitude, a killer by day and night, the only thing that brings me the smallest satisfaction are the shackles keeping me from her. Sure, I have Dom and Bryant, but we were a team because of our skills.

We share a taste for bloodshed and bourbon, and now, women.

"Do you want to talk about it?" Dominic asks me through the silence.

"No." I reach for the handle of the door and pull it the second the vehicle has slowed down enough. I hop out while simultaneously grabbing my pistol from its holster. Chambering a bullet, I run up the front steps and kick in the front door, wasting no time at all.

Dom takes his time, walking with less urgency to catch up to me. He's not bothered by my rampage; he's used to it.

There's a thin line between being reckless and efficient, and I walk that tightrope more often than I probably should. I guess that's why I'm good at my job, because I'm not afraid of taking risks. At least not when it comes to me. With June, that's an entirely different story.

Hence our efforts of finding the man responsible for the cuts and bruises on her porcelain skin. We've killed a dozen men, and will continue to slay them until we are satisfied she has been avenged.

Beckett has us exactly where he wants us, focused on retribution instead of the war. It's genius really, although I doubt he understood the lengths we would go to when he made his order. He will meet the same fate as the rest, it's only a matter of time. Dominic was right about one thing all those years ago, death follows in my wake and I welcome it with open arms.

"What the fuck," a man calls out from his spot on his couch. His disgusting stomach hangs out of the bottom of his shirt. He reaches for the gun on his side table, but I point mine at him.

"Move another inch, I dare you."

"Okay, okay. Fuck." His eyes go wide when he spots something behind me.

The typical reaction from the fear-inducing legend I share a home with.

Dominic's shadow is cast over me as he appears in the room. He skims his gaze over it and settles on the man. "Pull your sleeves up."

"What?"

I step closer with the barrel aimed at him.

"Fine, Christ." He complies, revealing two pasty, hair-covered arms.

"Anyone else in the house?" Dominic comes around to my side.

"No. What's this all about?" The man anxiously glances from me to Dom.

"We're looking for someone. Brown hair, beard, scars on his face." Dom strolls around the room, peering at anything he can for a clue. "Into knife play. Has a tattoo around here." He sticks his index finger on the spot June had mentioned it was located.

"Vincent, yeah. What'd he do?"

"You know him?"

The guy nods and relaxes a bit now that he assumes he's not the one in trouble. "You could say that. Why? What kind of trouble has he gotten himself into?"

Dominic ignores his questions and asks one of his own. "Where is he?"

He shrugs. "Last I heard he was holed up recovering from some knife wound. Went rogue and kidnapped some bitch who got the best of him. Fucking hilarious if you ask me."

My heart rate picks up speed. "What part of that do you think is funny?"

"All of it, really." He lets out a chuckle then his expression shifts to serious. "Oh, was she *your* bitch?"

I pull the trigger without another thought, the vibration of the recoil settling in my wrist, the bullet lodging itself right between the man's brows, exactly where I was aiming.

His eyes go wide and a bit of his blood splatters around, his head whipping back against the couch he's sitting on. Red trickles down his forehead and his mouth hangs open.

Dominic sighs. "You couldn't have waited, maybe, I don't know, another minute or two?"

"We got all we need. A name." With June's description of her assailant, we've made more progress tonight than we have since we found out she was taken. We had been going around blind, asking everyone we could about a man who might be into knife torture. And considering the crowd we run with, that could be a multitude of people. We had narrowed our search to a handful of suspects remaining, but without her help, who knows how much longer it would have been until we found the one guilty.

"I'll call it in." Dominic pulls out his phone, pushing a button and bringing it to his ear.

I leave him to give the details of our location to our clean-up crew—something that shouldn't seem so routine to a person, but is second nature to us. I just killed a man, spilled his blood onto the wall of his living room, and I feel no different than I did before. Not better, not worse. Just numb.

Is there something wrong with me for being cold with death, and careless to inflict it on others? For ten years, it's all I've known. The only thing keeping me remotely sane, if I can even still be considered that. I'm a murderer. A killer. A destroyer of evil. But doesn't that make me the most sinful of them all?

I don't care what happens to others. No part of me harbors guilt for what I've done. Every ounce of care inside my black heart is reserved for one person, and one person only. Her.

And yet she wants nothing to do with me. She hates me.

Still, I will continue on my mission to do everything I can to save her from this life that has consumed me, even if that means an ocean of bloodshed.

# CHAPTER 18

# June

T he last few days have fallen into a routine pretty easily.

I discussed the changes with Bram, letting him know I would be only working three days a week instead of whatever he would give me. We agreed to Monday, Wednesday, and Saturday, and decided that we may flex them if needed.

He was pleased with this, despite me originally worrying that he might not be okay with the lowered hours. He continues to surprise me with his kindness and consideration for my well-being. He's skeptical of the tattooed man that follows me around to and from, but I think he's aware he's keeping me safe.

What was once a strange annoyance has turned into me being grateful for the shadow that looks over me.

Magnus is protective, intimidating, and a total fucking sweetheart.

A drastic difference from Coen and Dominic. They're both too busy with whatever else they have going on to barely pay any attention to me. Which is fine, considering the sooner they end their war, the quicker I can be free from their constant surveillance. If only there was something I could do to speed up the process and help them out with their problem. It's the least I could do after they gave me ten large to live with them. I might have had to sacrifice my freedom, but what exactly did they gain other than a liability?

I carefully walk down the stairs in my heels and into the kitchen.

"You're not wearing that," is all Coen says.

"Damn, princess. You're looking fine as hell." Magnus hops up from his stool to take my hand and help me the rest of the way.

"These shoes are a bit much, you think?" I turn to the full-length mirror in between the kitchen and the living room, taking in my outfit. A long sleeve black dress, made of something close to heaven, with the most revealing plunging neckline, almost down to my belly button. The length sits mid-thigh, with a short slit on the left side. Thank God for my period being over, otherwise, I'd be worried about more than just my ass having the potential to accidentally hang out. Chains of various lengths line my neck, one all the way down between my breasts, and a few shorter ones with matching stones. The heels aren't too tall, maybe three inches, but it's more than I'm used to wearing.

"Not at all. I'd definitely do ya." Magnus folds his inked arms across his chest and leans against the wall. He sighs and shakes his head.

"What?" I tuck my sleek onyx hair behind my ears to reveal diamond studded earrings. All of which was located in my room, courtesy of my live-in bodyguards. Along with makeup I could never afford and a stunning leather clutch that I've tucked my lipstick, cell phone, and a few of the hundred-dollar bills I was given.

Coen steps forward. "You need to change."

"No." I stare straight at him. He hasn't spoken to me in days and now he's going to demand that I switch into another outfit?

"Yes." His jaw tenses but I don't care that he's bothered. He lost the ability to have any input on my life when he left and never came back. He's had numerous opportunities to open his mouth and communicate with me, and yet he remains painfully silent, reinforcing my belief that he doesn't actually give a shit at all.

"You realize this was upstairs. If I wasn't meant to wear it, it wouldn't have been there. Clearly you, Magnus, Dom, someone approved this. Maybe your fucking driver, I don't know. I don't care. Stop pretending that you do."

"You think I don't care?" Coen softens his resolve.

"It's pretty obvious, Co." I fight back the anger that rises, the one that threatens to ruin this potentially good night. He's had ample chances to talk to me, and he's choosing to do so now? "I won't allow you to ruin my evening."

Magnus pulls his ringing phone out of his pocket. "It's Dom." He presses the button and connects the call. "Boss." He nods through the muffled speaking as if Dom can see him. "Got it." He exhales and glances between me and Coen. "Um, so. Good news and bad news."

"What's the bad news?" I plant my hand on my hip and wait for him to tell me I can no longer go out with Cora.

He flinches like I might smack him. "You and Hayes get to hang out."

I narrow my gaze. "And the good news?"

"You and Hayes get to hang out." Magnus steps forward. "You two need some quality time anyway. I've got to help Dom with a thing, meaning Hayes is off the work hook and gets to escort you tonight."

"Why can't I help him?" Coen runs his hand through his hair.

"Calls for my expertise, not yours." Magnus shrugs. "Trust me, I'd rather take your place." He glides over and kisses my cheek. "Don't kill each other." He continues toward the door, snatching a set of keys off the stand. "Seriously." And with a wink, he's gone.

I swallow down the news and do my best to process it. Turning to Coen, I say,

"I'm not changing. You can't make me. If you don't want to go, stay here, but I'm leaving."

"June," Coen reaches for my arm.

I yank it away. "You know better than to try to control me, Coen."

"That's not what I was going to say." He motions to his body. "Give me a second to get out of these clothes."

"Oh. Right. Of course."

Coen nods toward the living room. "Make yourself a drink, I'll be right back." He vanishes up the stairs and leaves me behind.

My heels click against the floor as I stroll over to the mini bar, not because he told me to, but because some booze could take the edge off what I'm feeling right now. Various shades of brown fill three different crystal containers. I assume they're bourbon, given that seems to be their go-to. I pull the stopper off one of them and pour a bit of it into a short glass. Bringing it to my lips, I take in the aroma and sip it carefully. The taste is smooth, consistent with what they usually drink. Expensive, that's for sure.

The burn rolls down my throat and into my chest. I swallow another mouthful in hopes that it will calm my raging nerves.

Footsteps sound on the steps, and when I turn, my pulse picks up its pace.

Coen appears, black fitted jeans, pointed onyx shoes, a snug, white button-up that's hanging open, his chiseled torso exposed as he fumbles to fasten it. A v-shape leading down to his groin. His golden hair is messy but in a sexy kind of way. "At least you have good taste." He continues toward me, seizing the glass from me and taking a drink.

"I could say the same about you." I shouldn't, but I extend my hands and finish buttoning where he left off, leaving the top few undone. I fix his collar and pat it down where it stood, grazing my fingers along his skin. My gaze flits up to his, my heart nearly thudding out of my chest. I steal the bourbon back from him and down the rest of it in one swallow.

"Thanks." He rolls his left sleeve up and tucks it neatly in place.

"Mmhm," I mumble.

Coen fumbles with the right one but manages on his own.

Touching him like that was already dangerous enough, I can't risk it again. Being this close to him, the flood gates threaten to burst and send me over ten years to the past when our love was fresh, unbroken.

In a way, it feels no time has passed. That he is still the sweet, miserable boy in need of someone who understands him. He probably thought I was saving him then, but little did he know, he was the one that saved me. From my darkness. My depression. The nightmares that kept me up at night. But then he left, throwing me into the depths of the shadows—alone, damaged, and ruined.

I've worked every day since then to build up those walls. To disallow anyone the power to hurt me that way ever again. To maintain every ounce of control over my life, my body, my soul. And I've done exactly that. Never giving another the chance to betray me—always being two steps ahead, one foot out the door at all times.

I thought I had a grip on it, but inches away from him, I can sense my soul reaching out to his, begging to sever the distance between them. I've been angry with him for ignoring me since I've been here, yet maybe that's the only thing that we can do to ensure we don't go down that road again.

"Are you ready?" I walk away from him in an attempt to put that tumbling wall back up.

"Yeah. Are you?" Coen rinses our shared glass in the sink and heads toward the door, plucking a set of keys from the hooks with the others.

"Your driver isn't taking us?" I follow him into the garage, careful when I walk down the steps.

"I'm driving." He clicks a button on the key fob, the headlights of a dark matte-grey sports car lighting up.

It's then that I notice how big the garage actually is, with at least a half dozen other vehicles parked around the space. Dom's Mercedes SUV, a blacked-out Suburban and a matching sedan, a couple muscle cars, Coen's ride, and numerous motorcycles.

Coen strolls over and opens the passenger door, extending his other hand for me to use for support. "My lady."

I roll my eyes at him but accept his help anyway. If I'm going to eat shit in these shoes, it's going to be because I'm drunk, not because I trip before getting into the car.

My fingers on his are electric, sparking that fire from our past. I ignore it and settle into the bucket seat, adjusting my dress once I'm inside the elaborate thing. Four connected rings embellish the steering wheel and are sprinkled about the leather upholstery.

He climbs into the driver's side and presses the garage door button before turning the car on. It roars to life, along with a rather large screen in the center of the dash. Coen pokes at it and music comes through the speakers.

I side-eye him. "You still listen to The Broncos?"

The soft melody plays. A beautifully tragic song about heartbreak and loss. One of the many tunes that we had danced to on the rooftop of a pizza shop a lifetime ago.

"Yeah. I guess I'm a bit nostalgic." He extends his hand, but I hold mine out and stop him. "I can change it if you'd like."

"No. It's nice." I shouldn't allow it to play. Shouldn't let the notes weave their way in and tighten the noose around my heart. Maybe I'm yearning for the past, too. One track won't do any harm.

Coen puts the car into reverse and backs out of the space. He shifts it to first, his foot pushing on the clutch as he makes his way through the gears.

I focus out the window and ignore his hand gripping the gearstick. Something I didn't realize could be a turn-on until he was next to me doing such a mundane task. I pull out my phone and send Cora a quick text to let her know I'm on my way.

**Cora: Already here, two drinks in. Can't wait to see your ass!**

I'm only one behind her, but knowing Cora, she's already feeling a bit saucy.

The car ride isn't long, except once we hit the outskirts of the Haven, traffic slows to a crawl.

People gawk at Coen's car, mostly guys and the occasional girl. The windows are tinted enough that they can barely see inside, probably an added safety feature to attempt to protect their identity. Although with a car that sticks out like a sore thumb, I assume it's difficult not to be noticed. I wouldn't put it past him to have bulletproof glass just in case something happened.

We pull up in front of our destination and Coen pulls the parking brake and rests his palm across my thigh.

"I'll get the door." He jumps out and walks around the front of the car, tossing his keys to the valet and slipping him some cash. Running his fingers through his hair, he approaches my side and tugs on the handle, opening it up and offering me his hand again.

I step out of the car and adjust my dress from where it's riding up my thigh. "Do I look okay?" I'm not sure why I inquire, but the familiarity of him has me asking his advice anyway.

Coen sighs and holds out his elbow. "Yes, J. You're a masterpiece."

I weave myself around him. "You clean up pretty well, too, Co."

He glances down at me, his blue eyes peering into my soul. "I won't bother you tonight, but make sure you stay where I can see you. Don't take drinks from anyone you don't know. Actually, scratch that, only get them directly from the bartender, and under no circumstance do you leave with anyone other than me."

And just like that, the mood is ruined. Coen goes back to controlling body-guard mode, a switch that he so easily flips, reminding me that all I am to him is a job. A target to ensure their safety.

A bouncer opens the door for us, and we step through into the noisy place.

I pull away from him. "Got it." I take a few strides and scan the crowd for the beautiful blonde I'm looking for, not the one I came with. She waves her hand at me to catch my attention, a grin spreads across her face. I continue toward her, already feeling lighter at putting some space in between me and Coen.

"Dude, when you said *dress up* you really meant it, didn't you?" Cora holds me at an arm's length and studies my outfit. "You're like, super-hot, J."

I laugh. "Thanks. I'd be a lesbian for you, too."

"This is so pretty." She skims the necklaces laying on my chest. "Are those *diamond* earrings?" Her eyes go wide. "Did you hit the lottery and forget to tell me?" Cora's finger runs next to my face to move my hair out of the way to get a better look. Her touch floats against the makeup-covered mark on my chin. "What's that?" The bubbly vibe fades. "What happened?"

I tuck the clutch under my arm. "It's no biggie. I'm fine." I gesture toward the bar. "You want to get a drink? I'm buying."

"Okay, seriously. What the hell is going on?" She follows me over to the busy counter.

The bartender immediately walks over, something I'm not quite used to. She places two glasses filled with a golden liquid in front of us.

"I didn't order those," I tell her.

She throws a thumb in a general direction. "Pretty boy did. Said your tab was on him. Can I get you anything else?"

I glance where she had pointed and spot Coen standing there, his glass tipped in the air at me. I glare at him and he grins.

"Pretty is an understatement," Cora says. She raises her arm and signals for him to join us.

"No, wait." But it's too late, he's already on his way.

Coen stands close behind me, his fingers resting on the small of my back. "Is there a problem, ladies?"

"Not at all," Cora speaks up. "But it's tradition for us to start the night with a shot. I thought maybe you'd want to join us." She turns to the bartender. "Three of your cheapest tequila's, please."

Coen scrunches up his nose. "Come on now, we can do better than that."

"Nope, the cheaper the better," Cora corrects him.

I tilt my head toward him. "Can't fuck with tradition, Co. It's bad luck."

Cora passes the shots out to each of us. "What are we cheersing?"

"How about nostalgia?" Coen offers.

The rope tugs tighter around my heart.

"I can get down with that." Cora holds hers up in the air. "To nostalgia."

I sigh and make eye contact with her then Co, clinking our glasses together at the same time. "To nostalgia." I down the contents and bask in the warmth running down my chest, hoping it takes root soon and frees me from being so damn uptight.

"I'll leave you two be." Coen places his empty glass on the counter. "Have fun, but not too much." He gives my waist a light squeeze and then disappears into the crowd.

"Okay, so." Cora grabs the original two drinks we were given and leans into me. "Tell me everything."

I follow her away from the bar and over to a dirty but deserted high-top table that gives us a little shelter from the roaring crowd.

She eyes the dance floor then me. "Spill."

"Um, well, where do I start?" That I was kidnapped and tortured moments after I left here last week? That I stabbed a man, escaped with my life, only to get fired and kicked out of my house the next day. That a beautiful, knight in tattooed armor offered to let me live with him and his two housemates, all of which I have romantic feelings for in one way or another. Past and present. And they're all in the mafia, which means they can provide whatever I could possibly need or want, and that they seem to truly want to do that. Oh, and I agreed to stay with them and accept their protection for the next three weeks in exchange for ten thousand dollars.

No big deal. They're also currently in a war, if you wanted to add that, too.

"How about the hottie over there? He's friends with Magnus, right? Wasn't he at his house?" Cora wildly waits for me to give her any detail I'm willing to spare.

I sip my bourbon and scan the crowd for his stupidly handsome face. "Yep. They're roomies."

"That's crazy. All three of them, under the same roof."

"Four, actually," I add.

She reaches out to grasp my forearm. "Wait, there's another guy? This is getting good."

I laugh. "No, I meant *me*."

"*You're* staying there, too?" Cora brings that same hand of hers to her chest. "You realize how fucking lucky you are, right? People write books about this shit."

"What, no way?" I inadvertently avoid her question.

"Um, yes way. It's called reverse harem, google it. Seriously. Best smut money can buy. Any genre, too. You want some alien love? They've got it. Vampires? Yep. How about a little werewolf action? It's there. Obviously, there's biker gangs and mafia, too."

I hold my hand over my mouth to hold in the drink that I nearly spit out. I swallow down the liquid and cough a little. "Sorry, wrong pipe."

"You okay?"

I nod, my eyes watering a bit.

"Pretty soon you'll fall in love, someone will almost die, and then you'll live happily ever after. Sprinkle in a little conflict to keep the readers turning the page."

Great, I'm living in a mafia reverse harem book. Can I skip ahead and see how this one ends?

"You're the worst."

Cora rubs her chin. "I hope I'm not the one that bites it. I am the meaningless side character in the story."

"Meaningless my ass."

She smiles. "You're right, I totally have main character energy. I'll probably get a spin-off book of my own."

"A girl can dream."

"Wait, you changed the subject. Explain to me how you managed to *move in* with them since the last time I saw you?"

I want to confess everything. All the minor and major details that led to tonight, but a lot of them aren't my secrets to tell and that would be unfair of me to be that careless with the sensitive specifics of their complicated lives. "Well, if you recall, I was having money trouble." I reach into the leather clutch. "Speaking of." I pull out a couple of the bills and slide them across the table. "Here. I really appreciate you helping me when you did."

"Hey, what are friends for?" Cora glances down at the money. "That's more than you owe me, though."

"Consider it interest, and my meager attempt at reimbursing you for all the booze you've provided lately."

She laughs and holds up her glass. "Again, what are friends for?" Cora guzzles her drink and scrunches her face. "Back to your story."

"Right, so. I had a rather weird day. Got fired from that pizza shop I was working at. Dude was a real prick." To say the least. "I had run into Magnus by chance, and he offered to drive me home. And when I got there, Carter and Heather had thrown my shit on the little landing at the top of the stairs and changed the fucking locks."

"Damn, J, that's intense." She circles her chin with her finger. "What happened there?"

"Dumb accident. I was carrying stuff and missed a step. Cut my face and bruised my knees. Anyway, Magnus was still leaving when he saw me fall, and being the sweetheart that he is, he insisted I stay with them until I get things sorted."

Cora narrows her gaze and slowly bobs her head up and down. "You're totally a sugar baby now."

"Am not." I grin and down the rest of my bourbon, courtesy of my blast from the past.

"J, I love you and all, but you are oblivious. You're wearing designer everything from head to toe and those earrings..." She continues to study my appearance. "Wait, what did you say they do for a living?"

"I don't know, security or something." Isn't that what Coen had told me before I knew the truth?

Cora puts up both hands to use air quotes. "Security. Okay." She shrugs. "Whatever. If my bestie is happy and healthy, that's all that matters. The wealthy part is just a perk."

I can't keep continuing to talk about this unless I'm willing to risk confessing details I shouldn't. "You want to dance?"

Cora puts both palms on the side of her face and squeals. "Really?" She immediately grabs onto me and tugs me toward the steady moving group of people. "I'm not letting you change your mind."

The music gets louder the closer we get; the temperature rises under the strobe lights.

I shift my gaze to where Coen once was, but struggle to spot him. It's not that I mean to obey him, but he did tell me to stay in his line of sight. Surely, he didn't expect me to stay in one place all night.

Cora weaves us through the swaying bodies and further into the center of the floor. She spots an opening and settles us right into it. Spinning me in a circle, she lets go and laces her hands up her neck and into her hair, her hips immediately finding a groove with the song. Her heather grey crop top has a plunging neckline and draws the attention of nearly every surrounding human with a thing for females. Between my skimpy dress and her high-waisted, short black skirt, we have people gravitating toward us within moments of stepping foot onto the dance floor.

Cora beams, her bright white smile glowing with happiness.

A decent-looking man approaches her from behind, his body floating along with hers to the beat.

A cute, short, curly-haired brunette steps in front of me, grabbing my hands and putting them on her shoulders. We finish out the song and both the girl and the guy flutter away and out of sight.

Cora laughs and continues dancing her little heart out.

Two more guys get closer, more attractive than the last. One with dark brown skin, a jawline to die for, and beautiful green eyes. The other with fiery red hair and freckles galore. They take turns circling us, their hands gripping our waists and dancing along with us. They stick around longer than our last partners.

Every time I spin around, I scan the crowd for Coen, never once spotting him. I shouldn't care, and yet I can't help but wonder what he's doing, who he's talking to, if he's miserable by himself. Is he watching me? Fuming over the sexy men giving me their attention?

A hand latches onto my wrist, tugging me toward the person it's attached to.

My sights raise, settling on the man I was looking for. "Co. What the hell?"

"We need to talk." He continues to pull me, his expression unreadable given he's always in a grumpy mood.

Now? Of all the fucking opportunities he's had, he's choosing to communicate at this very moment?

I turn toward Cora and the guys. "I'll be right back," I call out to them, because it's not like I have another choice; Coen is practically dragging me away.

We thrash through the crowd, Coen not giving a shit about the shoulders he's bumping into and people he's disregarding. He leads me down the hallway that's labeled bathrooms, walking us past the few couples lining the space and making out. He stops at the very end of the dimly lit corridor.

"J." His expression is hard and stern. He grabs onto my hand, spinning me toward him and pinning me up against the wall with his body. One hand slams the surface beside my head, the other hovering just along my face. "You think this is a game?"

I blink in an attempt to figure out his angle here. "No. Do you?"

Coen's gaze trails mine, frantically glancing back and forth. His jaw is tighter than anything I've seen before, something that can't be good on his pretty teeth.

People don't pay us any attention when they pass, probably because they're drunk or assuming we're another one of the duos trying to get a little privacy.

"Do you have no idea what you're doing to me?" Coen's nostrils flare.

"Considering you won't speak to me, no, Co, I don't. Care to fucking enlighten me?"

His breath grazes my skin, a mixture of bourbon and mint. "I will not allow you to flaunt your ass around here and disrespect yourself by letting any random man put his hands on you."

"I have needs, Coen, desires that you know nothing about." I take a step, but he pushes me back.

He brings his palm on the side of my cheek, his touch warm and electric.

I can't be this close to him. Not if I stand any chance of maintaining my resolve.

Coen runs his thumb down over my bottom lip, his fingers wrapped around the base of my chin and neck.

"What are you doing?" My body comes alive with his every movement. The undeniable chemistry is still there despite our aversion to each other.

He continues his descent, tracing the area between my collarbone and my practically exposed breasts. "What I've wanted to do for years."

I have no will left to make him stop, because it's the last thing I truly want. He was the first person I ever longed for, and that craving never went away, no matter how hard I try to fuck it out of my system with anyone but him.

Coen makes his way over my waist and to the bottom of my dress, his body shifting to block the view from anyone who might glance our way. His growing hardness presses against my leg. He snakes his hand up and glides it over my panties. "Tell me to stop."

I exhale and bite my bottom lip, my body hungry with the need for more. I eye his mouth, the same one I've kissed a million times.

He stares at me, his eyes pleading like they're begging me to put an end to whatever is about to happen next. Because once we open those flood gates, what if there's no going back? It's been over a decade and yet I lust for him like no time had passed at all.

My body gravitates toward him, inching forward for just a little more.

He obeys, slipping his fingers under the hem of my panties and gliding them down. Coen's dick throbs against me as he feels my eager wetness. He presses a digit on my aching clit and slides it further until it's resting just along my hole.

I pulsate, my pussy impatient for him to penetrate me.

"Last chance," he tells me, moving his fist from the wall onto the base of my skull and tangling it in my hair.

My eyes roll at the layers of pleasure he's already providing with minimal effort. "Kiss me before I change my mind."

Coen brings his face closer, floating it next to mine. "I've missed you," he murmurs and finally closes the void between us.

His lips are everything I remember, except the passion has increased, like they're yearning to erase all the lost time. An endless apology in his kiss. Our tongues reacquaint themselves—two old lovers finally reunited at last.

I gasp as he inches his finger into me, slow at first, but then he shoves another one in, filling me a bit more.

We continue to make out without a care for anyone who might witness this indecent public act. The only thing on my mind is scratching that figurative itch that has plagued me for so long.

He rocks the base of his hand while sliding his fingers in further, inching them back and forth.

I pivot toward him to give him a silent approval to keep going, my leg raising and wrapping around the bottom of his to give us both a better angle. I grip his waist and pull him toward me, dying for him to be closer. If only there was a way to actually fuck in this hallway without causing too much of a scene.

Coen fills me with a third digit and positions his palm to apply pressure to my clit.

I dig my fingers into him and stifle a moan, my orgasm already growing near.

He's well aware of it, too, moving in just the right ways to keep me on that decadent path to explosion. His tongue goes deeper into my mouth, mine into his, the frenzy we've created becoming more out of control with each passing second.

Coen clenches onto my hair, pulling it tightly and kissing me harder.

I come undone in this dark hallway, my pussy clasping and pulsating around him while drunken people walk on by. I bite at his lip with a bit too much pressure and whimper as the pleasure of the entire experience cascades over me.

He carefully pulls himself out from under my dress and breaks away from our heated kiss. Coen brings his fingers to his mouth, gliding them in and sucking me off them, his blue gaze piercing through me. "You are not to flirt with another man in this bar. Do you hear me?"

If I weren't riding this wave, I'd protest, but watching him taste me, the little bit of blood I drew from his lip mixed with my lust, I find myself unable to object.

After all, I got what I wanted anyway—we can argue about my disobedience later.

I'll allow him to think he's in control for now.

## CHAPTER 19

# *June*

Ijust got finger-banged in public, and I kinda loved it.

Maybe it's the booze running through my veins, or the craving I've had for Coen since the first time we kissed when we were kids, but the adrenaline coursing through me makes me feel more alive than ever. Something is enticing about the line of danger we dance along, and it makes me want to dip my toes further on the other side, perhaps see how much risk-taking I can actually get away with.

Coen pulls his phone out of his pocket—Dominic's contact lighting up the screen. He presses the green button and puts it to his ear. "Yeah?" Coen flits his gaze to me. "She's fine." He winks and grins, the smile only lasting a second before Dom continues talking. "Of course, he's already on his way?" He pauses. "Right, I will."

"Who's on their way?" I ask him, not caring that it's probably not my business.

"An...associate."

"Simon?"

"No. He knows better than that."

I exhale, not quite sure why I was holding my breath on that one. The guys have made it clear that Simon is their rival—a threat—the man potentially responsible for what happened to me. It's a natural reaction to internally cringe at the thought of him just showing up out of the blue.

"Is everything okay?" I study the way his face hardens and returns to the cold and distant man from earlier. The robotic Coen, void of all emotions other than anger, unlike the soft and sweet boy I remember from my childhood.

"It will be. I'll make sure of it." Coen turns back to me fully. "Just because I will be distracted, does not mean I won't be watching. If you want to dance, that's fine, but tread lightly with who you choose to join you. Do not underestimate whether I will cut the throat of a stranger if they touch you. I don't care who sees it."

184

And somehow, despite it not aligning with the Coen I once knew, I believe him, because neither one of us are that person from forever ago.

"Got it." I adjust the necklaces on my chest.

Coen picks up my discarded clutch from the ground, something I didn't even realize I had dropped during our heated time together. I was more focused on his lips, his touch, his fingers sliding in and out of my pussy.

He hands it to me and leaves his palm hovering there for me to take.

I clasp onto it and allow him to guide me down the make-out hallway, passing the bathrooms and back out into the blaring nightlife. The music seems louder than it was, the crowd easily doubled in size while we were busy.

Coen points ahead to the blonde shaking her ass with another girl. "Your friend is there." He brings my knuckles to his lips, kissing them gently and releasing me to join her.

He walks away, a strange abyss filling me with the increasing distance. Regret sets in with it, reminding me that I potentially fucked up by allowing us to cross that line. I wanted it, he wanted it, but did we go too far? Did we reopen a wound impossible of closing? Something that will take us both down because of our complicated past and our unresolved feelings for each other?

Cora spots me and waves her arm to get my attention.

I'll leave the potential consequences of my few minutes of pleasure behind and worry about it another day. Tonight is for having fun with my friend.

I glide over to her, stepping around the many moving bodies and joining her on the dance floor. I lean in close. "Want to grab a drink?" I could use a minute to catch my breath and some booze to numb me.

"Um, yes." Cora latches on to my elbow and takes me with her.

I go with her, grateful that I've gotten used to these shoes by now. Otherwise, I might have just face-planted or twisted an ankle. I pretend they're an extension of my body, adopting the whole *fake-it-till-you-make-it* motto. I refuse to let a few inches make me look bad.

Cora pulls me to her side. "Was lover-boy pissed?"

"What?" I glance over at her. "Oh, Co? Well, when isn't he mad?"

"So that's his type." Cora squeezes into a spot at the bar.

The bartender looks directly at us and holds up a finger. She finishes pouring the drink she's working on and comes right over. "What can I get you?"

A couple dude-bros a few people down throw a few choice words our direction and shake their heads. I don't blame them, considering they were waiting ahead of us.

Coen must have used his influence to ensure our prompt customer service.

I step forward. "Can we get four Washington Apple shots and two Flokis on draft?"

Cora smiles and squeezes my hand, excitement running through her at the renewed alcohol source.

"What happened to those guys?" I ask her when the bartender starts making our drinks.

"I think your man scared them away." She shrugs. "Shit happens."

"He's not my man." And yet I scan the crowd for him anyway.

He's leaning against the wall in the corner, his arms crossed, staring directly at me. He pushes off, breaking eye contact with me, and shakes the hand of a man who approaches. They exchange pleasantries and Coen gestures toward a table for them to sit at.

"Ohh, who is *that*?" Cora joins me in watching them, her attention on the man with Coen.

"I don't know."

Decently tall, with soft features, a hint of red in his ashy hair. He follows the path where Coen was looking, grazing his focus on me for a second before settling on Cora. He appears young, too much so to be in that line of business.

"OMG, am I having a moment right now?" Cora nudges me with her elbow and continues to eye-fuck Coen's *associate*.

"Miller," Coen mouths, but I can't quite make out what he says next.

"His name is Miller," I tell Cora once she stops staring.

Her cheeks blush and she turns her back to the two of them.

"J," she grabs onto me. "Will you introduce us?"

"Introduce you? I don't even know that man, Cor." I reach for the drinks the bartender sets out for us. I hand one to Cora and keep another.

"Please?" Cora juts out her bottom lip.

"Let them do their business and if they're still over there when we're done with these, I'll consider it."

She holds out her shot glass. "Deal." She tips it back and downs it, not even making a face. That girl is on a mission.

I swallow mine, too, and leave the empty glass on the counter. I grab her the other shot and her beer, and take my own. "Thank you," I tell the bartender as we walk away and give room to whoever else needs to order something. I find another abandoned but dirty high-top and make a beeline for it.

"Listen, J, I know you have a way with the fellas, but you are seriously pulling some quality eye candy lately." Cora flips her hair off her shoulder. "What devil did you sell your soul to, because I'm ready to trade mine in, too?"

"Dumb luck?" I sip the beer and scan the crowd. "Enough about me. How was your week? How did the test go?"

Cora dramatically exhales. "Dumb. Super dumb. I mean, I probably did fine, but I swear, nothing from the study guide was on it. That should be illegal."

"One hell of a bait and switch."

"You're telling me. I scoured that thing for like three days straight." Her gaze locks onto something across the room. "Coen's friend is super hot."

I push her shot glass toward her. "They're business associates, Cor. I don't know if they have a relationship outside that." And I'm not sure if they're even on the same side of the war they're battling. Allowing Cora to get involved with someone from that line of work would be irresponsible of me.

But if she did, then I wouldn't have to hide anything from her, and could tell her the truth about what actually happened to me. It would be selfish, but I wouldn't have to lie to her.

"You'll find out though, right?" She picks up the glass and brings it to her lips, waiting for me to do the same.

"For you, yes." I'll get the scoop on whoever this Miller guy is, and see if he's worthy of my best friend.

Coen is protective of me, so I have no doubt he would tell me if Miller would be a threat to Cora.

"Otherwise, you're going to have to learn how to share." Cora tosses her shot back and immediately reaches for her beer to chase it down. "I'm starting to feel it, are you?"

The alcohol warms my chest and settles in my belly, spreading a residual warmth over my body. I expect my vision to blur or my speech to slur, but instead, I'm just slightly buzzed, an overall contentment flowing through me. "Not really."

Cora's eyes widen and she cups her hand around her mouth. "Boner alert. Don't look now, but Damon is heading this way." She averts her gaze and scratches at her neck like she didn't blatantly announce his arrival. It's safe to say the intoxication is hitting her harder than it is me.

I casually pick up my glass and hope that her drunken state is causing her to see shit that isn't there.

A hand on my lower back tells me otherwise. "Fancy seeing you here." The Damon lookalike comes between me and Cora. His black jacket hugs his shoulders, a matching shirt clinging to his chest. The darkness of his brows intensifies his stare, reinforcing that bad boy look he's going for. There's something dangerously seductive about him I can't quite put my finger on.

He scans my face, his gaze falling on my brow, my lip, my chin. All the places I tried my best to apply the expensive makeup that one of the guys I live with provided me. "What happened?"

I note his jaw tensing, a rather weird reaction from a stranger.

His last few words he spoke to me float through my head. *You will be mine.*

"What the fuck do you think you're doing?" Coen comes out of nowhere and shoves Damon away from me. He positions his body in front of me like this guy might be some kind of threat.

"Co." I reach out and place my hand on his shoulder. "Everything is fine." I step around him. "You two know each other?"

Damon smirks and crosses his arms. "Yeah, *Co*, we were just having a chat."

"The fuck you were." Coen brings his hand around toward his back, gripping the handle of a gun I didn't realize was there until now.

"Whoa." I leap to stop him. "Not the time or place."

Cora sips her beer and watches the drama unfold.

A few other people had turned to watch, but once their attention span deemed it less than exciting, they stopped observing.

Damon speaks up. "You should really take better care of her, unless you want someone else to step in and do it for you."

"I should end you right here for your part in this." Coen's hands form fists, a rage like no other consuming him.

Damon tilts his head. "Wait, you think I had something to do with that?" He points toward me.

"I thought you fell," Cora adds.

I shake my head at her, silently pleading with her to stay out of this. My Spidey-senses tell me this is not the appropriate time to be an innocent bystander. The last thing I want is for Cora to get caught in the crossfire.

"Someone want to tell me what's going on?" I motion between the two guys.

"I don't think we've had the pleasure." Damon turns to Cora. "Simon, Simon Beckett, and you are?"

My heart stops. My mouth drops open. Without thinking, I take a step back, all fight or flight buzzers going off inside me. My chest tightens and for a second, I forget how to breathe. All of it comes into focus when I see their hands touch.

"I'm Cora." She has no idea of the threat at the end of her grasp. "Anyone ever told you that you bear a striking resemblance to Damon Salvatore?"

Simon pivots his head toward me. "Doesn't he get the girl in the end?"

Coen charges forward. "So, help me God."

Simon throws his hands up in the air. "Now, now. Don't forget the level of amnesty we have in places like this."

"Cor, babe." I put on my best mom voice. "Hey. When was the last time you peed? Do you need to use the bathroom?"

She blinks at me and nods. "I do, actually." Her words slur a little. "Good idea. You want to come?"

"I'll meet you in there, okay?" Anything to get her away from the evil men in her close proximity.

"Okie." Cora walks off without any other coaxing. Her full bladder doing the work for me.

Once she's out of earshot, I turn to Simon. "You leave her out of this."

Coen extends his arm in front of me. "Let me do the talking."

Simon laughs. "What kind of man do you think I am?" He flips his thumb toward where Cora had disappeared. "You think I'd hurt blondie?"

"I wouldn't put it past you," I say despite being told to basically shut up.

Simon brings his fingers over his mouth. "I'm offended. You barely know me, *June.*"

"Don't you say her name." Coen continues to clench his fist.

"I know enough. And to order this." I point to my face. "That makes you a sick fuck."

Simon drops his faux wounded persona. "I had nothing to do with that. I swear it on my life."

"It was one of your men," Coen adds. "Claims the command came from you."

Simon steps closer. "I might see the same thing you do in her, but I would *never.*"

Coen bridges the gap, too. "One day, you'll drop your guard, and when you do, I'll be there to put a bullet right there." He presses his finger into Simon's forehead.

"Who was it?" Simon swats Coen's hand away. "Who did this to you? Tell me their name."

"I don't know." Because truly, I don't. And if I'm being honest, he doesn't either.

"Vincent," Coen says through gritted teeth.

Simon shifts to Coen. "You're sure?"

"Deadly."

"I'll get to the bottom of it." Simon rubs his neck. "I'll deliver him by nightfall tomorrow. Give me thirty-six hours of a truce."

What the fuck is going on?

"Why?" Coen asks the question in my own mind.

"Because I want to see this fucker dead as much as you do." Simon extends his hand. "Day and a half?"

I flinch when Coen reaches into his pocket.

He pulls out his phone, pushing Dominic's contact. It rings once and connects. "Thirty-six-hour cease-fire, going into effect now. I'll explain later. Beckett is off-limits, get the word out." Coen hangs up and glares at Simon. "Make the call."

Simon does as he's told, doing the same thing Coen did. The two of them shake hands and I brace myself for the world to implode.

"Oh, what did I miss?" Cora says as she stumbles over.

For the second time tonight, I'm unsure where to begin with her. She requests information I'm not capable of providing. Luckily though, she's too drunk to put much thought into it.

"I was just ordering you an Uber," I tell her. "It's getting late."

Cora pouts and grabs at her beer. "What? It's barely..." She reaches between her boobs. "Shit, I think I left my phone in the bathroom. BRB." She staggers back where she came from.

Coen tips his head down and glares at Simon. "If you so much as think of betraying this agreement, I will tie you up, peel off every inch of your skin as slowly as I possibly can until you beg me to end you."

Simon pats Coen's arm. "I expect nothing less outta you, Hayes." He walks around him and grazes his finger up my chin. "Don't worry, love. We'll get to the bottom of this."

He strolls past us and through the crowd, out the front door of the bar, leaving me with more questions than I have answers.

Coen slowly faces me. "J, please tell me you and Beckett..."

I shake my head, for no good reason desperate for him to know the truth. "No, absolutely not."

"You're messing around with the wrong men, June." He runs both hands up his neck and through his hair. "It's dangerous enough that you're involved with Dom, Bryant, and me...but Simon. I won't allow it. The guys won't either. They'll kill you and him both before they let that happen." Those familiar baby blue eyes of his stare at me. "I never wanted this for you. None of it. And now here you are, thrown right into the snake pit."

"Hey." I take his hands in mine. "I've made it this far on my own, put a little faith in me."

It's not me that I'm worried about anyway. Simon made it clear that he meant me no harm. And as long as I steer clear of him, the others won't either. But Coen, he's lost, a darkness has consumed his soul and it's only a matter of time until every ounce of his humanity is gone for good. I might have a mysterious killer after me, and four men doing what they can to track him down and end his life, but who's looking out for them? Protecting them from the lengths they're willing to go to get their revenge.

Coen is clearly battling a plethora of things I've yet to uncover.

Magnus is attention-starved and dying for companionship.

And Dom acts like he's unworthy of affection and understanding.

They're all broken in their own ways and none of them are equipped to handle it themselves.

Each one of them is stressed, under an insane pressure to constantly be vigilant to what's going on in their work-life because if they're not careful, it could mean the end to everything. Their lives, their livelihood, everything they've worked to achieve.

I feel this strange sense of obligation to help them see their situation through, because whether I want to admit it or not, I do care about them, and even when I push their buttons, they continue to keep me around, protecting me, providing for me. They offered me shelter when I had nowhere else to turn. They've given me more than I deserve and ask next to nothing in exchange for their generosity. I've defied them, gone against their wishes, and yet they have been noble and kind, despite their ruthless and brutal ways.

It doesn't mean I have to stick around forever, but the time I have left with them, I want to use it wisely and do what I can to provide them a little more value than what I have to offer between my legs. After all, I can't exactly leave without their war coming to an end anyway.

# CHAPTER 20

# *Dominic*

"Y̲ou have some explaining to do." I grip the edge of the countertop. "Should she be in here?"

"Listen, this whole talking about me like I'm not in the room thing has to stop." June crosses her arms across her chest, making her cleavage plump up even more than it already was.

A distraction I cannot allow right now.

"Can you at least change first?"

She drops her hands to the side and looks down. "What's wrong with what I'm wearing?"

Bryant speaks up for all the men in the room. "J, princess...come on. You're a walking boner magnet." He gestures to his groin. "I've got one." Then at me. "Dom's got one." He glances at Hayes. "All three of us, a freaking sausage fest in here."

He's not wrong.

"Take off your shirt then," June tells Bryant.

"Uh, what?"

June pulls the strap of her dress up and over her head and allows the dainty fabric to fall to the floor, leaving her in nothing other than her panties and heels. "Your shirt." She holds out her hand and waits for him to comply. "What? It's not like all of you haven't been up in this at one point or another, no sense in acting modestly."

"Bryant, shirt, now," I order. Because if I continue watching this spectacle, I'm going to bend her over the counter, slide her panties to the side, and fuck her in front of both of them without a single care in the world other than feeling her pussy around my cock.

Bryant drags the white thing over his head and tosses it to her, leaving himself topless with a shirt of tattoos covering his torso.

"Better?" She asks once it's hanging loosely on her body.

Somehow, it's not. Her nipples show through the white fabric, giving off an entirely new provocative appearance. Leave it to her to be sexy in whatever she puts on.

"Not really." Bryant goes over to the couch and pulls off the throw blanket. He walks to June and drapes it around her shoulders. "Here. Try to stop being so hot so we can focus."

"You know, there's an easy solution to the problem here." June leans against the counter opposite of me.

I recognize immediately where her train of thought is going. "June. Please. Save it for another day."

She grins and raises her brow at me. "So, the option is on the table." June bobs her head up and down with a smug look caked on her face. "Interesting."

"Are we talking about what I think we're talking about?" Bryant drops his mouth open. "Because I am *so* down."

"Guys," Hayes interjects. "Focus for fucks sake."

"Right. Group sex is on the back burner." Bryant makes an imaginary checkmark in the air.

June tugs the blanket around her. "I met Simon tonight. Well, I sort of met him once before, didn't know it though. Anyway, that part's irrelevant. Tonight, he made it pretty damn clear that he had nothing to do with what happened. Seemed just as pissed as you guys are. So, Co agreed to do that thing where you don't kill each other for a short window of time and Simon said he'd find the dude responsible."

I rub my temple. "How? Why? I..."

Hayes speaks up. "He snuck in when I was meeting with Miller. Must have noticed I was preoccupied."

So much for the head of security being on top of things.

"Legit surprised you didn't kill him right there." Bryant leans back in his chair. "I would have."

Hayes smacks Bryant's shoes off the table. "No, you fucking wouldn't have."

Bryant shrugs. "Guess we'll never know."

"He was going to." June chimes in. "I stopped him."

No one stops Hayes from killing anyone. That's an impossible task. And yet June somehow managed to pull it off, only further proving the power she has over us. The entire situation never should have transpired, but it's brought a few key points to light.

According to June and Hayes, Beckett wasn't involved. If that's the case, then who was? How could June have provoked someone else to do what they did to her? And why? It makes no sense at all, unless...unless he's working for another person. Beckett and I have been battling for the throne, but other factions have tried to overpower both of us. That couldn't be possible though, could it? Between the two of us, I was under the impression we killed off the other threats. Could some of them have slipped through the cracks?

"Hello." June waves her hand in front of my face. "You in there?"

I blink at her and catch her wrist in my grasp. "Yeah. Stop doing that."

Her soft skin is warm, inviting, and does wonders on completely consuming my attention. My cock throbs in my tailored suit pants, reminding me just how badly it wants to ravish this stunning creature standing in front of me.

"What are you thinking about?" June raises a brow at me.

"Strategizing," I lie.

She flits her gaze at my hand still gripping her arm. "Right."

Bryant clears his throat. "I could literally cut the sexual tension with a knife."

I glance over at him. "I could cut *you* with a knife."

He throws his tattooed arms in the air. "Just stating the obvious."

"You're all fucking terrible. Can we focus for five fucking minutes?" Hayes smacks his palm against the counter.

I drop June's wrist, immediately regretting the distance between her skin and mine. I shove away every thought of spreading her tightness wide with my cock and settle on the most pressing matter.

"Beckett claims he'll find the man responsible and deliver him by tomorrow night." Hayes continues going over business. "I named Vincent and he acted like he already knew the guy and how to find him. Making him that much more guilty in my opinion. Why else would he serve him up on a silver platter?"

June shifts her weight and tugs her bottom lip in between her teeth. "Um, well, that might be my fault."

"What?" A bit of a growl escapes me with the word.

"He..." She rubs at her neck. "I think he *likes* me."

My jaw tenses and I steady myself by taking in a breath. Despite my efforts, it doesn't calm me in the slightest. "No."

"I told you," Hayes adds.

"Told her what?"

"That you wouldn't approve." Hayes crosses his arms.

"Approve? Are you fucking serious?" I close the little bit of space to stand before June, my large frame towering over her. I steady my gaze at hers and find myself trailing my hand up her arm and cupping her neck, tilting her chin toward me. "Never. I repeat, never, will you entertain the idea of being with Simon Beckett, do you hear me?" I tighten my grip and wait for her to confirm.

Instead of the fear I expect to see from her, there's something else, perhaps intrigue, lining her features. June watches me through her lashes, her cheeks turning upward in a grin. "Harder," she breathes and licks her lips.

My erection betrays me, pushing through my pants and up against her leg.

How can I be the one physically dominating her, and yet she's in complete control? Never in all my years have I met someone who had this kind of power over me. Women typically cower to my darker side, but with June, it's like it matches and brings out hers. A deadly combination that will no doubt end disastrously. We are both raging fires that are doused in a gasoline of desire that will burn us to the ground.

"I have to go." Hayes pushes a button on his phone, disconnecting from the call I wasn't paying attention to. "There's been a breach at one of our buildings. I'll take care of it since I'm no use here."

"You're really going to miss the show? It's about to get good." Bryant states from his spot in plain sight of me and June.

June breaks away from my hold on her and turns to Hayes as he walks toward the door. "I could think of something useful you could do, Co." She drops the blanket wrapped around her shoulders.

Hayes glances back at her. "Maybe another time, J." He continues on his path, grabbing a set of keys and disappearing into the garage, leaving the three of us behind.

"As you were saying." June reaches down, latching onto my hand and returning it to her neck.

Oh, she knows exactly what she's doing and she's having fun testing me.

I glide my thumb along her chin and grip the base of her neck.

"Is this where you punish me for being a bad girl?" June's wild eyes bore into me, furthering the sarcastic teasing she's doing.

"Stop talking," I tell her, wasting not another second by forcing my mouth onto hers. I part her lips with my tongue, caressing it possessively. Claiming her, willing her to understand that she belongs to no one outside of this house. Sure, I'll share her with Hayes and Bryant, but if she thinks for a second that she can be with anyone else, she's mistaken. I will happily murder every single person who tries to blur that boundary.

I break away from June's luscious lips for only a moment when I notice Bryant's presence come toward us.

He approaches her from behind and reaches for the hem of the shirt he let her borrow, dragging it up and over her head.

She spins from my grasp and faces Bryant. Her fingertips skim his chest and settle on his neck, pulling him down to crash her lips on his.

He moans into her mouth and tugs her nearly naked body into him.

I drop to my knees, yanking her panties down and over her ass. They land along the last thing she's wearing, the heels I personally picked out for her.

Savoring the touch of her skin, I glide my calloused hands up her thighs and part her ass. I leave a trail of kisses in their wake and tease my tongue over her soaked folds.

June arches toward me, her body inviting and begging me for more. I want to stop, to slow down time and please her over and over, but I need her to know, to understand, who she belongs to.

I stand, unbuttoning my pants and reaching in to free my cock. "Mine." I rub the tip of it against her and she backs into it while sliding her own hand up and down Bryant's shaft, her mouth still on his.

His palms massage her breasts; his eyes unknowing of the sight from behind the woman that's pleasuring him.

I grip her waist and line myself up, shoving inside of her with a bit of force.

June lets out a whimper and Bryant pulls away, blood on his lip. His tongue darts out and skims the red spot. He grins and melts back into her for another heated kiss.

I thrust into her again, sparing no regard for how much of her I'm filling. Every single inch of her needs to comprehend how serious I am.

"Fuck," she mutters into him. June reaches between her legs, her fingers grazing her wetness and feeling my cock pounding in and out of her. She takes that same hand and with its new moisture, she returns to pleasing Bryant.

June rocks her body into mine, matching my intensity in a way that only blows my mind.

I shove my cock deeper and change the tempo.

She reaches around to place her hand on my stomach. "Stop."

Immediately, without another thought, my body halts completely. Did I hurt her? Was it too much? Was this all more than she bargained for? Did she finally realize the magnitude of the situation?

"What's wrong?" Bryant asks her first.

June slides me out of her and takes a step to the side. She lowers herself onto the sheepskin rug only a few feet away. "Nothing." She spreads her legs and pivots onto all fours, licking her lips and smirking. "Just getting more comfortable."

Bryant returns to his place in front of her, except he's on his knees now, too.

She grips him in one hand and runs her tongue along his length, bringing his erection back in full force. June swirls her mouth over his tip before gliding him into her.

Bryant collects her jet-black hair in his hands and pulls it away from her face. His fists guide her head deeper and deeper until she's almost choking on him.

I get into position between her legs, taking a moment to taste her first. This is for me, not for her. I lick at her dripping lust and glide my finger over her throbbing nub. I don't give her the satisfaction of lingering too long. She doesn't need much to send her spiraling over the edge and right now, I refuse to give her that.

When I don't continue, she groans and positions her hand on her clit. Instead of allowing her to finish herself off, I grab both of her arms and hold them with my left hand behind her back. She mumbles into Bryant's dick, but he continues to guide her with the control he has over her.

I shove inside of her, filling her once again with every inch of me. My need for release matches hers with each forceful thrust I slam into her.

Her body relaxes and tightens all at the same time, her legs widening to give me better access to fuck her. June slams her ass into me and her mouth opens wider to take more of Bryant in.

Bryant's eyes roll at the new sensation and his grip on her hair tightens. "Jesus, princess."

June moans and gags but we continue to ruin her pretty little holes in tandem. Her body, hungry for more.

I dip my thumb into my mouth and moisten the tip, resting it gently against her tight ass.

Bryant lets out one final moan and explodes in her, pulling out and stroking every ounce of his orgasm into her mouth and onto her face.

She gobbles it up greedily and tenses around my shaft.

I drop her hands and remove myself, shoving her to the side and onto her back. I return my hardness to where it belongs and grip her hands over her head while fucking her slow and hard. "No one else, June." I slam into her. "Do you hear me?"

She licks the remains of Bryant off her bottom lip. "I hear you."

"But do you swear it?"

Her eyes stare at mine, questioning them as if they're trying to figure out just how serious I am. Perhaps they're wondering if there will be consequences to her actions if she chooses to lie.

Her core tightens, her orgasm just on the brink, exactly where I mean to keep it if she won't comply.

Like a final remaining puzzle piece locks into place, she parts her lips and mutters, "I swear."

"Good girl," I tell her, the weight lifting from my shoulders at her submission. I position myself lower, my body lining up to grind against her in the exact spot I know she needs.

Her grip tightens on my hands, her nails digging into my skin and mixing with the pleasure of her cunt pulsating with my cock buried deep inside her. I allow her the pleasure of completion, cherishing the scream that leaves her at her climax.

With her body still shaking, she blinks up at me. "I want you to finish in my mouth."

How can I deny such a request?

I release her hands and she brings herself to her elbows as I slide my aching cock out of her. Bryant, watching us intensely, strokes his length.

June moves elegantly, her ass going toward Bryant this time, and her hand and mouth finding me.

He drops his dick from his hand and mimics her position, getting himself a face full of her sweetness.

She moans as she takes me into her small grasp and plunges the tip of my shaft between her lips. Gliding her tongue along the bottom, she grips the base and twirls her thumb and index finger in a perfect motion to bring me a heightened sense of pleasure.

Despite knowing I could finish at any moment, I hold off and let Bryant build her closer to oblivion. It doesn't take long until her labored breaths and hungry mouth alert me to her near completion.

I weave my fingers in her hair and orgasm into her mouth, allowing her to swallow down every bit of me while she climaxes against Bryant's lips.

I thought I'd have more control around her, that her living here wouldn't change things. But here we are, fucking on the rug in the middle of our house.

Here's to hoping that will satisfy us enough to focus our attention on pressing matters.

The war we're in.

Claiming the throne is that much more imperative now that her life depends on it.

If Beckett thinks he stands a chance to be with June, he'll have to come through me first.

The stakes are somehow higher than they've ever been.

# CHAPTER 21

# Magnus

"You're not going." Hayes crosses his arms tight over his chest like that will somehow convince June of changing her mind.

"You can't stop me." She folds her arms, too, and juts out her hip.

"Yeah, not happening," Dominic adds.

I shrug when she glances my way. "Don't look at me."

"What the fuck. I'm not a prisoner." June snatches Hayes' phone off the counter and brings it to his face before he can comprehend what she's doing. The thing unlocks with facial recognition and she pushes a few buttons while backing away.

"J, give me my phone." Hayes steps toward her.

"No, Co." With one more flick of a finger, she puts the device to her ear.

Hayes snatches it from her and disconnects the call. "Are you fucking crazy?" Immediately, the cell rings. Hayes sighs and pushes a button. "Sorry about that, Beckett, pocket dialed you. We'll be there soon." He hangs up and shoves it into his pocket, out of her reach.

June takes in a breath and exhales slowly. "Okay. I will give you guys two options. Either I go with you, or I wait until you're gone and follow you, which seems risky, given the circumstances. The choice is yours. I won't mind if you'd like to do things the hard way."

I walk over and put my arm around her shoulder. "I'm voting on the easy way."

"This isn't a fucking democracy." Dominic glares at me and if looks could kill, I'd be brutally dead.

"Maybe it should be." June grips my waist and tugs me closer. "Two against two."

"Listen," I add. "I hate the dude as much as you do, but I get the vibe he's not going to hurt her. I mean, he's fucking obsessed with her." I glance down at the sweet-faced vixen. "Can you blame him?"

"And you have what, like twelve hours or so with your truce?" June continues to stand her ground in front of two of the deadliest men I've ever met. "I won't forgive you if you don't let me go."

Her last statement cuts like a knife despite it not being aimed at me. Something about being on her bad side is enough to make my heart ache. How the fuck Hayes deals with it on a daily basis is lost on me.

"God knows how you hold a grudge," Hayes mutters under his breath.

"Oh." June tilts her head. "You're going *there*? *Now*? Okay. Let's do this then." She pushes his shoulder. "Come on, tell me what you really think, Coen. Share with the whole group how you made a bunch of empty promises and left, like a fucking coward. You couldn't be bothered to call, to check-in, to be a man, and maybe just admit you moved the fuck on? You know, I should have known you'd betray me, that you'd leave me without a second fucking thought." June shakes her head. "You knew what that meant to me. To be abandoned. And you did it anyway. Did you ever fucking care about me at all?" Her voice lowers. "Was I a joke to you? A quest?"

I knew it was bad, but I didn't realize how deep the wound was until I could *feel* the pain in each of June's words. She prides herself on being shut off, not letting anyone in to see her for who she truly is. She was damaged when she and Hayes got together, but he was the one person she decided to let in. She trusted him and he did the unspeakable. The unforgivable.

"It's not his fault." Dominic runs his hand through his hair. "If you want to be mad at someone, take it out on me. Not him."

"What are you talking about?" June asks the question in my own mind.

"Stay out of it, Dom," Hayes barks. "This has nothing to do with you."

"It has everything to do with me. She deserves the truth."

"Someone better start talking." June grips the edge of the counter.

Dominic looks directly at her. "It's my fault. I'm the reason he never came back to you."

June flits her attention from Dom to Hayes. "Co?"

For the first time ever, at least for my witnessing, tears well in Hayes' bright blue eyes. "I thought I was protecting you, J."

The excuse for leaving her behind, the most selfless of them all. June thinks her first love abandoned her because he didn't care, when in reality, he did it to save her from this dangerous life he would never escape. He put her in the past so she would never be put in harm's way. It's no wonder he's been so fucking mad at us for carelessly bringing her into it.

Hayes keeps his gaze trained on June; his tone hushed. "I never stopped loving you. Not for a second."

June wipes at a rogue tear that cascades down her cheek. "I, um, think we should talk about this later." She sniffles and regains her composure. "This has nothing to do with tonight. And if either one of you ever wants to be forgiven..." She points to Hayes and Dominic. "You won't stand in my way anymore."

"Okay." Hayes nods, accepting that maybe, just maybe, he has a chance of getting back in her good graces.

Dominic drives his SUV while Hayes rides shotgun. June and I silently behind them.

I study her while she stares blankly out the window at the passing scenery. I can't quite tell what she's thinking or feeling, a tornado of emotions and thoughts more than likely devastating her with each second. I can only imagine the torment she's going through at finding out something so haunting about her past and present, the two colliding and wreaking havoc on her life.

I don't want to overstep, but my soul begs for hers to understand that I'm here if she needs me. We haven't known each other long, and yet there's this undeniable connection we have, an invisible thread linking our fates to one another. It's cliché as fuck, I totally get that. Still, I'm convinced our paths crossed for a reason, that we were meant to meet. I'm equal parts powerful and vulnerable with her around, and if I'm not mistaken, I think she experiences that, too. Not just with me, but with all three of us. I never imagined someone like June would find me. I had accepted my fate of meaningless one-night stands and surface-level conversation. I never saw her coming, and somehow the first time I laid my eyes on her, it was like the heavens opened and quite literally dropped an angel into my life.

A beautifully broken one.

She is no damsel in distress. No. June is a walking enigma of beauty and strength and a dark femininity that only she could exude. She's been hardened by her past. She's guarded. She's smart. She's dangerous. She took everything that ever hurt her and molded herself into the most badass woman I've ever known. She strolls head-on into danger not because she's a fool, but because she can overcome anything this world throws at her.

She will absolutely be our saving grace, or our demise. Definitely one or the other.

Does she realize that the three men in this vehicle would literally do anything in their power for her? Give her anything she could ever wish for. Satisfy her every desire and still never shy away from wanting to do more for her to prove how much she means to them?

"We're here." Dominic glances at us in the rear-view mirror.

June grips the handle, tugging at it harder when it doesn't budge. "What the fuck, let me out."

Hayes turns to face us. "June. I ask that you put aside our differences for the next hour or so." His voice is calm and calculated, like he's talking his way through detonating a live bomb. "Our number one priority is all of us getting out of here unharmed, and we can't do that when you jump out of the car while it's still moving."

She exhales and leans back into the seat. "Fine. What's the plan?"

Hayes continues. "I'm going to get out first, assess the surroundings. Then, and only then, when I have assured it is safe, you may come."

"And you expect me to trust you that you'll come back?"

Ouch. That burn even stung me.

"He will." Dominic cuts the engine and looks at Hayes. "Now, go."

"You're one to talk," June mouths off.

Dominic doesn't bother taking the bait, he knows better than to add any fuel to this raging fire. Dom backs down to no one, but this calculated risk is more than he'd like to bargain with right now. I don't exactly blame him. The idea of June flying off the handle and doing something to get herself hurt or potentially decide she's had enough and leave us for good is what keeps me walking on eggshells. She can be mad at them, but if I lose her too, will she have no reason left to stay?

It's obvious she's not here for the money, or the financial security we provide. June is resourceful, and if I hadn't stepped in when I did, there's no doubt in my mind she would have found some other way to survive with the little she had. She has no shortage of male suitors, either. Any man on the west coast does a double-take when she walks by. Perhaps it's the safety we provide...the security. But that couldn't be, because June somehow outmaneuvered one of our kind and managed to escape with her life. Which only reinforces the fact that she can handle shit most people can't. Further proving that maybe, just maybe, she could survive this deadly world we live in.

June needs no one.

But what if it's that after all. What if June *wants* us?

Despite her past with Hayes, and her present anger with Dominic, deep down, she has feelings for them, for me, for us.

Would she be here if she didn't?

Hayes knocks on the window, snapping me out of my heavy train of thought.

June immediately grabs the handle, but I reach out and stop her.

"Hey," I say in my softest, most gentle voice ever.

"Don't try to stop me."

I shake my head. "I'm not trying to. I just wanted to tell you, at any point, if you want to leave, let me know. I'm here for you."

The one thing she's never had from an outside source. Stability. Someone who would actually be there, no matter what.

"Oh." She blinks at me a few times. "Thanks."

Half of my face turns up in a grin. "Of course, princess."

"I'm going to kick your ass." June chuckles gently, the tenseness in her shoulders leaving momentarily.

"Don't tease me with a good time."

We both hop out of our respective sides of the SUV and join Dominic and Hayes. The two of them are chatting but stop when we approach. Another thing for June to get mad about. Can these idiots be any stupider? Am I the only one who thinks the key to this entire thing with June is including her, not making her feel like an outcast? Why would anyone want to stick around when people treat them that way?

I guess if they can't get their shit together, I'll confess my love to her, and we can run away, just me and her.

"What's so funny?" Hayes asks when I let out a laugh I didn't realize was audible.

Oh, just imagining a fantasy life where June and I live happily ever after. Something that could never be possible, for a multitude of reasons.

"Was thinking about this cat meme I saw earlier."

"Get your fucking head in the game, Bryant." Dominic turns to Hayes. "Tell them what you told me."

Hayes glances between the three of us. "Perimeter is clear. Beckett and the suspected man inside." His jaw tenses before he continues. "He's asked for a few minutes alone with June."

The figurative rug is pulled out from under my feet. My heart thuds wildly in my chest. The idea of not being there, not having eyes on her, to confirm her safety, it nearly ruins me. But then an idea sparks, one that will give him what he wants, while maintaining some level of control. "Do you have your phone?"

June pats her pockets, coming up empty-handed. "No, I didn't think I'd need it. Why?"

I point to the other two. "Either of you have yours?" I pull mine out and unlock the screen. Grabbing Dominic's from his hand, I glance toward the building where Beckett is currently hanging out with a soon to be dead man.

"What are you doing?" June asks me.

The rest of our little group succumbs to whatever plan I haven't filled them in on yet.

"Give me a second." I push the video chat button on mine, connecting it to Dom's. I hit the mute button on my end and look at June from head to toe. "Turn around."

Her front pockets are small, too small. Women's clothing is stupid. Maybe if they had bigger pockets they wouldn't have to carry purses or juggle fifteen things in their dainty hands.

I run my hand over her ass, sliding the phone into her back pocket, leaving the camera part exposed to the outside world. I'd rather have a different vantage point, but this should allow us to hear everything that does go down and give us the advantage we need to intervene if Beckett goes against the truce and pulls something. Granted June wasn't necessarily written into the rules, it's obvious if he harms her, consequences will follow.

"You done feeling my ass up?" June looks over her shoulder at me.

"Never, princess."

The sound echoes through the cell in my hand, confirming that there's a decent probability this will work.

"We need a safe word; in case you want us to come in sooner." I shut out the sexual thoughts that come to my mind.

"I can handle Simon. Don't you think you guys are overreacting?"

Does June still not realize how dangerous the men in her life are? Or does she, and simply not care?

Dominic clears his throat. "June. There is a man in there, tied to a chair, waiting for death to come from any one of the guys standing in front of you. I assure you, we will find great satisfaction from ending his life. It won't be our first, and it won't be our last. The guy who brought him here is no different than us. He is a ruthless, dangerous, selfish criminal, and has little regard for human decency. He may have some fixation on you, but if you think for a second that it's comparable to an innocent crush, you are wrong. Men like us, we are possessive. When we see something we want, we take it. If we can't have it, no one else can. Beckett is no exception." He steadies his intense gaze on her. "Do you understand?"

June slowly nods her head. "Yeah, I..."

Dominic adds, "Do not forget, Beckett is the enemy. He will use his cunning and charm to persuade you otherwise. He cannot be trusted."

"And why should I trust any of you?"

"Don't." Dominic grips June's shoulder. "It's better that way."

June studies his hardened face and I wish I could do a deep dive into what she's thinking. Each second she spends with us is another that she learns the truth about how brutal we can be. How we have been. How we will continue to be. This life isn't something you ever escape from. The things that we've done—the sheer number of people we've tortured, killed, left for dead. All in the name of maintaining our reputation, keeping the business at the forefront of our priorities. The reason we're still standing when so many others have fallen is because we do what it takes to stay on top.

We are feared, we are powerful, we are lethal.

June has only gotten a taste of what it means to be with us, and yet she's never once shied away in the face of the unknown. She's either a fool or a perfect match for our chaotic disaster.

"Are we done here, or is this where you continue to try to 'scare me straight'?" June uses her fingers to wrap air quotes around her last few words.

I bite at my bottom lip to hide the smirk that would give away the immense satisfaction coursing through me. I fucking adore how she challenges each one of us and refuses to be a sheep, blindly walking its way to slaughter.

"Pineapple," Hayes announces out of nowhere. "The code word."

June runs her palm against Hayes' face. "Cute." She walks away without another glance and disappears into the old, abandoned warehouse that is identical to the countless others surrounding it.

Far enough from the city limits that people won't notice the screams of agony of those being tortured inside. We keep local police's pockets lined and they stay out of our hair. At the end of the day, everyone has a price for keeping their mouth shut. And luckily for us, we have plenty of funds to grease whatever hands we need to.

"You sure know how to keep a man waiting." Simon Beckett.

"What can I say, I'm a busy woman." June walks further into the building, the door latching shut behind her. She stops, her body tensing slightly.

My fingertips turn white from the grasp I have on the phone in my hand. Dominic and Hayes both peer over my shoulders, watching the minimal contents of the building we can see from this vantage point.

Beckett's footsteps approach June, his shadow cast over her. "Is it him? The man who hurt you?"

June sucks in a breath and exhales. "Mmhm."

"I'm glad I could find him for you." Beckett pauses. "Something the men you spend your time with were clearly unable to do." He shuffles closer. "You know...I could give you anything you wanted."

June stands her ground, unmoving from his advance.

All three of us tense and wait for this to be over. The clock to tick the seconds away and for him to finally reach the point of why he wanted to see her alone.

"Why did you request I come in without them?" June asks the question we're all thinking.

"A couple reasons, really." The volume of his voice changes as if he shifts his position. "One, to see the satisfaction on your face at having this man tied up and ready for you. That is definitely something I didn't want to share with *them*."

"And the other?"

Beckett lowers his tone. "Well, you, of course. You're heavily guarded. They even tag along when you go to work. And you haven't been to your apartment lately, which could only make a man assume you've shacked up with them permanently. Leaving me minimal options if I want to see you. Of course, I could rely on your weekly girl's night outs."

The sick fuck is stalking her. But am I at all surprised? We're kindred in that sense.

"Here I am. What do you want?"

Oh June, never ask a man like Beckett something so loaded like that.

Hayes whispers, "We need to get in there."

"Let him play his cards. She's got it under control," I reassure him.

Not to mention, Beckett won't harm her, not today. He wants the same pleasure we all do. To see the man who hurt June suffer.

Beckett continues. "I want to give you a choice. It's a simple one, really."

"Yeah?" June fakes intrigue.

"Be with me."

June laughs. "You know that will never happen."

"I don't know. I can be pretty persuasive."

"What makes you think I'd ever choose you?"

"It's me, or death."

June doesn't back down, instead, she steps toward him. "Then fucking kill me."

And on that note, the three of us bolt through the door and enter the building.

Beckett cautiously backs away and throws his hands up in the air. "Easy now, fellas. The truce is still very much intact."

June turns to us. "Seriously? I was fine."

I guess June's definition of *fine* is telling a psychopath she'd rather die than be with him. No big deal, totally normal. If it weren't for the cease-fire and thirst for revenge, she'd probably already be dead.

Actually, from the smug look on Beckett's stupid face, I'd say she just activated some ultimate challenge in his mind. A quest that he will spend the rest of his days on until he finally claims her as his own.

Does he not realize June is an untamable woman? Even if she didn't care for Dom or Hayes or me, I doubt she'd ever settle for this douche of a guy. Simon Beckett could never be man enough for a woman like June, let alone the vixen that she is. That won't stop him from trying though.

Hayes positions himself in front of June, his body like a shield blocking the douche rays coming from Beckett.

"You sure you're okay?" I ask her, my hand resting on the small of her back. I slide it down and click the button on the side of Dom's phone to shut the screen off.

She nods and watches Dominic while he approaches the man tied to the chair. A single bulb dangling from the air, illuminating the disgusting unconscious prick.

June should leave, she should go sit in the car, wait for us to do what we do best. She shouldn't see what's about to happen, for it might actually make her change her mind about how merciless we are.

"Love, you might not want to watch what happens next." Beckett approaches June but Hayes blocks his path.

"Don't tell me what to do." She walks over to where Dom stands and eyes the small cloth on the ground with a few shiny, sharp objects. Kneeling, she hovers her fingertips over them, grasping the switchblade on the end.

Her breath catches, something I'm not sure if the others notice.

Is that the weapon he used on her? The one that sliced through the delicate skin on her jaw. The same one she impaled in his thigh before fleeing his captivity?

I yearn to take it from her grasp and filet him over and over, allowing him to beg for mercy, only to be met with endless slices of the blade until he bleeds to death at my hands. A death that would never be justice enough for what he did to her.

Beckett takes a few steps toward her. "I can wake him, if you'd like."

A growl leaves Dominic's chest, something I'm not sure he intended on doing. His possessiveness is almost animalistic at this point. He extends his hand. "Give it to me."

"Very well." Beckett drops a small white packet into Dom's palm.

"What is that?" June asks him.

Dominic pinches the thing between his fingers and puts it under the captive man's nose.

The guy wrenches his head back, his eyes wide, his mouth gasping for air. "Fuck." He blinks a few times and steadies his gaze around the room, his sights lingering on June and then Dominic. "This can't be good." He wets his dry and cracked lips and relaxes into his chair.

June rises to her feet, the knife clutched in her small hand.

Dominic plants his arm in her path to block her from getting any closer. "Not yet."

I rush over to her, hoping that because I'm the only person in the room she's not pissed at, it will calm her a bit. This man has it coming, but first, Dominic would like to question him.

"It's no use." Beckett chimes in. "Already worked Vincent over. He's not spilling."

Dom tilts his head at Beckett. "Sounds pretty convenient coming from you."

"Have at it then." Beckett motions for Dom to go on.

"Oh, how cute. You think I'm working for Beckett." Vincent laughs. "While you two play a pathetic game of cat and mouse, you're none the wiser to what's really going on out here."

Dominic kneels where June was, grabbing the handle of a knife off the fabric laid on the concrete floor. He lightly points it on Vincent's thigh. "Which one was it, this one? The other? You know, doesn't matter." Dominic shoves the sharp edge through the man's jeans and into the fleshy part of his upper leg.

Vincent screams, a salve to my soul knowing he's in pain. "Fucking bastard."

"Who are you working for?" Dominic slowly pulls the serrated thing out of his leg and lines it up against the other.

"Like I'd fucking tell you." Vincent wretches back and forcefully spits at Dominic.

Dominic doesn't flinch. He slams his fist down, driving the knife into the man's leg.

I side-eye June, an unreadable expression on her beautiful face.

"Get her out of here." Dominic doesn't bother turning around.

"No." June comes to life, stepping around in his peripheral.

Dominic stands, this bloody knife remaining in his grasp, and wipes his face on his sleeve. His jaw tenses before he looks at June. "You're not going to want to witness this."

June calmly touches his shoulder, nudging him aside. "Allow me."

Vincent loudly laughs through his pain. "This ought to be good. Sending a *girl* to do a man's job."

June isn't just *some girl*. She's fucking fierce. And this fucking idiot has no idea what's in store for him. To be honest, none of us really know what June's capable of. Will she end him quickly? Will she decide it's too much and let one of us finish him off? Will she do what any rational person would do? Call the cops and let the system do its job?

I eye her every move, my heart steady as I prepare myself for what's about to happen next.

Using caution, June raises her knife-wielding hand toward the man.

Vincent glances down at the blade and then up at her. He snaps his head forward, biting at the air in his attempt to rattle her.

Just like Dominic, June doesn't budge. She inches the blade closer, dragging it along the man's cheek. At first, it's a small prick of blood, but she drives the thing in, sending a trail of red pouring down his chin. Her body relaxes, almost like she's done this before in another life.

"Fucking bitch," Vincent blurts out, ripping his head away from her.

June clicks her tongue and runs the blade along the other side of his face. Sloppier this time but still effective. "Someone hold him for me."

When the other three fail to act, I move, rushing over to latch onto Vincent's head and secure it as best I can. Now I can watch her face while she carves into his flesh.

He wiggles under my hands. "What the fuck, you're going to let this bitch do this?"

"Shut the fuck up unless you want me to cut your tongue out," I tell him.

June digs the thing into his forehead, slicing some kind of pattern I can't see from behind him. Not that I care. The satisfaction of witnessing this so intimately is enough to make my dick throb in my pants. What kind of sick fuck am I for being turned on by watching my girl inflict bodily harm on someone who deserves it?

"Shirt." She points the knife at his chest.

This time it's Dominic that steps up, ripping the collar of this man's top and exposing the thick, hairy grossness underneath.

Blood trickles onto his skin.

"Think I could cut out his heart?" June rocks on her hip, sizing up the potential in front of her.

Beckett approaches. "I'll do it for you."

"Wh-what? No. You people are fucking crazy." Vincent twists to get away.

"What did I say?" I grip his hair and tilt his head up to look at me. "Now you lose the ability to speak." I release him with a shove forward and come around to where Dom and June stand. "Anyone have any pliers?"

Beckett holds up his finger. "Hold please." He walks over to a nearby workbench and fumbles through a small bag. "Here we are." He pulls out a rusty pair that will do the job. Coming back, he asks, "I can do the honors, if you'd like?"

I glance over to June, noticing Hayes standing off by himself, a look of complete surprise on his face. Is he in shock? I never pegged him to be one to shy from bloodshed, especially with him being the man that he is, but with June involved, it must be rocking his world at how naturally she has adapted to this lifestyle. It's a bit mind-blowing for me, too, but I'm choosing to ride this wave of euphoria while it lasts.

Hayes clears his throat, getting June's attention. "He might lose a lot of blood when you cut out his tongue."

"You're not serious." Vincent continues to struggle despite being tied to his death chair. "I barely touched you. You made your point."

June turns back to him. "And what if I didn't get away? What would you have done then? Continued to carve me like a pumpkin? Would you have gone so far as to rape me? Do vulgar things to my corpse? The possibilities are endless, aren't they?

Who's to say when you would have stopped? If this doesn't end tonight, when does it? What other innocent people have you hurt because no one thought to put you down?"

"I-I...I'm no different than them." Vincent flashes his gaze at the guys in the room and then at June. "Than you."

"Maybe." June agrees. "But that's not why we're here. No. This is your doing. You are a sick and twisted man, and this world will be a much better place without you taking up one more breath of air."

His mouth drops open in disbelief.

June looks over her shoulder at me. "Do it."

I nod to Beckett, who moves forward and rips Vincent's chin open and latches onto his tongue with the pliers. He tugs it out of his mouth while Vincent writhes.

Dominic places the knife in my hand and I waste no time slicing it across the thick, meaty thing, partially separating it from where it spent at least forty years. I drag the blade back and forth to cut all the way through. With a final tug from Beckett and a gurgled scream, it flops onto the ground, and blood pools in Vincent's mouth, overflowing onto his exposed stomach and coating his lap.

Tears roll down the man's cheeks, either from the pain or the realization that he fucked with the wrong woman. June alone is wicked enough but mixing the four of us men into this is a nightmare he never could have imagined.

"Finish him," Hayes tells her.

June glides behind the man, taking a fistful of his hair into her hand. She shifts her gaze briefly to each of us, settling on me last.

Is it approval she's after?

I nod and semi expect her to hesitate, to process what she's done, and come to the realization that we've corrupted her. To stop and run out of here, getting as far from the madmen in this room as possible.

Instead, she continues to confirm just how well she fits into this madness.

June tilts Vincent's head up and with one final movement, she slices the blade across his neck, cutting him open from side to side. Blood gushes out, a bit of it spraying onto her face. Her crimson-soaked hand, still gripping the knife like she'll never let it go.

Is this when the other shoe drops? The recognition of the magnitude of what she's done setting in? Or maybe this is the evolution of June stepping into the new chapter of her life?

I felt it from the first moment I saw her. The darkness, the torment, the thirst for something more. There's this softness about her that people might confuse for weakness.

June isn't weak, she is no sheep, she is the wolf disguised to blend in and strike at a moment's notice. The force that no one saw coming.

She isn't fragile like a flower or a butterfly, no, June is fragile like a bomb. Explosive. Powerful. Capable of destroying anything she sets her sights on. Deadly. Like the four men standing here in complete awe of just how fierce she is.

"That was..." Beckett speaks first. "Hot."

He seems to snap the rest of us out of our stupor and get to action.

Dominic points to Hayes. "Weapons, now. I'll make the call." He tugs the handkerchief out of the pocket of his suit jacket folded neatly on the workbench and gives it to me. "Get her cleaned up."

Beckett walks toward us. "What do I do?"

"Shut up, that would be useful." Dominic reaches for his phone but it's still in June's back pocket.

I grab it for him and toss it over. Turning my attention to June, I take in her blood-splattered face. "You okay?"

She snatches the fabric from me with her one free hand and wipes at her cheeks. "I'm fine."

If I didn't know better, I'd assume June had an accident with a kitchen blender or something much more innocent than the wrath she just inflicted on the dead man beside her. But I do know better, and she killed a man. Sure, that's something that might be taken lightly by us, but for June, it was her first time. Shouldn't she be panicking or shutting down or showing *something* other than annoyance at me asking her if she's okay?

"It's done, a crew is on their way." Dominic puts his phone away and approaches. A bit of apprehension in his every move.

Hayes tosses all the weapons in a pile and hesitantly comes over to June. He eyes the switchblade still clutched in her hand. "J…"

"Oh, right." She extends her arm. "Here."

"Shall we discuss the elephant in the room?" Beckett shoves his thumbs in his pockets and taps his foot on the floor.

"The truce stands," Dominic confirms. "We are men of our word."

Beckett shakes his head. "No, not that. I'm referring to this sad sack of shit." He points to the dead guy. "Wasn't working for me, or you."

"Make your point, Beckett."

June states the obvious. "Someone else is trying to outplay both of you and you're too focused on each other to notice the power move to gain control."

Beckett smirks and Dominic clenches his jaw.

Dom tilts his head toward June. "When did you become an expert on these types of matters?"

She shrugs. "I'm a business major, it's not rocket science."

Beckett laughs. "A feisty one at that."

"Stop fucking looking at her." Hayes steps between June and Beckett, doing the thing that Dom and I both want to do, block her from that asshole.

I pivot my body to obstruct his view, too.

"You're all a bunch of children." June sighs and wipes her hands on Dominic's hankie.

We assisted her in murdering a man for harming her and somehow, we're juvenile? Has she completely lost touch with what just transpired?

"I do enjoy getting under all of your skin." Beckett cranes his neck to see June.

"But, considering we all have a vested interest in that murderous vixen, I think it's best if we put our differences aside for the time being."

Dominic slides his arms into his jacket carefully. "What do you propose?"

Is he seriously considering this? Has he lost his mind? Has his obsession with June fucked with his head so much that he's actually contemplating aligning with Simon fucking Beckett?

"An extension on our amnesty while we get the riffraff under control."

"And you want to work together to accomplish this?"

Beckett bobs his head up and down. "I do think it would be wise to pool resources, yes. Eliminate the target swiftly so we can return to the task at hand, gunning for one another."

This isn't a decision to be made in the heat of things. It's something we should discuss as a group, *without* the sneaky little shit present. Hayes and I both know that, hence why we're keeping our mouths shut and not giving Beckett the satisfaction of a reaction.

"We'll need a moment or two." Dominic joins me and Hayes where we block June from Beckett.

"Of course." Beckett glances at his watch. "Although, the clock is ticking. Do get ahold of me prior to our truce expiring if you'd like to extend the agreement and strategize."

"We'll be in touch." Dominic tilts his head toward the mess June made. "Think you can handle this?"

"Oh, this? This is nothing. Who's coming?"

"Drew and his guys."

"Perfect."

One thing our clean-up crews don't do, and that's choose sides. They're there for the entire organization regardless of affiliation and don't ask questions or play middleman. If they're getting paid, they don't give a shit about the political stuff. Because at the end of the day, whoever wins, there will always be bloodshed, meaning job security for them. It would be foolish of them to play favorites when the power dynamic can so easily shift.

I place my hand on the small of June's back and guide her behind the broad shoulders of Hayes and Dominic. "Let's get you out of here, princess."

Despite our best attempt to shield her, Beckett still manages to find a gap. "My offer still stands." He winks at her and watches us march her out of the old-dusty warehouse that many men have died in prior to tonight.

Vincent wasn't the first, and he won't be the last.

As I study her seemingly normal expression coated in the remnants of someone else's blood, I can't help but wonder, will he be June's last?

# CHAPTER 22

I didn't realize killing a man would be so...easy.

Each of these guys keeps staring at me like I'll break at a moment's notice. That my spirit will shatter, and I'll have some kind of breakdown. If anything, I feel empowered at having ended that life. I made him fear me, made him wish he never laid a single fucking finger on me. And then, I made sure he stood no chance of ever seeing the light of day again. I regained the power he thought he had over me and I loved every second of it.

Does that make me a monster?

And if it does, does that change the way these men feel about me?

Does it matter either way? Isn't this all a means to an end? A temporary safe haven while they claim their throne and get Simon out of the picture for good?

"Stop fucking looking at me like that," I tell them.

We stand around the kitchen counter in their massive house, a place we often congregate. Each of us spaced apart, exchanging glances at one another. Coen won't meet my gaze, almost like he's ashamed of me, afraid to go eye to eye and confirm I am the same woman from that warehouse.

"You're covered in blood, princess." Magnus reaches over and places his hand on mine. "Why don't you get cleaned up?"

"I don't get it. This is *normal* for you." I pull at my speckled tank top. "You act like I have a tail or something."

"We're...processing." Magnus sighs and squeezes me.

"You want to have your little meeting without me." I tug my arm away and cross it over my chest with the other. "Why, so you can talk about how disgusted you are with me?"

Dominic shifts his attention toward me. "Do you not recall our first *major* interaction?"

"I do, actually, so why is this any different?" Whether or not he killed that guy, I'm entirely unsure, but that minor detail is unimportant in the grand scheme of things.

"You don't get it, J." Hayes keeps his sights locked on the counter. "We didn't want this for you." He slowly looks up. "What we are, who we are, we don't want that for you."

"Simon sure as hell didn't mind." I bite at the inside of my cheek knowing damn well I shouldn't have said that. It was a low, hurtful blow in an attempt to get them to understand.

Dominic grips the edge of the stone "So help me God, if you even think..." He moves from his spot, stopping right in front of me. He grabs my chin and tilts it up toward him. "Do you think this is some kind of game?"

I lick my bottom lip. "Do you?"

I'm playing with fucking fire by taunting him like this. It's dangerous, but it's the only way I can seem to get them to respond in any other way than staring blankly.

Magnus shoves both of his forearms between Dom and me, breaking us apart. "Okay, okay. Take a breath. Both of you." He moves me a little further away. "How about we all try a bit of honesty at this point? Huh? I'll go first." He glances at Dom and then at me. "What happened tonight was...unexpected, but not entirely surprising. Can we all agree?" He doesn't wait for anyone to respond. "I think it's safe to say we knew June had a dark side, the shade of that darkness perhaps feeling a hair too familiar? That's probably why we're all in shock, because we didn't think we'd ever find someone to match our level of crazy. Or remotely come close." Magnus pauses and holds out his hand to me. "No offense, princess."

I shrug. "None taken."

Magnus continues, focusing on Coen. "You've known her the longest, I get it. You wanted to protect her. We all do. But did you ever consider the fact that maybe, just maybe, she can fucking handle her own?"

Finally, someone fucking gets it.

Coen meets my gaze, his jaw clenches, and his brows bunch, pain in every inch of the expression. "I didn't want this for you, J."

"You don't choose my fate, Co." I turn to Dominic. "None of you do. The sooner you accept that, the better. I won't be some second-class citizen here. Not when I'm fine on my own. If you want me to stay, you have to treat me as an equal."

"You're thinking of leaving?" Dominic's hardened exterior softens like I just kicked his puppy.

I want to reach out, smooth the worries from his face and press my small frame against his strong chest. To see such a brutal man show this side of himself jump-starts my cold, black heart. "Should I?"

"No, of course not. You're safer here, with me." He exhales. "With us."

"Is that all this is about? My safety? You feel obligated to protect me?"

Dominic runs his hand over his salt and pepper beard. "Do you really not see what you do to us, June? We care about nothing aside from our jobs. We don't take charity cases. This isn't some fucking obligation out of guilt, it's because we...we fucking care about you."

I narrow my gaze at him. "You...*care*? Like you care about your expensive suits and fancy bourbon?"

Dominic grunts and looks to Magnus. "Can you help me here for Christ's sake?"

Magnus grins. "I think what he's trying to say is that we're all in love with you."

My mouth drops open, my heart sputtering more than it did when I sliced that man's throat from ear to ear. "Um, what?"

"Bryant, what the fuck?" Dominic rakes his fingers through his hair.

"J...I..." Coen starts to speak but he's cut off by the phone ringing in Dominic's pocket.

Dom pulls it out, his cold, hard expression returning to his face. "Shh."

Who could be calling Dom to make him react that way?

"Winnie, hi. Is everything all right?" Dominic says into the speaker. He sets the thing on the counter and flashes his serious gaze at Coen and Magnus.

Magnus leans in close and whispers into my ear. "Don't say a word, princess."

The woman clears her throat. "Why yes, of course. You know I prefer the night hours to conduct business." She comes across formal, mannerly, like she's in charge of something.

"Very well. What can I help you with?"

"Actually, I'll keep this rather brief, but I wanted to call you personally to inform you before you heard from someone else." The speaker muffles as if she's switched it to the other ear. "There will be a gathering in three days where I will make a final decision on who is to take over. I have some rather pressing family matters to attend to out of town, so you'll have to excuse the rush on things."

"That's understandable. Is there anything I can be of assistance with?"

"No, I'm afraid my hands are tied but I do appreciate the thoughtfulness." She pauses. "Dominic?"

"Yes?"

"While you have always been a favorite of mine, you must recognize that I'm not the only one on the council. This decision could be easily swayed in any which way. You must bring a compelling argument if you'd like the reign to become yours. The wives are entertaining all parties."

The wives? What the fuck does that mean?

"Thank you, for the heads up. Please let me know if I can be of further help."

The woman sighs. "I'll be in touch with the details soon." The line disconnects and the room goes quiet.

"Someone want to explain?" I break through the silence. "And why did her voice sound so familiar? Who was that?"

"That was..." Magnus climbs onto a nearby stool and props his tattooed arms on the counter. "Winnie Sharp. Our late ruler's wife. The one who decides our fate."

Winnie Sharp? "Wait. Do you mean *Gwyneth* Sharp?" The puzzle pieces click into place.

"You know her?" Magnus perks up his eyebrow.

"Kind of, yeah. She lives over on Pinehurst?"

All the guys turn and stare at me.

"I take that as a yes?" I scratch at my arm, a bit of dried blood flaking off and going under my fingernail. Maybe I should take a shower and get these human remains off me.

"How?" Dominic asks the question I'm sure is on each of their minds.

"You forget I've worked at almost every takeout place around here. I've delivered food to her place like a dozen times." I nod to myself. "I was certain I knew her voice from somewhere." When they don't say anything, I continue. "Super nice lady. She adores me. Real *girl power* kind of woman." That's when it dawns on me. "Let me come to the event thingy she was talking about."

"What?" Dominic blurts out.

"No," Coen says at the same time.

"Yeah, it's genius. No one would ever see it coming." I tell them. "A council full of women, and their leader already loving me? It's a surefire way to get them to vote your direction."

"She has a point," Magnus adds on my behalf. "A pretty fucking good one."

"Absolutely fucking not." Coen cracks his knuckles.

"You need an advantage over Simon, am I right?"

Dominic exhales and nods.

"Voila, me. What could possibly go wrong?" Famous last words?

Coen leans against the counter behind him, crossing his arms over his chest. "Other than putting a permanent mark on your head for associating with us in a business setting? I could think of a few things, all of them resulting in danger to your life."

"Pretty sure me murdering someone in front of you and Simon tonight confirmed that."

"I don't know." Dominic rubs his chin.

"Extend your amnesty thingy with Simon. Get rid of your competitors, use the opportunity to get whatever leverage you can against him, and bring me to the event. You three are solid, Simon doesn't have that, but adding in a female element is something all of you are missing."

What the hell am I signing up for? Why am I so dead set on them allowing me to tag along? What if I'm wrong? What if they're a bunch of snobby bitches who don't give a shit about me? What if I'm completely misreading my cards and I'm setting us up for failure? Why does it matter to me that they claim the throne? How is it possible that the power dynamic of them being possessive over me has now flipped to me being possessive over them? The idea of them losing, and to such an arrogant shit like Simon, it's enough to make me play whatever role I need to ensure they win.

Even if that puts a target on my back. One that I will never escape.

For them, I'd do anything.

I owe them that much, at least, after everything they've done for me. If I help them with this, then we'll be even, and I can walk away without feeling like I owe them for saving me from the shit storm that consumes my life regularly.

In three days, I'll do my best acting performance ever and convince whoever needs to be swayed that they deserve to win this war.

"You don't know what you're getting yourself into, June." Dominic stares into my eyes, daring me to realize the severity of the situation.

It's like when he stood there silently in that bathroom, blood covering his face after beating that man who threatened me, and instead of running out of the door like most other women would have, I stood taller and pressed my lips to his, embracing the danger like it was an old friend.

Something stirs in my chest, that same feeling from that night, the one where I choose to walk right into his darkness instead of shying away from it.

"Let me prove myself."

"You have nothing to prove, princess." Magnus is the only one who thinks I can pull this off.

"To them I do." I tip my head toward Dominic and Coen.

They're too busy worrying about sheltering me than helping me embrace this world I've been brought into. If they expect me to make it out alive, shouldn't they teach me how to survive, not cower in fear?

"J...can I have a moment alone with you?" Coen surprises me with his forwardness. Usually, he does everything in his power to avoid me, except when he finger-banged me in the club. That was definitely unexpected.

"Um, sure. Yeah."

Magnus stands and kisses my temple. "Goodnight, princess."

"Night." I make brief eye contact with Dom before following Coen out of the room.

He leads me upstairs and into my bedroom, not stopping until he reaches my private bathroom. Grabbing a washcloth out of the cabinet, he says, "I can't keep looking at you like that." Coen dampens it under the faucet and approaches me carefully. Dotting it on my cheek, he moistens the blood and wipes it away.

I point to the shower. "You know it would be easier in there."

Coen nods. "Yeah. You're right. I'll..." He drops the rag on the counter and turns to leave.

I catch his forearm. "Co?" I should let him go, let him leave this room, and not ask the question bubbling on the tip of my tongue. Nothing he could say could erase the damage he's done. He betrayed me. He left. He did the very thing that ripped my heart out of my chest, causing irreparable damage that would mold me into the person I am today.

"Hm?" Those blue eyes of his bore into mine, and it's like I'm taken back to all those years ago when I fell for him the first time. A million memories flutter through my mind, reminding me of a much simpler, happier time in our lives.

When it was just me and him against the world. A teenage dream I never thought would end.

"Is it true?" My voice is barely a whisper.

Coen pivots toward me, his body towering over mine. "Is what true?"

I swallow, suddenly feeling so small in his presence. Like I'm shrinking down to the girl I once was, standing on a rooftop of a local pizza place, giving her heart to the sad boy who understood her often misunderstood nature. "Any of it? All of it?" I glance between those bright blue orbs. "Did you want to come back?"

Coen sighs, reaching up and brushing my hair off my face. "More than anything in the world."

My heart constricts. The pain of his absence swelling and exploding, silent tears I've held at bay for far too long rolling down my cheeks. I don't want to cry. Not here. Not right now. But it's a waterfall I cannot control. A dam breaking with the immense pressure of being strong for far longer than it was made for.

"J..." Coen brushes them away with his thumbs and pulls me to his chest. "I'm so sorry. I never meant to hurt you. I swear it." He rubs his hand along the top of my head and tries to shush the waterworks away.

I hold him close, breathing in his familiar scent. It's changed over time, but I'd still recognize the earthy aroma anywhere. Tilting my head, I glance up at him. "Kiss me." I'm caked in snot and blood at this point, but the desire to feel his lips on mine is overpowering.

He complies, only hesitating for a split second before lightly caressing our mouths together. It's soft at first, the fire burning brighter the longer they touch.

I lean into him, and him into me. Our bodies are not satisfied with the distance between them, no matter how small that gap becomes.

His tongue darts into my mouth, dancing along mine and tangling themselves together. It's been years and yet they remember each other like it was yesterday.

I skim my hands up under his shirt and run my fingers over the muscles rippling his body. My teenage attraction holds nothing to the torch I carry for him now. I grip the bottom of his top and drag it over his head, our lips parting for the brief moment to rid him of the thing. "I want you, Co," I breathe into him.

Coen wraps his arm around my waist and hoists me into the air, guiding my legs around his torso. "I *need* you, J."

With each kiss, every delicate and passionate movement, I sense how desperate he is to make me understand, to realize the answer to all the questions that have haunted me since the day he left.

"It's you, June. It's always been you." Coen slams my body against the glass wall to the shower. He reaches in and turns the faucet, water cascading down, a beautiful soundtrack for our heated moment.

But is that all it will be? A fleeting moment? A taste of what we missed and what we will never be able to hold onto? I didn't plan on sticking around once I help them win this war, but how can I be the one to walk away from him, after all this time? How could I say goodbye to any of them when I finally feel like I've found my home?

He lowers me to the tiled floor gently and steam fills the large bathroom while Coen and I remove our clothing. We don't take our eyes off each other, returning our mouths together the second we're fully undressed.

His erection presses into my stomach and he lifts me back into the air.

I grip his neck and lock my legs around him, reaching down to stroke his length in my free hand.

Coen walks us into the shower, water flowing down our eager bodies. The temperature stings my skin at first but acclimates quickly.

The water runs dirty with the reminder of what I did tonight. The man I killed without a second thought. I didn't feel remorse, or guilt, or any doubts about ending him.

Coen sets me onto the shower floor and reaches for the loofa hanging there. He pumps some soap out and lathers it up. "Here." Thoughtfully, he holds onto my hand and scrubs each of my arms until there is no more blood. He glides it over my chest, and neck, going lower and kneeling to clean my legs, too. "There, that's better."

I place my palms on the side of his head and pull him toward me. It's late and I can't decide if I'm exhausted or riding some adrenaline-infused rush from what went down tonight. Either way, I want what should have been mine a long time ago.

He breaks away and looks into my eyes. "Are you sure?"

I tug him closer and mutter against his lips. "Without a doubt."

Am I hurt? Yes. Does the wound of Coen leaving all those years ago burn like it happened yesterday? Absolutely. But does knowing a bit of the truth help repair that bond that might have never been broken after all? Definitely.

Coen kisses me back with a soft, gentle hunger. He weaves his fingers along my neck and into my damp hair. Gripping my hip, Coen backs me into the cold tile wall. His cock presses against me and I reach down and stroke it, a soft moan escaping him. He separates my legs with his knee, positioning himself between them.

I comply completely, arching my body to get a better angle.

Coen penetrates me slowly, the hot water tumbling down on us. Despite all the years spent apart, our chemistry is somehow fully intact, if not more than I remember. Time and space never stood a chance against us.

"I love you, June, I never stopped loving you," Coen mutters while thrusting into me.

His tongue dances with mine and it's as though for once, all is right in the world.

Only, that couldn't be further from the truth. But for now, I'm going to pretend.

# CHAPTER 23

# June

Am I crazy for being more mind-blown about the fact that I had sex with Coen than I am about having killed a man?

It's been three days, and yet I keep finding myself touching my fingers to spots on my body where his lips had touched. My neck. Just below my ear. My collarbone. Even the corner of my mouth. Soft, delicate, but full of a burning desire I thought was long forgotten.

I've officially had sex with every member of this house, and somehow, they're all okay with it. Or they're at least acting like they are. I've made it pretty damn clear that I'm not going to choose between them and although I thought that was pretty damn irrational, they haven't said a word about it. It's strange, really. I mention Simon and all three of them nearly jump out of their skin and bark off how they want to tear him apart, but I can openly sleep with any one of them without them batting an eye.

How did I go from never sticking around longer than a couple rumbles in between the sheets, to bunking up with three, I repeat, one, two, three men?

And if I'm being honest with myself, I'm not mad about it at all.

The thought of settling down with one man is unappealing. I'd go as far as to say it's suffocating to imagine. But with Dominic, Coen, and Magnus, they each bring something else the others don't bring to the table. Dominic is a brute with a dominant side. Totally fitting for his name. He's a softie, but only for me, which absolutely drives me wild. Magnus is a picture-perfect bad boy with the tattoos to go along with it. He has the sweetest heart and believes in me way more than the others do. His appearance and demeanor are the exact opposite of Coen's which is hilarious because Coen is supposedly this big tough guy, ruthless killer, and yet he looks like your typical surfer boy mixed with an Abercrombie model.

They're damaged, a darkness consuming their souls in an equal but somehow entirely unique way. It's familiar. Comfortable. And ignites a connection between us unlike anything I've ever experienced.

Each one of them treats me differently, even fucks differently, which provides a constant and well-rounded level of satisfaction.

Am I being greedy to not settle for just one? Is it unfair of me to keep them all on the hook and not choose between them?

What was it that Cora had mentioned at the bar that night? Reverse harem. Polyamory. Is that real? Something that would be doable for this odd situation I've found myself and three incredible men in?

"Princess." Magnus snaps his fingers in front of me. "You in there?"

I blink and nod. "Yeah, sorry, I..."

"Were you having a sex daydream?" Magnus plops himself onto my bed next to me. "Because...it could be arranged."

"You don't even know what it was." I teasingly bop his leg with my foot.

He catches and drags it across his waist. Magnus lowers his voice and raises his brows, giving off one hell of a seductive vibe. "There isn't anything I wouldn't do for you."

And somehow, I wouldn't put it past him to be telling the absolute truth.

"What?" Magnus tugs me even closer, pressing his lips against my ear. "You don't believe me?" In an instant, he flips me over, his ink-covered body on top of me, pinning me to the mattress. His shirtless torso begging me to reach out and skim my fingertips along his bare skin.

I can't help but stare up at him and admire his beauty. Instinctually, I bite at my bottom lip, endless ideas of what I'd like to do with him running through my mind.

A knock sounds on the frame of my bedroom door. A throat clears.

"Here." Dominic.

Magnus rolls his eyes dramatically and falls onto the bed beside me. "Uh. You ruin everything."

"The simple fact that you haven't gotten used to it by now is your fault, not mine." Dominic enters, his hand outreaching, a hanger dangling off his finger with a black dress attached to it.

"What's this?" I scoot off the bed and stand, eyeing the offering.

"If you insist on attending tonight, you will be dressed appropriately."

"Is that..." I softly touch the black fabric. "Armani?" I saw a dress similar to this a while back in one of those waiting room magazines that you browse mindlessly while wondering if your appointment will ever start on time.

Dominic scoffs. "Don't insult me, June."

"Armani is *under* you?" I glance up at him.

"You don't have to wear it if you don't want to." Dominic pauses before continuing. "But you can't come if you don't."

"An ultimatum, that's very like you."

Magnus props himself up on his elbows. "Don't worry, you're not the only one he's insisting on dressing. Hayes and I both have new suits."

I jut out my bottom lip. "I want a suit."

Dominic shakes his head. "Fine. Next time then. I'll just throw this out."

I catch his arm when he goes to turn away. "I'm teasing you. It's fucking gorgeous, are you kidding? Gimme." I wiggle my fingers to motion for him to hand it over.

"Do you need anything else?" Dominic folds his arms behind him, eager to be of service however he can be.

Is this nerves? The events of tonight finally exposing themselves in him as anxious jitters to fill the time between now and when the verdict comes in. I should have realized sooner how...*human* he is. Of course he's worried. The fate of his entire future rides on a room full of women who could easily choose an incompetent fuck boy as the new leader of their organization. If I can just sway Gwyneth then maybe she can convince the others, too. Having a female around might give the guys the edge they need to gain the upper hand over Simon and his new-age ways.

Over the last few days, the men have teamed up and eliminated their other threats, getting the competition narrowed down to Simon and Dominic. Two ruthless men, both drastically different in every way other than them having the same goal in mind. Claiming the throne. And well, claiming me. The last part, I'm not sure anyone has the power to accomplish.

As for winning this war, I never considered what would happen if he lost. Would they exile him? Would they strip him of his title, his assets, everything he's worked his whole life for? What happens to Coen and Magnus? Would they all go their separate ways? Get other jobs? Who the fuck would employ them with their resume consisting of primarily illegal activities? If Simon gains total control, do these three have to work for him? Bow down and be his bitch?

Or would they be deemed unnecessary and killed in order to eliminate any potential threats they could pose to Simon following through with the new advancement in his career?

I can't allow that to happen. None of it. There are too many variables if they lose. The only option is to ensure Dominic maintains his position as the fearless leader he is. And with him giving everything he already has, I'm going to have to be the one to pull a Hail Mary out of my ass and figure out how to secure his victory.

I will do whatever it takes because I can't stomach the idea of any of these three men not getting what they rightfully deserve.

After all, I'm obligated to live in this house until the battle is over anyway. If I want to be free, I have to liberate them, too.

"No," I tell Dominic finally. I choose a softer, kinder tone. "Thank you, though." I shouldn't have teased him about the dress. It was a thoughtful gesture, even if it was laced with him being a dominant control freak over the situation.

He wants me to look good, and that makes perfect sense, considering I'm the pawn being used to advance him into checkmate. I've used my body and mind for a lot of things, but tonight will take my skills to a whole new level. What if I fail?

Carefully, I step down the stairs, holding onto the railing for dear life. I've walked in heels countless other times, but I've never been so determined to not faceplant. I'd like to at least get out of the house and show this gorgeous dress off before I fall and ruin it. I suck in a breath and round the corner, swallowing every bit of my nerves and putting on my game face. I won't show my nerves, not to anyone.

My mindset for today is *fake it till you make it* because that will quite possibly be the only thing helping me keep it together. A few months ago, I was aware sketchy dealings were flying under the radar, but never did I imagine I'd be tagging along to one of the very events where a change in leadership would be decided. Let alone on the arm of the man who will hopefully take that reign.

I'm in over my head and if I allow it to show, everyone will see me as a weak link, not the rare driving force I need to appear to be. I will not be the flaw that loses this for them.

"Jesus fucking Christ." Magnus is the first to speak when I appear.

"Yeah?" I continue toward them, a sly grin on my face and one foot in front of the other. The strings on the gold heels that wrap around my ankle are the perfect contrast to the jet-black dress I'm privileged to be wearing tonight. Slits all the way up on both sides of the dark fabric leave a strip between my legs, showing them off with each step. Going commando was the only viable choice since the cuts go so fucking high up my thigh.

The entire thing fits like a glove. Dominic outdid himself, clearly somehow having the gown fitted to my body seamlessly. I wouldn't put it past him to have used his advanced skills to eyeball my naked figure while we were fucking to get my measurements.

I take in each of them, my gaze not quite sure which one to settle on. All three of the handsome men stare at me, their own bodies decked out in hand-crafted designer suits. Matching, but with their own individual embellishments. They're fucking breathtaking, a sight I cannot believe I've been allowed to witness these last few weeks.

My heart sputters in my chest, a feeling I've never felt before. Not even with Coen all those years ago. Sure, I loved him then, but this...this is something different altogether.

Now it's more...whole. And for once in my life, I don't want to run away from it.

What the fuck is happening to me? I'm going soft. I need to get my head back in the game and focus on the task at hand—helping them win this war.

Dominic slides a felt black box off the counter and opens it, holding it out toward me. "You didn't think I'd allow you to wear those department store earrings, did you?"

But he didn't just stop there. Next to the solid gold hoops are a matching necklace and tennis bracelet. I stifle the gasp at just how stunning each piece is. Hand-crafted for sure, and probably more expensive than I could even imagine. What hasn't he thought of? At this point, I wouldn't be surprised if Dominic pulled out a tiara to go with the entire ensemble.

"When did you have time to do all of this?" I glance from the jewelry up to him.

The wrinkles beside his eyes crease and I'd wager to say under his salt and pepper beard his cheeks flush. "I have my ways."

"You do, don't you?" These three, it's like they can pull anything off, no matter how extreme. Getting away with murder, securing the perfect dress and embellishments, mind-blowing orgasms...you name it, they deliver.

"May I?" Coen motions towards the box and waits for Dominic's nod before reaching in and gently taking the long delicate chain.

I scoop my hair to the side and make way for him to secure the thing around my neck. A section of it clings to me like a choker, while another layer creates a soft point a few inches below my collarbone, a long dangling piece comes off that making a home between my breasts, complimenting the plunging neckline effortlessly. A chill runs down my spine at Coen's fingertips brushing my skin as he finishes clasping it in place.

Magnus plucks the bracelet out without Dominic's approval, obviously not wanting to be excluded from this interaction. "You look radiant, princess."

I roll my eyes at him. "Haven't you had enough of the princess thing?"

Magnus smirks. "Never. Although tonight, you're more fit to be a queen."

"You sure you're up for this, J?" Coen skims my arm with the knuckle of his index finger.

It's not like I could back out now even if I wasn't. Sure, using me could definitely be a make or break for them, but they planned on doing this without me from the start. My fear of letting them down far outweighs going face to face with a criminal organization. Does that make me a fool? More than likely. Do I care? Not really. What do I have to lose? Aside from Cora, these guys standing in front of me have become the most important thing in my life. I'd do anything to secure their win, regardless of how dangerous and potentially idiotic it is.

I'd be lying if I said I wasn't concerned about what happens if they *do* win. What will that mean for us? For me? Will they no longer need me or feel obligated to keep me under their protection? Will I be tossed aside? A used-up pawn in a never-ending game of chess. It shouldn't matter though. My goal is to help them succeed, anything else is unimportant compared to the greater task at hand.

I managed just fine without them before all of this, I'll figure it out after. I can live with whatever the consequences are if I know I did my all to assist in this monumental battle.

Steadying myself for what's to come, I let out a breath. "Let's do this."

---

Dominic extends his hand to help me out of the blacked-out car we arrived in. "Remember, this is an amnesty zone. There will be no violence or bloodshed while on these grounds."

I glance at the dark tinted glass separating us from the driver. "Does someone need to tip him or something?"

"He's on the payroll, princess." Magnus hops out of the other side and appears next to Dominic in a flash, his hand outreached, too.

I slip my palms into both of theirs, using what I can to support me onto the brick-paved driveway we arrived at. My sights skim the massive structure behind these two, and then on the numerous bodies getting out of other vehicles around us. I swallow down the knee-jerk reaction to be intimidated and assume my fake it till you make it bravado. I refuse to allow these people to make me feel any less than them based on their status in this cold-blooded world.

I'm in over my head but they don't need to know that.

Coen takes his time walking around and joining us, his gaze scanning everyone around us, too. It's then that I remember he's the head of their security and this is him in his element, doing what he does best.

Once I've adjusted my dress and gathered my bearings, I slide my hand around Dominic's offered elbow and allow him to set our pace.

He doesn't hurry us, yet he walks with purpose and intensity, something that causes people to pause and stare.

I glance over my shoulder at Magnus and Coen leading up the rear, only further reinforcing how entirely badass we must appear. Pride swells in my chest. These men chose me to be here tonight, not some other female. It could have been anyone, but it's me. I'm either stupid or lucky, definitely one or the other. I'll decide that once this is all said and done.

"You okay?" Dominic mutters to me.

"Mmhm." I'm being stared at by potentially murderous strangers, what more could a girl ask for?

"You keep shaking that ass..." Magnus whispers from his spot in my wake.

Coen cuts him off. "Bryant, not the time or place."

I hide a smile that creeps up at their seemingly constant banter. Or well, Magnus being a perv at inopportune moments and Co snapping at him. If it's not Coen, it's Dom telling Magnus to keep it in his pants. Either way, I adore the dynamic shared between these three, no matter how serious or light-hearted it becomes.

We approach a rather large entrance with numerous men standing guard. I note the little clear earpieces they wear and their matching brandless black attire. One guy who looks like all the others nods approval to the couple ahead of us.

"Mr. Adler." The nameless man closest to us says.

Dominic tips his head only slightly, acknowledging him.

Is that Dom's last name? I guess I never paid much attention to the fact that they use Magnus and Coen's last names, but Dom's first.

"Your guest is aware of the house rules?" The man doesn't meet my gaze.

"Yes," is all Dom replies.

"You may enter."

Two of the men hold the large, oversized double doors open for us.

The air is thick with expensive leather and a plethora of other decadent scents. Rich tobacco, the finest perfumes, and something resembling apple pie. It's a bit overkill if you ask me. But who am I to judge in this mansion full of people way more accomplished than me? I'm a no-one here; my opinion doesn't matter.

Heads continue to turn, some of their sights lingering longer than others. It's almost as though people are surprised Dominic brought a date with him.

The number of men outweighs the women two to one, each of them wearing some kind of overpriced suit or dress. Between the luxurious vehicles they arrived in and their attire, I can only imagine the sheer amount of money spent by those in attendance tonight.

A few older women catch my eye. They chatter among themselves while staring right at us as we walk further through the massive foyer. One of them breaks away and comes directly toward us. It's not until she's within a foot of me that I realize who it is.

*Gwyneth Sharp.*

I steady my nerves, engaging every ounce of acting skill I have. I have to prove myself to her in order to secure her vote, to be sly enough to get her to convince the others, too.

"Oh my." She smiles kindly. "You bunch look handsome as ever. I'm not at all surprised." Winnie tilts her head around to glance at Magnus and Hayes behind me.

"Winnie, it's great to see you." Dominic releases me to kiss the older woman's cheek.

I run the numbers in my head, recognizing that they're probably closer in age than me and Dom are. Yet imagining the two of them together seems much more far-fetched.

"And who might we have here?" She continues to gawk at me.

"Winnie, this is June."

Winnie narrows her gaze. "June..." It comes across as more of a question than anything. "Your face is so familiar."

"Croissants, toasted, chicken salad with extra grapes on the side." I spit out the last order I delivered to her.

An imaginary light bulb flicks on above her head. Her cheeks turn up. "That's right. I knew I recognized you from somewhere." She reaches for me, tugging my hands toward her. "Come. We have much to discuss."

Holy shit, already? I didn't think she'd pull me aside quite yet, if at all. I thought I'd have to slip subtle hints in here and there. I didn't imagine she'd drag me away the first chance she got, giving me no time at all with my three guys watching over me so I don't shove my foot in my mouth.

What better time than now, though?

I note how stiff each of these men gets at her persistence to separate me from them. It's not about my safety, they made it clear that I wouldn't be harmed here, not with the rules in place about making it a violence-free zone. Other than a truce, like the temporary one they made with Simon, this giant home is one of the few places all these enemies can gather and not worry about having their throat slit.

Winnie points into a room that's just off the foyer. "Go have a drink, relax. I'll take good care of her."

Dominic stands there, not giving much emotion away. He can't break character in front of all these watchful stares.

Magnus winks at me—a silent gesture that tells me I got this.

Coen scans the crowd in search of any threat, even though I was told there would be none. His gaze halts and I follow it to see Simon leaning against the railing of a large arched staircase that leads to what I can only imagine is a beautifully decorated second floor. Everything about this place screams, I have too much money and don't know what to do with it.

It's fitting though, considering the things I've seen Dom blow his cash on without a care in the world. Me specifically. He brought out ten thousand dollars to dinner that one evening and dropped it next to my plate like it was no big deal at all. That's a life-changing amount of money for someone as broke as I am.

Winnie, which is weird to refer to her by considering I barely know her, continues to pull me through the expansive foyer and down a long hallway. She leads me into a closed-off room, latching the door shut behind us. The noise from the crowd dies down immediately. Are those soundproof walls?

The new space is clearly an office, with a large dark wooden desk off to one side, and floor-to-ceiling shelves lined with books opposite of it. A patio door leads to a darkened area that I can't quite make out from my spot near the entrance.

"Come on in." Winnie glides over to an elaborate drink station that resembles the one in the living room of the house I'm currently living in. "May I make you a drink? Bourbon, whiskey, rum, vodka...pick your poison."

I clear my throat and take a few cautious steps toward her. "Bourbon, please. Neat."

She raises a brow and cocks her head to glance at me. "Has that always been your choice or have those boys converted you?"

"I've always preferred it." Although I never knew what I was missing until I tasted a few of the brands they frequent.

"A woman with good taste." She hands me a glass with two fingers of golden liquid and extends the one in her hands. "What shall we toast?"

"How about new beginnings?" Because isn't she planning on being done with this life once someone else gains control? A strange retirement of sorts given her late husband is no longer ruling this criminal organization.

"To new beginnings, may they be worth the sacrifices." Winnie maintains eye contact with me as we clink our glasses together. I don't dare mention the old superstition about what would happen if you broke it. I'm not sure she'd get the humor in potentially having seven years of bad sex.

I bring the thick crystal to my lips, inhaling the delicious warmth of the bourbon. I take a sip and wait for her to make her next move. "Thank you, this is lovely."

Winnie sits on the plush couch and pats her hand on the spot near hers. "Now that it's just us girls, let's chat."

I do a quick scan of the room before sitting. I could easily dive right into how worthy Dominic is of claiming the throne but I decide to hold off and see where she goes with the conversation.

"That's a rather exquisite gown you're wearing tonight." She reaches forward and grazes her fingers against the fabric. This woman definitely doesn't know what personal space is.

I glance down at her aged hands. "I don't disagree. It's beautiful."

"It's in good company." Winnie places her glass on the small table next to her side of the couch. "I saw one similar to it at an Armani show."

I blink up at her and smile. "I think I know the one you're referring to."

"Fine bourbon, designer dresses. And what men you surround yourself with."

"I credit them for this outfit. Dominic specifically."

Winnie smirks. "He has an eye for detail, doesn't he?" She pauses. "But you already knew that."

An opening I can work with, despite it very much coming across like she's baiting me. "Dominic has a refined skill set, that's for sure. I'd venture to say it's rare even."

"Oh, June." Winnie relaxes into her seat, facing me. "You don't have to convince me of it. I've known Dominic since he was a boy. He's always had a knack for coming out on top, no matter what. Resourceful...something that comes in handy in this line of work.

"Tell me, how did you manage to allow him to bring you tonight? In all the years I've spent hosting these events, Dominic has never once brought a plus one."

I consider the question, determining which route I should take. I choose an authentic approach—honesty. "I insisted."

Winnie snorts. "A woman with a hold on the fearless, ruthless, Dominic Adler. Interesting."

His last name again. Somehow adding it makes him even sexier in my eyes.

"Is that a difficult feat?" I ask her, curious if I can run with this topic of conversation and use it to my advantage.

She inhales deeply. "Actually, yes. Taming any of the men here tonight is always an interesting task. There are some of the easier targets, obviously, but it takes a special kind of woman to stomach the things that happen in our world. Not just that, but maintaining their interest, that's a challenge in itself. With wealth, the kind we experience, any one of us could have whatever we desire, whoever we desire. To find something worth holding onto, that's rare for us."

"I thought I saw plenty of couples when I arrived here."

She shakes her head. "Most of them are keeping up appearances. Not many will maintain those relationships long term. Once the women realize how dangerous it is, they either leave or end up dead. Very few make it as long as I have, which leads me to wonder, do you plan on sticking around?"

What could be her reasoning for asking? Because she's curious about the role I'll play? If I'll weaken Dominic's ability to lead in the capacity he's currently managing. Or perhaps because she cares for Dom and doesn't want to witness me taking advantage of him?

"I'm not afraid."

"I didn't say you were." Winnie runs her finger along her jaw and then points at me. "That looks new. How did it happen?"

I avert my gaze, recalling the night where I was kidnapped and held captive by a man wielding a knife and threatening to carve me like a pumpkin. The same man I tortured and killed, spilling his blood without a second thought.

"This?" I touch the puckered scar. "This is nothing."

"And it will be...compared to what you might endure if you stick around."

"Are you trying to convince me otherwise?"

Winnie reaches for her glass. "No." She sips the liquid then places it back on the table. "I'm simply warning you of the risks associated with being with men like Dominic. There's only so much he can do to protect you."

"I can handle my own."

"I don't doubt that." Winnie's cheeks turn up. "Considering you're sleeping with three ruthless men."

My lips part, unsure of what to say to her blatant calling me out.

Winnie chuckles at having caught me off guard. "Oh, it's obvious. The way those three tensed up when I took you away from them. I'm not sure which one of them has it the worst." When I don't speak, she continues. "I'm intrigued, really. How they all fancy you and seem to be okay with it. And I mean, to each their own." She holds up her hands. "In this day and age, people can do what they want." She lowers them. "If you were any other woman who walked in here tonight, I wouldn't have pulled you aside. But watching them watch you, and having felt your presence personally in the past...there's something about you, June. Something I can't quite put my finger on. You bring something different out in them, like you've uncovered a layer of those three I didn't think was possible. You very well could be their secret weapon, but it's possible you could also be their kryptonite."

What happened to me coming in here and pitching myself as an asset? This woman has dominated the conversation and managed to shock me with her candor. I need to reel it in and show I can be of use, that I won't be their downfall.

I recall the question I sidestepped earlier. "You had asked me earlier, if I had planned on sticking around."

"Mmhm." Winnie waits for me to continue.

The one thing I've been sure of this entire time, that no matter what, when all was said and done, I would help them win their war, and I would leave. I don't stick around. It's not what I do. It's not in my DNA to commit myself to a person or situation. My job and relationship history speaks volumes for my inability to linger longer than necessary. Whether it's self-sabotage masked as a coping mechanism to keep myself safe, or not ever finding anything worth staying for, I'm not entirely sure. But that's not what she wants to hear right now. She's looking for confirmation that I'm not going anywhere. I'm not certain whether it's a good or bad thing in her eyes.

"I do." Am I lying to her or to myself? Am I capable of planting roots?

The idea of being without them somehow painfully outweighs any desire I have to run.

"June, the last time I saw you, you were delivering food for some mediocre restaurant. Now, you're wearing a twenty-thousand-dollar dress and hundreds of thousands of dollars in jewelry. Drastic change if I may say so."

"It's not about the money, if that's what you're getting at. I didn't ask for any of this." I glance down at the elaborate clothes clearly not fooling anyone. I don't fit in here and it's blatantly obvious.

"What is it then? Humor me."

"I..." I don't want to say anything else. I barely know her. Then I remember why I'm here. "I care. About each one of them. For many different reasons. I feel safe with them, but not in the way you might think." I shake my head. "They understand me." I glance off into space. "I've never really had much. Never needed much, if I'm being honest." I let out a breath. "Never really had a home, a constant. With them, I have that. Not their literal house, but *with* them, if that makes sense at all."

Winnie nods. "It does."

I swallow. "I guess for once in my life, it's like I'm looking in the mirror when I look at them. I see dark pieces of me in each of them, but with that darkness, they bring out my light. And if I'm not mistaken, I do the same for them. It's not one-sided. You might think they're protecting me, that I'm a liability, but who's looking out for them? Who has their best interest in mind? They're constantly fixing problems and cleaning up messes, always on edge and needing to think ten steps ahead. Other than themselves, there's no one watching their back. Not a single person, that would do all of that for them."

Winnie tips the drink back that I didn't realize she had grabbed. She watches me carefully. "And you're saying *you*, you'd be that?"

I never meant for any of this to happen. I thought Dominic would be a random hookup in the bathroom at the shitty dive bar I worked at. I thought Magnus was a stranger I would spend one glorious night with. And Coen...I thought he was gone years ago. If someone would have told me six months ago that Co and I would stumble into each other's paths, and that I'd get tangled up in Magnus' and Dom's, too, I'd never believe them.

And yet here I am, fully prepared to put myself on the line in the most dangerous of ways to ensure they get what they deserve. Because if it's not me, who will do it for them?

"Yes, without a doubt." I lift my drink to drain the rest of the contents into my mouth.

A knock sounds on the door, a second later, it cracks open and one of the women's heads from earlier pops in. "Winnie, we're ready for you. Dom is up."

"I'll be right there." She stands and smooths out the wrinkles in her pantsuit from sitting.

"It's starting already?" My heart picks up its pace.

"Ah, yes, dear. We thought it would be better to meet with the contender's first thing, that way we can deliberate over dinner and drinks, and make a final decision before dessert."

Will I get a chance to talk to my men prior to them going in? To tell them how much I believe in them and how proud I am for all they've already accomplished. That no matter what, I'll be here, regardless of winning or losing. It wasn't their expensive bourbons or fancy suits that caught my attention, it was their souls, calling out to me and telling mine that we don't have to face the darkness alone.

Winnie downs the rest of her drink, too. "I think you know what needs to be done then." She lingers near her desk for a long second, like she's willing me to understand something deeper to her words.

I desperately try to figure out what she means, internally punching myself to decipher the clue. Maybe it's nothing after all, and I'm just grasping for straws because of how badly I botched this meeting with her.

I failed. I massively fucking failed. I was supposed to convince her and all I did was stumble around my words and grow uncertain of my control of the situation.

"June?" Winnie says while walking toward the door we entered through. "We had spoken briefly in the past, during one of your deliveries. I recall you mentioning you're a business major?"

Was a business major. Now I'm just a dropout, but she doesn't need to know that. "A few credits from graduation, yes."

Winnie points her finger at me. "While they don't exactly teach our kind of profession, those skills will come in handy." She winks. "Don't be afraid to use them." Winnie slips out the door, leaving me behind in her office alone.

I suck in a breath and settle the raging nerves threatening to destroy me.

"Get it together, June," I say under my breath while I brace myself on the elaborately carved wood desk.

Opening my eyes, my sights fall on the case perched just inches away from me. I blink a few times and step closer, glancing back at where Winnie disappeared only seconds prior. Is this what she was trying to show me? To tell me? It can't be. This mansion is a violence-free area, why would she alert me to the weapon sitting here in plain sight? Is this a test? Some kind of game she's playing to see how far I'd be willing to go? If so, how do I know which is the right decision to make? I've been informed of the sanctity of the rules numerous times, it would be downright disrespectful and foolish of me to disregard them, wouldn't it?

When have I ever played by the rules anyway?

Carefully, I press my fingers against the glass and tip the lid to the case. I lower it gently onto the desk, careful not to make a sound, all while keeping my eyes trained on the dagger inside. I reach in and pull it out, somehow already feeling more powerful with it in my grasp.

The hilt is dark blue and could even be mistaken for black. On the end, a round, golden insignia. But where the handle meets the blade, there's a small skull, the same color, just a bit shinier. I run my finger along the length of the weapon, noting how sharp it is. I swivel the end of it on the tip of my index finger, pricking the smallest amount of blood. The entire thing is no more than ten inches but could do loads of damage.

With the door still ajar, commotion from outside the room gets louder. Instead of putting the thing back where I found it, I find myself flipping it upward and holding it out of sight against my arm.

I keep my arm tucked close to my side, careful not to draw attention to it or myself, and even more so not to slice my forearm open. I slip out of the room, immediately catching Coen's stare from across the room as he chats while walking with a man I haven't been introduced to yet. I turn, dipping into another place full of people, scanning the crowd for the person I'm trying to find.

There are only two people at this party that can alter the outcome tonight, and I will do anything in my power to make sure my men are on the winning side.

Dominic bumps shoulders with me. "You okay?"

I nod and force a smile. "Yeah. You?"

"A bit stuffy in here." His gaze flits around then lands back on me. "I've been summoned. I'll see you after, okay?"

A million thoughts cross my mind. The countless things I want to tell him. I bottle them up and save them for later, knowing we have plenty of time to say all the unspoken things between us. I reach out and grip his shoulder with my free hand, saying exactly what he needs to hear right now. "You've got this."

Either way, he'll have won fair and square, or I'll make damn sure of it.

Dom leans forward and brushes his lips on my cheek. "Thanks, June." He leaves me with the lingering touch of him along my skin, a feeling more overpowering than the one of the cold knife I'm still holding onto.

I continue through the rooms, everyone unsuspecting of the small, dark-haired girl wielding a weapon capable of slitting all their throats. To them, I'm just another pretty face wearing a dress way too expensive and sleeping with the three deadliest men in here. Little do they know, the reason we go so well together is because I'm their perfect match.

I spot my target up ahead, and he locks his gaze onto mine. He's surrounded by a group of his men, various sizes and statures. He stops his conversation abruptly, raising his hand to signal them to hush, and leaves them in the dust to approach me. I knew this would be easy. Like taking candy from a baby.

Turning on my heel, I glide out of the room, around a corner and into a quieter area. People are still coming and going, but nothing like the crowds out there. Here, I can talk, and he can listen.

"You couldn't stay away, could you..." He follows me exactly where I want him to, but when he steps into the space, I draw the knife and hold it to his neck, backing him against the wall.

"Simon."

"June." A wicked grin forms on his face.

I press the dagger further, pricking the skin and letting him know how serious I am.

"Such foreplay, I like it." He keeps his arms to his sides.

I lick my lips and slide the knife down and over where his heart is located. "Do you recall the time you told me...what was it...I could choose *you* or death?"

"Vividly." His wild green eyes stare into mine. "Having second thoughts, are you?"

"Not at all." I steady my footing. Who's fucking idea was it for me to wear stilettos?

"Oh?"

"I'd like to give you a similar offer. Back down, or die."

Simon tips his head. "You can't be serious." He glances in the direction we came. "Did they put you up to this?"

I push the blade through the fitted jacket he's wearing. It pierces through with ease. "Does it look like I'm joking?" I continue until the tip penetrates his skin.

He stifles a wince and clenches his jaw. "You know I can't do that."

"Then I have no other choice." I push it a little more.

Simon stares at me, really into my eyes. "Do what you have to do." It's like he's accepting this fate because the idea of backing down just isn't an option.

And because I refuse to accept the possibility of defeat, I apply my weight onto the handle and plunge it into his chest.

Only, a flash of light and a loud cracking stops me in my tracks.

Simon's expression shifts to confusion, something that I assume matches mine.

Pain ripples through my body, but that makes no sense. I was the one stabbing Simon. How could it be possible for me to be in pain?

I lower my gaze, along with the dagger, wondering how blood could be flowing from my chest instead of his?

Simon reaches forward, and while I expect him to take my weapon, he presses his palm onto the spot seeping red. "June. Fuck. June."

My legs fail me, buckling out from under my frame.

Simon softens the blow, holding onto me as I diminish to the floor of this elaborate mansion, ruining whatever upholstery I must be gushing onto. "No, no. Hang on. You're going to be fine." Genuine concern rattles his features, another thing that doesn't add up. "Help," he calls out. "Someone help."

A moment ago, I had a dagger poised on his heart and now, he's trying to prevent me from bleeding out.

My eyes close against my will, dizziness consuming me, darkness pulling me under.

"Stay with me, June. Come on." Simon tugs me to his chest.

I cough, the taste of iron filling my mouth. That can't be good. Each breath is labored and more difficult than the last, like there's a limited amount of air left in my lungs and there isn't enough left to survive.

I don't want to die like this. Here. In his arms. In the arms of the man that was supposed to die. Him. Not me. But I guess that's the thing about fate, you have no control over what that bitch has in store. And for me, this is it. Dying without the three men I love more than anything in this world and with the guy who could potentially take everything from them.

Me along with it.

"Please, I'll do anything." Simon brushes my hair out of my face. "June."

"Promise me…" I can barely spit the blood-soaked words out.

"Anything, just stay with me."

"Back down." I cough again. If I'm going to die tonight, I must make sure I go down with a fight, doing everything I can to secure Dominic's win.

"I concede, do you hear that?" Simon pushes harder in my chest. "June, I fucking give up. Now stay with me, okay? They can have the throne you crazy woman, don't die on me over it."

"Get out of the way," Dominic growls.

A thud hits the wall, people curse, and wind blows against my skin.

"What did you do?" Dominic's voice grows near.

"J…" Coen drops to the ground next to me.

"I'm going to fucking kill you," Dominic tells what I can only assume is Simon.

"Stop it, please," Magnus yells somewhere between them. "He's probably the only thing keeping her alive. Look."

I try to open my eyes, to see what Magnus is talking about, but everything is heavy, dark, too much for me to control. The world spins and hot and cold take turns alternating through my body. My mind only focused on one thing—the words Simon said. He gives up. And if his word counts for anything, Dominic has officially won, meaning my job here tonight is complete. It didn't necessarily go as planned, but the end result was all the same.

With that overwhelming relief, I lose what remaining strength I have to hold on, my entire world fading to black. I do everything I can to claw my way awake, to stay a little longer, but the pull to go into the darkness is far too strong.

"I…" I want to tell them how much they mean to me. To apologize for taking so long to realize it. To congratulate them for their win and kiss all of them one last time. I'd even settle for a hug, or a simple hand squeeze to bid farewell. Any gesture to make them understand I didn't want things to end this way—bleeding out in the lap of their enemy.

Instead, I dive deep into the abyss as it welcomes me with open arms.

For once in my life, I don't want to leave, but I don't have any other choice than to go.

# CHAPTER 24

# *Coen*

I rise to my feet, June's blood coated on my hands.

Rage, unlike anything I've ever felt, consumes me.

My world goes strictly into tunnel vision, the only thing on my mind is eliminating anyone and everything that could have been responsible for what happened.

Spotting a shiny and sharp object at the base of where June's body lays, I snatch it off the ground and go to work, doing what I do best. I swing my arm, slicing one man's throat immediately, more blood splattering and filling this hallway.

Screams let out, people scurry, but I have my sights set on my next target and they won't get away.

The guy backs into the wall, dropping his gun and throwing his hands in the air. "Dude, it wasn't me. I didn't—"

But I don't care that it wasn't him that shot June. It could have been, and for that alone, he must die.

I shove the dagger into his throat and yank it out. His eyes go wide and then he drops to the ground, clutching the spot that's gushing red.

I pivot, not caring about the continued muffled screams.

An arm reaches for me, but I shrug it off.

I snatch the man's discarded pistol and blast off two shots into another guy who looks a bit too guilty. One in the chest, another in the middle of his forehead.

"Who was it?" I scream. The voice sounds foreign and unfamiliar. "Who shot her?" I scan the gun through the crowd. Women duck and some drop to their knees, black tears streaking their cheeks. Some men remain, a few of them using their bodies to shield their dates. Others being cowards and hiding between their legs. Fucking pathetic.

I don't give a fuck about any of them. They can all burn for all I care. There's only one person in this house my heart beats for, and she's currently bleeding out in Simon Beckett's lap.

"Coen. Put the weapon down." Winnie Sharp. "You're making an already bad situation worse."

I turn toward her voice. "Someone better tell me who shot her, or I will end every person in here until I'm certain they're dead." My head pounds and my heart thumps wildly, an overwhelming helplessness taking hold of me.

I've only just gotten her back and now I'm going to lose her again because of this dangerous world I never wanted her to get involved with. This is the very reason I stayed away, because I never wanted her to get hurt. I didn't want this lifestyle to corrupt and damage her, let alone steal her from this earth prematurely. June deserves far better than to die like this—in a room full of sadistic criminals who don't give a shit about human decency. They're only in it for the power, the lucrative paychecks, and lavish existences. They don't get to live if June doesn't. None of us do. And I will make sure not a single person makes it out alive if June dies here tonight.

I blast another shot off at a man standing nearby, his hand resting in a position to conceal the gun in his other. Did he think he could hide that from me? My senses are heightened, and despite his best effort, he never could have kept that from me.

His stupid frame thuds against the hardwood floor.

Winnie flashes her gaze past me, a tell she's old and wise enough to know better than to give away.

I drop to my knees, turning and pointing my weapon behind me, firing off two shots into the chest of the man who approached me. I quickly lower it and fire another round into his partners. Dead bodies litter the floor and bring me back to a time when I was killing my way to freedom. Or at least, that's what I thought I was doing. Little did I know, I was setting myself up for a lifetime of misery with each life I ended. I killed with no mercy, finally collapsing onto the cold, hard concrete of that building, blood soaking through my clothes. I'm uncertain how long I was there until Dominic had found me and told me that there was no going back. I could either die or accept the role that was given to me.

I was too much of a coward to take the easy way out, essentially signing my soul away to be a murderous psychopath for the rest of time. I left June in the past as my only means to keep her safe. And look at her now. My efforts were wasted. The infinite torture of leaving her had haunted me every day, but it's nothing compared to the anguish I feel in this moment. Knowing that I could have had her in my life this whole time eats away at my soul. We lost time that we can never get back, and now I'm going to lose her for good because Dominic and Bryant couldn't just leave her the fuck out of it.

I should fucking kill them, too, for bringing her into this mess despite being well aware of the danger it would put her in.

I allow myself too much time in my thoughts, faltering slightly when I catch something moving in my peripheral. I don't react quick enough and the next thing I know, something blunt and hard smacks me in the side of the head, knocking my legs out from under me and dropping me like all the bodies I've destroyed tonight. My eyelids slow and become heavier as I fight the urge to get back up and annihilate whoever managed to land a blow to take me down.

Despite my best efforts, my world goes black.

---

"You can't fucking keep me here." I pound my fist on the metal door. The sound echoes into the small room I'm being held in. There are no windows, just the one exit I must have been brought through after I was rendered unconscious.

How I'm still alive, that's lost on me.

I should have been killed on the spot. I never should have lived past inflicting an ounce of pain on a single person in that house. Those are the rules, and they're pretty damn cut and dry. And yet, here I am, having killed a half dozen people or so and living to tell the tale. Although, considering my confinements, it's safe to say I won't be getting off easy.

They'd be doing me a favor if they followed through with protocol and ended my life, too. The idea of living in a world without June is unbearable, something I'm not capable of doing. It's one thing to not be with someone but still exist on the same planet as them. It's shitty, that's for sure, but it's tolerable knowing they're out there somewhere, potentially happy and healthy and safe. But for her to be gone, no longer breathing the same, looking up at the same night sky, I cannot accept that reality. I'd rather be dead.

June isn't just my first love, she's my fucking soul mate. She brings out the best and worst in me and never fails to make my heart beat a little harder and slower at the same time. She's a rare mix of daring and adventurous and manages to have a hidden softer side that she doesn't show often. She fools everyone into thinking she doesn't care and isn't bothered when in reality, she's one of the kindest and most selfless people I've ever met. I've personally witnessed her give her last dollar to a homeless person on numerous occasions. One time she rummaged through what little clothes she did have to see what she could spare to an old lady who was living in the trees out behind a discount store.

Not many notice how she hates watching others suffer, and does what she can to help them, even if she doesn't think it's much. And maybe that's because she's never really had anyone looking out for her. Instead of allowing her hardships to make her bitter and cold, it's formed this protectiveness over those she cares about that she keeps concealed.

June has changed over the years, there's no doubt about that, but she's still that same girl who pitied me for crying at my mother's gravestone when we were kids. I knew from that very first moment that June had claimed my heart for all of time. We formed a bond over shared trauma and being misunderstood and I can't imagine getting that close to someone ever again. It's been almost a decade and I've never once felt anything remotely similar to the spark I feel with June. I thought it was gone forever until I saw her in that bar a few months ago, the flame reigniting and burning brighter than ever before.

I need answers, I need to know if she's okay. If she made it. Or if the pit in my chest means that she really is gone forever.

I slam my fist against the door again and tug at the handle. "You're making a mistake by keeping me here." I run my fingers through my hair and let out an exasperated breath. Scanning the room, I search for any way out of this imprisonment.

A dingy twin mattress is pressed up along one wall and a bucket sits on the opposite. There is no toilet or sink, and the bed doesn't even have a pillow, just a ratty excuse of a blanket balled up in its center.

I glance down at my body, the tailored suit that Dominic had custom made still clings to my body, although now it's speckled with the dried remains of those I killed. The crusty dark red coats my hands, too, and no doubt if there was a mirror, I'd find some on my face.

Some of this is June's blood. My sweet, tortured girl.

"Focus, Co. You can do this." I tell myself while trying to gain control over my unruly emotions. "Everything has a weakness. Find this one."

I shove my hands into my pockets, turning them inside out and coming up empty. They rid me of my wallet and phone, which is no surprise at all. I pat all my hidden compartments, each one of them empty. Whoever stripped me of my belongings was thorough, and for that, it makes me want to add another person to my hit list. Anyone who stands in the way of me getting to June must die.

Skimming my hands over the wall, I check for any inconsistencies. Any fractures or hollowed spots that could assist in my escape. I spend what must be a half-hour on the first one, finding not a single thing to help me.

I unbutton my jacket and toss it onto the concrete. Dominic would scold me for that, but I'm sure I'm already in deep enough shit for going on a killing spree in an amnesty zone. I roll up my sleeves and get back to work on the second wall, hoping like hell something will budge.

Thoughts of June lying there, bleeding out in Simon's arms, continue to float through my mind and it's everything I can do to stay standing and not collapse to the ground. My heart aches at not being there for her in her final moments. My anger had taken hold and the only thing my body knew to do, was to react. To kill. To somehow manage to tip the scales and get even for what had happened.

As I finish up the second wall, the sound of metal from the door catches my attention. I rush over, but not quick enough. The person was able to shove a small plastic cup of clear liquid through and set it on a tray extended from the door.

"Fuck," I scream while slicing my hand at the cup and sending it flying across the room. Do I need to stay hydrated? Probably. But there's no telling if they laced that water with something to sedate or poison me.

I grip at the tray and do my best to pry it off. If I can detach it, maybe I can use it to force open the door. Wiggling it back and forth and up and down, the stupid fucking thing doesn't budge at all. Whoever designed it had considered that the person held captive might try brute force to remove and utilize it. This room was carefully planned and executed—a solid, unescapable chamber.

"How long are you going to keep me here?" I pound both of my fists into the door. "Someone just tell me if she's okay." I hit it harder. "Please." I rest my forehead on the cold surface, my aching hands still pressed against the impenetrable thing.

---

Countless hours go by and time becomes this strange elusive construct I can no longer keep a hold of. When the exhaustion is too much, I doze in and out, my nightmares no better refuge for my mind than my waking reality. I see red no matter what. June's blood, her dying body. I close my eyes and it's burned into my memory. Her demise haunts my dreams. I never get there in time, always running but never fast enough. She dies a thousand deaths, and I am not capable of saving her no matter what I do.

It's been at least a day. My internal clock is sure of that. I have no idea how much longer, but despite the protests of not eating or drinking anything I'm served, my body is fatiguing hard. Between the immense stress and lack of basic human needs, I find myself no longer functioning at my peak. I'm weakened, tired, and wish that someone would just put me out of my misery. Is this my punishment for what I've done? Leave me here to rot while I never know the truth about whether June lived or died?

It's fitting, really. Because this is the worst thing they ever could have done to me outside of hurting her, which they've already done. To rob me of the truth of June's condition is the ultimate torture.

Each time the little opening on the door creaks, I desperately plead with the person delivering what measly offerings they bring. Not once have they replied or hinted at what their plans with me are. No one will tell me anything. I tried to reach through the gap but was met with a crowbar smashing down on my hand. I was able to pull it away from doing any major damage, but the thing made contact with my index finger, breaking the bone and leaving a wound that wouldn't stop bleeding until I ripped off a part of my undershirt and tied it around it.

It's strange how numb I was to the pain. I *knew* it should hurt. But when you're already consumed with an incomprehensible agony, it's hard to feel much of anything else.

A mechanism sounds from outside the door, something I haven't heard this entire time I've been in here.

I push up from the floor and rise to my feet, readying my fists for whatever fight I'm about to face. I plant my feet and suck in a breath, eyeing the room to find anything I can use to overcome my contenders. I snatch my jacket off the ground and grip both sides of it, twisting it into a rope of sorts. It's not much, but if I can get it around the person's throat, maybe I can strangle them with it.

"Hurry up," a thick and familiar voice floats into my confined space.

My eyes widen and my grip on the designer thing loosens. Am I hearing shit or was that really him?

"Hayes," another person calls to me through the small gap that's formed when the door cracks open. He shoves it harder and steps into the space.

And for once in my life, I've never been so fucking grateful to see that tattooed idiot and that brute old man.

My dried lips part and regardless of my efforts, my voice comes out fractured. "June?"

"She's alive." Magnus nods. "She's alive."

I clutch at my chest, the wind knocked out of me. His repeated words offer me an immense relief I can barely process. I drop to my knees, the weight of everything caving in on me all at once. Tears I cannot control stream down my cheeks. "She's alive," I echo.

# CHAPTER 25

# June

"F uck," the word leaves my mouth without my approval. It's followed by a groan and my labored attempt to open my heavy eyes.

"June." A warm hand wraps tighter around mine. "You're awake."

I blink and grow impatient as my vision adjusts from nothing to the bright fluorescent lighting overhead. "Dom." I try to sit up, but he gently restrains me.

"Shh. You're okay. Don't rush it."

I wince, glancing down and spotting the bandage wrapping my chest under my thin hospital gown. "What happened?" I try to recall what caused all of this, but it's a giant blur.

"One of Simon's men, they shot you. You underwent surgery to repair the damage." Dominic swallows and a side of him I've never seen before shows through. "We weren't sure if you'd pull through."

I painfully take in a breath and relax into the bed. "I'm like a cockroach, you can't kill me that easily."

He forces a fake toothless smile. "I don't know what I would have done."

I give his hand a gentle squeeze. "Hey. I'm good, don't worry about me." Scanning the rest of the room, I focus back on him. "Where are Magnus and Co?"

Dominic's jaw tenses. "Bryant is getting you a change of clothes, and Hayes is..."

My eyes go wide, my heart immediately picking up its pace. "No..."

Dom shakes his head. "No, he's not dead. Although, he probably wishes he was." He pauses. "He's being punished."

Once I catch my panicked breath, I process what he said. "Punished? Why?"

"Hayes broke house rules. Honestly, he's lucky he's still alive. Anyone else would have been murdered on the spot. But considering the circumstances, Winnie convinced the council to grant him a bit of leniency." Dom rubs my palm with his thumb. "The outcome of his sentence would be determined by your condition."

"What does that mean?" What does any of this mean?

"Well..." Dom repositions himself in his chair but maintains a grip on my hand. "Given Hayes' abilities..."

Can he just get to the fucking point already?

"If you died, Hayes would have, too."

"What? Why? How does that make any sense?" I drag my free arm up to rest my palm against my chest. Getting worked up is not cooperating with the gaping hole in my chest.

"June, please try to remain calm." Dom glances at the monitors. "Hayes is a flight risk. He's dangerous, and while that might be a surprise to you, it's not to us who *know* him. If something happened to you, I mean, permanently, there's no stopping the lengths he would go to avenge you. He made that clear when he openly fired in an amnesty zone and took down those who were innocent and guilty."

Coen did what? He went on a rampage and murdered a bunch of people? Because someone shot me? It was my fault. I'm the one who was going to plunge a dagger into Simon's chest because he refused to give up. Shouldn't I be the one who's being punished? Not him.

"Wait." Bits and pieces start to come back to me. "Who won? Please tell me..."

Dominic sighs. "Simon Beckett might be a vile excuse for a human, but he is a man of his word."

"He is?"

"He conceded. Thanks to whatever it is you said to him, he made damn sure I and everyone else knew that he was stepping down from his position against me."

I may have almost died, but I did it, I fucking did it. I got Simon Beckett to admit defeat.

"I'm so proud of you," I whisper.

"I've wanted this most of my life." Dom stares at our intertwined hands. "I've never worked harder for anything. But the second I saw you bleeding out, I would have traded it all just to make sure you lived to see another day. I need you to know that, June. I don't know what tomorrow brings, but I refuse to ignore what I can no longer control. And maybe I didn't fully realize it until that moment, when I would have given up everything to save you from this nightmare. Or maybe it confirmed what I already suspected." He exhales and slowly meets my gaze. "Either way, the fact is, I'm in love with you."

I'm stunned by his declaration despite having the same exact one myself.

He continues. "I'm not expecting you to reciprocate those feelings. I know you and Hayes have a long history that far exceeds the time we've spent together. And Bryant has already made his intentions clear. I would never make you choose between us, but just know, I'll be here for you no matter what decision you make. I need to be a part of your life, no matter how big or small."

I open my mouth to speak but am interrupted by the door opening and a beautiful, tattooed man walking in.

His eyes light up the second he realizes I'm awake. "Princess." Magnus rushes over to my other side.

I narrow my gaze at him. "Seriously, still with that?"

"What? It's perfect. You're like a Disney Princess, but in a dark and twisted kinda way." He reaches over and brushes the hair off my cheek. "How are you feeling?"

I flit my attention briefly at Dom. I didn't get a chance to let him know that there is no way I could ever choose between the three of them. That the only way I can be happy is if I'm with all of them. That each one brings something different to the table and that for the first time in my life, I'm not scared of not knowing what the future holds.

Being with these three men is everything I want but didn't know I needed.

And now that I've had a taste, there's no way I could ever imagine my life without them.

I had my doubts about what would happen when Dominic won the throne, but he's made it clear that he wants me to be a part of this next chapter of his life. And if I had to guess, Magnus and Coen want that, too.

"Not bad, considering." I try to push myself up again, but my arms give out without much effort. "Does this thing move?"

"Yeah, here." Magnus pushes a button on the little remote off to the side. "That better?"

"Much." Although, there's one thing missing from making me feel complete.

"What is it?" Dominic stares at me like he can read my mind.

"Get Coen, please."

"Of course." Dominic releases my hand and stands, accepting the task I gave him without hesitation.

"Wait." I extend both of my arms toward him, hungry for his touch to remain.

His resolve softens and he complies, leaning down and as carefully as he can, hugs me. He presses his lips to my cheek and breathes in deeply.

"The feeling is mutual," I mutter into his ear.

He sighs, the tension in his body relaxing with the expelled air. "I'll get him back for you, I promise."

That alone tells me that Dominic will do whatever it takes to free Coen from the hell he's currently experiencing during his punishment.

"This is...fucking adorable." Magnus allows Dom to finish hugging me and then plants a kiss on my forehead.

A light knock rattles the door.

Magnus gets there first, granting entry to the person.

Simon Beckett walks into my decently sized hospital room.

Something that will probably end up costing me a fucking fortune. Part of the reason I didn't go to the hospital after I was attacked was because I didn't have insurance and couldn't afford the gnarly bill they would no doubt stick me with. A gunshot wound and an emergency surgery will likely cost me an arm and a leg but that's a problem for another day.

"Beckett." Dominic positions himself between me and the newcomer.

"Dominic." Simon nods at him and then at Magnus. "Bryant." He points and tilts his head to look around Dom. "May I?"

Is he politely asking for approval? What the fuck did I miss when I was busy almost dying? I guess Simon did concede. Does this mean that there is no more weird rivalry?

"He's fine, let him through." I tug my stiff hospital issue blanket a little higher and cover my chest with my gown. "Magnus, you should go with Dom to get Co."

"It's going to take both of you." Simon cautiously steps closer. "Pretty sure the council wants his head to set an example."

"Seriously?" Magnus glares at Simon. "You're going to stress her out."

"I'm good. I pushed that little red button for more drugs and they're starting to kick in. I'll be better once you're back, so hurry up." It's not a lie. I am feeling a bit loopy, a warmth coursing through me and tugging at my eyelids to carry me off to sleep. And the idea of knowing Dom will do everything he can to get Coen out of his imprisonment sets my soul at ease.

Soon enough I'll have my three men at my side, and then, there isn't anything we can't face together.

"Your phone." Dominic turns toward me. "It's at your side, under your blanket. Call me if you need anything. Okay?"

I nod and offer what I can of a smile.

"And you..." Dominic pokes his finger into Simon's shoulder. "I don't need to tell you what will happen if you pull anything."

Magnus slaps Dom on the back playfully. "He practically saved her life; he's not going to do anything. Come on, you heard the lady. Hate on Beckett some other time." He glances over at me on his way out the door. "Love you, princess." He disappears before I can even process his words.

Did he mean to say that? Was it some knee jerk reaction? Either way, my emotions swell with wanting to say it back. To him. To Dominic. To Coen. Each second my heart beats, my love for them grows. How did I go from never wanting to say those three words to anyone, to wanting to scream them from the rooftops?

Simon sits down in the seat Dominic had been in and scoots it forward. "You had us all scared."

"That's what I heard." I study his face, comparing the details to what Cora had said, that he resembled Damon Salvatore.

Same pronounced jawline, dark eyebrows, and captivating eyes. A touch of mysterious bad boy thrown into the mix with his leather jacket and devious stare. He's handsome, to say the least, but nothing compared to the three men who have ruined me for anyone else.

The old me would have slept with Simon in a heartbeat. Gone headfirst into the allure of his penetrating gaze and seductive tone. I would have eaten him up and spit him out, not a care in the world. But now? All I see when I look at him is someone who almost took everything away from the men I care most for.

The pain medication coursing through my IV and into my veins threatens to pull me under like a warm blanket and a sweet lullaby.

Simon runs his hand through his brown hair and leans back into the chair. "I don't know what it is about you, but you have us all captivated." He folds his arms across his chest. "I'm just the only one stuck on the outside."

A part of me feels sorry for him. Now that I've embraced the connection I feel to each of my men, to be on the opposite end of those feelings and not have them reciprocated, I'm sure that's a difficult truth to stomach. It would be a betrayal to my guys if I even considered bringing Simon into our circle. I've been fortunate enough that they haven't put up a fight sharing me between the three of them, introducing an outsider would only be a surefire way to make the whole arrangement implode.

"What was Magnus saying?" I ask him.

Simon rubs his temple. "About what?"

"You saved me?"

"Yeah. That. Um, well. After you tried to kill me..." He breathes in and leans forward. "One of my guys shot you, and I maintained pressure on the wound until help arrived. You lost a lot of blood, but it would have been a lot worse if I hadn't. You probably would have died."

"Why would you do it?" I shake my head. "I was going to stab you."

Simon laughs but the humor doesn't meet his eyes. "You did, actually." He raises his shirt to reveal a small, stitched section of his chest, right where his heart is.

And I'd do it again if it meant the same outcome—Dominic winning their war.

"They were going to crown him anyway, you know. There's no way I would have won against Dominic." Simon pats out the wrinkles on his top. "He has far more experience, obviously. The dude is like sixty."

"Fifty, but whatever," I correct him.

"Either way, the entire thing was a long shot. He's had Winnie wrapped around his finger for as long as I can remember."

"It wasn't just up to her though, there are others on the council."

Simon nods. "That's the angle I was playing, but her sway is still more powerful in the end. Especially with you added to the dynamic. She adores the shit out of you. Not that I blame her."

"You still didn't answer my question." I blink slowly as the medicine continues to take its hold of me.

"I couldn't do nothing, June. I couldn't watch you die, not when every inch of me was screaming to save you." Simon glances at his hands, rolling his thumbs along his fingertips. "There was so much blood." He lowers his voice. "I'm no stranger to violence, but that...that was something else entirely."

"For what it's worth..." I lick at my dry lips, my eyes shutting without my consent. "Thank you."

Simon reaches forward cautiously and pats my hand. "I'll wait...forever if I have to."

---

I wake up alone, the lights in the room dimmed and not a soul in sight. I blink through the fog and reach for that remote to raise my bed back into the upright position. Simon or one of the nurses must have lowered it when I dozed off earlier.

Sipping from the cup of water left on my tray table, I reposition myself slightly. Something hard catches my attention and I lift the blanket to find my cell phone in the spot Dominic had told me it was earlier.

I have seven missed calls from Cora and thirteen text messages. I know I should click the button and return her call, but what am I supposed to say?

*Oh hey, bestie, my bad for not answering when you reached out, I was just hanging out with a bunch of criminals at this semisecret event where the fate of their illegal organization was decided by a group of old ladies who have entirely too much money. Plus, the whole, me commandeering a dagger and almost killing a man, then being shot and nearly dying in said man's arms while one of the men I'm in love with went on a murderous rampage to avenge me. No big deal. I have a gunshot wound to the chest and I have no idea how long recovery will be, let alone how expensive my hospital bill will add up to, but I'm totally fine, how are you?*

Yeah, I doubt that would go over very well.

I skim her last few messages and decide to send one anyway.

**Me: Sorry I've been MIA, super hungover. I'll call you tomorrow.**

I sprinkle in a few choice emojis and hit the send button, hoping it will grant me a bit of reprieve from being a completely shit friend.

I was shot after all, I deserve a tiny bit of slack, right?

If anything, it will buy me a little time to figure out what the fuck I'm actually going to say to her. She's going to find out I'm injured one way or the other. We meet once a week, there's no way I'll be healed by our next one and it'll raise too much suspicion if I blow her off for too long, especially now that she knows the guys are funding our girl's nights.

I set the phone down and lay my head back, taking in a breath that makes me wince a bit. My hand reflexively goes to my chest, hovering over the place I almost bled out from. If it weren't for Simon, I would have. Although, if it weren't for Simon, I never would have been in that situation to begin with. I cannot blame him —it was my choice to risk threatening him. I knew there would be consequences, I just didn't think I'd get fucking shot.

The doorknob to the hospital room I'm posted up in jiggles and turns. Is it a nurse coming to check on me? Is it someone coming to finish me off?

I squint to see better through the dim light. Magnus pops his head in and spots me awake, opening the door even more. "She's up."

"Get out of my way." Coen shoves past him, wearing the same outfit from the other night.

What's it been, one, two, three days? I have no idea how long I was out after my surgery.

Blood coats him from head to toe—speckling his face and caking his hands. There's something wrapped around one of them, potentially splinting it in place. Dried tears remain on his cheeks and his hair is a mess. Somehow, he's more beautiful than ever. His blue gaze frantically searches my body.

"J..." He drops to his knees beside the bed and takes my hand in his, pressing his lips over and over on my skin. His sobs wreck me as new tears fall down his face.

"Co, come here." I tug at him despite how weak I am.

Coen complies, planting his butt next to me while still holding onto my palm. "I thought..."

"Shh. You thought wrong. I'm fine." I cup his face with my free hand. "What did they do to you?" I glance over at Dominic and Magnus, then back at Coen.

He swallows and kisses my fingers. "Nothing that knowing you're okay can't fix."

I drag him closer to me and hold him as tightly as my injuries will allow. Patting his head, I whisper into his ear, "I love you, Coen."

He sniffles into my shoulder and sighs. "You have no idea how long I've needed to hear that."

"It's true," I tell him. I lift my head toward Dominic and Magnus standing at the foot of my bed. "I love you all, more than anything."

Dominic reaches down and squeezes my foot, a look of relief plastered across his face.

Magnus grins from ear to ear and comes to the side opposite of Coen. "I knew you couldn't help but fall for us." He leans down and plants his lips on my cheek and then grips Coen's shoulder like he's letting him know that he's there for him, too.

I never thought it would be possible to fall for anyone, and here I am, head over heels, quite literally, irrevocably in love with these three men.

I nearly died for them, and I would do it all again in a heartbeat if they ever needed me to.

I guess that's the thing about love—you don't know it until it's knocked you on your ass and made you completely change your mind about everything you believed in up to that point.

If this is what it means to finally have something worth fighting for, I'll burn this city down and start a war to keep what we have alive.

# Epilogue – June

"**A**re you excited?" Cora sits across the booth from me, her head resting on her hand, her elbow propped on the table.

I sip my coffee and shrug. "Kind of."

She reaches for me. "You're graduating, J, that's a huge accomplishment."

Six months after I should have, though.

I had originally taken time off school because of finances, but once the guys found out I was so close to finishing my degree, they insisted I put pen to paper and mark that off my to-do list before fully jumping into the business side of their lives. In a way, I think they were trying to prolong the inevitable at my joining them in their endeavors—forever doing what they think is protecting me. Not only did they pay my tuition, but each one of them took turns helping me study my way into getting a nearly perfect score on all of my remaining classes.

An achievement I'm lucky to have completed between getting shot and committing a huge no-no in the criminal world. Fortunately for me, Simon had no hard feelings for my attempt to kill him, and he put up a rather convincing case to the council that I actually didn't hurt him and it was, in fact, his men that were in the wrong for shooting me. And given the circumstances, Coen got off the hook too, based on him acting in self-defense on my behalf. His reaction was deemed acceptable despite him brutally murdering numerous people that night during his rampage. Acceptable is a subjective term in that world.

"Yeah." The ache in my chest remains, an injury that will probably take years until I feel remotely like myself again.

"Are the guys doing anything special for you?" Cora takes a bite of her banana-nut muffin.

"I'm not sure." I pause. "I doubt it. They're really busy with work."

The whole, managing a criminal enterprise thing. All of which they're complete naturals at. The darkness suits them well.

I change the subject. "What about you? How's the new job?"

Cora smiles and it warms my heart. "Really great. I love it so much. They tasked me with doing the interior design of that new condominium complex across town. You know the one I'm talking about? It's super high-end, very exclusive."

"Damn, Cor, that sounds incredible."

She nods. "Minus Jenn, she's a total bitch."

I drink another swig of Bram's locally famous coffee. "What's up with her?"

Cora exhales dramatically. "So for this project, we had to submit portfolios, but the company requested a blind approach, meaning it wasn't clear who got the gig until they announced it. I've been there a whopping couple of months and Jenn's been there three years. Safe to say she was pissed when I got it over her."

I tilt my head. "But, clearly, you're better qualified then?"

"Exactly." Cora waves as someone comes through the door of Bram's diner. "She accused me of cheating the system."

Magnus slides into the seat next to mine and throws his arm over my shoulder. "Princess." He presses an aggressive kiss on my temple and turns to Cora. "What're we talking about?"

"Some bitch at Cora's new job," I tell him while leaning into his strong frame.

I'm still not quite used to being in a relationship, but my three men make it feel like second nature.

"Ohh." Magnus brings my mug to his lips and has a taste. "Want me to kill her for you?"

I throttle my reaction and elbow him in the ribs.

"What?" He looks over at me and then at Cora. "It could be arranged."

Cora breaks off another section of her muffin. "I love this kind of energy." She plops the bite into her mouth.

"Speaking of..." Magnus glances at the watch on his wrist. "I have a surprise for you, so I'm afraid I have to cut your little meeting short."

"You know, I'm not even going to ask how those two things are related." Cora continues to chew her food.

"It's probably best you don't." I roll my eyes at Magnus and poke him.

He grabs my finger and brings it to his lips, kissing it gently. "You love me."

Cora speaks up, "Magnus, hey, since you're giving out favors."

Oh shit, what is she about to ask him?

"Happy to be of service, what can I do for you?" He gives her his attention while continuing to hold onto my hand.

"I've asked June like twelve million times, but I was hoping to get an in with Coen's friend Miller. I think June said you guys were business associates. We've never formally met, but I think we shared a moment."

Magnus tenses slightly next to me.

Fuck. I've been meaning to tell her that Miller is off-limits, but haven't found the right time or way of getting that across without hurting her feelings. It's not like I can just tell her the truth, that he's one of the leads of the east coast market and that he's enemies with my men's old boss. Granted, that guy is dead and no longer in charge, it still adds a weird dynamic and isn't something I'd allow Cora to get involved with. He might be a decent man, but decent doesn't cut it with my best friend. I may have gotten lucky with the three dangerous guys in my life, but I was made from the same dark cloth. Cora is soft, bubbly, too fucking happy, and kind. The world I am now involved with would swallow her whole. What kind of friend would I be if I exposed her to that?

"About that..." Magnus drinks more of my coffee, almost like he's coming up with some kind of story. "I have a better chance with him than you do."

I blink at him, not fully processing the angle he's playing.

"He's...gay?" Cora leaves her question hanging in the air.

Magnus nods. "Yep. Super gay. The dude loves dick."

"Oh." Cora's shoulders slump. "Well, that's cool."

"Yeah. He's not fully out though, so it might be a sensitive topic if you bring it up to him."

Cora crosses her arms. "Of course, no, that makes sense."

Magnus checks his watch again. "Listen, don't beat yourself up about it. Plenty other men would be lucky to have you."

Cora glances up at Magnus and then at me. "Think so?"

Shit, the whole reason I refused to introduce her to Miller was because I didn't think he was good enough for her.

"Absolutely," I reassure her. "Without a doubt."

The smile returns to her face as Magnus bobs his head and agrees with me.

***

"Where are we going?" I ask Magnus once we're outside Bram's diner.

"It's a surprise, princess. Keyword, surprise." He tugs me closer to his body as we continue to stroll down the sidewalk.

"Miller isn't gay, is he?" Because there was no denying that he was checking Cora out when the two of them first saw each other.

"Super straight, but she doesn't need to know that." Magnus glances behind him. "He's not ruthless like we are, that's for sure. Still, he's involved with shit that is way too shady for that sweet girl."

"My thoughts exactly."

"You were right in not hooking them up." Magnus steers me across the street. "Be different if you didn't care about her, but you do."

We approach a dark alley, slipping into the shade and walking until the shape of a man appears.

Coen kicks off the wall when we get closer and comes over to us. "Only a few more minutes, give or take." He tucks a strand of my hair behind my ear and looks over at Magnus. "Dom should be here any second."

And like clockwork, the brute steps into the alley with us.

"Someone want to fill me in on what we're doing?"

Dom winks and presses his finger to his lips, signaling me to be quiet. He points the direction he came, toward a few run-down buildings on this sketchier side of town.

I shove my hands in my pockets and wait impatiently. Don't they know by now that I hate surprises?

Any normal person would be concerned about being led into a weird alley and yet here I am wondering what kind of fun these men have in store for me?

Magnus nudges my arm and nods ahead for me to focus.

It takes my eyes a second to adjust, but once they do, I lock them on a familiar figure ahead.

*Carter.* My piece of shit ex-roommate who made my life a living hell while I was stuck sharing an apartment with him and the rest of those losers. The pathetic douche who stole my rent money, propositioned me numerous times, didn't care when I came home brutally beaten up, and managed to convince his equally worthless girlfriend to change the locks and kick me out after I'd already given them my share of that month's rent.

My jaw clenches, along with my fists. With this new world I'm living in, I feel stronger than ever, and the idea of letting him off the hook is one I'm not willing to consider. He's gone long enough without having any repercussions for his actions and that stops here and now.

Except when I take a step forward, Dominic catches me from going any further. "Give it a minute."

I glare at him, part of me wanting to rip myself free from his grasp and making a beeline straight toward that fuckboy in the near distance.

"Trust the process, princess," Magnus whispers into my ear.

A year ago, I'd never put my faith in anyone except me, or maybe Cora, but things have changed. Hell, everything has changed. No longer am I a loner who refuses to settle down with a man. Instead, I'm romantically involved with three ruthless men who claim me as their queen.

And there's nowhere I'd rather be than at their side.

Carter turns his back to us, cowering in a nook of an old building stoop. He fumbles with something and does a terrible job at concealing himself from the outside world. Facing us, he presses his thumb to his nose and inhales numerous times, his gaze darting around at anyone who might be watching. He shoves his finger into the baggie in his grip, and then pops it into his mouth, rubbing the thing along his gums.

Leaning against the building, he tilts his head up and braces himself.

"Did he just do cocaine?" I ask quietly.

"Wait for it…"

Carter slumps against the wall, his body dropping out from under him. He falls onto his ass hard and steadies himself with his hands.

I hold in a laugh that threatens to expose our concealed position and continue to watch him have what must be one hell of a high.

A hand gently rests on my lower back, and when I steal a glance, Magnus's strong frame inches closer to me. I lean into him but glue my gaze back on Carter.

If the guys went through the trouble to bring me here, it must be for a reason.

Carter starts shaking. It begins slowly, then turns into a more violent rattle, like he's having a seizure. Wait, is that what's happening? Is he having a bad reaction to the drugs? Or is this something more serious—an overdose?

From my spot across the way, I still see the foam bubble up and out of his mouth, a look of terror caked across his hardened face.

All of a sudden, his body stops flailing and he goes limp. The entire process only takes a short moment, not long enough for anyone to walk by and notice and potentially offer help. This is probably why he comes to this location to do drugs out in the open, because he won't get caught. Little did he know, that very detail could have been the difference between him living and dying. For this sad sack of shit, his poor decision-making resulted in the worst possible outcome for him.

And the best for me.

A warm hand tugs me backward, further away from the lifeless body and into the shadows.

"Is he…?" I squint to keep my gaze trained on the still man who did his best to ruin my life.

"Yes."

A wave of triumph courses through me. It's sick of me to feel this way, I'm well aware of that, but Carter had it coming. Each day he continued to breathe was more than he deserved.

My men continue to guide me back in the direction we came, leaving Carter to lie there alone while his soul leaves his body. A death that still wasn't as cruel as he was.

"How did you know he'd…?"

Coen is the first to speak up. "He's predictable. Wasn't difficult at all to find a pattern."

Leave it to Mr. Head of Security to figure out Carter's every move.

"Or to give him a hot batch." Dominic runs his hand over his salt and pepper beard.

"I have to say, this is the most thoughtful gift I've ever gotten." I glance between them.

Magnus nudges me. "Just wait until your birthday."

A statement that would have normally turned me off and made me run for the hills. Planning for the future with someone was never in the cards for me. But now?

I want nothing more than to spend however many days I have left with these three men.

<hr>

Dying to find out what happens with Simon…flip the page to read the continuation of June's story in *Villain Era*!

# Villain Era

## A MAFIA REVERSE HAREM ROMANCE

# VILLAIN ERA

## LUNA PIERCE

# playlist

RIVER - BISHOP BRIGGS

FIGURE YOU OUT - VOILA

I TRIED - CAMYLIO

FROM THE START - MATT SCHUSTER

I LOVED YOU THEN - WOODLOCK

I BURNED LA DOWN - NOAH CYRUS

SOMETHING IN THE ORANGE - ZACH BRYAN

CINDERELLA'S DEAD - EMELINE

MIDDLE OF THE NIGHT - ELLEY DUHE

HAUNT YOU - X LOVERS, CHLOE MORIONDO

TILL FOREVER FALLS APART - ASHE, FINNEAS

CONSEQUENCES - CAMILA CABELLO

CAN'T FORGET YOU - MY DARKEST DAYS

BETTER OFF WITHOUT ME - MATT HENSEN

THIS LOVE (TAYLOR'S VERSION) - TAYLOR SWIFT

THE DEATH OF PEACE OF MIND - BAD OMENS

# Dear reader:

The contents of this book contain graphic material meant for mature audiences. Some situations and scenes are triggering, and I urge you to read through this list of triggers and make sure this book is suitable for you.

Murder. Death. Kidnapping. Gunshot. Alluded eating disorder. PTSD. Scars. Attempted murder. Panic attack. Mention of deceased parent. Mention of abusive parent/alcoholism. Mention of deceased grandparent. Nightmares/night terrors. Mention of assault. Torture. Mention of Stockholm syndrome. Lying. Self harm. Mention of deceased sibling. Mention of drowning. Mention of domestic violence. DVP. TVP.

For a more comprehensive list of WHERE the triggers are located (spoilers), please visit https://www.lunapierce.com/triggerwarnings

# CHAPTER 1

# June

I step out of the oversized shower, hugging the plush towel around my body and standing on my tiptoes to wipe the condensation off the mirror. The faded scar on my chin is a bit more purple than it usually is—a reminder of the man who had kidnapped me, tortured me, and then bled out when I slit his throat.

I never imagined murdering a man would have been that easy. And a small part of me worries that this isn't a normal human response, but I recall that day, when he almost succeeded in ending my life, and reassure myself that he got what was coming to him.

My gaze trails to the scar on my chest—a memory of another near-death experience. One minute I was piercing Simon's shirt with a knife, and the next I was bleeding out in his arms. His warmth had consumed me; his stare desperate and pleading for me to stay a little longer.

I manipulated him. I asked him to concede. I used my last breath to beg him to give up so Dominic would win.

I did what had to be done.

And it worked.

In those final moments, Simon kept his hand pressed against my wound, holding me together and allowing me to feel a brief flicker of hope. I was prepared to lose everything, but I wouldn't allow Dominic to lose, too. Not when I knew how much winning meant to him.

*Meant.* Past tense.

Because when he came to me, in the hospital, after I had come out of surgery and the doctors did what they could to repair the damage that had been done, Dominic confessed that he would have traded it all for me to live.

Becoming the head of a prosperous criminal organization was always important to him.

But at that moment, I was more important.

A priority.

Something I've never been to anyone else. Not in the *risk it all* way.

And not in a *burn it all to the ground* kind of way, either.

Co had gone completely feral when he saw me dying in Simon's arms. He slaughtered numerous people in an amnesty zone—shooting and slicing the throats of anyone who exerted a shred of guilt. He didn't care that he would be killed, too. He needed to inflict as much damage as possible in his attempt to right the wrong.

"Penny for your thoughts?" Magnus interrupts my rampant trip down memory lane. He leans against the doorframe, his tattooed arms crossed over his chest.

My heart stutters at the sight of him; it's the same effect he's always had on me. His love overflows from him and pours into me—it's pure and strong and endless. A constant I can rely on. He loves unconditionally, irrevocably, and unselfishly.

Magnus has never doubted me. He's never questioned whether I would fit into this dangerous world of theirs. He's open and honest and says the things no one else is capable of. He might boss me around in bed, but not for a second do I doubt that he would do anything I could ever ask of him.

That doesn't mean I haven't noticed his possessive body language when we're in public. How he positions himself in front of me. How his jaw tenses and his gaze scans every room, frantically looking, assessing the threat risk. How it's like he's on edge, worrying, waiting, afraid something will happen again.

It's been over half a year since I almost died. But sometimes, I think for all of us, it feels like yesterday.

"Do you know when Alec's birthday is?" I ruffle my damp hair with a towel.

"Alec? Driver Alec?" Magnus shoves off the wall and begins his approach toward me.

"Mmhm."

He grips my waist from behind and kisses my exposed shoulder. "Leave it to you to care about your driver's birthday."

I turn around to face him, extending my arms around his neck. "I see the guy every day. The least I could do is get him a card or something."

Magnus's lips pull up into a grin. "Don't worry, princess. It's taken care of. We give every employee holiday and birthday bonuses."

"Really?" I narrow my gaze at him.

He presses his lips on my forehead. "Promise." Then, he leaves another kiss on my temple, my cheek, and my nose.

Ravenous for more, I claim those lips on mine. My body melts into his, and we become one being fused together. His arms hug me tightly, and he lifts me onto the counter, my towel barely hanging on.

Magnus nudges my knees apart and positions himself in between them. Using one hand to grip the back of my neck and the other to skim the soft flesh of my inner thigh, he moves closer and closer until he reaches my entrance. He runs his thumb over my already aching nub and dips it inside my eager pussy.

I whimper against his lips and inch toward him.

He pulls away, bringing his thumb to his mouth and tasting my lust. "My God, princess." Magnus skims the same thumb over my bottom lip before he pushes it between my lips and into my mouth. "You taste so sweet."

I reach for his pants and unbutton them. "I want you to fuck me."

It's then that I realize someone else is standing in the doorway to my ensuite bathroom.

"Don't let me stop you." Dominic stands there, his jaw as tense as always, his shoulder pressed along the wall.

Magnus doesn't pay him any attention, opting to keep his focus on me. He slides his finger between my breasts to release the meager hold my towel had on my body, leaving me there, completely exposed. He pinches my left nipple between his fingers and then gives the other one the same amount of attention.

I swallow and keep my gaze on Dominic. "Join us."

"I just want to watch. I have to get to work."

I sigh and Magnus immediately picks up on my disappointment.

He releases my nipple and steps back, holding out his hand to me to help me off the counter. "On your knees, princess."

I hop down and comply, getting on my knees and looking up at him, ready for whatever command he's going to give me next. I've never been the obedient type—but with him, I fucking love being bossed around.

Magnus smooths the hair off my face and skims my cheek. "I'm going to fuck your face, princess. Is that okay?"

I nod, ready and completely willing to take him into my mouth. My own pleasure heightened at the idea of getting him off.

Finally, he acknowledges Dominic. "And Dom's going to fuck you from behind. Right, Dom?"

"I don't want to be late." Dominic remains where he stands.

I glance over at him. "Aren't you the boss?" I arch toward him, tempting him to follow through with what Magnus suggested.

Sex with any one of my men alone is fucking heaven, but two of them at a time is like sensory overload in the best way possible. Dominic and Magnus are murderous psychos but they love sharing me, and I love being shared. Co and I haven't gotten to that point yet. He's well aware I'm fucking multiple men, and he's accepting of our unusual arrangement, but the opportunity hasn't presented itself for *all* of us to be together. The wound from our years apart is still fresh—our moments of intimacy better suited for just the two of us...for now.

We'll get there, just not today.

Especially since he's already left for the day, anyway.

"You're wasting time," I tell Dom and then lick the tip of Magnus's cock. I stare up at Magnus as I take him into my mouth.

He moans and guides his shaft in and out, slow and steady, deeper and deeper.

My eyes water from the length of him, but I hungrily take every inch of him I can. I grip the base of his cock and revel in his hardness, not caring at all that we're being watched. If anything, it only turns me on more. Just when I grow certain that Dominic isn't going to join us, I hear the sound of a zipper, the crinkle of a wrapper, and feel the warmth of his presence coming up behind me.

I smile against Magnus's cock and continue sucking him.

Dominic doesn't waste another second; he slams his sheathed dick into my soaked pussy and latches onto my hips to steady me.

I tighten around him, his length stuffing me full, his girth spreading me open.

Dom kneels behind me and fucks me hard and fast. I rock back, my ass bouncing and slamming into him.

"That's our good girl," he says through gritted teeth.

Magnus holds my face and fucks my mouth. "Tell me if it's too much."

I open wider, letting more of him ravish me. I spread my legs, too, desperate for every inch these men will provide.

My core tightens and without even fully being aware of its approach, my orgasm crashes over me. I let out a muffled scream around Magnus's cock, and Dominic continues to thrust in and out, not letting up at my release at all. I tremble but remain upright, pleasure coursing through me. The tension builds again, this time a bit more under my control. I keep it at bay and savor the ecstasy of riding that post-orgasm and near-orgasm bliss.

Magnus stops fucking the back of my throat and slides some of his shaft out to grip it in his hand. He strokes himself and leaves the tip of his cock in my mouth. I open up and cup the bottom of his dick with my tongue, eager for him to finish.

"Look at me, princess," Magnus commands.

I stare up at him through my lashes, a bit of me grateful I hadn't put my makeup on yet, because my mascara would no doubt be streaking my cheeks.

He explodes in my mouth, and I gratefully lap up every drop of him. He drags the tip against my lips and then shoves it back under the band of his boxers.

I drop my head, my hands latching onto the ground to steady me as I focus my attention on the man fucking me hard from behind. Arching my back, I grip the rug we're on top of and slam into him, giving as much as he is, matching his intensity and holding out even though I could easily give in to my release at any given moment. I want to feel him explode inside of me when my pussy tightens around his shaft—my own climax waiting for his to come first.

But that's the thing about Dom and me, we're both greedy in our desire to satisfy the other, so what we want is often the same damn thing. The real question is, who will give in first?

I wasn't always like this. No, when we first started fucking, I was incredibly selfish in my attempt to make sure I came first. Because most men are stingy in bed and don't often reciprocate once their own satisfaction has been met. But the more time I spend with my three men, I realize that they would never allow my needs not to be met. That alone made me hungry to make sure theirs were, too.

Dominic slows his pace but maintains his depth. He grips my ass and gently digs his fingers into my flesh. "Come for me like a good girl."

And because I apparently have no fucking self-control, I do. My pussy clenches around him, and I scream into the rug. His cock throbs inside my hole as he follows me across the finish line.

I lie there, my face buried and my breath ragged. Dominic slows his pace until he's not moving at all.

He remains while I pulsate around him and shiver at the intensity of the climax.

Finally, he pulls out and rises to his feet, removing the condom and dropping it into the wastebasket under the sink.

"You okay, princess?" Magnus helps me stand on my shaky legs.

"Mmhm." I smirk at him and force myself to get it together. My entire body radiates bliss from head to toe. My mind spins in the euphoric orgasm-induced frenzy.

Dominic glances at his Patek Philippe watch. "We're going to be late."

I go into the private toilet area, not shutting the door all the way, and relieve myself. Through the crack, I ask, "Who are you meeting with?" I finish up quickly and go back into the main bathroom area to wash my hands. I flit my gaze at both of them in the mirror, wondering which of them will choose to be vague this time.

Ever since I met them, they've never been that open about the dealings of their business. There was this brief time between then and me getting shot that they were more willing to share information, but now, after *that*, they avoid the topic of work like the plague.

And honestly, it's fucking annoying.

The reason I got kidnapped in the first place was because they were keeping secrets. Don't they realize if I'm going to be a part of their life, I have to be a part of their business, too? I don't have to know every nitty-gritty detail, but they tell me next to nothing. It's as if they think if they don't acknowledge the elephant in the room, it doesn't exist.

But all they're doing is making me feel isolated and shut off from them. And it's only a matter of time until that bleeds into our romantic relationships.

I'm not asking to be nosey. I'm asking because I want to help. Maybe not to the same lengths that resulted in me getting shot, but in any capacity that could assist them in managing this empire. I have a business degree—one that they insisted I finish—and enough smarts to understand and be willing to navigate their corrupt ways. I should be an asset to their organization, not some liability they feel like they have to shield from it all.

"Nobody important, princess." Magnus kisses my cheek and tucks a strand of my wild jet-black hair behind my ear.

I'm well aware that Magnus is the most conflicted of them on this, but still, he doesn't budge. He was the one to advocate for the truth when we first started seeing each other, practically demanding that the other two confess a fraction of the truth. Yet now, he goes along with the secrecy. Getting shot and almost dying has a way of changing the dynamic of things.

Each of them is aware of how strong and capable I am, but there's still the need to protect me from their world. I'll just have to prove to them that I really do fit in and that I can handle my own.

Only, their continued secrecy, and the fact that I'm under pretty much constant surveillance makes that sort of difficult.

A chime sounds from Dominic's pocket. He retrieves his phone and returns it a second later. "Beckett's here."

The man who was once their enemy, who quite literally saved my life, is now my permanent bodyguard. It wasn't a decision they took lightly, but they insisted someone watch over me when they couldn't, and despite hating his fucking guts more than anything, they shared one thing in common with said enemy—the innate desire to keep me alive.

They vetted numerous other soldiers in their organization, coming up short after every interview. Sure, they were obedient and good at following directions, but none of them had a personal stake in the matter. Which left Simon Beckett to be the most qualified for the position.

"I don't need a babysitter," I huff while clasping the bra that matches the panties I'm wearing. Back when I had pretty much no money, I had to scrounge to find clean undergarments, let alone matching ones. The guys make sure I have anything I could possibly desire, giving it to me before I even know I need or want it. Well, everything but the truth.

I throw a plain white tee on and slide into a pair of ripped black skinny jeans.

"He's not a babysitter." Dominic approaches, plants a quick kiss on my lips, and stalks toward the door. "He's your detail, and whether any of us like it or not, he's necessary." He leaves without allowing me the chance to respond.

I sigh and shift my focus to the last remaining man.

Magnus shrugs and follows after him. "Necessary evil, princess." He pauses at the door, his tattooed hand gripping the frame. "Love you."

"Love you more," I mutter and turn to find a pair of socks.

"Never," he calls out on his way down the hall.

"Always," I holler after him.

A few minutes pass and a chill creeps over me. I glance over my shoulder to find Simon Beckett standing in my doorway. I press my hand to my chest and settle the start he gave me. "Christ, Simon. Warn a girl next time."

He remains there, stone-faced and solemn. "Are you ready for work?"

I snatch my phone off the nightstand and slide it into my back pocket. "Yeah." I stop right in front of him. "You're not allowed in here."

Another one of the rules made by the men I call mine.

Simon is not permitted to step foot into my bedroom unless there's an emergency. It's like they think if he does, he'll accidentally slip and fall with his dick out and it'll land in my pussy. I'm not entirely sure if they realize there are a million other places Simon could have his way with me, and that making my room off-limits doesn't actually prevent that from happening.

No, the thing that prevents it from happening is that I wouldn't do that to them. I know how much they hate him, how much he almost took from them, and I wouldn't sabotage my relationship with three incredible men because of some fuck boy.

Okay, that's a stretch. Simon isn't exactly a fuck boy. More like a wannabe fuck boy.

The more time I spend around him, the more I see through the façade he paints on heavily. He wants the world to see him as this carefree ladies' man, but he's not entirely terrible.

Or maybe the simple fact that I'm surrounded by morally grey men has me blurring the lines of what I view as good or bad.

Simon peers down at me, his emerald gaze falling to the floor and then back at me. "I'm not in your room." He swallows as I press closer to him.

"No, but you're in my way." I push past him and into the hall. I glance at him when I reach the stairs. "You coming or what?"

And just like that, my puppy dog of a bodyguard follows. His footsteps close but not too close. Always there, but with a bit of distance.

"Have you eaten breakfast?" Simon asks me.

"No, have you?" I say, a bit of condescension lingering on each word.

"You should eat before we leave." Simon ignores my question.

"I'm not hungry."

Simon broadens his shoulders when I approach, his frame blocking the door to get into the garage where Alec is waiting to take me to work. "You need to eat, June."

I stand taller in an attempt to mimic his bravado. "You going to make me?"

Simon's beautifully carved jaw clenches slightly. "I will if I have to."

My heart picks up its pace, and the tension between us grows thicker with each second we remain in this deadlock.

"I dare you," I mutter under my breath. "I fucking dare you."

Simon keeps his eyes trained on mine. "You're impossible, you know that?"

"I'm aware," I tell him, not backing down.

Simon finally breaks eye contact and brushes past me to snatch a banana off the kitchen counter. He cracks it open, peeling back the flesh, and holds it out to me. "Please?"

And only because I'm evil as fuck, I step forward, my gaze remaining firmly on his, and wrap my mouth around the tip of the banana, biting it off with every ounce of seduction I can muster. I chew it slowly while staring at him. "Happy?"

Simon swallows harshly like he's considering his words carefully.

Instead of responding, he steps closer, bringing the banana to my lips.

I take another bite, watching him watch me, and then take another. We continue this back-and-forth thing until only a small chunk remains.

"Now I am." He pops the rest of it into his mouth and nods to the door. "You may leave."

Here I was, thinking I was calling the shots, but in a matter of seconds, Simon completely flipped the script, and I played right fucking into it.

Him being my bodyguard might annoy the fuck out of me, but at least this is an entertaining game of who can push who more.

# CHAPTER 2
## *Simon*

I stand in the corner of Bram's diner, a quaint little place on the edge of town that serves the best coffee in the entire city. Hell, maybe the whole state. But that's not why I'm here. I'm here because I'm June's personal bodyguard. Because it's my job to make sure she remains safe at all times when she's not under the protection of her three boyfriends.

They hate me.

And I hate them.

But that doesn't change the fact that we have one common goal—keep June alive.

I almost failed her once, and I won't make that mistake again.

It was my fault she put herself in danger. I was the reason she got shot. Because one of my men got trigger-happy when they saw her press a dagger to my chest. I should have acted sooner, noticed the threat. But I was too damn captivated by the radiant beauty aiming a blade at my heart. If she would have succeeded, that death would have been far less painful than the one I'm experiencing now.

To be *this damn close* to her...but unable to call her mine.

To watch her, day in and day out, be with the three men I hate the most.

To know with certainty that she'll never feel the way she does about them, for me.

A large part of me wishes she would have succeeded that day. That she would have driven that blade into my heart, ending my life right then and there. It could have been me bleeding out in her arms instead, and I wouldn't be here, slowly tortured by the impossible distance between us.

But then I remember, I'm Simon fucking Beckett, and when have I ever given up so easily?

Dying that day would have been the easy way out.

When I went to visit her in the hospital, to confirm with my own eyes that she really was okay, I told her I would wait forever.

And that is what I'll do.

I'll play the long game. I'll suffer through the unbearable sight of her loving three other men just for the possibility that I might eventually convince her of the truth. That I'm better for her. That my arms are where she belongs.

Until then, I'll play the role she needs—a devoted bodyguard.

I nearly lost it this morning. I was perched just outside her bedroom door as the scent of sex lingered in the air. I wanted to breach that threshold and toss her onto the bed, claiming her for myself. But I didn't. I couldn't.

One: because that's not what she wants...yet.

And two: because if the guys kill me first, she'll never be mine.

I recall our interaction in the kitchen, her pushing my buttons and me pushing hers right back. I knew she hadn't eaten. She's terrible about skipping breakfast. I've noticed the weight she's lost since the accident. Her clothes hang a bit looser with each passing day. She's stressed, no doubt a result of the choice of men she keeps around. But there's something else going on. She doesn't talk about things much—keeping them bottled inside and letting them fester. There's no telling the level of post-traumatic stress that was caused by the accident. Adapting to this lifestyle alone is enough to derail a person's mental health, but she was thrown in headfirst and then hit with wave after wave. I was born into this world; it's all I've ever known.

I couldn't back down when she called my bluff about eating, but dear God, I was not expecting her to eat a phallic-shaped food mere inches from my face, with her very best set of bedroom eyes staring up into mine. It was everything I could do to keep my dick in my pants and not take her right there on the kitchen counter. But I maintained control, locking the image away in my mind to keep forever.

It was my fault; I could have easily grabbed something fucking else for her to eat, but it was the first thing readily available. And I had no idea she'd so easily gain the upper hand when I thought I was the one calling the shots.

Another reason I'm absolutely bat-shit-crazy for her. She's unpredictable. She's bold. She's so fucking strong-willed.

Which brings us here—to Bram's diner.

A job that she doesn't need, yet chooses to keep because she can. Because she wants to.

Any single one of her men could easily provide whatever she wanted, but throw all three of them together and the possibilities are endless. Money is of no concern. They have the power to make pretty much anything she could want happen. And here she is, working a barely over-minimum-wage job three days a week. None of this is about money for her. It's about holding onto any shred of independence she can.

She glides from one table to the next, taking orders and gathering empty plates in the process. She drops them off at the kitchen window and places two ticket orders on the little carousel for the cook. June grabs two stacks of pancakes and delivers them to the corner booth. Wiping her hands on her apron, she peers around the room to check on her other customers, assessing whether their needs have been met and anticipating any request they may have.

Her gaze trails over mine, and when she notices I'm staring directly at her, she does a double take. I don't look away. I keep my sights set on her, noting the subtle flush of her cheeks, the soft bob of her Adam's apple when she swallows, the nervous tuck of her obsidian hair behind her ear.

All of it is an act to draw me in even more.

And damn is she good at it.

She glances at the clock and then back at me, tilting her head to motion for me to come over.

Without skipping a beat, I march across the room and follow her to the counter.

I'd follow her to the depths of fucking hell if she asked.

"Your highness," I greet her.

She rolls those radiant brown eyes of hers. "What do you want to eat? Your usual?"

"Are we not going straight home?" *Home.* Hers and theirs. A place where I don't belong.

"No." She doesn't elaborate because she knows I already know where we're going.

"Usual is fine."

June slides behind the counter, gives Carlos an order, and turns her attention to the coffee station. She pulls out two to-go cups, filling both of them with coffee, leaving a little room in one. She tops it off with a bit of cream, and a single packet of sugar. She plops an ice cube in the other before putting the lids on both. She kneels down, her entire form almost out of sight.

My legs instinctually move so I can get a better view of her.

A second later, she returns to her upright position and puts the cups in a little two-cup carrier. She places it on the counter near me, pointing at one of them. "This one's yours."

But I already knew that. And not for a moment do I disregard the fact that she's memorized my *usual* and how I take my coffee. It should make me feel special, but when I remember that this is what she does for a living, that warm and fuzzy sensation quickly dissipates.

She's good at her job, that's why she knows those details.

Just like I'm good at mine. That's why I catch the little things—like the change of inflection in her voice when she talks to certain customers, the smile on her face when Bram arrives, the tenseness in her shoulders when something is bothering her. I see more than she thinks I do—more than I probably should. Each small observation makes my heart that much more hers than the day before.

We've been doing this for over six months. Every single day for the greater part of a year. In the very beginning, I was posted up at her house while she recovered from the gunshot wound to the chest. But then she went back to college, finishing her degree. I was there outside her classroom, silently waiting, watching, protecting. I walked her to and from without so much as a word—a shadow lurking, ready to strike at a moment's notice. I wouldn't allow anything to happen to her, and between my presence and that of her feared men, not a single threat has dared fuck with her.

That doesn't mean they aren't out there—they just haven't been stupid enough to fuck around and find out what happens if they touch our girl.

I've accompanied her to doctor's appointments, physical therapy, girls' nights out, and on occasion, when she's feeling a certain kind of way, we go to this little park on the outskirts of town where she sits on this one particular bench. I know she'd rather be there alone, but her safety doesn't permit such a thing. So, I do what I can to give her some space while maintaining my watch over her.

And today, that's what we do.

When her shift at the diner is over, we walk to her favorite spot in silence.

I assess every person that comes near her, searching for signs of potential threats, and I ready myself to act if needed.

We make it there without issue, just like every other time, and go straight to the bench she always sits on.

She lowers herself onto it and rummages through the bag of food.

I pull my coffee out of the holder and wait for her to give me my food so I can go to the other bench that's just a stone's throw away—my meager attempt at giving her some space. It isn't much, but it's the least I can do to make her feel like she isn't constantly under surveillance.

June pulls out my burger but doesn't give it to me. Instead, she nods at the open seat next to her. "You can sit here." She pauses and then adds, "If you want to."

"Are you sure?" I'm well aware that I nearly force-fed her this morning and like to fuck with her every chance I get, but in moments like this, when I can *feel* that something is going on, I back off. I can't afford to push her too far over the ledge when our entire relationship has never been on stable ground.

"Yeah, but you better hurry up or I might change my mind." She smirks and holds out the burger.

I take it and settle in on the opposite end of the bench from her. "Wouldn't want that to happen, now would we?" My sarcasm lingers in the air. All I could ever ask is for her to change her mind—about me, about them, about us.

She doesn't bother taking the bait, instead, she peels back the paper around her chicken wrap and bites off a small corner of it. She chews slowly, swallows, and then stares blindly off into the distance, seemingly at nothing in particular.

"Want to tell me what's wrong?" I dig into my own lunch, a bit afraid that I might be overstepping my boundaries by asking her something so personal when she's never been the one to open up without immediately shutting back down.

June draws in a breath, her chest expanding slightly before she exhales, her gaze skimming the ground in front of her. She nibbles on the inside of her bottom lip.

A bird flies overhead, casting a shadow over both of us temporarily.

She looks up to watch it pass, but I keep my eyes firmly on her.

"Nothing's wrong," she finally says.

I run my hand through my longish hair, dragging it off my brow. "I can't fix the problem if you don't tell me what it is."

"Why are you so sure there's a problem that needs to be solved?" She takes another small bite of her wrap.

"We wouldn't be here if there wasn't." I nod vaguely at the park around us. "You come here to escape the noise of the city—to think."

"Maybe I just come for the view."

"Maybe." Although we both know that's a lie.

"What's wrong with you?" she asks. It's a question I don't expect.

"What?" I stare over at her, reading her face to pick up anything I had missed.

"You're telling me nothing is wrong with you?" She positions her body toward me, her one bent leg coming up onto the bench and the other pulled up on top of it.

"Other than the obvious?" Instinctually, my body gravitates toward her, turning and facing her the way she had done to me.

"And what's the obvious?"

"I think you and I both already know the answer to that one." I grin at her. "But nice try changing the subject."

June rolls her eyes and reaches into the bag to pull out a box. "Can I have one of your fries?" She pops the top and snags one before I can even respond to her.

Not that I would have said no either way. That woman can have whatever it is she wants from me.

*Take the bleeding fucking heart from my chest if it pleases you, June.*

A thought that I keep to myself, silently begging her to comprehend what I refuse to say out loud.

"Sure," I tell her anyway. "Help yourself." I grab a fry and toss it at her. It bounces off her forehead and onto the ground.

Her eyes widen as she slowly glances up at me. "You did not."

I throw another one at her. "I did too."

June latches onto a fistful of fries and chucks them at me. She bursts into laughter, and it completely fucking paralyzes me from even reacting to the fact that I have French fries all over me, one of them stuck in my hair.

I pluck a fry off my lap and fling it at her. "You're lucky I'm here to protect you, otherwise, I'd kick your ass."

She catches the thing mid-air and pops it into her mouth, grinning from ear to ear. "You'd lose."

"In your dreams." My finger twitches to reach out and brush the hair from her cheek, tucking it gently behind her ear. I imagine the warmth of her skin against mine.

Soft...porcelain...scarred.

I sigh at the mark the blade had left behind, the one from the man that I helped her kill. He deserved that death ten times over for harming a hair on her head.

June brings her hand to her mouth. "What? Do I have something on my face?" She snatches a napkin and wipes at seemingly nothing.

"No. You're..." But I don't finish my sentence. I don't tell her that she's perfect. Instead, I tell her, "Actually, you have a booger hanging out of your nose."

"Oh my God, do I really?" She pats around her nose and then reaches forward and shoves me. "You're a jerk."

I revel in the reverberation of her touch long after it's gone, wishing like hell I could duplicate it and put it on repeat. I nod toward the wrap she's only taken a couple bites out of. "Eat your food."

"Or what? You'll feed it to me like this morning?" She raises a brow, clearly calling my bluff again.

"I'm starting to think you like me feeding you." I lean my arm over the back of the bench. "How about this, you either eat, or you tell me what's bothering you."

"I hate you, you know that?" June deadpans.

I take a bite of my burger and nod. "Mmhm."

She fingers some of my fries, looking for the specific kind she likes. Squared-off edges, extra crunch, the perfect amount of salt.

I pick one up and hand it to her. "Here."

She narrows her gaze but takes the offering anyway. "I don't need you."

Her words knock the wind out of me, even if I was already aware of the truth. "Thanks for the reminder."

June sighs. "That's not what I meant, Simon."

Fucking Christ. My name, her lips, a beautiful melody to my ears.

"Then what did you mean, *June*?"

She points between us. "This. This arrangement. The whole *bodyguard* thing. It's not necessary. I'm not in danger, not any more than any other random girl in this city is."

"You're mistaken." I sip my coffee and continue. "You're shacked up with three of the most notorious criminals on the entire west coast. Anyone who's anyone knows who you are. Could spot your face in a crowd."

"So what? That doesn't mean I'm in danger."

"And it doesn't mean you're not. The risk is too high. It would be foolish to underestimate the threat level."

June drags her food off her lap and stands up. She huffs and runs her hands through her hair. "This is fucking stupid." She turns toward me. "All because what, I got shot?" Her chest heaves up and down. "That was my fault, because of me. I had it coming. It wasn't some random attack; it was because I tried to fucking kill you." Her hands shake. "I deserved that. But this?" She rocks her head back and forth, tears welling in her eyes.

I'm on my feet in an instant, going against my better judgment, and latching onto her shoulders. "Look at me, June."

"This isn't what I wanted."

"Hey," I say softly. "Breathe."

Her chest continues to rise up and down at a steady rate.

"Take a breath for me, okay? In through your nose. Keep your eyes on me. Out through your mouth. Take another one, in through your nose, out through your mouth." I mimic the pattern with her. "Good, that's good."

After what feels like an eternity, she starts to calm.

"You know you're not being punished, right?" I keep my hands resting against her shoulders, selfishly not wanting to let go and grateful she hasn't yet pulled out of my grasp.

"It feels like it." She exhales and takes a step back.

The ghost of her touch haunts my empty palms.

"What's this really about?" I rub my neck in an attempt to busy myself from the loss of her closeness.

She lowers her voice. "I don't even know. Not really. I just feel so..." She pauses to find the right word to say. "Alone." June glances up at me. "Which is stupid, considering I'm never fucking alone."

I take no offense to the fact that she'd rather I not be around. It's not her fault she's stuck with me. Even though I'm grateful for every fucking second of it. Sure, there are other things I could be doing with my time, but when I lost the throne to Dominic, everything else paled in comparison to where I really wanted to be—at her side.

This isn't how I wanted it to happen, but beggars can't exactly be fucking choosers.

"What can I do? To help you not feel that way." I quickly add, "Except for no longer being your bodyguard."

"Probably nothing, considering the guys hate you." She crosses her arms over her chest but turns more toward me. "They don't tell me anything at all. And I mean, they never really did, but there was this short while where they kind of did. Like they included me, wanted me to be part of their world. Now? Fucking crickets. I can't even get minor details. Even Magnus is evasive, and he was never like that. He was always the one to put faith in me. He believed I could handle it. And honestly, it all just really pisses me off. They think they're protecting me, but all they're doing is..."

She doesn't finish her train of thought but I know exactly where it was heading.

"You almost died...can you imagine how terrifying that was for them?" For all of us. For me specifically. I held her in my arms, her blood pooling all around me as I maintained pressure on the wound, all while praying to any fucking God that would listen to keep her with me. Terrified doesn't even scratch the surface of the sheer magnitude I felt surging through me.

Moments prior, the same woman had a knife poised to my heart, and that was nothing compared to what I experienced when I thought I might lose her.

"But I didn't die. I'm right here. And I'm going fucking crazy." Her hands ball into fists. "I'm so angry, I just want to..."

"Punch something?"

"Not some*thing*."

"Someone?" My teeth clench. "Who?" Because whatever name comes out of her mouth, I will track them down and deliver them on a silver fucking platter the same way I had done to Vincent—the man that kidnapped and tortured her.

"That's the thing." June shakes her head. "I don't even know who. I just want to fucking hurt someone." She lowers her voice. "What the fuck is wrong with me?"

I breathe in a lungful of relief. "Nothing, June, you're just..." A grin forms on my face at the thought of this sadistic vixen in front of me.

"You're smiling, right now? Really?" She shoves me again, and I welcome the touch like it was a gift sent from the heavens. "You think I'm fucked up, don't you?"

"Not at all, actually." I skim my gaze along the delicate features of her face. Her entire exterior is a contradiction to the evil begging to be let out. I saw it that day in the warehouse when she took pleasure in carving up the man who had hurt her. I wondered whether it was an isolated incident—only an equal retribution, a settling of scores. But throughout our time together, I've seen it rise to the surface, pleading to be let free.

"Then what?" she asks me.

"You're stepping into your villain era."

"My what?" June plants her hand on her hip.

"You know, when the good guy turns bad. When the hero of the story realizes there's much more fun in being the villain."

"I was never the hero or the good guy."

"Said like a true villain." My mind races at the possibilities. "I think what you need is a little bloodshed."

Her eyes twinkle, the excitement showing through without a single word spoken.

"Give me some time." I reach out and even though I shouldn't, I place my hand on her shoulder. I keep doing things I shouldn't, but hey, things haven't completely blown up in my face yet, so what's the harm in one more boundary being pushed. "I'll figure this out."

*For you, June, anything for you.*

# CHAPTER 3

# June

I sit on a stool in the guys' mansion, picking at a blueberry muffin. The clock on the oven reads 5:08 a.m. and my tired eyes confirm to the world that I'm not built to be up this fucking early. But, if I stand any chance of getting face time with any of my men, I must beat them before they leave the house.

I rarely see them all at once, let alone for more than five minutes. I see Dom and Magnus more than Co, but even then, it's not much. One of them is always hanging back and waiting to pass me off to Simon, the man who I spend most of my hours with these days.

At one point, we all ate dinner together every night. Not with Simon, but with me and the rest of the men. It was nice getting those guaranteed moments with them. But one skipped meal turned into another, turned into nothing at all. I'm grateful for Simon's company, annoying as it is, but it's not what I truly want. I want to be with the men who supposedly love me.

And with each passing day where they're less and less present, I start to wonder if that was ever true at all.

I believe they care about me, but more in an obligatory way than anything else. I feel more of a burden, or a distraction, than the woman they claim they'd lay their life down for.

If I'm being honest, Simon's the only one who's actually proven that.

Even when Co had gone on his murderous rampage to avenge me, it was for his own satisfaction to fuel that rage, not because he thought it might bring me back.

I miss the old days, when it was pining and proving and groveling and *wanting* to be around me. I don't think I'm asking for that much. And that's why I think if they were to at least include me in their business dealings, I could co-exist in that world while they're busy doing whatever it is they're doing. They wouldn't have to pick sides because I would willingly join them on theirs.

Footsteps sound from behind me, a presence from a man I've been missing far too long.

Co places his firm hands on my shoulders and presses his lips to my temple. "J, what're you doing up this early? You're freezing." He takes a few strides to the sitting area and snatches a throw blanket from the couch, coming back and draping it over my back. "You okay?" He leans against the counter and stares at me. "What's wrong?"

If my eyes weren't so damn dry from being tired, I'm sure they would water. The emotions rolling through me threaten to overflow in whatever capacity they can.

"I just wanted to see you," I tell him.

"Aw, J..." Co grazes his thumb over my cheek, then pauses at the scar on my chin. He pulls away but latches onto my hand. "I've been busy lately, I'm sorry."

"Busy is an understatement, Co. You're gone when I wake up, and you don't get back in until I'm already in bed. I know you come in and kiss me sometimes when you get home, but I'm starting to wonder if you're avoiding me on purpose."

The beautiful, golden-haired boy shakes his head. "J...never." He sighs and squeezes my hand. "Things have been...less than ideal. But I promise it doesn't mean I love you any less."

His eyes dart to the watch on his wrist briefly. Something I'm not sure he wanted me to notice.

"See, right there. You're already about to bolt out of the room to whatever it is you have to do. Where do you go this early? Where are you in the wee hours of the night? When do you sleep, Co? I'm seriously concerned."

Despite his gorgeousness, his eyes are a bit sunken in. New wrinkles form in places that weren't there six months ago. My sweet, innocent boy is no longer. Instead, here stands the broken man who stole my heart all those years ago, a darkness to him that was never there before. One that was built from a decade of illicit activities and what felt like an eternity of lost love. No, not lost—*stolen*.

The tiny, delicate red thread connecting us was never really severed. It was stretched and twisted and pulled and even when I was certain it would snap, it remained steady. A slow and labored heartbeat that would forever remain ours. An impossible force that could never be breached. A torch that would never be snuffed out.

We had bonded over trauma when we were just kids—both of our mothers dead. Two children who spent more time in a cemetery talking to ghosts than other people their age.

I had been collecting wildflowers the day we met. Vibrant purple, some the color of sunshine, white, and crimson. I picked so many my fingertips were raw from accidentally going after too many with bristly edges. A sad reality that even pretty things can be laced with the ability to hurt you.

I saw the pretty boy with blond locks there before, but I had never spoken to him. I let him exist in solitude, to mourn over the woman buried in the grave he spent most of his time. The same thing everyone else did in cemeteries. It's not a place to socialize, it's a place to pay respect. Or whatever else people do there. I never really understood it, but I felt called to the solemnness and despair, like it was calling me home. Nobody judged me for my lack of smiles or the heaviness I exuded. It was there that I didn't have to put on an act to exist in the real world. Nobody questions why you're sad when you're surrounded by the dead.

But that day, I couldn't stop looking his way. And when I saw his shoulders quiver, and how he wiped at his cheeks, my body gravitated toward his. My feet took one step after another, until I was next to him, sitting cross-legged on the ground with a bunch of flowers in my hand. I set them in his lap and sat there with him, not speaking, just being there. I'm not sure whether he cared or not, but he didn't tell me to leave, and I found myself not wanting to go. I stood to walk away, to sit with my own ghost, and it was then that he finally spoke.

"Thanks."

One single word and that thread wrapped its way around my heart.

It was a different kind of love then. Not necessarily romantic. But visceral. I was too young to really understand the grown-up kind of love. Instead, it was this yearning to be near someone who understood what loss felt like. To share a common denominator—death. And to do so without judgment.

I was the sad loser girl at school. But there, with him, I was someone else.

That love grew and continued to blossom with each passing day. That thread binding us tighter and tighter. He was my constant. My safe space. My best friend.

We had picnics in that cemetery, we played hide and seek, we made it ours. We talked about the past like it was a lifetime ago, when things weren't always covered in darkness, and we allowed ourselves to be vulnerable. We shared things that we had never shared with anyone else. Not our remaining parent, not our so-called friends, not the school counselor that we were both forced to visit. Everyone else just wanted to fix us, to figure out how to put us back together.

We didn't expect that of each other. Not then, not ever.

And when the time finally came for us to part, it was like I lost the glue that had been holding me steady for all those years we were friends. I didn't just lose my best friend, my first kiss, my first love...I lost a piece of me. With the days that turned into weeks that morphed into months and months, I lost hope, too. I lost faith that I would ever *feel* again. I was numb and hurt and I was so fucking mad. Angry that I allowed someone the power to wreck me after I gave them my heart. Furious that I was dumb enough to think he would eventually come back.

We were kids, but our connection was everything.

At one point, I almost convinced myself it was never real, that it never happened. That I had created it as some weird coping mechanism to deal with the loss of my mother. To distract me from my abusive, alcoholic father. But there was proof, reminding me that what Co and I had shared wasn't a figment of my miserable imagination. Old polaroids of us at the beach, seashells we had collected, a tattered necklace he had made me out of string, a faded sweatshirt of his that he let me borrow one cold night that I never gave back.

And the biggest reminder of them all—the gaping hole in my chest.

Plus, massive trust issues.

Now, a decade later, that same beautifully broken boy, the one who helped me nurse a butterfly back to life we had found in the grill of his dad's old truck, stands in front of me, those ocean-blue eyes staring into mine.

"Don't worry about me." Co breaks off a piece of the muffin and pops it into his mouth.

That's all I've done since the moment I laid eyes on him when we were just kids.

"You're right, though." He cups my cheek. "We haven't gotten enough time together lately. What can I do?"

A throat clears from behind us. A bit of chatter following the interruption. I glance behind me to find Magnus and Dominic coming down the stairs and into our line of sight.

"Actually," I say loud enough for all of them to hear.

"What are you doing up?" Dominic's brows pinch together. "Did something happen?"

Magnus rushes around him to get to me first. He pulls my face between his hands and presses his lips onto mine. "God damn you're gorgeous in the morning."

I kiss him back. "But not in the afternoon?"

Dom reaches me, smoothing the hair that Magnus had tousled off my forehead. He plants his lips in the spot that he had cleared. "Really though, is everything okay?"

"Since I have you all here, and I have no idea for how long. We need to talk," I tell them.

"Oh shit, this is serious." Magnus hops onto the stool next to mine and holds his tattooed hands around one of mine. "Are you breaking up with us?"

The door to the garage area creaks open and Simon steps through.

"Am I interrupting something?" Simon stops with one foot still outside.

"Yes," Co tells him.

"No," I say louder. "You can come in."

Magnus leans in closer and whispers, "Are you going to break up with us *in front* of Beckett?"

I squeeze his hands. "No, goofball." I shift my gaze at Dom and Co. "But something does have to give. I hardly see any of you, and when I do, you're all evasive as hell. So, I propose, you carve some time out of your busy schedules for a date night. Actually, no, I insist. Non-negotiable."

Co and Dom exchange a look like they're communicating telepathically or something.

"Okay, that's way better than breaking up." Magnus brings my hand to his mouth and kisses my knuckles. "And I absolutely agree."

I turn to him. "Thank you." But the fact that Dom and Co haven't immediately joined in has me holding my breath and waiting for the possibility of rejection to rip me to shreds. I already feel weird enough that I'm asking my boyfriends for some quality time.

Magnus continues to smooch my hand. "I'll have my people get ahold of your people."

"Noted." I roll my eyes but am otherwise grateful for his humor in this incredibly tense time.

Simon remains quiet by the door, but I can sense his energy from across the room.

"How about tomorrow?" Co finally says. "Just you and me. I'll put something together. I promise."

Dom places his large hand on my back. "And I'll work on a date for next week. How's that?"

"Really?" I flit my gaze between both of them, those tears that almost formed earlier still wanting to rise to the surface.

"Yes." Dominic nudges my chin softly and tilts it up toward him. He kisses my lips with such ease that you'd never imagine he's the brutal man who murders people on a semi-regular basis. "I'm sorry you've been feeling neglected."

"It's okay," I mumble against his mouth. But is it? Is it really? I understand they're running a criminal conglomerate but they're the ones who insisted I be a part of their life.

Well, that's not totally true—it was my doing, too, but they could have said no.

All at once, multiple phones buzz. My three men reach into their respective pockets and check the notifications.

"Let me guess," I sigh.

"Sorry, princess." Magnus wraps his arms around me and hugs me tightly. He places a kiss on my cheek. "Love you."

"Love you more," I grumble.

"Never." He releases me and stands, slapping Dom on the shoulder. "You driving?"

"Always," I say, barely a whisper. And honestly, it feels like the truth.

Magnus turns back toward me and caresses my face. "I'll plan something, too, don't worry."

"We all will." Co grips my hand before following Dom and Magnus toward the door where Simon still stands.

Dom pauses on his way over. "I've got to make a coffee real quick."

"Already waiting for you in the car," Simon tells him. "Americano, black." He looks to Magnus. "Cappuccino, extra whip." Then at Co. "Tall coffee with a shot of espresso."

With all that caffeine, it's no wonder Co never sleeps. Or maybe it's just the fuel that keeps him up during his late nights and early mornings.

"You know, Beckett." Magnus latches onto Simon's shoulder and gives it a firm shake. "You're kinda growing on me."

Co shoves past Simon and leaves the space, his absence tugging at that invisible thread wrapped around my heart. Dom mutters a "thanks" on his way by. And with one more farewell, the door latches shut and leaves just Simon and me here alone in this massive kitchen.

His emerald gaze locks onto mine. "You okay?"

I nod slowly and hold the blanket Co gave me tighter around my body. "I'm tired, that's all."

He whips his head toward the stairs. "Why don't you go back to sleep? I'll be down here if you need me."

"I don't need a babysitter, Simon."

"You keep telling yourself that."

"I thought this place was supposed to be impenetrable. I'm not safe in their home?"

"Your home," he says without hesitation. "This is your home too, June."

"Whatever." I hop off the stool, dragging my feet over to the sitting room, and plop onto the expensive couch.

Simon walks into the kitchen and pushes a few buttons on Dominic's fancy coffee machine.

"Why didn't you get yourself something when you got the rest for the guys?"

Simon shrugs. "I would have gotten you something but I didn't think you'd be awake yet."

"Yeah, yeah," I mumble into the arm of the couch. "I think we've established that everyone knows I'm not a morning person."

Simon carries his drink over into the sitting area and takes a seat in the chair near the foot of the couch I'm in. "I'm not either." He blows on the steaming cup and takes a cautious sip. "Fuck that's hot."

Through my heavy eyes, I study the shape of his jaw, the hard lines and sharp edges. Even with the stubble from his beard coming in, his bone structure is fucking immaculate. My gaze trails to the coffee in his grasp, the veins prominent on the back of his hand. I don't mean to pay him this much attention, but there's no denying his maker spent extra time perfecting him.

"What's that ring?" I ask him.

"Which one?" He turns the black thing on his middle finger and fidgets with the other on his index finger.

"The bigger one."

"Family heirloom."

I close my eyes and wait for him to continue.

"My grandad gave it to me when I was ten. That was shortly before he passed..."

"I'm sorry," I mumble.

"He was sick."

"I'm sorry," I say again, as if the second time will somehow make the words actually mean something to him.

"He told me to hold onto it for him. He was paranoid at the time—used to go on about someone rummaging through his things. Pretty sure he was just losing his mind, ya know?"

"Mmhm," I mutter to keep him talking.

"He wasn't always like that. We used to have a blast together. He'd take me to ball games...basketball *and* baseball. Although, baseball was both our favorites."

He hesitates but continues, "I looked forward to those games with him." Simon laughs like he's recalling a memory. "We'd get hotdogs first. Without question. And then we'd get the biggest bucket of popcorn. I'd nearly puke from eating so much."

"I love popcorn," I tell him.

"And if I wasn't already full enough, he'd buy me a gigantic cotton candy."

"Which color?" I ask him.

"Blue, definitely blue."

"We should go sometime," I say.

"What?"

But instead of answering him, I accidentally drift to sleep.

---

I wake to the sound of screaming. My chest aches. My throat raw. I blink and try to catch my breath. My eyes finally focus, and I settle them on the man who's holding onto me, nothing but fear and concern caked on his face.

"You're okay," Simon tells me. "You're safe."

I steady myself and scoot out of his grasp. "I'm sorry." Bringing my knees up to my chest, I try to recall what I was even dreaming about.

Simon moves from the floor where he was kneeling beside the couch, and sits next to me while maintaining some space between us. "How long?"

I look over at him. "What?"

"How long have you been having nightmares?" His jaw tenses.

"Oh." I hug myself tighter. "Um, like...forever? I don't know. Don't you have them?"

"Every night." Simon twirls the ring on his index finger with his thumb.

"What about?" I ask him even despite it being such a personal question.

Simon sucks in a breath and exhales. "Well, for starters, you're in a lot of them."

I chuckle. "So, I'm not your dream girl, I'm your nightmare girl."

He side-eyes me and shakes his head. "Something like that."

"Am I chasing you around with a knife Michael Myers style?"

"Something like that," he repeats with a grin.

"And the ones I'm not starring in?"

"Uh..."

"You don't have to, it's okay." I turn toward him and lean my head on the back of the couch.

"Promise you won't laugh...or tell anyone?"

I hold out my pinkie toward him.

He locks his around mine and gives it a little shake.

Our hands lower onto the couch with our pinkies still intertwined.

"I can't swim. Not well, at least..."

I look for any indication that he's lying, that he's fucking with me. "Really?"

Simon bobs his head up and down. "Yep."

"Lots of people can't swim," I tell him in a weak attempt to make him feel better.

"Maybe lots of kids, but not grown adults."

"Why didn't you learn when you were younger?"

Simon looks away like he's recalling a memory. Every bit of him seems to tighten with the recollection. "I just didn't." He takes his free hand and runs it through his dark brown hair. "And in these nightmares, I'm drowning."

"That must be terrifying." I've had my fair share of nightmares: being burned alive, chased, attacked, cheated on, assaulted in any way you can imagine. I can't say I've ever had one where I was unable to swim, though. I guess our minds torture us with the things we're most afraid of or insecure about.

"It's not a good time." He turns his head back toward me. "Enough about me though. Are you okay? You were screaming something fierce."

"I don't even remember what it was." But that's a lie, because, with each passing second, pieces of it come into my head and taunt me with their memory. I won't admit that to him, though. Instead, I'll keep it bottled up and hope I never have to dream it, or live it, ever again.

"Even if you do..." Simon keeps his voice low. "I wouldn't let anything happen to you."

"Don't make promises you can't keep."

"Wow, are you really insulting my abilities?"

"Speaking of your *abilities*. You said you were going to—"

He cuts me off. "It's in the works. Give me a minute to figure out the details." Simon raises a brow. "Although, I may have to work it into your *date* schedule."

I grin at him. "Am I sensing jealousy?"

"Kinda, but honestly, sounds like they're the ones who should be jealous since I spend more time with you than they do."

"Touché."

He's not wrong. Simon and I spend every day together, and aside from fucking and macking on each other, we do pretty much everything me and the rest of the guys do.

If they weren't the ones who insist on keeping Simon around, I'd be concerned I was borderline cheating.

My gaze falls to our pinkies still interlocked. I release his and pull mine away, that line blurring too damn much for my liking. I would never do anything to jeopardize my relationship with the guys—but it's difficult to deny the friendship building between myself and their enemy.

# CHAPTER 4

# *Coen*

So help me God, if we do not finish up this meeting in the next five minutes, I am going to murder every fucking person in this room.

I check my watch and sigh.

It's either I kill them, or June kills me for being late for our date.

Especially after seeing the hurt on her face yesterday. I hadn't realized things had been affecting her that severely. But that's what I get for not paying attention. I've been consumed with more pressing matters and not focused on my main priority—her.

"Hayes, are you with us?" Dominic snaps his fingers in front of my face.

I smack his hand away. "Fuck off."

His jaw tenses, and for a split second there, I forget we're in a room with people other than just us.

*Fuck.* I just disrespected my direct superior.

I rise to my feet, shuffling the stack of papers in front of me. "Two shipments were intercepted. Four casualties. I got it."

"Where the fuck do you think you're going?" Dominic calls out to me as I make my way to the door.

"I have to go. It's important."

"You'll be dealt with later." Dominic's parting words don't shake me. He can punish me all he wants; nothing would be more severe than losing her again.

I rush outside, hop into the driver's side of my Audi RS4, and push the button to start the engine. The thing purrs to life, the exhaust crackling and sputtering. I waste no more time, throwing the thing into reverse and backing out of the parking lot. I slam it into drive and heave myself directly into traffic, darting around the meaningless vehicles that get in my way. The light ahead of me turns red but I thrust my foot onto the gas and blast right through it.

Flashing blue and red lights catch my attention in the rear-view mirror but I don't let up on the accelerator, instead, I push it down harder, the speedometer reading eighty-two in a thirty-five.

The police car struggles to keep up as I pop in and around traffic.

I poke the touch screen on the dash, dialing one of my saved numbers.

It rings once, then twice before a man answers. "Officer Bradshaw."

"You've got a man on Ninth near Parsons. Call him off."

"You're going—"

But I interrupt him. "If you want your paycheck, you better fucking earn it or I'll find someone else to do it for me. Call him off. *Now.*"

"Yes, sir, Mr. Hayes."

I disconnect the receiver and glance in my rearview, waiting and wondering if this incompetent fuck is going to do what's asked of him. It's either that or I stop this car and put a bullet in the cop's head. That alternative is a little messier to clean up than a speeding ticket.

But I'll do whatever it takes to get to her sooner rather than later.

I whiz through another intersection and turn left at the next, my car struggling to grip the pavement as I push it to its limit. The blue and red lights follow, hot on my ass.

Guess I'm going to have two cops to kill—the one behind me and the one who didn't do his job.

The idea isn't all that unappealing. I don't necessarily mind exterminating useless people but it's the fact that it might cut into my time with June that I'm concerned about.

Luckily for them though, that won't happen tonight, because when the flashing lights suddenly stop blaring in my rear-view mirror and the cop car stops pursuing me, I realize that I'm in the clear.

One obstacle down.

I skid to a stop at the gated entrance to our house. I fumble with the fucking switch, pushing and repushing buttons until finally, the thing cooperates and opens. I rush the rest of the way in, forcing my car into park in the garage and hopping out before it has a chance to cool down. I bolt around the other luxurious vehicles parked in here and burst through the door.

June stands there, a sight for sore eyes, wearing the dress I had picked out for her and the bracelet I gave her after she graduated from college.

Simon is next to her, entirely too close for my liking.

Both of them stare at me, a bit startled, like I may have interrupted something.

June is the first to speak. "You made it."

I continue into the house, stepping in front of Simon and pressing my lips to June's cheek. "With two minutes to spare. Give me five to get changed out of this?" I tug at the collar of my shirt.

"I think you look pretty damn good." June squeezes my hand.

"I'll be quick, promise." I turn to Simon and shift my tone. "You're dismissed."

"Aye, aye, captain." Simon avoids my stare and looks at June. "See you tomorrow."

"See you then," she confirms.

Once he's gone, a weight is lifted from my chest. It's our fault he's around but it doesn't make it any less intolerable. Simon Beckett is in love with my soulmate, and he's the reason she almost died. But he's also the reason she didn't.

I hate him more than I hate myself for losing all those years with her.

And here he is, spending more time with her than I am, because of a threat I haven't yet eliminated. A problem I'm desperately trying to solve so Dom, Magnus, and I can finally give in to our desires. So we can maybe breathe a little easier at having brought the woman we collectively love into our dangerous world.

Until then, it's early mornings and long, sleepless nights away from my better half.

"Is something going on between you two?" I ask her even though the second the question leaves my lips, regret courses through me.

June strolls over to the table where various booze lines the top. She pulls a crystal cup from the tray and pours herself a dram of bourbon. "Is that how we're going to start the night, Co?"

"No, you're right. I'm sorry." I follow her over, take the cup from her grasp, and sip some of the golden liquid. "I shouldn't have doubted you." I give her the drink back and kiss her cheek before disappearing upstairs.

It's not her that I doubt, it's me. Ten years ago, I never would have wondered whether she loved another, but that was when I gave her all of me. Now, she only gets the pieces and parts left over that I manage to scrounge together. She deserves someone whole, someone present, someone capable of giving her everything she could ever want. That time apart changed me, as did the person I morphed into in her absence. I turned cold, callous...murderous. And the worst part of all is that I didn't hate the person I became. It was easy once I flipped the switch, almost like that version of me was just under the surface the whole time. June was what kept the evil at bay, and without her, it consumed me fully.

I want to be what she needs, but what if I'm not capable of it? What if I'm too damaged, too broken, too fucking wicked to be the man that is worthy of her love? What if I'm too far gone to be saved? What if there's no coming back from the things that I've done?

If she knew the truth of what I'm capable of, she'd walk away.

And maybe that's why I busy myself with the tasks of eliminating threats; I'm terrified to admit that if she saw me, *really* saw me, then this fairytale would be over. But if I keep giving her less and less of me, she'll be gone either way.

It's only a matter of time until my worst fear is realized and I lose her again.

Because whether I want to acknowledge it or not, she's better off without me.

I'm just too damn selfish to let her go...not yet.

Not when I only just got her back.

I shower in record time and slide into the outfit I already set out for myself this morning. Taking the stairs two at a time, I clasp my watch around my wrist and count the minutes that have passed—four.

"I haven't even finished my drink," June says from her spot on the couch in the sitting room.

I grin at her and approach the bar. "Gives me a chance to have one, too, then."

"Aren't you driving?"

"I am." But I make one anyway, knowing damn well even if my tolerance to alcohol weren't so high, I'll still be under the legal limit.

As if laws applied to men like me.

I pour some amber liquid into a glass and sit on the edge of the chair near June.

She stands from her spot and strolls over to me, her body stopping between my legs. "Your hair's wet." June runs her hand along my damp locks.

"Is that a deal breaker?" I ask her, my heart picking up its pace at her nearness, an effect she will forever have on me.

From the moment she sat down next to me in that cemetery, I have been completely enamored with this girl. The butterflies I got that day still present today.

"It's kinda sexy, actually." She continues to play with my hair, her touch temporarily melting away my worries.

"Yeah?" I grip her waist and tug her toward me.

She leans in close, her mouth hovering near mine. "Mmhm."

I bridge the gap and hungrily press my lips on hers. My tongue darts in and dances with hers as she steps even closer to me, both of her hands gripping the back of my head.

She kisses me deeper and I match her intensity, setting my drink on the nearby table without even looking.

With one hand still on her waist, I run the other up her thigh and under her dress. I skim my palm up higher, noting the lack of panties, and continue on my exploration. I glide my hand between her legs and find her wet entrance. Using her moans against my mouth and the arch of her body toward me as permission, I trace my finger along the outside of her and dip it inside, paying attention to the way she tightens around me. I shove another into her and curve my fingers toward the softness of her G-spot, rocking them gently.

"Co," she breathes into me, her pussy clenching my fingers.

I dig my hand into her waist and stand, nudging her down and onto the chair. I break my mouth away from hers and drop to my knees before her, immediately bringing my head between her legs to taste her sweetness. I glide my tongue over her clit and drive those two fingers back inside but this time with a third to fill her even more. I suck on her nub, and savor the taste of her lust.

If someone would have told me a year ago that I'd be burying my face in her, I never would have believed them. But here I am, ready to suffocate myself with her pussy.

June scrapes her nails against my scalp and tugs me toward her, moaning and pivoting toward me. "Fuck," she breathes—her tautness telling me just how close she is.

I wiggle my fingers exactly how I know she likes it, and a second later, she pulsates around me, her body quivering under my touch. I stay there after she's finished, lapping up the sweetness dripping out of her, wishing like hell I could survive solely on her alone.

Finally, she scoots back and nudges me upward, pressing her lips against mine. "What was that for?"

I kiss her back and stand, holding out my hand to help her up. "Had to start the night on a good note."

"That wasn't good, Co. That was fucking great." She smooths out the wrinkles that have formed on her dress and reaches for her cup, draining the contents of it into her mouth.

"Don't give me that much credit." Having forgotten I had even poured myself a drink, I down it in one gulp, the warmth coating my mouth and trickling down my throat.

"Where are we going?" she asks while latching onto her clutch and shoving her phone inside.

"It's a surprise." I reach into the pocket of my pressed slacks. "Speaking of..." I pull out a silk tie. "Turn around."

June raises a brow but complies. "Kinky."

I wrap the thing around her eyes and secure it behind her head, ignoring the rampant thoughts that come to mind. Like I need any more ideas of the things I'd like to do to her.

I guide her through the garage, help her into the passenger seat of my car, and shut her in. Verifying the gun in my waistband holster is loaded, I shove it back in its home and climb into the driver's side.

A soft melody plays over the speakers, and June quietly hums along.

I'm transformed to a time long ago, when things were simple, untainted. When it was just a boy and a girl, falling in love one day at a time. I loved her from that first moment, but it was all the little ones that made it something truly powerful. Something I never thought I'd find again after I had lost her. I knew my feelings would always remain, but didn't expect them to be reciprocated. There were times over the years when I'd sneak away, when I would track her down, just to catch a glimpse of her. I watched her from a distance, my heart aching to be near her, but knowing it was impossible. That I missed my window of opportunity once all those years had passed. I told myself she was happy, better off without me, and that she would never understand what I had been through in our time apart.

I fucked up the moment I got into that truck with my father, and I continued to ruin things with each life I took trying to get back to her. I just didn't fully realize that until I stood in the bloodied aftermath of the massacre I created, and Dominic told me that there was no turning back. That I had two choices: death, or embrace the darkness.

I should have chosen the former, but I was too much of a coward. I took his hand and let him guide me further into the abyss, fully accepting the man I had become—reborn in blood.

He warned me that no one was safe. Anyone I cared for should be left in the past. So that's what I did. I left her where I thought she would never be harmed by the life that had taken its hold of me.

Eventually, the desire to see her overcame me, and that's when I finally tracked her down. I needed a glimpse of her, something to confirm that the decision I made was not in vain. She was having coffee with a friend at a café we used to go to. I watched her through the window, my heart being ripped to shreds at the sight of her. But when I saw her smile, could hear her laughter float through the space and to me, I knew I had done the right thing. That I had given her an opportunity at a better life than what I could have given her. That she could be happy without me, and that my presence would have done nothing but bring her down.

I was proud of her for moving on, even though it was like losing her all over again.

I would suffer through that loss over and over if it meant she would be okay.

And so I did, over the years, rip my heart to shreds to verify she was safe...happy.

Because at the end of the day, that's all I really cared about.

I almost spoke to her once, the urge nearly overtaking me. She was a freshman in college, wandering around the campus of the local university, her gaze darting from a map in her hands to the area around her. She was lost, unsure of where to go. My feet betrayed me, inching out from behind the building I was concealed by. But I was halted by another guy who approached her, mumbling what I can only guess was a question of whether she needed assistance.

The tall man pointed to a nearby building and she nodded, a soft smile of gratitude appearing on her face.

It could have been me but I was too weak, or maybe too strong, to give in.

The two of them shook hands, no doubt exchanging formalities, and went their separate ways.

I left town that day and didn't come back for a while, busying myself with whatever task I could to distract myself from the sad reality that she would never be mine. Pathetically trying to find comfort in someone else, I slept around, but I never felt anything more than a mild attraction to the strangers I occasionally fucked. I convinced myself I didn't have feelings—that they disappeared the same day she did from my life, but still, I was drawn back to this town and the brown-eyed girl who stole my heart.

I was a fool to tiptoe so close to the fire when I stepped foot in a bar I knew she sometimes went to. I just wanted another glance, another morsel of her to tide me over until the next time I couldn't stand to be away from her any longer. I never meant to bump into her, to talk to her, to hear the sadness—the *anger*—in her voice. She was bitter, and honestly, I deserved that. I deserved much more. I didn't expect to feel *so much* though. Her touch was electric, her presence like a defibrillator to my heart. I had told myself over the years that I could handle it, but it wasn't until that moment that I realized I was sorely mistaken.

Everything I thought I had shut away came rushing back in, and my love for her overflowed like it had never stopped in the first place.

But just as I had all those other times, I swallowed down the painful reality that the June I fell in love with was no more, and that the version of me that once existed died along with the men I slaughtered in my feeble attempt to get back to her.

I had doomed us without even knowing.

June reaches blindly over toward me, nudging the shifter in her attempt to locate me. "Where's your damn hand?"

I chuckle and place my palm on hers, resting them both on her leg. "I'm right here." *I always have been, June, even when you thought I wasn't.* I'll never go anywhere—not as long as I live.

"How much longer?" She glances over, despite having a blindfold still wrapped around her eyes.

"No peeking," I tell her. "We're almost there."

"I was trying to track where we were but I got lost after Seventh Avenue."

"We'll have to practice that sometime. It's a good skill to have." Just in case... because in our world, you'll never know when it's the difference between life and death.

I disregard the buzz of my phone in my pocket and pull into the parking lot.

"Hmm," June mumbles, no doubt trying to figure out where I'm taking her.

I hop out, rushing over to open her door and help her from the passenger seat. Her cool hand fits perfectly in mine and manages to calm my anxious heart. No amount of time will ever make those nervous jitters go away. It's like every time I'm with her, I'm transported back to that self-conscious pre-teen who's bubbling with insecurities. What if I do the wrong thing? What if she doesn't like me? What if I mess something up?

But the worst damage has already been done. I broke her trust. I left her—the worst crime of all, especially knowing how that was the ultimate offense. She had abandonment issues, and all I did was exacerbate them. Even if it was against my will, I hurt her either way. And I'll forever be paying the price.

"What's that smell?" June sniffs at the air.

I guide her through the front door of the place and once we're inside, I tug the fabric of my tie to release it from shielding her eyes.

She squints, blinks a few times, and brings her hand to cover her mouth. "You didn't."

I don't take my gaze off of her as she breaks out into a huge smile and throws her arms around my neck, hugging me tightly.

"Co, are you kidding me?"

I still don't look away when she releases me and takes in the candlelit pizza shop that we spent many evenings in when we were kids.

The shop is empty aside from us and a couple workers in the back. A lone table sits in the center of the room, decked with more candles and a chilled bottle of champagne.

"This..." She strolls back toward me and pulls me into her. "This is perfect."

"Yeah?" I tuck a strand of her black hair behind her ear.

"Yeah." June stands taller and presses her lips on mine.

The single kiss melts the tension from my shoulders.

"I didn't think you remembered," she tells me, her face just an inch from mine.

"I could never forget. Not a single detail of us."

"Oh my god." June holds me at an arm's length and laughs. "That fucking pizza challenge."

I shake my head, the recollection of that day coming to me in an instant. "Can we not?"

"Co." She continues to giggle. "That was brutal. We ate so much pizza I thought we were both going to die."

Back then, neither of us had much money. We came here because the pizza was cheap and good and the owner wasn't mean to us like a lot of the other shop owners were. He served dollar slices, and sometimes, he would even give us two for one.

We devised this idiotic plan where we were going to do the pizza challenge—eat a gigantic pizza in thirty minutes and if you succeed, it's free. Otherwise, it's forty bucks.

To us kids, the idea of eating that much money in pizza was a fucking dream. We had no doubts going into it that we could pull it off, but when June and I hit the halfway mark, the doubts started flowing in. A crowd had gathered, random strangers cheering on the two dumb ass kids stuffing their faces with pizza. People clapped and encouraged us, and just when I thought we wouldn't be able to pull it off, June and I got our second wind and shoved so much pizza into our mouths that I wasn't sure I'd ever crave it ever again. The last ten seconds ticked by as the crowd yelled, the owner joining in, every single person in that place wanting us to win.

And because we were both too fucking stubborn, and too broke to pay the tab if we didn't, we won.

Everyone yelled and I tried to force a smile, but the amount of pizza filling me kept my celebrations at bay. June and I locked eyes from across the table, a sort of telepathic stare saying, *we did it, we did the impossible.*

And maybe eating a massive pizza wasn't impossible, but to us, it felt like it, and in a way, it was like a sign that we would get through anything—together.

We had spent the rest of the day suffering from our brilliant idea, but as the fullness wore off, a renewed bond had formed between us.

"Let's never do that again." She places her hand on her stomach. "I can still remember how stuffed I was for what felt like days. I thought cheese and pepperoni were going to come out of my nose."

"I'm surprised it didn't." I take her hand and guide her to the table. "Hopefully you're back in good standing with pizza, otherwise, we can go somewhere else."

She sits onto the seat but reaches over to squeeze my forearm. "I'm not kidding when I say this is perfect, Co."

The door to the kitchen opens, and a bright-eyed older man comes out with a steaming pie in his grasp. "My two favorite customers," he greets us.

After all this time, the same guy runs the place. When I made arrangements for tonight, I had asked him why he's never retired but he insisted he loves his job so much that retirement was never something he considered. He said he hoped that someday, one of his children would take over, but that he wasn't holding his breath.

"Jovi, you're still here?" June rises and hugs the round man after he's set the pizza on our table.

"Until the day I die." He embraces her and pulls away to look her over, but not in the creepy way that most men do. "You're all grown up, kid." He smacks my shoulder. "You both are." Jovi glances between us. "But don't let me interrupt. You two have a wonderful evening, and if you need anything don't be afraid to holler. I'll send Jonah out in a bit to check on you."

"Thanks, Jovi," June calls after him.

The two of us settle into our chairs, cutesy grins on our faces like we transformed back into those kids who were scrounging for change to get a slice of pizza to share. And now I have more money than I know what to do with, my heart still belonging to that same girl from all those years ago.

June digs into a slice, closing her eyes and moaning as she chews. "This is exactly how I remember."

"You haven't been back?" I ask her.

She wipes at the corners of her mouth and swallows the bite. "Nope. Have you?"

I shake my head. "No."

"I avoided anything that reminded me of you." June sips from the glass of water near her. "It honestly took me a long time to go back and visit my mom, afraid that her ghost wouldn't be the only one I'd find."

"I never meant to ruin *that* for you."

She shrugs. "That was the past."

"I'm sorry." I reach for the champagne bottle. "Here's to the future."

"Co?"

"Hm?" I fill her glass and then mine.

"You never really told me what happened."

"With what?" I respond, afraid to meet her gaze. There are few things in this world I'm afraid of and she's at the top of the list.

"With everything, really. Your dad, why you had to leave, why you never came back, why you're...*different* now. I mean, you've told me bits and pieces, but never the whole story." June nibbles the edge of her pizza and waits for me to say something, anything.

But where do I begin? And how can I prepare either of us for the truth of it all?

That the sweet boy she fell for ten years ago transformed into a murderous lunatic.

"Why didn't you come back? Tell me that, at least."

"I thought I was protecting you," I confess the only truth that isn't too ugly to admit.

"How?"

"I...I did some terrible things, J. Things I thought I had to do. Things that changed me. Things that were supposed to bring me closer to you, but ended up being the very thing that made returning to you impossible."

June stares at me, her gaze scanning my face. "And I thought it was because you didn't love me."

"Exact opposite, really. Everything I did, that I still *do*, is because I love you, maybe too much."

"You know I waited for you?" She continues to look directly at me, her eyes glistening. "I went to your house every day for months. I sat on your porch, glancing up at every vehicle that went down your road. I broke in through your window and slept in your bed, hoping and praying that I'd wake up to find you there. I couldn't tell you how many times I checked and rechecked our answering machine to see if it still worked. If I ever hear the automated words, *no new messages* ever again, I'll probably lose my mind.

"I was sad for the longest time. And then my sadness turned into anger. It was easier to be mad at you than anything else." June chuckles. "My whole personality is based around being constantly pissed off. I'm not even sure if I could fix it if I tried."

"I thought you were happy."

"How would you know? You never bothered to find out."

I recall all the times I stalked her. That I lurked in the shadows to catch a glimpse of the girl I would never move on from. But I don't dare admit the truth. Instead, I say, "You're right."

"I'm not going to judge you for what you did, Coen, whatever it is, I can handle it." She reaches across the table and latches onto my hand. "I know you still see me as that fractured girl in the cemetery, but I outgrew her a long time ago. You might think you've changed, but so have I."

I consider my next move, a large part of me wanting to confess everything, but all of those underlying insecurities rising to the surface telling me to keep my mouth shut. I fight both versions of myself and study the gorgeous face of the woman in front of me. She really is right. We're not those same kids from before. Our love for each other is the only thing that truly remains from that time long ago.

"My dad," I begin. "He pissed some really powerful people off." I unravel the story one piece at a time, glossing over the details that aren't totally necessary. "He didn't tell me everything, but from what I gathered, they threatened him...something so bad that he shoved everything he could into the bed of that old pickup and nearly dragged me out of the house kicking and screaming. It wasn't until one drunken night that he confessed what happened with my mom."

June holds onto my hand tighter, an anchor keeping me from spiraling at the recollection of my life being turned upside down.

"He's the reason why she died, J. My fucking dad."

"Co..." A tear rolls down her cheek.

"He said those same people were after him, that they were after me, too, and that we had to run." I take a breath in and exhale. "We hopped around different motels, never staying more than a couple nights at a time. We were running out of money, not like we had much to begin with…" I look at her. "You remember what it was like growing up."

June nods. "Yeah."

"I found a dollar that day. I was kicking rocks in the parking lot of a run-down motel, and saw it peeking out from under some leaves. I couldn't believe it; thought I had hit the lottery. I was so fucking excited that all I could think about was the vending machine I had passed twenty times already. I ran right to it, straightening the edges of the bill on the side of the machine before shoving it in the little slot. I even remember the button I hit, D3, and the sound of it whirling to life, the swirly thing pushing the bag of powdered donuts closer and closer to the edge. They thudded when they hit the bottom, and I nearly got my hand stuck when I reached inside to pull them out. It was stupid, really, to be that excited, but it felt like the first good thing that had happened in a while."

I let my gaze trail to our interlocked hands, hoping like hell it'll give me the strength to continue the story, to reach the plot twist that set my life spiraling out of control.

"But when I was on my way back, this pit formed in my stomach. You ever get that? When something is about to go wrong?"

June bobs her head in agreement.

"I could hear commotion, people screaming at each other. Which wasn't all that uncommon considering where we usually shacked up. But this one felt different. Bigger." I think back to that day, the scent of the damp air so strong it's like I'm there now. It was dark out, but there were overhead lights, some of them flickering, some not on at all. "I paused at the corner of the building, poking my head around it and trying to figure out what it was. That's when I saw him…"

June seems to hold her breath in anticipation of what I'm about to say next.

"My dad, kneeling on the ground, his hands tied behind him. A man, easily twice his size punched him across the face. Blood and spit went flying everywhere. The guy grabbed my dad's collar and pulled him up again. But this time, he didn't use his fist. For a brief second, my dad looked directly at me and shook his head. It was subtle, barely even recognizable, but I could tell he was warning me not to come any closer. And like the coward I was, I stayed concealed in place, my hands gripping that wall and watching as that stranger put a bullet between my dad's eyes."

"Co…"

"I wanted to scream. I wanted to fight them, do something. But I couldn't. All I could do was watch as the other guy with my dad's murderer ransacked our motel room, probably looking for me. They climbed into a white panel van and drove away, leaving my dad there to bleed out."

June moves from her seat and comes over to me, wrapping her arms around my head and hugging me to her chest.

"I was so mad," I tell her. "They took my mom, they took you, they took my dad."

She tilts my face up at her. "I'm right here, Co, I'm right here."

"I couldn't let them hurt you, J. I had to stay away; it was the only way I could keep you safe."

"Shh, I know." She presses her lips to my forehead over and over. "I understand."

She might understand but does she believe me? Does she realize that all I ever did was want to protect her? That bringing her into this world was never an option in my mind, and that doing so has only made me fear for her that much more? I wanted more than anything to be with her, but I could never be selfish with her, not when it meant risking her life. There was no escaping this for me, but for her, there was hope.

I bring her onto my lap and hold on tight, never wanting to let my sweet girl go. "All I had was a license plate number and enough rage to burn down the entire city."

"Is that what you did, Co? The thing you're afraid to tell me about?" June runs her fingers through my hair and settles her hand along my cheek.

"Dominic was the one to find me, after I went on my rampage." I swallow and play the memory in my mind. Blood everywhere. Caked on my hands. Pooled around my feet. Dead bodies lying haphazardly around. Something from a horror film, caused by a teenager hellbent on getting revenge. "He should have killed me right there. But he didn't, he saw my potential."

"For what it's worth, I'm glad he didn't."

I stare into her eyes, willing her to really understand what I'm about to say. "If you saw what I had done, I'm not so sure you'd feel the same."

# CHAPTER 5
## June

Just when I think Coen can't surprise me anymore tonight, he guides me onto the rooftop of Jovi's pizza shop where a blanket and more candles are set up. Glistening string lights are strung about, and a soft melody flows through the nighttime air.

"This is beautiful," I tell him while clutching his hand.

We used to sneak up here when we were kids. Giggling and shushing each other as we climbed the ladder in hopes that we wouldn't get caught for trespassing. Part of me wonders if Jovi knew all along and just looked the other way. A small gesture since we didn't have much. We were never the type to destroy anything, always leaving things the way we found them—except for when we would break in and steal ice cream from the shop down the way. That's another story entirely, though.

Here we are, ten years later, a million things changed but one constant remains —our love for one another.

I held so much resentment and anger, letting it bubble and fester into every aspect of my life, when in reality, Coen had suffered more torment than I had. Sure, I had to deal with my own fatherly shit, but that's nothing compared to what Coen went through. To learn the truth about his mother's death *and* witness his dad be murdered? That's enough to drive someone to the lengths he took. I can't say I wouldn't have done the exact thing, given the opportunity.

Coen did what he thought he had to do, and what kind of person would I be if I blamed him for that?

I just wish he could have found some way to tell me, to come to me sooner. But I blame myself for him feeling that he couldn't trust me with this information. That I wouldn't have done everything in my power to protect him the same way he did for me. We could have figured it out together, just like we had done with everything else. But at the end of the day, it's not some pizza challenge. It's life and death.

"Here." Co takes my hand and guides me over to the blanket. He sits next to me and grabs the bottle of bourbon that was already up here. "You want a drink?"

I slide my heels off and pull my feet up toward my butt, turning toward him. "Sure."

He pours a couple fingers' worth into a glass and gives it to me.

"This is no Dixie cup." I smirk and take a long swallow of the golden liquid. "And it sure beats that cheap shit we used to drink."

"I'm sorry about all of our lost time, J. I think about it and it kills me. I wish we could go back to that day and start over again. I would never get in that truck with him, I would have insisted I stay. We could have figured it out." He latches onto the glass in my hand and downs the rest of its contents, then pours some more in.

"You realize we were kids, right, Co? I know you're a few years older than me, but you can't blame yourself for what happened. For any of it, really." I sigh and lean back. "There are countless things I regret doing in my life, but no matter how much I beat myself up about them, it won't change what's already happened." I reach out and skim my finger along his brow. "You give the past too much power when you do that."

I snatch the cup from his grasp and drink some of it. The same thing I did when we were kids too young to be drinking in the first place.

"Is this too weird? Being here?" Coen snatches it back from me.

I sigh and relax backwards on the blanket, looking up into the night sky. "Not one bit." Okay maybe a little, but not in a bad way. I've missed these moments with him, and until recently, I had suppressed them in hopes that they wouldn't continue to break my heart every time I remembered them. But now that I have him back, the real Coen, not some figment of my imagination, I don't ever want it to end.

I tug on his shoulder and get him to lie down with me, both of us staring up at the same stars, a reality that I had wished for a million times over in all the years apart. Even when I hated him the most, I still longed for him. I had hoped that fate would bring us back together but I never imagined it would be like this—under these extreme circumstances.

Him *and* two other men.

Am I greedy for not choosing just one of them? I'm not sure I could even if I was forced to. Sure, Coen and I have the most history, but that doesn't invalidate my intense feelings for Magnus *or* Dominic. It's three different kinds of love, and I don't want to be without any of them.

Coen turns toward me and props himself onto his elbow.

"Take a picture, it'll last longer," I tease him.

"I missed you, J." Coen traces my arm with his finger. "More than you'll ever know."

"I think I have an idea, Co." I point to the sky. "There's the big dipper. Isn't it beautiful?"

"Yeah," Coen breathes, although he's still looking at me. He leans down and tilts my face toward him, pressing his lips to mine.

Soft, gentle, with such finesse.

But the second I melt into him, I'm overcome with an insatiable hunger to be closer. I tug him on top of me and immediately reach for the belt around his waist.

He sits back on his heels and watches me. "Are you sure?"

I yank at my dress and pull it up to give him access. "Why wouldn't I be?"

"Uh." Coen glances around. "We're on a rooftop, J."

I laugh and sit up, bringing his face to mine and kissing him again. "You can't tell me you never thought about it back then."

"I wanted to wait until you were older," he says between panted breaths.

"Guess what? I'm older." I unbutton his jeans and lie back.

He pulls a condom out of his pocket and secures it over his hard cock.

I inch toward him, impatiently waiting for him to be inside me.

Coen glides his erection over my soaked folds and then enters me so fucking slowly.

We moan at the same time, his hardness filling me to the brim.

He leans down, wrapping his arm around my waist and tilting my body up toward him. Coen plants the other hand above my head and thrusts himself inside me. He's methodic at first, but then picks up his pace, slamming his cock deeper.

I shove my hands up under his shirt and dig my nails into his back, pulling him closer and begging him silently for more. More closeness. More of him. More of his cock.

"God, J, you're so tight, I'm afraid I'm going to hurt you."

"You need to stop worrying about hurting me all the time." I pivot myself closer toward him, letting him know with my body that I can handle whatever he gives me. "Here, let me on top." I nudge him to move.

He reluctantly complies, and I straddle his lap, gliding carefully up and down on his shaft, adjusting to the change in position. Still moving, I drag the straps of my dress over my shoulders and expose my chest. I latch onto his hands and cover both of my breasts with them.

Coen swivels his hips and fucks me while I ride his cock. "You feel so good."

"Still afraid you're going to hurt me?" I lean forward and plant my hands on both sides of his head and give myself something to push against. I slam myself onto his cock and revel in the pleasure it gives us both.

Coen cups my face in his hands and kisses me with so much passion I could die right here and now and be completely okay with it. Oh how I've longed for these lips, this broken boy, the way he makes me feel.

"I love you, June."

My core tightens at those words. The ones I wanted to hear for so long. The ones that I had doubted for a decade, only to be proven wrong, that he really did love me after all. "I love you, Coen."

I shove my mouth onto his, our tongues dancing wildly, ravenously. My pussy tightens around him, and I bite at his lip as my climax rattles through me.

Coen grips my waist and fucks me all the way through both of our orgasms, his happening in tandem with mine. "Fuck," he moans.

I quiver on top of him, both from the pleasure and the cold air nipping at my exposed skin.

"I love you," he tells me again, like I might not have believed it the first time.

A car alarm goes off in the distance, reminding me that we're out here in the open, just barely above eyesight range. Only someone on another rooftop or a passing plane might spot us, but still, the adrenaline rushes through me from fucking in public like this.

Coen kisses my forehead, then my nose.

I climb off of him and collapse on the blanket, completely grateful for this entire night. Although, even after everything he's told me, it still feels like there's *something* he's not saying. It's only a matter of time until I figure out what it is.

I just hope it doesn't ruin us like last time.

# CHAPTER 6

# Dominic

I put out one fire, and another ignites.

The shitstorms are endless.

They consume my waking hours, and plague any chance I have at sleep.

I knew that stepping into this role would mean taking on more responsibility, I just didn't anticipate I'd be juggling so many things at once. I like to think I'm pretty damn equipped at handling situations, but this, this is something else entirely.

The leader of our organization was murdered in a war with his brother, which resulted in his death, too. And if that weren't enough, his brother was the rival head from the east coast syndicate. Leaving both coasts in shambles to pick up the pieces and scramble to find a foothold. His new predecessor used to be a runner for our organization, but after a faked death and secrets that continue to unravel, he found himself on the east coast, heir to a massive fortune and criminal empire. He's inexperienced, unqualified, and in over his head.

Between that, the feuds with factions here, and the pressure from the north and the south sectors, there isn't a direction that isn't coming at me with their hand out or a gun pointed to try to push me out of my position.

The stakes have never been higher. Only, I'd be wrong if I thought things couldn't possibly get worse.

"Someone on the inside must be tipping them off," one of my men tell me.

I turn toward him. "What's your name?"

He shifts his gaze to the guy next to him. "Uh, um."

"You have to ask your friend for your name?" I slam my palm onto the table in front of him. "You have one second."

"John, my name's John, sir."

"John." I roll it around on my tongue. "How long have you worked for us, *John*?"

I've never seen his face prior to today. There's no telling if *he's* the fucking rat.

"Six years, sir."

"Hmm." I take a step back and look him over.

Six years is a long time to commit to something, but that doesn't equate to loyalty. He could have easily turned but stayed here to help whoever gain an upper hand. Or, I could just be fucking paranoid. It's difficult to determine who to trust, and the constant issues that keep coming up have me questioning literally everyone except Hayes and Bryant. Hell, I put more trust in Simon fucking Beckett than I do any of these men sitting in front of me today.

"Where are we at with intel?" I ask the small group of men.

John clears his throat. "Sir, we've taken the biggest hit on the northwest quadrant. Followed by the southwest. If I had to guess—"

"Guess?" I crash both fists on the table.

He flinches but otherwise remains there.

"This is not a fucking guessing game, *John*."

John lowers his gaze to the paperwork in front of him. "Sir, yes, sir."

Bryant kicks off the wall and approaches, placing his hand on my back. "Clear the room, give us five," he tells the men.

They quickly scurry out of the room like their fucking lives depended on it.

Once they're gone, Bryant latches the door shut and sits on the edge of the table next to me. "What's going on, dude? You're about to blow a blood vessel."

I run my hand over my beard and exhale. "This John guy, what's your read on him?"

"Well, I'm pretty sure he was about to piss his pants."

I clench my jaw and turn toward him. "Not fucking helpful, Bryant."

Bryant throws his hands up and slaps them on his thighs. "He's just a guy, Dom. He's worked for us for a long time. No infractions. No reason to suspect him of treason. I didn't get a vibe, only that he's afraid of you." He scoots onto the tabletop. "Everyone is fucking afraid of you, Dom. You can't mistake that for disloyalty just because they tremble in your presence. Because if that were the case, we wouldn't have anyone left."

"We can't keep taking these hits."

"I know."

"We have bigger problems to worry about."

"*I know.*"

"Any update?" My hands clench into fists.

"Nothing new, no."

I cross my arms over my chest. "How did we let this happen?"

"You know how."

"We've been distracted." And because of it, our distraction is in danger more than ever before. "Where the fuck is Hayes?"

"Probably living his best life with the girl of our dreams." Magnus pulls his phone out of his pocket and pushes a few buttons.

I wait for him to continue, but he doesn't. "Well?"

"Oh, sorry, dude, I was checking the weather."

"The weather?"

"Yeah, I was thinking of taking June up in a hot air balloon for our date."

*Their date.* Shit. I haven't made arrangements for my time with her yet. I need to somehow navigate the balancing act of being a good boyfriend and making sure June stays alive—and prevent the business I'm running from crumbling.

"Everybody wants us—and June—dead, and you're going to send her into a fucking flying bucket in the sky?"

Magnus nods. "You're right, bad idea." He pinches his chin between his thumb and index finger. "Hmm."

"Does Beckett know?"

Magnus blinks at me a few times. "About flying buckets?"

"About the threat, dumb ass."

"Oh, no. You said to keep it between the three of us."

"Good. The less he knows, the better."

"I still think we should tell him...tell her. The last time we tried to keep secrets, the shit blew up in our faces."

And admit that we're not capable of taking care of her? That we made a mistake? Maybe I'm not actually cut out to be the man she needs in her life?

*Never.*

"I'll handle it."

"You don't have to do this all on your own, Dom."

But if I don't, who will? It's clear that if I'm not the one micromanaging every fucking thing, shit slips between the cracks. Problems arise with no possible solutions. People get hurt. *My* girl gets hurt. There has to be a way for me to do it all, because that's the only way I can ensure it gets done.

"Where are we at on putting a team together?"

"It's already done. They'll be following all shipments in and out."

"This better not be a waste of resources."

Magnus shrugs. "It's more of a waste if they intercept them and kill more of our men."

"And Johnny, when's the meeting with him?"

Magnus pulls his phone back out, and so help me God, if he's checking the fucking weather again. "Miller is working with the schedule. I'll have to let you know later."

"Miller." I pause and add, "Do you think he's equipped for the job?"

"More so than, Johnny, yeah. Dude was Luciano's right hand."

"I don't like this; I don't like any of it."

"Me either, but we'll handle it. We always do." Magnus rolls one of his rings around on his index finger. "I think you should hear John out, see what he has to say. Could be a useful asset."

I drag my hand through my hair and smooth down the sides. I adjust my tie and straighten my suit jacket. "Bring them in."

We spend the next hour discussing strategy, figuring out the best routes, and coming up with numerous alternative paths. Because we keep getting hit on the west, we're moving shipments further east. There's concern that this is what our attackers want us to do—that perhaps they're pushing us farther from the coast, but it could just be that the coast provides easier targets for them, and that's why they haven't been hitting our more inland routes yet. I'm still not convinced that we don't have a mole, but Magnus is certain that it isn't within the small group of men in this room. I put my faith in him since reading people is kind of his forte.

He's always had a knack for picking up on tells and minor shifts in mood. He notices body language and is able to make swift and usually spot-on judgment calls. It's an incredibly useful resource to have, but with pressure coming from all directions, it's impossible to have him in multiple places at once. The guy is already overworked and spread thin—hell, we all are. But this won't let up until we get the attacks under control and we eliminate the bastard responsible for attempting to overthrow me.

One hour turns into another, and the next thing I know, it's nearly two in the morning. My eyes burn from being awake for almost two days straight but I push through the pain and focus on the dry-erase board in front of me.

"Here." I circle a spot on the haphazard map on the board. "I say we send dummy cargo out. Try to catch them in a trap. We need bodies to interrogate to get more information. This is our best shot." I look at the thing again. "They're hitting us in spots where surveillance is spotty. That's why we take those routes. But this one, there's none. Tell all the men you can without making it too obvious. Don't let on that it's an empty shipment. We need our mole to spread the news."

"But..." John speaks up. "That's a death trap for whoever's driving."

I turn toward him. "I'll do it, don't worry. I won't put any more of my men at risk."

Bryant clears his throat. "I'm coming with you."

"Fat fucking chance." I stare directly at him. "And that's an order." I point to the other guys. "You can ride in the convoy, be my backup."

"What the fuck, Dom?" Bryant climbs out of his seat and approaches me, as if standing in front of me will somehow get me to change my mind.

I slap his shoulder. "Glad we came to an understanding."

He lowers his voice. "Are you trying to get yourself killed?"

I look into his frantic eyes. "Are you?"

That's twice in one day these two fuckers have disobeyed me in front of others. First, Hayes when he left a meeting after he zoned out of the whole thing, and now, Bryant, questioning my authority with these men to bear witness. They're setting a bad fucking example and making me look like I don't have control over my subordinates. It's no wonder someone is trying to overthrow me—I look weak as fuck.

But how do I make an example out of what they've done when I know June will have my ass for laying a finger on either of them. What's worse—June being mad at me, or the threat to her life gaining the upper hand because I went soft?

I can't keep her safe if people start walking all over me. A decision needs to be made, and none of us are going to like it.

In one solid movement, I draw in a breath and force my hand around Bryant's throat. I walk him back and slam him into the wall.

"What the fuck, Dom," Bryant sputters.

But I shove him harder and tighten my grasp. "Who calls the shots here?"

Bryant struggles to speak but manages to spit out, "You do, you fucking psycho."

I release him and he coughs, clutching at his throat.

"Christ, man."

I flex my hand and turn back to the men sitting silently in their chairs. "If any of you think for a second that I am taking this threat lightly, you are sorely mistaken. I will find and punish anyone who dare tries to take what is mine. I call the shots here, no one else. That's why the council voted me into this position. And that's why Franklin appointed me in the first place. These people will not go unpunished, and when we figure out who is behind all of this, I will skin him and send his body parts back to his family piece by piece. *Anyone* involved with this movement will be taken care of. Do you hear me?"

A few heads nod and there's a collective murmur of agreement.

"I want a list by tomorrow of everyone who was in the run for my title. I don't care if they conceded or not. We need to scour every single person until we figure out who's responsible." I point to the door. "You're dismissed."

Magnus stalks past me but I grab his arm and hold him from leaving.

"I had to," I tell him.

"Whatever."

Great, now I have to deal with the consequences of hurting *his* feelings, too.

"If they think I'm weak, they get the idea that they can join this usurper or take the position themselves. People were defecting to Beckett until I started smashing heads in public. You and Hayes were the ones that suggested it. Hayes already showed his ass in the meeting earlier, I can't have you both defying me every chance you get."

"No, I get it, loud and clear." Bryant crosses his arms over his chest. "I'm still not okay with you doing this mission on your own. And no amount of showing *your* ass is going to make me change my mind. What would June think if she found out? Or is this just another secret you're going to keep from her?"

"That's not fair."

"Isn't it? Neither is making me lie to her." Bryant brings up a solid point, but it doesn't change the fact that I'm not okay with telling her any of this.

Not that I'm potentially putting my life in danger. Not that I put Bryant in a chokehold to assert my dominance. Not that the throne she helped me win is being threatened with each passing second. And surely not the biggest secret of them all.

That the man who ordered the hit to have her kidnapped and tortured, eventually to be killed—the man who we thought we eliminated...he's very much alive and well.

# June

"Don't you get sick of sitting in the corner of a diner three days a week?" I wipe up spilled orange juice off the table and put the salt and pepper shakers into their home with the various packets of sugar, making a mental note that the blue one needs to be refilled. "Doesn't your back hurt? That can't be good for you, standing all day."

Simon smirks at me. "It's almost like you care."

"You're right, I don't. Forget I said anything." I move around him and service the table to his left. "Wouldn't want you to get the wrong idea."

"You can admit it, you know." Simon looks away, out the door, scanning the group of people that walk by the front of Bram's diner.

He might fuck around a lot, but he's actually pretty damn good at his job. Or, there just aren't any threats that need neutralizing. The fact that the guys still insist on having him around is enough to make me think that there are, though. Because why else would they allow someone they hate to spend every fucking day with me.

Unless, they're using Simon to distract me from the fact that they don't want to be around me. Maybe the newness has worn off and the feelings they felt in the beginning are no longer. Maybe they see me as nothing but a liability they have to protect out of guilt.

"What's for lunch?" Simon asks me.

I glance over at the clock—almost quitting time. "What were you thinking?"

"Pizza?"

"I had pizza with Co last night."

"Oh right, how was your *date*?"

A pack of loud college kids bursts into the diner, and without hesitating, Simon throws himself in front of me, one of his hands pinning me behind him and the other gripping the gun in his waistband.

The guys walk over to the register and place an order with the other waitress on duty. They settle onto stools at the counter and wait for their order.

Slowly, Simon releases his weapon and turns around, his grip settling on my shoulders. "I'm sorry, I didn't mean to scare you." His stare scans my face as he reaches up and moves my hair off my cheek.

"Scare me? I thought you were going to have a heart attack." I plant my hand on his shoulder and give it a few taps. "Down boy."

"One of these days you'll be glad I'm here to protect you."

"And until then, I'll be annoyed about having a babysitter." I tug the apron over my head and stroll to the counter, putting it on the hook with the others, and punch my timecard. I wave a quick goodbye to Carlos, the cook, grab a few of those blue packets of fake sugar, and pop them into the holder before it completely evades my train of thought. "How about tacos?" I weave my arm around Simon's and pull him toward the front door.

Simon tenses under my grasp. "I know a place."

We walk outside and Simon scans the vicinity. He places his hand on my lower back and guides me down the sidewalk, his gaze assessing every person around. He scans the windows of the building nearby and the parked vehicles.

"I thought you had a Lambo?" I ask him.

"What?" He flits his attention to me for a brief second.

"Yeah, the guys had told me you had a Lamborghini and were this big playboy."

"When would I have time to be a *playboy*?"

"We're not *always* together," I remind him.

"But even before this *arrangement*, I had other obligations that required my attention." Simon keeps his hand on my back as we cross the street. "And I sold the car. It wasn't practical."

"Simon Beckett, a practical man?" I nudge him with my elbow.

"You shouldn't listen to what everyone else says, especially about me." Simon latches onto my hand and pulls me out of the way of a speeding car that runs the red light. "Christ, love, are you okay?" He loosens his grip and skims his fingers over my wrist. "Did I hurt you?"

My heart pounds, the sound of the blaring horn of oncoming traffic still ringing in my ears. "I'm fine." I tug my hand toward me to conceal the growing red mark where he grabbed me.

The appetite I thought I had disappears with the closeness of yet another near-death experience. I shove away the memory of that man putting something over my mouth, the choking sensation as I inhaled, a reaction I couldn't stop myself from having. I clawed and wiggled but it was no match for the debilitating toxin. I woke to screams, but they were my own. The scar on my wrist, a reminder of the cigarettes he burned me with. The one on my chin making me forever uneasy around knives. I was able to enact my revenge...but at what cost? Things changed the day I murdered that man. Within me, and within the relationships I hold most dear. I could see the terror on the guys' faces when I was speckled red with the blood of the man who hurt me. I slit his throat without question, and the craziest thing of all—it was fucking easy. Too easy. I took a life, and I don't know what's more alarming, the fact that someone was dead at my hands, or because of how unbothered I am by it.

Does that make me a monster, too? No better than the man who wanted to carve me like a Halloween pumpkin.

"Let's get you out of here." Simon puts his hand on me again, nudging me to move.

I hate how it steals my train of thought, the warmth of his touch overpowering the rampant visions attacking my mind. But if I focus on him, I can escape the wrath my brain creates on a constant loop.

If it's not a waking nightmare about the events that took place in the past, it's the constant worries of the growing distance between me and each of my men. Ever since Coen broke my heart all those years ago, I've spent the rest of my life avoiding situations like this. Ones where I allow myself to be vulnerable, to care, to be hurt. It's served me well, keeping me from dealing with the uncomfortable realities of heartbreak. But I was no match to the way Dom, Co, and Magnus came barging into my life. It was swift and unexpected, and I fell for them harder than I imagined possible. Only, with that, those insecurities I've worked so hard on masking behind one-night stands and fake phone numbers come bubbling to the surface.

There's no coming back from jumping headfirst over the edge into that kind of love.

If I thought the pain of losing Co all those years ago was rough, I can't begin to fathom what losing my three men would be like. I would die from a broken heart, and that alone is what plagues me. I insisted on being part of their world, and now that I am, they've shut me out.

I was hesitant to let Coen in, too. I was riddled with the loss of the only person I ever loved, and losing such an integral part of your life at an early age has a way of fucking with your head. I didn't want to suffer through that loss again. I picked up the pieces of my broken heart and held onto it tightly. I never meant to give it to the boy who shared the same trauma. Our mothers gone, and with them, shreds of our humanity we would never get back. We were thrown into a life of pain that we would never escape, not then, not now. We found comfort in each other, and whether I'm proud to admit it or not, we trauma bonded—something one of the therapists I had for a short stint told me is an unhealthy coping mechanism.

*"It may look and feel safe, but those types of relationships can be extremely volatile,"* she had said.

Coen did make me feel safe. And what we had was real. But when he was ripped from me, so was the warm blanket of his love, leaving me cold and alone and exposed to the violence of what love can do once it's gone.

I don't know if I can go through that again. I pretend I'm strong, that I can handle anything, but what if the guys are right—what if I really am weak?

Simon orders us food, and it's only when he's telling me to sit that I snap back to reality.

Completely unaware of my surroundings, I anxiously glance around. I press my hands to the picnic table, grounding myself to the here and now. I close my eyes, taking in a breath and paying attention to the oaky scent of Simon's cologne, the crispness of the air, and the remnants of saltwater lingering in from the coast.

"I got you a Dr. Pepper." Simon pops the top of the can and places it in front of me.

"Thanks." I take a sip of it in hopes I'll appear somewhat normal despite having such a strange out-of-body experience.

Simon fidgets with the ring on his thumb. "The guys are going to be busy tonight."

"Of course they are." I roll my eyes and sigh. "I get one night with Coen and they think they have a free pass to ignore me for a week." I clamp my hand over my mouth. "I didn't mean to say that out loud."

"I didn't hear anything." Simon drinks from his bottle of water. "For the record, I don't think they're ignoring you, not on purpose at least."

"You're giving them the benefit of the doubt, really? Since when were you on their side?"

Simon grins, exposing his excessively white and perfectly aligned teeth. "I'm not."

"Sure seems like it."

"I'm on your side. Always have been, always will be."

I shake my head and lean on my elbow, resting my head in my hand. "Why?"

"Why not?"

"You know we can never be together, right?"

"I'm aware." Simon tries to hide the hurt that washes over his face briefly. "But that doesn't change the way I feel about you."

He only wants what he can't have. If I decided to give Simon the time of day, the thrill of the chase would be gone, and I'd have ruined everything with Magnus, Dom, and Co for a man who only pursued me for the fun of it.

"Do you think they're hiding something from me?" I ask him.

"Yes. Without a doubt." Simon gets up from the table to walk a few feet over to the food truck to get our order as it comes available. He returns a second later, never having actually taken his eyes off me the whole time he left my immediate presence. "But that's their nature. They can't tell you everything."

"They don't tell me *anything*." I pull a few napkins out of the holder and give a couple to Simon and keep the rest for myself.

"What do you want them to do? Come home from a long day of torturing people and be like, *hey honey, killed that traitor from the second division today. Might bust another guy's kneecaps in front of his family tomorrow if you want to come watch*." Simon takes a bite of his taco, some of the filling falling onto the other taco in his basket.

"I mean, no, not specifically that, but *that* would be better than nothing. I get the silent treatment at best. Even Magnus is vague as fuck, and he used to be the one who includes me in everything." I poke at the food in front of me but pull my hand away when I notice a faint bruise forming from where Simon had pulled me from the street just a little bit ago.

"If it makes you feel better, they don't tell me shit either." Simon wipes at his mouth with his napkin and points to my uneaten food. "I'll force-feed you if I have to."

"I hate you."

"I know." He nudges the basket toward me. "Don't make me have to come over there."

I take a bite of the taco to comply with his demands, the flavors melting into my mouth and reminding me of the appetite I once had earlier. "These are better than the last ones we got from here."

"Carne asada," Simon tells me.

I've eaten more meals with this man than I have my own boyfriends. Not just lately, but in general. If you don't count sleeping hours, Simon and I have spent more time together, too. He's their enemy, which makes him my enemy, but somehow, he's become my most trusted ally. The one person who I can *actually* count on being there if I need him. There really is something to be said about keeping your friends close and your enemies closer.

I can't imagine this is what the guys wanted, or even anticipated, but what did they expect when they pushed me away and into the arms of this man who would do anything for me?

I would never act on it, or betray our relationship, but it does make me question who cares for me more—my men, or their enemy?

"So, you have no idea what's been keeping them extra occupied lately?" I eat more of the food and hope that Simon has some kind of information he's willing to give me.

He pops the rest of his taco into his mouth, chews, and swallows it before speaking. "There's been some shipment issues. I'm guessing they're navigating that."

I nod like I have any clue what that might entail. "Isn't that something the logistics department should handle?"

"That's not how these things work. Not on this scale. There were casualties. And the product wasn't stolen, it was destroyed, like a message was being sent." Simon tells me more than I bargained for, and I'm grateful for every word of it.

"What kind of message?" I try to get as much out of him as possible until he realizes he's sharing details they probably don't want me to know.

"A threat of some kind maybe. Probably one of the rival factions testing Dom's new authority, see if he has the chops to handle the situation."

"And does he?" I ask the question even though I know the answer. Of course Dominic is more than qualified to handle whatever is thrown at him.

"That's why he has the job and not me."

"You conceded," I remind him. "My dying wish, remember?"

Simon's pretty face tenses. "I'd rather forget if I'm being honest."

"Ah, losing hurt that bad?" I tease him.

But he doesn't take the joke, instead, he stares directly at me. "Losing you, yeah."

A chill rolls down my spine, and my heart pounds harder at the intensity of those emerald eyes of his. "Well, here I am." I try to make light of the situation. "Looks like you got what you wanted after all."

"Not yet." Simon winks at me and turns his attention back to his food. That feisty version of him returning and masking the vulnerable version he doesn't let out often. "I said I'd wait forever if I had to. It's only been a few months."

But it's been longer than that, more than half a year. And soon enough, it'll be a full year, and at this rate, it'll turn into two, or three. Who knows how long the guys will insist that Simon watch over me. Maybe long enough for them to figure out how to get rid of me without having to carry the guilt of it. Maybe their plan all along was to get me to fall for Simon and then make this look like it was my fault.

Or, maybe I'm being fucking paranoid and they really are busy with work and it has nothing to do with me. I only wish I could get rid of this nagging feeling that *something* is going on they aren't telling me about. The suspicion continues to morph into irrational thoughts that eat away at me, and if something doesn't change soon, I worry that the distance might cause irreparable damage between us.

"The shipments," I say, bringing us back onto business talk. "I assume the routes are constantly changing, right? To avoid detection from the police or whatever."

Simon downs some of his water and nods. "Yeah."

"So then someone on the inside is tipping them off?"

"Has to be." Simon points to my food. "You have two minutes to eat one of those or I'm coming over there and shoving it down your throat."

I narrow my gaze at him. "Doesn't that go against the whole protecting me thing?"

"I can't protect you if you starve to death, love."

"I'm not going to starve, you're being dramatic."

"You think I don't notice, don't you?"

"Notice what?" I swallow the lump that forms in my throat.

"Nothing."

"Don't do that."

Simon reaches across the table and moves the basket of food closer to me. "Eat. The. Taco."

"Tell me what you notice and I will."

"I see everything. All the little and big things." He draws in a breath and exhales. "And if you don't eat that taco, you will witness me up close and personal." Simon raises his brow. "Unless that's what you want."

"Fine, I'll fucking eat it." I shove half the thing in my mouth and with some of it hanging out, I ask him, "Are you happy?"

"Yep." A smug look of satisfaction appears on his stupidly handsome face.

I chew the ginormous bite and swallow it down with a gulp of the Dr. Pepper. I burp, not caring at all how unladylike it may be, and eat the rest of the taco. I go to work on the other one, knowing damn well that he isn't going to let me off that easy. I manage to choke half of it down and shove the thing across to him. "That counts, right?"

He pinches his gaze at me, assessing whether he's going to accept it or not. Luckily for me, he does. Simon drags the basket toward him and eats the rest of my taco, licking the juice from his fingers when he's finished.

I catch myself staring and do anything I can to avoid looking at him any longer. "If the guys are gone tonight..." The realization finally dawns on me. "Does that mean you're stuck with me?"

"Stuck isn't really the word I'd choose." Simon cleans his mouth off with a napkin and drinks the rest of his water. "But yes, until one of them gets home. Although, I do have plans for us."

I ignore the flutter of my heart. "Plans?"

"Mmhm. But it's a surprise."

"I hate surprises." Okay, that's a lie, I just hate *knowing* about surprises. That weird limbo of anticipating what it could be drives me fucking insane.

"Too bad."

"I hate you," I tell him for what must be the tenth time today.

"Keep telling yourself that, love. Maybe one day you'll actually believe it." Simon gathers our trash and carries it over to the nearest bin. He points to the can of soda. "You done with your pop?"

"My what?"

"Don't make me repeat myself, are you done or not?"

I rise from my seat and grab the *soda*. "Did you just call this *pop*?" I walk over to him. "Simon fucking Beckett, did you just say *pop*?"

"Pop, soda, whatever the fuck you want to call it, are you done?"

I laugh and shake his shoulder. "Are you from Ohio or something?"

"June, I'm going to take back my vow and murder you right here if you don't give it up."

His persistence only makes me laugh harder.

"This is the best day of my life." I toss the can into the trash. "There, I'm done with my *pop*. Are you satisfied?"

Simon latches onto my hand and spins me toward him. "You'll know when I'm satisfied."

I press my palms against his chest, the warmth of him coursing through me. Jesus Christ, I cannot be this close to *this* man. He's sinful and alluring, and if I'm not careful I will get caught in his flame, burning us all to the ground.

"You have an eyelash." Simon picks it off my cheek, his finger like cool electricity along my skin. "Make a wish."

I purse my lips together, forming said wish in my mind, and blow gently, but enough to send the thing flying.

He swallows, and with one hand still holding me close to him, asks, "What did you wish for?"

"If I told you, it wouldn't come true." I should move from his grasp, but instead, I stay firmly in place, a strange comfort coming over me with his nearness that I'm not ready to give up just yet.

"If you told me, maybe I could help make it come true." Simon brings his hand toward my face, hovering it just along the edge of my skin. His green eyes dart from my eyes, to my lips, back to my eyes.

Green, an eye color to signify greed, malice, danger. Sure, they're fucking radiant, but they're capable of mesmerizing and distracting me from the fact that Simon is still the enemy.

Being this close to him isn't only distracting, it's wrong.

I wiggle out from under his hold. "That's not how wishes work, Simon Beckett."

It's fun playing with fire, but soon enough, someone is going to get burnt.

"So tonight," Simon doesn't push the issue anymore and allows me to escape with my wish tucked deep inside me. "Do you have a baseball cap?"

# Simon

I should be nervous because I'm breaking the rules, but instead, I'm anxious for an entirely different reason. I pace outside her bedroom door, waiting for her to finish getting ready.

I try to think about all the ways tonight could play out, coming up with backup and escape plans, excuses and cover-ups. The guys can't find out where we went or they'll murder both of us for sure.

But they can't continue to keep June under a rock, tucked away in some massive tower where she's withering away from stress and neglect. It's not in my job description to notice these things, but there's no way I could ignore the truth of the situation.

And the longer they ignore her wants and desires, the worse things are going to get. For her, for them, for all of us.

Someone has to be the man she needs, and if they won't do it, I will.

June steps into view—tight black pants, a matching fitted tee, her obsidian hair straight and cascading down her back. She glances over at me, and I try to pick my jaw up off of the floor.

"I couldn't find a hat," she tells me as she approaches. June stops in front of me, her feet on one side of the doorway, mine firmly planted on the other, that invisible barrier keeping us apart.

That rule forbids me from entering her space. What a stupid fucking rule.

"Why do I need one, anyway?"

"Here." I pull the cap out of my back pocket and unfold its bunched condition. I place the thing on her head and move her hair out from her eyes. I tug the hat down and step back to look at her. "Perfect."

"That didn't answer my question." She makes her own adjustments before stepping across that forbidden barrier.

"Do you trust me?" I ask her, but the second it's out of my mouth, I'm afraid to know the answer.

She rolls her eyes. "With my life."

I let out a relieved breath. It's not with her heart, but her life is just as important.

June strolls down the expansive hallway, and I follow her closely, savoring the scent of her shampoo wafting back at me. It's such a small thing, but knowing this is all I get from her is enough for now.

"Can I drink?" She walks over to the selection of booze between the sitting room and kitchen on their first floor.

"One."

"Do you want a drink?"

I shake my head. "I'm driving, love."

"We aren't taking Alec?"

"No." I study her features, watching as she tries to put the pieces of this evening together.

"Well, I won't either then." June sets the bottle of bourbon onto the tray and heads straight for the door. "Are we leaving through the garage?"

"Yes," I catch her arm on the way. "But you're allowed to have something if you want it."

She stares up at me. "It's my decision, not yours."

That feisty girl I adore is rising to the surface.

I grin and let her go. "As you wish."

We step into the garage, walking by all of the guys' various luxurious vehicles. We pass an Audi, a Land Rover, a Maserati, and then finally arrive at my car.

"You drive a Volvo? How did I not know this?" June turns back to me.

I reach for the handle and open the door for her. "It's practical." Although, the blacked-out bulletproof windows and steel-reinforced doors were an addition I don't mention. One can never be too careful in this line of business.

The ride across town is quiet, my nerves getting the best of me the entire time. Is she going to like my surprise? Is it going to be what she wanted? Is she going to regret coming along and think this entire night was stupid? I chuckle at the fact that of all the concerns I could have, what she thinks is a priority over the guys finding out and having my head for taking her to a place like this.

June finally speaks up. "Magnus just text me, what do I say?"

Guilt hits me like a ton of bricks. I don't want to ask her to lie, but I can't allow her to tell the truth. Not that she even knows where we're going yet. Magnus might be the only one of the three that would understand or even accept what we're doing, but I can't risk him freaking out or letting the other guys know.

"Be as vague as possible. Tell him we're going to get something to eat and we'll be home later."

"Okay..." She thumbs a response and hits send. A second later, her phone buzzes. "He said to have fun, and to tell you to keep your hands to yourself."

My fingers twitch, the single order going against everything my body wants to do. If she were mine, I'd have my palm resting against her thigh. I'd kiss her at every traffic light, hell, I wouldn't even wait for the red to give me permission. I'd smother her with so much fucking love that she'd never question my intentions the way she does with them. I'd put her above my career, above my fucking life. I'd never take her for granted, and I'd spend every day making sure she knew just how much she meant to me.

*Three* God damn men, and none of them make her feel secure in their relationship. Not a single one notices the post-traumatic stress that plagues her dreams and haunts her waking hours. They don't see the weight she's lost, the way her light has dimmed since they came into her world.

She loves them, but at what cost?

Instead of being what she needs, they push her away, keep their secrets, and make her question whether they want her around at all. It's not fair. To her, or to me, when I'd so willingly be the man she deserves.

I'd nurture that light instead of letting it burn out. I'd listen to all the things she doesn't say and give before she can even ask for what she wants. I would anticipate her every desire and fulfill her fantasies.

I might not be responsible for her heart just yet, but that doesn't mean I won't do what I can to make sure she knows she's seen, that she's heard.

And maybe tonight is the first overstep of the boundary put in place, but someone has to give in to her darker side before it consumes her completely.

I pull my car down a dark alley and park it under a flickering light. Reaching into the middle console, I pull out a pair of sunglasses. "Put these on."

She eyes me suspiciously but decides to comply. "Any chance you're going to tell me where we are?"

"That would ruin the surprise. You'll find out soon enough." I nod toward her door. "Wait for me to come around. Don't talk to anyone inside the building. The fewer people who know we're here, the better. If the guys find out I brought you here, they'll murder us both. Stay close to me, and whatever you do, you do not leave my side. Understand?"

June nods sharply. "Okay."

"And at any time, if you want to leave, all you have to do is tell me."

"Okay," she repeats.

I take a deep breath in and exit the car, slamming my door shut and walking over to hers. I reason with myself on the way, allowing for a small window of opportunity where I change my mind, where I drive her away from here and go back to complying with the guys' rules. I guess this isn't directly disobeying them—they didn't exactly tell me I *couldn't* bring her here, just that I had to keep her safe at all times, and away from mafia business.

As long as she does everything I asked of her, her safety remains intact.

Plus, this isn't mafia business per se—more like a side hustle.

I reach her door, opening it and sealing our fate. I extend my hand, reveling in the softness of her skin when she places hers in mine. "This way, love." I guide her through the dampness of the alley and through a back door.

The noise of a bustling crowd fills the space and grows louder as we approach.

I tug her down a narrow corridor where people are gathered, some chatting in small groups, some waiting in an excessively long line.

"Stay close to me," I remind her.

She tightens her grip on my hand and steps closer, her body only inches from mine as we weave our way through the throng of people. I pretend for a moment that this is what it would be like, us against the world. Me and her, together, at fucking last. But then I'm quickly reminded that this is a fever dream, a night that will exist only in my memories once it's over. Either way, I'll gladly take whatever I can get with her.

"Move," I tell a middle-aged man standing in my way.

He hesitates and for a second I'm unsure whether he's going to actually comply. But like a sense of realization hits him, he steps back and gives me the space I demanded.

I shove my key into the door he was in front of and turn the handle, pulling June in with me and shutting out the chaos of that crowd. It takes my eyes a second to adjust to the darkness of the room, and then again when I flip the light switch on.

"What is this place?" June pulls the glasses off of her beautiful face and looks around.

I pull back the curtain on the large one-way window, revealing a room filled to the brim with people.

June approaches and glances over at me. "Can they see us?"

I shake my head and walk over to the refrigerator in the corner. "No." I pull out two bottles of water and give her one of them. "It won't be too long."

"I don't understand."

I press a button on the wall, a speaker in our room crackling to life.

A man's voice comes through the end. "Settle down everyone." He clears his throat. "The boys are making their final rounds on bets. If you'd like to place a wager, you have...." The announcer from across the way checks the clock near him. "Sixty-two seconds."

"What are they betting on?" June asks me.

The man continues. "Our first fighter of the evening is three-time champ Bradshaw Cleary."

Cheers call out for the welterweight-looking kid that appears from the back corner. The crowd parts and allows him to walk to the center of the room where the mass of them automatically create an open square about the size of a boxing ring without the ropes and pads. Instead, it's just a bare area with remnants of old blood staining the concrete floor.

"Is this a fight?" June perks up her brow.

At least intrigue is a better sign than her being ready to leave already.

"Just watch, *Miss Impatient*." I twist the cap off my water and down some of the contents. "And drink that, you need to stay hydrated."

She rolls her eyes. "What are you, my mom?"

I glance over at her. "I can baby bird it if you'd prefer."

"You're going to...spit in my mouth?" June blinks at me and it's moments like this I wish like hell I could read her fucking mind.

My cock twitches at the thoughts that run wild in my head.

"And his opponent," the announcer says into his mic. "The four-time undefeated Axel Covington."

"Shit," I mutter. I hadn't looked at the roster for the evening, not even entirely sure if I would have been able to pull this off at all. But the stars aligned when the guys told me they were going to be occupied, and that June would need to be watched. She's had a hankering for a little bloodshed, and what better than some gruesome underground fighting?

Axel is one hell of a brute, and he's bound to put on a damn good show—making this the perfect setting for a bloody good time, giving my girl exactly what she wants. Or at the very least, a taste of it.

"He kind of reminds me of Magnus." June watches the tattooed man as he strolls into the center of the room.

He punches his right fist into his left hand and jumps a few times. His feet bare and his knuckles wrapped in white tape.

"Axel's a good fighter," I tell her. A damn good one, actually. And I hope he continues that streak because we can't afford to lose someone like him, not like this. "It's a pretty even fight." I'd know for sure if I paid attention to the lineup when I decided to bring her here. But the betting wasn't even a blip on my radar then, and still isn't now.

June presses her palm against the glass and watches the men circle each other in the makeshift ring. "Why aren't we out there?" She nods toward the thick crowd of people.

"Too many prying eyes." These aren't the type of men who are hungry for *only* blood. They crave carnage in any capacity, and having a beautiful woman like June in their vicinity is a recipe for disaster. I wouldn't dare threaten her safety by having her out there with those vile creatures. Instead, I keep her tucked away in here with me, where I can manage the level of monster she's around. I'm no better than them, but the difference between them and me is that I actually care about the dark-haired vixen in this room. I'd rather die than let anything happen to her.

Bradshaw throws the first punch, landing his fist across Axel's jaw. Blood goes flying, and Axel turns to Bradshaw with a shit-eating grin on his face. Axel keeps his arms low, not blocking any of the blows that Bradshaw sends his way. The crowd goes wild, people screaming at Axel to react.

June stays firmly in place, her gaze glued on the fight unfolding in front of her.

We aren't super close, but we're elevated from the rest of the people, making this the perfect vantage point to watch from. Only a few people have a key to this room, and three of them are occupied with something else tonight.

Bradshaw shoves Axel but all Axel does is laugh at him. That guy is a fucking lunatic. He's got nearly every person in this place on edge, clutching their fucking balls and wondering if their bets were appropriately wagered.

Something shiny skids across the concrete to Bradshaw, and I hear someone shout through the speaker, "Fucking finish him off!"

June looks over at me. "Is that allowed?"

I step closer to her, our bodies just a few inches apart. "Yep. No holds barred." I press my hand along the edge of the window and brace myself.

Bradshaw does a double take but grabs the knife, gripping it in his hand and swiping it at Axel. He manages to slice the blade across Axel's forearm, blood splattering onto the floor. He aims at him again, but Axel manages to dodge the attack.

Axel bounces on his toes and shoves his arm forward, blasting Bradshaw in the throat with the heel of his hand.

June latches onto me, her fingers wrapping tightly around my hand.

Whether it was a conscious action or not, I don't bring attention to it out of fear that it will end all too soon.

Bradshaw recovers from the hit and jabs at Axel with the knife.

The crowd screams, their demands impossible to make out through the incessant chatter. They collectively roar when Axel spins and kicks Bradshaw in the stomach, sending him backward and clutching at his gut all in one fluid movement. Bradshaw takes a few steps to get away from Axel and regain his composure. He lands a punch across Axel's face, his blade nicking Axel's brow. Blood trickles down and Axel whips his head to rid himself of the obstruction in his line of sight. Axel wipes at it and glances down at his crimson-soaked hand. He laughs and spits some of the blood that trails down into his mouth.

Axel motions for Bradshaw to attack and Bradshaw does exactly that.

He lurches at Axel, the blade poised in his grasp. Axel dodges him at the last second and sends Bradshaw falling into the crowd. They shove him back into the center of the ring and scream obscenities and demands at him.

"Come on you fucking pansy!" some guy screams loud enough for me to make out above the rest of the noise.

Bradshaw runs at Axel, tackling him and causing everyone to yell even louder. Bradshaw pins Axel to the concrete and punches him in the face over and over again. He traps Axel's arms under the weight of his body and does not budge when Axel tries to buck him off of him.

"Fuck," I whisper. If Axel doesn't do something soon, Bradshaw is going to win this fight and we're going to lose one hell of a soldier.

"When do they call it?" June doesn't move her hand from mine but shifts her gaze slightly to glance at me before returning it to the match before us.

I bite at the inside of my lip, unsure of whether or not I'm ready to tell her this part just yet. The real reason why I thought this might satiate that hunger she's been craving lately.

Bradshaw grips the knife firmly in his grasp and raises it dramatically in the air above Axel. With one hand around Axel's throat, he readies himself to end this fight once and for all.

"He's going to fucking kill him." June digs her fingers further into my skin. What should be pain only floats through me as pleasure.

The crowd screams louder than ever—people angry over their wagers about to be lost, and people begging to win their bets.

But, just like everything else in this world, it's not over until it's over.

And when another weapon is tossed into the battle, Axel frantically scrambles to gain an inch and reach the lifeline he was given. He tries to buck Bradshaw in an attempt to advance even slightly toward his target. He drags his legs up, bending them at the knee and throwing his weight into moving the man pining him down.

Bradshaw laughs at Axel's attempt but doesn't quite realize *why* he's doing it. He must assume Axel is just trying to get free, not latch onto the other knife tossed onto the battlefield. And when his cockiness finally gets the best of him, Axel digs deeper, his fingers ultimately wrapping around the handle of the blade.

Another smile forms across Axel's face, and a split second later, he drives the knife into Bradshaw's side, yanking it out and slamming it back in. Once, twice, three more times. Blood fucking splatters everywhere and Axel doesn't let up, not even when Bradshaw falls off of him and stops moving. Axel continues to jab the sharp edge into his chest, making damn sure that Bradshaw can never recover.

It's not until three men from the crowd grab his shoulders and drag him from Bradshaw's dead body does he finally stop.

"Holy shit," June mutters. "That was…"

I hang on to that last word, dying a little myself waiting for whatever it is she's about to say. The one word that will alert me to whether this was a mistake in bringing her here. The word that will tell me if I got this all wrong and I don't actually know her after all.

But June doesn't continue that sentence. She doesn't say the single word that has the power of making or breaking this entire night. Instead, she turns toward me, a sort of glimmer in her eyes that wasn't there before.

"Is there another fight?" She asks me.

A hopeful glimmer, that's what it is.

"Two more, yeah."

June grabs my shoulder, shaking it and then turning toward the crowd, her gaze expectantly waiting for things to start again. "I wish we could be out there."

"Maybe another time, love."

"Yeah, maybe." June cracks open the bottle of water I gave her before the first battle to the death and takes a drink.

I settle onto the couch near the window, throwing my arm over the back of it. "You can sit while they clean up and prepare for the next one."

June glances back and laughs. "I didn't even notice the couch."

"You were a bit preoccupied."

She joins me but not as close as I'd prefer. Hell, she could have chosen my lap as a seat and it still wouldn't be close enough.

"So like…" June turns toward me, pulling her leg up onto the couch and putting her arm over the back, too. "Are you dating anyone?"

This time it's me that lets out a chuckle. "What?"

She shrugs. "It's a reasonable question."

"What do you think, love?"

"I think you're a relatively attractive man with a solid set of teeth and a prominent hairline. According to the current dating pool, I'd imagine you have a plethora of women suitors."

I trail my finger along her hand. "You think I'm attractive?"

She swats at me. "That's really all you heard?"

"It's what you said."

"Still doesn't answer my question." She rests her head in her hand.

What do I say? No, June, I'm not dating anyone. Because all I can think about is you. I eat, sleep, and breathe you, and from the second I fucking set my sights on you, I knew you had to be mine. What I thought was going to be a fun game of fucking with my rivals' girl turned into me being completely captivated by a woman I could never have.

I point to the open window area. "Another fight is about to begin."

"Do they teach avoidance at mafia training school?" June rises from the couch and strolls over to her spot at the window.

I follow her over, my heart aching at the immediate shift in dynamic in the room. I gently latch onto her forearm and pivot her toward me. "I'm not dating anyone, love."

She swallows harshly and stares into my eyes. "Why?"

"Because I don't want to." The honest truth, aside from one obvious exception.

"Maybe you would if you weren't forced to be around me all the time."

I shouldn't, but I take a step toward her. "I am *not* forced."

"Stockholm syndrome," she mumbles.

I can't help but focus on her lips, wishing I knew what they felt like on mine. "I want to be here," I tell her. No, it's more of a need than a want, but I don't tell her that.

"Why?" Her dark brown gaze darts between mine.

"I think we both know the answer to that question." I bring my hand slowly up her arm and hover it next to her face. "And don't you dare compare me to them."

"I..." June starts to say something but struggles to find the rest of her words.

My attention flickers to the crowd on the other side of the window. Protective mode always enabled and ready to go into action when she's around. A large man creates a path as he moves, his presence alone keeping people at a short distance. He approaches and I focus on the shape of him, nearly having a fucking heart attack when I finally realize who it is.

"Shit, J, we have to go." I grab onto her hand and yank her in the direction we came.

"What? Why?" Disappointment and shock no doubt coursing through her.

But we'll have bigger problems than her temporary frustration if we don't get the hell out of here.

"Dom is here," I tell her, hoping she'll get the urgency of the situation.

Her eyes widen, an appropriate response to the untimely arrival of her ruthless boyfriend.

The door opposite of us jingles. Dominic must be entering the room from the other side.

If he makes it inside, he'll murder me on the spot. Any of her men will kill me if they find out, but death at their hands could never be worse than seeing June longing for something she can't have or that they won't give her.

I yank the door we came through open, but that throng of people from earlier remains. Well, maybe not the *same* people, but yet an endless supply of men that are trying to get a spot inside to watch the fights.

"Get the fuck out of the way," I tell the two assholes not bothered by us at all.

June flits her attention to the other side of our room and then shoves the man in our path. "Move, dick head." She doesn't waste another second, no, June balls her hand into a fist and blasts it across the guy's face.

"Fucking bitch," he yells and grips the spot she hit.

I yank the gun out of my waistband and point it at his fucking head. "What did you just say to her?"

Within an instant, the crowd parts for us. The man mostly in our way throwing both hands up and mumbling an apology.

June grabs onto my arm and pulls me through the opening, the door Dominic is at opens as ours closes and latches behind us.

"Love." June shakes me. "We have to go."

I'm brought back to reality, the warmth of her touch and the softness of her voice searing through me. I shove the gun back in its home, weave my hand around hers, and rush us down the hall.

We burst into the alley, the chilly air hitting us in the face.

Laughs bubble out of both of us but it doesn't stop me from hurrying to my car and opening the door for her. "Quick, get in."

June complies and I dart around to throw myself into the driver's seat.

A second later, my wheels spin and shoot us out onto the main road, my car blending in with all the others.

I look over at her reddened cheeks and watch the steady rise and fall of her chest.

"Did you just call me *love*?"

"I thought we were flying under the radar. I didn't want to say your name," she explains.

"Pretty sure everyone will have known that was me after I pulled a gun."

But a part of me feels like she already knew that—or at least, a part of me hopes that's the truth.

"That was so fucking close." June flips down the mirror and pats down her unruly hair.

At the next light, I brake and reach over to pull her seatbelt across her lap. "Buckle up, love." I latch the thing in place, our breaths mingling at the closeness.

Her phone rings, snapping us both out of our trance.

The signal changes to green, and I push on the accelerator. "Who is it?" I ask her and wonder which of her boyfriends I'm going to envy.

"It's...Gwyneth." She holds the phone out and looks at me as if silently questioning what I think she should do.

"Answer it." I pause and add, "Put it on speakerphone."

She pushes a couple buttons and the line connects. "Hello?"

"June, hello. It's Winnie Sharp. How are you, darling?"

"Hi, Winnie. I'm good. How are you? Is something wrong?"

"Not at all, sweetheart. I was just calling to check in; see how things were going. It's been a while since we last chatted."

But there's something else she isn't saying.

"Things are fine. Pretty much the same," June tells her.

"That's good to hear."

An awkward silence falls between them.

Finally, Winnie speaks again. "Listen, I'm in town this week, and I'd love to get together. What do you say, brunch on Tuesday?"

June glances at me again and I nod.

"Yeah, that works."

"Great, I'll send you the details Monday."

I drive the speed limit while I attempt to dissect any hidden meaning within the call.

"How are your men, darling?"

"Um, they're good, I think. They're pretty busy."

"Mmhm. Yes, I can only imagine. Dominic has his hands full." A muffled sound comes through like she's switched the phone from one side to the other. "And Simon, how are things with him? I understand you two have been spending quite a bit of time together."

June's cheeks flush. "Per the guys' request."

I shove away the bitter rejection caused by her defensive tone.

"Yes, of course. Your safety is their highest priority. And Simon is fit for the job. He's rather fond of you, June. But that's not why I called. I'm sure you've got other things going on this Friday evening. I'll let you go, but I'll be in contact about Tuesday. Do let me know if something comes up and you cannot make it. I look forward to seeing you and getting a chance to catch up. We have much to discuss."

"I look forward to it, too."

They say their goodbyes and the call disconnects.

June steadies her gaze on me. "What the fuck was that about?"

I shrug and turn onto a side street. "I have no idea. But you'll find out soon enough."

# CHAPTER 9

I push around the soggy cereal in my bowl and reminisce about last night.

Simon had surprised me, like really fucking surprised me. In a way that was totally unexpected and so fucking wonderful.

It's been a while since I've felt the type of adrenaline I did from the second we pulled into that sketchy, dark alley. I had a hunch that he would take me somewhere fun, but I had no idea it would have turned into *that*.

I witnessed someone nearly die, and that same man murder another.

The entire atmosphere of that building was buzzing with a darkness I haven't felt in a long while. It was familiar and foreign all at the same time, and I was living for every second of it.

And then the cherry to top it all off—almost getting caught.

I hate lying to my men, but something about being that damn close to Dominic finding out was a thrill I hadn't anticipated either.

It's not like I'm *lying* lying. I'm just not telling them the whole truth. And isn't that exactly what they're doing to me? Only, none of them have questioned where Simon and I went last night. Do they even care? Do they not wonder where some other man has taken their girlfriend? I ask questions and get vague answers—they don't ask questions at all.

Simon and I didn't do anything bad; we just did something they wouldn't approve of. It's not like I fucked Simon or went running through town naked. But they also don't approve of me doing pretty much anything outside of existing within this house, so it's difficult to tell what really *should* be off-limits.

They can't keep me locked away forever.

Not that I would allow myself to be caged anyway.

The confines they have on me are almost too much to handle, but if I were able to have more moments like last night, maybe I could balance the line of being their good girl while still dipping my toes into my bad side.

Something has been missing from my life, and for a blip of time tucked away in that room with Simon, I felt like I had finally found it.

My gaze falls to my knuckles, swollen and bruised from punching that guy in the face when he wouldn't get out of the way. I recall the rush that came over me, the pull to inflict pain on this arrogant asshole. I wanted to do more than just hit him, and a large part of me wished that we weren't in a hurry and that Simon would have used the gun he had pulled out on him.

Watching Axel and Bradshaw fight to the death unlocked something from within me. Or maybe it just shined light on a darkness that had been hiding all this time. Either way, witnessing them have the raw, unrestricted ability to beat the living shit out of each other made me want for a chance to...

My mind trails off at the endless possibilities. What is it that I want?

To hurt myself? To inflict pain on someone else? To kill?

Whatever it was, the drive to make it happen was higher than ever.

I have to talk to Simon, to convince him I needed more.

"Good morning, princess." Magnus approaches me from behind, wrapping his ink-marked arms around my frame. He hugs me tightly and kisses the side of my head. "How did you sleep?"

"Pretty decent actually." I turn and catch his lips with mine. "You?"

"Could have used about ten more hours, but I'll survive." He shoves his hand into the box of Cheerios and pulls out a handful, tossing them into his mouth. "Where did you and Simon eat last night?"

"Um, uh, some Mexican joint."

"Word." He releases me and strolls over to the coffee machine, pushes a few buttons and waits for his cup to brew. "How was it?"

I shrug. "Decent."

Two lies already told in a ten-second conversation.

"What had you out so late?" I ask him, even though I know he won't tell the truth either.

"Work stuff. The usual."

"It's usual that you're out all hours of the night?"

Magnus sighs and comes back over to me. He takes my hands in his, cupping them together on the marble countertop. He steadies his serious gaze on mine. "I promise it won't always be like this. We're just dealing with some changes. Once we've handled it, we'll be more present."

Is he referring to those shipments and the men who died in the process? Why can't he admit that's what has them busy? What is the harm in saying what's really happening? How could *that* possibly put my life in danger? And why is that something that has to remain a secret? How do they think I would possibly react that causes them to refuse to tell me? The whole selling point in involving me with their business was so they could keep me in the loop and *not* exclude me from everything. I was supposed to help them, provide insight into situations that they hadn't already considered. Even Gwyneth thought my business degree would give them a fresh new perspective on how to run things. They insisted that I finish my schooling, but I didn't realize it was just another way for them to bide their time of keeping me in the dark.

"Why won't you tell me, though, Magnus? I don't understand. You were always the one who wanted to include me, but even you hardly talk to me these days." I chew at the inside of my lip, my emotions bubbling up to the surface even though I want nothing but to keep them at bay. "Did I do something wrong?" *I mean, other than almost dying.*

"No, no no no." Magnus brings both of his hands from mine and places them on my cheeks. "My sweet girl, no. You didn't do anything wrong."

"Then what is it?" I ask him. "Why won't you tell me? Do you think I can't handle it?"

He tucks my hair behind my ear. "You know better than anyone that I think you can handle anything. You're the strongest person I know, princess."

A low beep alerts us that his coffee has finished brewing.

"Who's making you keep secrets from me? Is it Dom or Co?" I lean into his touch, savoring the comfort it brings me.

"It's not that simple." He runs his thumb along my skin. "But I promise it's for your safety."

Anger courses through me. "My safety." If I have to hear something is for my fucking safety one more time, I'm going to lose my Goddamn mind. "Fuck my safety." I shake off his hands and push back from the stool.

The garage door opens and someone walks into the kitchen. I don't bother looking to see who it is, because like clockwork, I already know.

"Have a good *fucking* day at work!" I call out as I stomp up the stairs and into my bedroom.

A few minutes pass and even though a bit of guilt starts to trickle in at having scolded Magnus, the fury I feel continues to overpower any other of my emotions.

A soft knock sounds on the door, and when I look up from my spot on the floor next to my bed, I spot Simon standing there in the hallway.

He leans against the frame and crosses his arms over his chest. "Want to talk about it?"

"No." I clench my fists even tighter than they already were.

Simon stiffens in place and his brows furrow. "Let me see your hands, love."

I pull them toward my body. "What?" Why? No."

He kicks off the door and stands as close to the inside of my room as possible. "Damn it, June, let me see your hands."

"Just let me leave, Simon."

"Fuck it," he mutters and barges into my bedroom, not giving a shit about the stupid rule that he isn't allowed in here. Simon kneels next to me and pries one of my fists from me, peeling my fingers away from my palm and revealing the crescent shaped cuts lining my skin. He sighs, his resolve softening. "Give me the other one." He takes it into his hand, gently pulling back the fingers on that one, too. "Come on, let's get you cleaned up." He lifts me off the floor with ease, helping me rise to my feet.

I want to shrivel back down and crawl under my bed, hiding and wasting away into nothing, because that's how I feel. Like nothing. One minute, I'm confident and on top of the world, and the next, I'm insecure and doubting everything. I'm furious and sad, and I just want something to make sense. I thought I had finally found something stable, a constant in my life, but it's like once I found solid footing, the rug was pulled out from under me. The only steady part of my life is gripping my arms and helping me down the hallway to the bathroom where he's not forbidden from entering.

Simon puts his firm hands on my waist and raises me onto the counter. He turns on the faucet and looks under the sink for what I can only assume is a first aid kit.

I study his face while he goes to work, not paying attention to the burn of the water or the sting of the ointment he puts on the tiny cuts. Instead, I focus on his meticulously crafted bone structure, the delicate shape of his lips, the wispiness of his long eyelashes. The same man who brought me my abuser so I could get my revenge, who had a smile on his face when I sliced the guy's throat, is the same guy who is tender and kind and caring. He pulled a gun on some random stranger last night and here he is, delicate as a flower.

"I didn't realize you hurt your hand either, love. Why didn't you tell me?" He turns my wrist and runs his thumb along my swollen knuckles. "I think you should have this looked at."

"You're looking at it right now."

He tilts his head slightly. "You know what I mean." Simon applies soft pressure to my hand. "Does this hurt?" He moves around, applying more pressure and bending my fingers carefully.

"No," I lie. But I wouldn't erase it if I could. It's a reminder of the first time in a long while that I've felt relatively *normal* and I welcome the pain with open arms. "I'm fine, really."

Simon continues to work my hand. "You may be able to fool them, love. But you don't fool me."

How is it possible that a man that isn't even mine knows me better than my own boyfriends? I guess that's what happens when you spend day after day with someone. Simon isn't just here to hang out, he's here to watch my every move and anticipate any threat that may come my way. His job is to pay attention to me, and that is exactly what he does.

"Thanks," I tell him and hop off the counter. "I'm going to take a nap." I hold my bandaged hands close to my body.

He follows me down the hall but stops at my door.

"Will you stay?" I ask him.

"You know I can't do that." Simon's jaw tenses.

"Then I'll sleep on the couch." I go to leave the room but he raises his hand to stop me.

"No, you'll sleep in your bed, love." He points to the floor outside my room. "I'll stay out here. Okay?"

"That won't be comfortable."

"And neither would the couch." His gaze stares into me. "I'll be fine."

I want to protest, to tell him that the rules the guys put in place are stupid, and that if they didn't want Simon in my room, they should be here to prevent it from happening. Maybe they shouldn't have hired him to watch over me because they're too busy to do it themselves. But that would involve more energy than I'm capable of expending right now, and all I really want to do is curl up in a ball and drift off to sleep. I only hope it will be nightmare free and grant me the tiniest bit of rest.

I crawl into bed, bringing the covers up to my neck and smooshing my face against the pillow. I train my attention on the man outside my doorway, his back pressed along the wall, his one knee brought up toward him and the other out flat. He fiddles with the ring on his thumb and he's the last thing I think about when I finally drift into sleep.

At some point, a person moves me, their body coming under mine.

I settle into them without question, assuming it's probably Magnus coming to have an apology cuddle. He's the most snuggly of all my men, and definitely the most affectionate. His love is a warm blanket that soothes my aching soul.

I don't open my heavy eyes, instead, I keep them closed and welcome the comfort my company brings. I wrap my arm around their chest and listen to the steady but boisterous beat of their heart. *Thump-thump...thump-thump.*

It lulls me into a restful sleep, keeping the nightmare that was plaguing me moments ago away.

It's not until I finally wake up that I realize it wasn't Magnus at all.

I breathe in that familiar and forbidden scent of a man that isn't mine.

"Simon?" I mutter.

He smooths the hair off my cheek and looks down at me. "I'm here, I'm right here."

"You aren't supposed to be in here." Am I dreaming, or is this real?

"You were shaking, love." Simon pulls the blanket over my shoulder.

I blink a few times and sit up, my body immediately growing cold at the loss of his touch.

Simon sits there, his back resting against the headboard of my bed, his shirt wrinkled from where I was nestled into him. This whole time, I thought he was Magnus, I thought one of my men came to me and rid me of the terrifying scenarios that my brain conjures when I try to sleep. But no, it wasn't—it was their enemy who brought me comfort when they couldn't...or wouldn't.

"Simon?"

"Yes, love?"

I sit back, bringing my knees to my chest and pulling the blanket around my body. "Do you think there's something wrong with me?"

"Your taste in men, maybe." He smirks and tugs the blanket over my exposed foot.

"No, I'm serious. Do you think they had some epiphany, and that's why they're so distant and shutting me out? You're around me more than anyone. You'd notice if I did something wrong, right? If I was defective."

I shouldn't be asking him things like this, but who else am I supposed to talk to when I barely get five minutes at a time with my so-called partners. I can't even talk to Cora about it, either. One, because of the complexities of the situation; it would be too difficult for her to understand. And two, because she's been out of town the last three weeks at some work education enrichment program. She won't be home for another week, and by then, I'll have gone crazy dealing with this situation myself.

Simon repositions himself closer and places his hand on my cheek. "You, my love, are not defective. There is nothing wrong with you. You have done nothing wrong. I assure you, you are perfect in my eyes. All these doubts, these insecurities, you shouldn't be having them."

My phone buzzes on the nightstand and Simon breaks away to hand it to me.

"It's Magnus," I tell him. "He said he's made plans for us tomorrow."

"That's good, right?" Simon shifts in his seat, moving closer to the edge of the bed, away from me.

"He's only doing it because we had a fight." I sigh and drop my phone onto the bed. "It's a pity date."

The thing buzzes again, only this time, it's a text from Dom.

"And now Dom is saying he's arranging something for Wednesday." I bury my face in the blanket and let out a muffled groan. "I shouldn't have to force them to be around me." I sit up and look at Simon. "Even you're here out of obligation."

Simon frowns. "That isn't entirely true."

"But it is partially true, there's no denying that."

"That's not fair, love. You chose them, not me. I would…"

I wait for him to continue but he doesn't.

"I think it would be better for all of you if I weren't here," I tell him. "Then none of you would have to be bothered by worrying about me. You could go back to the life you had before. Hell, you'd have time to date, or do whatever it is you wanted to do. This isn't fair to you either, Simon. You didn't ask for this. You were in the running to take over a criminal enterprise and now you're a glorified babysitter."

"June…" Simon runs his hand through his hair and settles on the base of his neck. "You've got this all messed up. And you're comparing me to them again. I *want* to be here. More than anything, *really*. There isn't anywhere I'd rather be. Not a single person I'd rather spend my time with. Coming here, being with you, protecting you, it's the only reason I wake up every day, and I go to sleep every night counting the minutes until I can be back by your side. How do you not see that by now? I would have nothing if I didn't have this, if I didn't have you."

"That's even worse, Simon." I yearn to reach out and touch his arm but I don't. "Because you don't have me. This will never be what you want it to be, and what kind of person am I to sit here and torture you with the details of my relationships. I'm not being fair to you. None of this is."

"If you think for a second that it isn't all worth it, you're wrong."

"You're delusional, you have to be. You can't possibly be okay with this arrangement."

"God damn it, June." Simon stands from the bed so suddenly I accidentally flinch. His demeanor immediately shifts and he lowers his voice. "I'm so sorry." Simon drops to his knees next to the mattress and stares up at me, his hands reaching up toward me but not landing on their target. "I'd never hurt you; you need to know this."

"I..." My heart pounds wildly and I'm not entirely sure which of the many things going on it's from. "I believe you." And I'm telling the truth, because Simon has never given me a reason to doubt him. Not once has he proven to be a liar. Maybe he was a little deceptive in the very beginning but it was more him being cryptic than him lying.

"They'll come around eventually, love. And if they don't...I'll always be here for you. No matter what. Even if you never feel the same, I'm not going anywhere." He flits his gaze behind him, at my door. "But I do need to get out of here before one of them appears and decapitates me."

I softly smile and inch my hand toward him. I rest my fingers just along his, our skin barely touching. "Will you do something for me?" I shouldn't ask him for anything, but I cannot resist the allure of the adrenaline rush the night out with him gave me.

"Anything."

"Can we have another night like last night? You and me."

Simon pulls his left hand back and runs it through his hair, leaving the other one next to mine. "We almost got caught. That could have been bad."

"But we didn't." I continue to push the boundaries and wrap my index finger around his.

He draws in a breath and sighs. "You're killing me."

"Please."

He studies our interlocked fingers, and I can't help but wonder what's going through his mind and if it's the same thing that's on mine.

"I'll think about it, okay?"

I let out a squeal. "Thank you, thank you, thank you."

Simon shakes his head and stands. "God damn you're cute."

Just moments ago, I got a text from both Magnus and Dom about arranging dates for this week, my excitement for that nowhere near the thrill of Simon possibly taking me somewhere dangerous again.

# CHAPTER 10

# Magnus

I kind of want to murder Dominic.

I mean, it would make things *so much* fucking easier.

I wouldn't have to lie to June. I wouldn't have to suffer through the wrath of disappointing her, letting her down.

I could speak freely, the way I want to, and she wouldn't be left in the dark, questioning things left and right.

And honestly, I don't fucking blame her. I would, too. We went from a solid and inseparable unit to this detached shit show that keeps her at an arm's length. I want nothing more than to pull her into our darkness, not because I want to put her in danger, but because she can handle it. Hell, she very well could even help us navigate our way through this shit storm that is consuming our life right now.

Maybe she'd even cut us a little slack and understand *why* we're so occupied with business dealings. But how can she understand anything when Dom insists on keeping her in the dark?

But, killing Dom would create a nightmare itself. Our entire organization would crumble beneath us and we'd lose the minimal hold we currently have. He is the glue and without him, things would absolutely fall apart.

Plus, June is in love with him, and I can't imagine she'd take too kindly to me murdering one of her boyfriends.

I don't exactly hate the guy, either.

He just gets on my fucking nerves from time to time.

Coen isn't any better. He's the first to want to hide things from her like it'll somehow shield her from the threats if she doesn't know about them. Part of me thinks that he truly believes if he avoids telling her, maybe it'll stop the bad thing from happening.

That's not how these kinds of things work, and the longer we harbor this secret, the more damage it does. To her, to me—to *us*.

Hell, Dom doesn't even want to inform Beckett, who spends the majority of each day protecting the girl we all love. He's too insecure that it'll cause Beckett to doubt his authority and give him an opportunity to steal the throne from him.

As if June didn't do everything in her power to make sure that wouldn't happen.

The woman nearly died for him to secure that win, and he repays her by lying to her and being secretive as fuck.

He claims he's doing it to protect her—that this is what's in her best interest—but Dom can be a giant fucking idiot sometimes.

I flip the very last pancake and turn off the burner. My phone buzzes from a notification that one of the people I've hired for today is pulling into the driveway. I grant them access, send a quick message, and rush to the front door to unlock it. I go back to the kitchen and finish arranging the breakfast I've prepared for my sleeping beauty. Once I've tweaked things about twenty-seven times, I grab hold of it and carefully walk toward the stairs.

"You can set up downstairs," I tell the woman who comes through the front door. "It's straight through there to the left."

She nods and carries a long table at her side.

I'm not supposed to let strangers into the house, especially when times are tough like they are now, but I spent hours between—and even during—meetings vetting numerous companies and ensuring this one would pass Dom's insane security protocol. Okay, maybe not *pass*, but close e-fucking-nough.

I go the rest of the way to June's room, nudging the door open with my elbow and stepping inside.

She stirs and opens her eyes, blinking a few times and rubbing at them. "You're home still. What time is it?"

"About eight." I place the full tray on her bed and sit on the edge. "Breakfast for my princess."

"This smells fucking heavenly." She sits up but then focuses her sights on me. "What if I was craving something else for breakfast?"

My heart skips a beat. "That could be arranged." I lean over and kiss her cheek.

She turns toward me and catches my lips with hers. "Thank you." June focuses back on the assortment of food and beverages. She picks up the steaming cup of coffee and takes a cautious sip. "When do you have to leave?" A sort of sadness lingers in each of her words.

"I took the day off for you."

"You're not serious."

"Deadly."

"The whole day? How?" She pops a green grape into her mouth and chews it slowly, her gaze fine-tuned on mine.

"I insisted."

"And Simon?"

"He has the day off, too, to do whatever he pleases."

"Interesting." June drinks more of her coffee and holds out her arm. "Pinch me, I must still be dreaming."

I skim my hand along her skin but when my sights trail down to her hand, my stomach drops. "What happened to your knuckles?" I rush over and flip on the light then make my way back to her. I trace my thumb over her bruised and swollen hand. I turn it over and take in the small cuts on her palm, too.

"Nothing." June tries to pull away but I latch onto the other hand, examining it, too.

"That's not nothing." I try to remain calm even though my first initial response is to burn the whole world to the ground. "Please, tell me what happened. I won't be mad, I promise."

For a second I worry that she isn't going to give in, but she surprises me by sighing and turning both palms toward me. "I got mad."

"So you punched something and dug your nails into your palms." It's not a question but more of a clarification of the damage that's been done.

"Yeah," she confirms.

I push around the edges of her knuckles. "Does this hurt?" I move her fingers to make sure everything is where it should be. "I can have our doctor come to the house and check this over."

"No, I'm fine, really. I don't want to make a big deal out of this."

How can she not realize that her health and well-being is our main priority? But in being so focused on her overall safety, we've neglected and ignored how she was actually feeling.

"I'm so sorry, princess." I bring her hand up and press my lips softly to the swollen and discolored spots. "You have every right to be angry with me. With all of us."

"It won't last forever though, right?"

"No." This would be the perfect opportunity to confess it all. To tell her the truth. That the man who ordered her to be kidnapped and tortured, the man responsible for almost taking her from this world, is still out there. That we made a mistake. We were so focused on our feud with Beckett that we missed the signs when they were right in front of our faces. We thought we eliminated the target, that all of the main threats were neutralized, but we only eliminated what he wanted us to think was him. Something much more sinister was at play. Even Beckett was convinced we had removed the other main person who could potentially overthrow either him or Dom for the top spot. But instead, the guy is hiding behind a false identity and waiting for the opportune time to strike. Only emerging from the shadows long enough to tease and taunt us with the mystery of who he really is, and the constant threat that he will take the two things that matter most to us.

June. And the throne.

Dom has been teetering on a dangerous balancing act of maintaining both, but in doing things the way he thinks is right, he's not only continually losing men to the attacks, and product that is being stolen or destroyed, he's pushing our girl away, too.

But because we insist on this stupid fucking united front, Dom has made both Hayes and I vow that we will not tell her the truth. Not until the real threat has been neutralized and things can return to somewhat normal.

My concern is that if things don't fucking change soon, it's going to be too late.

Our businesses are suffering, but more importantly, so are our relationships.

June isn't the only one who's angry—I'm consumed by an insufferable rage, too.

"You see this right here?" I point to a spot just to the left of my middle knuckle. A jagged and faded scar is covered with black ink. "And right here?" Another scar just along the other side of the knuckle. "I used to punch shit all the time when I was mad." I take her hand and run it over mine. "Feel that? They're all permanently knotted."

June skims her fingers over mine and examines my hand. "I never noticed that before."

I chuckle. "The tattoos cover more than you think."

"Really?" Her dark gaze looks up at me and it's like her soul is reaching out in hopes that mine will respond back.

I lift my shirt and bring her fingers to my side. "This one was from being stabbed." I trace a few more on my torso. "I can't even remember what some of them are from. It's like they all blur together." I stick out my arm and point to my biceps. "I got shot here. Flesh wound, nothing serious. Bled like a mother fucker though." I laugh and bring her hand to my face, trailing it along my nose "I've broken this thing countless times." I skim it down to my upper lip. "This little one is from the time I was driving like an asshole and wrecked my car. Fucking tooth went through my lip when I hit the airbag."

"Damn, Magnus, how are you not already dead?"

I laugh again dryly. "Your guess is as good as mine."

"You never really told me how you came into this line of work." She grips her coffee but keeps her other hand in mine.

"Well, I'd say it was a long story but it's really not." I think back to all those years ago. What seems like a lifetime ago, really. "We're all pretty much orphans, and those make the best candidates for this line of work. People who don't have anyone else are typically pretty desperate to fit in somewhere. I was a reckless kid…"

"I'm not at all surprised by that." She grins and takes a drink of her coffee.

"Somehow, I was probably worse back then. Anyway, I was a delinquent. I fucked around and vandalized everything I could. I trespassed; I stole shit to pawn. Anything I could do to earn a few bucks to eat. I bounced around at aunts and uncles, cousins, fuck, I used to crash on random strangers' couches. I did anything I could to survive."

I've never been one to talk about my past, but with her, right now, it's like she needs this story more than my desire to keep it in.

June pours syrup on her pancakes and eats a small bite. Without really thinking about it, I reach over and wipe the syrup from her lip with my thumb, licking it off and continuing my story.

"I was fucking around at this construction site one day. Trying to find tools to steal. I heard a commotion, some yelling. Nothing crazy, but then there was a gunshot, and I froze in place. I hid up against a slab of sheet rock that hadn't been hung yet. It was just propped up along the wall. I remember pressing up on it, trying to fucking disappear. But I leaned back too far and my head went in between the studs and into the insulation. That shit itches like a mother fucker, and I could barely sit fucking still. I had a crowbar in my hand, like it would somehow outpower a gun. I was a kid, ya know?"

June nods and takes another forkful of her pancakes into her mouth.

"Anyway, this big brute of a man rounded the corner into the unfinished room I was in. I held my breath, thinking I could pretend I didn't exist if I didn't move. He held a pistol at his side and stared right fucking at me. I nearly pissed my pants. He looked from the crowbar to me like four times and then he finally spoke. He had asked me what I was doing, and in all my years running around various types of criminals, I knew there was no way I could bullshit this guy. I had spent my whole life reading people, figuring out who I could fuck with and who I couldn't. It's probably the only thing that's kept me alive this long. Well, that and I can run really fast." I chuckle and accept the bite that June offers me.

"Was it Dom?" June asks.

I nod slightly. "Dude was intimidating as fuck. Like pure evil had stepped through the door. He asked me what I was doing and I told him the truth. That I was stealing tools to take to the pawn shop. He asked me why and I said I needed money to eat. I remember there was this moment where I swear he was deciding whether or not he was going to kill me right there. I contemplated going after him with the crowbar but I knew I'd never outmaneuver him. Finally, he spoke, but it wasn't what I expected. He motioned with the gun for me to follow him, turning around on his way out and telling me to leave the crowbar.

"I thought that was it, that he was going to just take me somewhere else to shoot me, somewhere that it would be easier to clean up. I had seen and heard about shitty stuff that happened in and around that neighborhood, but I had never been that up close and personal to it. To the fucking grim reaper himself. I followed him through the house, past the room he had shot that other guy, where a couple dudes were cleaning up the mess. He led me out front and told me to get into his car. I still didn't know what he had planned for me, if he was going to sell me into human trafficking or had something more sinister in mind. In those few minutes, I ran every possible worst-case scenario through my head. I couldn't fucking believe it when we pulled up in front of a diner. I thought it was fucking weird, like why bring me here to off me? But he put away his gun before getting out of the car, walked me right into the place, sat me down at a booth and told me to order whatever the fuck I wanted. On him."

June's eyes widen a bit like she's hanging on my every word.

"I got the biggest fucking cheeseburger of my life. French fries *and* onion rings.

A chocolate milkshake. I nearly puked. I ate so much but I figured, I'm going to die anyway, what the hell. But I didn't die. Instead, Dom remained stiff as a board in the booth across from me. His suit was perfectly pressed and his cufflinks were shiny as fuck. He asked me about where I was staying, how I got money, if I had any family. But then he asked me why I told him the truth. I didn't have an answer really, just that my gut told me to."

I pop a slice of bacon off the tray and munch on it.

"Then what happened?" June swallows down some of the orange juice I brought her.

"Well, he asked me if I wanted to make some cash. Told me that it would probably be sketchier than how I was already acquiring my funds, and that it was still illegal, but that he would be there if I ran into any trouble. Obviously, the pay was better, too, and more consistent. He told me I'd never have to worry about where I'd get my next meal."

June sighs. "That explains why you're a little obsessed with food."

"Yeah, probably." I shrug, not having ever really put the two together. I'm damn good at reading other people but I'm kind of an idiot when it comes to dealing with myself. The only thing I really know for sure is how much I fucking love this girl sitting in front of me.

"You want another bite?" She holds out the pancake stuffed forkful, her other hand below it to catch any of the syrup that falls.

I allow her to feed me and reach for her coffee to wash it down. "Dom and I had a pretty sudden understanding of one another, and it wasn't long until I started picking up little tells from the people he associated with. I caught a couple of them in a lie, and once Dom really realized how good I was at reading people, he brought me in even closer. I was like a fly on the wall for a lot of meetings. No one understood why he kept me around, but Dom kept weeding out traitors and growing the ranks. I never once betrayed or gave him a reason not to trust me, and there wasn't anything I wouldn't have done for him, and vice versa. Loyalty is a hard thing to come by, especially in our world. Dom was the first person to ever really give a shit about me, and as foreign as it was, I wasn't about to fuck that up. I think it was like five years later when he came across Hayes, the poor kid was fucking traumatized and psychotic but Dom saw his potential, too. The dude doesn't spare many, if any, really. But Hayes and I were lucky enough that Dom took us under his wing and gave us this life. If I'm being honest, I probably would have either ended up in jail or dead if it weren't for him. The same goes for Hayes. I know he did it for his own gain, but we would have never amounted to anything without him."

June reaches for my hand. "I can't imagine a world without you or Coen or Dom. I'm glad you three found each other. It's like you were the family you always needed."

"Found family, for sure." I weave my fingers around hers. "But we were even luckier finding you, princess."

"It's kind of strange how it all worked out. My history with Coen, meeting you and Dom separately, waking up in this house, and seeing you all standing next to each other. Fucking Coen pointing a gun at me." She pauses like she's recalling the memory. "I couldn't believe any of it. I was in shock. The Coen I knew, from ten years ago, he would have never hurt a fly. Then I run into him at a bar and he tells me he's in *private security*." She forms air quotes with her fingers around the last two words. "He nearly broke my date's arm. Slammed him into the bar and didn't let him go until I told him he was with me."

"A date?" I do a poor job of disguising my jealousy.

"It lasted for a whole five minutes. I got the guy's name wrong like four times. I think that was the day I delivered food here." She rubs at her temple. "Feels like an eternity ago."

"It does, doesn't it?" I skim my thumb along her cheek.

"I missed this," she tells me, her gaze boring into mine. "Us."

I exhale and wish like hell I could continue spilling all the secrets, tell her every little detail about every little thing until there was nothing hidden between us. I want her to know everything—my past, my present, my future. Because none of it matters without her. I didn't come alive until she showed up on my doorstep all those months ago. They say love at first sight isn't real, but I knew from the very fucking moment I laid my sights on her that she had stolen my heart.

"I miss you even when I'm with you." I lean toward her and press my lips to hers. I breathe her in and kiss her deeper, the intensity of her touch growing with each eager advancement. I climb onto the bed and push her gently back as I position my body between her legs.

She holds herself up with her elbows until I'm fully on top of her, her body relaxing back onto the mattress.

I tug the pillow down and position it under her head and then grab a second one and place it under her ass. Pulling up her oversized tee shirt, my mouth instinctively finds her bare skin, and my lips leave a trail of kisses on her stomach. Inching farther south, I make my way to her center and nudge her panties to the side with my nose, licking at the crease of her thigh. I slide my tongue along her wetness, too greedy in my own desire to taste her sweetness, and flick her clit, popping it between my lips and sucking on it.

June arches toward me and moans, her hand gripping the top of my head and pushing me into her.

I shove two fingers inside her and grin when she tenses around me. I rock them back and forth and curve them upward. My cock hardens in my pants, and I reach down to reposition it as it grows against my jeans. I ache for it to be buried deep in her but this day is about her, and right now, her pleasure is my highest priority.

It doesn't take long for her climax to build. We've done this dance long enough for me to know just the right way to lick and suck and finger fuck her to oblivion. And no matter how familiar I get with her pussy, I'm grateful for every fucking moment of it.

"Magnus," she moans.

I spread her legs and throw one over my shoulder, giving myself a better angle to shove my fingers deeper. I spit onto my hand before pushing another within her, filling her even more.

"You're so fucking tight, princess."

She quivers under my touch and explodes around me, her juices coating my fingers and tongue as I lick it up.

I flip over onto my back and drag her still-trembling body on top of me. "Sit on my face, princess."

June giggles but complies. "I'm going to crush you."

I rip her panties completely off, tearing them to shreds, and loop my arms around her ass to encourage her to straddle my face. "Good, don't let up." I yank her down until her pussy is finally within reach. I slide my tongue across the length of her and nibble her throbbing clit. "I want you to fuck my face, princess."

June leans forward, gripping the headboard and pressing herself on me. She's subtle about it at first, but finally finds her groove, my grasp encouraging her to give me more.

I dig my fingers into her and bask in the life force of her pussy. I swirl my tongue and dip it into her while she rocks back and forth on my mouth. I run my hand up her back, gliding it along the arch of her delicate body.

Just when I'm sure she's about to come for a second time, she slows her pace and straightens her body. She spins and positions herself facing the opposite direction but keeps my face covered with her.

I moan against her as she grips my cock through my pants and strokes it. I throb in her grasp and do everything I can not to explode right here and now. But between the taste of her coating my mouth and the warmth of her hand around my girth, I'm ready to fucking go.

June unbuttons my pants and slides them over my hips, freeing my cock from its confines. She leans forward and drags the tip along her lips before circling her tongue and taking just an inch of me in her mouth. Clutching the base of my shaft, she takes me into her mouth, a little at first but then nearly gagging on my length.

I continue to grind her pussy onto my face, wishing I could crawl up inside there and fucking live forever.

June sucks my cock like there's no tomorrow, her lips cupping my shaft and her hand sliding up and down with them, only intensifying my pleasure. She pops me out of her mouth and strokes me against her lips, the softness of them enough to make me fucking climax. But I've never been the one to give in this quickly. She glides her tongue up me and then scoots down my body, her pussy inching farther away. With her ass still facing me, she glides herself along my pounding cock. She positions it at her entrance and slides down onto me.

With the best fucking view in town, I watch her take every inch of me inside her. I clutch her thighs and spread them apart, pivoting my hips up and fucking her. "God damn, princess. You feel so fucking good."

She leans forward, giving me somehow an even better look. June rocks back and forth on my cock, and I can't help myself from touching her from behind. I reach under her, positioning my hand at the base of her pussy as it rides my shaft. I glide my thumb along her wetness and up toward her tight asshole. I push along the edges and she lets out a whimper and spreads her legs wider for me.

"You're such a good fucking girl," I tell her as I pop the tip of my thumb through her puckered ass. "You're taking me so well, princess." I grip her thigh with my other hand and thrust in her from below, increasing my intensity and fucking her harder. I glide my palm up to her ass cheek and move it in a circle before bringing it back and slapping her.

She tightens both around my thumb and my cock but leans down even more, her face smashed into the foot of the bed and her hands weaved through her own hair.

"Harder," she begs of me.

I circle that soft spot again and crack her ass once more, then again, and again until her butt is flushed red and swollen. "You like that, don't you?" I thrust inside her. "Do you want more? Or do you want me to stop? Just tell me to stop." I fuck her harder.

"Keep going, please," June breathes.

My cock throbs deep within her, my orgasm too fucking close. I smack her ass harder this time and she rocks back on me, her body quivering as her climax consumes her.

She screams out and pushes back on me, her pussy tightening around my cock and practically fucking milking me.

I explode inside of her and lean my head back as my pleasure fills her.

It's only after I've come that I realize we weren't wearing a condom. I knew this felt too fucking good, I was just too fucking stupid to realize it sooner. There really is something to be said about thinking with the wrong brain.

Once June stops moving and pulsating, I press my hand against the warm red spot on her ass. "Um, princess. We, uh...weren't wearing protection."

June perks her head up. "Oh shit. I, um, I'm on birth control so we should be fine, right?"

I slide out of her aching hole and sit up to drag her onto my lap. "We should be, yeah, but I'll pick up a Plan B just in case." I kiss her cheek. "Unless you want a baby Magnus running around."

I'd never wanted kids before but somehow, sharing that with her doesn't at all seem that terrifying. But the reality is, we live in a world that's too dangerous to bring children into it. If I thought I was worried about her all the time, bringing a kid into the mix would only make me die early from massive heart failure. I'm pretty sure Dom and Coen would agree—as appealing as knocking her up is, it's not a risk we should take. Although, I have no idea where she stands on reproducing, and if that might be a deal breaker for her.

Suddenly, I'm overwhelmed with the thought of her leaving because we can't give her the family that she's always wanted.

"As adorable as you are..." June leans her head against my chest. "I don't think I could handle a miniature version of you." She laughs. "Or Dom or Co." She presses her hand against my unwieldy heart. "I'm good with what we have." June peels herself away and looks right at me. "Unless you wanted kids. Did you? Do you?"

I grin at watching her experience the same fear I had just seconds ago at not knowing what she truly wanted. I shake my head. "I want you, that's all."

It's hard enough keeping one additional person alive, let alone a smaller human who doesn't understand that their three daddies run a criminal syndicate.

"Magnus, I have to tell you something."

My heart lurches and I do what I can to remain calm and collected. "Anything, princess."

"I don't think I can walk." She breaks into a huge smile and laughs. "Seriously. My legs are inoperable. You'll have to bury me in this bed. And let everyone know you fucked me to my death."

I shake my head and poke her in the side. "You had me sweating bullets there for a second thinking I did something wrong."

"You did." She giggles. "I can't move." June pokes at her thigh. "These things are fucking Jell-O."

Still holding her in my arms, I stand from the bed and wiggle my pants the rest of the way, completely stepping out of them and advancing toward the bathroom. I carry her over to the toilet and set her down gently on it. Giving her the tiniest bit of privacy, I leave her to relieve herself and go over to the shower, turning the faucet and stripping out of the rest of my clothes. Once the temperature is good and the toilet has been flushed, I go back over to her, tugging the baggy shirt over her head and tossing it aside.

"You're stunning, princess." I lift her into my arms, cradling her and carrying her into the massive shower. I sit her down against the wall and adjust the jets to hit her without splattering her in the face. I lower myself onto the tile next to her and let the weight of her body melt into mine. "You sure about the kid thing?"

She tilts her head over at me and pinches her brows together. "Yeah. Are you?"

"I was just going to say, if you are, I could get a vasectomy. That way we don't have to worry about anything happening."

"You'd be willing to do that?"

"If that's what you wanted, yes. Without question. We have options now, but we—you—might not always. If it meant your safety, and getting to have sex with you without a condom, I'd let them chop my arm off, too."

"But how would they ever decide?" June runs her hand along each of my arms. "They're both so nice."

I press my lips to the top of her head. "So, it's decided? You're totally sure? Or do you want some time to think about it?"

"That's not my decision to make, Magnus. It's your body. What if you..." She doesn't finish her sentence but I know exactly where her train of thought is going.

I cup her chin in my hand. "Never, not for as long as I live, will I ever want to be with someone other than you. Do you hear me?" I glance back and forth between her eyes.

"I hear you."

"I love you."

"I love you, more."

"Never," I tell her, knowing damn well her next word.

"Always," we say at the same time.

I kiss her lips and then her nose. Water droplets cascade down her body and make me jealous of how much closer they are to her than me. I shouldn't, because she's already complaining about being worn out, and because the next phase of our day is set up and waiting for us in the basement, but I weave my hand between her legs and guide them apart. I trail my finger along the inner crease of her thigh and dip it inside her soaked entrance.

June moans and leans her head back against the wall. Her gaze locks onto mine. "You're not serious, are you?"

I lick my lips and nod my head. "Lay down and let me do the work."

She reaches for my cock and it immediately hardens in her grip. With a smirk on her face, she rises to her knees and turns around, backing herself right onto my shaft.

I grow harder inside of her, stuffing her full and stretching her tender pussy. I go slow at first, pumping my hips into her ass. I weave my arms around her body, holding her close to me, one hand finding her clit, the other reaching up and pinching her nipple between my fingers.

June moans and tilts her head toward me, her lips desperate to find mine.

We kiss, our tongues lavishing each other and our bodies desperate to gain any more proximity.

She bounces onto me and matches my rhythm, my finger circling her pulsing nub.

"Come for me, princess," I breathe into her mouth. "I want to feel you shatter around me." I slide my hand from her nipple over her wet chest and grip the base of her throat.

June places her hands on both of mine, guiding my pressure on both her neck and clit. She continues to thrust back onto me, her pussy tightening the grip it has on my cock. "Fuck," she mutters.

"That's my girl." I squeeze her neck and bury my cock inside of her so deep I'm afraid it'll hurt her.

But all she does is sit back further and let me do as I please.

I flick her clit and pinch it between my fingers, rocking them from side to side. The shift in sensation sends her spiraling into an explosive orgasm, my cock spewing inside of her pulsating pussy. We come together, our breaths ragged and our bodies quivering.

She exhales dramatically with the lingering shudders that come over her. "I think I'm going to need a Plan B after that one."

After a two-hour couples massage and a hilarious pedicure where June managed to talk me into painting my toenails purple, we take a break to relax from our relaxation in the living room. It's been the perfect day—one I didn't realize I needed just as badly as she did.

In our line of business, there's hardly any downtime, and when there was, there wasn't anyone to share it with. Having a meal with your live-in criminal partners isn't comparable to what we're doing now.

"How are your legs?" I ask her teasingly.

"Barely functioning, thank you very much."

"You're so very welcome." I grip her hand and tug her toward me. "I'll have to run out and make a stop at the pharmacy."

"What? You don't want to send Alec after a morning-after pill?" She leans into me and I welcome every bit of her body close to mine.

"I didn't think of that, actually." I kiss her forehead. "Good idea."

June glides her fingers under mine and weaves them around each other. "I'd just rather be the cool aunt, you know. Cora can have all the babies, and I'll sugar them up and dip when they're bouncing off the walls."

"Is Cora even dating anyone?" I ask her.

"No," she chuckles. "She still swears she and Miller had a moment and is trying to convince me that he's bi and not gay."

"I wonder how long we can keep up the act before she figures it out."

"Forever, hopefully." June sighs. "I don't want you to take this the wrong way, because I'm forever grateful you guys finally told me the truth, but..." She trails off leaving the rest of her sentence up in the air.

I finish it for her. "You don't want this life for her."

She turns toward me. "Is that bad?"

"No, not at all." I tuck her hair behind her ear. "Not everyone is cut out for it. I think it's smart of you to want to protect her."

"But?"

"Well, how did it make you feel when that decision was made for you?"

"Like shit."

I nod. "It's an impossible situation. Someone is going to get hurt either way." Like right now, the secrets I've been carrying haven't just been eating away at me, they've been harming June, too. No matter what we do, no matter how hard we try to do what's right, we keep fucking up. Maybe one day we'll figure out how to keep her safe without fucking lying to her.

My phone buzzes and without meaning to, I glance down at the notifications that pop across the screen.

**Dom: I have a lead. You need to get here now.**
  **Dom: Right fucking now.**

. . .

"You have to go, don't you?" June pulls away, her mood immediately shifting.

"I...I don't want to." I'd do anything to stay here with her for the rest of my life.

"It's fine, I'll call Simon and let him know." She hops up from the couch and grabs her phone from the table.

Simon answers on the first ring.

I can't make out what he says, but she tells him, "You're on babysitting duty." She hangs up without another word and comes back over to me. June plants her hands on my shoulders. "I love you, a lot, Magnus. But I don't know how much more of this I can take. This isn't a warning, it's not a threat, it's just the truth. You should try it out sometime." She kisses my lips before walking away and leaving me here alone to wonder about the implications of her declaration.

# June

I'm not sure what's worse—knowing that something has the potential to be great or realizing it's never going to happen.

That's my life. A balancing act of always coming close but never being close enough.

In life. In death. In love.

And aren't they one and the same, really? Love *is* life, but ultimately ends just like death.

All of the words have been spoken. The feelings have been felt. Nothing is new and fresh, and every bit of it eventually fades into the abyss. Only for the cycle to repeat again and again, claiming anyone who dares gamble the greatest wager of all —their heart.

Bloodied, beaten, shattered—no matter what you do to avoid it from latching hold of you and sinking its vicious claws into your chest and ripping the thing out. If you're lucky, maybe you'll make it out of it alive, but sometimes, if you do, you'll have wanted to die anyway.

"June," Gwyneth says from across the table. "You've barely touched your ceviche."

"Sorry," I tell her and shovel a bite into my mouth, chewing it with a forced smile on my face. "It's delicious," I murmur once I've swallowed and patted at my lips like a proper, polite lady.

"As I was saying, I do think you'd adore Italy. The northern coastline is truly magical with its lakes and vineyards. And Treviso is just stunning. Has this old charm to it with the cobbled lanes and canals. Enough about me, though, what have you been up to since we last got together?"

My gaze flits to the man standing post at the far corner of this empty room. Simon's stare catches mine and he glances away.

"Other than being under constant surveillance?" I nod to the beautiful body-guard. "I don't do much with everyone treating me like a child who can't be left alone."

Gwyneth tilts her head to the side. "And if you had your freedom, what would you do with it?"

I exhale and ponder her question. "I don't know. Maybe walk into town on my own. Eat a meal by myself. Go out dancing with my best friend without feeling like I'm the freak who has eyes on her at all times."

"But that's the life you chose, June. For as long as you live, there will never not be someone looking in your direction. Whether they are friend or foe depends on the day."

I sip my water and focus on the droplets that roll down the side of the glass. "I'm being selfish, I understand."

Gwyneth shakes her head and holds out her hand. "No, you have every right to be. But things are different now, and I'm not entirely sure if you were aware of those stakes when you sealed your fate."

"I..." I push around the seafood with my fork. "I think I could deal with that, really, but..."

"Listen," she continues where I left off. "I'm going to be honest with you, June. I didn't think you had it in you. I had my doubts about what you were capable of. But seeing you take initiative and attempt to settle the score on your own accord... I didn't know whether you were plain foolish or brilliant. Those men lost their minds, all four of them. And I've never witnessed them care about anyone other than themselves or what kind of advantage they could get. They would have willingly given up everything they had to see you have one more day."

Here I was, risking my life for them to have everything, when they would have given it all up for me.

"Can I tell you a little secret?" Gwyneth leans into the table and lowers her voice. "Just between us girls."

I nod. "Of course."

"Up until that very moment, when Simon conceded, he had a strong chance of winning."

My heart pounds in my chest. "What?"

She smirks and grabs her wine glass. "I didn't figure you knew."

"I was told otherwise."

"I don't know what the outcome of that day would have been had you not intervened, but I do know this for sure—you're the one who solidified Dominic's win."

I helped him win his fucking war and he repays me by shutting me out?

How is that fair?

"The...what shall I call them? Adjustments. The adjustments that they're experiencing right now are only the beginning of a much bigger storm that is coming. Times are changing and pressure is approaching from each direction. It's part of the reason I made the decision to leave when I did. I'm getting too old to handle such situations, and after losing Franklin, it made me realize how much of my life it had consumed. He wasn't always a ruthless man, my Franklin, but his ambition and greed got the best of him and turned him into the monster he was when he died. Dominic didn't just take over the entire enterprise, he inherited all of its enemies and liabilities, all of its demons, too. There is no escaping for him. Dark days are looming ahead."

She says it all with conviction, like there is no avoiding this predestined outcome. That Dominic no longer has a say in the matter except to accept that he will succumb to the darkness that is waiting for him.

How can I sit back and let that happen?

But how can I do anything when he refuses to let me in?

I guess I'll find out tomorrow during our one-on-one time. I will make him talk to me even if it means sacrificing a time that was meant to be romantic, to bring us closer when we've never felt further apart.

"I believe in him," I tell her.

She nods. "I know you do, and maybe that will be his saving grace."

A waiter comes out to take our plates and make room for our next course.

"Thank you," I say while he avoids making direct eye contact.

Does he know who she is? Does he know who the man standing near the door is? Does he know who I am—and the men I surround myself with? Is this what it means to be with them? A threat by association?

"Your studies have concluded?" Gwyneth asks me.

"Yes, a while back, actually."

"I see. And what do you intend on doing now that you've finished?" She takes another drink of her wine—so ladylike and pretentious.

Just drink the fucking wine already.

Another waiter brings our dishes but as he walks away, I catch his forearm. "Can I get a bourbon, neat, whatever you have back there?"

"That sounds delightful, I'll have the same," she chimes in.

A whistle sounds from across the way. Simon waves the waiter over to him. They exchange a few words that I can't quite make out.

"I'm sure he's just insisting he get you the best or he'll end his life." Gwyneth winks at me. "That one...he's always been a wild card, but with you, he's different."

"How so?" I ask her even though I know I shouldn't. I should let it go and avert the conversation back to her trip to Ireland or Finland or wherever the fuck she went.

*Italy.* That's right, it was Italy. *Silly me.*

"Well, for starters, he quite literally gave up his ambitions for you to become a glorified babysitter."

I chuckle. "That's exactly what I said."

She smiles, too. "Although, I don't think he quite minds."

"He claims he doesn't." I steal a glance at him and sure enough, he's staring directly at me. I shift my gaze behind me just to confirm there isn't something else he's looking at. There isn't.

She keeps her voice lower than it was before. "Simon was born into this life. It's all he's known. But after what happened with his sister, nothing was ever really the same."

"His sister?"

"Tragic accident. They were at the lake, the two of them. She fell in, hit her head under the dock, drowned. Simon went in after her, almost drowned, too. A fisherman pulled him out of the water."

My heart breaks at remembering him tell me he was afraid of water, that he couldn't swim. It's no wonder he has reoccurring nightmares of drowning.

"Anyway, he went from being a loving and sweet child to this closed-off boy I no longer recognized. He was consumed by his dreams of taking over the company. Rose through the ranks quicker than most. But Dom always stood in the way. He had more years, more experience. Dom was always going to be next in line—that's what Franklin had put in place. Didn't trust Simon's new-age antics. Thought he'd never cut it. But when Frank died, it opened up that opportunity for Simon to prove to the council that he had what it took. And I'll be damned, the kid nearly pulled it off. If it weren't for you, he very well could have."

In helping Dominic win, I caused Simon to lose. Both men were deserving, but one of them already had my heart. Had I not interfered, maybe it would be Simon in Dom's place, but then what would have become of Dom, and what would have happened with me? Would Simon have let the guys walk away? And what would he have done with me? It's clear he's obsessed, but where would that line have been drawn if he was the one in control?

I guess we'll never find out because I did step in and threaten Simon's life with that blade from Gwyneth's office. Only, isn't that what she wanted me to do all along?

In the various instances where she and I have gotten together for these occasional chats, I've never asked her about that day. But the more I learn about these men and the layers of this world I uncover, revealing the truth has never been more appealing.

"Was it a test?" I ask her.

"What do you think?" She doesn't bother pretending like she doesn't know what I'm referring to.

"I think..." I fiddle with one of the many spoons in my place setting. Whoever thought someone needed this many utensils clearly never did the dishes a day in their life. "It was," I continue. "I think you wanted to see what I'd be willing to do for them, and if I had what it took to take risks, to put myself on the line, and how far I'd take it. You brought me into that room for a reason and dangled that dagger right in my line of sight. And I think you wanted to see how *they* would react to me taking that risk. You weren't just testing me, you were testing them, too."

"Sounds like you're pretty confident in your reasoning." Gwyneth picks up the glass the waiter sets down in front of her, and she holds it out toward me. "To taking risks."

I raise mine in the air. "And to them paying off."

But did they, really? Maybe for Dominic, but it's obvious Magnus is caught in the middle of this back and forth, and poor Simon had his life completely ripped to shreds when I poised that dagger to his chest. Even Coen is more flustered than usual. And here I am, wondering where things went wrong and why none of my men want to tell me the truth about a Goddamn thing.

I sip the amber liquid and savor the expensive taste. "Was I right?" I ask her.

"Well, you sure weren't wrong."

Her strangely deceptive answer causes my head to spin at the other possibilities I may have left out. What other reason would she have had for leading me to that weapon? Unless...

Unless she wanted to eliminate me.

That house had rules, and it was a violence-free zone. The use of such weapons was prohibited. Maybe in bringing me in there, she wanted to see how stupid I really was. To see if I was capable of following orders and doing what was expected of me. And if I didn't, she was within her right to have me killed. To make sure that the guys weren't distracted by some random female. I had already caused them to have a few mishaps, and with me in the picture, their work wouldn't be their constant priority. But maybe Simon really was the wildcard, and his actions were the only thing that stopped her from following through with her diabolical plan.

But, like anything else in my life, I'll never know the truth—her lips are just as sealed as Dominic's are.

"Do you have what it takes, June?"

"Excuse me?"

"To make this work." Her menacing stare goes right through me.

Do I? I thought I did, but with all of the secrets, I'm not so sure. I can't force them to be honest with me, and the more they push me away the harder it makes things. I can't build a bridge with only half of the supplies. And until they decide to bring me into the fold, my doubts will only continue to fester.

"Do you?" I ask her.

"I guess we'll find out."

# Dominic

"*Don't forget about me, tonight,*" I recall June saying this morning when I kissed her goodbye.

All I ever think about is her, how could I forget?

I threw our date together last minute, but she's right in insisting we get more time together. It's not that I don't want to, I've just been a bit preoccupied with tracking down the man responsible for ordering her hit and disrupting our business. I hate that I can't be honest with her, but the less she knows, the better. It's safer that way. As long as Simon keeps his word and protects her like his life depends on it, she will remain out of harm's reach.

I drag the edge of the baseball bat across the concrete and approach the man tied to the chair in the middle of the room. "How do you feel about your knees?" I nudge him in the chest and lift his chin with the bat. "Or those teeth of yours." I step closer and reach for a pair of pliers off the tray. I shove them into his mouth and yank one of his molars out as he whines and moans.

He hacks bloody spit onto the floor next to me. "You fucking psycho. I don't know anything."

I discard the tooth on the tray and set the pliers back in their place. "That's the thing, you wouldn't be here if you didn't." I take a deep breath and exhale. "Just between you and me, I don't give a shit if you die. I'll stay here all day ripping you apart piece by piece. I'll pluck every tooth from your head. I'll peel your fingernails off one by one. I'll break every single bone in your body until you tell me what you know. Or you die. It's as simple as that. And if you think for a second that I won't enjoy it, you're wrong. Oh, I'll get great satisfaction in watching you suffer."

"You're fucking sick, man!" the guy cries out.

"I never said I wasn't." I grab the hammer and kneel before him, tugging his shoe off his foot and looking up at him. "Do you have anything you'd like to tell me?"

"Go to hell, asshole."

I drive the thing back and slam it down onto his foot, crushing every bone it comes into contact with. He screams out but it only fuels me to hurt him even more. Eventually, he will break, but in the meantime, he's going to be a fun one to crack.

Despite him thrashing in his seat, I manage to yank his other shoe off. "You'll probably never walk again after this. But, once I'm done with you, walking will be the least of your concerns." I steady my aim, hesitating to give him an opportunity to speak. When he spits in my face, I thrust the hammer down harder than I did on the other foot. I stand, ignoring his cries of agony, and stroll over to the table with various torture devices. I pluck a rag off the end and wipe at my face. "This is fun, no?"

I turn toward him, tears streaming down his red-hot cheeks. His face is somehow so pale yet so full of color. What a twisted contradiction.

"You'll pay for this." He moans, his head struggling to stay upright. "You'll fucking pay."

I toss the rag aside and consider his meaningless words. "I doubt that, but I appreciate your tenacity." I scan the tools and assess my options. "I could make this quick if you'd like, all you have to do is use that voice of yours for something other than crying."

"I'm dead either way," he blurts out. "Why would I tell you a damn thing?"

"Do you not know who I am? Do I need to remind you of the rumors whispered about the man with no remorse? The one who takes great pleasure in inflicting pain." I clasp onto the pliers again and go behind him, latching onto his index finger. "This." I press the thing under his nail and rip it from his finger. "Is just another day at the office." I ignore his screams and crush the same finger. "I could do this in my sleep."

Once he finally gathers his breath, he says, "He'll gut you like a fucking pig."

"Yeah?" I lean down, my hand pressed against his shoulder. "All you have to do is tell me a name and I'll give you a swift death. I'll even let you choose." I motion to the table behind me. "I'd probably pick a bullet in the head if I were you, but I'll be kind enough to let you decide."

"I don't have a fucking name," he yells at me. "Don't you think I'd have told you by now?"

"No, not particularly. I haven't even really gotten started." I take the spoon-looking thing from the table. "I think I'll pluck your eyes from your skull next. Actually..." I toss it aside. "I think I'll get my hands dirty for this one." I unbutton and roll my sleeves up. "I wonder what the chances of you dying are?" I pause and think this through. "Possibly high. I may have to hold off on that and save it for later." I face him. "What do you want to do next? What about electrocution? That could be fun."

"Savini," he blurts out. "Talk to fucking Savini. I don't know anything else, but Savini does."

I sigh and cross my arms. "Lorenzo Savini?"

He nods aggressively. "Yes. If anyone has any information, it will be him."

One of our organization's most notorious hitmen. A shadow like me that people fear. A man I respect because he's so damn good at his craft. He isn't afraid to get his hands dirty, but he has standards, a set of moral codes and boundaries he doesn't cross. I never considered he would have anything to do with June's kidnapping and torture because women and children are typically out of his scope of work. But that doesn't mean he doesn't know who did it.

"I am a man of my word," I tell the man I've been tormenting. "Pick your poison."

"Just shoot me and get it fucking over with. Please, for the love of—"

But I don't let him finish; I grab the pistol and fire a round straight through the center of his forehead and one in his chest for safe measure. "That wasn't so hard," I say to what's left of his dead body.

I pull out my phone, dialing one of my saved contacts.

"Sir?"

"I need a location for Lorenzo Savini and a clean-up crew over on Ninth."

"I'll have that to you immediately, sir."

I disconnect the line and shove the device back into my pocket. I secure the gun into my side holster and unfold my sleeves, smoothing them out and putting them back in their place. On my way toward the door, I slide my arms through the sleeves of my suit jacket.

---

The drive across town isn't long, but the traffic is more than I hoped for. I check the time as I'm leaving my SUV, my head spinning with all the things I need to accomplish before night's end.

"Your keys, sir?" The valet holds out his hand.

"No, it stays there. I won't be long." I rush past him and into the hotel. Ignoring the staff that attempts to greet me, I march across the polished floor to the restaurant beyond. I take one look around the various patrons and spot my target in the back corner. I almost overlook him in his nearly concealed position, but my eye is sharper than the average person's.

Upon my approach, he stands. "Mr. Adler." The man, about ten years my junior, extends his hand.

Pressed suit, similar to mine, lesser quality. Greying beard and that familiar murderous glimmer in his eyes I know all too well.

"Mr. Savini." I shake his hand firmly, his grip matching mine.

"What can I do for you? It must be of great importance if I'm graced by your presence in person." He motions for me to sit.

I unbutton my jacket and slide into the booth. "I believe you have information that could prove valuable to me."

He sits across from me. "I see. And what might that be?"

"Before I speak freely, I must ask that you tread lightly with what you choose to do with it."

Savini nods curtly. "Your reputation precedes you, Mr. Adler. I assure you; I have no reason to betray your trust. It's within my best interest to maintain our professional relationship."

"It's my understanding that you have your own reputation. That's why I feel confident you'll grasp my concern about the situation." I swallow and ignore the strong desire to keep my fucking mouth shut. I won't gain any insight if I don't follow up on any possible lead. And after I pulled Magnus away from his date to chase a dead-end, I have to keep pushing if I want to finally uncover the truth about who is responsible for hurting her.

"Please, continue," he tells me.

"I'm sure you've heard stories of what happened at the council choosing ceremony."

Savini bobs his head. "I was there."

"Ah, so you witnessed the shooting, and then the aftermath of it all."

"Yes."

"That woman, the one who was shot, she means a great deal to me. In our line of business, you can comprehend how significant and dangerous that is."

"Absolutely."

"That wasn't the first time her life was put in danger."

Savini raises his eyebrow, clearly intrigued by where this story is taking us.

"Not too long before that day, she was kidnapped and tortured. She was innocent then, and she remains that way to this day. She's not a part of this world, she's just someone caught in the crossfire of a war that was never meant for her."

"And you're trying to locate the man who harmed her?"

"No," I shake my head. "He's been dealt with." I take in a breath and exhale. "I'm trying to find the person who ordered the hit. He has evaded me, and I will not rest until he's brought to justice."

"I see."

"She was lucky enough to escape with her life, but with him still lurking in the shadows, I cannot afford to allow him to live." I consider how much more I should tell him but decide to leave it there. He doesn't need to know that this same man is also disrupting routine shipments and picking off my men left and right.

"You love this girl?"

"Does that part matter?"

"No."

"She didn't deserve what happened to her. I understand that being with me causes countless other threats to pop up, but this one is of great urgency."

Savini rakes his hand across his beard. "I don't have immediate information for you, but that doesn't mean I cannot find it for you. I'll do some digging and see what I can locate."

"And in return?"

Savini checks his watch and glances up at me. "I could use your influence on something urgent. You don't even have to do anything, just ride over there with me and your presence alone should be enough."

"You're sure you can get me a name?"

"Nobody hurts a woman and gets away with it. You have my word." He extends his hand across the table to solidify our agreement.

"Let's go."

He said it would be quick. An in and out job that wouldn't take long.

But when the ignorant little strung-out drug runners refused to stop harassing the women at the local strip club, Savini and I had to get our hands dirty.

The smartest of the bunch ran as soon as I stepped out from behind Savini's shadow.

A few stragglers smacked each other, loudly whispering amongst themselves and questioning whether I was real or not. Some of them evaded us, too.

But then there were the stupid ones. The fucking idiots who decided to get cocky and pull out their guns and take a handful of the strippers hostage.

It wasn't the cleanest operation, but Savini and I managed to slaughter every single remaining fuck boy with only a few injuries to the women. We worked well together, our backs to each other as we maneuvered through the dimly lit place to eliminate each of our targets.

I had shot the last one in the leg, his scream rippling through the air. He dropped his gun and clutched at the gaping wound as I shoved him onto the sticky floor and punched him over and over until blood dripped down my face. I rose from his dead body, and the women who were cowered in the corner gasped.

Savini reassured them that I would bring them no harm and told them to leave. He threw a quick bandage on the last woman's arm where a stray bullet grazed her and told her to get to the hospital. He shoved a fistful of cash into her hand and turned toward me.

"Are we good?" I had asked him.

He nodded and I left, which brings me to the here and now, where I'm speeding across town and running every red light to get to the woman I did this all for. The one that's going to fucking murder me for being late.

I burst through the garage door and into the house.

Magnus and Simon stop chatting and look right at me.

Magnus is the first to speak. "You can't go up there. Not like that."

"You don't understand, I have to." I glance at the clock, noting the three hours that have passed since when I told her I'd be here.

Simon puts his hand out to stop me. "Look in the fucking mirror, Dom." He nudges me toward the one near our bourbon bar.

Blood streaks my cheeks and speckles my hair and beard. My knuckles are tender and painted red, too. The shirt that was perfectly pressed earlier today is now ripped and destroyed, stained with remnants of the evening.

"She's already made it clear she wants to be left alone." Magnus comes over and slaps me on the back. "Your best bet is to get yourself cleaned up and beg for forgiveness when she cools down tomorrow."

"I didn't mean to..." I don't finish my sentence, because if being here was what I really wanted, I would have been. I might think I'm doing this all for her, but it's pointless if I lose her in the process. If I must lose her, I'd rather it be this way than in death. I'd rather her hate me than be dead.

I can live with that, but I can't live with doing nothing when I know her tormentor is still out there.

The only way to salvage this entire situation is if I come clean and tell her the truth about why I wasn't here.

But what if even that isn't enough to bring us back from the cliff I've thrown us off of?

# CHAPTER 13

# June

I'm so fucking mad I can't think straight.

I thought I would sleep it off, but no, what little rest I did get was taunted by nightmares I couldn't wake up from. Luckily, my obsessive bodyguard shook me to reality and cupped my face in his hands.

He isn't supposed to be in my bedroom, but that hasn't stopped him from crossing that line and coming in here when I've needed him.

After a long shower where I stood under the water until my skin turned red from the temperature, I towel dry my hair and moisturize the fuck out of my scalded body. I dress quickly, throwing on the first thing I find in the expansive closet, and step into the hall.

I run smack dab into Simon's strong chest. "Shit, I didn't see you there."

He steadies my shoulders. "Sorry, I should have stepped out of your way. Didn't realize you were still on a warpath."

I roll my eyes. "I'm not one to get over things easily."

"I've noticed." Simon motions for me to go ahead and walks beside me as we descend the stairs. "How are your palms?"

I show him the right one. "They're fine." The marks have scabbed over and started to fade. And I'm sure within a week or so, the cuts will be gone completely.

"And your knuckles?" He turns the same hand over. "Looking better, too."

"I told you I was fine." I march over to the coffee maker and grab a mug. "Do you want one?"

"Sure, yeah, thanks."

"Before you badger me about breakfast, can you give it a rest today? I have a gnarly headache and the thought of eating literally nauseates me."

Simon clenches his jaw and hesitates before responding. "Fine, but can you at least drink some water?"

I turn, stand tall, and reach for a glass from the shelf. I put it under the faucet and fill it, downing the entire contents in one go. I drop the thing into the sink. "Happy?"

"Something like that." He points to the fridge. "You know there's filtered water over there, right?"

I shrug and go back to the coffee machine. "Did you forget I was a broke college kid before I came to live here?"

"Never."

I go still and listen to the sounds of the house. "Is anyone else here?"

He shakes his head. "No."

I laugh dryly. "Did I scare them all off?"

"Pretty much." Simon pulls the creamer out of the fridge and brings it over to me. "Bryant came in and kissed you before he left, but Dom and Hayes were already gone when I got here."

Even his name is enough to send my blood boiling again.

All I asked for was one fucking date. He was the one that insisted it be last night. Made plans and promises and fucking broke them. Didn't even bother to call and tell me he wouldn't be here. Not even so much as a text or a carrier fucking pigeon. He didn't trouble himself with telling Simon, either. Instead, I had to wait around like a fucking idiot while my heart shriveled up in my chest. I was going to give him the benefit of the doubt; I was going to attempt to hear him out and see if he would finally tell me the truth. But no, he didn't show up, which only made me that much more confident that he doesn't actually care as much as he pretends to.

Whatever he was doing was clearly more important than the obligation he made to me.

I refuse to continue to beg someone to want to be around. From here on out, I'll do the bare fucking minimum, too.

My phone buzzes and I almost ignore it, but when I glance down and see the photo of a beautiful blonde pop across my screen, I nearly jump out of my skin.

"Holy shit, is everything okay?" Simon stares at me like I have a horn growing out of my forehead.

"Yes, sorry, it's Cora. I haven't talked to her in fucking forever."

**Cora: Dude, to say I missed you is the understatement of the year. I just finally got into the service area and had like 47 notifications from you. ARE YOU OKAY?!**

**Cora: Also, the second I get back into town, we are going out. Non-negotiable.**

I quickly thumb back a response.

**Me: I'm great now that I have proof of life. Do not ever go out of town ever again. K thanks.**

I smile at my screen when the dots appear and impatiently wait for her response.

**Cora: I'm taking you with me next time, how about that?**

**Me: Deal. Srsly. I miss you so much you stupid asshole.**

**Cora: Ditto, you dirty slut lol**

**Cora: Reception is still spotty. I'll get ahold of you soonish.**

She adds a handful of sad and crying emojis at the end, and I match the amount and double them, sending them right back.

Simon pushes a coffee I didn't realize he had made me across the counter and finishes stirring his.

"Hey, I was supposed to make those," I tell him.

"You were busy with something more important."

I bring my mug to my lips and blow on the scorching liquid. I take a cautious sip and look up at the guy watching me intently.

"What?"

"Nothing." Simon turns away and walks over to the island, leaning against it.

His biceps bulge his black tee and hug his shoulders tightly. I force myself to look anywhere other than him.

"So..." I walk over and nudge him in the side. "After work, how about you and me get into some trouble?"

Simon tilts his head toward me. "You *are* trouble."

"Ah, come on. You promised." I hop onto the counter and dangle my legs off the edge. "And if I don't fuck something up soon, I'm going to lose my mind. Especially after last night."

"I don't know what it was, but I'm sure he has a good reason."

I shake my head. "Don't want to talk about it. Don't want to think about it. I just want to do something reckless, and unless you want me to run off and do it alone, here's your chance to be involved."

Simon's whole body goes tense and he stares directly at me, his body towering over mine even though I'm on the counter. "You will *not* go anywhere without me."

I tilt my head. "Don't make me."

Simon inches toward me, his body pressing between my legs. He reaches up and puts his palm under the base of my chin. "You wouldn't."

I stare up at him, my heart racing in my chest. "I would and you know it."

He licks his lips, and I don't mean to, but I flit my gaze down at them. Plump, full, right there for the taking. Time seems to slow down and gravity threatens to move me closer to this man. I push against the pull and fight the urge to do what my body begs me to do. But I know better, and crossing that line with him would be wrong. Just because my men are pissing me off doesn't mean I'm allowed to do the unforgivable. I might be a spiteful bitch but there are some lines I won't cross— and kissing their enemy is one of them. Even though I really fucking want to.

I won't dare ever admit that out loud though.

My phone buzzes, snapping both Simon and me out of our trance.

He drops my face and takes a step back, shaking his head. "I shouldn't have done that."

I hop off the counter. "You didn't do anything wrong," I reassure him. *We* didn't do anything wrong.

I check my notifications.

**Cora: We have so much to catch up on. Talk soon, babe. Love you.**
**Me: Yes, we do. I can't wait to hear it all. Love you!!**

Simon doesn't try to hide his stare my entire shift at Bram's. I feel it pierce through me every second of the six hours and even though we're forbidden from being anything more than what we already are, I welcome his hungry eyes anyway. He might just want what he can't have, but still, it's nice to be wanted for a change. And if we never cross that line, what's the harm in letting him distract me from the gaping hole in my chest.

Because if I think about it too long, tears well in my eyes and an emptiness consumes me. I have shit to do, I can't be falling apart because the men who are supposed to be my partners want little to nothing to do with me. I thought getting a chance to spend some time with them would somehow make things better but all it did was remind me that what we have is great, just impossibly out of reach.

Maybe the timing is all wrong. Or maybe some things aren't meant to last. People come and go in your life to teach you a lesson. To help you learn about yourself. What if that's all this was? The universe reassuring me that love is out there, but that it's fleeting and difficult to hold onto. Maybe I haven't found the person who is willing to fight for my heart the way that I deserve to be fought for. I had hoped it would be Dom and Co and Magnus, but with each passing day, I continue to grow unsure of what any of this means to them.

Coen and I have history—a past that was stripped from us. But what if it was never meant to be? What if our forever was exactly what it was—powerful and temporary? Magnus is the only one who shows genuine remorse for his part in things. He's distant and allusive but he's put forth the most effort. I believe that he wants to tell me the truth, but something stronger than his love for me stops him from following through.

"I have a proposition," Simon tells me as he approaches.

I raise my brow and smirk. "Yeah?"

"Perv." He shakes his head and blushes.

"Hey, you thought it, not me." I finish wiping off the table and toss the rag into the bin behind the counter.

He follows me every step of the way. "If you eat, we can go do something."

"Like what?"

"I don't know, pizza or burgers or..."

"No." I chuckle. "*What* would we do?"

"Oh." Simon rubs his neck and glances around the room before settling his sights back on me. "Something stupid, probably."

I hold out my hand. "Deal."

He slides his palm around mine, his warmth enveloping me. "Deal."

"Let me clock out and we'll get going. How about tacos from that food truck?"

I manage to choke down a taco and a half, my usual at this place. It's not that they aren't delicious, I just don't have much of an appetite these days. After a bit of pushback, Simon finally accepts that as having had enough. He threatened to feed me again after I refused to touch the second one, but I gave in and had a few bites to satiate his desire to boss me around.

"How about go-karting?" Simon scrolls through his phone and glances up at me.

I narrow my gaze. "You're going to have to try harder than that."

"Paintball?"

"Glorified babysitter." I scoff. "Listen, I held up my end of the bargain, now you need to hold up yours. I want danger, not bumper cars at the mall."

"That reminds me, we could go bowling?"

"Simon, do you have a knife by any chance?"

"Uh, no. Why?"

"Because I'm going to stab you." I laugh. "Actually, no really, can I stab someone? That might make me feel better."

I think back to when I slit that guy's throat, and his blood splattered onto my face. Simon had smiled through the whole thing. Where's that version of him? The one who teased me with the danger he could provide every chance he got.

"Calm down, Cujo."

"Are there any fights tonight? That was perfect the other day. We can do that again."

He sighs. "They haven't announced when the next one will be. And that was almost too close, love."

"Do they have those for girls? I'd love to kick some ass. Maybe not to the death." An idea sparks in my head. "You should teach me how to fight."

"What?" Simon peels his attention from his phone to me.

"Yeah. You guys are all bat shit about my safety. Shouldn't I know how to defend myself? Maybe the next time I get kidnapped I'll have a fighting chance, literally."

Simon's nostrils flare. "If I have any say in it, next time will never happen. Don't you dare talk so carelessly about your life like that."

"Geez, who's the one who needs to chill? Why are you so against me knowing how to defend myself?"

"Because that's what I'm here for. You should never have to lift a finger."

I raise my hand in the air. "What about five? Wait..." I point to my thumb. "Unless you don't count this one, then I guess there's only four."

Simon pinches his eyes shut. "You are so frustrating."

I bop him on the nose. "I know."

A group of motorcycles whizz by us and revs their engines.

"Fucking tool bags," I mutter. "Letting everyone know how tiny their penises are."

Simon glances in the direction they went and then at me. "I have an idea."

"If it's not better than finger painting, I swear to God…"

"Trust me." Simon downs the last of his water and tosses his bottle into the recycling bin. He clears off the rest of our trash and discards it. "Come on."

I follow him, because what other option do I have? My only hope is that he doesn't let me down. But I guess with how things are currently going, the bar isn't exactly that high.

---

We drive in Simon's Volvo across town and pull into a parking garage. He punches in an access code and the gate opens, granting us access.

"Where are we?"

"My place."

So much for those boundaries. Simon is really going all out with the things we aren't supposed to be doing.

"Don't get any ideas," he tells me before my mind can run too rampant. "We aren't staying."

"Oh, no. I totally wasn't." I release the grip I had on my knee. "What are we doing here?"

"Switching rides." He pulls into a spot at the far end, where no other cars are parked. Simon puts the car into park, cuts the engine, and hops out, darting around to my side before I can get my hand on the door handle.

I step out onto the pavement and look around, wondering what the heck his intentions are. There aren't any vehicles near us but maybe he plans on having us walk to whatever we're swapping to.

But Simon doesn't lead us away from here. He fumbles with the keys on his chain and unlocks the small garage we're next to. Simon's shirt rises as he lifts the door, a bit of his torso exposing itself in the process.

I blink to see into the darkness of the small enclosure and settle my sights on what he must have in mind.

Simon strolls inside and pushes the two-wheeled machine out into the open.

"A motorcycle. You own a motorcycle?"

He chuckles. "This isn't just *any* bike, love. It's a Ducati Panigale."

"Am I supposed to know what that means?"

"No, probably not." He turns the key and pushes a button to start the bike. The thing roars to life, and the sound alone is enough to send a chill down my spine.

Okay, maybe Simon might actually pull tonight off.

He revs the throttle but not as excessively as those douchebags in town. No, Simon does it like doing so has a purpose.

Still, I can't help but find an opportunity to tease him. "Is this your way of telling me you have a tiny penis?"

His seductively green stare locks onto mine. "That is for me to know, and for you to find out." He winks at me.

I swallow and internally shake off that flutter that flickers in my belly. Or maybe it was between my legs, I can't really tell with the reverberations of the bike rattling through me too.

Simon goes back into the garage and brings with him two black helmets to match his blacked-out bike. "Here, put this on."

"Really? You're going to make me wear this?"

He glares at me. "We can be reckless, love, but your safety is still my utmost concern."

I groan and slide the thing over my head. "Fine." I fumble with the little straps, unsure how to fasten them the way he does his.

Simon swats my frantic fingers away. "Allow me." In a quick second, he's secured the thing on my head, the heat from his touch lingering after it's gone.

"Thanks," I say loud enough for him to hear.

He gives me a thumbs up but then pushes something on the front of his helmet, then reaches to do the same to mine. A crackle comes through the inside of my helmet followed by his voice. "Save the screaming for later, love."

"You wish," I say with a grin through whatever microphone is installed in these things.

Simon tugs down the garage door, letting the thing slam shut. He throws his leg over the bike with ease and holds his hand out to me. "You ready?"

I slide my palm into his, step onto one of the foot pegs, and climb onto the back. Unsure of what the fuck I'm supposed to do with my hands, I keep them to myself.

Simon tilts his head slightly back toward me. "You're going to want to hold on tight, love."

I wrap one arm around his waist, my body pressing up against his.

He does something with his foot, or maybe his hand, I can't really be sure how these things work, and gives the bike some throttle while we slowly take off. It's a clutch, or something, I think, that he lets out to make us move. Maybe I can convince him to teach me how to operate this thing so I don't feel so fucking stupid trying to figure it out. Or I could just accept that I don't need to know *everything* and just roll with it. I mean, if we're going to be stuck together, I'm sure it might come up sooner or later.

Simon moves us through the garage, the vibration of the bike purring like a fucking cat. He stops us at the gate, waits for the thing to open, and then shoots us out onto the street.

The air is a mixture of a warm breeze with a slight chill—perfect conditions for a night ride.

He glides through traffic with much more ease than we do in his car. He's not exactly a grandma in his Volvo, but on this, it's like he's someone else entirely.

We go around a corner at what feels *probably* too fast. Naturally, I grip him tighter and lean from the opposite direction of the pavement.

"Lean with the bike, love," he says through our headsets. "I won't let anything happen to you. I promise."

"Sorry," I tell him, because what else am I supposed to say at potentially almost killing us both for moving in the wrong direction. It's not like I got a passenger manual.

Of all the guys I've screwed around with in the past, I've never once gotten on the back of any of their motorcycles. I was stupid enough to follow them to their apartments and fuck, I wasn't going to cross that line of danger even further and get on their bikes. I'm reckless but not completely foolish. And here I am, never having had sex with Simon but playing the role of backpack on his crotch rocket.

"I want to show you something," Simon tells me before twisting the throttle and weaving around cars. We speed through intersections, maneuver traffic, and get across town quicker than I ever have in my whole life.

I take turns positioning my helmet on the left or right side of him, taking in the view as I can. Buildings blur and people seem so unrecognizable, but all of it is a different kind of beauty. It's new and fresh and so fucking exhilarating. It's not exactly the danger I had in mind, but it's a thrill I didn't know I needed until I was shooting down Third Street with my hair whipping behind me.

I'll worry about all the tangles later.

I don't doubt the guys will be livid when they find out, but they didn't state specifics about getting on a motorcycle with Simon—and considering Simon insisted on me wearing a helmet, he's following through with his promise of my safety. No one said we couldn't have a little fun.

"Aren't you worried about cops?" I ask Simon.

He chuckles. "Most of them are on the payroll."

"So, you're above the law."

"How else do you think your boyfriends get away with as much as they do?"

"Touché."

"Plus, lane splitting is legal in our state. The speeding not so much, but I can outrun them."

"Think so?"

"This thing goes almost 200 miles per hour, so yeah, I'd say so."

I grip his waist tighter at the idea of going that fucking fast on these two wheels. If we wrecked, I'm fairly certain my body would just explode on the pavement. At least then there wouldn't be anything left of me for the guys to murder.

"Don't worry, love. I'd never go that fast with you on the back."

"You shouldn't go that fast with you on the front, either."

"Watch out, love, it almost sounds like you care about me."

*Almost?* Does he really think I don't? Just because we can be nothing more than what we are doesn't mean I don't *care* about him. He might be my boyfriends' enemy but that doesn't mean he isn't my friend. I refuse to still acknowledge him as my enemy when he's done everything in his power to make me feel anything but alone.

"Who's going to protect me if you get splattered across the road?" I tell him while doing my best to avert the focus from my feelings for him.

"Touché."

We hit the outskirts of town and traffic dies down. The overhead lights from the street start to fade and we're left with only a few cars and the headlight of the bike. Salty air, a cool breeze, and the warmth of Simon's body. His touch is forbidden, but right now, it's a complete necessity.

"Hold on, love. Things might get bumpy." He steers us off the road and into a parking lot. He continues through the entire length of it, and when I'm certain he might finally stop, he maneuvers us onto the grass and goes around the no-trespassing signs.

I don't ask questions because I'm confident I won't get answers. Instead, I wrap my arms around him and wait for whatever he has in store for us. My ass thuds on the seat, and I hold on tighter as we traverse the rockier terrain. I close my eyes, not out of fear, but more out of trust. I lay my helmet-covered head against his back and savor this thing that will not last. The closeness I've dreamed about but never allowed to happen.

The bike crawls to a stop, and Simon cuts the engine.

"We made it." He runs his hand along the arms that are gripped around his torso.

I peel myself off of him, holding onto his shoulder to hop off the bike. "Where are we?" I glance around at the cityscape in the distance, the ocean in sight, and the night sky that's visible. It's nearly impossible to see the stars from home, but from here, holy shit it's mesmerizing.

"Come here, love." Simon motions for me as he approaches. He weaves his fingers along the strap under my chin and unbuckles the restraints.

Plucking the helmet off my head, I give it to him to set on the foot peg of the bike.

He laughs and pats down the side of my head. "Your hair is fucking wild."

"You're one to talk." I reach up and shuffle his hair around to match mine. "There, twins."

Simon rolls his eyes. "Thanks, I appreciate you."

I turn my attention from him to the place he brought me, scanning the horizon. "This is..."

"Something else, isn't it?" He steps beside me. "I come here, sometimes, when I need to clear my head. Like the park, for you."

"The park has nothing on this." I crane my head up to take in the night sky. "Holy shit, there's the big dipper. It's so much brighter than down there."

He points his long hand at a big bright star. "See that reddish-orange-looking one?"

"Mmhm." I stare right at the one he's referring to.

"That's Mars."

"No fucking way." I glance over at him.

"I swear." He shifts his arm in another direction. "And I'm pretty sure that's Saturn."

"Shut up, you're fucking with me."

"You're going to make me prove it to you, aren't you?"

"Maybe," I smirk at him but look back up into the sky.

Simon pulls his phone out of his pocket and pushes a few buttons, pulling up an app with every star imaginable on it. "See for yourself, love." He puts the device in my line of sight and points it toward the glowing orange thing. Sure enough, he was right.

I take the thing from him and hover it over the other one—Saturn. My eyes widen with disbelief. "You're a freaking astronomer and didn't tell me?"

Simon grins. "There's a lot you don't know about me, love."

"I'd say so." I spin and continue directing the thing at the sky. "Look at that one."

"That's Vega, the fifth brightest star in the sky. Twice the mass of the Sun."

"How the fuck do you know that?" I gawk at him but turn back to the app, clicking the star and confirming that he was correct. The thing explains something about the northern constellation Lyra.

"By doing what you just did. Every time I see something interesting, I click it to read more. After a while you just sort of retain the information." Simon shrugs. "Plus, I've spent enough time up here to have a general idea of where things are."

"Is this where you bring all your hot dates?" I side-eye him.

"Are you saying this is a hot date?" Simon tilts his head to the side.

"You know what I mean."

The smile melts away from his face. "I've never brought anyone up here."

"Why?"

"I've never wanted to."

"Oh." I focus back on his phone, scanning the sky and distracting myself from what he just told me. A notification pops across the top of the screen. I don't mean to, but I glance at the message, the name Sarah with some hearts in the text. Immediately, I give him his phone. "Uh, I think your girlfriend just text you."

"What? No, I don't have a—"

I cut him off. "You don't have to lie, Simon. You're allowed to have a life outside of this." I motion between us. "And you don't owe me an explanation." I cross my arms over my chest and walk away while looking up at the sky.

Simon stalks after me. "Are you jealous?"

"What? No. That's ridiculous." I roll my eyes and continue to move away from him, anything to get some space between us.

"You're acting jealous, love."

I turn toward him, my cheeks flushing hot. "I'm not *jealous*."

Simon throws up his arms. "If it looks like a duck, and quacks like a duck."

"I'm going to punch the duck in its face."

"What did the duck do?"

"You know what the duck did." I lean against a large boulder and stare at the sky to distract myself from him and his accusations.

*Jealousy*. Is that what this is? But why...Simon and I aren't dating, and the possibility of that ever happening is zero. Still, I can't shake this strange feeling coursing through me, and the more it festers, the more it pisses me off.

"June..."

"Simon..."

"Sarah is just—"

"Nope." I hold my hand out in front of him. "I don't need to know. Don't tell me."

"Fine." He huffs. "Make things more difficult than they need to be."

"Don't you dare sass me."

Simon steps forward, pressing me harder into the giant rock I'm already pinned against. "You want to talk about *sass*?" His gaze trails mine, drops to my lips, and then back up. His chest rises and falls, his breath ragged. He places both hands beside my head, caging me in.

My heart races, and I grow uncertain about how far he's going to take this, and how far I want him to. What's wrong with me? I shouldn't be thinking, or *feeling*, any of this. I have a boyfriend—three of them. I am satisfied with my relationships. But am I really? When they keep pushing me away, practically shoving me into the arms of this man in front of me. Still, that's no excuse for straying, and even though my body practically begs me to stop teasing this forbidden line between us, my mind knows this isn't right. I might be in an open relationship with three men, but Simon is their enemy, and that means he's off-limits.

That whatever he's about to do next is off-limits.

"Simon..." I warn him.

He lowers his voice. "You should have been mine."

A chill rolls down my spine. "But I'm not. And I never will be."

Not as long as I'm with my men. They would never tolerate it. They've made that much clear from the second they found out I knew who Simon was. They may insist that he be my bodyguard, but they would never be okay with anything more. Even if, lately, he is proving to be better for me than them.

They had warned me that they'd kill us both if we entertained it. And either way, whether Simon means something to me or not, how could I allow him to get hurt if I decided to be selfish?

Because of my feelings for him, I'd never risk it.

I guess at the end of the day, we both care about each other's safety more than anything.

"You think I don't know that, love?" Simon's breath touches my cheek. "That no matter what, you will always be out of reach..."

"I'm—"

Simon interrupts, "Don't you dare say it."

Lights flicker up the hill, and the sound of motorcycles alerts us that Simon isn't the only one who knows about this place.

"God damn it." He shoves off the rock and puts distance between us.

Distance that I am grateful for, because if he hadn't, I don't know what would have transpired. I don't want to be wrong, but how can I resist something that *feels* so fucking right?

"Simon..."

"We need to leave, love." He stalks over to his bike, latching onto the helmet he let me borrow and holding it out toward me.

I take it into my hands and wonder who else has worn this thing before.

*Sarah. Heart emojis.*

I clench my jaw and shove the thing over my head.

Simon reaches for the straps, but I shrug him off.

"I'm fine, I'll get it myself."

But after a few failed attempts and the sound of the bikes getting closer, Simon insists that he secure it. "I shouldn't have snapped at you," he tells me and meets my gaze through the visor. "I'm not being fair."

"None of this is fair."

The headlights of the bikes crest the ridge of the hill and point directly at us.

"Get on the bike. *Now.*" Simon throws his leg over and immediately reaches for my hand while using his other to turn the thing on. He repositions the gun at his waist as he puts the bike into gear.

One of the bikes cuts us off and blocks our path. The dude without a helmet seems pretty fucking harmless, but with Simon and the guys, you can never be too cautious.

"Sick bike dude," he says to Simon.

Simon lifts up his visor. "Thanks. We were just leaving. The cliff is all yours, man." Simon walks the bike back to clear a path but another bike approaches from our rear.

A few more come up the hill, dust and dirt filling the air.

"Do you know another way down, dude?" the guy asks Simon. "We've got a moto cop on our asses."

Simon sighs and glances toward the group of bikers. "Yeah, follow me."

Once his visor is shut, I say through our shared headset, "I thought you said you were good with cops?"

"That doesn't mean I want to deal with them, especially when you're with me. Imagine having to explain this one to the guys."

The guy in front of Simon gets out of our way and Simon darts through the gap he creates.

"Hold on, love. It's going to be rockier than earlier."

Sinewy and rigid, he is the anchor I grip onto tightly, my arms locked around him.

"You're safe, I promise."

"I never questioned that, not with you."

"Then why are you trying to squeeze me to death?" Simon chuckles.

I loosen my hold on him. "I hate you."

"Just admit it, you like feeling my body up against yours."

We hit a bump and then another. The other bikes hot on our tail.

"Hey, Simon?"

"Yeah?" A hint of intrigue lines his tone.

"How would you feel if I let go and fell off the back of your bike? Think they'd run me over? Or maybe I'd snap my neck first? What do you think?"

Simon releases the handlebar with his left hand and pins it around my hands on his chest. "If you even fucking think about letting go."

"Okay, okay," I call out. "Focus on getting us the hell out of here."

"Promise me you won't let go." He keeps his palm pressed on mine.

"I promise."

He exhales and returns his attention to where it belongs—the rocky terrain ahead.

We continue to descend the uneven grassy slope, my ass growing numb from all the bumps we keep hitting until finally, we approach solid land. Simon drives us straight toward the lights of the city, coming into town from a direction I've never been before. We pop out onto a street and he glances back at the bikes behind us.

The guy from earlier catches up and comes to our side. "Thanks, man, that was a fucking close one!" he yells across to us. "Let me buy you a beer to thank you." He points ahead. "I know a place up here."

Simon lifts his visor to talk to the guy. "It's all good, man. No sweat."

"Ah, come on," I tell him. "What else do we have going on?"

"Are you sure, buddy?" He motions again. "It's just a couple blocks away."

"It'll be fun, let's do it." I clasp onto Simon's torso. "How dangerous could it be? Don't make me squeeze you to death."

"Lead the way," he tells the guy and snaps his visor back down. "Don't make me regret this."

"More than you already do? Impossible." I loosen my grip, letting one arm completely free of my hold on Simon, and let the wind rush through my fingers.

It only takes a minute to get to where the guy told us to go, and the second we arrive in the dark parking lot behind the bar, I hop off the back of Simon's bike and fumble with the stupid straps of the helmet. Finally, I figure it out and pop it off my head before Simon can intercept.

"Look who doesn't need my help anymore." He takes the helmet from me and secures it to the bike with a little locking mechanism thingy.

"Maybe eventually I'll grow up and you won't have to babysit me anymore either."

"Never." He cups my chin between his thumb and index finger. "One drink, then we're leaving. Stay close to me, okay?"

"Fine," I sigh while still being relieved that he gave in at all.

"Sup, man? I'm Derek." The biker guy extends his hand toward Simon.

Simon shakes it and says, "I'm Brad, this is Shelly."

*Brad. Shelly.* What the fuck.

I narrow my gaze at Simon but go along with it anyway and offer a nod of acknowledgment. "We'll be right behind you," I tell them.

We let the group of biker people enter the bar while *Brad* and I hang back at the entrance.

"Do I look like a fucking Shelly to you?"

Simon shrugs. "Do I look like a Brad?"

"No, not even a little bit." I laugh and shove his shoulder. "Next time I'm picking the names."

"Hopefully there *isn't* a next time, love. You can't trust strangers like this. If one of them found out who you are, who I am…"

"Then what, *Brad*? What would happen?"

"You could get hurt!"

"Nobody gives a shit who I am. You just worry too much."

"And you don't worry enough. Someone has to do it for you."

I roll my eyes. "I'm fine." I wrap my arm around Simon's and tug him toward the entrance. "Come on, Brad."

The bar is thick with smoke and cheap booze. A billiards game begins when we walk in, and a group of drunk women wiggles around in a circle on the dance floor. This place is quaint, to say the least.

"There he is," Derek yells from his spot with his arm outstretched toward Simon. "The man of the hour, Brad."

The little group of bikers cheer and slap Simon on the back. I can sense his aggravation at the whole situation and eat every second of it up. If only these men knew who he was, then they probably wouldn't put their hands all over him. I guess his reputation doesn't stretch to this side of town. Or maybe the name really was enough of a disguise to conceal his true identity.

"What'll ya have?" Derek asks him.

"Tequila and a bourbon." He turns toward the bartender who's awaiting his order. "Top shelf." Simon shoves his hand in his pocket and slides a hundred-dollar bill out and puts it on the counter.

"Ah, shit, man, I woulda got that for ya." Derek frowns and throws his arm over Simon's shoulder.

Simon shrugs him off. "No worries, man. I appreciate the sentiment, a drink can still be had together, regardless of who pays for it."

Derek sighs heavily but seems to accept Simon's answer. He reaches for his huge mug of beer, a bit of it sloshing over the sides. "You're a good dude, Brad." From the sound of his voice, he's already been throwing them back long before he stumbled upon us. Probably why that cop was after him and their group.

The bartender sets our drinks on the counter and takes the bill Simon had laid on top and makes change.

"Keep it," Simon tells the older woman working behind the bar.

Her eyes widen and she smiles, a few of her teeth missing. "Thanks."

Simon hands me my glass and takes the other into his hand. "To Brad and Shelly."

I grin at him and clank my shot glass against his. "To Brad and Shelly." I down the contents of the bourbon in one swallow, noting how it's nothing like what we have at home. Not too long ago, this would have been out of my price range, and now here I am, a bit of a snob at the lower quality. Funny what being around wealthy mafia men will do to a gal.

"High roller, are we?" Derek slurps some of his beer and wipes his mouth with his sleeve. "What do you do for a living, Brad?"

Simon tenses, his eyes pinching shut before turning around. "Security."

The same answer that Coen had given me when we ran into each other in that bar all those months ago. I thought it was strange. *My* Coen, sweet innocent Co who slow danced with me on top of a pizza shop, did something dangerous for a living. Little did I know, that job was much more deadly than he let on. And that version of him no longer existed. I see it sometimes, a ghost of who he once was, but that part of him is gone, as is the young girl from my past.

"Like mall security?" Derek gulps down more of his beer.

I hold back a chuckle at having said the same thing to Coen.

"Yeah, like mall security," Simon confirms even though he's blatantly lying.

"Sick. I didn't know those gigs paid so well; I'll have to look into it." Derek grabs onto one of his friends and drags him over. "This is Brody. He works at the mall, too." Derek aggressively rubs the guy's head and shoves him away. He settles his sights on me. "How long you and pretty little Shelly been together?"

Simon stiffens, his body gravitating in front of mine.

I weave my fingers around his and hold on tightly. "A few years." I place my other hand on Simon's chest.

Derek bobs his head up and down. "I was in love once...shit, feels like forever ago."

Simon grips my hand and runs his thumb over mine. He glances down at me. "Has it really been a few years? Time flies when you're having fun."

"What happened?" I ask Derek since he's clearly zoning the hell out while he goes down memory lane.

He blinks back to reality. "Bitch cheated on me. Went through her phone and found some texts she had been sending my buddy. I went home, beat the shit out of her and never saw the slut again."

My breath catches and Simon and I both hold onto each other tighter.

"She called and threatened to have me arrested but I told her about the tittie pics I still had saved from her." Derek laughs. "Shut her up real quick."

"Listen," Simon announces. "We should get going, it's getting late."

Derek picks up his beer. "What, gotta curfew or something?"

"Yeah, or something." Simon backs us from the crowd, and I let him.

I thought coming here would be fun, not fuel my desire to snap this fucking asshole's neck. First, he admits to abusing his girlfriend, then he blackmails her out of having him arrested with revenge porn.

He doesn't deserve to walk out of here, let alone continue breathing. But just because I think he's a piece of shit doesn't mean there's anything I can do about it.

And asking Simon to step in when we're in unfamiliar territory, using fake names, at a bar full of strangers, would be even more wrong.

"Sure, yeah. Let me walk ya out." Derek slams his mug on the counter.

"Not necessary," Simon tells him.

"Ah man, I insist. Give me a chance to check out that sick bike of yours before you leave." Derek slaps Simon and me both on the shoulders and guides us toward the door.

I cringe under his touch and wonder how much more of this Simon is willing to take. He has much more self-control than I do.

Derek calls out to his friends. "I'll be right back, boys."

We step out front of the bar, the fresh air a gift to my lungs.

Simon pivots me in front of him, his hands on my waist as he guides me toward his parked motorcycle.

"You're a lifesaver, man," Derek tells him while stumbling with each step.

The parking lot is dim, nearly pitch black. I can only make out a couple feet in front of me. The only light is from the residual glare of the bar's neon sign floating into the space. Whoever is in charge of maintenance around this place is slacking at replacing the bulbs in the lamp overhead.

Still, that doesn't stop Simon from leading me directly to his bike.

"This a nice rig you got here," Derek says while trailing his finger over the dash of Simon's bike. "What this run you, about forty, fifty grand?" He glances up at Simon. "Where's the key? Start this bad boy up."

When Simon doesn't comply, Derek reaches into his pants and draws out a knife, somehow at the very same time as he snatches me by the arm and puts me in front of him. He presses the blade against the base of my throat. "Get the key, pretty boy."

Simon doesn't have time to get his gun, at least not enough that he's comfortable risking my life for it. There's no telling how much this asshole has had to drink and if he'd drive the knife into my throat on accident.

"It's in my pocket, Derek. Come get it yourself. Don't you dare touch a fucking hair on her head." Simon keeps his hands out in front of him. "Let her go and get the key. You can have the bike."

Derek chuckles. "Like I fucking believe you." He presses the blade into my flesh, almost breaking the skin. "Why don't you grab the key out of his pocket for me, sweetheart?"

My stomach turns at the disgusting tone of his voice. I lock my gaze onto Simon's and inch toward him as Derek moves me in that direction.

"Any funny business and I gut her right here." Derek keeps his arm around my waist and the knife at my throat. Even if Simon wanted to pull me away from him, Derek would be able to kill me before I'd have the chance to get free.

"Love..." Simon whispers, his whole body tense.

"Which pocket?" I ask him, my mind focused on getting the damn key.

"My right." His gaze searches for a way out, anything to free me from this man who holds me captive.

"No fucking funny business." Derek shakes me as if that's going to make this go any fucking smoother.

I reach my hand into Simon's pocket, moving past a wad of cash and locating the key. But that isn't all I feel, and he and I both know it.

Simon slowly shakes his head, his gaze frantically on mine.

But that's the thing...I've never really been good at following directions.

So, the second Derek and I step away and place the key in his hand, I use his momentary triumph to spin myself in his grasp, facing him and shoving the blunt edge of Simon's gun into his side and pulling the trigger.

Derek's eyes go wide. The knife falls from his grasp and his hold no longer remains on me but on the blood gushing out of his side.

Simon reacts immediately, kicking the knife from his reach and yanking the gun from my hands. "Jesus Christ, love. What the hell were you thinking?" He grabs my shoulder and steadies me toward him. "Are you okay?" Simon tilts my chin up and examines my neck. He runs his hand behind my head and tugs me into his chest, hugging me with one arm while the other holds the gun toward Derek. Simon kisses the top of my head and releases me.

"I'm fine, I'm fine." Even though I just shot a man, I'm weirdly very much okay. Maybe it's shock, or adrenaline, or just the pure desire to kill this fucking bastard, but I'm not at all shaken up. I know I should be scared, afraid, terrified that I was held at knifepoint, *again*, or that I fired a gun, but even with Simon standing there unable to do anything, I still felt safe in his presence. Maybe it was the reassurance of him nearby that gave me the power to act so fucking irrationally and get myself out of the situation. Whatever it was, I'm grateful for it. Because here he is, the bastard that doesn't deserve to be alive, bleeding out in this dark fucking alley.

Simon shifts his attention toward the end of the dead-end lot and then back at Derek who's choking on his own blood. "You got him fucking good, love."

"He had it coming," I tell him.

"He did," Simon reassures me. "But you can't always take things into your own hands." He tucks my hair behind my ear. "I have to call this in. We can't just leave him here."

My heart nearly jumps out of my chest. "You're going to call the cops?"

Simon sighs. "No, love. I'm going to call a clean-up crew."

# CHAPTER 14

# Coen

What do you get when you have a room full of ignorant men who can't solve a problem?

Total fucking anarchy.

My phone vibrates in my pocket and when I pull it out, my heart thumps fucking harder.

**June: Missin you, Co x**

At least she doesn't completely hate me for all of the secrecy and distance. But the longer I keep this up, there's no telling how much she'll deal with.

I'd be mad at me.

Hell, I *am* mad at me.

It shouldn't have been this difficult of a situation to handle. We have the best of the best on our side and with having full control over the organization, we should have been able to pull any resources we needed to figure this out.

But Dom is too fucking proud to make it a companywide problem and insists we handle it in-house with our own limited team.

He's too afraid someone will doubt his power, that they'll come for his precious throne.

Well, they're not only coming for his throne, but his woman, too, and that actually means something to me. I couldn't give a shit less if they burn every last ounce of product to the ground and kill every man that works for us—but the second they involve her, it becomes my business.

"Out, all of you," Dominic orders everyone in the room.

I remain in my seat, my phone in my hand. I thumb a quick text back to June and let her know I'm missing her, too, even though there are no words to string together to prove to her exactly how much.

I only just got her back, and this situation calls for my full attention, leaving her left alone, with Simon fucking Beckett as her personal bodyguard.

I'm the first to admit he'll do what it takes to keep her alive, but it doesn't make it any easier to fucking stomach. When all of this is said and done, I'll gladly put a bullet in his head.

Bryant is the first to speak once it's just the three of us. Me, him, and Dom. "If you don't tell her soon, I'm going to. This can't keep going on." He drops his feet from the table onto the floor and slams his hands on the hard surface. "This is bullshit." Bryant rises from his chair. "It's fine if neither of you gives a shit about losing her, but I fucking do, and I refuse to stand by and let it happen."

Dominic stands, too. "You will do no such thing."

"What are you going to do? Fire me? Go for it. I don't care." Bryant empties his pockets on the table—his wallet, keys, and gun. "What do you want from me? The clothes off my fucking back? Take the house. I've got savings. I can provide for her just fine."

Dominic makes fists with his hands and if this were a cartoon, steam would no doubt be spilling from his ears. "No one is leaving. And no one is telling her. Not yet."

"Then when? Huh?" Bryant crosses his arms over his chest. "Give me a fucking deadline then. Because I'm not going to keep doing this. I'll tell her my fucking self. I'll take the blame. I'll deal with her being pissed at me, but I will not fucking lose her." He glances over at me. "Dude, come on, you have to have a say in this. You lost her once. Do you really want to do that again?" He turns back to Dom. "Do none of you care about her the way I do?"

I sigh and run my hand through my hair. "Don't speak for me, Bryant."

"You know what's fucking hilarious?" Bryant chuckles dryly. "You both hate Beckett so fucking much, and yet he's the *only* one she can count on. The only one who actually shows he gives a shit. Honestly—"

"Don't you fucking say it," Dominic growls.

Bryant throws up his arms. "But it's true." He points to Dom. "You know it." Then at me. "And you fucking know it." He pauses for a second and continues. "I'm not a fan of the guy, but right now, as of today, he's more of a man than the three of us combined. He conceded because it was her dying wish. Would either of you do the same? No? I didn't think so." Bryant kicks a chair across the room. "I wouldn't even be mad if she chose him over us. He prioritizes her. What do you do? Shove her aside to figure out who's stealing your fucking contraband?"

"This"—Dominic tries to keep his tone even—"has nothing to do with the business, and everything to do with her. How do you not see that?"

"Oh, I'll explain." Bryant draws circles on the table with his finger. "This is you. This is the business. This is you caring about the shit that happens. This is June running away with your so-called enemy because you were too stupid to do anything about it." He looks up to Dom. "Are you that fucking dense?"

"I will tolerate this lack of obedience because I understand how you're feeling—"

"Do you? Do you really?" Bryant motions to Dominic's chest. "Do you even have a fucking heart in there, Dom? Have you been in this industry so long that you're so blind to what's right in front of you? Tell me, truthfully, do you not care if you lose her? Because I do. I'd rather fucking die. And let me fucking warn you, if I do lose her..." Bryant stares right at Dom. "You better put a bullet in my head because if you don't, I'm coming to put one in yours."

"Enough!" I tell both of them. "Sit fucking down, Maggie." I drag the chair he kicked back over to him. "Sit. We're not losing her, okay? Not today." I turn to Dom. "Wipe that murderous glare off your face. Nothing he said wasn't anything you didn't already know." I stand at the edge of the table. "What we need to do is figure out what we're doing here. The time to act is now. We need to handle this situation with urgency."

"You think I haven't been trying to do that?" Dominic asks me.

"I don't know, Dom. Have you? Because this fucking guy has been running amuck for over six months and hasn't been captured." I scratch at my neck, hesitant to say the next words that leave my mouth. "You're right to be concerned. About what people will think of you. About what will happen when they find out. But what are you more concerned about—that or June? Because you have to decide. If you choose to not involve everyone, this will only take longer. And time is not on our side. I think you forget that you're human. You can't do everything, and it's showing. Asking for help is not a weakness. There's only so much that Maggie and I can do. We have a small team, but even they have limited information. We have to pull more resources. We need all hands on deck if we're going to take this fucker out. Savini is a great asset, but we need more."

Dominic lowers himself onto the seat, his cuffs unbuttoned and rolled up to his forearms. His entire outfit is disheveled and nothing like the put-together man I've grown accustomed to. He's stressed, and it shows.

Is this what he would be like even if June weren't in the picture?

Taking over a multi-billion-dollar criminal enterprise is a lot for one person, especially given the circumstances of our late predecessor. Factor in the fallout of his brother, the leader of the east coast syndicate, and you have a recipe for fuck-shit-pie. But finding the love of your life in the midst of it, at the ripe age of fifty-something, and it's bound to take a toll on a man.

Dom is a powerhouse, but there's only so much he can handle.

I'd be losing my mind if I were him, too. Hell, I am in my position and it's nowhere near as important and influential as his.

But something has to change. Because if it doesn't. We're going to lose everything. The business. The money. The girl.

And even though I hate agreeing with Bryant, I'm on his side on this one—about her being the priority.

"Give me a week. That's all I ask. Another week. If I can't neutralize the threat, we come clean." Dominic looks up at me, his hand resting along his scraggly beard.

"When was the last time you fucking ate?" I ask him.

He looks like shit. Sunken in eyes, pale, a bit thinner than usual. All of it is so very unlike him.

"Does it matter?" Dom shakes his head. "I don't know. Earlier. Yesterday."

"What do you think, Maggie?" I turn toward Bryant who's fuming in his seat. "Can we handle seven more days?"

Bryant glances at me then Dom. He sighs. "Seven fucking days. No more. Then me and June and Simon are running away together. Not a fucking second more."

At this point, I'd go with them if it meant escaping from this fucking nightmare.

I used to live for this shit. The chaos fueled my restless soul. But now, I just want it to be over.

When we finally involved June in all of this, I thought that was going to be the turning point. No more lies. No more betrayal. No more hiding who I am. She would know the truth about my past, what I did, and why I had to leave her behind.

But the second Dom got wind that her attacker was still out there, he ordered us to keep our mouths shut about our business. Said the less she knew the better. He's not wrong, but if that's the decision he was going to make, he should have kept it that way from the start and let her go her separate way.

Instead, she took a fucking bullet to secure him the win and then he pushed her into the arms of our enemy because he didn't know how else to handle things.

I'm usually on Dom's side about business matters—but this was the stupidest choice he's ever made. And his judgment might be what risks everything we've worked toward. Our careers, and her love.

"You need to fucking stop with the Beckett shit," Dominic tells Bryant.

Bryant shrugs. "You can't get mad about the truth."

I roll my eyes. "Seriously, the both of you, just shut the hell up." I glance at my watch. "When's Johnny going to be here?"

Bryant checks his phone and must get distracted by something shiny because he doesn't answer me.

"Soon," Dominic confirms. "Any minute now."

A knock sounds on the door, like fucking clockwork.

"Get your shit together if you want to be taken seriously," I tell them both. "Enter!" I call out toward the door.

A young guy walks into the room, about medium build, not much to him. A baby face and a stone-cold stare. Yeah, he's definitely been in this world long enough to have the light stolen from him.

The meeting was scheduled to be with Johnny Jones, but this is his advisor, Miller.

With my hand outstretched, I stalk toward him. "Afternoon. When should we expect Mr. Jones?"

Miller shakes my hand, firmer than I anticipated him to. "You won't. He's occupied with other business. You'll be dealing directly with me."

Dominic stands but doesn't come any closer. "This isn't what we agreed to."

"This is what you'll have to accept because Johnny is away on other business." Miller doesn't back down despite Dominic easily doubling him pound for pound. "With all due respect, Mr. Adler, I've been with Luciano since a young age. I know the ins and outs of the organization better than anyone alive, and there isn't a person more capable of handling today's affairs than I am. Now, with that being said, shall I leave, or can we continue?"

Dominic chuckles. "Audacious young lad, are we?"

"Please don't insult my intelligence because of whatever biased impression you have of me based on my age and appearance. The late Luciano and I ran a successful operation with next to no issues for many years until your predecessor came to kill his own flesh and blood." Miller stares directly at Dominic with each word. "I don't question the way you run things, now I'd appreciate you doing the same."

Bryant finally rises from his seat and walks over to Miller. "We've spoken before." He extends his hand. "Magnus Bryant. At your service."

"Miller Rossi." Miller grips Bryant's hand and then extends it to mine. "Coen Hayes." And then turns toward Dom. "Mr. Adler."

Dominic hesitates but takes the young man's hand.

"Alright then," Miller announces. "Let's cut right to it." He claims a seat and sits in it without asking permission.

I kind of appreciate the balls on this kid.

"I believe we have a common enemy." Miller glances between us. "We can talk shop all day long until our faces are blue, but I think we should focus on the core issue here. I did some digging and found your profit margins are down, did a little more digging and uncovered you're having some transit issues."

Dominic clenches his hand into a fist. "Who?"

Miller shakes his head. "You're asking the wrong question, Mr. Adler."

I sigh and take the bait. "Why are our profit margins important to you?"

"Yes, thank you, Mr. Hayes. Great point you bring up." Miller taps the manila folder he sat down on the desk in front of him. "Because ours are, too. And if I'm not mistaken, whoever is attacking your business is also after ours."

But that's impossible, isn't it? I thought ours was a personal attack.

I catch Bryant's stare and feel Dom's boring into me. All of us thinking the same fucking thing.

"Whoever is targeting us..." Miller folds his hands together on the table. "Is on the inside. Deep inside. Someone who knows both of our operations well enough to make this happen. Someone with connections on both the east and west coast. Someone who can pull strings from wherever they are. And someone who can do so completely undetected."

Everything he's saying makes complete sense, but how does that connect to June? What angle would this person be playing that they would involve the east coast syndicate? Is it a ruse to confuse us and get us off their trail?

"I'm going to need to see proof," Dominic finally says. "Are those your records?"

Miller slides them across the table. "See for yourself. I have nothing to hide. Our numbers have been down for six months. Slow at first. Then the attacks started hitting heavier about a month ago. We're not just losing product, but we're losing men, too. And that's not something that I, or Johnny, will stand for. That is not the legacy that Luciano left behind."

Dominic studies the paperwork then looks up at Miller. "Who do you think it is?"

Miller shrugs. "That's what I'm here for. To figure it out. To cross-examine every piece of data we have and see if a pattern shows up. If we can identify that, I think we can solve this mystery once and for all."

"I'm following up on a few leads," Dominic tells him. "We have a small team canvassing, and I've brought Lorenzo Savini on board."

"He's a great asset." Miller nods and continues. "As do we. Along with myself, Johnny, and a couple trusted assets, we've been chasing every possible lead. His wife, Claire, is tracking down a source as we speak, and their close friend and business partner Josey Romano is assisting her. I believe you may know him."

I run his name through my head, considering where I may have heard it before. "Wait, he works for Johnny? I thought..."

"Yes, he was a former associate of Franklin Sharp. Now he works with us on the east coast."

"Hold on," Bryant chimes in. "Johnny's *wife* is involved?"

"Very much so," Miller confirms. "She's an invaluable asset to the organization."

Bryant narrows his gaze at me and then Dom. "See."

"With her being so...hands on." Dominic repositions himself in his seat. "Have there ever been instances, and forgive me for being so specific, where she has been kidnapped?"

Miller doesn't hesitate. "Yes."

"Lately?"

"No, not since the fallout. Franklin was the one who ordered the hit."

"Why?" Dominic asks him.

"Because Johnny had done something that no one else except his brother had done before. He outsmarted him. I'm sure you heard all about this on your end."

"Yes, we have heard rumors of what happened." Dom rubs at his beard. "It was my understanding there was a longtime feud between brothers. That came to a head, both dying at the hands of each other. If I'm being honest, things have been so chaotic in the fallout that the specific details have been lost in the shuffle."

"It's a much longer story than I bargained to tell, but the importance of it is not relevant today. Perhaps another time I will correct the erroneous details."

"Dominic has a point," I tell them.

Dom looks at me with a tilt of his head and a warning stare.

"I'm sure you heard of the council meeting where Dom was crowned the successor of the west coast."

"Hayes," Dominic says with a quiet but vicious urgency.

"Let him talk, Dom," Bryant interjects.

Miller remains focused on me, not paying much attention to either of the other two men in this room. The kid has the ability to stay completely stoic in the face of danger.

"*Our* partner took a bullet that day. She almost died. And that wasn't the first time her life was in peril. A few weeks prior to that, she was abducted, tortured, and had she not gotten away, I don't think she would be here with us." I focus on each word and do my best to continue. "We were under the impression it was ordered by our enemy, our competition. But upon him finding out what happened to her, he tracked them down and brought her attacker to justice. We witnessed it with our own eyes.

"We continued a cease-fire until we eliminated what we thought was the group of people responsible for the attack—another faction that was trying to gain control over who won at that council meeting. But threats have been coming in from time to time, threats against her life. Very specific threats left at these transit sites that have been seized. They point directly at this person from before, the one we were sure we had purged."

Miller blinks a few times like he's processing the information. "And you're sure it's not a copycat, someone just picking up where the other left off?"

"We aren't sure of anything, other than these things are tied together, and that she isn't safe."

"This information cannot circulate." Dominic stares right at Miller.

"Understood." Miller sighs, something weighing on him. "I have something I'd like to share, too." He reaches into his pocket and pulls out a slip of paper. He slides it across the table to Dominic. "This was at the last cargo van that was compromised."

I walk over and stand behind Dom to get a better look. Bryant joins me.

Dominic clears his throat and reads the paper. "You took what is mine, now I will take what is yours." We all turn to Miller.

"What does this mean?" I ask him.

Miller shakes his head slowly. "I have no idea; I was hoping you could tell me."

---

Dominic and I ride across town to one of the warehouses on the outskirts of town. A run-down old thing that doesn't have much security or prying eyes—a perfect place for pickups and drop-offs.

As much as he insisted to be a part of this stupid fucking mission, I was even more persistent in demanding that I go with him. He needs backup, and if he isn't willing to bring one of our men, there isn't anyone more suited to be at his side than me.

Bryant and I played rock paper scissors to determine which of us would go, but even if he had won, I'd have hogtied him and left him with no choice. If something happens to me or Dominic, I want Bryant to be the one to comfort June. He'll know what to say and how to handle the situation, and he'll provide her more stability than I ever could. I hate admitting someone else is more capable of being the man she needs, but when it comes to her heart, I cannot be selfish. I never have been, and I never will be. For her, she deserves the whole fucking world.

And that's exactly what she will get—even if I'm not the one to give it to her.

If Dominic didn't agree, he wouldn't be so carelessly risking his life.

We pull into the parking lot, dust picking up in our wake, and park near the white panel van we're taking on the route.

I hop out of the car we borrowed from one of our trusted runners, Axel, and assess our surroundings. I reach into my waist holster, pull out my gun, and verify that it's loaded. After sliding one into the chamber, I assess the rest of my weapons. Another pistol on my ankle, another in the waistband of my jeans. Various knives secured around my body.

Dominic does the same, checking each of his weapons and climbing into the driver's seat of the van. "You ready?" he asks me.

"Yeah. Are you?"

"Let's fucking do this."

He turns the key, starting the engine and securing whatever fate has in store for us.

I ignore the thoughts that run through my head, the regrets I have for all the lost years with June. They fester and try to force their way in but if I want to make it back to her, I cannot afford to allow the distraction. I have to be sharp, vigilant, and focused on the task at hand.

We aren't on the road for more than five minutes before I spot a vehicle tailing us. This plan is almost too fucking easy, too fucking quick.

"We've got one on our six."

"I've got eyes on him," Dominic confirms. "Any others?"

"Just the SUV for now. Keep with the route."

Dom maintains the speed limit while following the path we spread word of that this envoy would be taking. It's clear we have a mole within our organization, we just aren't sure who.

"You think they'll take us on sixth?" Dom asks me.

"Yeah, that's where I'd do it. Minimal witnesses, no traffic cams." I continue to scan our surroundings, noting the distance the vehicle maintains behind us.

The small car signals, gets into the other lane, and speeds up. Was I wrong? Was this a random car on this random street going about its random business?

But when they pass us, my doubts are erased by the barrel of a rifle that is pointed our way.

"Dom, get down," I scream, throwing myself over him and reaching for my own weapon. I shoot it out Dom's window, nicking the passenger of the car but not before he fires a few rounds our way.

Dom swerves the van, almost side-swiping a parked car, and pushes on the accelerator. "Fucking bastards," he spits out. "Are you hit?"

"No," I steady my breath. "Are you?"

The car that attacked us veers and hits us in our back corner.

"They're trying to pit maneuver us, Dom. Don't let them." I steady my aim behind him, waiting for the bastards to get back up in my line of sight again.

"Give me the AK."

Our plan was to save the heavy artillery until we needed it, but there's no time like the fucking present.

I reach under the seat, pull out the weapon, and shove it across to Dom.

"Take the wheel," he tells me.

I comply, doing my best to steer from the passenger seat.

Dom releases his pressure on the throttle and we slog back, the car trying to hit us coming into view. He aims the AK straight at them, blasting at least a dozen rounds into the car.

Shots fire back and I swerve to avoid them from hitting Dominic.

"Gas, Dom!"

He pushes while continuing to shoot, and I yank the steering wheel to turn us down a side street where there will be fewer civilian casualties.

These fuckers fired on a semi-busy fucking street, no doubt causing more chaos than was necessary. They want us dead, but that doesn't mean innocent people need to die, too.

"Shit, we've got two more on our ass, Dom."

He heaves the gun into my chest and takes the steering wheel from me. "Do your worst, kid. I'm going to try to shake them."

Because this wasn't the plan, not here, at least. We were going to guide them where we wanted them and attack where we knew we had an advantage. Not go to war in the middle of a fucking road.

One of the vehicles, an SUV with blacked-out windows, approaches from the passenger side of our van. I roll my window down and shove the AK out, firing it directly at the hood. Bullets ricochet off and do minimal damage.

"Bulletproof," I yell at Dom overtop the loud road noise.

"Aim at the tires."

"I'm fucking trying." I pull the trigger, the shots reverberating through my chest and body. The noise blares in my ears. The shell cases buzz past my face and singe the skin of my cheek. "Yes!" I call out when I finally fucking land one in their tire. "Take that you fucking prick."

But when a bullet hits me, I know I've celebrated all too soon.

I fall into the van, my hand clutching my arm. I pull it off and glance down at the blood gushing out of the wound. "God damn it."

Dominic flits his attention toward me. "Did it go through or is it still in there?"

"I don't fucking know, but it hurts like hell."

"We've got to stop the bleeding." Dominic presses on the gas but uses his knee to steer while he shifts his attention to me. "Your shirt, take it off."

I drag the thing over my head, barely able to get it around my injured arm. "Here."

Dominic rips the fabric with ease, his hands going back to the steering wheel for a second to navigate us around traffic and then onto me. "Hold this." He circles the wound with the remains of my shirt and ties it tight, applying enough pressure to hopefully stop the excessive bleeding. "There, that'll have to do until I can get you out of here."

"No," I tell him through gritted teeth. I latch onto the AK and stare right at him. "We've started this, now we end it. There's no turning back now."

"You're one crazy son of a bitch."

"Thanks."

"What do we have? Two on our tail still?"

I glance in the mirror and assess the situation. "Yeah, the one I hit isn't back there anymore."

"Hang on, I'm going to do something stupid." Dominic slows down, letting the cars gain on us. At the last second, he shoves his foot onto the throttle and goes left into oncoming traffic.

"Jesus Christ," I call out while bracing myself on the door.

"I told you to hold on." Dominic keeps checking his rearview and darts around the oncoming traffic.

Horns blare, people slam on their brakes, and some cars crash into each other to avoid us.

He continues going the wrong way, his hands gripping the steering wheel like his life depends on it. Because well, it sort of does.

I push away the pain and focus on staying alive. I knew this would be dangerous, but this would be a hell of a lot easier if I weren't gushing from a gunshot wound. We haven't even gotten to the fun part, and I'm already down for the count. I refuse to let a little blood stop me from following through with our plan. I've been through and survived worse.

Dom cuts down an alley, blaring his horn at the people that are walking in our path of destruction.

They jump out of the way in the nick of time.

We cut through another side street, demolish the mirror of a car as we pass, and continue on.

"They still on us?" Dom asks as he navigates this ride through hell.

"Yep."

Dom slams on his brakes and turns left. My whole body slams against the door no matter how hard I try to brace myself.

I can't help but laugh at being thrown around like a fucking rag doll.

"You doing okay, kid? You're not losing it on me over there are you?"

I chuckle. "No, I'm good. Never better." I grab onto the handle and wait for the van to come to a stop. The second it does, I jump out with the AK in my grasp, slam the door shut, and rush to a dark corner of the warehouse we just pulled into.

Dom no doubt does the same, grabbing his own rifle and positioning himself in place.

I steady my breath, willing myself to hold it together even though the blood loss is making me a bit woozy. "Come on, Hayes," I whisper. I don't mean to, but I allow my mind to wander to June...the girl I fell in love with when I was just a broken-hearted kid. She was everything to me then, and everything to me now. Will she ever truly understand how much she means to me? And how I would give anything to make sure she's safe? I'd rather die than let anyone hurt a single hair on her beautiful head. And even though he has a shit way of showing it, I think Dom feels the exact fucking same.

That's why he's here today—risking his life to come one step closer to finding out who has threatened her. He won't stop until they're six feet in the ground, and I will be with him to see it through. My only hope is that we succeed, because I can't leave this world knowing that threat is still out there, lurking in the shadows and waiting for one of us to slip up so they can finish what they started.

The sound of tires skids along the pavement as the vehicles approach. My heartbeat pounds in my chest, and I bite at the inside of my lip as I steady myself for what's to come. No matter what happens here today, I will not go down without a fight. And I will take out every single person who stands in my way.

Concealed in my spot, I watch both of the vehicles roll to a stop and park behind our empty van. I squint to look across the way, to where Dominic should be. But just as I am, he's done a good job hiding himself in the darkness that lies beyond.

Three men exit one vehicle and two come out of the other.

Five to two. Not great odds, but we've had it worse and managed to make it out alive.

I wait, not yet moving and showing my cards. I'm at a disadvantage being injured so I have to be strategic about how I attack.

Dominic does the same, biding his time for an opportune moment.

"Spread out," one of the men says to the others. "They could have gone on foot."

"I fucking clipped the passenger," one guy reveals arrogantly.

"Doesn't mean you fucking killed him, asshole." The first guy shoves the other. "Come on, they're just runners. Follow orders, finish them off, and burn the product. Then we can get the fuck out of here."

"Whatever." The guy who shot me holds his gun in hand and turns in my direction but doesn't spot me kneeling out of his line of sight.

Two of the other guys head toward where I assume Dominic is, and the other two make their way to both sides of the van.

They reach for the handles as a smile forms on my face.

I close my eyes and shield my head from the explosion that fills the building. The van was rigged to detonate when the driver's door was open. I'm just fucking grateful Dom was able to set it in place as he darted the fuck out of sight.

Things were sloppier than we planned for them to go, but at least *that* fucking worked. And if we're lucky, two of the five have just been blown to smithereens, or at the very least, knocked out and giving us a better set of odds.

I blink through the thick smoke and debris that pollute the air, completely missing the fact that the guy who came my direction is right in fucking front of me.

"Oh shit," I blurt out and raise my gun, blasting him in the head with the butt of it.

"You mother fucker," the guy yells at me. He swings blindly and grabs me by the waist, yanking me to the concrete.

We wrestle around, my arm blazing fierce pain through me with each blow I take, but my willpower to live stronger than the agony to let it take me under.

"Stupid. Ass. Fucking. Fuck." I punch him in the head, my fist aching at how hard his fucking skull is. "Are you a fucking robot?" I groan and scramble for either his gun or mine, something to end this once and for all.

"You fight like a little bitch," he spits out and lands a fist on my side.

That's when I see it, my saving fucking grace. I latch onto the grip, kicking him in the face and freeing myself to fully grasp onto the gun, pointing it upward and shooting him right under his fucking chin.

His head snaps back, blood splatters onto me and the floor around us, and he falls right fucking on top of me.

"God damn it," I groan and shove his lifeless body off of me. I stand on solid ground and scan the vicinity, my eyes straining to see through the thick fog still filling the dark space. "Where the fuck..." I spot a body near the exploded truck writhing in pain. I put a bullet in his head for safe measure and continue on.

That's a confirmed two out of five.

I go around the front of our van and shoot the other guy who was hit by the explosion. He wasn't even moving but one can never be too sure. Half his face was missing, and I'm fairly certain part of the door was impaled in his chest, but crazier things have happened, and that's not a risk I'm willing to take.

Three out of five down.

I pause, listen, and try to locate the rest of the party. Commotion carries from deeper inside the empty warehouse, and I follow it like a dog with a fucking bone. Dom has taken on more than two guys at one time, in a non-sexual way, and it's not like he was shot in the damn arm. He's probably faring well, taking his sweet ol' time inflicting the kind of torment that only Dom is capable of. Still, I go after him anyway. Might as well have a little fun myself.

Gripping the tourniquet around my arm with my teeth, I tug it and try my best to tighten it back up from my romp with that guy with the hard head. I climb up a metal flight of stairs toward the noise, my hand leaving a bloody print in its wake. I'm going to need a bottle of Aspirin and bourbon when I get home if I stand any chance of relief. My ribs ache, and upon further inspection, there's blood coming from the back of my head, too.

How am I going to explain any of this to June?

*Oh hey, J, don't mind all the blood, just a little occupational hazard. No big deal. The bullet? Yeah, it's probably still in my arm, it's fine. Totally fine. Just a normal Monday at the office.*

Or is it Tuesday? Or Wednesday? Hell, I don't fucking know what day it is anymore. They all blur together. No weekends or nights off. Just one constant shit-storm of problems to solve and people to kill.

By the time I reach the top of the stairs, I'm winded.

Two men have Dom cornered, their fists landing punches every chance they get. One of them spins and kicks him in the ribs. Dom grunts but remains firmly rooted in place, giving back as many blows as he's receiving. He slams his elbow across one guy's face and the guy stumbles a few feet.

"Down," I yell. I pull the trigger of the gun and take down one of the men.

That makes four.

Is Dom fucking going soft on me or is he hellbent on dying today?

I'm a murderous lunatic but usually he matches or at least gets close to the same number of kills.

While still crouched from my command, Dom reaches for the pistol near him but the last remaining guy kicks it away from him. They both leap toward it, scrambling to be the one to clasp onto it and end the other one's life. Dom punches the guy across the face and blood and teeth splatter about.

I search for a clear shot, but none comes. I move closer, but I'm not fast enough.

The man dives at the gun and latches onto it, spinning on his back and pointing it up at Dominic.

"No, don't!" Dominic shouts.

I aim, shooting without a second thought, my bullet hitting the man at the same time his hits Dom square in the chest.

That makes six men down.

I rush over to Dom and attempt to soften his fall to the concrete, but with my own injuries, I'm not as strong as I once was.

Speckled red from head to toe, Dom clutches at his chest. "Fuck," he mutters, looking down at where he was shot. He fingers the hole in his suit and yanks out the smashed bullet. "He ruined a perfectly good suit."

"I fucking told you these vests would come in handy." I shake him and grin.

Dom exhales and turns toward the dead guy next to him. "We needed one of them alive."

"That's why you were pussy footing around up here?" I release him and stumble onto my ass, glancing at the blood-soaked wrap around my arm. "It's better than being dead, dude. Imagine having to explain that one to J."

Dom rakes his hand through his hair. "At least we've got the bodies and their vehicles to search. Better than nothing."

My head grows fuzzy. "Yeah, for sure." I lean all the way back and look up at the ceiling. "I'm just going to..."

But instead of finishing my sentence, I pass the fuck out.

# CHAPTER 15

## June

"Dude, but have you had the Thai over on Front Street?" Magnus asks Simon.

Simon scoffs. "It's good but nothing compared to over on Ballard and Hazel."

"Bullshit." Magnus wraps his arms around my shoulder and tugs me toward him, almost like a natural reaction he doesn't even realize he's doing while he's so lost in the conversation of who knows where the best food is with Simon.

It's kind of strange how well they get along considering they *hate* each other.

But the more they talk, the more they have in common. Their interests align with food, business, and women.

Okay, maybe not *women*, but *woman*. Singular.

I've never asked about any of the guys' exes. I haven't wanted to know. Because no matter how much I pretend I wouldn't care, I'd compare myself to each and every one of them. It's basic human fucking nature, and I want no part of it.

I'm already in my head enough about their feelings for me, I don't need that to add to the insecurities, too.

*Sarah...heart emojis.*

I should have heard Simon out when he tried to explain who she was, but I didn't want to know that either. I shouldn't be possessive over him, or remotely jealous of some other woman having his attention, but I'd be lying if I said I wasn't.

Maybe it's because Simon and I have evolved from enemies to friends; our forced relationship molding us into some weird, platonic relationship. But is that all these feelings are? Platonic? A friend caring about another friend?

Simon steals a glance at me, a smile on his face as he talks to Magnus. He winks at me and turns his attention back to Magnus.

That flutter in my chest telling me otherwise about my friendship theory.

We're both aware this can be nothing more. It's forbidden—practically fucking borderline illegal. Dominic and Coen would decapitate us if we even thought about it. Magnus, on the other hand, might be down. Still, there's no way the other two would be.

The door to the garage opens and my heart completely comes to a stop.

Dominic and Coen, speak of the fucking devils, walk through the door, blood and gore covering their bodies.

I slide off the stool at the kitchen island and rush over to them, not sure which one to focus on.

"What happened?" I stare between them.

Coen is shirtless, but wearing what looks like a bulletproof vest. At least he's fucking careful. But there's white gauze wrapped around his forearm with a center of red.

I press my hand on Dom's chest to confirm he's wearing a vest, too. "Are you okay?"

Dom nods but doesn't hold my gaze. Instead, he looks to Magnus. "I thought everyone would be in bed by now."

I snap my fingers in his face. "Hello, I'm right here."

"I, uh—" Coen starts. "I'm going to get some sleep." He points to the stairway past me.

I raise my arm and stop him. "Not until someone tells me what's going on."

"June." Dominic sighs. "Can we not do this tonight?"

I cross my arms. "Then when? Huh? You mean tomorrow morning, when you sneak out of the house before I wake up? Or maybe when you come home after I've gone to sleep? All you do is avoid me. You don't respond to my texts; you don't bother to call. You make plans with me and miss them, knowing damn well how important it was to me that we spent some time together. Listen, I'm trying to be fucking patient here—be the *understanding* girlfriend to the big bad mafia man, but you've got to give me *something* Dom, a fucking crumb to signal that you still care."

Dominic's jaw clenches, and if I didn't know better, I'd think his eyes were glistening. But I do know better—and Dom is fucking heartless. His emotions are reserved for being a merciless psychopath with only his endless pursuit of ambition on his mind.

He doesn't give a shit about me, and he continues to make it known each day as he pushes me farther away. And when he looks away, his feet taking him around my body and toward the stairway, my concerns are proven correct.

If that's how he wants to be, two can play this fucking game.

Dom leaves the room, Coen's eyes unsure of where to focus.

I sigh and glance up at him. My sweet, tortured boy with blood all over him. "Let me guess," I tell him. "You're not allowed to say anything."

"I'm sorry, J." His apology is so genuine it makes me want to hug him and never let him go.

I reach up and run my thumb along his cheek. "I know, Co."

He turns toward me, leans down, and kisses my forehead. "Give him a week, okay? We'll come clean then." Coen flits his gaze toward Magnus. "Right?"

Magnus nods. "Promise."

At least two of my men don't completely want to keep me on the outs. How is it that Simon is so unaware of what's going on? He'd tell me without question, not giving a shit what Dominic or any of the guys had to say. He's always been honest with me—in the ways that matter. He recognizes how hurt I've been by them shutting me out, there's no way he would withhold information if it meant my unhappiness.

But I guess that's the difference between Simon and the rest of the guys. Simon understands the darkness within and doesn't deny that part of me. No, he helps me embrace them and nurtures those illicit tendencies. Simon isn't a good guy by any means—he's no hero. He's the villain who extends his hand and guides me into the depths of my deepest desires, even when they're twisted and sinister as fuck. I knew it from the moment he brought me my abuser and was willing to cut his fucking heart out just because I asked if it was possible. He proved in that moment he would do anything for me, no matter how fucking insane, and has only continued to with each moment we spend together.

"You sure you're okay?" I ask Coen.

"Yeah," he mutters. "I'll be fine."

"Get some rest, we'll talk tomorrow." I stand taller and press my lips to his. "Thanks for texting me back earlier."

Dominic is old as fuck, but it only takes two seconds to respond. If Coen can do it in the condition he's in, there's no reason Dom shouldn't have been able to, too.

Coen heads out of the room, and I go back over to Magnus and Simon. They both stand there like they're waiting to get in trouble. A house full of feared mafia men and not a single one of them will look me in the fucking eyes. If I had it in me, I'd yell *boo* just to see if they'd jump.

"A week?" I state.

Magnus bobs his head up and down, finally meeting my gaze. "Not a moment longer."

"Hell hath no fury than a woman scorned." I pause and add, "Or something like that."

"On that note, I'm gonna go," Simon announces and slaps Magnus on the shoulder. "Glad I'm not in the dog house with ya."

I narrow my gaze at him. "It can be arranged."

Simon winks at me again. "Have to be in the house before I can be thrown out."

"Something will change in a week's time. Either way, you'll know the truth, and we'll all live happily ever after, or the three of us will run away together." Magnus shrugs. "It's a win-win in my book."

"Wait." I chuckle. "Us three?" I motion between us and Simon.

Simon raises his brow and cocks his head to the side. "I'm down."

Is that a flicker of hope I spot on his face?

Dominic and Coen will snuff that out quicker than they can pull a hairpin trigger.

Magnus shrugs. "Why not?" His question comes out a bit rhetorical.

"Okay, before I wake up from this dream, I really am leaving." Simon points to me. "I'll see you bright and early, love."

"Bright maybe, but not early.

"Don't worry, I won't wake you." Simon walks backward toward the door. "I'll just watch you like a serial killer while you sleep."

"Oh, that's not creepy at all."

Simon slips out the door and leaves me and Magnus behind.

Magnus rubs my shoulder. "Let's get you to bed." He pulls me toward him and buries me in his chest, his arms holding onto my body tightly. "Man, I love you so fucking much." He kisses the top of my head over and over.

"So much you're willing to suffocate me?" I say into him while enjoying every second of it.

He releases me but only slightly. "Is that better?" Magnus tilts my head up toward him and finds my mouth with his. He swirls his tongue around mine and ignites a fiery passion within me.

I deepen the kiss as he tangles his hands in my hair.

Magnus pulls away, his breath lingering with mine. "You should get some sleep, princess."

"Actually..." If he's insisting on going to bed, I have something else in mind. "I think I'm going to torture Dom."

"Yeah? That sounds fun." Magnus yawns. "Will you film it for me so I can watch it in the morning?"

I laugh and give him a quick peck on the lips. "The things I have in mind shouldn't be recorded."

"You're really making me wish I wasn't dragging ass right now." He rests his chin on top of my head. "I could make coffee. You could tape my eyes open."

I spin out of his grasp, latching onto his hand and pulling him toward the stairs. "Let's get you to bed, sleepy boy."

His tattooed arm reels me back into him, his body pressing against mine as we make our way toward the stairs. "Will you tuck me in?"

"I'd have it no other way."

I finish with Magnus, quite literally nudging him onto his mattress and bringing his blanket up to him. His eyes close the second his head hits the pillow, and I wouldn't be surprised if he had fallen asleep before I even got to the edge of his room.

I tiptoe the long hallway to Dom's room, entering without permission, and going straight into the bathroom where the water is running.

Despite the elaborate and expensive house, the door creaks when I push it open.

I drag my shirt over my head and drop it to the floor, the steam in the room kissing my bare breasts. Yanking down my bottoms, I kick them off and leave them in the pile with the rest of our clothes.

"What are you doing, June?" Dominic asks me as I approach.

"Whatever I want."

He might want nothing to do with me, but I don't ignore the twitch of his cock upon seeing my naked body.

Dom rinses the rest of the shampoo out of his hair and turns toward me.

I step into the shower with him, my nipples hardening at the shift in temperature. I walk right up to him, craning my neck to look up at him as I reach down and grip his shaft. I stroke it, maintaining eye contact with him, and internally rejoice at how he immediately grows in my grasp.

"What are you doing?" he repeats through gritted teeth.

I turn around and press my ass against him, nudging his cock between my legs and gliding it over my wet pussy. "I want you to fuck me, Dom. Fuck me like you mean it."

He steadies his hand on my waist and digs his fingers into my side. "I don't think you want that, June."

I guide him to my hole and penetrate myself with the tip of his cock. "You don't know what I want, Dom, that's the problem."

He shoves into me with force, giving me exactly what I asked for. Dom tilts me forward, bending me at the waist and holds onto my hips as he thrusts inside me. Our bodies slap together, the mixture of tempo and water playing the perfect soundtrack.

I push into him, taking every inch of his wrath and reach between my legs, circling my clit between my fingers and using my other hand to brace myself against the wall. My pussy clenches around him, my orgasm building already at the intensity of the entire situation.

"Is that all you got, Dom?" I taunt him.

Dom slams into me harder and grabs my hand from pleasuring myself. "You'll come when I say you will."

I grin and bite at my lip, reveling in the bliss of getting him to do exactly what I want him to without him even realizing it.

"Stop," I tell him, reaching back and putting my hand against his stomach.

He complies immediately. "Did I hurt you?"

I turn toward him, my gaze locked onto his. "You're going to have to try harder than that."

Water trickles down on both of us, our chests heaving at the passion and angst between us. I love this man so fucking much but damn it he pisses me off.

Doesn't he see that I can handle him? I can handle this life? I can handle whatever fucking secrets he's keeping from me? We don't need the distance, the lies, the pushing each other away. We are better together, all of us are, and I don't know why he can't just fucking see that.

I prop my foot up on the bench and tug him toward me.

He wraps his arm around my waist and rubs his cock over my soaked pussy. Dom slips his thumb inside, and as he's pulling it out, he thrusts into me with his shaft. He brings the same thumb up and traces it across my lips before popping it in my mouth.

I rock my hips toward him and suck on his thumb, biting down when he slows down his thrusts. I nibble on the tip of it as he drags it out. "I told you to fuck me." I drop my leg and nudge him to the bench. "Sit down and I'll show you how it's done."

Dom is anything but submissive—he's dominant in every single fucking way, but right now, he is butter in my hands and he cannot gain an ounce of control over me—not when I'm so hellbent on giving him a taste of his own medicine.

I climb onto his lap and lower myself onto his rock-hard shaft. I move slowly at first, but then clench my pussy and ride him harder and faster.

With one hand on my waist, and the other gripping my tit, he sucks on my nipple and pulls it between his teeth.

I moan and hold onto his shoulders, my ecstasy just around the corner.

Dom moves his palm from my side and onto my ass. He slides his pointer finger down until it's resting on my puckered hole. He applies pressure, penetrating it gently.

I arch toward him, giving him permission, and savoring the heightened pleasure.

"One of these days." He brings his other hand up to my throat and tilts my chin toward him. "We are going to fill every one of your holes." Dom slides the tip of his finger in and rests it there.

I lean down and moan, my face just against his. "Why stop there?" Because after all, I have three holes and two hands...

He grips a fistful of my hair and forces my attention on his. "What is that supposed to mean?"

I fuck him harder and pull against his restraint. The pain only fueling my orgasm that much more. I grind his shaft, the pressure just fucking right to hit my clit at the same time. I dig my fingers into his shoulders and climax around him, my body nearly convulsing with tremors. But instead of riding him through until his hits, I stop moving and plant a kiss on his lips. "This, right here"—I climb off of him, his aching cock throbbing with want—"is what it feels like to love you."

He stares at me, a look of complete fucking bewilderment on his face as the water still flows onto him. "Where do you think you're going? I'm not done with you."

I don't return and give him what he wants. No, I walk away and leave him there yearning for more and not understanding why I left him when he needed me the most.

It's more difficult than I thought it would be, especially when I steal another glance at the beautiful man with flecks of silver in his beard and hair.

If this is what it takes to get through his thick skull that something needs to change, then so be it. He doesn't listen or pay attention to any of my other tactics, and if this is the only way to make him see something is wrong, then I'll fuck him until his balls are blue every day of the week. Maybe then his cock and balls will feel what my heart does when he gives me a little just to take it away.

# CHAPTER 16

# Simon

"Why are you all dressed up?" I ask June even though I know exactly why. Well, the numerous reasons.

One—it's the first night she's seen her best friend Cora in far too long.

Two—she's trying to make anyone with eyes fucking jealous or horny.

I'm sure there are more but my brain cannot comprehend words when she looks this fucking good. And after Magnus made a joke about us three running away together, I can't get the possibility of actually being with her out of my mind.

It's impossible, so fucking unlikely, but still, my heart has beat a little bit harder from the second he brought it up.

Magnus has always been the most open-minded in June's life. He's the one who insisted she be brought into our dangerous criminal world, and he was the first to advocate that she could handle it. He's also been the only one who holds more than a two-second conversation with me and treats me with some common decency. I wouldn't go so far as to say we're friends, but it's definitely a step up from enemies.

And with him on my side, it gives me a slightly better hand than I was playing.

If only I could get him to tell me whatever secret it is that they're hiding from her, then maybe I would finally have the leverage I need to convince her she's better off with me.

"If you forgot about going out with Cora, I am going to unalive you." June stares right at me.

I can't help but chuckle. "You're going to do what, love?"

She makes a fake gun with her hand and bends her thumb, insinuating a shooting motion.

"You do realize that's not how guns work, right?" I reach for her, pulling her toward me and gripping her hand. I fold her fingers back into the faux gun position. "These two, that's where the trigger would be, not here." I wiggle her thumb.

June rolls her eyes and sighs. "It doesn't have to be anatomically correct, Simon. You knew it was a gun, I knew it was a gun." She puts the fake thing to my chest and pulls the wrong trigger. "And there, you're dead."

"Wouldn't be the first time you tried to shove something into my heart," I tell her. The scar lingering just below the surface of my black button-down shirt.

"And it probably won't be the last." She winks at me, and I swear to Christ it's like my whole world is set on fire with just that simple blink of an eye.

I fucking hate this effect she has on me when there isn't a damn thing I can do about it.

Oh, what I would give to graze my fingers up under the base of her head and pull her all the way to me. I'd savor the closeness of her skin, the scent of her like it was the only thing that could keep me alive. I'd melt my lips onto hers and pray that I could restrain myself from not taking her right here and now. In another world, maybe, but not this one. At least, not today.

So instead, I say a silent prayer that my cock stops pulsing in my black pants and takes a fucking nap.

June stares up at me, that fiery gaze melting a hole through my fucking soul. "What are you thinking about?"

I inhale and consider telling her all the terrible things I'd love to do to her, but instead, I exhale and say, "You'll find out eventually." Because that's all I can really do. Hope that there's a chance in hell this will happen.

And even if it doesn't, I still have this. I still have us. Just not exactly how I'd prefer. But it's better than nothing.

"Simon Beckett, such a tease." She shoves my shoulder and walks to the door. "Come on, we're going to be late."

---

"Bye, Alec," June calls out to the driver who she keeps insisting on being on a first-name basis with.

"Stay behind me," I tell her as I help her out of the blacked-out SUV. I nod a farewell to *Alec* and scan the vicinity as he drives away.

"Simon..." June tries to go around me but I don't allow it.

I stand firmly in place and peer down at her. "My rules or we go home now. Do you hear me?" Fuck I hate being stern with her, but does she still not realize her safety is my primary concern? After almost losing her, there's no way I'd let that happen again, especially after my feelings have evolved into what they are today. Back then it was a mild obsession, now I'm fully fucking consumed by her. I eat, sleep, and breathe June and would go full on *Romeo and Juliet* if something happened to her.

I knew she was special, but it wasn't until I spent six solid months at her side that I started to unravel pieces of her that she doesn't share with anyone else. She doesn't even share them with me, not on purpose. But that's the benefit of spending so much time with someone, eventually your walls come down whether you realize it or not. You start to see the version of them that's unfiltered and raw. You get a sneak peek at who they are without the lens of the public eye. Hell, I'd go so far as to say I know more about her than her own boyfriends do.

Her shoe size, her to-go order at every fucking restaurant in town, the side of the bed she prefers to sleep on. I might not know what she prefers in bed, but I'm a quick study and willing to do anything to please her. And that's why when Magnus mentioned the three of us, I didn't hesitate to immediately jump on board. Do I prefer to keep her to myself? Yes, absolutely. But what fucking idiot wouldn't. I'd be a fool to think that I would be enough for her though, and I would never try to trap her in a box that she didn't want to be in.

The shackles they try to keep on her are proof that she isn't satisfied with their current situation.

"I hear you," she huffs and adjusts her shirt to expose more of her chest.

I tug the sides of her leather jacket to cover her.

June narrows her gaze. "Seriously?"

"It's a distraction, love," I tell her, because it's the fucking truth.

"Aren't you worried about snipers or something?"

"What?"

She motions to the buildings behind us. "I don't know. You act like I'm going to be assassinated."

I laugh. "You're a mafia queen, not the fucking president."

"Then let's go. Cora text me five minutes ago that she's already here. Get the stick out of your ass and come on." June pushes me but I don't move.

"Aw, that was cute. Why don't you try again?" I know I'm supposed to be playing the role of bodyguard, but man is it fun to fuck with her.

"Don't make me get out my gun." June tilts her head and raises her brows.

My face drops. "You did not fucking bring a gun." I start to pat her down, but she stops me.

"Here..." She reaches into her coat pocket and pulls out her fake finger gun. She draws back her middle and index fingers. "Pow." Then she shakes her head. "No, that doesn't feel right, I'm sticking with the thumb, sorry. "Bang." She brings her hand to her chin. "Which do you prefer, *pow* or *bang*? I could go for a *pew pew*. What do you think?"

"I think...you have lost your mind."

"Yeah." She shoves me again. "Because you're making me stand out here on the sidewalk all fucking day." June cranes her head around me. "Like twelve people have gone in while we were out here."

"Promise me you won't sneak off."

"That was one time, Simon." She sighs dramatically.

I fold my arms over my chest. "Promise me or we aren't going in."

She rolls her eyes for what must be the fiftieth time today. How they haven't gotten lost in her head yet, I'll never know. "Fine, promise."

"Good," I grin. "Have a wonderful time. If you need me, just say my name. I won't take my eyes off of you." Not even if I wanted to. I take her hand and turn around, holding her close to my backside. Her warmth flows through me, and I wish with all my might that when we step into this bar we would also be stepping into an alternate universe where we're here together—like really together. I'd still do everything in my power to protect her, but at least I'd be able to kiss her before she ran off with her best friend.

"Simon," she whispers once we're inside.

I turn to her immediately and evaluate the potential threat. "Yes, love?"

"Do you want to get a drink with us?"

My heart lurches forward, and for a second there I think I'm about to lose all sense of fucking gravity. How is it possible she does so much by doing so little?

I ache to reach out and touch her cheek, but I don't. I'm her bodyguard, not her boyfriend. I spot her blonde friend across the way and focus back on the stunning vixen in front of me. "Maybe after I've done my scan of the place. Okay?"

She bobs her head, and if I didn't know better, I'd say there was a hint of disappointment on her features. But I do know better and the only reason she asked was because she pities me for having to stand here all night watching over her.

If only she knew there's no place I'd rather be. Other than by her side, obviously.

I nod toward Cora. "Your bestie is that way."

June reaches toward me, surprising me when she latches onto my forearm. She gives it a squeeze before she turns and walks toward Cora, the spot she touched burning even when she's no longer near.

I make quick but thorough work of making my way through the bar and scanning the place for anything unusual while maintaining my sights on June. I manage to check the entire place out and watch her the whole time, something I've grown to be pretty fucking good at. I wasn't always the best at this kind of gig, but I've never had a person I've been more concerned with keeping safe. Nothing out of the ordinary sets off my Simon-senses so I go to the bar, the bartender immediately approaching me.

"What can I get for you?" the guy asks me.

"Those two," I point to Cora and June. "Whatever they order is on me."

He glances over at them and nods. "Sure thing."

I settle into the corner I usually lurk from. It gives me a clear vantage point of the front door, the one that leads to the staff area, and the hallway that goes to the bathroom, where another door leads out the back.

It only takes about two minutes before a random drunk girl starts eyeballing me from across the way. I avoid her stare and try to seem as uninterested as possible. I wouldn't have even noticed her in the first place but paying attention to every little thing is kind of why I'm here. Unfortunately, that opened up a small window of opportunity for this unsuspecting female. Cracking my neck, I readjust my stance and attempt to get out of her line of view. Maybe if she can't see me, she will stop fucking staring.

She's not ugly by any means—some might consider her conventionally attractive, but there isn't anyone that holds a fucking candle to June. It's like once she unknowingly reached in and ripped my heart out, I can't even stomach thinking of another woman that way. Sure, I might notice someone pretty, but it doesn't do the same thing for me that it used to. It's like my heart, brain, and cock all have this June filter that is impossible to bypass. Not that I would anyway. She's fucking radiant, and not just on the outside. She's funny and charming and kind, and damn if she isn't fucked in the head just like me. June has this immense soft side, but then this darkness that could swallow her whole if she's not careful. She tries so hard to hide it, but there's no escaping the flicker in her eyes when she's faced with danger.

June isn't afraid of danger; she fucking craves it.

And right now, she's staring right at it.

I hold her gaze and breathe through the way my heart picks up its pace. Something so intimate about her sultry eyes on mine from across the room. She could be looking at anyone else, and here she is, focused on me.

Cora says something and pulls her attention.

I'd love to be a fly on the wall for her conversations with Cora. But I respect her enough to give her some privacy with her friend, considering she doesn't get much of it with me being around all the time. It's a fine line to balance between protecting her and not making her hate me.

Her guys sort of do enough of that on their own—I don't want to be included on the shit list.

I recall Dom's bloodied face, the hole in his suit that was caused, no doubt, by a bullet. Coen was injured on his arm, and if I had to take a guess, I'd wager he was shot, too. They were both dirty and worn out from an extensive battle. But isn't that what they have their grunts for? Why were Dominic and Coen dealing with that kind of situation to begin with? Unless it was something they don't trust anyone else with. Which would make sense why it isn't common knowledge.

They've been dealing with some shipment issues and trying to keep it under wraps, but even if it was that, other qualified people would have handled it instead of them.

What happens in a week? They told June they would tell her the truth then, but I have no knowledge of anything going down in that time frame. I've been so wrapped up in her that I haven't paid much attention to the inner workings and politics of the criminal world. I stay up-to-date enough to get by, but my concern is her and nothing else. I still have my small team, my investments, my sources of income. But outside of that, I've kind of fallen off the radar.

I've been fortunate that some people have remained loyal to me despite Dominic having taken over. Sometimes discretion is needed, like the other night when June shot and killed a man in a bar parking lot. I was able to contact my clean-up crew and get the situation remedied without alerting any of the guys. People die all the time, and that aspect of our jobs isn't usually something that brings up much concern unless it's a high-profile person. And the dude June murdered was a low-life piece of shit that I can't imagine anyone will miss.

It was risky, using someone in our organization to handle it, but so far, nothing has come from it, and I hope it stays that way. I don't really need her guys to be breathing down my neck for letting her kill someone.

We haven't really talked about it—me and June. She seems relatively unfazed by it, almost like it was a pretty normal thing to do. I'm sure that would alarm a normal person, but she and I are a different breed.

If anything, it's as though a temporary weight has been lifted from her shoulders. I noticed it after the fight night; the way she came to life in that illicit place and felt more at ease than when she's just going through the motions elsewhere.

I cringe when the girl who was gawking at me earlier stalks across the room toward me. I avert my gaze and hope that I can pretend to be invisible, but it's hard when you're a guy like me in a place like this.

"Shit," I mutter to no one but myself.

She steps right in front of me. Golden blonde hair, tits bulging out of her tight blue dress, ruby red painting her lips. "Hey." She puts her hand on her hip. "You want to dance?"

"No." I shift away from her, hoping she'll pick up on the body language and leave me alone.

I keep my attention on the dark-haired woman who has my heart across the room.

"I'm Carli, what's your name?" She extends her hand, but I don't take it.

"Uninterested." I finally look down at her for a second. "Shit," I whisper again as I watch June push her way through the crowd toward me.

She shoulders Carli on her way by and weaves her arm around mine. "Oh, so sorry," she tells Carli then glances up at me. "Didn't mean to keep you waiting, *love*." She throws extra emphasis on the last word.

I grin at her possessive bitchiness. "You know I'd wait forever for you." All truth, not a hint of a lie.

"Uh," Carli finally speaks. "You two are..." She points between us. "Together?"

"Mmhm, yeah, why?" June feigns ignorance then laughs. "You didn't think you had a chance, did you?" She holds onto me tighter. "*Brad* would never."

"Brad?" Carli furrows her brows. "I thought your name was Simon." She shakes her head. "I must have you confused with someone else."

"Simon?" June chuckles. "That's a silly name." She pulls me away from Carli and toward where she and Cora were sitting at a high-top table.

"What was that all about?" I ask her.

She doesn't release her hold on me but keeps moving us through the crowd. "You looked miserable." June glances up at me through her thick, dark lashes. "Was I wrong? Because if I was, I can be one hell of a wing woman." She stops walking. "We can turn this ship around and go get you a piece of that plastic Barbie."

This time it's me that pushes us forward. "Don't be foolish," I tell her. "Although..."

"I knew it, you had a thing for blondes." June halts us again.

"You really are completely oblivious, aren't you?" I peer down at her. "What I was going to say before you rudely interrupted me, was that was the best place in here to keep an eye on everything."

"I literally invited you to hang out with us. Isn't next to me the best possible option?"

It depends wholly on the reasoning, but without question, yes, absolutely.

June drags me the rest of the way to Cora, who's frantically thumbing something on her phone. She angrily fingers a send button and slams the thing down on the table, looking up to greet us.

"Simon, how kind of you to grace us with your presence. I thought you were just going to lurk in the corner all night like a fucking psychopath." Cora grins and teases me like I'm not the most dangerous man in the room.

"Aw, go easy on him, he was being attacked by a gold digger." June pats my arm. "There, there, you're safe now."

I shake my head. "You're something else, you know that, love?"

Cora rests her head on her hands. "What's it like?" She stares at me and June.

"What, being a gold digger?" June climbs onto the stool she was sitting on earlier and pulls out the one next to it.

"Oh, hush, you're practically a sugar baby."

"Am not," June protests. "I work!"

"Even mister *not your boyfriend but is around more than your boyfriends* picks up your tab."

June glares at me. "You did not."

I shrug and take a look around from where we are. I don't like not being able to see everything, but at least I'm next to her if anything *were* to happen. It's been six months and there hasn't been a threat to her life, but one can never be too sure. The second you get complacent, that's when shit happens. And with her, I cannot afford to take foolish risks.

Cora perks up. "Are you expecting someone?"

"No," I tell her without explaining anything else. Because what would I say? That I'm assessing for threats to her best friend's life? I don't know what all June has told her, and I don't think I'm the appropriate person to bring it up. I'm all for honesty, but those are not my secrets to confess.

"I thought maybe you had a friend coming." Cora doesn't question my lurking, and I'm grateful that she doesn't pry into things I'm not able to discuss. "Do you have any single friends, Simon?"

"I don't have any friends." What I have is more like business acquaintances that I occasionally eat a meal or get a drink with. No one that I trust or would call for anything other than cleaning up dead bodies or handling professional matters. Truthfully, June is the only person I'd even consider a friend, but I'm not stupid enough to realize she wouldn't have me in her life if I didn't completely persist. What I feel for her is real, what she feels for me is strictly based on the habit of me always being around.

If I disappeared it wouldn't take her long to get used to her life without me. I don't doubt that she'd prefer it, especially with how much she lets me know she dislikes my company.

"Oh, that's not true," Cora says. "You're a popular guy."

I laugh dryly. "It's not that."

June hit the nail on the head earlier. The only reason that girl came up to me earlier is because she thought I was Simon Beckett. The notorious playboy who lives a lavish lifestyle of luxury. A fake fucking persona I accidentally created when I went through my rebellious phase and tried to fill the void in my life with booze, girls, and spending money. It didn't work, obviously, but that didn't stop people from craving what I could offer. I had more fake friends than I knew what to do with, and for a while, I thrived on the high of being the center of attention. But even with every bit of notoriety it gave me, I was still an empty fucking pit inside. Nothing could fix the emptiness and the more I took, the worse it made me feel.

And to top it off, that's the lasting impression I have on every single person I interact with. They think I'm this fuckboy who doesn't have feelings, who doesn't care, who has no intelligence, but yet only cares about bottle service and boobs. Everyone underestimates me, and that was one of the main reasons I wanted to prove them wrong and win the throne that Dominic now holds.

Is he qualified for the position? Without a doubt.

But so fucking am I.

And it was just within my grasp until June came charging into our lives.

I could have had it. I could have had everything. I was prepared to use my power to eventually claim her, too, but when she was bleeding out in my arms, everything that I worked so fucking hard for felt impossibly unimportant. It was overwhelming, the flush of emotions that went through me. Rage. Agony. Terror.

I went from almost having it all to nothing and I didn't know how to react other than to give her my word that I would concede as her dying wish. Because if I was going to lose everything, I wanted her final moments to be filled with the understanding that I would have chosen her. Her above the lifestyle, the money, the only thing I've ever really cared about.

I held my hand against her chest as her blood slipped through my fingertips, leaving with the only chance I'd ever have to prove to everyone that I wasn't the immature boy they thought I was.

I could have let her die. I could have pushed to have the council overthrow Dominic's position. I could have convinced them he was distracted by a female and wouldn't be fit for the job.

But I knew all too well the pull she had on him, because I felt it, too.

He's just the ignorant bastard that's taking it for granted.

"Listen," I tell the girls. "I don't want to interrupt. I know how long it's been since you two got to see each other."

"Are you kidding?" Cora laughs. "I word-vomited my entire trip in like four minutes flat. And June here is a closed book, so it's safe to say we're caught up enough for you to join."

I side-eye June and consider my options. I don't want to leave her, but I don't want to impose, and I sure as shit don't want to impede the real reason I'm here, to protect her.

"Everybody, down!" someone yells.

Two shots ring out.

I react without thinking, shielding June with my body and yanking her off of the chair and under the table. My heart races, those memories of that night in the council home rushing back over me. I fumble my hands over her, frantically searching for the blood.

"I'm fine," June reassures me. "Simon, I'm fine."

But I don't believe her. The image in my mind is too vivid to shake, and I can't suppress the fear that she's going to die on me again.

Cora responds much slower than I do, joining us under the table and cowering next to us.

I grab her and pull her toward June, covering them both with my frame. "Are you hurt?" I ask her.

"No." Cora's chest heaves. "What the fuck is going on?"

I shake my head. "I don't know. Active shooter. I won't let anything happen to either of you, I promise." I rip my shirt out from its tucked-in position and pull out one of the guns on my body. I verify that it's loaded and press it into June's hands.

She eyes me seriously and takes it.

"If anyone approaches that isn't me, you fucking shoot them. Do you hear me?" I slide the other gun out of my ankle holster and check the chamber. "Do not leave each other, and whatever you do, do not try to run. You'll make yourself an easy target."

"Where are you going?" June asks me.

"To kill the bastard."

Cora stifles a gasp, but I ignore it and focus on the sounds happening within the confines of this death trap. A woman screams, feet shuffle against the floor, furniture creaks as it's moved. Panicked whispers spread and somebody muffles something incoherently.

"Simon?" June meets my gaze. "Be careful, please."

I run my hand along her cheek, not giving a shit how fucking inappropriate it might be. "I will, love." I push the gun in her grasp toward her. "You know how to use it."

She nods stiffly and I turn, still crouched but trying to get a better look before I rise completely.

A shaking couple stares at me from their spot under the table closest to us.

I press my finger to my lips to signal them to be quiet and scoot myself over near them. I scan the crowd ahead, looking for anyone who isn't pissing themselves with fear. That's when I spot the set of legs walking carelessly around the cowered patrons. I point my gun toward him but can't find a clean shot. I glance back at June before I move closer to the danger zone.

Her hand clenches the gun, but not in a way that makes her appear weak, but more so that she's ready for whatever comes her way. Her face is set in a hard line and her body gravitates toward keeping Cora concealed.

That's my girl, protecting those she loves.

"You," the gunman yells. "Get on your fucking feet." He points his gun at a scrawny man hiding behind a woman. "Both of you."

The man and woman hesitate but comply with the gunman's demands.

She mumbles something but I can't quite make it out.

The attacker is wearing common clothes. His hair is unkempt and if I had to guess, he hasn't showered lately. I mean, why would you if you planned on shooting up a bar? His hands shake, the gun trembling in his grasp.

I let out a sigh of relief. He might be here for blood, but I'm fairly certain it isn't June's. This is just a terribly unfortunate case of wrong place, wrong time. Still, I can't let him get away with this, not when my girl is fearing for her life under a fucking table. He ruined her night, and for that, I will ruin his entire fucking existence.

I rise to my feet slowly and hold my arms up in front of me. I tuck the gun along my hand and hope he doesn't notice it in his frantic state. "Hey, buddy." I inch toward him.

He peels his attention from the couple for a split second to look at me. "Sit down, fucker. This is between them and me." He shoves the gun forward like some silly threat.

"Name-calling is a bit unnecessary; don't you think?" I continue in his direction and try to get him to shift his focus to me.

He takes the bait and points the gun right at me, his hands still quivering.

"What's this all about?" I ask him.

The guy yanks his arm toward the ceiling and fires off a warning shot. "Don't you come any closer, you fucking hear me? I'll shoot every person in here."

"I don't think you have enough ammo for that, buddy."

"I-I—" he stutters while trying to come up with something to say.

"Cat got your tongue?" I move two inches to the right and finally get the window I've been searching for. I bring my arm down and pull the trigger in one swift motion, the bullet from my gun penetrating the man's chest.

His eyes go wide and a ring of blood pools through his shirt. The arm that he was holding his own gun in lowers and his legs give out from under him.

I stalk toward him, my pistol still trained at his pathetic frame. "Why don't you pick on someone your own size?" I blast another round into his temple for safe measure.

Sirens sound in the distance, and I'm reminded that I'm in a public fucking place, and I just killed a man. God damn it, this is going to take more effort to handle than usual.

Warm arms wrap around my torso and latch onto me.

I raise my elbow and hug her back. "You're safe, love," I reassure her.

She looks up at me, tears welling in her eyes. "I wasn't worried about me, you fucking idiot."

"Shh." I hold onto her and pull her close. "Where's Cora?" I turn where I had left them, Cora standing in my shadow.

People shuffle about, their heads peeking out from under tables to see if the coast is clear.

The woman who was targeted meets my gaze. "Th-thank you."

I nod and while still locked onto June, I grab Cora's hand. "Come on, both of you. We're getting out of here." I pull them toward the door and kick the pile of shit that's barricading it shut. I drag them onto the sidewalk and motion to the SUV parked down the road.

The headlights flicker on immediately and the thing heads in our direction.

"Cora," I steady the blonde and tilt her head toward me. "I'm going to take you to June's place. Okay? You're safe now. You don't have anything to worry about."

Her blue eyes blink a few times, and she nods. "Yeah. Okay."

She's in shock and dealing with that here isn't the best thing for her. She needs to be somewhere completely protected from the outside world.

June wraps her hand around Cora's and pulls her to her.

"How did you..." Cora pauses and stares at me. "How did you know to do that? Why do you have...guns?" She lowers her gaze to the one still in my hand and then to the one June is holding. "You have a gun, June."

"I'll explain in the car, Cor." June shoves the gun in my direction and guides her friend to the blacked-out SUV.

Alec jumps out and opens the door. He helps Cora inside then June. His concerned stare meeting mine. "Is everything okay, sir?"

I lift my shirt and tuck one of the guns into my waistband and lean on Alec's shoulder to put the other one in my ankle holster. "Yeah. We need to get out of here before the cops arrive."

# CHAPTER 17

# *June*

"What do you mean, you fucking shot someone at the bar?" Dominic clenches his fist so hard I worry it will break his entire hand if he applies any more pressure.

I stand in between the sitting room and the kitchen. My best friend is being comforted by Alec in one room, and Dom's considering murdering Simon in the other. Both are equally important.

"You would have done the same thing," Simon tells Dom, but with much less anger in his voice than Dom. "He ruined June's night out."

Wait a minute, Simon killed the guy because of *that*?

"Plus," he adds. "He was about to shoot some lady and her dude. I think it was a lovers' quarrel or something."

"A lovers'...quarrel?" Dominic pinches the bridge of his nose between his fingers. "You opened fire in a public place because of a little relationship drama?"

I step forward. "He had a gun, Dom. Simon did what he had to do to eliminate the threat." I sigh. "Isn't that what you hired him for?"

He ignores me and focuses on Simon. "And you didn't think you should stay? Deal with the cops yourself? Do you know how big of a headache this is going to be to clean up?"

"My priority was getting June out of there safely." Simon glances down at me. "That's always going to be my priority."

Dom's phone buzzes on the counter. He glares at it. "And so it begins." He grabs it and points at Simon. "I have to take this. Don't fucking go anywhere."

Simon leans against the counter and folds his arms over his broad chest.

"You did the right thing," I try to reassure him.

He shrugs. "Maybe."

I stalk toward him, my hand resting on his shoulder. "You did."

Simon flits his attention to my best friend in the other room. "How's she doing?"

If I'm being honest, I've been partially unsure of how to handle the situation. Cora has been on a need-to-know basis with pretty much everything that's happened since the guys have come into my life. But with that, it makes stuff like this difficult. I don't know what to say, what to do, how to comfort her when it's laced with secrecy and lies. She's one of the most important people in my life, and the truth will only put her more at risk.

But if I'm okay with keeping her in the dark, should I be allowed to be mad at the guys for doing the same fucking thing? Is what I'm doing really any different?

I don't have a romantic relationship with Cora, though. I don't live with her, share space with her, and avoid her at all costs. I don't sneak out before she wakes up and come home when she's asleep, and I don't lie when she point blankly asks me a question.

Okay, maybe about Miller—but that's for her own good. Miller is deep in the criminal underworld, and if she got involved, it would pull her into it, too.

There's a large portion of me that welcomes it. To have a best friend I could confide in, to actually have proper girl talk and explain *everything*. It would be amazing. But that would be selfish of me, and Cora staying in the dark is for her best interest.

"I don't know what to say to her," I whisper to Simon while looking over at her.

"You'll figure it out." He nudges me in the direction of where she and Alec are sitting on the couch together. They're close, too close, and in my focus on Dom and Simon, I may have missed another potential relationship I need to steer her away from.

Alec isn't nearly in the life as much as the rest of the guys are, but he still has his foot in the door and knows way more than I'm comfortable with her finding out. He's a good guy, but good isn't the only standard that my best friend deserves. I guess he scores a few points in the looks department too, with his dark eyes and matching hair. That isn't enough to get a chance with my best friend, though.

I walk over and lower myself onto the couch next to Cora. "Hey, you."

She tugs the blanket over her shoulders tighter and turns toward me. "Hey."

"Crazy night, huh?"

Cora nods. "Yeah."

"You doing okay?"

"Yeah. Alec and I were just talking about this course at the university we both took."

"Oh, you went to college?" I ask Alec.

"I'm getting my graduate degree now."

"Cool," I say with a bit of surprise showing through. "What in?"

"Architecture."

"That's dope, dude." Simon comes over and sits on the edge of the couch behind me.

Something so fucking comforting about his nearness.

"Thanks." Alec smiles while averting his gaze, his cheeks reddening.

"But yeah, we had a lot of similar undergrad classes. And I think we were in the same econ my last semester." Cora turns to me. "Remember that stupid bitch who kept rounding my grade down even when it was like a tenth of a point from going up?"

"I wanted to stab her for you."

Cora grins. "He dealt with the same shit. Almost cost him a point on his grade point average."

Alec clears his throat. "I contacted the Dean about it and a week later, she fixed everyone's scores."

"I thought I was going to fail that class." Cora chuckles. "Thanks to you, I didn't."

A man was just shot and killed, and Cora is in our house chatting about college with a boy she barely knows. I don't know if I should be relieved or concerned, but either way, I don't want to bring it up unless she does. I wanted to come over here and diffuse their conversation but if it distracts her from the ugly parts of this evening, what kind of friend would I be to put a stop to that?

I reposition myself on the couch and twist my neck to the side in an attempt to get it to crack. I must have crouched in a weird position too long and cramped something in my back, the tightness and pain spanning my entire spine and up into my neck. My head aches, and I'd do anything for a hot shower and about twelve hours of sleep.

"You okay?" Simon asks me without hesitation.

I swear, I could breathe weirdly and he'd notice.

"Yeah." I wiggle my back a little. "I think something needs to crack but it won't."

Cora and Alec waste no time picking their conversation up and chattering about professors at the university they both attended.

If it were any other night, I'd plop my ass between them and break it apart, but I welcome the temporary distraction he brings.

"Stand up." Simon nudges me and rises to his feet. "Come here."

I comply even though I have no idea what the fucking standing up is going to do for me.

"Turn around." He spins me so I'm facing away from him. "First, take this off..." Simon drags my leather jacket over my shoulders and tosses it onto the couch. "Cross your arms." He leans in close, his breath on the back of my neck sending a chill down my spine. "Like this." He grips my forearms and directs me exactly how he wants me. Simon wraps his own arms around me and presses himself into me from behind. "Relax, love." Those two words are a whisper that only I can hear.

I close my eyes and exhale, fully melting into his embrace.

He squeezes me tight and lifts me off the ground like I weigh nothing at all. He applies a bit more pressure and leans back.

A million pops and cracks sound and it forces a moan out of my chest. "Oh my God, Simon. That was fucking amazing."

He chuckles and sets me on the floor. "I'm not done, yet." Simon turns me toward him and tosses my arms over his shoulders. He weaves his under mine, and he picks me up in a giant hug. Simon intensifies his hold on me, and my back pops in ways I don't think it ever has.

"Fuck," I mumble. "I think I just died and went to heaven."

The door to the garage slams shut.

"What the fuck is going on here?" Coen calls out, clearly fucking pissed off.

Simon releases me, and I move my shoulders and revel in the relief of tension already there.

Cora and Alec both look in Coen's direction but don't say anything.

"Chill, Co," I tell him, still rolling my arms.

"Chill?" Coen slams his keys on the counter by the door. "I could hear you fucking moaning from in there." He points to the garage.

"Moaning?" I laugh. "Are you serious?" I point to where my best friend is sitting. "You think I'm in the middle of the house fucking Simon out in the open?"

"So, you're saying you do it behind closed doors?" Coen's entire body tenses and part of me wonders whether he's going to self-implode. The veins on his forehead bulge.

"What has gotten into you?" I move around Simon and toward my angry boyfriend.

"More like *who's* gotten into *you*." Coen steps back when I approach.

"Don't make accusations you know nothing about."

His anger seeps into me with each word he fucking speaks.

"You think I'm stupid, don't you? You think I don't know what's going on here?" Coen glances over at Simon and then back at me.

"Tell me, genius, what is it you claim you know? Because I'd love to fucking hear it," I snap at him.

Dominic stomps into the room. "What the fuck is going on in here? I can hear you from my office."

I jut out my hip and cross my arms. "Coen here was about to enlighten us."

"You're allowing this type of behavior?" Coen says to Dom.

"Excuse me?" Dominic stiffens in place, assuming his defensive stance.

"You think I don't know, but I do." Coen stares right at Simon. "I know exactly what you're trying to do."

"Dude, I think you're overreacting," Simon finally tells him.

"Whatever you think is going on, you're wrong." Dominic steps closer to Coen. "I could hear the whole thing. He was cracking her fucking back. You're going to lose your shit over that, of all things? If anything, you should thank him, it sounded like she needed it."

"You're standing up for him now? Is that what this is? You've joined Bryant in..."

Dom cuts him off. "Do not put words in my mouth. If you know what's best for you, you'll shut yours and take a fucking chill pill."

Coen's chest rises and falls so dramatically that I can see it from my spot six feet away from him. His whole body is tense, and I haven't seen him this fucking mad since...ever, really.

"You're being paranoid for no reason, Co," I attempt to reason with him despite wanting to punch him for having such bold accusations.

I have never crossed the line with Simon. Sure, we've flirted and had little moments here and there, but *nothing* like Coen is insinuating. He has no right to treat me like this, especially when his avoidance, all of their avoidance, is the reason Simon and I are as close as we are.

They've insisted Simon be with me every fucking second they aren't. And he has been—right at my side for over six months. Something none of them have done. He's foolish if he didn't expect some type of relationship to have never naturally grown.

"Am I? Am I, J?" He steps toward me with his wild stare trained on me.

In all the years we've spent together, and all of them apart, I have never once been afraid of the man standing in front of me. Not when we were young, and not when I found out he was a murderous psychopath. Not even when he pointed a gun at me when I walked down those stairs after my first night with Magnus. But here, right now, watching something unfamiliar consume him, I'm not so sure anymore. The Coen standing in front of me isn't a version of him I'm accustomed to, and if I'm being completely honest with myself, he kind of scares me.

Simon steps around and positions himself in front of me. "Don't take that tone with her."

"Yeah, what are you going to fucking do about it?" Coen comes even closer.

"Enough!" Dominic blares. He stalks over and shoves his forearm into Coen. "Get the fuck out, *now*." He pushes his palm into Coen's chest, nudging him again. "Don't come back until you've calmed down."

"Fuck this." Coen huffs and snatches his keys off the counter. "I don't want to fucking be here anyway." He doesn't look back as he reaches for the garage door, disappearing on the other side and slamming it shut.

I startle at the sound of it and hold my hand to my chest. Tears unwillingly spring from my eyes, and it's like Coen ripped part of my heart out when he left. I stand there, silently crying and wondering what the fuck I did wrong to deserve that from him.

Did he find out Simon and I have been going behind their back to do sketchy shit? And even if he did, why is he acting like that's any worse than coming home with a gunshot fucking wound and covered in blood? If he gets to act recklessly and do dangerous shit, why can't I? Because he's a man? Because he's been doing it longer? Because he gets paid to hurt people?

None of that is reason enough to disallow me from having a little fun.

Simon and I have never shared a kiss. Never once had sex like Coen fucking thinks we have. Is he questioning my loyalty because I'm with Dom and Magnus, too? He agreed he was okay with our arrangement, but now he thinks I'm slutting around with Simon because he's fucking insecure and making wild assumptions?

I thought we were finally on solid ground, but little did I know our foundation is rockier than ever. I've tried to forgive him for the past, accepting that he never meant to hurt me the way he did, but when he acts like this, it makes me want to scream at him and remind him that he's the one who *fucking. Left. Me.*

I had started to heal from that decade-old wound, but now, I'm torn open and bleeding as the sweet boy who stole my heart all those years ago walks out on me once again. Leaving me here wondering and aching for an explanation.

"Love," Simon mutters and reaches for me.

I shake him off and wipe at my cheeks. "No." I turn and bolt across the room and take the stairs two at a time to put as much distance as possible between me and anyone else. I cannot afford to show another ounce of myself in front of people who are capable of ripping me apart.

Dom has shut me out, leaving me in the dark alone.

Simon is only around out of obligation because he feels bad that I almost died.

Cora and I are separated by a wedge of secrecy I don't know how to navigate. Not to mention how fucking embarrassing that whole interaction was. If she ever wondered how dysfunctional having three boyfriends was, she's seen it first-hand now.

Not a single relationship in my life is healthy, and I'm not in a place where I can handle another sad stare or dismissive tone.

It's times like this when I wonder if things would have been better had I never met any of them. Then, at least, I wouldn't be this giant fucking burden in their life.

I close myself into my room, not bothering to turn the light on, and go straight into the bathroom where I slide down the wall and sit in the dark. I clench my fists, the desire to break open the flesh of my palms strong. I place my hands on my legs and dig my fingers into my thighs, the fabric from my jeans protecting my skin. I lean my head against the wall and exhale, the weight of my fingers not enough relief from this overwhelming feeling taking hold. I run my hands through my hair and tug it to provide a different kind of stimulation. Something, anything, to distract me from the hole in my chest.

A knock sounds on my bedroom door.

"Go away," I call out to whoever it is and hope like hell it isn't Cora. She's the only one who doesn't deserve to be shunned for the distance between us. That alone is my fault.

Maybe if I came clean I could repair the damage I've done to our relationship.

Whoever it was doesn't listen, instead, they open the door and enter anyway.

"June?" Dominic says in the dark of my room. "Where are you?"

"I need some space, Dom, please." I sniffle and wipe at my nose.

He continues toward me, ignoring my request. "Oh, June." Dom manages to find me through the darkness and lowers himself onto the cold tile floor in front of me. "Come here." He reaches for me, but I pull away.

"I don't want your pity, Dom. You ignore me every day, why can't you do it when I actually want you to?" I don't mean for the words to come out as harsh as they do.

"I don't mean to…to ignore you. It's just…" Dominic keeps his hand on my knee. "There are things going on that I can't talk about." He sighs. "Not yet."

"Did you change your mind? Is that what it is?" I fight the tears that continue to roll down my cheeks.

"God, no." Dominic grabs me and this time I don't stop him, because as much as I can't stand him, I need him more than I want him gone. He pulls me into his lap and kisses my forehead. "Never, June. Never will I not want you with every piece of me."

I bury myself in his strong chest and let myself accept this fleeting closeness.

He moves my hair from my face. "My love for you has never faltered, I promise you that."

"It feels like it," I mumble into him.

"I'm sorry," Dominic says. The weight of those two words so fucking heavy.

"I don't know how much more of this I can take." I lean into him and listen to his thunderous heartbeat. "This isn't what I signed up for."

But who ever really knows what they're going to get when they begin a relationship—let alone multiple, with three incredibly complicated men?

I just didn't expect it to be *this* fucking hard. I can handle the violence. The illegal activities. The entire criminal side of things. I don't even mind the late nights and early mornings. But it's the pushing me aside and disregarding me like I don't exist. Like I don't matter. That's what hurts. And that's what I cannot accept. They don't trust me and it shows in every hushed conversation they have and the way they refuse to include me in literally every aspect of their lives outside of this place. I only matter to them when I'm down on my knees or having a laugh with their so-called enemy.

I never asked for Simon to be a part of my life. I never insisted I spend every fucking day with him. That was them. And now they're mad at me for treating him decent. For having a relationship with him. One that is strictly platonic. One that makes me wonder what life would have been like if I had met him first. But I'd never even fucking have that thought if they didn't shut me out and shove me toward this man they hate.

How did they not realize how entirely fucked this whole plan of theirs was?

Then they have the audacity to blame and accuse me of being unfaithful.

"I know it isn't," Dominic tells me. "None of this is fair. And the way Hayes just spoke to you was completely unacceptable. I will deal with him later, but right now, you are my concern. Do you hear me?" He holds me closer like he actually cares.

I mumble a half-assed acknowledgment.

"I just need a little time." Dom sighs. "And then I'll tell you anything you want to know. But until then, you have to trust me."

"Trust you?" I sit up and glare at him through the darkness of the bathroom. I can barely see his outline, but if looks could kill, I'm sure he'd be dead. "That's all

I've ever done. What does it get me, Dom? Fucking nothing." I try to remove myself from his lap, but he holds onto me. "You didn't even bother to let me know you were going to stand me up the other day. How do you think that made me feel? Huh? You knew how important that date was to me and you didn't even bother to call." I wriggle under his strong grip. "You left me with Simon."

"I'm sorry." Dominic holds onto me.

"Sorry doesn't cut it, Dom. You hurt me. You continue to hurt me." Tears roll down my cheeks, months' worth of emotions spilling over the surface.

"I'm here now, okay?" Dom keeps his strong arms around my body. "I'm going to make it up to you. I will."

"How? The only thing I want from you, you won't give it to me." Sobs wreck through me and add to how fucking frustrated I am. I don't want to feel this way. I don't want him to see me like this. I don't want to be this fucking weak—all because of a man. Three men. Who refuse to keep any of the promises they've made.

"It's not that simple." Dom sighs. "But I'll fix this. I'll fix everything. And then we'll get our happily ever after."

"What if it's too late for us?"

Even in the dark I can spot his jaw tense. "It will never be too late for us." Dominic places his large hand on my cheek. "Don't give up on me, not yet, please."

There's a desperation, a tenderness to his tone that's so unfamiliar that it actually makes my heart skip a beat. I've gone six months in the dark, what's another week? And if he breaks yet another of the vows he makes, then I'll know for sure where we stand. I love him enough to give him that.

"Okay," I whisper.

He rests his forehead against mine. "You are the only thing in this world I cherish. Give me some time, and I'll prove that to you."

"Okay," I repeat, because what other options do I have.

I don't want to be without him. I don't want to be without Coen or Magnus, either. I don't even want to lose Simon, whatever we may be. He is my friend. My constant. And without him, I don't have anything else I can count on. He's been there for me more than anyone else, and it might be strictly out of obligation, but it feels like more than that. Like maybe I matter to him, too. In a perfect world, the guys would stop being so fucking controlling and distant, and Simon would still be around. But that's the thing about life, it's far from perfect.

"I'll call my pilot and make arrangements for tomorrow," Dominic says.

"What?"

"Me and you. Let's skip town for a day. We can go up north. I know a good bed and breakfast in Washington."

"Washington, like the state?" I ask him.

"Yeah, you ever been?" He skims his thumb over my cheek.

"No, never." I leave out the part where I've never been out of California, let alone traveled to another state.

I grew up poor, and I've remained that way until they came into my life.

Surviving was always the main goal, not going on trips. Hell, the only reason I've seen the ocean is because we live sort of close to the coast. Coen and I spent a lot of our time together there, getting burnt during the day and laying under the stars at night.

I guess that's one of the perks of having a dead mother and deadbeat dad—lack of parental supervision. I'm not entirely sure if my father knew I wasn't home, or if he would have cared if he found out I was with a boy.

It wasn't just any boy, though. The majority of my childhood years were spent with the blond-haired, blue-eyed kid who would have risked his life to ensure my safety. Not much has really changed, aside from him turning into a massive prick.

A shudder runs through me at the memory of him glaring at me like he hated my guts earlier. I shove the thought aside and focus on the man holding me in his arms.

I'm so small here, tucked away in his grasp. Oh, how I've longed for this much attention from him. It's a different kind than when we're fucking. Even with our clothes on, this is somehow much more intimate.

"What do you think?" Dom glides his finger to tuck my hair behind my ear. "Want to run away with me?"

I draw in a breath and consider my options. I could say no—break both of our hearts, or I could say yes, and put mine on the line to be broken once again.

"Yes..."

A sly grin forms on his face.

"But," I add. "If you so much as even think about no-call-no-showing me, I will hunt you down and make you wish you never met me."

Dom presses his plush lips against mine, his beard bristling my face. "I would expect nothing less from you."

I chew at the inside of my cheek. "I left Cora out there alone."

"She's with Alec, she's fine."

"They're flirting," I tell him. "That's not good."

"Alec's harmless."

"But he's..."

"He wouldn't be your driver if I didn't think he was a stand-up guy."

Dominic assures me but it doesn't make me any less suspicious about someone from this world infiltrating my sweet best friend's life.

The light in my bedroom flicks on and someone enters. The illumination fills the entry of my bathroom enough that I'm sure Dom can finally see my swollen eyes and red cheeks.

"Princess?" Magnus calls through the empty space.

"In here," I tell him while remaining on Dom's lap.

Magnus pops his head around the bathroom door, craning it one way, and then at us. "Christ, there you are." He kneels beside us. "What are you guys doing down here?"

I sigh. "Long story."

Magnus holds out his arms. "I can take over." He glances up at Dom. "You're needed elsewhere." They exchange a look like they're telling a secret that I'm not supposed to know.

I roll my eyes and stand, Dom finally letting me go. I flip the switch to turn the vanity light on. "Fuck." Me and crying are not friends.

Some girls are cute when they cry. Me on the other hand…I'm a mix between stung by a bunch of bees and haven't slept for thirteen years. And with my pale complexion, the crimson gives off an unpleasant *what the fuck happened to her* kind of reaction.

"Tomorrow." Dom points at me in the mirror. "Have a bag packed by noon. Okay?"

"Don't make me regret saying yes."

He strolls over and kisses the top of my head. "I won't." Dom leaves the room, and Magnus makes his way over, gripping my shoulders and turning me toward him.

"Who do I need to kill?" He studies my fucked-up face.

"I'm fine, don't worry, no one needs to die today." Although, I wouldn't mind putting a flaming bag of shit in Coen's bed for him to find when he comes home.

Maybe I'll mail him one of those glitter bombs or add his phone number to every single spam website I can find. I might really fucking dislike him right now but I can't imagine actually doing something that would harm him, even if he did rip my heart out of my chest and stomp on it—not only once, but twice.

"I heard Simon shot someone tonight." Magnus keeps his hands on me. "Are you okay?"

I nod and steady my blurry gaze on him. "Yeah, why wouldn't I be?"

"Um, because he fucking murdered someone, princess. And you sort of got shot once upon a time. That's a massive trigger." Magnus releases me and reaches for a washcloth, dipping it under running water and bringing it to my face. He blots at my cheeks and tries to remove the mascara streaking them black. "You're allowed to be human and feel things."

"That's why you think I'm a wreck?" I take the rag and wipe my face more aggressively than he was.

"What else would it be?" He leans against the counter and watches me in the mirror.

"Coen freaked out on me earlier." I shouldn't tell him, but I do, because I don't want him to assume I'm emotional about some dead guy I don't give a shit about. That asshole deserved to die for all the chaos he was trying to cause. And if Simon hadn't done it, I would have.

Magnus balls his hand into a fist but remains otherwise collected. "What happened?"

"He accused me of cheating."

"With Beckett," he adds.

"Yeah."

Magnus shakes his head. "What a fucking idiot."

"My thoughts exactly."

"I'm sorry, princess." He stands and wraps his arm around my shoulder and tugs me toward him. "You didn't deserve that."

"Maybe I did," I confess.

Magnus tugs his bottom lip in between his teeth and rolls it out. "Have you and Beckett..." He stops himself. "No, fuck it, I don't give a shit if you did. It doesn't change things between us. Right?"

I let out a big breath and turn toward him. "For the record, we haven't. I'm not romantically interested in Simon. He's my bodyguard, that's it."

A throat clears in the doorway of my bathroom.

Simon stands there, his gaze trained on me. "I was, uh..." He rubs at his neck. "Coming to check on you. But I'll go."

He turns to walk away and I call out to him. "Simon."

But he doesn't stop.

"Simon," I say louder.

Magnus puts his hand on my shoulder. "I think you hurt his feelings, princess."

Great, as if things weren't rocky enough, now he's upset with me, too.

# CHAPTER 18

# *Dominic*

I check my watch, noting the time and wishing this meeting would end so I could get on with my fucking day.

"Analysis is inconclusive," the man tells me.

"That's not helpful." I tap my finger along the mahogany desk. "And not what I paid you for."

"My apologies, sir, I was unable—"

"To do the job you were hired to do, I understand." I snap my fingers to signal to the guy standing guard near the entrance to this room. I point to the guy in front of me. "Have him dealt with."

The first man widens his eyes and lurches forward. "Sir, I can run it again."

"You've been nothing but a waste of my resources. If you could have done it, you would have the first time around." I nod to the other guy. "Get him out of my office."

The guard latches onto the man who kicks and screams, but I pay them no attention as I turn back to the paperwork in front of me. Deliveries that need to be signed off on. Potential revenue ventures that need my approval. The endless to-do's that come with running this kind of business. There is always something that needs done or looked over or assessed. Threats pop up left and right, and there are constant fires that need put out. This job is all-consuming and nonstop.

But today, I refuse to allow that to get between me and my girl.

It's already done enough damage, and I will not be responsible for pushing us off a cliff I cannot save us from.

Plus, getting June out of town serves a dual purpose.

I have a small group of guys running point on following up a lead that might actually bring some closure to this mysterious situation, and I want her nowhere near when shit goes down. I'm not sure why I hadn't thought of it sooner, but holding her in my arms and wracking my brain on how to do two things at once, it dawned on me that this was the perfect plan.

I'll be there to ensure her safety, and give her some of the quality time we both desire. It'll be a challenge to micromanage the situation from another state, but it's the challenge I will endure to be the man she needs me to be. Especially when things are rocky with her and Coen. If that bastard doesn't get his shit together soon, he'll be the first to lose his relationship with June. I'm treading a thin line with the secrecy but in a matter of days, I will finally come clean about what's been going on and why I've done what I have. Then she will understand this was all for her and we can get back to how things were.

I'd be lying if I said I didn't want to keep her out of our business, but if we're going to be with her, long term, that would be impossible. I don't want to see her turn into another council wife who is constantly in danger just because of who they're married to. And with June being involved with four made men, it only puts her more at risk. She might only be in a relationship with three of us, but Simon has made it clear to everyone in our organization that he would give his life for her.

My cell rings, and I answer it immediately. "Yes?"

"Mr. Adler. The jet is fueled and ready for departure. Should I send a driver to your location?"

"No, I'll be there in an hour."

"Very well," the older man says.

"Did my package arrive?"

"Yes, not too long ago."

"Great, I'll see you soon."

I disconnect the line and snatch my keys off my desk. I may have fucked up last time, but I refuse to be late and ruin things again. This organization can run for a day without me, and if it can't, I'll pick up the pieces tomorrow.

I stalk out of my office and a young man jogs to catch up to me, a clipboard and pen in his hand.

"Hold all my calls today, and forward anything of importance to my cell. Hire another analyst to go over the data from the delivery. Get a location on Hayes, and send it to me immediately."

"Yes, sir." He makes notes and follows me down the corridor. "And Mr. Bryant, sir?"

I stop and turn toward him, pressing my hand into his shoulder. "He is not to be bothered. Do you hear me?"

The kid averts his gaze and nods. "Yes, of course, sir."

"Good." I immediately start moving down the hall again.

"Is there anything else you'd like me to handle while you're away, sir?"

I latch onto the door and pause. "The coffee machine is on the fritz. Have that fixed by the time I get back." Sixteen grand and the thing wants to stop working on me after a year. "Call the company, they should send someone out."

I rush across town, rolling through every stop sign and turning on every no-turn-on-red, not giving a shit about the petty laws that I'm breaking. I do worse daily; a little traffic violation is nothing in the grand scheme of things. I end at least one life a week, sometimes a dozen. Consequence means something different for a man like me. I'm not necessarily above the law, I just have it in my pocket.

Parking in the garage, I note that Coen's car isn't in its normal spot. Simon's is here, something I've grown rather used to in the last six months. Magnus's isn't, but I knew that already. He's in charge of today's mission and the reason why I'm able to get away with June. Coen was supposed to head this one up, but no one has heard from him since he stormed out last night. When I told Magnus I might have to cancel my evening with June, he threw himself into the volunteer position to make sure I could still go. I'd rather have both of them on the job, but if I have to settle for anyone, Magnus is a solid alternative.

He's a fucking lunatic, don't get me wrong, but Magnus has more heart than Coen, which makes Coen the perfect soldier. I've never not been able to count on either of them to come through when shit needed to be handled. Coen skipping out on us is new and has me questioning if I ever really knew him at all. This is unlike him. He's a battered soul but never once did I think he'd get *that* fucking mad at June and assert his dominance that way in front of her.

If we didn't have a strict no violence in the house rule, and she didn't love him as much as she does, I would have put a bullet in his head just for his fucking tone.

I step into our house and toss my keys onto the counter. The main floor is quiet aside from the faintest instrumental music playing in the background. I make my way past the kitchen, and up the stairs to our second story. Chattering floats back to me, and when I reach the top, Simon nods at me from his post just outside June's door.

June pokes her head out and grins. "You're here."

"I am." I approach, Simon moving out of my path, and I press my lips to hers. "You can go now," I tell him and focus on her. "I have to throw a few things in a bag then we can head out."

Simon hesitates like he's waiting for *me* to leave. "Right, yeah. Um, see you later, love."

I glare at him without really meaning to, watching as he waves and exits the hall, disappearing down the stairs.

"You don't have to be so mean." June nudges my arm.

"How was I mean?" I huff and press my hand along the doorframe.

"*You can leave*," she mocks me in what she considers my voice.

"I do not sound like that."

"*I do not sound like that.*" She does it again.

I narrow my eyes. "You're being a brat."

"You like it." She grins and goes to turn around.

But I grab onto her hand and spin her toward me, pressing her into my chest. "Brats get punished."

She flutters her lids at me. "Oh, no," she feigns innocence. "How will I ever survive?"

"You're asking for it, little girl."

June stands taller and tries to kiss me but I remain out of her reach.

"It's no fun to not get your way, is it?" I graze my finger over her cheek and rest my hand along the base of her neck.

My cock pulses in my suit pants and tells me if I don't end this soon, I'm going to make us late for our flight. I imagine pushing her against the wall, ripping her pants down and burying my face in her tight little pussy. I'd spread her folds and dip my fingers into her honey pot, licking up every drop of her until she begged me for her release. And once she was breathless from ravishing her, I'd slam my cock into her and fuck her with no restraint, making her come over and over again.

"Whatever you're thinking," June breathes into me. "Do it." She reaches down and strokes me through my pants, my shaft reacting and making me wonder how it's possible to do anything while she's around.

I lean toward her, my mouth resting against hers. "Maybe later." I trace my tongue along her bottom lip and kiss her briskly before turning around and going to my room.

"Suit yourself," she mutters.

I make quick work of distracting myself with tossing some clothes into a bag, not giving a shit about how haphazard they are. Usually, I'm more meticulous about things like this, but the sooner we get out of here, the sooner I can give in to our carnal desires.

Only, when I finish packing and return to her room, my cock rages even more at the sight before me.

June, completely fucking naked, legs spread and hand sliding up and down her slick pussy. She uses her other hand to grip her breast and pinch her own nipple. Her head leaned back, her eyes closed, a moan leaving her mouth.

I swallow and watch her, reaching to adjust my throbbing cock as it pushes to get free.

She glides two fingers into her hole and arches upward, her hips rocking gently. June stops moving, barely glances over at me, and brings herself onto all fours, her ass in the air.

I nearly lose all sense of reality when she buries her face in the comforter, extends one arm behind her and one under to circle her clit. She whimpers and the sound goes straight to my fucking shaft.

I stroke myself through my pants and sigh. Glancing at my watch, I count down the minutes until I said we would be arriving at the tarmac. This isn't exactly how I intended our date to start, but who am I to deny this beautiful specimen the fucking she deserves? Quicker than I prefer is still better than not at all.

I leave my place in the doorway and enter her room, going straight over to the edge of the bed and climbing up toward her. With her hands still in place, I grip her thigh and lick her dripping wetness. She moans louder and inches toward me, a sign that she's okay with me interrupting her solo time. I shove two fingers in alongside hers, both of us filling her tight hole. I thrust them in and out and put in another to spread her even more. I rise to my knees and straddle her left leg, my three digits still fucking her little pussy. I use the other hand to latch onto the arm teasing her clit and remove it.

"You come when I say you come."

She arches her back and pops her ass out even farther.

"Good girl," I tell her. "You're such a good fucking girl."

June spreads her legs and takes her free hand to weave it up the bed and grip the sheets.

"Open up," I command with my hand hovering next to her mouth.

She complies and I pop them inside. She sucks and swirls her tongue, and I touch the base of her throat before pulling them out and rubbing them along her pulsing nub.

I show it no mercy as I pinch it between my moistened fingers. I remove her hand from inside her and toss it aside. "You're going to want to hold on to something." I force another finger inside her and dive them deep into her hungry hole. My cock, still encased behind my pants, rubs up against her leg, begging to be set free.

I drive my hand back and forth, finger fucking her harder than I ever have. I swivel my pressure on her clit and revel in the tightness as she clenches around me.

"Come for me. *Now*," I growl.

June screams and clenches the bedsheets, her entire body pulsing as her orgasm crashes over her. I don't let up, my fingers still pinching her throbbing clit. Her climax lengthens and another bolt of pleasure flows through her. When her second orgasm isn't even finished, I remove my hold on her clit and unbutton my pants.

"Dom," she whimpers.

"I'm not done with you yet." My cock springs out, precum lacing the tip. I rub it over her juicy, stretched-out entrance and slam it in; I'm not being gentle at all. I grip her hips and thrust into her, her face smashing into the bed even more.

June shoves her body into me and spreads her legs wider apart.

"That's it," I mutter. "That's fucking it." I pump harder, lengthening my strokes and slamming into her. "You're taking me so well."

"Oh God," she mumbles.

I shove into her. "If you're going to be screaming anyone's name, it's going to be mine."

"Dom...Dominic."

My cock throbs in response, ready to spill over and fill her full.

"That's my good girl."

I clench her ass, circling one hand and pulling it back to smack her. She flinches but doesn't tell me to stop. I do it again, her cheek turning blood red.

June brings herself onto her elbows, and I slow my tempo to let her change positions. She sits on my lap, her back pressed against my chest. She reaches around to grab onto my arms, putting one hand on her breast and the other on her clit. June moves up and down, her pussy tensing and her clit throbbing against my touch.

I rock my hips and thrust into her from this new angle, my mouth finding and kissing her neck. I drag my teeth over the tender skin and bite down. Not hard enough to break the flesh but enough to leave a mark.

She moans and her nipple hardens between my fingers.

I pinch and roll it the way she likes, her whole body coming undone in my grasp. She shudders and tightens her pussy so much that I worry I'm going to explode from the pressure. I hold off, fucking her through her orgasm, and once she's finished, I release my hold on her.

"On your knees," I command.

June obeys, her breath ragged as she turns herself over and drops down. She licks her lips in anticipation.

I run my hand over my rock-hard cock, her juices coating me. Gripping the base of her head, my fingers tangled in her hair, I tilt her toward me and skim my wet fingers over her lips and into her mouth. "That's what a good girl tastes like." I tighten my hold on her and slide my index and middle finger farther along her tongue and to the back of her mouth.

She doesn't gag, she just takes as much as I give her and reaches down to stroke my shaft while I do as I please.

If we weren't pressed for time, I'd keep making her come until her legs gave out.

But we are, and this needs to end soon. Not before I've fucked that pretty little mouth of hers, though.

I remove my fingers and take my cock from her. "Open up." The same thing I told her earlier, but this time I'm going to fill her fuller than just two fingers.

June glides her tongue along her lips and swirls it over the tip of my shaft. She moans and closes her eyes but I tug on her hair and tilt her toward me.

"Keep your eyes on me," I command, guiding my cock into her enthusiastic mouth. "That's a good girl." I sway back and forth, going easy on her to start.

But the second she gets her groove, she takes more of me until I'm hitting the back of her throat, her eyes watering with each inch of me she swallows up.

I hold onto the sides of her head, my fingers weaved through her hair, and force her onto my cock. I slam down her throat, and she doesn't protest one fucking bit.

Instead, she opens wider and spreads her tongue over the bottom of my cock.

June braces herself with one arm and uses her other to grip the base of my shaft, circling and tightening her hold on me. She moans against me, and it's everything I can do to stay fucking put together.

"You like the way I fill you, don't you, my pretty girl?" I thrust into her.

"Mmm," she mumbles against my shaft, the vibration of her voice nearly sending me over the edge.

"You feel so fucking amazing." I fuck her face deeper. "You're doing such a good job."

June moans and it's my undoing. I slam into her, spilling my load down the back of her throat. I pull out to give her a chance to fucking breathe and finish coming on her pretty little face. She swallows and licks her lips, her mouth hungry to get every last drop of me.

I exhale and let the bliss course through me, my cock still throbbing at the edge of her mouth.

She wipes at her cheek and dips her fingers into her mouth. "Mmm."

I shake my head. "You, are something fucking else." I exhale and sit back on my heels.

"Yeah, but you love me for it."

There are a million reasons why I love this beautiful woman in front of me, and that one is very high on the list.

June props herself up against a pillow and rubs her wet fingers over her still-soaked pussy. "Want to go again?"

I grin at her and a chuckle flows out of my chest. "You're kidding?"

She teases her entrance and then spreads it open. "What do you think? Am I joking?" Her sultry gaze doesn't leave mine.

I flit my attention between her and her glistening pink center. "We're going to be so late." I stalk forward, press my lips to hers, and shove my already hardening cock back into its home—deep inside her.

# CHAPTER 19

# June

Dominic and I finally arrive at what I thought was an airport, but it's not what I expected, not really. Instead of long security lines and a bunch of tired people waiting to board their flights, we pull straight onto the runway and get out of the blacked-out SUV and walk directly to a small plane. Small being super relative considering planes are fucking massive in general. I thought we were flying first class or something, not on a private fucking jet.

"This way," Dominic tells me while holding my hand and slinging my bag over his shoulder. He passes it off to the man standing at the base of a set of stairs that leads up to the plane.

"Afternoon, Mr. Adler." The man nods at him.

"Frances," Dominic greets him. "This is June, she'll be accompanying me today."

Frances tips his hat. "Pleasure is all mine, Miss June. Please let me know if I can be of any assistance to you."

"Uh, thank you," I say, unsure how to greet this man. There are so many random people I come into contact with because of the guys' work, and they all side-eye me when I try to befriend them and care about stuff like their damn birthdays. I still haven't figured out Alec's, and he drives me around almost every day. I'll have to just ask him myself and deal with the guys being mad at me about it, not like it puts me in danger by asking a simple question.

I realize they're employees or whatever, but they're still human beings. And it's not like they get days off for special occasions or holidays. The least I could do is get them a Christmas card or something.

"Go on," Dom tells me. "I'm right behind you."

I latch onto the cold metal of the railing and make my way up the stairs. It creaks under me and the more I get off the ground, the more unsteady I become.

I've never had an issue with heights in the past. Hell, Co and I used to climb onto rooftops to look at the stars, and one time we were nearly arrested after we climbed the local water tower. We were able to get down before the cops came, but damn was it a close call. The idiots had their flashing lights and sirens on, and we could see them from miles away, giving us plenty of time to escape.

*Coen.* Memories from another life—from another boy. He is not that same person anymore, but neither am I. I shouldn't fault him for changing, but what if the new version of him is something I cannot live with? The idea of losing a love I've held on to for so long aches something fierce in my chest. I used to think there wasn't anything we couldn't get through, but I'm not so sure anymore.

I step inside the plane and turn to my right, considering I don't exactly plan on flying this thing. I glance at the cockpit but all the buttons and knobs immediately send panic flowing through me. How can someone possibly remember what all of those do? I guess it's like driving a car though, right? When I was little, I couldn't wrap my head around the levers and steering wheel and gearshift. But now, I do it without effort. Maybe I'm only rattled by the idea of operating a plane because I have no idea how to do it. And unfamiliar territory is bound to stir up some uncomfortable or irrational thoughts.

Like falling out of the fucking sky.

Dom places his hand on the small of my back and guides me farther in. "Sit wherever you'd like."

"Anywhere?" I take in my options. There are numerous single seats, with a polished table separating them from another seat. There are a couple double options, and then couches in the back of the plane. I didn't even know planes had couches. How was I was living off of sips of booze at Jack's and packs of Ramen about a year ago, and now I'm deciding which level of luxury I'd prefer on my private flight with my mafia boss boyfriend?

Life is fucking strange.

Dom dips his head into the cockpit and chats with the pilot while I make a decision.

I settle on one of the double chairs because it seemed like a midline rational decision. In between the single seat and couch. A happy medium of sorts. Dom could sit opposite or next to me. Heck, we could play musical fucking chairs if we wanted.

I lower myself onto the plush leather and revel in how damn comfortable it is.

Frances appears at my side, startling me a bit at how prompt he is. With his hands folded so fucking properly on top of each other, he says, "Care for a beverage, Miss June?"

"Yeah, uh, sure. And, just, just June is fine."

"My pleasure, June. What would you like? I could bring you a fine Merlot, or perhaps a Shiraz. I do have a wonderful Bordeaux I personally picked from France. I've chilled Mr. Adler's Hawks Mark."

"I'll have that, please. Neat."

Frances grins. "Ah, similar tastes, I see."

I smile politely even though I would have easily settled for a cheap bottle of bourbon over Dom's preferential thousand-dollar bottle. Don't get me wrong, it's fucking delicious, but holy shit is it expensive. I don't think I'll ever get used to this lavish lifestyle. Although, it is nice to not have to worry about where my next meal will come from or if I'll be able to work enough to pay my portion of the rent. I don't have monetary worries with them. They insist I have the best of everything, even though I'm okay with "off-brand shit," as Magnus would call it.

I don't need their spoils though, and it's not why I'm with them. Their love is all I want, and lately, that's been the hardest thing for them to give me. I'd easily trade all the lavish shit for more of their time, but I know that isn't possible. I just didn't think it would be this difficult. It wasn't supposed to be. I was going to be a part of their world. Help them with the daily operations and give them business advice, potential ways they could scale and grow their empire. I was told I would be their queen, but all I feel like is their hidden mistress who barely gets an ounce of their attention.

They tell me it will change, that it will get better, but what if it's only a lie to keep me on the hook for longer without any real promise of things being different? What if we never really do get that happily ever after they promised me?

Frances returns from the door he had disappeared behind in the back of the plane. Two glasses in his grasp. He sets both of them on the table in front of me. "Are you hungry? Or would you like me to wait for Mr. Adler?"

"I'm good, thank you, but he might be." *Especially after the sex-capades we had before we came here.* I leave that part out though. Frances doesn't want to know about the dirty things Dom did to me only a half hour ago.

My body still tingles from Dom's touch, my pussy aching from the pounding it took.

Dom usually gives it to me good with his dominant bedroom antics. I eat it up like the good girl I am, but damn do I like pushing his buttons and being the brat I truly am at heart.

"Very well, Miss June." Frances motions toward the direction he came. "The lavatory is that way, and if you need anything…" He shows me a little button on the side of my armrest. "You can simply push this."

"Thanks." I want to correct him about my name again but I don't force the matter. Formalities sort of seem like his thing.

Dom finally leaves the front of the plane and comes toward us. He grips Frances's shoulder. "Franc, man. How are you? How's the family?"

Frances smiles warmly. "Doing wonderfully, thank you, Mr. Adler."

"That's great to hear. And your grandson? How did the trial go?"

"We have seen much improvement, sir. I cannot thank you enough." Frances's eyes glisten.

Dom gives him another firm squeeze. "Don't hesitate to let me know if anything changes or issues arise. I'll make a phone call."

"You are a good man, Mr. Adler."

The two of them exchange a silent nod and Frances goes toward the front of the plane.

I raise a brow at Dom. "What was that all about?"

My Dom, a good man? Ruthless, murderous, cold as ice Dom...

Dom reaches for his glass of bourbon. "He had a problem and I solved it, no big deal."

"Sounds like it was a very big deal, Dom. What did you do?"

"His grandson has cancer. I pushed to get him into a trial he otherwise wouldn't have been accepted into." Dom lowers his glass onto the shiny table and spins it around. "That kid shouldn't have to die just because he doesn't have resources."

I stretch across the surface to latch onto his hand with mine. "That was very kind of you, Dom."

His gaze trails up and a smirk forms on his handsome face. "Don't get any ideas, I am not a nice guy." He rakes his other hand through his beard and leans back, still holding my hand.

"Why do you pretend you're not?"

"I'm not pretending. Sometimes I do good deeds, but that doesn't change who I am, June. You might get to see a side of me that no one else does, but don't for a second equate that to me being kind, or noble, or *good*. I am a bad man. I always have been, and I always will be."

Why is he trying so hard to convince me that he has no redeeming qualities?

This theory of good and bad is strictly that—a theory. No single person is inherently one or the other. Doing good things doesn't make you a good person, and doing bad things doesn't make you bad. I've done my fair share of both, and I lean much more toward the darker side of things, but I doubt any of the few people in my life would say I'm *bad*. That's all that really matters—how those closest to you view you and the things you've done. If people can choose to love you knowing all the terrible acts you've committed, how could a person truly be evil? Or maybe the evil is just that alluring and makes them blind to the depravity.

Engine sounds fill the cabin and a second later, we slowly move from our spot.

"We'll be wheels up shortly," Frances says on his walk by us.

Dom reaches into his pocket to pull out a buzzing phone. "Shit, I've got to take this." He gives my hand a gentle squeeze. "I'll be right back."

Isn't he supposed to put that thing into airplane mode? Isn't that why the damn button is there? Because we're on an *airplane*.

"Adler," he answers the call. He moves to the back of the plane where I can no longer make out the words he says into the receiver.

My heart thumps harder, and I grip the seat, no longer lulled by the presence of my strong man. Instead, I'm left to consider the endless list of things that could go wrong. I never should have watched *Final Destination* a month ago with Magnus. The image of the side of the plane bursting open and my body being sucked out and mutilated by the rotating blade thingies fills my head. Are those the engines? What happens if we hit a bird? Or a fucking goose?

I'm moved back into my seat as the plane picks up speed. I close my eyes, my fingers digging into the expensive leather seat. At least, I think it's leather. I'm not really familiar with upholstery. It kind of looks like leather, but it's much softer and plush than one would assume leather to be.

*That's it, focus on fucking seat upholstery to distract yourself from the ridiculous idea of death by a plane crash.* I've been tied to a chair and tortured by a man I didn't know the identity of, and yet *this* is somehow more terrifying.

A warm hand grips mine and peels my hand from the seat. Dom throws his arm around my shoulder and tugs me into his chest.

"I didn't know you were afraid of flying," he says softly.

"Me either." I lean into his body and remind myself that if Dom truly thought I was in danger, he never would have brought me here. Because after all, that's what he claims is his biggest concern—my safety.

"I've got you, there's nothing to be afraid of." He kisses the top of my head and his beard prickles me.

I breathe in his musky scent and savor the warmth of his embrace. Dom isn't often very soft, but lately, he's held me more than I expected, and I am so fucking grateful for it.

Things have been rough, with all the secrets, but it's moments like this that make me hopeful that we might actually make it through this.

The plane finds a horizontal space in the sky, and I breathe a sigh of relief at having made it through one aspect of this flight. Now I have to manage the in-air time, and the landing. I swallow down the reminder that we'll have to do this on the way back, too.

I peel myself from Dom's chest and tuck my hair behind my ear.

"Have you never flown before?" Dom keeps his hand on my back.

I shake my head. "No."

"Oh, June. I...I'm sorry." He skims my cheek with his palm. "I shouldn't have taken that call."

"It's fine," I tell him. How was he supposed to know I'd be a big baby about flying? I didn't even know until we were going a billion miles per hour on a runway and lurching ourselves into the sky. My stomach twists at how impossible it is that we're up here in the first place. "I'm fine."

Dom leans forward and latches onto the glass nearest me. "Here, drink this." He pushes it into my grasp. "But don't have much more. The altitude will make you feel drunker than you really are. This should be enough to calm your nerves."

I sip the golden liquid and settle back into my side of the seat. "Who was on the phone?"

"One of my assistants. Small fire needed to be put out. Nothing to worry about."

A generic and vague answer just like all the others he gives me. You'd think I'd quit asking by now but I cling to the hope that eventually he will be open and honest about what it is that consumes almost all of his hours.

This is usually where I make some smart-ass remark but I don't have it in me.

Not when we're however many feet in the air and I'm unable to escape him. Jumping out of an airplane isn't exactly on my bucket list.

I nod and down a little bit more of the bourbon. "I didn't know you had access to a private jet." I change the subject because if I don't, I'll stew on how secretive he is.

Dominic reaches for his own glass. "Mmhm. I bought it a while back."

My eyes widen. "Oh, you like, own it. A whole fucking airplane."

"Along with a few homes across the United States, and a Villa in Portugal."

"You're not serious." I stare at him.

"Why would I lie about that?" Dom sets the glass back down.

It's a valid question. Why *would* he lie about it? But how did I not know that? He's such a fucking closed book, and it only makes me wonder what else I haven't unearthed about him.

"Some days, it feels like I don't know you at all," I tell him.

"I don't understand." Dom tilts his body toward me.

"You wouldn't, because you know my every move." I leave out the things that Simon and I do behind their back. But maybe if they didn't shut me out so fucking much, I wouldn't be doing that shit with him. "And I don't have much history. I've never left California, let alone bought a house in another country."

"I'll buy you a house wherever you want."

I sigh. "That's not my point, Dom."

"Then what is it?"

"My point is, is that you're closed off. You hardly ever actually tell me anything about *you*. I find out in these nonchalant moments where you just randomly say you have a house in France."

"Portugal."

"Same thing." I throw up my hand. "I don't even know if I could differentiate them on a map."

"Well, Portugal is west of Spain."

"For a really smart man, you sure are dense sometimes, Dom."

He narrows his eyes for a brief moment, then relaxes them. "What would you like to know, June? Ask me anything."

"Other than work things, obviously."

"Obviously."

"What about how you got into the life? That doesn't cover current events. And I already know the story of Magnus and Coen."

"I grew up in it." Dom latches onto his bourbon again.

"Great story."

We hit a little turbulence, and I accidentally grip Dom's leg.

"That was nothing to worry about." He places his hand on top of mine. "As far as my involvement, it began when I was a child. I don't remember a time when things were any different. I had family that were made men, and I idolized them. Franklin had seen potential in me from an early age. He shaped me into the son he never had, and in a way, he was like a father figure to me. But even though his method was the only one I knew, I still questioned his authority left and right. There were numerous times when I thought he'd cast me out and find someone else to mold into his protégé, but I was always able to reel him back in. Franklin was intelligent and a damn good businessman, that much was certain. He was also stubborn, hot-headed, and paranoid as hell."

I hold still and hope that if I don't move, maybe Dom won't realize he's sharing so much and he'll continue telling me his story.

"I knew if I played my cards right, I would eventually take over his reign when he retired, I just didn't anticipate his demise when it happened. It came to a head abruptly and without everything set in stone. It complicated things and gave others the opportunity to take what I had worked my entire life for.

"Anyway, you know how things ended, but how things began? Nothing crazy. Just a kid who grew up on the wrong side of town and seized a chance to escape from poverty and homelessness."

"I...I had no idea," I confess when he doesn't continue. "What about your parents?"

Dom shrugs. "Never knew them. They put me in the system when I was a baby. And the family I mentioned, I didn't mean blood. But we all know family is much more than DNA. They were older kids in the system who aged out and had other friends older than them that were runners or soldiers or just people who would do anything for a buck. I hung around them any chance I could. Some of them took me in when I didn't have anywhere else to go. It didn't take long for me to pay attention and figure out who Franklin was. The rest was history."

It's no wonder Dom is a cruel bastard—he quite literally had no parental figure in his life aside from a psychotic criminal who manipulated and brainwashed a child into joining their organization. He never got to have a warm mother, or a protective father.

I may have had a screwed-up childhood, but at least I have some memories from before my mother died. She was the light of my life, and my dad's, too, but once she was gone, she left behind nothing but darkness to swallow us whole. My dad resorted to drinking, and I hid in the shadows as the booze turned him into something that eventually became completely unrecognizable. My adult self sympathizes with his loss, but he never should have neglected his child, and that's unforgivable. I was never safe, loved, or cared for, not until the equally broken blond-haired, blue-eyed boy showed up in that cemetery. I felt his loss from a mile away and knew that only he could understand the agony of being abandoned.

It's a harsh thing to say, that my mother's death left me abandoned, but that's what it felt like. I was discarded, thrown to the wolves, and meant to fend for myself. I was a child, and I had no one to rely on. I stole change from my dad's coat pockets and walked barefoot down the street to buy whatever clearance food I could from the local mart. He bought groceries on occasion, but it was usually beer and chips, nothing a growing kid could survive on. I dug through trash bins behind the shops to scrounge for anything of substance. One of the shop owners near my house took pity on me, and when they set expired goods out to the trash, they would leave them on the step instead of putting them in the bins. It wasn't much but that act of kindness helped me through a time when I wasn't sure if I'd make it through or not.

The kids at school made fun of me for getting the free lunch but that was my only chance for a hot meal and there was no way I was passing it up.

It honestly wasn't until years later that I realized how fucked up I had it. Because when you're a kid and that's all you know, you don't consider much else. The memories of my mother faded into something from so long ago I started to doubt she had ever really existed. The only thing holding her in this dimension were a few of the Polaroids I kept tucked under my mattress.

One drunken night, my dad had set fire to her clothes in the front yard. He was carrying on about living with her ghost and that the only way to get rid of her was to burn her belongings. He ripped every picture off the wall, grabbed anything that remotely held any resemblance to her time with us, and lit it ablaze.

I ran to the drawer in the front room when he wasn't looking and snatched those few photos, hugging them tight to my chest as I ran out of the house and hid in the bushes next door. I watched with bated breath as the police came and arrested him. They searched the house, which I can only assume was for me, and I didn't see him for three days.

I was six years old, and that memory is only one of the few that is painted vividly in my head.

The rest of them are a muddled mess that makes me wonder whether I had any decent memories from my childhood at all. Or maybe my mind fucked up and repressed the good instead of the bad ones.

But even as bad as I thought I had it, I can't imagine being indoctrinated into a criminal organization before I could learn how to read.

Dom might have a great-ish life now, but he's lost so much in the process. His childhood, his innocence, his sense of self.

I'm fortunate enough that he's capable of the love that he does give me. Despite his upbringing, Dom has moments of being soft and kind and good.

I see it when he does something for others without expecting it in return. When he took Magnus and Coen under his wing—sure he had a greater plan for them, but he could have killed either one of them. When he cut his call short because he saw I was in the middle of a panic attack during take-off. When he burst into the bathroom during our first major interaction to save me from that disgusting drunk who tried to force himself on me. He didn't have to do any of that. He could have looked the other way or carried on with his life without intervening.

"Did you ever try to find them?" I ask him. "Your parents?"

Dom's jaw tenses. "I did, actually." He averts his gaze like he's recalling a memory.

"Were you able to meet them?"

He shakes his head slowly. "They had been long dead by the time I found out who they were."

I cup his hand with mine. "I'm so sorry, Dom." I am all too familiar with the pain of loss.

Frances approaches from the back of the plane, distracting us from the weight of this conversation. "Mr. Adler, would you like me to prepare something for you and Miss June?"

Dominic checks his expensive watch. "No, I think we're fine for now." He tilts his head toward me. "Unless you'd like something."

"No, I'm good." The idea of eating anything while stuck in this flying death trap is completely unappealing. I haven't had much of an appetite lately in general, but being up here, it's definitely nonexistent.

"Some water would be nice, though," Dom tells Frances.

Frances does that tipping of his head and slow blink thing that he seems to always do before he dismisses himself and turns on his heel, trailing back in the direction he came.

"I..." I try to find the words to say but know nothing will be right, so I say the first thing that pops out. "I didn't mean to bring up such a sensitive topic."

Dom clenches my hand and forces a toothless smile. "That was a lifetime ago. No need to fret."

"Thank you though, for sharing it with me." It might not be his whole past, but already I feel the space between us shrinking as I learn more about this mysterious, older man I love. Maybe my soul already knew that we shared a similar trauma, that our darknesses were alike, and that eventually I would uncover one of the reasons why we're drawn to one another.

"I don't mean to be this way," Dominic mutters. "I know it's hard to be with a man like me."

My heart breaks at watching this vulnerable side of him show through.

"Trust isn't something that's given freely, especially when this line of work is filled with traitors and scheming bastards." Dom takes another drink of his bourbon.

"You have Coen and Magnus..." I study the hard lines on his aged face. "You have me."

Dom's serious gaze bores into mine. "For now."

I sigh and grip his hand tighter. "For—" I start to speak but he cuts me off.

"Things have been unforeseen lately, June. This isn't how I wanted our life to be. But there are matters that need my attention, and until I handle them, I beg you to know that none of this means my feelings for you, or *their* feelings for you, have changed. We aren't pushing you away for any reason other than to keep you safe. I assure you that."

It's not that I don't believe him, but I just don't understand why it has to be this way. What could possibly be so dire that they couldn't tell me? I already know about their dangerous world, the issues they've been having lately, what more could be going on? And how does it have anything to do with my safety? Unless there's a direct threat to my life that they aren't disclosing. But who the fuck would want me dead? I could easily be used as a pawn to control any of my men, but that's a risk we all knew when I became involved with them.

"I need a little more time, June." Dominic runs his hand along my cheek.

"Okay," I whisper, because what else am I going to say? They've backed me into a corner that I cannot escape from. The only way out is to see this thing through.

Dom exhales and smiles softly. "Thank you."

And because I'd do anything to shift the dynamic of this conversation, I ask him, "What's your favorite color?"

"What?" He tilts his head.

I nudge him playfully. "Your favorite color, sir?"

"Uh, I don't know. Green, perhaps."

"Green is a great color," I tell him. "Favorite food?"

"These are difficult questions, perhaps we should go back to discussing my business instead."

I chuckle. "Come on, it can't be that hard."

"Well, if we're talking type of cuisine, I would have to go...French."

"Like French fries?"

This garners another grin from him. "You are so uncultured it hurts my soul."

"What?" I shove him. "I can't help it, I don't have a *private jet* to fly me to get some French fries whenever I want them."

"Those are not French food, sweetheart. I'm talking croissants, ratatouille, beef bourguignon. Simple ingredients turned into something beautiful and flavorful. It's art, really."

"I had no idea you were such a connoisseur."

"There are a lot of things you don't know about me."

"I've gathered. Why do you think I'm hounding you with silly questions?"

"Fair enough." Dom pulls my legs into his lap. "What's your favorite food?"

"Pizza."

Dom shakes his head. "I worry about you."

"What's wrong with pizza?"

"Nothing, we just really need to broaden your horizons. We'll add Italy to the list of places we'll take you."

"You're going to have to drug me before I get on a flight that goes over an ocean."

Dom's phone buzzes in his pocket but he ignores it. "I wouldn't let anything happen to you."

"You can't control acts of nature, or freak accidents. What if an engine fell off or something?"

"That's actually not as big of a deal as you would think. Plus, Sarge is trained to deal with situations like that."

"Sarge?"

"My pilot, yes."

He says it like he's a shirt hanging in his closet, so fucking nonchalant that he has a freaking pilot. Will I ever get used to any of this?

"Okay, next question."

Dom takes a deep breath in and braces himself. "I'm ready."

"Would you rather have...feet for hands, or hands for feet?"

He blinks a few times, almost like he's considering if I've lost my mind. "Hands for feet."

"Why?"

"Because I can't shoot a gun with my foot. At least, I've never tried."

I let out a laugh. "You would find a way to turn this violent."

"It's what I do."

Dom's phone vibrates again, this time on my leg.

"Do you need to check that?" I ask him.

"Yes." But he doesn't reach for it yet. "Does it matter if I don't *want* to?"

"Yes." I pull myself off of him. "Go, and hurry back before I think of other weird shit to ask you."

He stands from the seat and immediately my heart tugs at his absence.

"Adler," he greets the person on the other line.

I down the rest of my bourbon in an attempt to warm myself in another way. I turn toward the window and hug my knees to my chest while looking at the earth so far below. A few clouds flutter past, and I think of what it might be like to reach my hand out and feel them slip between my fingers.

That's sort of what love feels like, something that's there but just out of grasp, unable to be latched onto and held, fleeting and dissipating with just the change in barometric pressure.

A temptress to make you believe it's something you could have but is always out of reach.

I close my eyes and pretend Dom is finished with his call; his arms wrapped around me. I place Magnus here, too, his beautiful smile lighting up the whole plane. My mind flits to Coen, and even though I'm pissed at him for the way he treated me, I still want him here. I think I always will, no matter what happens. I hate myself for that, but it's hard to go against the gravitational pull we have on each other.

I don't mean to, but in this imaginary scenario, Simon is here, too. His attendance brings me comfort and a sense of fullness.

It isn't long until I trick myself into feeling Dom's arms around me and revel in his comfort as it lulls me to sleep.

---

A vehicle is waiting for us on the tarmac when we touch down. It's kind of strange to exit a plane and immediately be escorted into a blacked-out SUV. It's like we're celebrities or in the secret service, or both, really.

Dom keeps his hand on my thigh the entire ride to our destination. I don't know how long to expect, nor do I really care. Just being here with him is enough.

Away from the city that consumes him and the place that feels heavier with each passing day.

Mountains line the distance with lush greenery scattered throughout. The air *looks* clearer here, like if I were to roll down the window and breathe it in it could spark new life in my lungs.

"It's beautiful," I say to no one in particular.

"It really is." Dom throws his arm over my shoulders and tugs me toward him.

We stay like this for what feels like forever and somehow not very long at all. Our chauffeur turns us onto a gravel drive, and after a couple minutes down the winding path, we arrive at a picturesque structure. I wasn't sure things could be any more stunning but when I step out onto the ground, I'm struck by the gorgeous views from this place.

"Wow." I stare off into the distance at the open water ahead.

The building is tucked near the coast with nothing else in sight for as long as I can see in both directions. Trees block any potential neighboring places from being in sight, leaving this building completely off on its own.

So very like Dom to pick something so secluded. He's a man of privacy, and he intends on getting it every chance he can, and when he can't, he makes it happen anyway.

"Let me guess," I glance over at him. "You own this, too?"

Dom grins but shakes his head. "No, but it isn't from lack of effort." He nods toward the woman walking toward us. "Family owned and operated. It's been passed down from generation to generation."

"I'm surprised you didn't take it by force," I tell him, only partially being sarcastic.

"They're too nice of folks."

"Dominic," the woman greets him with rosy cheeks, her wiry gray hair fluttering in the wind. She immediately focuses on me. "You've brought a...woman." The lady latches onto my hands and holds onto them. Her face is kind and innocent but shows the gentle lines of her old age.

"Priscilla, this is June. June, Priscilla," Dom introduces us.

"It is so very nice to meet you, my dear." She continues to clasp my hands. "How lovely it is that you're here."

"Thank you," I tell her. "Your property is absolutely breathtaking."

"Come." She tugs me with her. "I will show you all around."

"Cill," Dom calls after us.

I glance over my shoulder as she takes me with her, Dom shrugs and lets it happen. I guess this is an instance where my life isn't in danger so he allows her to kidnap me.

"I like to say this is where the sky and the mountains and the water all meet to gather into this incredibly magical place." Priscilla points around the building. "There are lush gardens around every corner. And over there"—she motions in the distance—"is a lavender field. You smell that?" She sucks in a breath and exhales. "I just love it here."

I take in a lungful of air and revel in how pure it is.

"You two will be staying in the Lavender Suite, but you'll have the run of the place. Feel free to wander around and get lost." She cups my hand and smiles up at me. "You'll always find your way back, don't worry. Just close your eyes and listen to the water, it will guide you home."

We walk along a stone pathway that trails the massive building.

The landscaping is immaculate with its rich lawns and vibrant flowers and perfectly trimmed shrubbery. Each section is carved with precision and shows how much detail was put into every aspect of this place.

I take in the building, noticing all of the windows overlooking the still water.

"There are bikes all over the property. Hop on one and explore if you feel called to it. Make yourself right at home, okay, June?"

"I will, thank you." I continue walking with her and wonder how this place can continue to get any nicer. It's no wonder Dom comes up here to disappear. This is nothing like his day-to-day life. Back home is dark and dangerous and gloomy. Here, it's like anything is possible, or at least you can distract yourself long enough to believe it is.

"Are you running off with my girl?" Dom catches up to us and weaves his fingers through mine.

"I haven't shown her the Azaleas yet," Priscilla tells him.

"I'm afraid they are going to have to wait. I have to steal her for a few." Dominic tugs me away from her but she releases me with a warm smile on her face.

"I'm just happy you're here, June. It's nice to see Dom with someone other than those two boys of his."

I chuckle. "Coen and Magnus?"

Priscilla nods. "I do adore them, but it's about time Dom gets himself a lady."

If only she knew I wasn't *just* Dom's lady, that I was theirs too. But I don't mention it because I don't know how she would react to such a thing. Having multiple boyfriends isn't something that's quickly accepted in our society. They might have a whole fictional sub-genre associated to it, according to Cora, but that doesn't mean this sweet old lady wants to hear about me having three brutal mafia boyfriends.

"I will have Russ send something to your room to tide you over until supper."

"Thanks, Cill," Dom wraps his arm around my waist and picks me off the ground.

"Thank you for the tour," I say as he playfully carries me away. Once we're out of earshot, I poke him in the side. "Let me down, you big buffoon."

Dom throws me over his shoulder and smacks my ass.

I beat my fists lightly against his back. "Unhand me you giant."

"We're going to have to work on your self-defense." Dom continues to walk with ease toward his destination.

"I asked Simon to train me but he gave me some excuse that that's what you hired him for." I watch the ground pass upside down and wonder how much blood has rushed to my head already.

"To protect you, yes. But it would be useful to have some skills." Dom finally slides me over his shoulder and releases me onto a patio.

I blink to steady my vision. "Maybe I could learn how to shoot a gun." Properly, not half-assed like I have in the past. Although, I did recently kill someone, so I must not be entirely terrible at it. Granted, I was at point-blank range. How could I have fucked that up? Only, Dom doesn't know that, and I'm not about to tell him and ruin this incredibly romantic getaway.

"After you." Dom pushes the door open for me to enter.

I step inside the suite, and my eyes immediately find the massive bed posted along the wall. Across from it is a swanky couch poised in front of a huge window overlooking the ocean in the near distance. Rich greenery fills the view from the window where a large patio wraps around the front of the room. Tucked in one corner is a fireplace, and in the other is a large Jacuzzi tub, hopefully big enough for both of us. Two sets of doors are on opposing walls, and by my guess, are a closet and a bathroom.

"This is beautiful, Dom."

He steps around me and into the place. "You said that already."

I narrow my gaze at him. "I can't believe you've been holding out on me."

"I haven't been up here in over a year. I honestly forgot about it until the idea struck me yesterday. Thought we both could use the change in scenery." Dom strolls over to the table with a bucket of ice and a bottle of something tucked inside. He pulls it out and pops the top, filling two glasses and bringing one over to me. "To us."

I take it from him and clink my glass with his. "To us." The bubbly liquid tickles my tongue. It isn't exactly my go-to beverage but damn does it taste expensive.

Dom and I fuck on the bed, we fuck against the wall, and we fuck on the table the fancy champagne was on. We take a break to eat some of the charcuterie board that was brought to our room and then we make our way to the bathroom and fuck in the shower, my legs giving out as I climax for what must be the twentieth time today.

"Did you bring me here to fuck my brains out, Dom?" I lean my head against his chest and relax as the water cascades down us.

He drags my hair out of my face and kisses my forehead. "Wasn't exactly my plan, but I'm not mad about it."

"Me either." I grin.

"You hungry?" Dom slowly trails his finger from my chest to my center. He glides it down my slit and rests it there.

"For more sex? I don't know if I can stand."

Dom spreads my folds and circles his finger in place. "For dinner."

I tilt my head up toward him. "I think you and I have a different definition of dinner."

He presses his lips to mine, parting them with his tongue. He pushes into my already soaked entrance and grins when I tighten around him. His cock pulses against my back as he keeps guiding his fingers in and out of my pussy and applying pressure to my clit.

He kisses me deeper, and without so much as a thought, my orgasm builds once again. My nipples grow hard under the flicker of water, and Dom fingers my eager hole until I climax around him and pant into his mouth.

"Fucking Christ." I whimper, my body shaking under his authority.

Dom leaves a gentle kiss on my lips and removes his fingers to bring them up to his mouth. He dips them in and sucks my juices off of him. "You taste heavenly."

I scoot away from his chest and back myself into the wall. "All-you-can-eat buffet." I spread my legs toward him. Just when I think I've had enough, I'm filled with an endless desire that is impossible to satiate.

And thankfully, Dom is ready and willing to give me as much as I can take. His libido is off the charts, and it makes me wonder what his sex life was like before we met each other. I don't want to think about him being with other women, but how the hell did he satisfy all of his carnal desires prior to me?

Priscilla made it seem like Dom had never brought a female here, so at least there's that. This special spot was never tainted by him bringing someone else to this romantic place, Magnus and Coen, but not a woman.

Dom inches toward me and runs his beard from my ankle to the center of my body. He hovers his face near my pussy and darts out his tongue to slide it teasingly over my folds. He wraps his lips around my still-aching clit and dips his tongue into my hole. Dom buries himself in me and uses his arms to wrap around my legs and maintain a hold as he consumes his appetizer. He mentioned dinner, but maybe this is just his first course. We've already fucked countless times since being here, but what's one more?

My pussy is raw from him relentlessly pounding it, but somehow it isn't fully satisfied.

Dom licks and sucks on every inch of my sensitive bits and moans against me. Deep, guttural, and immediately sends shockwaves through my body.

I latch onto his hair and guide him closer, submerging his face even more. It's a wonder he can still fucking breathe. But I wouldn't put it past him to not give a fuck if he lives or dies down there.

"June," he mutters and breaks away to glance up at me. "Can you handle me again?" He glides a finger into my hole and gently rocks it in and out. "You're so swollen already. I don't want to hurt you anymore."

"Don't worry about me." I find the strength to bring myself to my knees and nudge him backward. I climb onto his lap and cup my hand around his shaft, rubbing it against my aching pussy.

"Are you sure?" He drags the wet hair from my cheek.

I sit down on his cock and lean back. "I'm sure."

Dom pinches both of my nipples between his fingers before gliding his hands down and gripping my waist. He pivots his hips up and down and hardens fully inside of me. He watches me intensely, his eyes leaving a burning trail in their wake. "You're so fucking beautiful."

I drag my fingers through his hair and settle them at the base of his neck. I lean down and whisper into his ear, "Fuck me like a good girl."

Dom's grip on me tightens and he weaves a hand up to press on the back of my head. He meets my lips with his, an intensity to him that wasn't there a moment ago. Before, he was taking it easy on me, but now, with my permission, he unleashes his true nature. One that I never wish for him to restrain.

Dom manages to wrap his arm around my waist and pick me up from the ground while rising to his feet. He pins me against the wall and thrusts into me, not holding back at all.

I keep myself tight around his neck and take every inch of him that he gives me.

"You take me like such a good girl, June." Dom thrusts in me harder. "I'm going to destroy your little pussy."

"Yeah?" I moan through the blissful pain of his cock spreading me wider.

Dom isn't just long, he's fucking girthy, too, and my pussy loves every bit of his thick and juicy shaft.

"God damn you're so tight around me." Dom holds me close to him and buries himself deep inside of me.

"That's it, right there," I tell him. "Fuck. Don't stop."

We come in tandem and stay glued together until our breaths grow more consistent.

I exhale and lean my head on his shoulder. "What are you wearing?"

He peels himself away. "Right now? You."

I give him a quick peck. "No, I mean to dinner."

"My William Westmancott suit."

"Only your suit would have a first and last name."

Dom slides out of me and sets me down on the tiled shower floor. "I didn't *name* my suit. That's the designer."

"Oh." I laugh. "That makes more sense." I step into the water that still runs warm and wonder how fancy their hot water tank must be for it to not have lost its heat.

"Don't worry." Dom rinses himself off for what might actually be the final time. Each other instance led to us having sex again. "I had something flown in for you."

I raise a brow at him. "What does that even mean?"

He kisses me before stepping out of the shower and leaving me to finish up in privacy. "It means that I think of everything."

I turn off the faucet and I'm welcomed by my strong man holding out a towel waiting for me. He rubs it over my body to soak up the droplets littering my skin and then wraps it around me.

"I brought a dress with me," I tell him.

"Yeah, but you needed a new one."

"I only wore the other one once."

"Then it's old." Dom cups my chin in his hand. "You deserve the best of the best. Let me spoil you."

And spoil me he does. All of the guys do—even Simon. I haven't paid for anything—other than an occasional meal I've had to sneak to pay for—since I stepped into their lives. But they learned about my sneaky nature and started taking care of the tab almost immediately and ridding me of any chance to use the money I actually earn. It isn't much, but it's *mine*. About a week after the council incident, Dom strolled into my bedroom and placed a black American Express card on my nightstand. Told me that when I was better, I could buy whatever I wanted, and insisted that any of my purchases either be made with that or the cash they give me, if they haven't already taken care of it themselves.

Not only do they insist on paying, but they ensure I have top shelf, the newest, and the highest quality, no matter what it is.

They have access to anything I could possibly want, but at the end of the day, the only thing that really matters to me is them. And that's been the hardest thing for me to get. Honestly, I think asking for a house in Spain might be an easier sell.

Dom leaves me in the bathroom to towel dry my hair and apply some lotion. I follow him into the main room a few minutes later to find him buttoning up his shirt. My gaze flits from him to the long dress dangling from a hanger in the open closet across the way.

"What do you think?" Dom asks me.

I slowly walk toward it and gawk at how fucking gorgeous it is. Every other dress I own is beautiful in its own way, but this is so pretty it makes my heart hurt.

"I sent your measurements off a while back to have a bespoke Givenchy made, but I called in some favors to have it expedited for tonight."

"Dom." I clasp my hand over my heart and turn toward him. "I love it." My eyes glisten with the thoughtfulness of his gesture. He wanted this evening to be special, and damn if he didn't pull it off. He might be massively fucking things up lately but he wouldn't have gone through all of this trouble if we didn't matter to him. If I didn't matter to him.

"Fit for a queen." Dominic tucks a strand of my wet hair behind my ear.

"I love you," I tell him. Not because of the dress. Not because of this trip. But because he carved time out of his chaotic schedule to finally give me exactly what I wanted. What I needed.

What I think he needed, too.

And more importantly, he gave me something without even realizing it.

*Hope.*

Hope that we might actually make it out of this nightmare together.

# CHAPTER 20

# Magnus

"So how was it?" I poke June in the side and tickle her.

She wiggles out from under me. "I am going to pee on your bed if you don't stop."

"Sounds kinky." I continue to tease her.

"Magnus Bryant." June slaps my arm. "Why do I not know your middle name?"

"I'll never tell." I laugh like an idiot and climb on top of her, pinning her to the bed and using one of my hands to hold hers above her head. I press kisses all over her face and down her neck. "I missed you so much, princess."

June tries to buck me off but it's no use. Instead, she manages to give me more of a boner than I already had. "It was good, it was great," she finally blurts out. "If you stop torturing me, I'll tell you."

I sigh, releasing her hands and plopping down onto the mattress beside her. "Fine," I say, dragging out the end of the word.

June props herself onto her elbow and turns toward me. "It was very romantic. So not Dom-like at all. He had this custom Givenchy dress made. Had a candlelit dinner prepared, which oh, my, God, it was delicious. Have you ever had duck before? I mean, so sad, but also, so fucking tasty." She bites at her lip and recalls more of the evening. "We danced." She looks right at me. "Dom, slow dancing, right?"

I grin at her and bask in the happiness pouring out of her. It's a strange thing to feel good about another man spoiling your girl, but because it's June, I want her to have every bit of happiness this world has to offer. She deserves it, even if it isn't with me.

"Then, we soaked in this giant fucking Jacuzzi. It was so relaxing I fell asleep and almost drowned."

My eyes widen. "What?"

June nods her head. "Yeah, Dom said he just thought I was chilling but then I started sliding down his chest and into the water." She lets out a laugh. "He didn't let me go all the way under but still, it was pretty fucking funny."

"I am very glad you did not die."

"Hmm, what else?" Her eyes light up like she's remembering more. "Breakfast the next morning, you would have loved it. Best waffles ever. And they had this honey that Priscilla said was local. It was infused with lavender."

"So, you met Cill?" I ask her.

"Yep. She kidnapped me the second she set her sights on me. Dom had to literally snatch me up and carry me away."

"She's a hoot."

"I loved it there." June meets my gaze. "We should go some time. All of us." But then there's a slight shift in her mood I recognize immediately.

"What is it?"

"Have you heard from Co?"

"Yes." I swallow down the uncomfortable turn our conversation took but refuse to lie to her. "He was with me last night."

"That's..." June tries to find the word she wants to use. She finally settles on, "Good." She studies my face and narrows her gaze. "Wait."

I blink at her. "What?"

"Are you wearing makeup?" She licks at her thumb and wipes at my cheek, no doubt revealing the fucking bruise I attempted to cover up. "What the fuck is that, Magnus?"

"I...I didn't want you to worry."

"Worry?" She looks me over. "What else are you hiding?" June latches onto my hand and studies the swollen and purple knuckles hidden underneath my tattoos.

"You should see the other guy," I laugh and try to make light of the situation.

"Magnus." She glares at me. "You guys have been into more dangerous shit lately than you have in a long time. Co and Dom come in all fucked up the other night and now this? Don't think I didn't notice Dom's bruised chest. What the hell was that from? And Co, did he get stabbed or something? He was bleeding a lot through his arm bandage."

"Umm..." I don't want to lie but I can't exactly tell her the truth. She's already pissed at us, if she knew that Dom and Co had both been shot, she'd lose her mind. But the way she's looking at me right now, she might already be on the verge of it.

"Why can't you just be honest with me for a change, Magnus? I know you want to."

"Promise me you won't freak out, princess?"

"I'm going to fucking stab you if you don't tell me." She punches my shoulder.

I lean in closer to her and lower my voice. "They got shot." A weight immediately lifts from my chest. "But they're fine, really. They were both wearing vests. That's why Dom had that bruising on his chest. But it isn't anything you need to worry about. Please don't say anything."

June's nostrils flare, and for a second, I imagine hot steam piling out of her ears. But a moment passes and her resolve softens. "Thank you for your honesty."

"Thank you for not murdering me." I lean forward and kiss the tip of her nose.

"So where were you and Co last night?"

"Handling a situation while you and Dom were away."

"Yeah?"

I bob my head up and down. "Yeah, he figured it would be safer than when you were around."

"Who did?"

"Dom, duh."

"Hold up. Let me get this straight."

My heart races as I realize I may have just fucked up. I spilled one secret and now they're all flying out of my mouth. *This* is why it doesn't pay to be dishonest with the people in your life. Honesty is the best policy. I'm shit at lying, and despite being a damn good poker player, my bluffing face is shit to those I love.

"Dom got me out of town so you and Co could do this *thing*?"

I chew at the inside of my lip. June is one hundred percent on the head on this one, but if I confirm it, she's going to lose her goddamn mind for sure. It isn't that Dom *didn't* want alone time with her, but he definitely made it happen in order to ensure her safety while Hayes and I followed up on a lead.

"I'm right, aren't I?" June frantically glances between my eyes in a wild attempt to locate the truth. But she and I both know that my silence speaks much louder than words.

"Princess..."

"That fucking bastard." June sits up and clenches her hand into a fist. "I'm going to..."

I place my palm on her back but she shrugs me off.

"Do not touch me right now, Magnus. I don't want to hurt you."

I scoot to the edge of the bed. "You're not going to hurt me, princess."

Her jaw tenses. "I am not mad at you, but I am trying very hard to regain my composure."

Hayes walks past my door at the wrong fucking time.

June lurches off the bed before I can grab her and calls out after him. "Where the fuck do you think you're going?"

"Can we do this another time, J?" Hayes continues down the hall.

"No." She latches onto his shoulder and tries to tug him toward her.

He stops in place, and I inch in their direction just in case I need to intervene. I know June well enough to know that she isn't going to let this go, and I don't want to get between her and whatever she needs to say to Hayes.

"Where were you yesterday?" she asks him.

With his back still to her, he says, "Out."

"Really, Co? That's what you're going to say? You act like an asshole and then leave for a day and that's all I get? No apology. No explanation. No nothing."

Hayes slowly turns toward her, his face finally in plain sight. Bruised, swollen, and with cuts on his brow and lip.

"What happened to your face?" A hint of concern lines her tone.

"I'm not doing this, J."

But the little bit of worry she had is quickly erased with anger. "Fucking fine, me either." She spins on her heel and stalks away from him, blasting past me and down the hall.

"Where the fuck do you think you're going?" Coen calls out after her.

But June throws up her middle finger. "Out."

I rush behind her and nearly fall down the stairs to catch up.

"Love," Simon greets her. "What's wrong?" He latches onto her shoulders and tries to stop her. "Hey, look at me. What is it?"

"I just need some fucking space."

Simon releases her without question. "Okay." He flits his attention to me briefly and focuses back on her. "Let's get some air."

"No," she blurts out. "Not you." She turns toward me. "Not you." And points up in the direction we came. "And sure as shit not him. I need five fucking minutes to myself. I'm not asking for much. For the love of God, just leave me alone. All of you."

My heart aches but I knew this was coming. The moment when she wouldn't want any of us around. She's only asking for five minutes, but how long until she wants it to be longer or more permanent?

June bursts through the garage door and slams it behind her.

I stalk toward where she disappeared but Simon cuts me off. "I think you should stay here," he tells me.

"Get the fuck out of my way, Beckett," I mutter only inches from his face.

"She's pissed at you guys, not me. I'm not the one who keeps lying to her. It's better if I go."

I hate that he's right, but he fucking is. June might have said she wasn't mad at me but that doesn't mean it's true. I'm just as guilty as Hayes and Dominic are for keeping June in the dark and harboring all these secrets and distance. Simon has been there for her the whole time and has done nothing but mend the wound that we keep ripping open. As much as I want to be the one to comfort her, it's possible I might only make things worse.

"Fucking go," I tell him. "Hurry up before she gets too far."

# CHAPTER 21

# *June*

Dominic lied to me. More so than he normally does. He took advantage of how much I wanted alone time with him and manipulated me into thinking he actually wanted to get away with me.

He fucked me. Over and over and over again. And what finally put the nail in the proverbial casket was when I realized all that fucking was to distract me from his ulterior motive. Leave it to him to have one. He's conniving, scheming, and infuriates the ever-loving shit out of me.

I rush through the opening of the entry gate before it closes and slip out onto the sidewalk. The night air is cool and warm all at once, but littered with pollution from the city. It's much different than in Washington, that's for sure.

I huff and stomp my feet down the empty sidewalk and try to shake off the entire experience. I can't believe I fell for Dom's charade. I ate up every minute of it and thought he cared. That he missed our time together and wanted some of it to tide him over until whatever made-up fucking deadline he created.

Was the whole making me wait another week even real or another one of his elaborate lies to prevent me from begging him for the truth?

Has any of this been real? Or was I just a game to him? A quest that he conquered and no longer is bothered with?

"Love, wait up," Simon calls out to me from the shadows.

I startle at the sound of his voice—I was so lost in my own fucking head I didn't hear him running to catch up to me.

"Leave me alone, Simon, please." I continue down the dim street.

"Sorry, love. No can do." He joins me at my side. "You can be pissed. I'm not telling you otherwise, but you'll have to do it with me."

"I can't fucking think with you around!" I yell at him. "You're all..." I point at him. "You." I push forward. "It's fucking distracting."

"Um, well. Sorry?" Simon strolls beside me, his steps slow compared to my choppy, short ones. It's almost like his pace is insulting mine because of how much shorter my legs are than his.

"I don't want to talk about it."

"Then let's not talk about it."

"It just pisses me off so much."

"I thought you didn't want to talk about it?" He glances over at me.

"I'm fucking mad. I don't know what I want."

Simon throws his arms up. "That's fair enough."

"Do you know where they were last night?" I stop and face him, studying every single feature I can make out on his beautiful face to see if he's lying.

"No. Do you?"

I sigh. "No. But it was something sketchy." I cross my arms over my chest. "Dom got me out of town so they could do it." I pause again. "Where were you last night?"

"Simmer down, love. I watched the new Keanu movie and took a freaking bubble bath. I was in bed by ten."

I narrow my gaze and assess his words—the pitch of his voice. I've been around Simon enough to know when he's lying. There's this trivial twitch of his lip and sometimes the octave of his voice changes ever so slightly. It isn't much, but I can tell. And I don't see any of that here. He's never lied to me about anything major, just silly stuff, like how he liked a certain food or his preference for something. Nothing life or death or that would make me lose my trust in him.

"I promise," Simon adds.

"Well," I start forward again. "I'm glad you got an evening to yourself."

"You know I would have rather been with you."

I side-eye him. "I've been lied to enough today, Simon."

Simon wraps his arm around my shoulder and tugs me to his chest. "I missed the shit out of you, love." He squeezes me tightly and then releases me, not wanting to overstep the boundary any more than he already has.

"Believe it or not, I kind of missed you, too." I nudge him with my elbow. "But if you tell anyone, I will cut you."

He pretends to zip his mouth shut and throws the key into the bushes next to us. "Lips are sealed, love."

Headlights illuminate the street and Simon steadies his hand on his gun as they pass. They drive down the road and disappear from sight.

"You're awful jumpy tonight," I tell him.

"Well, you're always finding yourself in dangerous situations, love."

"Maybe it's the men I keep around."

"Without a doubt, but I think we both know you go looking for trouble."

"Obviously." I skim my fingers along the leaves of the tree I pass below and pluck one off. "Speaking of." I pick at the leaf in my grasp. "Can we go do something again? Take a ride on your bike or something?"

Simon clutches his hand to his chest and gasps. "Are you using me, love?"

I deadpan. "Using, utilizing, whatever. We have fun together, are you denying that?"

"Not at all." Simon drops his hand along with his act of fake hurt. "But it's only a matter of time until one of your boyfriends finds out and puts a stop to it. What if they hire someone to replace me? Then you'll be stuck with some stick-in-his-ass grunt who has no personality."

"You have a personality?" I tease him.

Simon shrugs. "I'm the coolest person I know."

"You wish."

Another set of headlights brightens the street and passes, only this time, they distract me from the other set that comes at us from the right, and the ones that drive up onto the sidewalk behind us and block our path completely.

A man jumps from one of the vehicles and Simon reaches for his gun but it's too late, the guy tackles him to the ground and hits him across the face, knocking him out cold.

I watch in horror as the man I was taunting a mere moment ago lies motionless on the ground. I swing to hit the person who comes toward me, but I don't land a good enough punch. They overpower me and press a cloth against my face, the same thing that had been done when I was kidnapped all those months ago. I claw at my attacker, digging my fingers along their skin, but it's no use, whatever lines the fabric renders me unconscious within seconds.

---

I wake in a foggy state, my eyes blinking and desperately trying to see through the dimly lit area. I tug at my hands but they're tied to the armrests of the chair I'm sitting in. My legs are secured to the chair, too. All of my limbs held in fucking place. My shoes crinkle against the plastic covering the ground. I take in my surroundings, finally settling my sights on a few feet in front of me.

The beautiful man I've spent nearly every day with for the last six months is bound to a chair, too. His face is bloodied from the blow to his head and his nose is bent like it's broken. His head hangs loosely in place, and I've never wanted more than to reach out and touch him. I stare at his chest, holding my breath in hopes that his will rise and fall. It's shallow, but I sigh in relief at seeing there still be life in him.

A single bulb dangles between us, giving off minimal light to fill the eerie space. With its metallic and dirty scent, it leads me to believe we're in an industrial building. I pause and listen intently in hopes of picking up any clue as to where we are. Water sounds from a distance, and the second I recognize it, I pick up the faintest trace of it in the air.

"Ah, I see the little bitch is up," a man calls out as he moves toward me.

"Why don't you untie me and say that again?" I wriggle against my restraints.

"That's fucking cute." He comes into my line of sight. His hair is a mess, matted down on his head. His rancid fucking breath turns my stomach. He holds a knife in his grasp and points it at me.

I swallow the familiarity of the situation. Same way of kidnapping me. Same type of weapon to torture me. If I didn't already kill my attacker, I'd venture to say this is the work of the same man. But I sliced his throat and carried his blood home on me until I showered it off, rinsing him and that experience down the drain. That was the night something sparked to life within me. Simon had witnessed it as I sliced the blade through that man's neck. My men try to ignore what awoke inside me but there's no denying that kind of darkness. The more you try to snuff it out, the wickeder it gets.

And now here I am, face to fucking face with a copycat version of that man I killed. My past is coming back to haunt me and test whether or not I'll make it out again. Only this time I'm not that same weak girl. No, I'm a sadistic bitch with enough anger coursing through me to burn this whole place down.

I just have to bide my time and figure out how the fuck I'm going to get Simon and me out of this.

"Come back," I tell him when he walks away from me and toward Simon. "I thought we were going to have a little fun."

But he doesn't listen. "Have to wake your boyfriend up first." He pokes the tip of his blade into Simon's cheek until blood runs down his neck, and he snaps to life.

Simon gasps and writhes, and within a second, his eyes lock onto mine. A million emotions flash over his face, and I recognize every fucking one of them. *Concern. Anger. Fury.* They struggle to take their turn in the spotlight. "Let her go and take me."

I narrow my gaze at him. Like fucking hell.

The man laughs. "I will do no such thing. This was a two-for-one deal, and I will not lose out because of some pathetic bargaining."

"You don't want her. She's nobody to you." Simon continues to beg. "I can give you whatever you want. Money. Cars. Women. Anything you want, name it, it's yours. Just let her go."

"You think I came for you, son?" He chuckles dryly. "The hit was on her, not you, pretty boy." He draws his arm back and slams his fist across Simon's face. "Now shut up before I cut out your tongue."

That's what I had threatened that man with before I asked if the guys thought I could cut his heart from his chest. Simon had been the first to step up and volunteer to do it for me. In the end, we never tested the theory, but I sure as hell would like to with this guy.

I continue to squirm and try to find some weak spot in this plan of his. But neither my hands nor legs budge at all. This fucker made sure to not make the same mistake as the other man who dared to take me hostage.

"You'll fucking pay for this. You don't know who you're messing with." I spit at the man when he gets close enough.

He hits me with the back of his hand and sends blood trickling down my nose and onto my chest. He trails the tip of the blade down and slices through the fabric on the front of my shirt, exposing more of me than was already out in the open.

"I will fucking kill you!" Simon yells at him. "Do not fucking touch her or I will snap every single one of your fingers off and shove them into your eye sockets."

"Is that so?" He glances over at Simon and then at me. "What do you think?" He walks behind me and grabs a fist full of my hair, holding me securely in place with the blade poised to my neck.

"Look at me, love," Simon whispers. "Just look at me. Keep looking at me." His eyes shimmer the brightest green I've ever seen as he stares at me like my life depends on it. Because in a way, it does.

Maybe dying won't be so bad when the last thing I see is him. The one man who actually told me the truth and tried to do everything he could to protect me. My men claim they do, but everything they've done has only hurt me more and more with each passing day. Their deceit was what drove me out of the fucking house in the first place and led me and Simon to this fateful place.

If I die today, then my death is on their hands. Not this man's. The men who claimed to have my best interest in mind yet pushed me away until I quite literally ran from them.

And here I am, staring into the eyes of their enemy and feeling nothing but fucking hatred in my bones.

Hate for the lies.

Hate for the distance.

Hate for making me believe they would be something they could never live up to.

And perhaps that was my fault for putting that kind of pressure on them or for having unrealistic expectations, but I made it known from the start that I didn't want a relationship and they insisted. They tricked me into thinking they cared enough to put me first and all they did was prove me right.

Coen did me a favor when he walked out on me a decade ago. He reinforced my belief that nothing good lasts. I experienced it first when my mom died and closed my heart off to ever being hurt again. I was young but I knew I had to protect myself from the anguish her loss left me with. But when I saw that broken boy in the cemetery who had the same trauma as me, I chose to give him a chance. I let him in because I wanted to put faith in love—and when he disappeared in that truck and never came back, my heart froze over more than it ever had before.

I should have kept it that way. Hardened and guarded against caring and feeling and trusting. I had for so long, but when they randomly stumbled into my life and brought my heart back from the dead, I foolishly put that same faith in those three men and gave them a gigantic opportunity to ruin me worse than I ever had been before.

I promised myself I would never hurt that way again, but I betrayed the only person who had ever been there for me through every bit of the heartache—me. Not only that, but I served myself up on a silver platter.

Part of me really does wonder what would have happened if I had met Simon first. Would I have given him the same chance I gave them? Would it be me and him sitting on that throne, ruling the organization together, creating chaos in our wake and loving each other without conditions? Or would I have shut him out? Would he have never shown interest because I wouldn't have been some object he needed to take from Dominic in his attempt to overthrow him? Maybe he only wants me because he cannot have me.

But when I look into his eyes, so frantic and desperate for mine to stay locked on his, it makes me question everything.

"Love, I'm right here."

Simon's arms and legs are bound to a chair and somehow, it's like he's right with me, hugging me despite being restrained. So much of his love pours out and over to me that I wear it like a protective cloak, temporarily shielding me from the danger of this room.

"Love," the man mocks. "Wah wah wah." He drags the tip of the blade against my cheek and slices a thin layer of my skin. The blood trickles down, warm and sticky.

"Dominic is going to fucking gut you for this."

He laughs. "I have protection from higher up. Dominic Adler cannot touch me."

A phone rings, and I flinch at the sound.

The man shoves my head forward, releasing me and turning his attention to the chiming device. "Bronco, here."

Who the fuck names their kid Bronco? Or is that some stupid ass nickname he chose for himself to try to be cool? Either way, it's stupid as fuck.

"Love," Simon calls out toward me. "I'm going to get you out of here."

"If I could just get—" I struggle with my right hand and the rope binding it to the chair. It frays slightly but more than it had been before. Minimal progress but progress all the same.

Simon wiggles his chair, inching it toward me.

But when I glance to my side, I realize it's not that he's trying to get closer to me, he's trying to reach the table full of weapons beside me. Knives of various lengths and sizes, two handguns, various tools that belong in a garage, not here.

If I could just free my hand, I could extend my arm and attempt to grab something, anything from this sick man's arsenal. Maybe I'd have a fighting chance of getting us out of here.

I look behind me and try to settle my sights on our kidnapper. I can't locate him, but I can hear his hushed voice floating back toward me. I twist my wrist back and forth, the rope rubbing my skin raw. I grit my teeth and power through the uncomfortable pain.

"I almost have a leg free," Simon tells me. "Wait."

I pause and watch him as he tilts his chair to the side, almost tipping the thing completely fucking over as he maneuvers his leg down and jiggles the leg of the chair out from the restraint holding him in place.

"I fucking got it," he cheers quietly. "Love, I need you to do the same thing." He starts to lean over to the other side, this time with the help of his newly freed leg, but he's interrupted by the man sauntering toward us.

"Well, well, well. I've got new orders." He sighs and glances between us. "I'm to kill the boy and have my fun with you." He strolls over to the selection of weapons. "I guess a bullet to the head would be effective." He latches onto the gun and pulls back the slide.

"Wait," I call out to him.

He turns toward me and raises a brow. "Yes?"

"Let him go and I'll let you do whatever you want to me."

"Oh sweetheart, I'm going to do whatever I want to you anyway." A grin coats his disgusting face.

"But," I interject before he can turn toward Simon. "I'll cooperate." My skin crawls at the idea of allowing this man to do a fucking thing to me, but if it's what I have to do to save Simon, it will all have been worth it.

Simon has done everything in his power to protect me these last six months, it's my chance to return the favor.

"June," Simon stares directly at me. "Do not even think about it."

I mouth to him, "It's okay."

"Hm, it would be rather fun to have a willing participant for a change." The man looks me up and down, his gaze hot and repulsive.

"Why don't you put that gun down and come over here?" I give him my best fuck me eyes despite wanting to hurl at the sight of him. "Come on, I'll make it worth your while."

He complies, eating right out of my hand as he lowers the gun onto the table and glides over to me.

"Don't you fucking touch her," Simon yells at him.

The guy holds out his hand with his sights trained on me. "You'll be dealt with shortly, son."

I glance through my thick lashes at the dirty man in front of me. "Come here."

He places both hands on the armrests of my chair and leans down toward me. His breath is sour and turns my stomach even more than it already was.

I bide my time, waiting for him to get even closer.

Close enough to draw my head back and slam it directly into his, crushing his nose from the impact and sending blood gushing down his face. I rip my hand free of the restraints I had been working on and shove him onto the concrete floor. I reach as far as my fucking arm will stretch but I cannot latch onto the weapons just out of my grasp.

Simon acts at the same time, lurching forward and throwing himself and his chair onto the man, part of the wood frame buckling but not enough to completely free him.

I follow his lead and throw myself at the table of weapons, clipping it with my hand and tipping it over as I tumble to the floor with a great thud. I smack my skull against the hard surface and blink through the stars forming in my vision. I frantically search for any weapon within my reach, settling on a small knife only inches away.

Simon and the man wrestle on the ground, both of them muttering obscenities at each other that I can't quite make out.

I dig my fingers into the concrete and drag myself toward the knife. Finally, I latch onto it and immediately free my other hand, cutting my wrist in the haphazard process of getting out as quickly as possible.

The man shoves his knee into Simon's chest, pinning him down, and punches him across the face. He throws another blow and Simon is forced to take it, his hands still attached to the chair.

I drive the knife across my ankle restraint, freeing one leg, and then finally, the other. I scramble toward the men and shove the knife into the back of the man on top of Simon and yank it out. "Get the fuck off of him!" I yell.

Bronco falls to the side in agony, and I rush to free Simon from his restraints.

The sound of a vehicle hitting pavement makes my heart pick up its pace.

"We have company," I tell Simon.

He takes the knife from me once I get one of his hands out of the confines and goes to work on the other.

"You fucking bitch." Bronco grabs a fistful of my hair and tugs me away from Simon.

My eyes water at the hold he has on me, and I reach to free myself but his grip is too tight.

He tosses me onto the concrete, relieving me of his grasp, but then climbs on top of me and pins my arms down with his knees. "I'm going to make your boyfriend watch while I have my way with you, you little cunt." He wraps his hand around my throat and squeezes it.

My vision blurs, and I fight for air, the end seeming so fucking near.

"Over my dead fucking body." Simon comes out of nowhere and yanks Bronco off of me, slamming him down and shoving the knife I had left with him into the asshole's throat. He lifts me off the ground and stares into my eyes. His emerald gaze is a comfort to all of the throbbing pain flowing through me. "Love, we have to get out of here."

A car door slams, then another. At least two people are on their way toward us now.

"I'll kill you both," Bronco whimpers from his spot on the floor where he's bleeding out.

I rush over to him, pull the knife out of the gushing wound, and stab it into his chest repeatedly. "You. Will. Do. No. Such. Thing." Each word another gash through his torso. "You. Fucking. Bastard."

Simon grips my shoulders and drags me away from him.

I throw the bloodied blade onto the man and turn toward Simon, red dripping down the entire front side of me.

He weaves his fingers through mine, not giving a shit that I'm covered in blood, and tugs me away. "Come on, love."

We take off, but not before those people from outside step into the building and train their sights on us. "Hurry, they're going to get away."

Escaping death once might have been possible, but what are the chances we can do it again on the same night?

# CHAPTER 22

# *Simon*

I hold onto June and run as fast as her legs will take us.

A gunshot rings out, and I throw my body over hers.

We burst through a door and into the night, the entire area pitch fucking black aside from the moon giving us minimal light.

"This way," June whispers.

We dart behind cargo containers and continue pushing forward to put as much distance between us and these people as possible.

Another gunshot, but this time it isn't near us. We must actually be losing these assholes.

"Where the fuck are we?" June asks.

"I can't tell, not yet. All these fucking warehouses look the same."

We slither along the storage container and pause at the end.

I poke my head out to make sure the coast is clear and nod for us to continue.

"I hear water," June tells me quietly.

"I do too."

"Could we steal a boat?"

"Yeah." I swallow harshly. "Maybe." I'm not a huge fan of open bodies of water, but if getting on a boat is what it takes to get her away from here, I'll do it in a heartbeat.

"Over here!" someone yells. "There's a blood trail."

I grip June's shoulders and steady her toward me. "I'm outmanned and outgunned. We have to run, love."

She nods. "Together?"

I tug her hands up to my lips and kiss her knuckles. "Together."

We take off, darting around another container and weaving through this industrial maze.

The stale air whips over my cheek and burns the cut that asshole gave me. Luckily for him, June finished him off, because if she hadn't, I would have tracked him down and gutted him for what he did to her—and what he planned to do.

*Bronco*, I recall. A name that proves as a hint to who the fuck hired this bastard to abduct and torture my girl. Whoever is responsible will fucking pay—in blood, with their fucking life.

I will burn this city to the fucking ground to find the person who dares to try and take her from me.

Nobody considers laying a finger on her and gets away with it.

The open water comes into sight. For a split second, I hesitate, but continue pushing forward. We run along the edge of it and frantically search for a way out. Anything to give us reprieve from the men chasing us with guns.

A bullet darts by my head, and I move to position myself behind June to shield her from any attack. I don't care if I die, as long as she gets away, that's the only thing that matters.

We run closer to the edge of the water and use the few smaller storage containers lining the area to block us from any bullets that might come to us from the side. It isn't much protection but it's better than nothing.

Only, our rear and side aren't all that are vulnerable.

And when a man shoots at us from up ahead, clipping June's shoulder, spinning her around and toppling over the edge of the shipyard and into the water, I do the only thing I can think of—jump in after her.

# CHAPTER 23

# *June*

The last thing I see as my head is pulled under the water is Simon jumping in after me.

Simon—the man who is terrified of water and who cannot swim.

My shoulder screams from the bullet that grazed me, but it's nothing compared to the panic coursing through me at knowing Simon is here, somewhere, fighting for his life.

I burst through the surface of the water and suck in a gasping breath of air, frantically searching the surface for any sign of him. I thank a god I don't really believe in for sending us in near a loading area, giving us the docks as somewhat of a concealment from the men after us.

But none of that will matter if I cannot find him.

I dive under, my blood no doubt pooling around me, and crane my eyes through the darkness to spot him. I swim in circles and ignore the pain radiating in my body. I will cover every inch of this fucking bay to find him or I will die trying. Leaving him behind is not an option.

Erupting to the top again, I scan and scan. My heart picks up its pace as the men's feet shuffle against the pavement near us.

That's when I spot him, face down, his body floating along the water.

I gasp and swim faster than I ever have toward him, wrapping my arm around him and dragging him out of sight and under the pier. It's everything I can do to move him, but with the adrenaline in my veins, I make it happen. "Simon," I whisper, moving the hair from his lifeless face. "Stay with me, Simon."

"I shot the bitch!" one of the guys calls out. "If she ain't above the water yet, she's fucking dead."

"You don't fucking know that, Harold."

*Harold.* Another name to add to the list of men to kill.

I hug Simon tightly to my side and keep him afloat as I hold my breath and wait for them to leave. If I try to resuscitate Simon now, it will only bring attention to us and ensure that we both die.

"They're both gone. Now let's go clean up the fucking mess they made. We'll send a team to recover their bodies so we can get paid."

A lifetime passes, and finally, they decide to leave.

I don't move for a full minute, and when I do, silent tears roll down my cheeks. I shake Simon's limp body and move us out from under the pier. I try to lift him up, but it's impossible from this angle. I'm not strong enough to get him out of the water without any assistance.

"Simon!" I pound on his chest and kick my feet to tread water. "Do not leave me, damn it." I hit him harder, the full brunt of my weak fist clobbering him. I hold onto the edge of the pier with one hand, and with one arm under his to keep him up, I suck in a breath and press my lips to his, pushing air into his lungs.

My injured arm gives out and he slips from my grasp. I fight through the agony and latch onto him again. "Simon, please. Come back to me." I sniffle through the sobs bubbling out of me. "I'll do anything, just please don't leave me."

Simon flinches, his eyes flicking back and forth. He spits out water and coughs, his gaze frantic as life finally returns to him.

I burst into more tears and struggle to keep my hold on him. "Simon."

"Love," he mutters and reaches up to grab onto the pier to hold himself steady. "I thought I lost you."

"I thought I lost *you*!" I cry.

Water splashes up onto our faces.

"Where did they go?"

"They're gone," I say breathlessly.

"Let's get out of here." Simon climbs out first, his soaked clothes clinging to his body. He reaches out, offering me his hand.

I take it and allow him to pull me out of the water because I don't think I could have gotten out by myself. My left arm hangs to my side and blood spills out of the wound.

"Christ, Love." Simon presses his palm to it. "Can you apply pressure for a second?"

I nod.

He removes his hand and pulls his shirt over his head, exposing his muscular upper half. Simon rips the fabric and ties it around my biceps to stop the bleeding. "Here, that should hold you over until I can get you to a doctor."

"Okay," is all I say, because there are too many things running through my mind right now to focus on any single one.

I thought we were going to die. I thought Simon was going to die. I thought I was holding his dead body above the water and that he was never going to come back to me.

But at that moment, I realized exactly how much I cannot live without him. And that alone leaves me riddled with fucking guilt. I never meant to feel this way.

It's forbidden. Simon is my boyfriends' enemy, and he is my bodyguard. This wasn't supposed to be anything else.

I'm not even entirely sure if these are romantic feelings, but whatever this is, I cannot fathom the idea of living in a world where he is not.

Is this how he felt when I was bleeding out in his lap? *Helpless, terrified, infuriated.*

"Can you walk?" He steadies his grip on my shoulder and stares into my eyes.

Tears roll down my cheeks, and there is nothing I can do to make them stop.

"Are you in pain somewhere else? What's wrong?" Simon wildly looks for another source of my torment.

"I—I..."

"What is it, love?"

"Let's get out of here," I tell him. There isn't time for me to have a mental breakdown when those who wish us dead are still so near and more are on their way. It won't be long before their recovery team arrives and finds us very much alive.

"Together?" He wipes at my cheeks with his thumbs.

"Together."

Simon weaves his hand through mine and leads us out of this death trap.

We walk in silence for a few minutes until we arrive at a street.

"Come on, love. I think I know where we are." Simon tugs me across the empty street and onto a sidewalk. He makes a beeline through a residential neighborhood, cutting through backyards instead of leading us down the road.

My pace slows as the energy leaves my body. I don't mean to, but I trip over my own feet.

Simon catches me before I can hit the ground. "We can take a break, love. Here." He shifts me toward a picnic table in an unsuspecting person's yard. He kneels in front of me and rests his head on my leg. "This is all my fault."

I blink at him. "What?"

Simon glances up at me. "I should have protected you. I failed you, love. And I am so sorry."

"Would you stop blaming yourself?" I tilt his face up toward mine. "This is not your fault. If anything, it's mine. I'm the one who stormed off. You got hurt because of me. Because I got mad and left like a child and demanded space. Hell, it's just as much *their* fault as it is mine." I steady in a breath to calm my raging nerves. "I'm the one who's sorry, Simon. I haven't exactly made your job easy."

"My job?" Simon leans back. "Is that what you think this is? Me doing my job? June, love, I would do anything for you."

"Because of your obligation to me, yeah. I know."

"No." He shakes his head, his hair still dripping wet. "If you, for one second, think this has to do with anything other than my feelings for you, you're mistaken."

"Your feelings for me?" I laugh. "Simon, you're forced to be with me. And the only reason you *think* you want me is because you can't have me."

"Is that so?" Simon stands and runs his hand over his face. "Is that why I know more about you than anyone else?"

I sigh. "Because you pay attention, that's your job."

"It's my job to notice the anguish you've felt these last six months? That you've lost weight because of the stress you're under. That you have nightmares almost every night and the only thing that stops the tremors is when I sneak into your room and hold you. It's my job to see that you prefer the color green over anything else, and that wearing red lipstick gives you more confidence than you already have? It's my job to recognize you have a bigger heart than you let on, and despite being this raging bitch on the outside, you're a hopeless fucking romantic? Being alone in nature is what calms your wild mind, and holding a knife in your grasp is how you cope with losing that control to some asshole who held you hostage."

He lowers himself back down and presses his hands around mine. "You think I don't see the struggle when you look at me? That fleeting moment when you consider what your life would have been like if you would have met me first? You think I don't beat myself up about it daily, knowing that I could have been the one you loved instead of *them*? You think I don't want to blow my fucking brains out every time they touch you, knowing damn well that I'll never be that lucky. But I choose not to because this, whatever this is, is better than nothing at all."

"Simon, I..."

He draws in a long breath and exhales. "I would never ask you to feel the same, but do not for a moment question whether my love for you is based on something so foolish as a job position. I do not get paid for this. They've tried. But I refuse. I do this because I cannot stand the idea of someone else spending each day with you. There is no one else that cares more about your life than me, and I have failed you. For that, I'm so goddamn sorry, love."

This is the moment where I finally take all those months' worth of pent-up tension and press my lips to his and taste the sweetness of his kiss. I would wrap my fingers in his hair and let him pull me close, our bodies smashed together after what has felt like a lifetime of push and pull.

But I can't. Not like this. Not now. Not when it's still so wrong to cross that line.

Simon wraps his hand around mine. "Come on. We only have a little farther to go."

# CHAPTER 24

# *Magnus*

**M**y phone rings, and despite it being an unfamiliar number, I answer it immediately. "Bryant."

"We're at a gas station on the corner of Britton and Marley." Simon's voice flits through the receiver. "Send a car and call for a doctor. We're fine, but June needs medical attention."

He disconnects the line, and I reach for my keys, rushing toward the door.

"Who was it?" Hayes calls out. "Was it them? I'm coming with you."

I turn toward him and stop dead in my tracks. "No, you fucking won't. You've done enough."

He and Dominic are the reason June left in the first place, and despite my better judgment, I've contributed to the situation as much as they have. June is hurt because of me, and I cannot allow him to make things any worse.

I pull the gun out from my side and hold it to Hayes's forehead. "If you so much as move a fucking inch, I will blow your fucking brains out right here."

His eyes narrow like he's considering whether or not I'm being serious.

But I've never been so fucking certain in my life.

"Call my bluff," I tell him. "I fucking dare you."

"Fine." Hayes backs down, stepping out of my way.

I rush out the door and hop into my car, pushing a sequence of buttons—one to start the engine, and the other to dial a number.

The speaker sounds in my car as I shove it into reverse and push the gas. My tires spin, and I whip it around and throw it into drive.

"Dr. Murphy," the man answers on the other end.

"I need you at the house. It's urgent. I don't have any information other than it isn't life-threatening."

"I will be there shortly."

"Thank you," I tell him and hang up the phone, focusing on driving a million miles per hour to the intersection Simon had instructed me they were at. I break every possible traffic law, blasting through red lights, turning down one-way streets, and passing cars illegally. I blow my horn as I weave through oncoming traffic and dart back across to the correct side of the road. My tires skid across the pavement when I turn down the final street that leads me to the gas station where the love of my life is. I slam on the brakes and hop out before the car is fully shifted into park. With the engine still running, I run into the establishment and frantically look for her.

Standing there, one arm at her side and the other gripping her stomach, June stares at me.

I rush toward her and take her in. "Princess."

"Magnus," she breathes, and it's like life is blown into my own lungs with the sound of her saying my name.

"Let's get her out of here," Simon tells me.

I don't ignore his arm draped behind her, holding her to his shirtless body. But in this moment, nothing matters more than the fact that she's okay.

"What the fuck happened?" I say as we're walking toward the door.

Simon waves at the clerk. "Thanks for letting us use the phone, Boston."

The man nods and continues whatever the hell he's doing, seemingly unbothered by the urgency of this situation. But I guess on this side of town, crazier things go down on a daily basis.

"Did you call the doctor?" Simon asks while latching onto the passenger side door and opening it.

I rest my palm along June's soaked back and guide her into the seat. I shut her in and face Simon. "Yes. He's on his way now." I reach for my gun. "If you want to live, you better start talking."

Simon drags his hand through his hair. "You guys pissed her off and she left. I went after her. We walked a little bit then got bamboozled by multiple vehicles. They took us to a warehouse out near Crescent Valley." He points in the direction. "We both woke up tied to chairs, some bastard named Bronco—that alias sound familiar to you?"

I shake my head and grit my teeth.

"Dude had the same MO as Vincent." Simon glances away, like he's recalling a memory. "We managed to break free but not until he had already started." He motions to the cut along his cheek. "We ran, they were shooting at us. June got nicked in the arm, fell into the water. I dove in after her but..."

That's when I remember the story I had heard about his sister. She drowned when they were kids in some freak accident. If June's life being in danger didn't already frighten him, her nearly dying the same way his sister did was sure enough to instill terror in him.

"Sorry, Beckett."

June knocks on the window to draw our attention.

"We'll talk more about this at home," I tell him. "Get in the car."

I rush around and hop into the driver's seat, reach for the thermostat, and crank it as high as it will go. I push on June's seat warmer and turn it full blast, too. Anything I can do to rid her of the shivers coursing through her. I reach across and grab her seatbelt, tugging it across her chest and under the arm she holds close to her body.

The fabric is stained red but is no doubt stopping blood from gushing from the wound. Simon made the right choice in taking his shirt off and tying it around where she was shot. And it's only a matter of minutes until our doctor will assess it to make sure it's properly treated. That, and the fresh cut on her cheek and the skin that's torn away on both of her wrists. She must have struggled beneath her restraints, and from the look of the slashes along her skin, she used a blade to free herself. If it were Simon or someone else, the pattern would come from the opposite direction, not the way it is now.

No, my girl fought for her life and saved herself from her tormentor.

And judging by the marks on her forehead, she must have blasted the asshole in the face, too.

Simon has his fair share of bumps and bruises and cuts, too, but June's are just as much offensive as they are defensive. She wasn't going down without a fight, and despite that ripping a hole straight through me that she had to resort to that, I'm so fucking grateful for her strength.

I rush back across town, but this time, obeying a few more laws that I broke on my way to her. I still speed and run stop signs, but I do it with more caution as to not put her life in any more danger than it already is.

We pull into the driveway, and I park the car back in its spot in the garage.

The doctor pulls in just after us, his timing impeccable.

"Who is that?" June glances in the mirror.

"Dr. Murphy. Remember him from a while back?"

"What is he driving?" She continues to stare until he gets out of the driver's seat and approaches.

"He got a new SUV, no need to worry, princess." I grip her hand and unbuckle her.

"Who's here?" She looks up at me.

"Hayes was here when I left," I tell her.

"I don't want to talk to him. I don't want to see him."

"I don't think that's possible, princess."

Another vehicle pulls into the drive behind the doctor and darts around to enter the garage.

Dom jumps out of his SUV and rushes over to where we're parked. He almost rips the passenger door off my car to get to June. "You!" he growls at Simon in the back seat. "You fucking did this." He goes toward the back of my car and June reaches out to stop him.

"Dominic. If you know what's good for you, you will not make another fucking move." June slides her feet out and presses them to the ground. She's wobbly but remains upright.

I dart out to steady her. "Leave him alone, Dom. Things could have been worse without him."

June moves between Simon's door and Dom, pressing her small frame in to block Dom from doing anything else. "Get out of my way," she tells him. She glares at him with a force that could wreak terror in any man.

Dom surprisingly takes a step back, giving her the space she demanded.

She shuffles out of the way and struggles to open the door.

I grab it for her and watch in wonder as Beckett steps out of the backseat of my car.

"Let him through or I'm leaving." June marches toward the house.

I motion for Simon to follow her and head in behind them, blocking the path from Dominic. There's no telling what he will do, and this isn't the opportune time for him to completely lose his shit. We're dangling by a thin thread as it is, and we cannot afford for him to set June over the edge. He's already done enough, and it's a wonder she's here at all. She has more patience than a fucking saint.

I spot Coen the second June opens the door.

His eyes widen and his entire face tenses. "What the fuck happened?"

That's pretty much on par with how I reacted, too. Although, I don't know if I have that harsh of a wrinkle between my brows. I may have a few years on him, but damn if our job doesn't cause him a hell of a lot more stress. Or maybe it's just that I handle mine differently than he does.

"Step aside, Hayes," I call out to him before he can cause any trouble.

We all funnel into the large area between our sitting room and kitchen. It's definitely the most trafficked part of the house, being that it's located near the garage and has most of our food supplies. Our second-floor kitchen has most of our backup rations and shit that doesn't fit in this fridge, but it's seldom anyone is up there for anything more than grabbing a drink or snack in the middle of the night because they're too lazy to walk downstairs.

June gravitates toward Simon, and he to her. It's clear he's the only one she wants to be around, and I don't blame her at all for that. But it doesn't make my heart hurt any less.

I go the rest of the way in and stand next to Simon, providing somewhat of a buffer between him and the rest of the idiots. If anyone is less likely to murder him, it's probably me. It's not that it hasn't crossed my mind from time to time, but he's proven himself these past six months, and whatever hatred I had toward him back then has faded into a distant memory.

He's mostly tolerable at this point.

And if that's how *I* feel about him given our minimal interactions, it's no wonder June has developed feelings for him. The two of them spend nearly every day together. He gets to be himself with her, even when he's playing the role of bodyguard. He doesn't have to lie or deceive her. Honestly, I kind of want to trade places with the dude and give up my role in the company to spend every waking moment with her. Hell, all the sleeping ones, too.

I fucking hate leaving the house before she's up and coming back when she's fast asleep. I still go in there and kiss her good morning and good night but it's nothing compared to her falling asleep or waking up in my arms. Some nights I crawl into bed with her, but knowing how difficult getting a good night's rest is for her, I don't want to disturb her any more than I already do. And sometimes it takes me longer than I like to scrub the blood out from under my fingernails and come completely clean from the things my job forces me to do. It feels wrong to slide into bed with an angel when I'm nothing but a devil.

"Who needs my medical attention?" Dr. Murphy breaks the awkward silence.

Everyone points to June who remains in place, her arm hanging limply at her side, dried blood coating the skin around Simon's make-shift tourniquet.

"Very well." Murphy approaches her. "Is there somewhere more private we could go?"

"Yeah," June speaks. "This way." She turns, but not before grabbing onto Simon's hand and tugging him down the hall with her.

I feel the tension radiate from Dominic and Hayes but neither of them does a damn thing about it. They turn to me once the three have disappeared from sight.

"Details, now," Dominic growls.

I sigh and recall the information Simon gave me. "Well, she's fucking pissed at you, to say the very least."

"Why?" Dom furrows his brows. "We were fine earlier. We had a great time yesterday."

"Yeah, until she found out that you got her out of town so Co and I could shoot that fucking building up."

"You told her about..."

I hold up my hand to stop him. "No, not the details. She just knows *something* went down."

"Why the fuck would you tell her?" Dominic balls his hand into a fist.

I glance down at it and then at him. "You need to slow your fucking roll, dude. You're the one insisting on lying to her left and right. And now you're pissed because I blurt out one fucking truth. No." I shake my head. "I told you to be honest with her from the start, Dom. This is on fucking you. Don't you blame me for this shit."

Hayes clears his throat. "Explain to me how this goes from her being mad at Dom to whatever the fuck happened?"

I close my eyes and inhale deeply. When I open them again, I spill every last word that Simon had told me. They listen intently to every bit of it until I stop.

"Whoever it was is connected to the original hit ordered against her."

"No, shit. Sherlock." I pinch my brow. "Is that really all you fucking gathered?"

Dominic doesn't say anything, instead, he seems lost in thought—like he's trying to puzzle the pieces together.

"You need to tell her the truth." I cross my arms. "You're going to lose her if you don't. We're all going to."

"Tell her the truth about what?" June says as she enters the room, a new and proper binding wrapped around her biceps and various bandages covering her face and arms.

Simon follows behind her, his own wounds treated by the doctor. Still, he remains shirtless and sopping wet.

"Why don't you get changed?" I tell him. "There's probably something in my room that would fit you. Help yourself." I make eye contact with June, pleading with her to give me a few more minutes alone with the guys. "Both of you should get out of those clothes before you catch a cold."

She stares at me for a long second, and I worry that this simple request will put me on the shit list with Dom and Co, a place that seems impossible to escape from.

"Fine." She latches onto Simon and pulls him toward the stairs, the two of them leaving us here with the doctor.

Murphy approaches and sets a vial on the counter. "She'll need to take four of these daily for the first seven days. And I'd like to check the wound in a few days to make sure there's no sign of infection. You guys can keep an eye on it. You know what to look for. Change the bandage in twenty-four hours unless it becomes wet or dirty. And don't hesitate to call if you have any questions or concerns." Murphy sighs and points to Coen. "And how is yours healing up?"

Coen shrugs. "It's fine, I've had worse."

Murphy approaches him anyway. "Let me have a look." He peels back the bandage and cranes his head to check it out. "More swollen than I'd prefer. Are you taking the antibiotics I prescribed?"

"Yeah, I think so."

"It isn't the wound you need to be concerned about. It's the infection that can come after." Murphy turns toward all of us. "This isn't our first rodeo, boys. Don't let this be the thing that kills you." Murphy closes his little briefcase full of supplies and walks toward the door. "I'll be in touch."

When he's finally gone, I say, "Swell guy, that Murph."

"Yeah," Dominic agrees. "But I don't think this is the time or place for the conversation you're suggesting."

"Then when?" I grip the counter of the countertop. "After what happened tonight? It's fucking proof that not telling her is only putting her in even more danger. If she knew the threat then maybe she wouldn't have stormed out. She would have stewed safely upstairs in her room instead of barging outside for any of our enemies to snatch her."

"I can't believe you two are okay with him being up there with her right now," Hayes mouths off.

I tilt my head toward him. "I'm sorry, did you miss the part where he saved her life, *twice*? I don't care if the two of them are upstairs fucking, as long as she is safe, that is the *only* thing that matters."

Coen kicks off from his place at the island and gets right in my face. "Say that again, I fucking dare you."

I push my chest into his. "Don't fucking test me, Hayes. I've been in this world longer than you, and you might think you're this Billy fucking badass but you've got another thing coming. I will fucking ruin you."

Coen reaches into his waistband and pulls out a gun, but not without acting too slow and giving me a chance to rip mine out, too.

"Enough!" Dominic yells and slams his fists onto the counter. "Guns. Down. What the fuck do we have rules for if you're not going to follow them?" He steps in between us and uses his forearms to push us apart. "No fucking killing in the house."

I lower my weapon not because he demanded it, but because he's right. That kind of mess isn't something you want to deal with inside a place like this. That's part of the reason we made the damn rule in the first place. Blood stains stuff and it's difficult as fuck to get out. And aside from the few people we let into our home to do miscellaneous things, we'd prefer not to have to invite a clean-up crew in here.

"Fine." Coen huffs and holsters his gun.

"What's all the commotion down here?" June appears from the stairwell with an oversized tee and a pair of my sweatpants on.

I always knew they were her favorite, but every time I see her wearing them, my heart nearly lurches out of my chest. *My girl.*

Simon follows her like a fucking puppy dog. He's in my clothes too, but it doesn't quite have the same effect on me as it does when she's in them.

"I think everyone needs to sit down." I motion toward the sitting area. "I'll make us all a drink."

"Bryant," Dominic snarls.

"I'm done, dude. I'm not doing it anymore. It's time we come clean."

If we lose her, we lose her, but it will have been with her finally knowing the truth.

# CHAPTER 25

## *June*

I ache all over, from head to fucking toe, but it's nothing compared to the sensation rippling through my body when the men who I thought loved me sit me down and tell me that the person who ordered the hit on me last year, that started the chain of events that led me to be with them, is still fucking out there.

"What?" I say, not quite understanding. "I thought you figured out who it was and killed them all."

Dominic rubs at his neck. "We were under the impression we had."

"How could you make a mistake like that?" I glance between each man in this room and settle my sights on the beautifully broken one beside me. "Did you know about this?" I ask him.

But from the shocked expression on Simon's face, it's safe to say he didn't have an idea either.

He shakes his head. "Why wouldn't you guys tell me? How could you possibly think this wasn't important information? I'm her fucking *protective detail* for Christ's sake."

"I feel like I don't know you," I whisper, my attention flitting from Dom to Coen. It lingers on Magnus. "I knew you wanted to tell me. But I don't understand why you didn't. You could have told me." Tears well in my eyes but I beg for them to stay firmly rooted in place.

I will not cry, not here, not ever again. I have shed too many fucking tears for these men, for this fucking life that I never asked for.

I was dragged into it, an unwilling participant who bared her heart to these men, only to be pushed aside when I needed them most.

But isn't this what they worried about? That I wouldn't react well. Am I giving in to their concerns by being mad at them? How could they expect any other reaction from me? Am I supposed to be grateful they kept this massive secret from me and pushed me aside while they handled such a situation on their own?

They put my life in danger every single day when they refused to tell me that my attacker was still out there. Sure, I may have murdered the man who hurt me, both of them, but they were only puppets with their strings being pulled by someone much more sinister.

"It's my fault," Dominic admits. "I'm the reason Bryant didn't tell you sooner. I demanded he keep his mouth shut. He was only following orders." He sits up straighter in his chair. "Same goes for Hayes. I ordered both of them to remain silent."

"I would have told you, love. If I knew, I promise." Simon's pinky twitches like he wants to reach out and touch me but he doesn't.

"Isn't that fucking convenient," Coen blurts out. "Seizing a fucking opportunity when he sees one."

"Is there something you'd like to fucking say?" I stand and force my attention on the beautiful blond boy that I no longer recognize. "What the fuck is wrong with you?" I point behind me. "What has Simon done to you to make you hate him so fucking much?"

Coen rises to his feet. "You know exactly what he's done. What *you've* done."

My chest heaves with anger. "Fucking say it, Coen."

"I don't have to say it." He glares down at me. "We all know you've been fucking the enemy."

I have never been one to let my frustrations get the best of me, not ever in a domestic situation. In a bar fight, maybe. When someone shoulder checks one of my friends, for sure. When I'm kidnapped and have no choice, absolutely. But never with a partner.

So when my hands reach out and shove every bit of their strength into Coen's chest, I no longer recognize myself either. Pain ripples through my left arm and if I'm not mistaken, I've torn one of my sutures. I lower that arm to my side because I have no other choice, and shove him again with my right. "How fucking dare you."

I had barely moved him but he regains his footing long enough for Simon to jump around and get in front of me.

"You lay a fucking finger on her and I'll snap your fucking neck," Simon tells him.

"Oh, you think you're a tough guy." Coen pushes Simon.

Simon holds his ground and doesn't budge. "Get your fucking hands off of me, Hayes."

"For fuck's sake, will you two cut it out?" Dominic slams his glass on the table.

Magnus steadies his palms on my shoulders and guides me away from the confrontation. "Come on, princess. Sit back down."

Dominic drags his hand along his beard. "Listen, we're all stressed, tense, whatever you want to call it. But if there is one more fucking childlike outburst, you're out of here. Done. That's it. I will not tolerate you disrespecting June like that."

Dom settles his serious sights on me. "But I do think you owe it to us all to let us know if you're sleeping with Beckett."

"Ay," Magnus calls out. "That's not any of our business." He focuses on me. "You don't have to answer that, princess."

"I'll answer it for her," Simon interrupts. "You guys are the worst profilers ever. We're not fucking. We never have. We haven't even so much as kissed."

"Well..." I add.

"See!" Coen exclaims. "I fucking knew it."

"Who are you?" I crane my head toward him and then glance at Simon. "I gave you CPR when I thought you had drowned."

Simon brings his fingers to his lips. "I had to drown to get you to kiss me?"

"It wasn't a kiss," I tell the entire room. "It was life or fucking death. I would have done it to a stranger." I exhale and tug my arm toward me and hold it with my other hand. "But Magnus is right, it is none of your business. Especially now, after everything you've put me through. I never crossed that line with Simon because I was trying to be respectful, but it doesn't seem we have a mutual understanding of things here. On our relationship, or my fucking life."

I reach for the glass of bourbon across from me and down it in one gulp.

"Sit your fucking asses down before I leave," I tell Simon and Coen, but mainly Coen. "You're all fucking lucky I'm still here." I point my thumb toward the garage. "I could walk out that door and not look back but I'm here because *I* love you. Not because *you* love me, but because I fucking choose to love *you*." I skim my gaze across the room, even hovering it on Simon temporarily. "Now if you don't want me to walk away, there can't be any more lies. When I ask you a question, you answer it, and you answer it truthfully."

I don't know what's finally gotten into me, but I've had enough. Enough of the lies, the deceit, the being pushed aside. This is the moment they finally show me if they actually do care, and the moment I decide what I'm going to do with that.

Leaving would be easy, but staying would be more work. Nothing good in life is ever simple, but should things really be this Goddamn difficult?

"What do you want to know, princess? I'll tell you anything you want to know." Magnus rubs my shoulder.

"Everything. I want to know everything. Start from the beginning."

The guys finally settle back into their seats. Simon at my side and Coen in the chair opposite Dom's across the way.

They do their best, or what I think might be their best, in filling me in piece by piece. It's a lot of information to dish out spanning more than six months. They go over how they found the people the first time, how they thought they had eliminated the threat, and Simon even chimes in on how he was certain they had squashed the people that were responsible.

"So, hold on," I tell him. "If someone was able to orchestrate a cover-up that good, they had to be higher up in the organization, right? Since when do you not know of shit like that?" I train my sights right on Dom.

Dom nods. "Exactly. That's why I called in Lorenzo Savini."

"Who's that?"

"He's a mercenary with a specific set of skills. He knows almost every hit that gets ordered and who and where it happens. The inner details that aren't made common knowledge."

"Why? Why does he have all that information?"

"Because he's that good." Dominic drains more of his bourbon. "He can make anyone disappear. Not the type of person you want to be on their bad side."

"Does he even have a *good* side?"

Dom shakes his head. "No, not really. Although, he's got this thing against women and children."

"He's like a sexist pig or something?"

"No, I misspoke. He doesn't kill women or kids, not unless it's absolutely necessary. And he doesn't take kindly to men abusing their power against a woman."

"Interesting that a serial killer has morals, but go on."

"He's looking into the hit ordered against you. It's been difficult to locate, which only confirms our suspicions that it was someone deep in the organization."

Simon chimes in. "But you said the same attacks are happening on the east coast, aside from their obsession with June?"

Dominic nods. "Cryptic notes about taking what was theirs. Which is the opposite of what ours have said."

"Well, what was it?" I ask when he doesn't continue.

"That they will take what is *ours*." Dom sighs. "At first, I didn't place the attacks with what had happened to you. I was convinced we eliminated that threat. But the notes got more specific. There were several detailing the things Vincent had done to you. Others about certain clothes you had worn or the way you'd wear your hair. I kept the information concealed because I didn't know who I could trust. I wasn't sure who the mole was, but it had to be someone close to us. I was confident it wasn't Hayes or Bryant, and..." Dom looks at Simon. "Well, after Beckett gave up everything for you, I never questioned whether it was him."

"At least you were right about one thing," I tell Dominic. "But you were wrong in not telling me. Of all the people that should have known. Do you not realize how many times I potentially put myself in danger because you chose not to tell me someone wanted me dead? I assumed it came with the territory of being with you three, but this is something else entirely. This is personal."

"I see the error now," Dominic admits.

"But that isn't all of it, is it?"

Dominic's jaw tightens like he's holding something back.

"That's not how the truth works," I tell him. "You don't get to pick and choose."

Dom avoids my stare. "It's more complicated than that, June."

"Don't patronize me with that tone." I point to Coen and Magnus. "You might have these two scared into obeying you but the difference between them and me is that I'm not afraid of you."

Magnus places his hand on my thigh. "Princess, cut him some slack, please."

I peel him off of me. "No, I've cut you all more slack than you deserve. Six months you kept this from me. What else are you hiding?" I focus on Coen. "You keep accusing me of fucking Simon. Maybe you're projecting that you have something going on I don't know about? You can't honestly tell me all the late nights and early mornings were just because of this."

Coen's blue gaze trails up to meet mine. "I would never."

"And guess what, I fucking believe you. But how does it feel to be accused of something you didn't do?"

"J..."

I hold out my hand. "I'm not interested in anything you have to say, Coen."

Simon remains still and quiet beside me like a kid who's stuck in the room while his parents are fighting. Just trying to blend in until it's time for him to make his escape.

"I think I need some time to process this. For me to figure out what I'm going to do with this information, this situation." My head swims with questions, and if I don't take a break soon, I'm going to pass out from the exhaustion of the day slamming into me.

Finally, Simon speaks up. "You're not leaving, are you?"

"No, not the house. I'm going to bed. I need to be alone for a while."

"Okay," he breathes.

I stand from the couch and glance at each of the men that hold a piece of my heart. "We'll talk more about this tomorrow." I settle on Simon. "Walk me to my room?"

His eyes widen before he rises to his feet. "Uh, yeah, of course, love."

I ignore the seething stares of the rest of the guys and walk out of the room, their whispers fill the space by the time Simon and I reach the stairs. More secrets, no doubt.

Simon places his hand on the small of my back on the way up, and keeps it there down the hall. We stop in front of my room and when I turn to him, I don't hesitate wrapping my arms around his torso and burying my face in his chest.

He stiffens slightly but then his resolve softens. "Love..." Simon folds me into him and presses his cheek against the top of my head.

I breathe into him and sigh. "Sorry, I needed this."

And from the way he grips me tighter, I think he did, too.

"You had me worried today," I tell him. "I thought I lost you." I try to push away the memory of Simon's body floating face down in the water but the image is burned into my memory. I'd never felt fear like that in my entire life before. Not even when I was staring death directly in the eyes.

"I'm not going anywhere, love." He rubs small circles on my back and kisses my hair. "Never."

"I'm really sorry," I whisper into him. "About everything."

"Shh." He tilts my chin up toward him. "Please stop apologizing." Simon flits his gaze down to my lips, his attention lingering far too long.

My heart skips a beat, and I swallow at the possibility floating between us. Is this it? Is this the moment we finally cross that boundary? When we step over the line that we can never come back from?

But when Simon presses a soft kiss against my forehead, it disappears into thin air.

"Get some rest, love. I'll be here when you wake up."

I do as he tells me, only because I'm too fucking exhausted to protest. Between my normal sleep deprivation and the rather vexing day, my energy levels are at an all-time low. And if I'm being completely honest, I don't remember what I ate or drank today, either. Only, I don't say that out loud because I know Simon will insist that I eat something, and even though I probably should, I don't want to. Not when I'd rather bury myself in my bed and hope like hell that when I wake up, I will be rid of this nightmare I'm in.

I climb into my massive bed and pull the blanket all the way over my face, wondering how long it would take for me to suffocate under it. When it gets too fucking hot, I tug it down and let out an exaggerated sigh. I turn on my side, wincing and shifting to the other instead. Fucking gunshot wound. Hopefully, that was the last time I get shot in this lifetime.

At least an hour or two goes by as I relentlessly doze in and out, wondering if I'll ever actually fall asleep. I lick my lips, my mouth dry as fuck. I kick off the blankets and slide out of bed, tiptoeing out of my room to get a drink from the kitchen down the hall.

But when I unknowingly bump into something solid, I stop dead in my tracks and lower myself to the ground, feeling for what I hit.

"Love, what's wrong?" Simon mutters half asleep.

"What the fuck are you doing out here?" I whisper and ask him.

"Sleeping." He yawns and sits up all the way. "What are *you* doing out here?"

"I was getting something to drink, but..." I feel around in the dark. "You don't even have a blanket or anything. Are you crazy?"

"Yeah, probably."

"Come on." I reach my hand out and stand. "You're coming with me."

"Wh-what?"

"I said, come on."

"I'm not supposed—"

"I don't care what you're not *supposed* to do. We aren't fucking, you're just coming in to sleep. I refuse to let you sleep in the hallway like a dog."

"Love, I'm fine, really. It's not the first time—"

"Simon Beckett, I am inviting you into my bed, do not refuse my offer."

He brings himself to his feet within seconds. "Let me get you that drink first. What do you want?"

"I can get it. Go get in bed."

"Hey," he says while finding my cheek with his hand. "Together?"

I lean into him and smile. "Together."

We walk the rest of the hall side by side, silently working to get a glass and fill it with water. I take a sip and offer it to him. There's something so intimate about our lips touching the same cup. Once we're finished, we go back the way we came, not another sound filling the house other than the gentle patters of our footsteps on the wood floor.

I pull myself onto the bed and scoot far enough over to give Simon room.

"Are you sure?" he asks me. "I shouldn't—"

"What are they going to do? Shoot me?" I pat the spot next to me.

"Don't joke about something like that." Simon exhales and kicks off his shoes. He lowers himself onto the mattress and extends his arm. "If I'm going to die, I might as well enjoy it. Come here."

I grin and melt myself into him, resting my head between his collar and jaw.

"Are you comfortable, love?"

I mumble into him, my eyes already growing heavy by the second.

He places his hand on my waist instead of my arm, being careful not to bump my bandage. Simon drags his finger along my forehead to tuck my hair behind my ear. He kisses my temple. "Good night, love."

"Good night, Simon."

And for the first time in as long as I can remember, I sleep without nightmares.

# CHAPTER 26

# *Coen*

I fucked up. Big time. And everything I do only continues to dig the hole bigger and bigger with no chance of me ever dragging myself out.

I've ruined things with June. And with her slipping further out of my grasp, I feel my humanity tumbling out the door with her.

If only there were a way to turn back time. I'd snap my fingers and be back on that street and never get in the truck with my dad. I'd demand that I stay with her. I would have put my foot down and insisted that he go on his own. He would have died either way, he didn't need me there with him. I didn't have to witness his murder. I didn't have to become a part of that world. I didn't have to lose the last remaining years of my adolescence to a life of crime.

But that's the reality of it—I was just a kid. And here I am, blaming that kid for the situation I'm in now.

I could have made the choice to find her, to come clean about why I had left. I could have made things right, and we could have picked up where we left off. But I chose to stay away. I did that, not anyone else. And I chose to keep my distance until there was no other choice.

Even when she sat down next to me with that handful of wildflowers, I knew that I would be the worst thing in her life.

And I'd be lying if I said I didn't think a part of me was purposely sabotaging this all because I've known from the start that I was never good enough for her.

If I just push her away, she'll never find out the truth about who I am and the things I've done. I wouldn't ruin her, corrupt her, or shape her into something she wouldn't recognize.

I could save her from a life of torment if I bottled it all up and kept it for myself. She wouldn't have to see the darkness if I carried it for both of us.

But no matter how hard I try, nothing I do stops the darkness from dancing closer to her.

She hates me, and I don't blame her. I'd hate me, too. For the past, for the present, and for the future I can never give her. I don't know how to be the man she deserves because I am incapable of being good.

She is everything to me, but to her, I am nothing.

June would have been better off never meeting me. Then I never would have ruined her idea of love—I never would have broken her heart, and it never would have set her on the path to finding us. Maybe she would have fallen for a nice guy, a reliable guy, someone who could love her and keep her safe. Truly safe, protected from this life of crime we will never be able to escape from.

Bryant keeps making sure Dom and I know that Simon is better for her than us, but he's just as corrupt as we are. And according to what happened last night, he's incapable of protecting her.

I can't eat. I can't sleep. I can't fucking function knowing I've fucked things up this bad. To the point that I no longer recognize the person staring back at me in the mirror.

I don't want to be this version of me, but there is not a damn thing I can do to stop him from taking complete control. My only saving grace is knowing that there is someone out there who will pay for what they have done to her. I will make it my life's mission to bring June the justice she deserves, and then I will disappear into the shadows, never to be seen or heard from again. I refuse to continue plaguing her. I can't stomach watching her lose faith in me—in *us*.

She's better off without me, and I will make sure of that once I've enacted my revenge.

I can't stand another moment of watching her slip away into the arms of a man more capable of giving her what she needs than I am. It's not even about jealousy—I've grown familiar with sharing her. It's about recognizing that I am not a suitable choice for her. And maybe *that's* why I hate Simon so much. Because he loves her in a way that I will never be able to.

The things I have done are not redeemable—I'm well aware of this. But there is one thing I can do, and that's kill the bastard responsible for hurting the only girl I've ever loved.

Even if it kills me, I will make sure it's done.


June walks down the stairs with Beckett on her heels.

He slept in her bed, and even though it's something we all would have killed him for two days ago, we don't push the issue. June said it herself last night, we're lucky she's still here. And if it takes Simon being that fucking close to her, I'll accept those terms.

She clutches her arm to her side and comes closer, putting somewhat of a distance between us and them.

Simon and June on one side, Dom, Magnus, and me on the other.

A line in the sand.

"I've slept on it," she says, her voice raspy from a heavy night's sleep. "I will stay on one condition."

"What is it, princess?" Magnus blurts out immediately, nearly chomping at the bit to do whatever it is she asks of us.

I internalize that same exact feeling without acting on it. Dom, no doubt, does the same.

"You let me help." She glances between us. "You let me help figure out who wants me dead." June chews at the inside of her lip. "It's either that, or I walk out of here and never come back."

## CHAPTER 27

# *June*

The guys agree to my terms, but demand that I take at least one day to recover from my traumatic experience. They actually pushed for a whole week, but we negotiated down to one day.

*"We need to seem unbothered by what happened,"* I had told them.

Whoever attacked Simon and I are banking on the fact that we're trembling in our boots and afraid it might happen again. And it's not that we aren't, but that isn't the front we're going to let them see.

They'll be expecting us to be rattled, to put more of a divide between us. To anyone in the organization, they're aware our entire relationship is rocky. We're hardly ever seen together. And when I'm out in public, I'm usually with Simon. That has to appear suspicious for anyone with a set of eyes and a fucking brain.

I want whoever might be watching to witness all of us, all five, getting along and acting completely fucking normal. Well, as normal as a criminal poly relationship can be. Simon isn't my boyfriend, and we still haven't *truly* crossed that line, but after almost losing him, I'm well aware he's so much more than just my bodyguard. Only time will tell what comes from it, but for now, he's part of this family whether the guys want him to be or not.

*Non-fucking-negotiable.*

"Are you going to call Bram, or do you want me to do it, princess?" Magnus leads me through the garage toward his car.

"I already did," I tell him. "He sounded worried but told me to take as much time as I needed."

"He's a good man, that Bram." Magnus opens the passenger door and glances at the man behind me. "You coming, Beckett?"

Simon hasn't left my side other than to take a shower or use the bathroom. He hasn't even gone home, but instead has been borrowing clothes and necessities

475

from Magnus. I'd venture to say there might be a friendship budding between them.

"Yep." Simon slides into the seat behind mine. "These windows reinforced?" He taps his knuckle against the glass.

"Mmhm." Magnus shuts me in and strolls over to the driver's side. "Dom and Hayes said they'd meet us there."

"This is the first time I've ever seen the office." I fidget with a thread on my jeans.

"United front, right?" Magnus pushes the button to start his car and reverses it out of the garage. Once he's done shifting, he settles his palm on my thigh.

The ride across town isn't too long, and I spend most of it just staring out the window and pondering ways this entire thing could go sideways.

What if the mole is in attendance? What if the person who wishes me dead is there? What if I say something stupid or act dumb and embarrass myself or my men? What if I don't actually have what it takes to fit into their world?

What if Winnie was right after all and I can't cut it?

Maybe I could ask her for advice on the situation? I'm sure she's handled numerous death threats in her tenure as council seat holder and wife to the prior boss of the organization.

But telling her would be giving her details that the men don't want to be shared with just anyone. And if she found out that Dominic wasn't able to handle things on his own, wouldn't that bring up questions as to whether or not he was proficient for the job?

No, we have to deal with this on our own and prove that Dominic has what it takes to run this business.

Magnus pulls us into a secured parking garage and finds a spot near the exit. "Wait here," he tells me and then hops out. Simon follows him and the two of them linger outside for about a minute then approach my door.

Simon opens it and holds out his hand. "My love."

I gratefully take it and step onto the pavement. "Is the coast clear?"

"For now, yes." Magnus shifts his gaze across the open area.

"I was just being a smart ass," I tell him.

Do they often have people trying to shoot them before they can even get inside?

"I knew that." Magnus scoffs. He keeps his eyes peeled as we walk into the space and through a keycode entry door.

His guard lowers slightly when we go inside, but he remains aware of his surroundings.

Magnus is usually the most careless of my men; he's always joking and pissing Dom off by ordering endless take-out to the house. He's the one to lighten the mood if things get tense and be the voice of reason when Dom and Coen are being hard-headed assholes. This Magnus though, is more on edge, like a switch has been flipped and he's now in work mode.

It's kind of hot.

Which isn't really something I thought could be possible. Magnus Bryant is already supermodel bad boy sexy as fuck, but this is something else entirely.

And with Simon trailing behind me and Magnus in front, I'm surrounded by seductive testosterone.

My heels click across the floor as we make our way through the building. Voices carry down the hallway until we finally reach them.

People hush their chatter and poke their heads around cubicles to catch a glance of us as we walk by. Magnus doesn't seem to acknowledge them, but I can't be too sure from this angle.

The few people I do make eye contact with quickly look away, like they might burst into flames if they stare at me too long.

I follow Magnus down another hall and spot Coen and Dom waiting for us inside a large room with massive windows. Their lips move but I can't hear a word of what they're saying.

Coen flits his attention at me and forces it back on Dom the same way the others did. At least I know why *he's* ignoring me.

I would ignore me too if I was a giant asshole.

A large conference table sits in the center of the room with various cabinets lining the walls. In the far corner is a small kitchen suite. Everything is very sterile and tidy, and if I had to guess, Dom had some say in designing the space. He's all about quality and efficiency and this is very much his brand of control freak.

The door clicks shut behind Simon, sealing the five of us in here.

"Soundproof," Magnus tells me and strolls over to pull out a chair at the head of the table. "Princess."

I take another glance around before walking over and sitting in the seat. "What do those people do out there?" I tip my head toward the cubicles of random folks.

"Mostly accounting, financial things. Investments. Business operations stuff."

"Interesting." I settle in and adjust my blazer. The thing sticks to my bandage but I manage to tug it free. I wouldn't have worn it at all but the guys thought it best that I conceal the gunshot wound as to not cause anyone any more reason to question why the heck I'm here.

Dominic claims the seat at the opposite end of mine. He unbuttons his jacket and looks in my direction. "We have a plethora of legitimate businesses if that's what you're wondering."

"I mean, it is." I glance through the large window. "I sort of just thought you killed people for a living."

"We do that, too, princess." Magnus sits to my left.

Simon takes the one to my right and Coen walks down the table to find a place near Dominic.

"Did we have to have a room with such a massive table? I feel like you guys are a lifetime away. Do I need to scream or can you hear me?" I cup my hands over my mouth but before I can say anything, Dom interrupts me.

"This is the only sound and bulletproof room with all the amenities to accommodate us." He nods toward a closed door. "There is a restroom there if you need it." He checks his watch. "We should be expecting Johnny in about a half hour."

"Johnny Jones?" I ask him.

He nods bluntly. "East coast leader. You know him?"

"Kind of, but not really. I met him a couple times with Claire, back when she lived here. She and Cora were closer than I was with her, but he was always around. Lurking from the shadows, you know. I, uh, I couldn't believe it when he died. Or when I found out he was still alive." I chuckle. "I thought my life was complicated."

Magnus chimes in, "He's a good dude."

I meet Dom's gaze. "But Dom doesn't think so?"

Magnus sighs and leans back in his chair. "Dom is impossible to please."

Dom clears his throat. "Dom is very much in the room."

I tilt my head to the side. "Oh, you don't like when people talk about you like you're not in the room?" I smirk at him.

"Point taken." He rolls his beautiful eyes.

"If you don't like Johnny, why is he coming?" I ask.

"Because they've been doing an investigation of their own to figure out who's responsible for these attacks," Dom explains.

"Have you ever considered that they're involving the east coast sector to throw you off?" I rub my chin.

"Yes," Dominic tells me. "That is a possibility."

I lean forward. "This person knows intimate details about both organizations' inner workings, right?"

Magnus plants his hands on the table and stands. "Coffee?" He shifts his focus around and then settles on Simon. "Want to help me?"

"Sure." Simon rises from his seat and the two of them go over to the kitchen suite in the corner.

"Yes," Dominic continues where we left off. "And to have that kind of classified information would be incredibly rare if not completely impossible to obtain."

"Who has that level of clearance?"

He shakes his head slowly. "That's exactly it. No one does. I don't discuss matters with the east, and they don't with me. As of last year, we were rivals."

"But you're not anymore?"

"Things have...what's the word I'm looking for...*evolved* since leadership has changed."

"And what do you think?" I stare at Coen.

It takes him a minute to realize I'm talking to him but once he does, he shrugs. "I think I'd like to kill whoever it is."

"You and me both, buddy," Magnus calls out from across the way.

"What if it's not one single person?" I suggest. "What if it's a group working together?" An idea sparks in my head. "Simon, would you have been able to pull this off?"

His brows perk up at the sound of his name. "Um, well, maybe, but I doubt I would have been able to get the east coast intel. Why?"

"Because that pretty much wipes out anyone lower level than you, right? You guys mentioned you thought the person who took me in the first place was your rival, but what if it wasn't? I mean, not in the way you think it was. What if you're thinking about this all wrong?"

Simon places a cup of coffee in front of me. "One ice cube, how you like it."

"Thanks." I smile up at him.

"And that's a solid point," he tells me before returning to Magnus.

"Because this seems a lot less about claiming the throne and more about sabotaging both sides. Is this an enemy? Someone you crossed somewhere along the line. Maybe someone who worked for both sides at one point? Johnny used to be a runner for Franklin, now he's leading the east coast. It doesn't seem completely unheard of that someone would have access to both."

Dominic runs his hand over his beard and considers my theory. "But Johnny was an errand boy. He didn't have access to the inner workings. Although…"

"What? You can't leave me hanging like that." I take a cautious sip of my coffee and wait for Dom to finish.

"Do you guys remember that big dude that used to work for Frank? What the fuck was his name?" Dom wracks his brain trying to remember.

"You're going to have to be more specific than that, boss," Magnus tells him.

"He was alley muscle over on Brantley."

"Josey," Coen announces.

Dom snaps his fingers and points to Coen. "That's right, Josey." He bobs his head up and down. "He worked for Franklin for a while until the restructuring. Now he's with Johnny."

Simon speaks up. "A lot of people switched sides once they realized they wouldn't be killed for it. You know how many people were displaced from their families but found their way back once Franklin was dead? The list is too long to track." He sets a cup of coffee in front of Dom. "Plus, Josey is Johnny's right hand. He wouldn't do that. That would be like accusing me of doing it."

Dom glares up at him. "Did you?"

Simon sighs and moves away. "Clearly."

"What about the group you *thought* was responsible? Is there anyone you can question?" I try to think of any possible angle we could take to figure this out. There has to be *something* they haven't thought of. That's why I insisted on being here—to be in the loop and to help solve this mystery.

Coen doesn't look at me when he says, "We killed everyone."

"Okay, well, there goes that lead."

"The Santorini's were always doing shady shit, but that never sat right with me," Magnus says.

"Who benefited from getting rid of them?" I ask the guys.

"Us," Dominic answers. "They were flight risks and abused our pull with the police. Countless offenses were thrown out between the lot of them. I was glad when they were gone."

"So, the organization benefited. Who else knew about what they were up to?" I continue following every thread that might lead me to answers.

"Everyone." Dominic sips his coffee and turns to Magnus. "Anything stronger in there?"

Magnus grins and reaches into a cabinet to pull out a bottle of bourbon. "I knew it was five o'clock somewhere." He grabs a handful of glasses off the top shelf and pulls the cork out of the bottle with his teeth, spitting it onto the counter. He pours some into each glass and distributes it around the table. First to Dom, then to Coen, then to me.

Simon puts his hand up. "I'm good."

"You sure?" Magnus presses.

"I'm more of a tequila guy, anyway." Simon glances at me briefly.

"They're here," Coen mutters as he stands from his seat.

A knock sounds on the door and a second later, it opens, Johnny Jones stepping through, very much alive and well. He's not exactly what I remember. He seemed more depressed back then, like the life had been sucked out of him.

His dark chocolate hair falls onto his forehead and a pair of bright green eyes flit across the room, scanning each of us. Not a second later, Claire, his wife, follows him in.

I rise to my feet and greet her halfway, both of our arms outstretched toward each other.

"J!" Claire calls out.

"Claire." I wrap her in a hug and ignore the shooting pain in my arm at the embrace.

We may not have spent a ton of time together before everything went down, but being in *this* life together makes you appreciate those friendships even more. I don't have another girl, other than Gwyneth, that I can talk to. And she isn't exactly my first, or last, pick.

Having someone my age, and who understands what it's like to be newly introduced into this world has a way of making you feel not so alone. If only Claire was on the west coast more, then maybe I wouldn't struggle with this situation as much as I do.

"You look amazing," I tell her and touch her hair. "Did you go lighter?"

She grins and nods. "Thought I'd change things up." She steadies my shoulders. "And look at you, wearing designer everything." Claire narrows her gaze at the men behind me. "I see you're taking care of my girl."

Magnus puts his arm around my waist. "Your girl, I thought she was mine." He kisses my cheek and then releases me to hug her. "Claire. How are you?"

"I'm well, Maggie." She nudges his shoulder. "Still causing trouble?"

He grins and nods. "You know it." Magnus holds his arm out to Johnny. "Mr. Jones."

Johnny and Magnus shake hands.

I feel the weighted presence of the rest of the room as we exchange our causal formalities.

Dominic clears his throat a bit too aggressively. "Shall we commence?"

Claire weaves her arm around mine and walks us over to the table. She leans in close and whispers into my ear, "We need to get together soon and catch up." She eyes Simon and winks at me before patting my hand and claiming a seat of her own next to my bodyguard.

"Do you two want coffee? Bourbon?" I glance at the kitchen area where I have no idea what other options are available.

"What are you having?" Claire rises up on her elbows to look into my two cups. "Are you having coffee *and* bourbon? My kind of girl."

Johnny strolls over and kisses the top of Claire's head. "I'll get you something, babe."

Claire grips Johnny's hand, and the two of them hold on until he's no longer within reach. Pure fucking love radiates off of them and makes me so envious of being that close to someone. I wonder what it's like not to have secrets. To love unconditionally, and fully, without restraint.

They've been through so much together and it's like nothing can tear them apart. The issues that arise only seem to bring them closer together, forging an unbreakable bond.

"I'll show you around," Magnus tells Johnny on their way over to get drinks.

"Hey, sorry I'm late." Miller walks into the room carrying a large paper bag with a logo that can only be from one place. "But I come with donuts."

At least I'm not the only one who loves Bram's Diner. My heart aches a little at knowing I won't be back there until things settle down, but I'm grateful he's holding my place for me. I don't need to work, and the guys would rather I didn't, but I love being at the diner. I'm not exactly a people person, that much is certain, but there's just something about Bram's that feels like home. He was the first person to be kind to me without expecting a damn thing in return, and for that, I will forever be indebted to him.

"I hear you're running a café back east?" I say to Claire.

She smiles and nods. "Yep. Coffee isn't quite as good as Bram's but I'm working on it." Claire takes the cup that Johnny gives her. "It's like he makes it with love or something."

Johnny slides into the seat next to her and opens up the bag that Miller brought in. "Thanks, buddy."

I sit at the head of the table, glancing around the room, and wonder if this is what it's like to have friends. Like a group of people who know things about you that you cannot share elsewhere. A forbidden secret that we keep because sharing it would only put us all in danger. It's not that *no one* knows the truth about these men and their criminal doings, but it's not exactly common knowledge.

I bite the inside of my lip as I watch Miller pass around donuts. I lied to Cora and told her that Miller was off-limits. But what if she could be here too, experiencing a level of comradery that is unmatched? Is it fair of me to keep this from her when knowing the truth might be what brings us even closer and gives her a chance at love?

But what if Miller tore her apart? What if she had more issues with him than I've had with my guys? What if he has enemies? What if she faces similar shit like I have and isn't strong enough to escape it the way I did? But who am I to question whether Cora is capable enough or not? Is it my place to put limitations on her life when she's the one who wants to take those risks?

Claire did it and made it through hell to be with the man she loves.

And here I am, living proof that it's possible to overcome this dark and dangerous world.

But with my life still on the line, perhaps I shouldn't speak so soon on whether I have what it takes or not.

"Claire is an incredible detective." Johnny reaches out to brush the hair from her cheek. "She's helped me solve more mysteries than I can count. If anyone can figure out who's responsible for what's going on, it's her."

Miller settles into a seat between Magnus and Coen and bites into a donut. The crumbs spill over onto the napkin in his grasp. He seems so...not what you would expect from someone with so much knowledge of this industry. He's not jacked or tattooed like Magnus. Or big and scary like Dom. Simon exudes *I'm here to fuck shit* up energy. Even Coen has this murderous stare to his surfer boy exterior. And Johnny, well, he's got a bad boy vibe about him for sure. He's softer than shit for Claire but he rules an entire criminal faction. And then there's Miller. He's good-looking, that's for sure, but lacks that psychopathic aura that the rest of the guys have. He appears too young to know everything he does, too. Still, I wouldn't cross him, because the ones that look like *that* are usually the worst of all.

Miller is a pandora's box full of secrets waiting to be spilled.

And if I'm even going to consider letting him anywhere near my best friend, I have to do some digging first.

But, that's for another day. Maybe one day I can pick Claire's brain and see what she thinks about the mysterious man that is her husband's advisor.

Today, we have a bigger problem to solve.

"You haven't been able to successfully apprehend any of the hired hands?" Claire brings the mug to her lips and sips her coffee. She glances at Johnny and whispers, "Mmm, cinnamon."

He winks at her as Dom speaks up.

"No, but it's my understanding you haven't either."

"No, we haven't. We came close, but one man actually bit off his own tongue, swallowed it, and choked to death before we could interrogate him."

I shudder at the thought of being that fucking desperate to end my own life. Was it because the person thought the torture methods would be too extreme, or that the ramification of speaking would be too great?

Either way, such drastic measures bring awareness to the magnitude of the situation. If that person was willing to die instead of speak, we're dealing with someone heavily influential here.

"You've been around longer than anyone else on the east coast," I say to Miller.

"And the notes said you took something. Do you have any idea what that might be?"

"Luciano was a ruthless, but fair man. He didn't leave much to chance. If he had an enemy, he either eliminated them or turned them to his side." Miller pats his mouth with his napkin and looks at Johnny briefly. "Franklin, on the other hand, made enemies out of friends any chance he got. He ruled cruelly and maliciously. His list of enemies spans every coast and continent."

"Whoever it was wants to destroy both sides and take me down with it."

"Who's to say *you* don't have enemies?" Miller suggests.

I laugh. "Because I'm a nobody. The only thing I'm guilty of is being a bitch."

Simon pushes a donut toward me. "This has nothing to do with her."

"I wouldn't be so sure," Claire points out. "One thing is certain. They go after you when they think you're alone, or at least, unsuspecting."

I nudge the donut out of the way but Simon pushes it right back. I lean on my elbows. "I'm listening," I tell her.

"*Eat,*" Simon whispers.

I break off a piece of it and shove it in my mouth. "*Happy?*"

He grins and nods.

"What if..." Claire glances around the room at my men. "And hear me out before you shut me down. What if we use June as bait?"

"Absolutely not," Dominic is the first to speak.

"Not happening," Coen follows him up.

Magnus and Simon exchange a look like they're speaking telepathically.

Johnny reaches for Claire's hand. "I don't know..."

"I'm in," I announce.

"No." Dominic stares right at me.

"This isn't your decision to make." I stare right fucking back. After everything he has put me through, there's no way I'm going to let him call the shots. This is my life on the line, not his.

"You're injured," Coen tells the room.

*Fucking bastard.*

"I'm fine." I move my left arm and circle it around. "See?" But does he notice the tense of my jaw or the way I can't exactly get a full extension without the pain piercing through me?

Probably not, he's pretty fucking oblivious lately.

Simon on the other hand, he sees everything. Even the things I don't want him to. And the things I don't even know myself.

"Only if we can take certain measures," Simon suggests.

Because of course, he would be the one to actually think I was capable of pulling this off.

"Absolutely," Claire confirms. "I would be with her the whole time. I've dealt with my fair share of hostage situations. I know what to look out for."

"Claire..." Johnny sits up in his seat to force Claire's attention. "This is crazy."

She smiles softly and cups his cheek. "We've done crazier."

"I don't like this," Magnus finally chimes in. "But this might be stupid enough to work."

Now that I know a threat is imminent, I'll be able to actually prepare for it. A privilege I haven't been fortunate to have since the guys have insisted on keeping me in the dark. Maybe if I knew the magnitude of what was going on, I would have kept that bastard alive instead of killing him. *Bronco.* What a stupid fucking name.

"Wait," I blurt out, a memory floating in. "I remember another name from the other day." I dig through the pieces of that dreadful night to uncover what it was. "Harold." I blink up at the group gawking at me. "One of the men's names was Harold. And the other guy, Bronco."

"I have Savini working to see what he can find. I'll give him that name, too," Dominic says. He tilts his watch face up toward him. "Speaking of, I have a meeting soon."

Of course, he would. When we're finally all together, he would leave. Makes total fucking sense. How can we show a united front when he isn't even present?

"I won't be long, though." Dominic meets my gaze. "I'll only miss appetizers."

My heart flutters. Is this his way of finding some common ground between us? A compromise of sorts? It's not much, and he's going to have to dig a hell of a lot deeper, but for now, it works.

"So, it's settled?" Claire fills the awkward silence.

"Yes," I answer before anyone else can.

"Okay." Claire leans forward and props her elbows on the table. "We'll need to pick a place where they'll think you're vulnerable. Where the security is lax, and the chance of someone gaining access to you is great. Crowded, so it would be easily overlooked, but not so much that they couldn't take you if they make a move."

"I know the perfect place." I take a deep breath and prepare myself for the possibility that this all might be over soon enough.

Maybe then I will get my happily ever after.

But knowing how things go down in this world, the chance of one of us making it out alive isn't great.

# Simon

I hate all of this.

The only fucking silver lining is that I get to be near her. Which isn't much different than any other day, but now, things are different. She's more relaxed with me. Less on guard. We haven't done anything more than a little innocent cuddling. My morning wood pressing into her wasn't exactly innocent but aside from that, things have been very PG. Luckily, I woke before her and was able to get it under control before she realized my dick was pressing into her leg.

Between her small, warm body fitted perfectly against mine, and finally having her in my arms, how was I supposed to resist the desire pooling in my groin?

Still, being with her isn't primarily focused on wanting to have sex with her. No, just being near. Feeling her breath on my skin, basking in the scent of her, and knowing that maybe, just maybe, she might eventually want me the way I need her.

"You look radiant, love." I watch her in awe as she spins in a circle and walks toward me.

"Think so?" She stops in front of the full-length mirror in her room. "It's not too much?"

The black dress hugs her in all the right places, leaving almost nothing to the imagination, but it's enough to give her exactly what she needs. Protection, concealment, and a look that no one will question her intentions. She's dressed to kill—quite literally.

The plan is to blend in. But I'm not sure June could do that if she tried.

"Not enough, maybe." I chuckle and close the space between us. I reach into my pocket and pull out a long, thin box. "I got you something." I open the box and turn it toward her.

Her eyes widen and her mouth falls open. She glances from the necklace to me. "Simon, it's beautiful. You didn't have to—"

"Hush, love." I pluck the necklace out of its plush home. "Turn around." I drape it around her neck as she holds her hair for me. I clasp it in place, my fingers brushing her skin in the process. I settle my hands on her bare shoulders and pivot her toward the mirror. "What do you think?"

June grazes the dainty rose gold chain that rests just below her collarbone. Sitting right in the middle is a teardrop emerald with a quarter-carat diamond atop the green stone. It's simple, understated, but alluring and radiant.

"It's perfect, Simon. Thank you." She meets my gaze in the mirror.

I fix her hair behind her and kiss her shoulder. "As are you, my love."

Claire appears in the doorway, looking ready to break hearts, too. "June, holy shit." She walks into the room. "You clean up well."

The two of them exchange a hug, and not for one second would anyone think they're about to dangle themselves as bait for a criminal. Hell, if I didn't know better, I would assume they're just going out for girls' night.

Even Cora is tagging along to sell the whole thing.

She's not aware of what's going on, because everyone decided that was for the best. Not only would she potentially risk exposing the plan, but then it would open up room for a conversation that would be far longer than our window of opportunity.

We want to strike while things are so fresh, and that means doing it now.

## CHAPTER 29

# *June*

Cora literally squeals when she sees that Claire is in the limo with me.

"Shut the fuck up! I didn't know you were in town." Cora wraps her arms around Claire immediately and hugs her tightly.

"Surprise!" I give her a squeeze, too.

Do I want to put my best friend in danger? Absolutely not. But the fact that all of this time has gone by and she *hasn't* been compromised tells me that whoever is doing this shit doesn't care to involve her. It was a risk I was willing to take in an attempt to make this whole night that much more believable.

We do girls' nights often. And it's no secret that the three of us are friends. Going out is something that is totally within the range of our usual norm. And the fact that Claire is in town makes the perfect excuse to get together.

A week ago, I wouldn't have even questioned this setup.

Why would anyone else?

And because Simon has been with me non-stop for over six months, that doesn't change tonight. He will remain nearby, along with Johnny. Not a thing about that is potentially alarming for anyone who might be watching. The rest of the men are in position; lurking from their respective corners in wait for whatever might happen.

Half of us might hate this plan, but we've never been more unified than we are tonight. And maybe that will finally be the upper hand we need to take down this bastard once and for all.

Cora and Claire make small talk on the way across town. Johnny joins in here and there when he can get a word in.

I tune out most of their conversation and lean into the strong man beside me, hooking my pinkie around his and enjoying this simple but intimate grip we have on each other.

487

Simon throws his arm over my shoulder and tugs me toward him, replacing his pinkie with his other hand, fully enveloping my palm with his. It's moments like this when I feel capable of overcoming anything this stupid world throws at me.

The limo comes to a stop in the Haven District in front of Cora's favorite place.

The door opens a moment later, and Alec greets us on the other side.

Simon steps out first, assessing the vicinity, and then reaches for me.

I allow him to help me out and adjust my dress once I'm on the sidewalk.

"Are you sure I look okay?" Cora follows me and glances down at her outfit.

She's wearing a sheer black long-sleeve shirt that hangs off the shoulders, exposing a black push-up bra underneath it. Her black satin bottoms hug her curves tightly, and the heels she's wearing only makes her legs appear longer and her ass bigger. Her golden hair falls in loose waves on her shoulders.

Alec clears his throat. "You're, uh, beautiful." He avoids eye contact like he might be reprimanded for speaking to her.

"Thanks, Alec." She grins and her cheeks flush red.

Simon leans in close to Alec and whispers something into his ear.

Alec nods sharply and waits for the rest of our party to exit the limo before shutting the door. He and Cora exchange a bashful glance.

Once he's out of sight, she tells me, "He's so cute."

I elbow her and smile. "You're out of his league, sweetheart."

"Oh whatever, I don't believe in leagues." She weaves her arm around mine, and I ignore the ache that still radiates from the healing gunshot wound that's covered up by a flesh color bandage our fancy in-home doctor brought over.

It blends in so well that Cora doesn't even notice it.

The club buzzes with energy and loud music as we approach.

My heels click against the pavement, a pace matching that of my heart. Steady. Calculated. Prepared. Whatever this night brings, we will handle it together.

Completely bypassing the long fucking line outside the place, Johnny walks us straight to the doorman. The massive guy takes one look at us and opens the door, leaving an opening for Claire to step into the booming place.

We follow her in and are immediately greeted by a young kid with a clipboard. "Right this way," he tells us.

Simon nods his approval and places his hand on the small of my back to guide me. His touch travels a bit, resting just along my hip. It's electric and inviting and completely fucking distracting.

The worker leads us to a roped-off area. He lifts the thing to let us through and then secures it behind us.

"Shut up," Cora says. "I've never been in VIP." She spins in a circle in the open space and plops down onto the plush couch.

This girl has no idea what kind of things she's missing. If only her best friend would bite the bullet and tell her the truth about what her men do for a living, then maybe Cora could get a taste of this life, too.

"If you need anything else, don't hesitate," the worker tells Simon.

"Look at all these bottles." Cora rummages through the vast selection on the table in the center of our little area. "Who's paying for this?"

Simon rubs his neck. "I'm uh, part owner."

"Of this entire fucking place?" She throws her arms up dramatically.

"I didn't know that," I whisper to him. There are so many things about each of my men that I'm unaware of. Like the fact that Dominic owns multiple homes across the country and one internationally. He has a private freaking jet, too. What kind of secrets are Coen and Magnus hiding?

"Yeah, it's not a big deal," Simon tells Cora. "Drink up."

Cora grabs the bottle of tequila and yanks out the cork. She pours five shots and hands one to each of us. "A toast."

Claire smiles at her. "What are we toasting, Cor?"

"To friends." Cora holds hers up in the air. "The best of friends."

"To friends," we collectively say and then down the warm liquid.

The heat spreads down my chest and into my belly. I settle into the spot next to her as she fills her cup back up. "You getting shit-faced on me tonight?"

"So are you! It's the only way I can get you to dance with me." Cora refills my shot glass.

"You know I'm not a tequila girl." I take it, because I don't want to draw any unwanted attention, and down the contents.

Cora pours more into Claire's empty glass, too. "I'm seriously so happy you're both here. That we're here. I needed this. More than you know."

My heart tugs at the fact that I haven't been as good of a friend as Cora has deserved lately. I've been so focused on everything going on in my life that I haven't been paying attention to hers. Just because someone wants me dead doesn't mean her problems are any less important than mine.

"What's been going on, Cor?" I ask her and swallow down the guilt of being a shitty friend.

She sighs. "It's fine. Everything is fine."

But that couldn't be further from the truth.

I guess me and my men aren't the only ones with secrets.

"Talk to me, Cora bora." Claire drinks her shot and sets the glass on the table.

Simon and Johnny sit on the opposite end of our roped-off section and have a conversation of their own. But from the music blaring in this place, not a blip of what they're saying carries over to us.

Simon winks and my pulse picks up speed. I force myself to look away and focus on my best friend.

"Just the usual. Work. Life. Boys. Family. You know." Cora shrugs and paints a smile on her beautiful face. "But tonight is about forgetting our worries, right?" She pours herself another drink and tips it back.

Her eyes light up and I follow her attention to spot Alec walking toward us. Cora grips my arm and reaches for Claire. "Would you kill me if I asked him to dance? Oh my god, I'm going to do it." Cora rises to her feet and adjusts her boobs. "I'm going in."

And before either of us can stop her, Cora walks with confidence right over to him, their bodies separated by the rope between them. They exchange a few words and apparently, she convinces him because he unhooks the barrier and lets her out.

Alec glances over his shoulder at Simon and Simon gives him a thumbs up.

Simon turns toward me and mouths, "It's okay."

I draw in a breath and sigh. "I hate keeping her in the dark."

"Me, too." Claire leans back into the couch, throws her arm over the back, and turns toward me. "I haven't been around enough to have the conversation with her though. You know? And there are so many unpredictable variables. It could be the best or worst thing for her."

"That's my thought, too. I feel selfish not telling her, but I'd be selfish *for* telling her. It sucks not having someone to talk to. She's my best friend, and she's completely in the dark. Part of me wants to keep her there, to protect her."

"Yeah," Claire says. "It's not always the best choice though." She faces me more. "I told my best friend, Rosie."

My eyes widen. "No shit? How did that go?"

"Well." Claire exhales. "I was forced to, really. She got caught in the war, almost died. I didn't have a choice at that point. We went through a rocky period, but I think it brought us closer."

"Wow, I had no idea."

Claire grabs one of the bottles of water off the table and twists the cap off and takes a sip, returning to her position toward me. "We've all held our fair share of secrets in an attempt to protect those we love."

"Even you and Johnny?"

Claire laughs. "*Especially* me and Johnny." She shakes her head and smiles. "The shit we kept from each other was unreal. And there's still times when I have to shake information out of him. A relationship like ours isn't without its complications."

*Complications.* Is that what my guys and I are going through? Just a natural rough patch that is exasperated by being with multiple men who are also running a massive criminal syndicate?

I've honestly never been in a relationship before. So even if this was normal, I wouldn't know. It doesn't *feel* like shit everyone else goes through. But who am I to make assumptions like that?

"I had no idea," I tell her. "I thought you guys were solid."

"Oh, we are. There isn't a damn thing that could get between us. But that doesn't mean we haven't gone through hell to get here. We both kept secrets, some much darker and more dangerous than others. Some I had no idea how we would ever overcome." Claire chews at her lip. "But there comes a point where you have to make a decision. You have to decide if bearing it all is worth risking everything in hopes of making it work. Love is more powerful than you think, J. And if there's enough of it, there isn't anything you can't conquer."

Claire glances over her shoulder at Johnny for a moment.

I consider her words, letting the weight of them sink in.

There is no lack of love when it comes to how I feel about my men, but what if I'm the only one pouring my heart into us? I can't do it on my own. Not when they push me away every chance they get, only to pull me close when I'm one foot out the door. They hook me back in just enough to keep me on the line, letting me drift away until it's time to do it again. We can't maintain a relationship like that. And I can't deal with the mental mind-fuckery it brings.

Simon is right—this situation has been impacting me in more ways than I let on. I have lost weight. I have been more anxious and depressed than usual. I have resorted to harming myself when I need to feel *something*. And I've only felt relatively at peace when I've been inflicting pain on someone else. There's a darkness that's settled over me, and I underestimated just how intense it was.

"Did Johnny ever doubt you?" I ask her. "Like question whether you had what it takes to be in *this* world."

Claire nods. "Yep. Pissed me off, too. Especially when I proved myself more times than not."

"Exactly." I reach out and grab her forearm. "They do the same shit to me."

"Oh, and I'm sure it's even worse coming from four of them."

I pull my arm away and tuck my hair behind my ear. "Three, more so. Simon and I aren't together."

"Could have fooled me. The guy is in love with you."

My heart thuds wildly in my chest. "That obvious?"

"Pretty sure he's trying to stare a hole through my head to get a look at you right now." Claire chuckles and sets her bottle of water on the table, exposing Simon, who is doing exactly what she had said.

I reach up and graze my fingers along the necklace, skimming them over the scar on my chest, the one that matches the entry wound in my back from the night I was shot trying to kill Simon.

His men were only doing what they thought was right, but Coen and Simon made sure not a single person responsible for that near-death experience lived another day. I didn't learn about Coen's rampage until after I had come out of surgery, and it was a few months before I heard Simon had eliminated the guy who actually pulled the trigger.

He had fled that night, sneaking out a back door when the commotion erupted in the council mansion. That man never should have had a gun to begin with, but he did. And when he saw me about to drive the dagger into Simon's chest, he shot me in the back.

Luckily for me, his aim wasn't the best. Had he been a hair farther to the left, he would have hit my lung straight through. He still nicked it, causing me to nearly bleed out, but the surgeon was able to repair the damage and patch me up before I could drown in my own blood.

"Hey," I say to Claire. "Have you ever met the council wives?"

Claire rolls her eyes. "Stuck up bitches with too much money and ego if you ask me."

"It's like you're reading my mind."

"I'm so glad that's just a west coast thing. Why they give power to those women, I will never know."

I always thought it was a rather strange set-up they had. To give the wives the power to make massive decisions for the organization the way they do. Some of them don't even have the knowledge of the inner workings more than just surface level. It seemed flawed, but who was I to raise those concerns when I barely knew anything myself?

Claire hasn't been in the life much longer than I have, but given her intimate relationship with the head of the east coast, she's knowledgeable enough to have that kind of opinion.

"Supposedly," Claire continues. "Franklin's wife was the one who stuck her neck out for Johnny back in the day. But something always felt off about her. About her motives, you know?"

"I'm so sorry for what he did to you guys." I shake my head. "I've heard stories, and I don't know how much is true, but the shit he put you through. It's terrible."

Claire repositions herself. "Franklin was a sick man. The world is a better place without him."

"June!" Someone calls out from across the way.

I scan the crowd to find the culprit and latch my sights on the beautiful blonde we came with. Cora raises her arms and waves aggressively at us and then motions for us to join her.

"We have been summoned," Claire says while looking at our shared friend.

"You ready for this?" I ask her, rising to my feet.

She stands and adjusts her tightly fitted black bodysuit. "Born for it, baby."

I pour tequila into a few of the glasses and top them with a splash of orange juice before digging through the rest of our selection to find something more my taste.

Simon walks over and plucks a bottle of Hawk's Mark from under the table. "Is this what you're looking for, love?"

Johnny comes over and wraps his arms around Claire's waist and kisses her cheek from behind. "I love you," he whispers, but loud enough for me to hear.

Her lips meet his and I steady my attention on the man in front of me.

"Yes. How did you know?" I stand and come face to face with him.

"Because I know you." Simon pulls the top off and pours some of the golden liquid into my empty cup, his seductive stare making my heart pound harder.

"Do you want something?" I pause and then add, "To drink."

He winks and shakes his head. "I'm good, love."

I give Claire one of the tequila's and offer another to Johnny. I take the last one for Cora and pinch it between my fingers with my drink, leaving my other hand free to latch onto Simon.

We walk as a group out of the roped-off area and into the throng of people crowding this place. I've been in here countless times and never had any inclination that Simon owned part of it. I just assumed everyone treated him the way they do because of who he is. There isn't a place in this town where any of these men can go without them getting special attention.

Simon's hand weaves its way along mine as I lead us toward where Cora and Alec are standing along the edge of the dance floor.

She beams as we approach and gratefully takes the cup that I give her, a sheen covering her glowing face. Cora sips some of it and offers it to Alec. He flits his attention at Simon, who gives him a curt nod. Does he have to approve his every move with Simon before acting?

Alec hadn't been part of the plan, but I'm glad he's here to keep an eye on Cora. With Johnny focused on Claire, and Simon on me, it's nice to have Alec here looking out for her.

With just one glass in my grasp, I sip the decadent bourbon.

"Come on!" Cora yells over the blaring music. She takes Alec's hand and drags him through the crowd.

The rest of us follow her to a spot near the middle of the dance floor. The lights flicker and turn a shade of dark blue. I turn toward Simon, his body close to mine.

"Are you going to dance with me?" I shout at him.

"Do you want me to?" Simon raises a brow.

I take another drink of my bourbon and nod.

He grins and his strong grip finds my waist, tugging me close and swaying me to the beat.

It doesn't take us long to find our rhythm, dancing like our bodies were made for each other. I turn in his grasp, my backside pressing against his front. I weave my hand up and around his neck, holding him close to me. His hips move with mine, his cock only separated by the clothing that we're both wearing.

His hands glide over my body, exploring cautiously.

We stay that way for a short infinity. Cora and Alec dance a few feet from us; Cora's arms draped over Alec's neck, his hands holding onto her waist. I spin, catching a glimpse of Johnny and Claire, who are moving to the beat, too. Their mouths locked on each other's, a fiery passion between them unlike any other couple in this place. Their love is powerful enough to set this whole place ablaze.

I face Simon again and look up at him.

"What's wrong, love?" he asks me, concern lining his brow.

I stare into his emerald eyes. "I don't want to regret anything."

Simon skims his knuckles along my cheek. "What could you possibly regret?"

"Not saying yes." I swallow and flit my attention to his lips for a brief second.

"Yes to what?"

"You."

For a moment, the whole place quiets down, the sound muffles and fades into the background. Everyone is gone, except for us. Just me and this beautiful man who has done everything for me since the moment I met him. The one who declared that I would be his before I even knew his name. The one that vowed to wait forever. And that gave up everything on the off chance that it could bring me back to life. The guy everyone views as an arrogant fuck-boy happens to be one of the kindest and most considerate men I've ever come across. He puts my needs above his, and he's been there for me when no one else was.

"What do you want, love?" Simon keeps moving our bodies together to the distant beat.

"You." I stand taller. "I want you." And right now, with the whole world watching, I refuse to miss this opportunity to finally take that step.

"Love..." Simon hesitates.

"We might not get another chance, Simon." I hover my face closer.

He rests his forehead against mine. "I don't want that to be the reason you kiss me."

I graze my nose along his. "You know that's not why." With my hands draped around his neck, my grip barely hanging onto the glass of bourbon, I step closer to him. "Kiss me, Simon."

And because he never fails at giving me what I want, he presses his lips to mine, melting them softly at first, but then picking up his pace. He tilts his head to the side and parts my lips with his tongue. He keeps one hand on my waist and the other gripping the base of my skull, angling me up toward him. He moans into my mouth, and I swear to God if we weren't in the middle of this fucking dance floor, I would rip my clothes off to get as close to him as humanly possible.

He snakes his knee between my legs and continues to move us to the beat with his mouth not daring to leave mine. He deepens the kiss and tightens his grip on my side. I grind on his thigh and my core binds at the pressure of him on me.

Simon presses on the small of my back, applying more pressure between my aching center and his leg. He swirls his tongue along mine and bites at my bottom lip. "Love," he breathes into me. "You're sweeter than I imagined." He kisses me again, but this time it's soft and gentle and nothing like the inferno only moments ago. But despite it not being as forceful, it's intense in its own way. And when he rocks me on him just fucking right, I orgasm right here in the chaos of this nightclub. His mouth bears the brunt of the moan that leaves me. He trails a few soft kisses on my lips and then my nose, and grins triumphantly.

I breathlessly pant and pretend I didn't just grind against his leg so hard I climaxed in public. My cheeks flush at the thought that either of my friends just witnessed me pleasuring myself on Simon's damn thigh.

"No one noticed, love." Simon drags the hair from my cheek and tucks it behind my ear, leaning in to whisper, "But if a show is what you want...we can give them one."

"Simon!" I playfully smack him and adjust my dress before standing all the way up. My legs buckle slightly but I regain my composure.

*That* was definitely not part of the plan.

And honestly, it's not something that I should continue to think about because all it's going to do is distract me from what we're trying to accomplish here.

It was exhilarating, but it was forbidden and off-limits. I crossed a line that I cannot take back, and there will be consequences for my actions. Not just with me and Simon, but with my men, too. They've made it clear how they feel about him, and I went ahead and took what I wanted anyway. We never exactly discussed the exclusivity of our open relationship, not in great detail, but Simon has always been their enemy.

That will be a conversation for another day. One where my life isn't hanging so much in the balance, and when I've thought about how I want to handle the things they've put me through these last few months. I may be working with them on this, but that doesn't mean I have forgiven or forgotten how badly what they've done has damaged us.

I glance at Claire and tip my head toward a suspicious-looking dude. "I think we have a bite," I tell Simon.

His jaw tenses and the carefree nature that was once on him is no longer there. "You remember what I taught you, right?"

I nod and stare into his mesmerizing green eyes. "I've got this." I release my hold on him and down the rest of the bourbon, leaving my glass with him and latching onto Claire's hand and tugging her away before Cora can realize we're leaving.

Simon keeps his gaze pinned on mine until the crowd swallows him up.

"Think this is our guy?" Claire leans over and asks me, glancing behind us briefly.

The man I spotted trails us, only a few feet in our wake.

We turn down the hall toward the bathroom and lead him along the dim corridor.

He picks up his pace, my skin crawling at his nearness. The mystery man reaches into his suit jacket and I prepare myself for the familiar fabric that will be pressed over my face and rendering me unconscious.

I look over at him when he gets beside me and tell him, "Just don't smudge my makeup."

"What?" He cranes his head as he passes. "Were you talking to me?" He pulls his phone out of his pocket and doesn't wait for me to respond as he slips into the men's restroom.

"Wow." I laugh and grip Claire's arm. "I was fucking wrong on that one."

Claire shrugs. "Can't help it, all men look creepy." She points to the women's door. "I'm going to pee while we're back here. You coming?"

"You think I'm going to leave you alone?" I follow her into the bathroom where there surprisingly isn't a wait.

Claire goes straight into a stall, and I make my way to the full-length mirror.

I'm fixing my dress when another girl walks into the bathroom. I flinch at her arrival but soften my resolve when I see her walk over to a sink near me.

"June?" she says to me.

The noise from the club flows in here and makes me do a double-take. I turn toward her and nod, stepping a bit closer. "Yeah?"

"Listen," she bridges the gap and lowers her voice. "Some guy paid me a grand to come in here and tell you that if you don't walk out of here and turn right down the hall, he'll put a bullet in that pretty blonde friend of yours."

*Cora.*

"Wh-what?" I blurt out and shift my gaze at the stall Claire had gone into.

"He said if you don't come alone, he'll kill all your friends, starting with her."

And because there's not a damn chance in hell I'm going to risk Cora's life, I do exactly what this girl says and slip out before Claire is none the wiser.

# CHAPTER 30

# Coen

"What the fuck do you mean *you lost her*?" I shove Bryant. "You were in charge of lookout." I furiously point at Dominic. "The fuck were you doing when she was taken?" I don't even look at Beckett because if I do, I will fucking murder him just for putting his grimy fucking hands on her.

"Explain to me again what happened?" Johnny steadies Claire's shoulders.

Claire shakes him off. "She thought it was that guy. It wasn't. So we went into the bathroom. I went into a stall and when I came out, she was gone. There was someone in the stall next to me but she came out after me. I checked under every one before I rushed out here to find you guys."

"I have my team pulling surveillance as we speak." Dominic latches onto Bryant's shoulder. "You come with me."

Beckett opens his mouth to speak but Dom cuts him off.

"You two, canvas the place again." He points to me and Beckett. "You two, find something fucking useful to do instead of killing each other."

They all leave me and Beckett behind in this alley. My desire to follow through with what Dom had said stronger than ever.

Beckett takes off in the opposite direction.

"Where the fuck do you think you're going?" I call after him.

"To get our girl back." He doesn't stop walking, just continues stomping down the damp alley.

I rush to catch up to him, grabbing him by the arm and stopping him. "What the fuck does that mean?"

He turns toward me slowly. "If you touch me again, I will put a fucking bullet in your head. If you try to make me waste another second of her being out there, afraid and alone, I will—"

"Yeah, I fucking get it. Big bad Simon Beckett." I throw my hands up. "What's the plan, Sherlock?"

Beckett taps at his chest. "The necklace she's wearing. It has a tracking device."

"Why didn't I know about this?" I say as I slap his arm and move in the direction he was headed.

"Because it didn't concern you. It was *my* insurance because I didn't trust this fucking plan you guys came up with." Beckett glances both ways before turning left and crossing into another. He reaches into his pocket and pulls out a key fob. He pushes a button, and in the distance, lights flicker along the brick building. "If you're coming with me, you better fucking hurry up." Beckett takes off in a sprint toward the car.

I chase after him, desperate for whatever lead he possibly has and grateful that he was prepared enough to think of something we hadn't.

Just another one of the ways I have failed her and he has come out on top.

It's hard to even be mad at the relationship forming between them. If anything, I'm mad at myself, not him.

Beckett yanks the passenger door open and reaches into the glovebox of his car. He pulls out a cell phone and pushes a sequence of buttons, the thing lights up and something blinks on the screen.

"Is that her?" I crane to look over his shoulder.

"Yeah." He clutches it to his chest in relief, and glances at it again. "She's going south on Fifth."

"Are you driving, or am I?"

He shoves the device toward me. "I am. You can give directions." He pauses before releasing it. "Don't make me fucking regret this, Hayes."

"We both want the same thing." I pry the device from his grip. "To end this."

I don't just mean this threat to her life. I mean the plague that I cause her. But I can't rid myself from her world until I know for sure that she is safe. Until then, I will do everything in my power to overcome this obstacle in the way of her and her happiness. And then I will step out of the way and give her a fighting chance to get exactly that.

There's no way I can atone for my sins, and the best thing I can do for her is leave.

I would only be doing her a great disservice if I continued to stick around.

I see the disgust on her face when she looks at me. Or when she won't meet my gaze. She hates me, and I don't blame her. I never will. Not for everything I have put her through. All those years ago and still to this day. Her biggest mistake was sitting down next to me that day in the cemetery. Each bit of light she breathed into me was only sucked out of her. I have leeched on her long enough, and I refuse to be a drain on her anymore.

Beckett skids the tires of his Volvo as he darts out onto the main street and shoots us into traffic. He speeds across town, dodging cars and going left of center to take the quickest route possible. He blares his horn when we get stuck behind two vehicles and ends up driving on the sidewalk to bypass them.

"West on Beachwood," I tell him as I watch the flashing red dot on the screen with every ounce of my concentration. "What the fuck is over in that direction?"

"Warehouse, maybe? That's where they had us last time." Beckett presses on the throttle and speeds through a red light, a semi honking at us and nearly clipping our ass end.

"They're on Casa Bella now." I stare at the glowing red and wait for it to move.

"Come on you fucking cock sucker!" Beckett yells at a car and darts around it. "Fucking bastard." He clips a parked SUV but keeps going, not a care in the world about the traffic violations.

"Still on Casa, slow-moving north." Where in the fuck are they headed? I try to think of any places up there where we would take a prisoner, drawing a blank every time. We don't venture that far into residential areas. We tend to keep things within the outskirts of the city where no one can hear the screams or power tools as we torture people into telling us what we want to hear.

"Wait," Beckett says but doesn't continue his train of thought. Instead, he pushes harder on the gas and stares directly ahead, gripping the steering wheel. "I know where they're going."

He flits his attention toward me and it's like he's seen a fucking ghost.

"Where are they going, Beckett?" My heart thuds at the anticipation.

"Get ahold of Dom, *right now*, and tell him to get to Castleberry Court."

"No," I say, my voice barely a whisper.

"Where the fuck else, Hayes?" He darts us down a side street and lurches us onto the main road. The car's suspension buckles beneath us and tries to take the brunt of his wrath. "Contact anyone you trust within a ten-mile radius and have them get there immediately."

But what if I *don't* trust anyone? What if the only person I actually believe prioritizes her safety is sitting in this vehicle with me?

I thumb a quick group text to Dom, Bryant, and Johnny.

**Me: Castleberry Court. NOW!**

"It makes perfect sense," Beckett says. "This whole fucking time."

How could we have been so fucking stupid?

"Can't you drive any faster?" I grip the device in my grasp, no longer needing to look at it now that we know where she's heading. My sweet fucking angel about to be destroyed by this dark and dangerous world I could not protect her from.

"It's not for lack of effort." Beckett makes a beeline through a set of slowing cars and blasts through the intersection they were stopping at. Horns honk, tires skid, and vehicles crash into each other to avoid us.

Sirens sound and it's only a moment later when they appear behind us.

"Keep fucking going, do not stop," I tell Beckett and reach into my pocket to pull out my phone. I press one of the numbers in my contact list.

"Officer Bradshaw," the man answers.

"The guy tailing a Volvo, call him off."

Bradshaw sighs. "You're killing me, Hayes."

"Trust me, I will if you don't call him off. You and every fucking person you love."

"You can't just threaten a cop, Hayes."

"I did, and I will again." I clench my jaw, the next words out of my mouth something I'm not proud of. "How old is that daughter of yours? Sixteen? Sure would be a shame if..."

"Alright," he cuts me off. "I understand. Consider it done."

I hang up the line and wait for him to do the damn job he's paid for.

"That was a low blow, even for you, Hayes." Beckett side-eyes me.

I wouldn't have actually followed through with the threat, but neither Bradshaw nor Beckett need to know that.

"Desperate times..." I focus on the route ahead of us. "How are we going to get into the place, it's a fucking fortress?"

"I could crash the car through the front gate."

"You're not serious." I glare at him.

"Deadly." He steers us around another car and slams on the brakes to avoid hitting another, then speeds right past them.

"What kind of firepower do you have in here?" I open the glovebox but come up empty-handed.

"Under the back seat." Beckett tilts his head in that direction.

I climb onto my knees in the front and reach into the rear of the car to tilt up the bench seat. I drag myself through the opening, accidentally kicking Beckett a bit on the way.

"Come on man, watch the feet." He shoves my leg.

I kneel there and examine the selection of guns. There isn't much, but it's more than what I thought we had a minute ago. I shove a pistol under my front waistband and another behind, near the one that was already holstered there. I tuck a dagger into my sock and place a switchblade into my pocket. "Is this what I think it is?" I pull out a small black box and glance at Beckett.

"Yeah, do you mind? I'd rather not die just yet." He cranes his neck to take a better look at the selection left. "Christ, couldn't save some for the rest of us?"

I toss a gun and a sheathed knife into his lap. "There. Happy?"

He uses his knee to steer and shoves the gun in the same frontal spot I had put mine. "I wasn't kidding about the gate." Beckett nods toward the road ahead. "I'd buckle up if I were you."

I move as quickly as possible, throwing myself into a seat and reaching for the seatbelt. I barely get it fucking buckled when Simon veers us off the road and through the lawn.

He shoves his foot all the way onto the floor and says, "This is going to fucking hurt."

His cute little Volvo crashes right into the gate at the house we were heading to, buckling it and sending us both flying forward in our seats. The airbags deploy and his horn won't stop fucking blaring. I see fucking stars for a second and struggle against the belt that won't come undone.

"You good?" I cough and cut through the thing keeping me locked into place.

Simon doesn't move and for the first time in the history of knowing the fucker, I actually worry that he might be dead. I shake his shoulder and his head falls.

*Oh shit, June is going to kill me.*

But I let out a sigh of relief when he turns toward me, blood trailing from his forehead to his chin.

"You've seen better days," I tell him.

He spits blood onto his dash. "I told you it was going to hurt." Beckett unbuckles his seatbelt and shoves his door open. "I can't fucking move. My leg is pinned."

"God damn it, Beckett." I pull myself across the back of the car and exit on his side. There's no telling how quick security will get here and if we don't want to die within seconds of forcing entry onto the property, we need to fucking hurry.

"You act like I got myself stuck on fucking purpose." He pries at his leg but it doesn't budge.

I yank open his door and fumble around with his ankle. "I am way closer to your dick than I'd prefer." I smash my face into the side of him to get a better angle on his foot. "Got it." I pull a little too hard and when his foot pops free, he falls out of the fucking car and on top of me, caging me onto the ground.

"Listen, I know I'm tolerating you right now, but this is not what I had in mind." I shove him off of me.

"For a second there it was almost like you had a sense of humor." Simon dusts his pants off and reaches for the knife I had given him. "Where's that box?"

I grab it from the back seat and hand it to him. "What did you have in mind?"

"Pure. Fucking. Chaos." Simon reaches in and pulls out a grenade, handing it to me and taking the other one that's tucked in the box with it. "You know how to use one of those?"

I roll my eyes. "This isn't my first fucking rodeo."

"You've got about three to five seconds max to get rid of that thing. Don't cook it too long or it'll blow your fucking arm off."

"I told you I was fine."

Beckett limps from the car and crouches behind a bush. "We need to get the fuck away from here."

"Follow me." I take off in a zig-zag pattern toward the house, stopping periodically to assess my surroundings.

A group of men wearing all black and sporting assault rifles runs toward the smoking car at the gated entrance.

"Think you can chuck that thing that far?" I ask Beckett.

"I played football once." He yanks the pin free and sends the grenade flying through the fucking air. It bounces along the ground near the car and explodes a couple seconds later.

Some of the men are hit but from the smoke and debris floating about, I can't tell exactly how many.

"How long until we have backup?" Beckett glances over at me.

"Depends who's driving." I shrug. "Could be ten minutes."

"That's too much time." He sighs and scratches his lip with his teeth. "Here's the plan." Beckett points to the grenade still in my grasp. "We're going to find her, then you're going to throw that and buy me enough time to get her free. You can cover us."

"The fuck I will."

Beckett steadies my shoulders and looks me dead in the eyes. "Coen. You are a better shot than me. And you are June's first love. Do you understand me?"

I narrow my gaze. "What does that have to do with anything?"

"Losing you once turned her into a cold-hearted bitch. What do you think is going to happen if she loses you again?" Beckett shakes his head. "Not letting that happen."

"But I thought..."

"You thought wrong." Beckett yanks out one of his guns and checks the chamber. "I love her more than anything, but that means I can't be selfish with her." He holds out his hand. "Give me that switchblade."

I pull it out of my pocket and he snatches it from my hand, taking off along the exterior of the house and peering into the windows.

I rush to catch up and get my head back into the game. I never expected him to say *that*. To put what he assumes are her desires over his. Doesn't he realize that he's the better man? That she should be with him instead of me? He just proved it when he said he was willing to risk his life instead of mine. A man that he hates more than anything. He would put his life on the line to give me a chance with her instead of him.

I can't even tell her the truth and here he is, ready to die to allow another man to be with her.

"There." Beckett points through a window. "There she is." He runs away before I can say another word, darting around the side of the house.

He shimmies the door handle and makes a cupping motion like he's holding something and then throws it. His way of telling me to follow through with the plan, and because he isn't wasting any more time, there's nothing I can do but go along with it.

Beckett nods and gives me the go ahead, the door creaking open with his grip on it.

I jerk the pin out of the grenade, running back in the direction we came, holding onto it for far too fucking long before using every ounce of strength I have to throw it as far as I can. It explodes a second after I release it and I dive into the ground to avoid the brunt of the explosion. Part of the stone structure shatters around me, pieces of it falling to the ground and hitting me. Talk about a fucking distraction, I blew a hole in the second story of the fucking house.

I scramble to my feet and sprint toward where I left Beckett. Bursting through the door, I run in the direction I can only assume they're in and spot him there, kneeling at June's side, the knife in his grasp frantically cutting through the binds that hold her to the chair.

Her gaze trails up to lock onto mine, and for a split second, I think all of this is going to work out. But when I catch movement in my peripheral and turn to find Gwyneth Sharp pointing a gun at Simon fucking Beckett, I do the only thing I can think of.

I run. I push my legs harder than they ever have been pushed and dive to shove him and June out of the way. The shot rings out and fear washes through me. Fear that I didn't make it in time. Fear that I did the wrong thing. Fear that I only put June in more danger.

But when I blink down at my chest and see the blood pooling from the wound, I realize that one part of this plan worked. The man June loves is safe—but that man is not me.

And that is a reality I will take into the next lifetime. Because as much turmoil I caused her, the pain and torment and heartache, at least I could have given her that.

My redemption.

Trading my life for Simon Becketts.

# CHAPTER 31

## June

"No, no, no," I blubber and drop to my knees, the hard surface slicing them to shreds but I don't care. Not when blood is oozing out of a wound in Coen's chest. "Damn it, Co. You do not get to leave me like this." I shove my hand onto the hole.

"J..." He mutters, red spattering out of his mouth. "I—I'm so, sorry."

"No," I cry. "Not like this, Coen. You don't get to say sorry like this." Tears roll down my cheeks, and I glance up to see Simon with his hands up, Gwyneth holding a gun toward him too.

"It wasn't supposed to be him," she tells me like it's somehow supposed to make me feel any fucking better. "It wasn't supposed to be any of them. It was supposed to be you." She jabs the gun at me but immediately trains it back on Simon when he inches toward her. "You can't waltz into this life and cause as much anarchy as you have. You don't get to have multiple boyfriends. That's not *natural*."

"You, you want me dead because, because of *that*? You fucking animal." I shake my head. "You had me kidnapped and tortured because..."

How does any of this make sense? Why does it matter that I'm in a relationship with three different guys? I thought she was all about female empowerment and ruling this organization better than before. Or was that just a lie to get me to trust her? To let her weasel her way into my presence and give me the false sense of friendship to fuck with me even more.

"Co." I hold him in my arms, blood coating the floor around us. "Please, just stay with me." My teardrops fall onto his beautiful face. The face that I've kissed a million times. The face I never thought I'd see again when his dad drove him away. The face that changed and turned into something I no longer recognized days ago, but now the face that I cannot imagine never seeing again. "Co!" I sob. "Listen, we can get through this, okay? This shit we've been going through. We'll make it work." I nearly choke on my words. "I don't know how, but you have to believe me. We'll figure it out. You and me. Remember, it's supposed to be us against the world. It used to be. It can be again. You just have to hold on a little longer." I move my hand and blood gushes around it. I shove it back down. "I'm not done being mad at you yet, Co."

Earlier today I considered walking away when this was all said and done. I wasn't sure if I could stay when they've done nothing but push me away. But Claire's words made me realize that this was never going to be easy. It wasn't for her and Johnny, and they're just two people. Why did I ever expect things wouldn't be this fucking hard? I should have never considered giving up, not when I still have so much fight left in me. I know Simon wants this. Magnus does. Dom needs to man up and make a choice about what he wants, but Coen, Coen just proved all my doubts wrong when he jumped in front of a bullet to save Simon Beckett.

His sworn enemy. The man who he hates more than anything. If Coen can change, maybe Dom can, too. And if that's possible, maybe so is figuring out how to be together. All of us. Because I cannot live without any of these men. Not even Coen, the man who I had the most doubts about this morning.

When Coen had made that explosion, a few hunks of the ceiling rained down and distracted her long enough to give Simon a chance to cut the ropes holding me in place. It just wasn't enough time to get us out of here before she realized it was a diversion. And if Coen hadn't jumped in the way, it would easily be me or Simon bleeding out instead of him.

"Put the gun down, Gwyneth," another person demands.

I blink through my tears to see Johnny Jones stepping through the door Simon and Coen had come from.

Johnny continues into the room, and she steadies her aim at him.

"You!" she blurts out.

"I never liked you," Johnny tells her.

"You would be dead without me."

"Doesn't mean I like you."

"You took Franklin from me." Her hands shake with the gun pressed between them and her finger on the trigger.

I don't trust the fact that she won't accidentally shoot one of them because she's so fucking old and stupid.

Johnny steps in front of Simon, blocking him from her line of sight. "Franklin was a disgrace and you know it. He deserved to die. I was thrilled watching a bullet go through his skull."

Simon backs away slowly at her new distraction and then breaks away to rush over to me.

She tosses her attention toward us but quickly focuses on Johnny.

"God damn it, Hayes." Simon slides his hand under mine and applies pressure to the wound. "We've got to get him out of here." His emerald gaze trails up to my face. "Are you injured?"

I shake my head, the tears still silently falling down.

"You took Franklin, and *she*"—Gwyneth seethes—"took Vincent."

"Excuse me?" I rise to my feet now that Simon is clutching Coen, his grip much stronger than mine ever could have been. "*You* sent that sick fuck to kidnap me. *You* did this." I point to the scar on my cheek. "And *you* were the one who showed me that fucking dagger and basically dared me to kill Simon."

A sadistic laugh bubbles out of her chest, sending a chill down my spine. "And it was like taking candy from a baby." She chuckles more. "You fail to realize the man who shot you, how he got that weapon to begin with. If only I had hired someone with a better aim, we wouldn't be in this mess, and your precious *Coen* wouldn't be dead."

"You fucking bitch," I say through gritted teeth and step forward.

"June," Johnny warns.

"And you're just as much to blame." She steadies the gun at Johnny. "You just had to poke and prod at Franklin. I should have let him kill you when he first wanted to."

I inch closer to Johnny. "Give me the gun," I tell him. "This is between me and her." I look at Gwyneth. "You hear that, you stupid old hag? This has nothing to do with them. Let them go." I whisper to Johnny, "You have to get Coen to a hospital, *now*. I can't lift him. Please, Johnny, I'm begging you."

"June, don't you fucking do it," Simon calls out from his spot with Coen.

I put him in an impossible situation when I let him take over the pressure on Coen's wound. If he releases his hold and comes after me, Coen will no doubt bleed out. But if he does nothing, I put myself back in the line of fire.

Johnny effortlessly slides the gun from his grasp into mine. "Backup is coming soon," he mutters before he rushes away.

Gwyneth struggles to know where to focus her aim but I move farther away from the men to shift her focus to me.

I could easily shoot her, but she'll get a shot off before I can move out of the way, and she knows the same goes for me. We're at a standoff of who will get distracted first, and I fucking refuse to be the loser.

I've gone through too much and come too far to let this bitch be the reason I die. Her life will end one way or another, even if I have to stand here all fucking night waiting for her to make one tiny misstep.

"Get out of here," I tell the guys but keep my sights set on her. "Move that gun toward them, and I swear it will be the last thing you see. Do it, I fucking dare you."

"I'm not going to fall for your antics, girl. My qualms are with you, not them. They will be dealt with later." She takes a step back and I match her by taking one forward.

Is she baiting me? Is she trying to walk me into a trap? Or is she trying to escape?

Simon and Johnny lift Coen and drag his lifeless body away.

I ignore Simon's seething stare and focus on the bitch. "Who was Vincent to you?" I ask the question that's burning through my head. "Why did his death matter?"

Her nostrils flare and she inches toward me, stiffening her arms. "He was...*my son.*"

I pinch my brows. "What? I didn't think Franklin had..."

She rocks her head slowly.

"Oh," I say as the realization dawns on me. I let out a laugh. "You chastise me for having multiple men but you had a bastard son with another man. Is that why you hate me so much? I have something you wanted but never had? You're mad because *you* had to choose and I don't."

Gunshots go off in the distance. A sign that others are coming. That our time here is limited. My only hope is that Simon and Johnny can get Coen out of this hellhole before any more harm is done to them.

Coen has to live. He has to. Because if he doesn't, I don't know how I will survive the permanent loss of him. Just because I have gained one man, doesn't mean I'm okay with letting another go.

"You," Gwyneth spits out. "You are a selfish and greedy bitch. Everything would have been fine without you. Dominic and Simon would have had a fair battle and *none* of them would have fallen victim to your disgusting seduction."

I laugh again. "You realize *they* pursued me, right?"

"You baited them!" She clenches her jaw. "You were after their money! The empire! You gold-digging bitch!"

"Wow." With blood coated all over my body, I stand there, completely dumbfounded. How could she possibly be any more wrong? None of this has *ever* been about the money. Is not having to worry about how I'll scrounge up enough money for rent nice? Definitely. Is knowing I don't have to worry about my next meal a luxury I'm grateful for? Absolutely. But I have never asked them for a single thing. Not once. The only thing I want from them is their time—their love. The rest is theirs to do with what they want. I don't need the lavish lifestyle—I just need them.

And I would trade every bit of it for a chance to walk out of here with all four of those men.

I would go back to working three jobs, to dealing with shitty bosses who objectify me and treat me like garbage. I would live in squalor and struggle to make ends meet. I would walk through fucking hell and back to get our happily ever after.

Gwyneth turns on her heel, spinning so fast I barely recognize what's even happening. She darts around a corner and runs.

I start after her, but a second later, she stalks backward with her hands in the air. I keep my gun aimed at her and wait for the reason for her retreat.

Claire appears, a pistol in her grasp, looking like the baddest bitch I've ever laid my eyes on. "Not so fast, *Winnie.*"

"Drop the gun," I tell Gwyneth. "This is over." I stalk toward Claire.

"Sorry it took me so long," Claire mutters. "Took the scenic route."

"You're here, that's all that matters."

Gwyneth lowers her arms, and for a second I think she's going to use the opportunity to shoot one of us, but she actually complies and sets the thing on the floor. "You're going to kill a defenseless old woman?"

More gunshots, this time closer.

I flit my attention in the direction it's coming and hold my breath. Are those *her* reinforcements coming to finish us off? Are Claire and I about to be outnumbered and taken out by this stupid hag?

But instead of her goons, Dominic Adler bursts through the fucking door, one gun in each hand. He quickly turns around and shoots at his rear, hitting his target and sending them falling through the door behind him.

"Dominic," Gwyneth whines and fakes innocence. "You came. These two have made horrible accusations against me. And she..." The pathetic actor points at me. "*Shot Coen.* She's trying to pin it on me."

Dominic lowers his right hand and shoots her in the fucking leg. "Stop the antics, Gwyneth. I've heard enough from you."

Gwyneth cries out and falls to the floor, clutching her thigh. "Wh-why? Dominic. I was li-like a mo-mother to you."

"A mother?" Dominic sneers. "A mother would never do the things you've done." He rushes over between me and Claire. "Are you two okay?" He hugs me to his chest briefly but releases me, holding me at an arm's length and studies the blood covering my body.

"It's Coen's, not mine."

"I'm fine," Claire says and steps toward the whimpering lady. "But I'll be better once she's dead." Claire fires off a round into Gwyneth's leg. "That's for Franklin." Then another. "That's for Johnny." Another. "That's for hunting us down." Another. "That's for Luciano."

I join Claire at her side, pointing my gun at Gwyneth. "This is for Coen." I hit her in the stomach. "This is for Vincent. This is for Johnny and Claire. This is for trying to ruin my life."

"And this," Claire says while Gwyneth foams at the mouth with blood. "Is to end it." She blasts a bullet straight through Gwyneth's forehead.

Gwyneth's body shakes with the impact of the shot but then stills, blood pooling from the various holes we put in her.

I don't take my sights off of her. No, I empty the fucking chamber into her chest and hope that if there were a chance for her in the afterlife, that this will be enough to kill her in any lifetime. "Fucking. Bitch."

Dominic grabs me by the shoulders and turns me toward him. "She's gone, June." He takes the gun from my hand and tosses it aside. "Here." He shoves one of his into my grasp and glances at Claire. "We need to get out of here."

We may have defeated the evil bitch, but her minions are still out there, ready to defend her even in her death.

CHAPTER 32

## *Dominic*

"BP ninety over sixty. Pulse one fifty. We need another bag of blood."

I shove into the room as people in scrubs dart around.

"We need to find the tear," a woman says. "There's a compromised artery."

"Sir." A man approaches me. "You cannot be in here."

I settle my sights on Coen. Tubes and IVs and bags and monitors attached to him. Shit beeping at various rates. This isn't right. He shouldn't be there. Not like this.

"We have to cauterize it or we're going to lose him."

The man grips my shoulders, and with the help of another bigger guy, they shove me out the way I came.

I burst into the room to get answers for June, but how am I supposed to tell her what I just heard? That if they don't act quickly, her first love is going to die.

She hates me enough as it is, and now I have to give her that news.

If I would have come forward sooner, maybe none of this would have happened.

Why was I so fucking afraid to be honest with her when honesty might have been the only thing that could have saved us from this nightmare?

She was built for this. This life. This world. This fucking darkness.

I didn't want it for her. Neither did Coen. But now here she is, covered in multiple people's blood and not for a second crumbling from the things she's done. Maybe she's just in shock. The potential loss of Coen making her forget that she just brutally murdered a woman and shot numerous others to escape.

I should have known from the start. That moment when I was the one covered in blood, had just beaten her attacker in front of her, and instead of running out of there or shying away, she stepped forward and took my hand in hers. She reached

509

forward, pressing her palm along my crimson-speckled face, and did something I never expected. She fucking kissed me.

I was over twice her age. Had hardly spoken to her in the weeks I had been going into that bar. There was an undeniable chemistry but I assumed it was just on my end. I had put my brutality on display for her only for her to step into that darkness and embrace it. I figured it was a one-off. That she was just being curious, that the thrill of it would wear off and she would come to her senses and realize how bad of a man I was. But with each passing moment, she continued to defy the limits I had put on her.

She handled the truth then, why did I ever assume she couldn't?

Maybe it was that deep seeded fear that eventually I would wake up and this would all be over. That if I kept her from the life that I could stop that from happening. I could prolong whatever time I had with her if I just separated her from the dark parts of my world.

But in doing so, I built a bridge and tore down the pieces before she could cross it with me. Here I am, standing in the rubble with no hope of ever getting back across.

I walk through the corridor of the hospital, with my head down, and turn into the waiting room.

June paces the small space but rushes over to me immediately. That tight little dress ripped to shreds and dried blood coating most of her exposed skin. "How is he? Is he okay? Where is he? Can I see him?"

I swallow and put on my best face. "He's in surgery." I meet her gaze. "We should know something soon."

"No." June rocks her head back and forth. "I know that look, Dominic. What aren't you telling me?" She tilts her head to look around me. "I want to see him. *Now.*"

"They kicked me out of the room, June." I drag my hand over my beard. "The bullet hit an artery. They're doing what they can to find the tear and patch him up." I choose honesty because anything else will only make the situation worse.

June's eyes glisten as new tears form. "That's...that's bad. The mortality rate is..."

I place my hand on her shoulder. "You can't think like that, June. Not now. He needs you to be strong."

"Strong?" She shoves me off of her. "That's all I have been, Dominic. And where the fuck has *that* gotten me." June pokes her hand into my chest. "This is *your* fault." She shoves me harder. "*You* did this. With your lies. Your secrets." She balls her hand into a fist and slams it into me. "If Coen dies, this is *your* fault." She hits me with her other fist. "Do you hear me?" June sobs and pounds her fists against my chest. "*Your fault.*"

I wrap my arms around her and she collapses into me. "I'm sorry," I tell her. "You're right. Every word of it." I hold onto her and hug her for what might be the last time. Because even if Coen doesn't die, the damage has already been done, and there is no coming back from what I have put her through.

"Love," Simon approaches and peels June from my chest. He drags her into his arms. "Come on. Let's take a walk. You and me." He offers me a sympathetic glance but it does nothing to soothe the aching in my chest.

Magnus bursts into the waiting room and frantically looks around before rushing over to June. He plants his hands on her cheeks and tilts her face up toward him. "You're okay."

But she shakes her head. June might be uninjured, but she is the furthest thing from okay.

And it is my fault.

I glance over at Johnny and Claire who sit in the corner of the room, quietly chatting between them, their hands interlocked together. If it weren't for those two getting to that fucking house, I'm not so sure any of us would be standing here right now.

I once questioned whether he had what it took or not, but I was wrong about him, too.

I was wrong about Johnny. About June. About Simon. I was wrong about everything.

And maybe I was wrong to think I would be the best fit for running this organization. Maybe I was overzealous and foolish to assume I had what it took.

Because being here, watching June hate me, and Coen dancing so close to death—I want none of it. My whole life has been me working toward gaining that position, but I'd trade it all in a heartbeat to fix any of this. To make her hate me any less. To be the man that she deserves. But that ship sailed a long fucking time ago, and if I give up the throne, I give up the only remaining thing that I still have.

I will lose her. I will lose Coen and Magnus, and the alliance I had with Simon.

My heart, my soul, my fucking humanity. It will be gone and the only thing that will be left is a shell of a man.

Minutes pass. They turn into an hour. Maybe two. We take turns pacing the room.

June gravitates toward Magnus and Simon, and sometimes joins Johnny and Claire. She avoids me at all costs, and I don't blame her. I hate myself, too.

Alec arrives at some point to tell us he got Cora home safely. Tells us that she was worried about everyone leaving but that she had a good time. He brought a change of clothes for June, who despite wearing something a little less revealing, is still covered in someone else's blood.

Bram must have been notified, because he shows up, too. Carlos, his cook, at his side with two big bags of food and a vat of coffee.

June rushes over to Bram and buries her face in his chest.

He doesn't pay any mind to the blood and hugs her, muttering something as he makes small circles with his hands on her back.

I've never felt more like an outsider than I do at this moment. Like I'm not even here, just a fly on the fucking wall.

More minutes pass. Simon persuades June to take a few bites of a sandwich. She nestles a cup of coffee in her grasp, her knees pulled up to her chest in her chair. She periodically takes sips of the coffee and stares blankly ahead.

Magnus and Simon take turns trying to comfort her, then break off to have a conversation of their own before returning to her side.

Finally, after what feels like a fuckin eternity, the door opens again. Only this time, it's a man dressed in hospital attire and a clipboard in his grasp. He lowers the face mask and glances around the room, unsure of who he's supposed to focus on.

June rises to her feet and stares directly at this man like he holds all the answers to the universe.

Because to her, he does. Coen was her first love. And he is her universe.

Even if he's been a royal fucking prick to her lately.

But how can I fault him when I have been no better?

I hold my breath and wait for him to speak, to say anything to let us know if Coen survived.

"I apologize for keeping you waiting. The surgery took much longer than we expected," he explains. "The damage was more extensive once we opened him up. But we were able to successfully repair what had been done. Mr. Hayes has a long road of recovery ahead of him, and he's still not out of the woods yet."

"But, he's...alive?" June manages to mutter.

The surgeon nods. "Yes, he's in critical but stable condition."

"Can I see him?" Silent tears roll down June's cheeks, and I ache to reach out and wipe them away.

Magnus goes to her side and puts his arm around her shoulder, holding her tight and keeping her legs from buckling out from under her.

"He's being transferred from surgery now. You can visit him in about an hour. But not all of you." He shifts his gaze around the room. "Only one until he's more stable."

But it doesn't matter. One person is enough.

I let out a breath of relief and when the surgeon has left and June is buried in the chest of a better man than me, I leave the room. I am not wanted here, and now that I know Coen is going to survive, I will distance myself from putting June through any more unnecessary torment.

Walking away is the best—and only—thing I can do for her.

# CHAPTER 33

# June

I don't take my hand off of Coen from the second I get to his side.

"Oh, Co," I whisper and brush the golden hair from his brow. "What have you done?"

I lower myself onto the bed next to him, careful not to disturb him too much. I glance at our hands and wish he would squeeze mine back. Seeing him like this, it brings back a feeling of helplessness I cannot stomach. I would give anything to trade places with him. To be the one on the verge of death. I've only ever wanted the best for Coen, even from that very first moment.

I was just a kid but when I *felt* his anguish and watched as his shoulders shook, I knew I would do anything to make that go away. I didn't have much, but I picked those stupid wildflowers and handed them to him, hoping the tiny gesture would make a difference. To show him that in a world full of darkness, there was some light.

I could tell he was resistant to letting me in, but I pushed and he didn't stand a chance at how determined I was to show him kindness. I needed him to know he wasn't alone. Not then, and not now. Not even when I thought all hope was lost between us. That flicker of hope had dimmed these past few months, especially the last week, but it sparked back to life when I thought he was going to die.

Nothing had ever terrified me more, and I might want to strangle him myself for what he's put me through, but the thought of actually losing him, for real, was too much to bear. I would rather hate him and have him around than lose him forever.

What a fucking contradiction.

I sit there for a while, just watching him intently. I move into the chair next to the bed, still keeping my hold on him as I scoot it closer to his side. I rest my head next to his hand and sigh. "You are so easy to love, Coen Hayes, but Christ do you make it so fucking hard." I kiss his finger and close my eyes, letting the steady beeping of his machines lull me to sleep.

Dozing in and out, I flicker between reality and dreams that morph into nightmares. Coen being shot. His blood pooling around me. Simon getting shot, too. Magnus and Dom next. Their bodies falling to the ground next to mine. My hands frantic to reach each of them in time to save their lives. But I never make it in time, and every single man I love dies and I'm to blame.

If it weren't for me, none of this would have happened. They wouldn't have been in this situation at all. I was the catalyst that set this whole fucking thing in motion. I am the common denominator to all of their issues. I should disappear from their lives and give them a chance to turn this around. But I can't. And I won't. No—I claim I am not selfish, but I don't know how to be without them. I once thought relationships were stupid, and I refused to get into one. I guarded my heart like a feral cat does a scrap it finds in a dumpster. But I gave in. I opened myself up to these men and allowed myself to be vulnerable and I fell for every single one of them. How could I ever give that up?

Coen's fingers twitch and I shoot up to stare at his face.

His eyes dart back and forth, and finally, like a whole fucking eternity has come and gone, they open.

"J..." His voice is ragged.

"Co." I grip his hand tighter.

"You look like shit," he tells me.

I laugh and shake my head. "Thanks. So do you."

Coen reaches down and tries to sit up but his arm gives out from under him.

"Here," I say as I reach for the remote control to his bed. I push a few buttons until I find the right one and bring him upright. "Is that better?"

He struggles to reposition himself. "Yeah, thanks."

"I can't believe you tried to die on me." I stare into his beautiful blue eyes.

"I can't believe you wouldn't let me."

I scoff. "How dare you try to get off the hook that easily."

Coen sighs. "J, I owe you an apology."

"For almost dying? Yeah, you do."

"No." He wraps his hand around mine. "For so many things." Coen clears his throat. "For leaving you all those years ago. For not coming back sooner. For doubting you. For treating you like shit. For making you doubt *me*. I-I can't tell you how hard this has been. To watch you fall in love with the most dangerous men in this entire state. I still see you as this sweet little girl who gave me a handful of flowers. I never wanted that to change. I thought I was protecting you. I thought that if I pushed you away, that maybe you'd figure it out for yourself. That you were better off without us. With someone else. Someone safe. Someone *good*."

"Co..."

"No, J. I'm not finished." He coughs and the pulse on his monitor rises. "I understand if you can't ever forgive me, but I need you to know how sorry I am. For everything. I am forever a better man because of you, and I have done nothing to earn that love. I don't deserve it. I don't deserve you. And I'm so fucking sorry I ever took it for granted. I don't expect you to respond or even give me an ounce of your time, but Magnus, he never wanted to keep this from you. He's never doubted you from the start. You can be mad at me. You can be mad at Dom. But Magnus had nothing to do with it."

My heart matches the frenzied rhythm of his.

Coen continues, "And as much as I hate to admit this, Simon had nothing to do with it either. He's the man you should be with. Not me. He cares about you more than anything and he would never do the things I've done to you. You're safe with him. Your heart is safe with him."

"Co..."

"You don't need my permission, J, you're smart enough to make decisions on your own. But you need to know, all I want is for you to be happy. And if being with him is what it takes, then I will step aside and let that happen." He pauses and adds, "Okay, I'm done. I'm sorry for interrupting you. I just needed to get that off my chest before I pass out or something."

I hold onto his hand and look up at him while chewing the inside of my lip to stop the tears that want to break free. "I do have feelings for him, Co. You're not wrong. Simon was there for me when none of you were. He never pushed me away or lied to me. He gave me space when I needed it, and he was there when I didn't know I needed it. He's probably been the only thing to keep me from completely losing my mind these past few months. I never meant for us to become anything other than what we started out as, and I never intended on crossing that line with him.

"And you're right. I am pissed at you. And Dominic. I don't know if I'll ever be able to forgive him, especially when he refuses to acknowledge that he's done anything wrong. Magnus has made it clear what he wants. And he's apologized every step of the way. He's even tried to form some kind of relationship with Simon, treating him more like an equal than his enemy. I don't blame him for being coerced by Dominic. But you, you acted on your own. Pushing me away and saying cruel things. You were unrecognizable, and I don't know if that was an act, or you doing everything in your power to make me hate you." I bite at my lip, tugging it into my mouth and rolling it between my teeth. "I'm not afraid of dying, or being kidnapped, or even tortured. But the version of you lately, the one you've insisted on being. He's scared me, Co. And it worries me that that's the real you."

"J..." Tears well in Coen's eyes. "You know me. You know the real me. I would never..."

"Hurt me?" I tilt my head to the side. "But you did." I nod. "And you keep hurting me. And I don't know what to do with that, Coen. I love you, I always have, but Christ, should love be this painful?"

"No." He wipes at my cheek with his thumb. "It shouldn't. And I will forever be sorry for that."

I sniffle. "You did a foolish thing by jumping in front of that bullet, Coen."

"I disagree."

"Why?" I stare up at him. "Why did you do it?"

His blue gaze trails back and forth between mine. "Because he's the better man, J. And if it had to be me or him, I'd do it again in a heartbeat."

"I can live without you, Co, I did it for a decade. But I don't *want* to. Not ever again. Don't you see that?" I swallow down the pain I've suppressed these past ten years. "You can't leave me."

The door to Coen's room opens and a nurse walks in. "Mr. Hayes. Nice to see you're awake. How are you feeling?" She checks his chart and writes something on it.

"Fine," he lies to her.

"I see." She glances up from the clipboard of his paperwork. "Another dose of morphine should be settling in any second now." She steadies her gaze on me. "You should let him rest."

"Right, yeah." I release his hand and snatch a tissue from the box on the table and blot my nose. "Of course."

Coen reaches for me, his eyes growing heavy from the exhaustion and medication taking hold. "I love you, J," he manages to get out before his arm falls to his side.

"Is that normal?" I ask the nurse.

"To be in love?" She raises a brow at me.

"No, for him to pass out like that."

She marks something else off on his chart. "Yep. He had a cocktail mix of sedatives and pain medication. In this early stage, he should rest as much as possible."

"Oh, okay." I try to remember what it was like during my gunshot wound recovery but that period of my life is fuzzy. Maybe I was asleep the whole fucking time, too.

"I would use this opportunity to go home and get yourself cleaned up. He's in good hands here."

I know she's just trying to help but her condescending tone isn't doing her any favors. I'm well aware that despite having new clothes on, I'm still caked with fucking blood. How I haven't been questioned about the shooting is beyond me, but I assume it has something to do with the fact that Dominic still holds so much power.

Claire and I murdered one of the council heads of a massive criminal organization. Is that just going to be swept under the rug? Will there be consequences to my actions? Or will we be able to prove that she was out to get us from the start and take control of the narrative? Has Dom already started taking care of all of this? Not like he would tell me anyway, since he likes to keep me in the fucking dark.

I guess I'll leave that problem for him to solve since he insists on handling fucking everything.

"Okay, yeah," I finally say to the nurse because honestly, I could use a hot shower and a fresh set of clothes that aren't immediately soiled by my disgusting body.

I lean down and press my lips to Coen's forehead and whisper in his ear, "I love you more." I follow the nurse out of the room and make my way down the corridor to the waiting room we spent countless hours in, waiting to hear if Coen had made it through surgery.

Magnus and Simon sit in the corner, both of them asleep. Magnus's head rests on Simon's shoulder and the two of them use each other's weight to support themselves. If I had my phone I would take a picture but instead, I'll have to settle for this mental image.

Simon blinks a few times and steadies his sights on me. He slaps Magnus in the chest and Magnus nearly jumps out of his seat.

"What? Huh?" Magnus steadies himself. "Oh shit, princess. Hey." He rubs his eyes. "I wasn't sleeping." He rises to his feet. "Totally wasn't sleeping."

Simon stands, too, and dusts off his shoulder. "I think you drooled on me, man."

I approach them both, my arms folded over my chest. "Just admit it, you two were cuddling."

Magnus drags me toward him and suffocates me with his embrace. "Would rather be snuggling with you, princess." He sniffs the top of my head. "You could use a shower though." He hugs me tighter. "I still love you when you're dirty, but I don't know whose blood that is."

"Is there like...a hotel around here or something?" I lean into Magnus. "I don't really want to go back to the house. Not if Dom's there."

"You can shower at my place, love," Simon tells me. "And you can stay there as long as you need to."

"I can, uh, I can stop by the house and get you some stuff," Magnus offers.

"Yeah. That would be good."

I haven't heard from Dom since he walked out of the hospital, and I don't have the energy or mental capacity to deal with him. Eventually, we're going to have to speak, but for now, I'd rather give him a taste of his own medicine and ignore him for a change. Maybe then he'll come to his senses and realize how badly he fucked up.

He's lucky Coen is alive. Because I would have never forgiven Dominic if he had died.

There's only so much I can take, and that would be more than I could bear.

"Although..." Simon rubs his neck. "I sort of totaled my car so I'll have to call a driver."

"Nah, dude." Magnus tugs his keys out of his pocket. "I'll drop you guys off at your place and circle back to the house. No worries."

<hr>

Simon sits in the back seat with me as Magnus escorts us to Simon's place. He doesn't take his hand off of me, not even when we exit the car and walk up to his building. We take a private elevator to his penthouse and the doors open right into the front of his unit.

Floor-to-ceiling windows cover two of the walls in the far corner, the view over-looking the city below. A massive skylight opens up above it to add even more natural light to this spacious area. Everything is tidy and minimalistic, but with a modern vibe to it. Dark wood floors span the entire length of the place with deep grey furniture and lavish green plants strategically placed about. A charcoal metal staircase leads to another level and various doors line the walls.

"This way, love." Simon walks me up the stairs and leads me into a room that smells just like him. "You can shower in here." He takes me through to the attached bathroom and finally releases his hold on me. "Towels." He points to a stack sitting neatly on the vanity. "Um, you should be okay with the shampoo and conditioner in there." He nods toward the large open shower. "What else?" He snaps his fingers. "Clothes, you need clothes. I'll get you something to wear in the meantime."

I stand there as Simon leaves the room, goes into the other one, and returns a moment later.

"I hope this is okay." He sets a pair of grey sweatpants and a white tee on the counter next to the towels. "And..." Simon strolls over to the shower and turns on the faucet. "This is pretty self-explanatory." He goes to leave but I catch his arm.

"Simon."

"Yes, love?" He turns toward me.

"Stay."

He blinks as if he's unsure of what I said.

"Please." I chew at my lip. "I don't want to be alone."

"Love," he sighs and pulls me into his chest. "I'm not going anywhere."

I tilt my head up toward his. "Kiss me."

"Are you sure?" He skims his fingers along my cheek.

"Yes."

Slowly, he presses his lips onto mine, moving them with gentle ease.

My heart skips a beat and I melt into him, kissing him back and enfolding my arms around his neck. I tug him toward me, desperate for the closeness of his body.

Simon glides his hands down and hooks them under my thighs, gripping tight and pulling me off the floor.

I wrap my legs around him and part his lips with my tongue, dipping it inside and dancing it along his. I skim my fingers up into his hair and wish there was a way to bottle up what it is I'm feeling right now.

*Hope? Happiness? Love?* I can't be sure, but it feels like a mixture of all of them.

Simon backs us into the shower, both of us fully fucking clothed. He kicks off his shoes and I do the same, multitasking as best as I can. Both of us giggle as we haphazardly rid ourselves of the apparel keeping us apart.

He shoves me against the wall and stares into my eyes. "Love..." With his chest rising and falling, he releases me to my feet. He grips the hem of my shirt and drags it over my head.

I raise my arms to help him but grit my teeth at the contact the fabric had against the bandage on my arm.

Simon's gaze immediately falls to my ribs. "What happened?" He hovers his fingers just along them without applying hardly any pressure.

I wince in anticipation of the contact. "It's fine," I tell him. "I'm fine."

"Don't lie to me, love." He turns me to get a better look. "Is that from a boot?"

I nod and recall the memory of the man who took me to Gwyneth's place kicking me in the side when I tried to get away. He had tripped me, knocking me to the ground, and then slammed into me with his steel-toed fucking boot with enough force to send me onto my back. He gripped my ankle and dragged me screaming into the house where he tied me to the chair. It wasn't long after that Gwyneth entered the room and all of my suspicions had been proven right. It was her orchestrating the whole fucking thing—a truth I realized all too late.

Simon kneels and presses his lips to my bruised and swollen ribs. "I'm so sorry, love." He tugs my leggings over my ass and peels them and my panties down, sliding my feet out of each side and tossing them with no regard to where they land. He stands before me, reaching around and unclasping my bra with one hand, the other pressed along my cheek.

I grab his shirt and inch it up upward and over his head, revealing his perfectly chiseled chest and abdomen. I skim my fingers along every ridge and settle them at the button on his jeans.

He undoes and pulls them down over his hips, stepping out and throwing them with our other clothes.

I keep my gaze trained on his as he comes forward and brings me to his chest.

We stand there, completely fucking naked, just holding each other in this massive shower. There's something so intimate about our embrace despite it not being sexual at all.

Simon steps into the water and massages my scalp, moistening my hair and no doubt ridding me of the aftermath of what happened at Castleberry Court. "Turn around." He spins me at my waist so my back is to him.

"What are you doing?" I ask him.

"Washing your hair." He reaches for a bottle from the shelf that's on the wall and squirts some of the stuff into his hand. Simon lathers it into my hair, going in cautious circular motions and making sure he gets every inch of my hair. He grabs one of the many faucets spraying us and uses it to completely rinse the shampoo and bloody mixture down the drain.

"You don't have to do that." I stop him from grabbing another bottle.

"You're right, love. I don't *have* to. I want to." He latches onto it anyway and spreads conditioner through the ends of my hair, carefully pulling out any tangles that he finds. "And while that's sitting." He goes to grab the shampoo but I stop him.

"No. Allow me." I plop some of it into my hands and even though he persists slightly, he allows me to shampoo his hair. I run my fingers along his scalp and do as thorough of a job as he had done for me. I make a little mohawk and giggle at him. "Sorry, I had to."

He grins and shakes his head, wiping his hand through it to get rid of the silly styling and tilting his neck to rinse himself of the suds. Simon wipes his eyes and focuses back on me. He washes the rest of the conditioner from my hair and puts the shower head onto its hook.

Simon foams up some soap in his hands and steps toward me, starting at my collarbones and caressing his touch over my shoulders, paying special attention to each bump and bruise, and cut on my body. "We have similar scars." He hovers his finger along the one on my chest and grabs my hand to feel the subtle one on his, right above his heart, where I had tried to stab him.

"I'm sorry," I tell him.

"I'm not." He goes back to work cleaning me and there isn't a spot he doesn't cover, even going so far as to kneel before me and prop one of my feet onto his leg so he can get every inch of me. He wets his hands and applies a little bit of soap to rub over my thighs and inches toward my center. He stares up at me as he trails his fingers over my folds and tilts me toward the water.

I clutch his face in my hands and drag him up toward me, my mouth finding his within seconds. "Take me to bed," I breathe into him. "Please."

Simon rinses the rest of the suds from us and shuts off the water. He reaches for a towel but I stop him, grabbing his arm and turning him toward me. As if he reads my mind, he picks me up like he had done earlier, only this time we're soaked and completely nude.

I kiss him again and wrap myself around him on our way to the bedroom.

He lowers me onto the mattress carefully and lays me back. "Love, are you sure?"

I reach down and grip his cock in my hand, finally getting a look at what he's working with. I swallow and glance up at him. "I'm sure."

Simon cages me in, his hands on both sides of my head. He melds his mouth onto mine and kisses me with a fever that he's never done before. He drags his lips down my neck, sucking and licking my tender skin. Grazing one hand down my chest, he settles his grip on his shaft as he slides it along my entrance.

He positions himself in place and stares into my eyes. "Have you changed your mind?"

"In the twelve seconds since you last confirmed my consent?" I sigh. "No." I inch toward him and latch onto his waist, shoving him into me.

Simon moans when his cock barely penetrates me and continues to enter my eager hole ever so slowly.

"Fuck," I blurt out, his girth stretching me wider.

"Am I hurting you?"

"No," I breathe. "Not at all."

He picks up his pace, filling me even more. "You feel even better than I thought you would, love."

"Was it worth the wait?" I ask him, my hands dragging him into me.

He leans down, his face hovering above mine. "Without a doubt." Simon drags his thumb over my bottom lip, tugging it down. "Open up." He stares right into my eyes as he spits into my mouth, and if I thought something else was the hottest thing someone had ever done, I was sorely fucking mistaken.

No, Simon fucking Beckett spitting in my mouth definitely tops the list.

I clench around him, my orgasm nearing closer by the second.

"Together?" He asks me.

I smile up at him and drag him onto my lips. "Together." I swirl my tongue over his and he pumps into me harder, his climax filling me and mine happening in tandem. I tremble in his grasp and he remains inside me long after both of us have stopped shuddering.

"God damn, I love you, June." He pecks my lips, my nose, my forehead. "So fucking much."

"Hello," a voice calls out from downstairs.

I blink up at him. "Was that Magnus?"

"Yeah." He chuckles.

I crane my head toward the door. "We're upstairs," I yell out.

"Are you guys decent?" Magnus hollers back.

"No," I tell him truthfully.

"Sick." He climbs the stairs, his footsteps thudding on each one. "Can I join?" He rounds the corner and I watch him upside down. "Oh shit, you weren't joking." He leans against the doorframe. "About time you two boned down."

"It's been a long time coming," Simon says, a bit bashfully.

He and Magnus have become friends these past few weeks, but I guess this *is* the first time Magnus is seeing him naked, and with his dick inside Magnus's girlfriend. I can understand the coyness now that I fully process what's going on.

But when I feel Simon's cock grow harder inside of me, I realize he might not be as modest as I thought he was.

I reach my right arm back toward Magnus. "Come here." I look at Simon. "Is that okay?"

He nods and rocks his hips gently.

Magnus kicks off from the wall. "Don't have to tell me twice." He instantly unbuttons his jeans and tugs them over his hips, freeing his already rigid erection. He kisses me before kneeling behind me.

I lick at my lips and tilt my head closer to him as he guides the tip of it over the edge of my mouth. He plunges his cock between my lips and fucks my face tenderly. I keep my arm reached back, gripping his tattooed thigh and suck every inch of him that he gives me.

Magnus extends his grasp and places his fingers on both sides of my aching clit. He slides his hand farther, gripping the base of Simon's cock as Simon thrusts in and out of me.

The sensation and the fullness of both of my holes send my core tightening. I moan against Magnus's shaft and gag when he fucks me a bit deeper.

Simon leans down and to the side to pinch my nipple between his teeth. He sucks it into his mouth and rolls it over his lips.

Magnus pulls himself free of me. "You okay, princess?" He strokes his shaft above me, the moisture from my mouth lingering on his cock.

"Mmhm." I reach for him and grasp him in my hand, spinning and circling and tugging.

He collapses onto the bed next to me, giving me better and more comfortable access to him.

"Do you want to ride him, love?" Simon licks my neck and nibbles on my ear. "Do you want to sit on his cock for a little bit?" He slides himself out of me and swirls the tip up and over my throbbing clit.

I climb onto my elbow and then to my knees, spreading them over Magnus and sitting on his shaft.

Simon watches with his lust-filled gaze as the woman he loves fucks another man.

Magnus reaches up and cups both of my breasts in his hand. "God damn, princess."

I pivot up and down on his shaft, reveling in this new angle and cock filling me. I follow Simon's stare as he rises from the edge of the bed and comes behind me.

I lean down to Magnus, pressing my lips to his, and give Simon a better view.

Simon climbs onto the bed between Magnus's legs and nudges mine apart. With a palm resting along my hip, Simon rubs the tip of his shaft over my already full hole. He holds me in place, stopping me from moving anymore, and slides Magnus's cock out of me. A moment later, he fills me again, but instead of just Magnus's cock, both of them shove into my tight pussy.

"Oh my God," I whimper.

"I know, princess." Magnus drags my face down and onto his. He kisses my lips and rocks his hips. "You're taking us both so good."

Simon keeps his pace steady until I ease back onto him and have adjusted to the mass of having them both in the same hole.

"Fuck," I moan into Magnus and bite his lip.

"You're such a good girl, love." Simon fucks me a little harder, his cock growing stiffer against Magnus's.

Magnus brings his hand up and dips his index finger into my mouth. I suck it and he drags it down to my clit, rubbing a circle with the moist digit.

"Oh god, guys, I'm..." I pant.

Magnus grips the back of my head and melts his lips onto mine, his tongue forcing its way into my mouth. He gasps and is the first of us to climax, spilling over inside of me.

I come next, my orgasm shattering over me and my entire body shuddering with pleasure. I tighten around both of them and Simon moans, pumping his orgasm into me, too.

We lay there, a pile of sweaty sex.

I twitch and smile into Magnus's mouth as he kisses me one last time.

He leans his head back. "Fuck."

Simon crawls out from behind me, slowly pulling himself out of my stuffed pussy.

I climb off of Magnus and fall onto the bed beside him.

Simon lays on the other side of me, and I outstretch my arms to both men, one on each of their stomachs.

"That was fucking intense," I tell them while looking up blankly at the ceiling.

Magnus leans up on his elbow and stares at me. "You're definitely going to need a Plan B after that one."

I laugh and exhale, a million emotions floating through me all at once. Simon is in my life. Magnus is okay with it. Hell, Coen is even on board with it. And he's safe. My sweet Coen is going to live. But then my heart tugs at the seams of thinking of Dominic.

The distance between us has never been greater and no matter what I do, I can't help but feel like we might not make it through this.

# CHAPTER 34

# Dominic

I haven't eaten anything in three days. I'm not even sure if I've slept. For the first time in my life, this pit in my chest takes hold, and I don't know if it's grief or a fucking heart attack.

I pop an aspirin and swallow it down with a thick gulp of bourbon.

June hasn't been home. Magnus comes and gets her some clothes, but he prevents any reason for her to come here.

*Home.* I throw the bottle of aspirin across the room. "This isn't her home, you fucking idiot."

Coen is supposed to be discharged soon, but is he going to want to come back to an empty house? He risked his life to save Simon fucking Beckett—there's no way he's going to be without June during his recovery.

Will he go there? The same place that Magnus has spent most of his time, too?

This house is so fucking empty without any of them here.

All of them abandoning me for the man who was once my enemy.

I snatch my keys off the counter and take off toward the garage. If they're going to leave, so am I.

I drive without a care across town, not stopping at lights or stop signs or using a single fucking turn signal. I speed carelessly and don't give a shit about whether a semi fucking crashes into me or not.

What's the point?

How did I go from being on top of the world, having it all, a multi-billion-dollar criminal syndicate, and now I'm a man without a fucking purpose?

I had *her.* The strongest, most fearless, bravest woman I have ever known, and I let her slip through my arrogant fingers. I lied, I pushed her away, I did everything wrong and nothing right.

Maybe I just have one of those hearts that's bound to break.

I pull into the parking garage and hop straight out of my SUV, not bothering to shut the door or lock it. Someone can steal it for all I fucking care.

I push the button and wait for an answer. A second goes by, then two. I sigh and rub my hand through my beard. I knew this was a terrible fucking idea, but yet, I did it anyway. I lean my head against the building, my fist balling and tapping it, defeat washing through me.

But when the buzzer sounds and the door unlocks, I'm renewed with the tiniest bit of hope.

I barge straight into the building and go for the elevator, pushing the code in and waiting for the door to open. I climb inside and ride the thing all the way to the top. It opens, revealing Simon's immaculate penthouse and June, Simon, and Magnus all in the kitchen.

June turns toward me, the smile on her face dimming at the sight of me. "Dom, what are you doing here?"

Simon pulls his gun out and sets it on the counter, turning it toward me like a warning. "Don't make me regret letting you in."

"I thought it was the takeout." Magnus crosses his arms over his chest.

All three of them are on the defensive.

"I just came to talk." I inch forward, noting how June tenses with each step I take toward her. "Please."

She hops from the stool and steps around Magnus. "Then talk."

My cold dead heart beats at this ounce of a chance she gives me.

"June." I sigh. "I can't eat. Or sleep. Or breathe. My entire body hurts like someone ripped my heart from my chest."

"Then you know what I've felt for the last six months."

I take another step and ignore the blow to the gut. "I do. It's terrible. I never meant for you to feel like that. I..." I stare into her eyes, begging her to meet my gaze. "I was wrong, June. About everything. I was fucking wrong. And I know it's too little too late but God damn it, I need you to know how sorry I am." I drop to my knees in front of her, not giving a shit about the two men who are bearing witness to this pathetic act. "I'm so sorry about lying to you. Treating you like you didn't have what it took to be in my world. I was just afraid. I didn't want that life for you. I didn't want you to think I couldn't protect you. I wanted to solve the problem, *before* you were put in danger. I didn't want you to doubt me.

"I vowed to protect you, and even though that's what I thought I was doing, I did it all wrong. I should have told you. I should have let you in. I should have been the man you needed me to be. But I swear to you, I know now how fucking wrong I was. And I'm done, I'm done with it all. I have a council meeting scheduled next week to tell them that I'm resigning. I don't want it. None of it. Nothing means anything if I can't have you. I spent my whole fucking life working toward that position. It was the only thing I had ever wanted. But it's nothing compared to losing you, June. I...I don't want it. I don't need it. I need you. I want you. And I will spend every day for the rest of my life begging you to forgive me. Because you're the only thing I give a shit about, the only thing that matters. Whatever you want. I'll do it. Just tell me what to do."

I grip her hand in mine and watch the tears roll down her cheeks.

"I never meant to hurt you. And I will never forgive myself for that. You are strong. You are capable. You are worthy of so much more than this life has to offer you. You made me feel something I have never felt before, June. Unconditional love. And I am so fucking sorry that I didn't give you that in return. I was selfish. I was foolish. I was a fucking idiot. I don't deserve you. I know that. But please hear me when I tell you, I am sorry."

I drop my head as a single tear rolls down my cheek.

June doesn't speak. The penthouse is quiet aside from my haggard breaths.

I've said so many words and yet none of them feel like I've even scraped the surface of letting her know just how regretful I am. And now I kneel here, half a man with my beating heart bleeding out in my hands, offering it to her in hopes that maybe, just maybe, she harbors a shred of love for me still.

June releases my hand and it's like a stake is driven straight through my heart.

She places her palms on my cheeks and tilts my head up toward her. "Was that so hard?"

"Wh-what?" I stare up at her in disbelief that she's even speaking to me.

"All I wanted was for you to apologize, Dom." She sighs, her thumbs skimming my beard. "This whole time. That's all I wanted. But I was done begging you, you had to figure it out on your own."

"You still...?" But I can't get the last words out.

"Love you?" She smiles through her tears. "Yeah, I still love you."

And like I've been struck by fucking lightning, my heart pounds life back through me. I rise to my feet, picking her up and wrapping my arms around her waist. "You love me!" I spin her around in a circle and slowly lower her to the floor.

June stares up at me. "I'm still really fucking pissed at you, but I can be mad and love you at the same time."

I cup her face in my hand. "I'm okay with that. I am so good with that." I sigh and cherish the feel of her skin on mine.

"Well," Magnus says. "Are you going to kiss her or not?"

June and I both smile, and I waste no more time, bridging every bit of distance between us and pressing my lips to hers.

She wraps her arms around my neck and pulls me closer.

I bend her at the waist and tip her backward, my mouth on hers every second of the way.

Someone claps and I grin against her and straighten us to the upright position.

"I'm sorry it took me so long," I tell her. "I should have never kept you waiting."

"Just don't do it ever again." June reaches up and touches my cheek. "I missed you."

"I missed you." I press my hand over hers.

Her eyes widen. "But I'm still mad at you. Don't forget that." June smiles and it's like the heavens open up and an angel shines its light down on me.

"Don't worry," I tell her. "I'll spend the rest of my life making it up to you."

She points her finger at my chest. "I'm holding you to that."

"I'm just glad I didn't have to shoot you." Simon puts his gun back into his holster. "You know how messy that can get."

I extend my arm toward him. "I owe you an apology, too."

He glances down at my hand like it's a bomb waiting to detonate.

"I'm serious. I gave you a much harder time than you deserved. I'm sorry."

Simon raises his brow but decides to take my offer. "Apology accepted. But on my behalf, not June's. You have your work cut out for you on that one." He shakes my hand firmly.

"You're not really quitting, are you?" June tilts her head up toward mine.

"I called for the meeting, yeah. If it's going to get between us, I don't want it."

She places her hand on my shoulder. "Then let's not let it. You can have both, Dom, but you have to *choose* both. You can't shut me out again. We have to do this together. All of us." She nods toward Simon and Magnus, too.

"Really?" I ask her. "After everything I put you through, you're willing to give it another shot?"

"On *my* terms this time. Not yours." June crosses her arms. "And I don't know how it works exactly but my first order of business is getting rid of that fucking council. No one should give that much power to a group of money-grubbing old ladies."

I laugh for what feels like the first time in forever. "Deal." From the start of our organization, the council has been put there to ensure the men didn't have total authority over the business, but June is right, it's an outdated method that no longer serves us. It will take some convincing and shifting of roles, but we'll figure it out, because I can't fail her at the first thing she asks of me.

For as long as I live, I will make it my life's mission to please her.

"But first," June says. "We have a welcome home party to plan. Coen is being released tomorrow and this had better be epic."

And if epic is what my vixen wants, epic is what she will get.

# Epilogue – June

I glance up from overtop the paperwork I'm going through and meet Dominic's gaze. "Hey, quarter three projections are off by about two percent. You need to get them to run the numbers again."

Dom grins and strolls over, pressing his lips to my forehead. "Business major my ass, did you specialize in accounting, too?"

"I specialized in not fucking up a business because people don't know how to math." I crane my head and pucker my mouth toward him. "You better kiss me before my lips fall off."

He chuckles and plants a sloppy one on me. "Uh, I fucking love you so much." Dom scoops me into his arms and drags me away from my desk.

"Whoa, I said kiss, not whatever this is." I kick my feet and try to get free of this strong man. But who am I kidding, I eat up every bit of affection he showers me with.

Ever since Dom came to his fucking senses, things have been *completely* different between us. And not just he and I, but my relationship with all four of my men. There is no incessant animosity, arrogance, or excessive displays of toxic masculinity.

If anything, they go above and beyond to show me as much love as they can, leaving my heart fuller and fuller with each passing day.

It was a transition at first, but isn't every new relationship? And adding Simon to the mix of an already testosterone-heavy situation was definitely a fun thing to navigate.

We've had our speed bumps, but nothing like when they were keeping secrets, and I was stewing all by myself.

They were pretty livid when they found out Simon and I had gone to that underground fighting match, and they were more shocked when they learned that I had shot that man in that alley. But they embraced my secrets and accepted them as their own. They stopped keeping things from me, and instead of trying to solve every problem themselves, we deal with it as a group. Because we work better when we put all of our minds to it.

We deal with bad days and stubborn patches, but we go into every day with love and an open mind, and that is what helps us through. Each of us are insecure and dealing with our own traumas, stemming from our childhoods to things we have dealt with as adults, but instead of being broken alone, we do it together.

Because isn't that what relationships are all about? Being vulnerable and allowing yourself to love without restraints, even when you're not so sure you feel worthy of it?

"Where are you taking me?" I pound on Dom's back playfully.

"You've been a bad girl, June. You need to be punished." He smacks my ass and carries me up the stairs to the second floor of our house.

"Wait a minute? Is today Tuesday?" I wiggle excitedly. "Are you finally giving in?" When he doesn't answer, I squeal. "I knew it, I fucking knew you'd give in."

He pauses in front of my bedroom door.

Yes, my bedroom. We all have one. Each one of us. Even Simon. That way we have our *own* space, and then there is a shared bedroom that belongs to all of us. Simon still has his penthouse, and we stay there sometimes. But we're free to move about while still respecting each other's privacy. We might be super fucking open, but we allow that.

"We took a vote," Dom tells me. "Unanimous, obviously."

"Obviously," I grin so wide my fucking cheeks hurt.

"Group sex Tuesday is officially my new favorite day of the week." I wrap my arms around his neck and kiss him. "Screw Taco Tuesday, that shit is overrated."

He carries me into my bedroom where Simon, Coen, and Magnus are waiting for me. They're chatting amongst themselves, something that I'd never thought I'd witness six months ago. Let alone be hanging out in preparation for what's about to go down.

Dom plops me onto the mattress.

I hop up onto my knees. "Can we try it today?"

"I don't know, princess." Magnus leans on his elbows and tilts his head back toward me.

I kiss his lips and glance at the rest of the men.

Simon winks at me. "You know I'm down for anything, love."

Coen sighs. "Whose dick am I touching?"

Simon nudges him. "Probably mine, you little perv."

Coen narrows his gaze at him. "You're the one who tried to make a move on me back at Castleberry."

"I fell out of the fucking car, you're the one who was fondling my leg and shoving your face in my crotch."

"You know," I point between them. "You two bickering like this makes me think you're secretly in love or something."

"I tolerate him," Coen insists.

"Says the guy who wants to touch my dick," Simon teases.

Magnus scoffs. "How come no one wants to touch *my* dick?"

"Well," Dominic chimes in. "No one better touch my dick."

I tug my shirt over my head and toss it onto the floor. "Someone better give me a dick to touch or I'm going to get rid of group sex Tuesdays." I lay back and unbutton my black jeans and slither out of them. "This pussy isn't going to eat itself."

"Dibs!" Dominic calls out, grabbing me by the ankles and pulling me toward him. He yanks my panties off but keeps them balled in his fist.

"Ah, no fair." Magnus hops off the bed and rips off his clothes as quickly as he can, returning to the bed and plopping down next to me. He kisses my mouth while Dom swirls his tongue over my already wet slit.

Dom surprises me by shoving my panties inside of me with two of his fingers. He sucks on my clit and pulls himself away for a second. "What do you think, go for ten?" He takes his other hand and rocks it over my clit while fingering me with my panties.

Magnus grips my throat and kisses me harder.

"Ten would be pretty solid for a Tuesday afternoon," Simon says from somewhere above me.

I reach for him and he grabs my hand, guiding it onto his already-hardening cock.

My core tightens and before I can even fucking stop it, I climax under Dom's pressure and moan into Magnus's mouth.

"There's one." Dom tugs my panties out of my throbbing pussy, and when I break away from Magnus to glance over at him, he's shoving them in his coat pocket.

I shake my head. "You naughty boy."

He shrugs. "Little souvenir for later." Dom rises to his feet, drags his pants down, and climbs back onto the bed, shoving his thick cock into my ravenous hole.

I take his wrath and spit on both of my hands, one of them reaching toward Magnus, and the other for Simon. I tilt my head to locate Coen who is approaching me with his sprung cock, too. I open my mouth and lick at my lips, an open invitation for him to fuck my face.

Magnus sucks on my nipple and plucks it between his lips, pinching and applying pressure to it while I stroke his cock.

Dom fucks me harder, bringing my legs up to rest on his shoulders. He, or someone, I don't fucking know, rubs on my clit.

Coen slides his cock in and out of my hungry mouth, bouncing it off the back of my throat.

There are so many sensations I don't know where exactly to focus, especially when my next orgasm is riding so fucking close to crashing over me. But I'm no match to the wrath these men inflict on me, and when I come, it's harder than I did the first time. I pulsate around Dom's cock and he keeps pounding into me.

"Two."

"Not fair," Magnus declares. "You're having all the fun."

Dominic pulls himself out of me, leaving my hole raging with want. I've already come twice and yet I can't wait to see what else they have in store for me.

"Have at it," Dom tells him. "Let's see what you can do."

I release all of my men and scoot myself further onto the bed. "Magnus." I pat the spot next to me.

He sits down, grinning from ear to ear as I climb on top of him and straddle his waist, sliding myself onto his shaft while these three other men watch.

I bob up and down on him and he rocks his hips into me.

Dominic comes around the side of us and tugs my face down and onto his cock.

"You taste yourself on him, princess?" Magnus grips my waist and fucks me hard. "You taste so sweet."

I eye Simon and Coen who both stand there with their cocks in their own hands. Simon nudges Coen and motions for him to go.

Coen surprisingly complies and climbs up behind me on the bed. "Listen, I don't understand how you got two in there, let alone three."

Simon chuckles and gets on the bed next to him. "Just find the opening and shove your dick in there."

I laugh, too, causing my pussy to tighten around Magnus's shaft even more, and without meaning to, I come for the third time.

I stop sucking Dominic's dick long enough to say, "That shouldn't count. I accidentally orgasmed."

Dominic shoves back into my mouth. "It counts." He grips the side of my cheeks and thrusts into me.

Fingers feel their way around Magnus's cock and my pussy, and a second later, another cock joins us, stretching me open.

"Atta boy," Simon says.

"Dude, don't try to high-five me. You're going to make me go soft." Coen goes easy on me and seems to get acquainted with the feeling of his cock rubbing up against Magnus's.

I moan against Dom and look up at him with tears in my eyes.

He grins. "You're taking us like such a good girl."

Simon kneels beside me and reaches his hand between me and Magnus to rub my clit. "You going to give us number four, love?" He applies more pressure.

I rock back onto Magnus and Coen and revel in the fullness of them stretching me open.

Coen grips my ass and smacks it gently. Then a little bit harder.

He's not usually *this* adventurous, but he's been coming out of his shell the more time we all spend together.

He lands his palm another time, the sound crackling through the air and sending my pussy tightening around him and Magnus. I gag on Dominic as I breathe through yet another orgasm.

"Four," Simon declares. "How about five before we try to fit another cock in you, love?"

"I've got five right here." Magnus grips my hips and picks up his pace, fucking me harder and deeper from underneath. "Pinch her clit, Simon." He slams into me harder and Coen equals his force from behind. "You going to give us five, princess?"

And because I cannot contain myself when *this* much is going on, I shatter on top of him again and pulsate around two cocks.

"That's our good girl," Dominic tells me, his hands still gripping my cheeks and fucking my face. He slows his pace, deepening his strides. "Do you want filled even more?"

I nod and wonder how it's possible to desire anything more than they've already given me.

Dominic pulls himself out of my mouth. "I think you should flip her over onto her back."

Coen and Magnus both stop moving and wait for their direction.

"Good idea," Simon tells him. "You mean with Bryant still below her?"

Dominic nods and rubs his beard. "Yeah. Hayes can stay in the same position." He tilts his head slightly. "And you can come in at an angle." Dominic squints. "I think it'll work." He grazes my chin. "That still leaves your pretty face to be fucked by me."

"Aren't I going to crush you?" I ask Magnus as I turn and lay on his chest.

"Princess, if this is how I die, I would be honored." He slides my body down onto his shaft. "There's one. Who's next?"

Coen pushes himself back into place next to Magnus. "That okay?"

I nod and lick my lips.

"You sure about this, love?" Simon strokes his cock.

"Yes."

Simon manages to climb over both me and Magnus and glides his cock over my clit. He glances behind him at Coen. "Don't stare at my ass dude."

"I wasn't fucking looking."

Simon elbows him. "I'm just fucking with you, dude, lighten up."

"Do you think you can do it?" I ask him, the anticipation brimming at the seams.

"Love," he presses his lips on mine. "Don't doubt what I would do for you." Simon glides his dick farther down and shoves it in along Coen's and Magnus's, filling me more than I've ever been stuffed in my life. "Is that too much?"

I swallow and clench my teeth. "No, it's..." I tilt my head back and moan. "Amazing."

Dom takes the opportunity to trail the tip of his shaft over my lips. "Now you can say you've had four cocks at one time."

I open my mouth and let him slide himself between my lips.

He inches closer and doesn't hold back as he fucks the back of my throat.

All three of my other men rock their hips and fuck my greedy pussy, their girth stretching me so wide I wonder how I'll ever fucking recover. But this was my idea.

After Simon and Magnus fucked me both in the same hole, it sort of became one of my favorite things to do. And it made me consider whether I could take three at once, but now I guess we know the answer to that question.

Simon licks and sucks on my neck and fucks me from his position on top of me. "You're doing so good, love."

"Guys," Magnus says from under me. "I don't want to ruin the party, but unless someone switches positions with me, I'm going to bust soon." He pivots his hips gently. "I keep thinking about baseball and dirty socks but it's not working."

I drag my arm back and run it through Magnus's hair, scraping my fingertips along his scalp and tugging it in my grasp. A sort of silent permission that he's allowed to climax, too. But with Dom's cock shoved into the back of my throat, I can't exactly verbalize my approval.

Magnus moans against my touch.

"I'm pretty sure you're allowed to enjoy yourself, Bryant," Simon tells him. "I sure as hell am." He grunts and fucks me a little harder. "You doing good back there, pervert?"

Coen mumbles something. "Mmhm. Baseball. Or something."

Every single one of their cocks hardens, stretching me wider than I already was. I close my eyes and suck on Dominic's shaft and reach my other arm up to grip his base.

Magnus moans and whimpers, his body rocking harder into me.

Coen follows the motion and pounds my pussy until he explodes inside of me, too. He slows his pace and pulls out, leaving Simon and Magnus still penetrating my hole.

Simon wiggles down farther and shifts position now that Coen has left his spot. He reaches forward, skimming his hands over my breasts, and settling them on my waist. He fucks me deeper, Magnus's cock still coming down from his orgasm next to Simon's hardening shaft.

"God damn, love. You take us so well." Simon guides one of Magnus's hands up my body and the other down onto my clit. The two of them move in unison on my aching nub.

Dominic fucks my face and doesn't let up until I whimper around him with my next orgasm crashing over me.

"Six," Simon breathes while pounding into me. He lengthens his strides and turns my sixth orgasm into a seventh. "Good girl, love."

Panting and breathless, I suck on Dom's cock, tightening my lips around him and swirling my tongue.

"That's it," he tells me and gets a fistful of my hair. "You ready to swallow me down?"

I do my best to nod and mumble approval.

Dominic must understand, because he latches onto the base of his shaft and strokes his load into my mouth, filling the back of my throat. "Such a good fucking girl." He drags the tip of his shaft out and glides it over my lips. I lick at it and take in a breath of air.

"You good, princess?" Magnus cups my tit in one hand and my nub in the other. "Can you take much more?"

"Mmhm."

Simon reaches down, his hand wrapping around my neck and his mouth falling onto mine. "You're perfect, love." He tightens his grip and swims his hips over me, changing the friction between us. "You going to come again for us?"

Magnus grows harder, recovering from his climax and filling me alongside Simon.

Simon notices Magnus growing next to him and grins against my lips.

"Spit in my mouth," I tell him.

He smiles again. "You hear that, boys?" Simon drags my chin down and complies with my demand. "God damn, I love you." He pounds into me again and shivers as his orgasm crashes over him and sends me spiraling, too. He slows his pace and pulls himself out of my aching pussy. "Eight."

Magnus wraps his arm around my waist and lifts me into the air so quick I don't even know what happens until I'm on all fours and he's behind me, fucking me with a renewed sense of self. He shoves my face down into the bed and pounds into me.

I grip the blankets but they do nothing to keep me in place as Magnus fucks me harder.

He slams into me and I savor the satisfaction of his control.

Magnus reaches under and applies pressure to my clit. He pumps into me, and I shatter around him, my face buried in the sheets and my pussy pulsating with a new intensity.

"Nine," I whimper and collapse to the bed. "I'm tapping out," I tell them before anyone else can insist on climbing back up into place.

Magnus falls to the side and extends his arm.

I climb into his chest and scan the rest of the men in the room. "I love group sex Tuesdays."

---

Simon and I train at least two days a week. We do weightlifting, boxing, self-defense, and a mix of cardio and yoga or whatever else we manage to include in our regimen.

It's helped me build muscle mass from when I had lost weight, and it allowed me to put on more. My muscle is functional and purposeful and will hopefully prevent me from being overtaken by another shit bag ever again. I argued how important it was that I learned how to defend myself, not just with a gun, but with my body, too.

We spend time at the shooting range, too, and Simon has taught me how to break apart, clean, and put together most of the weapons in our arsenal. Some of them have more steps than others and I sometimes have to cheat and look over at what he's doing, but I haven't managed to shoot my hand off, so I call that a huge plus.

Things with Cora have been tense. She can tell that I'm withholding information from her, and the more I do, the more she pulls away. I fucking hate it, but I haven't exactly had the best opportunity to tell her what's going on. She's been dealing with some shit in her home life, and I haven't wanted to completely throw her life for a loop when I tell her that her best friend is dating four made men who run a massive criminal organization and the two guys she currently has a crush on are also part of the criminal underworld.

How does someone tell their best friend that?

I'll figure it out, but right now isn't the best time. Maybe next week when we get together for girls' night.

I'm planning on meeting with Claire prior to that, so perhaps she and I can sit down and come up with a game plan to break the news to Cora and navigate any potential outcome that might not go in our favor. The goal is to keep her safe, not have her fly off the handle and potentially put herself at risk.

Now I see how much of a struggle it was for my men to come clean with me. But I'm well aware that the truth is what finally brought us all together.

But what if Cora doesn't handle things the way I do? What if she's too sweet and innocent for this world, and I just happened to be a psychotic bitch who loves killing people?

I guess I won't know until I find out. And because Cora means the world to me, I'm going to have to find out.

"Hey," Dominic calls out across the room. "Bryant, you're with me."

Magnus glances up at him. "Where we going?"

"Knock some heads." Dominic winks at him.

"Sounds like a good time." Magnus hops to his feet and walks by Simon and me to kiss my lips. "You're all sweaty, princess." He licks his lips. "I like it."

"Can I go?" I ask Dominic and bat my eyelashes.

"Maybe next time." He strolls over and kisses me quickly. "I need Magnus's expertise. I can read people, but Bryant is a human fucking lie detector. Plus, you need to finish your session with Beckett."

Magnus glances back on his way out. "Thai for dinner, don't forget."

"I would never."

Magnus and Dom leave Simon and me behind.

Simon raises his padded hand. "Come on, love. Hit me."

I throw a punch then surprise him with a spin and a kick. "Can we be done for the day? I'm fucking beat."

He tilts his head to the side and steps forward, pressing his lips to mine, but not before rubbing his wet face all over me.

"I hate you." I glare at him.

He grins like an idiot. "I fucking love you, too."

Coen calls out from his spot on the bench. "You two going to finish or fuck?"

"Definitely one or the other," Simon tells him. "Why? You want to join?"

Coen rolls his eyes and goes back to his paperback.

"Want to hit the shower?" Simon asks me.

"Together?"

"Together," he says, that single word holding so much more weight than he could ever know.

---

That might be the end of *Villain Era* but that isn't all from this universe!

Love reading June's story and want more from this dangerous world? So much to choose from you never have to leave!

Already missing Dominic? Here's your chance to find out what was going through Dom's heading during chapter one of Untamed Vixen! *Join my newsletter to hop right into this exclusive bonus scene. Scan this QR code to take you straight there!*

Dying to get your hands on Cora's book? *Ruin My Life* is right around the corner!

Want to read Johnny and Claire's epic love story about how they overcame the impossible? *Broken Like You* is available now!

Or you could take a quick, spicy break with Axel and Lorenzo as they meet the feisty Banks in *Wings of a Devil* (a standalone novella set in the Sinners and Angels Universe).

Read everything and still want more? Come join us in my private reader group on Facebook!

# Acknowledgments

Okay, so, this book is absolutely FOR THE READERS. And a little bit for Simon. A LOT OF BIT, actually.

Untamed Vixen was written as a standalone, with what I thought was a HEA. But Simon disagreed, and so did a plethora of readers.

Almost every day for the past year, someone commented that they wished Simon had been included in June's harem.

I never meant to make him so dreamy, but I'd be lying if I said I didn't think Simon planted that seed on purpose.

His love for June runs deep, so much so that YOU felt it enough to want his story.

Thank you for pushing me, for begging for this book, and for taking your chance on June and her men.

And thank you for being patient and cheering me on as I wrote this MASSIVE book that never wanted to end.

If I'm being honest, I didn't want it to. But Simon got his way. And we all got the HEA we wanted and they deserved. Even if it was torture getting them there.

I cried, I laughed, I got so damn frustrated with these characters, but I truly hope you loved this insane journey they went on.

Writing Villain Era was the most fun I have ever had while writing a book.

I have so many people to thank for this one, but I had to start with YOU, the reader!

To my alpha readers (Sam, Michelle, Grace)—I legit would not know what to do without you. I adore you immensely and am so grateful to call you my friends.

Tiffany Hernandez, my assistant, my friend, you are the glue that holds me together. I appreciate you more than you'll ever know, and I am so glad you're along for this wild ride with me.

My Patrons over on Patreon—Heather, Emma, Mandi, Selena, Laura, Brittany, Stephanie, Paige, Grace, Ellie, Ashley, Michelle, Clayton, Tyler, Victoria—your support means the world to me. THANK YOU. I hope you love all the secrets we share as much as I do!

SJ Fowler, for spending entirely too much time helping me with the chapter headings for this book. You are an incredible friend, and not just for that!

My team—Tori at Cruel Ink Editing & Design. Complete sentences are so out.

Frags and commas for the win. Cady, thank you for adding some of those commas back in and catching that eye color error.

Vivi—I love you, always!

Kate—my manifestation partner.

Mini me—thanks for thinking I'm a cool mom.

And again, the readers, this wouldn't be possible without your love for this book! Especially those of you over on Tiktok who shared and commented and dueted until I was coerced into writing this book! Make sure to tag me and let me know how hard you fell for Simon!

Now it's time to give Cora her HEA.

*Together?*

*Together.*

# AMA featuring...

ANIANNA: "I'D ASK ANY OF THEM TO MY BEDROOM."
SIMON: "THAT SEEMS DANGEROUS."

MARCIVETTEG: "DOMINIC, WHAT CHARACTERISTICS IN A WOMAN ARE YOU DRAWN TO?"
DOMINIC: "JUNE."

FROMTHELIBRARYOFZEPHYR: "I WOULD WANT A TOUR OF MAGNUS' MANY TATTOOS!"
MAGNUS: "FOR JUNE'S EYES ONLY."

KAYLA: "ASK MAGNUS WHY HE WAS SO QUICKLY OKAY WITH SIMON BEING PART OF THE GROUP DYNAMIC?"
MAGNUS: "I'D NEVER RISK LOSING JUNE."

LAUREN: "JUNE, WHY DID YOU WAIT SO LONG TO BONE SIMON?"
JUNE: "TRUST ME, IT WASN'T BECAUSE I DIDN'T WANT TO, BECAUSE I DID. BUT I NEVER FELT LIKE THE TIMING WAS TRULY 'RIGHT', UNTIL IT WAS."

"JUNE, HOW DO YOU VIEW LOVE?"
JUNE: "IT'S MORE OF A FEELING THAN ANYTHING..."

"COEN, DO YOU THINK LOYALTY CAN BE UNCONDITIONAL, OR DOES IT HAVE LIMITS?"
COEN: "TO ME, LOYALTY IS SOMETHING SACRED. I BELIEVE IT CAN BE UNCONDITIONAL—AT LEAST, I WANT TO BELIEVE THAT. BUT THERE'S ALWAYS A LINE. IF I'M LOYAL TO SOMEONE, IT'S BECAUSE I TRUST THEM WITH MY LIFE. BUT LOYALTY SHOULD NEVER MEAN BLIND OBEDIENCE. LOYALTY HAS TO BE EARNED. IT'S A RARE GIFT."

"SIMON, IF YOU COULD CHANGE ONE THING ABOUT YOUR PAST, WHAT WOULD IT BE?"
SIMON: "MEET JUNE BEFORE THE GUYS DID, DUH." ~THE GUYS GLARE AT HIM~
SIMON: HE THROWS UP HIS ARMS. "IT WAS A JOKE."

"DOMINIC, IF SOMEONE WERE TO BETRAY YOU, WHAT WOULD BE YOUR RESPONSE?"
DOMINIC: "I THINK WE ALL KNOW THE ANSWER TO THAT QUESTION."

"MAGNUS, WHAT DO YOU THINK IS YOUR BIGGEST STRENGTH?"
MAGNUS: "BEING ABLE TO READ PEOPLE. STRENGTH ISN'T ALL ABOUT FORCE, IT'S BEING ABLE TO PERCEIVE PEOPLE INTO THINKING THEY'RE IN CONTROL WHEN THEY REALLY AREN'T. THE GAME IS ABOUT TIMING, AND I PLAY IT BETTER THAN ANYONE ELSE."

"JUNE, WHAT'S ONE THING YOU WISHED MORE PEOPLE KNEW ABOUT YOU?"
JUNE: "THAT I'M TIRED OF PRETENDING I DON'T CARE. I'VE GOT LAYERS LIKE EVERYONE ELSE, I JUST HIDE THEM A LOT BETTER THAN MOST PEOPLE."

MAGNUS: "CAN WE GO GET SOME FOOD NOW?"

# Also by Luna Pierce

**Sinners and Angels Universe**

(Dark romance with MF, RH, and MFM)

Broken Like You (Standalone MF)

Untamed Vixen (RH Part One)

Villain Era (RH Part Two)

Wings of a Devil (MFM Standalone novella)

Ruin My Life (RH Standalone)

**Brothers of Sin Series**

(MF billionaire romance)

Dangerous Haven (Standalone)

Book two (Standalone)

Book three (Standalone)

Book four (Standalone)

**The Harper Shadow Academy Series**

(Paranormal academy reverse harem)

Hidden Magic

Cursed Magic

Wicked Magic

Ancient Magic

Sacred Magic

Harper Shadow Academy: Complete Box Set

**Falling for the Enemy Series**

(Paranormal reverse harem)

Stolen by Monsters

Fighting for Monsters

Fated to Monsters

# About the Author

Luna Pierce is the author of gritty romance, both dark contemporary and paranormal. She adores writing broken characters you won't help but fall for on their journey to find themselves and fight for what they love. Her stories are for the hopelessly romantic who enjoy grit, angst, and passion.

When she's not writing, you'll find her consuming way too much coffee, making endless to-do lists, and spending time with her daughter and cats in small-town Ohio.

Join the exclusive reader group: Luna Pierce's Gritty Romance Squad

Join Luna's newsletter to receive updates at: www.lunapierce.com/subscribe

If you enjoyed reading Simon's book, please consider leaving an honest review on Amazon, Goodreads, Tiktok, and/or BookBub.